P9-DNZ-019

TO SLEEP IN A SEA OF STARS

ALSO BY

CHRISTOPHER PAOLINI

THE INHERITANCE CYCLE

Eragon

Eldest

Brisingr

Inheritance

The Fork, the Witch, and the Worm

TO SLEEP IN A SEA OF STARS

CHRISTOPHER PAOLINI

A TOM DOHERTY ASSOCIATES BOOK

NEW YORK

This is a work of fiction. All of the characters, organizations, and events portrayed in this novel are either products of the author's imagination or are used fictitiously.

TO SLEEP IN A SEA OF STARS

A Tor Book
Published by Tom Doherty Associates
120 Broadway
New York, NY 10271

www.tor-forge.com

The Library of Congress Cataloging-in-Publication Data is available upon request.

ISBN 978-1-250-76284-9 (hardcover)
ISBN 978-1-250-79366-9 (signed)
ISBN 978-1-250-79050-7 (international, sold outside the U.S., subject to rights availability)
ISBN 978-1-250-76290-0 (ebook)

First U.S. Edition: September 2020
First International Edition: September 2020

Printed in the United States of America

10 9 8 7 6 5 4 3 2 1

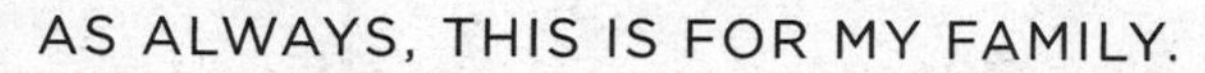

AS ALWAYS, THIS IS FOR MY FAMILY.

And also for the scientists, engineers, and dreamers working to build our future among the stars.

CONTENTS

A Fractalverse Novel

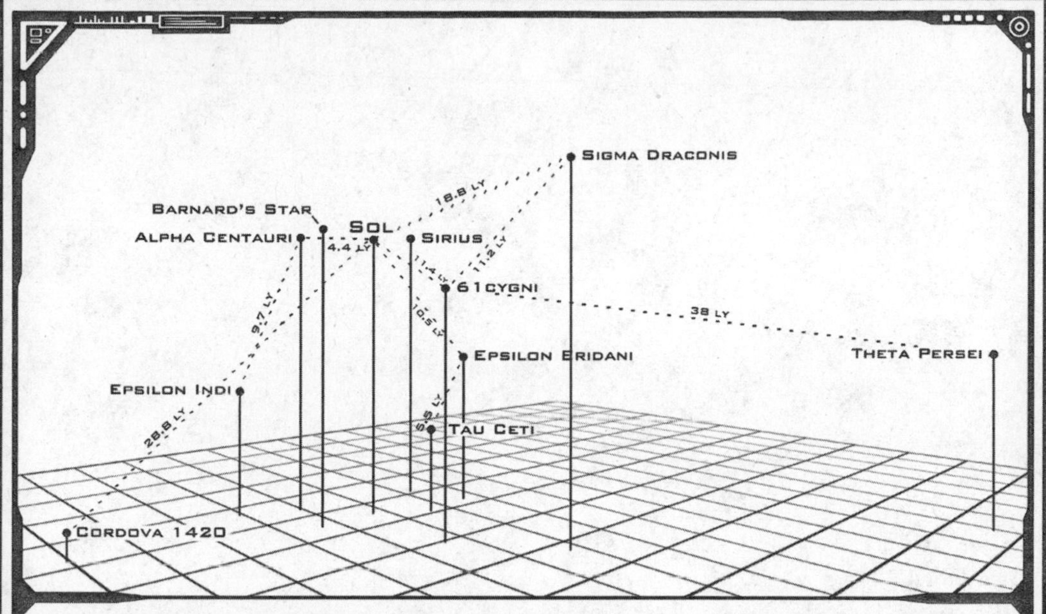

League of Allied Worlds

- Sol
- Alpha Centauri
  - Stewart's World
- Epsilon Eridani
  - Eidolon
- Epsilon Indi
  - Weyland
- Sigma Draconis
  - Adrasteia
- Theta Persei
  - Talos VII
- 61 Cygni
  - Ruslan

Non-Allied

- Cordova 1420
- Tau Ceti
  - Shin-Zar

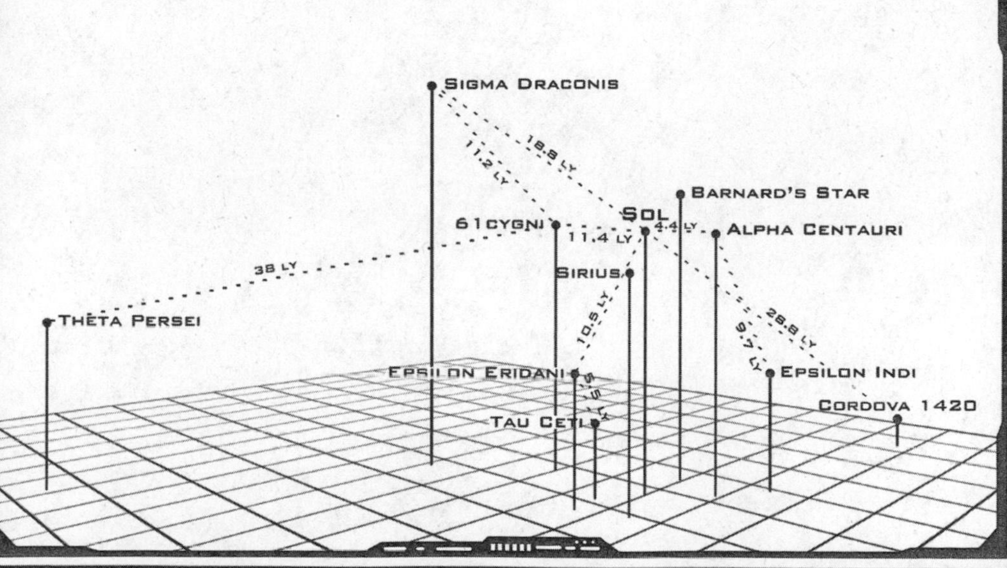

PART ONE

* * * * * * *

EXOGENESIS

O goddess-born of great Anchises' line,
The gates of hell are open night and day;
Smooth the descent, and easy is the way:
But to return, and view the cheerful skies,
In this the task and mighty labor lies.

—*AENEID* 6.126–129
JOHN DRYDEN TRANSLATION

CHAPTER I

* * * * * * *

DREAMS

1.

The orange gas giant, Zeus, hung low above the horizon, huge and heavy and glowing with a ruddy half-light. Around it glittered a field of stars, bright against the black of space, while beneath the giant's lidless glare stretched a grey wasteland streaked with stone.

A small huddle of buildings stood in the otherwise desolate expanse. Domes and tunnels and windowed enclosures, a lone place of warmth and life amid the alien environment.

Inside the compound's cramped lab, Kira struggled to extract the gene sequencer from its alcove in the wall. The machine wasn't that large, but it was heavy, and she couldn't get a good grip on it.

"Dammit," she muttered, and readjusted her stance.

Most of their equipment would stay on Adrasteia, the Earth-sized moon they had spent the past four months surveying. Most of their equipment, but not all. The gene sequencer was part of a xenobiologist's basic kit, and where she went, it went. Besides, the colonists who would soon be arriving on the *Shakti-Uma-Sati* would have newer, better models, not the budget, travel-sized one the company had stuck her with.

Kira pulled again. Her fingers slipped, and she sucked in her breath as one of the metal edges sliced her palm. She let go and, upon examining her hand, saw a thin line of blood oozing through the skin.

Her lips curled in a snarl, and she hit the gene sequencer, hard. That didn't help. Keeping her injured hand knotted in a fist, she paced the lab, breathing heavily while she waited for the pain to subside.

Most days the machine's resistance wouldn't bother her. Most days. But today, dread and sadness outran reason. They would be leaving in the morning, taking off to rejoin their transport, the *Fidanza,* which was already in orbit around Adra. A few days more, and she and everyone else in the ten-person survey team would get into cryo, and when they woke up at 61 Cygni, twenty-six days later, they would each go their separate ways, and that would be the last she would see of Alan for . . . for how long, she didn't know. Months, at least. If they were unlucky, over a year.

Kira closed her eyes, let her head fall back. She sighed, and the sigh turned into a groan. It didn't matter how many times she and Alan had done this dance; it wasn't getting any easier. The opposite in fact, and she hated it, really hated it.

They'd met the previous year on a large asteroid the Lapsang Trading Corp. was planning to mine. Alan had been there to conduct a geological survey. Four days—that was how long they'd spent together on the asteroid. It had been Alan's laugh and his mess of coppery hair that caught her attention, but it was his careful diligence that impressed Kira. He was good at what he did, and he didn't lose his calm in an emergency.

Kira had been alone for so long at that point, she'd been convinced she would never find someone. And yet seemingly by a miracle, Alan had entered her life, and just like that, there had been someone to care for. Someone who cared for her.

They'd continued to talk, sending long holo messages across the stars, and through a combination of luck and bureaucratic maneuvering, they'd managed to get posted together several more times.

It wasn't enough. For either of them.

Two weeks ago, they'd applied to corporate for permission to be assigned to the same missions as a couple, but there was no guarantee their request would be approved. The Lapsang Corp. was expanding in too many areas, with too many projects. Personnel were spread thin.

If their request was denied . . . the only way they'd be able to live together long term would be to change jobs, find ones that didn't require so much travel. Kira was willing—she'd even checked listings on the net the previous week—but she didn't feel as if she could ask Alan to give up his career with the company for her. Not yet.

In the meantime, all they could do was wait for the verdict from corporate. With how long it took for messages to get back to Alpha Centauri and the slowness of the HR Department, the soonest they could expect an answer was the end of next month. And by then, both she and Alan would have been shipped off in different directions.

It was frustrating. Kira's one consolation was Alan himself; he made it all worthwhile. She just wanted to *be* with him, without having to worry about the other nonsense.

She remembered the first time he'd wrapped his arms around her and how wonderful it felt, how warm and safe. And she thought of the letter he'd written her after their first meeting, of all the vulnerable, heartfelt things he'd said. No one had ever made such an effort with her before. . . . He'd always had time for her. Always shown her kindness in ways large and small, like the custom case he'd made for her chip-lab before her trip up to the Arctic.

The memories would have made Kira smile. But her hand still hurt, and she couldn't forget what the morning would bring.

"Come on, you bastard," she said, and strode over to the gene sequencer and yanked on it with all her strength.

With a screech of protest, it moved.

2.

That night, the team gathered in the mess hall to celebrate the end of the mission. Kira was in no mood for festivities, but tradition was tradition. Whether or not it went well, finishing an expedition was an occasion worth marking.

She'd put on a dress—green, with gold trim—and spent an hour fixing her hair into a pile of curls high on her head. It wasn't much, but she knew Alan would appreciate the effort. He always did.

She was right. The moment he saw her in the corridor outside her cabin, his face lit up, and he swept her into his arms. She buried her forehead into the front of his shirt and said, "You know, we don't *have* to go."

"I know," he said, "but we should put in an appearance." And he kissed her on the forehead.

She forced a smile. "Fine, you win."

"That's my girl." He smiled back and tucked a stray curl behind her left ear.

Kira did the same with one of his locks. It never ceased to amaze her how bright his hair was against his pale skin. Unlike the rest of them, Alan never seemed to tan, no matter how long he spent outside or under a spaceship's full-spectrum lights.

"Alright," she said in a low voice. "Let's do this."

The mess hall was full when they arrived. The other eight members of the survey team were crammed in around the narrow tables, some of Yugo's beloved scramrock was blasting over the speakers, Marie-Élise was handing out cups filled with punch from the large plastic bowl on the counter, and Jenan was dancing as if he'd had a liter of rotgut. Maybe he had.

Kira tightened her arm around Alan's waist and did her best to put on a cheery expression. Now wasn't the time to dwell on depressing thoughts.

It wasn't . . . but she couldn't help it.

Seppo headed straight for them. The botanist had pulled back his hair into a topknot for the night's event, which only accentuated the angles of his thin-boned face. "Four hours," he said, coming close. The drink slopped out of his cup as he gestured. "Four hours! That's how long it took me to dig my crawler free."

"Sorry, Seppo," said Alan, sounding amused. "I told you, we couldn't get to you before then."

"Bah. I had *sand* in my skinsuit. Do you know how uncomfortable that was? I'm rubbed raw in half a dozen places. Look!" He pulled up the fringe of his ratty shirt to show a red line of skin across his belly where the lower seam of his skinsuit had chafed.

Kira said, "Tell you what, I'll buy you a drink on Vyyborg to make up for it. How about that?"

Seppo lifted a hand and pointed in her general direction. "That . . . would be acceptable compensation. But no more sand!"

"No more sand," she agreed.

"And you," said Seppo, swinging his finger toward Alan. "You . . . know."

As the botanist tottered off, Kira looked up at Alan. "What was that about?"

Alan chuckled. "No idea. But it's sure going to be strange not having him around."

"Yeah."

After a round of drinks and conversation, Kira retreated to the back of the room and leaned against a corner. As much as she didn't want to lose Alan—again—she also didn't want to say farewell to the rest of the team. The four months on Adra had forged them into a family. An odd, misshapen family, but one she cared for all the same. Leaving them would hurt, and the closer that moment came, the more Kira realized just how much it was going to hurt.

She took another long drink of the orange-flavored punch. She'd been through this before—Adra wasn't the first prospective colony the company had posted her to—and after seven years spent jetting around from one blasted rock to another, Kira had begun to feel a serious need for . . . friends. Family. Companionship.

And now she was about to leave all that behind. *Again.*

Alan felt the same. She could see it in his eyes as he moved around the room, chatting with members of the team. She thought perhaps some of the others were also sad, but they papered over it with drink and dance and laughs that were too shrill to be entirely genuine.

She made a face and downed the rest of the punch. Time for a refill.

The scramrock was pounding louder than before. Something by Todash and the Boys, and their lead singer was howling, "—to fleeee. And there's nothing at the door. Hey, there's nothing at the door. Babe, what's that knocking at the door?" and her voice was climbing to a wavering, saw-blade crescendo that sounded as if her vocal cords were about to snap.

Kira pushed herself away from the wall and was about to start for the punch bowl when she saw Mendoza, the expedition boss, clearing a path toward her. Easy for him; he was built like a barrel. She'd often wondered if he'd grown up on a high-g colony like Shin-Zar, but Mendoza denied it when she asked, claimed he was from a hab-ring somewhere around Alpha Centauri. She wasn't entirely sure she believed him.

"Kira, need to talk with you," he said, coming near.

"What?"

"We have a problem."

She snorted. "There's *always* a problem."

Mendoza shrugged and mopped his forehead with a handkerchief he pulled from the back pocket of his pants. His forehead reflected bright spots from the strings of colored lights draped across the ceiling, and there were blotches under his arms. "Can't say you're wrong, but this needs fixing. One of the drones down south went dead. Looks like a storm took it out."

"So? Send another one."

"They're too far away, and we don't have time to print a replacement. Last thing the drone detected was some organic material along the coastline. Needs to be checked before we leave."

"Oh come on. You really want me to head out *tomorrow*? I've already cataloged every microbe on Adra." A trip like that would cost her the morning with Alan, and Kira was damned if she was going to give up any of their remaining time together.

Mendoza gave her a steady, *are you bullshitting me* look from under his brows. "Regs are regs, Kira. We can't risk the colonists running into something nasty. Something like the Scourge. You don't want that on your conscience. You really don't."

She went to take another drink and realized her cup was still empty. "Jesus. Send Ivanova. The drones are hers, and she can run a chip-lab as well as I can. There's—"

"You're going," said Mendoza, steel in his voice. "Oh six hundred, and I don't want to hear any more about it." Then his expression softened somewhat. "I'm sorry, but you're our xenobiologist, and regs—"

"And regs are regs," said Kira. "Yeah, yeah. I'll do it. But I'm telling you, it's not worth it."

Mendoza patted her on the shoulder. "Good. I hope it isn't."

As he left, a text popped up in the corner of Kira's vision: *<Hey, babe, everything okay? – Alan>*

Subvocalizing her answer, she wrote: *<Yeah, all good. Just some extra work. Tell you about it later. – Kira>*

From across the room, he gave her a goofy thumbs-up, and her lips quirked despite herself. Then she fixed her gaze on the punch bowl and made a beeline for it. She really needed another drink.

Marie-Élise intercepted her at the bowl, moving with the studied grace of an ex-dancer. As always, her mouth was pulled off-center, as if she were about to break into a crooked smile . . . or deliver a scathing witticism (and Kira had heard more than a few from her). She was tall to begin with, and with the shiny black heels she'd printed for the party, she was a whole head taller than Kira.

"I'm going to miss you, *chérie,*" said Marie-Élise. She bent down and gave Kira a kiss on each cheek.

"Same here," said Kira, feeling herself getting misty. Along with Alan, Marie-Élise had become her closest friend on the team. They'd spent long days together in the field—Kira studying the microbes of Adrasteia while Marie-Élise studied the lakes and rivers and the deposits of water hidden deep underground.

"Ah, cheer up now. You will message me, yes? I want to hear everything about you and Alan. And I will message you. Okay?"

"Yes. I promise."

For the rest of the evening, Kira worked to forget the future. She danced with Marie-Élise. She swapped jokes with Jenan and barbs with Fizel. For the thousandth time, she complimented Yugo on his cooking. She arm-wrestled

Mendoza—and lost—and sang a horribly off-key duet with Ivanova. And whenever possible, she kept her arm around Alan. Even when they weren't talking or looking at each other, she could feel him, and his touch was a comfort.

Once she'd had enough punch, Kira allowed the others to talk her into pulling out her concertina. Then the canned music was put on hold and everyone gathered round—Alan by her side, Marie-Élise by her knee—while Kira played a collection of spacer's reels. And they laughed and they danced and they drank, and for a time all was good.

3.

It was well past midnight and the party was still in full swing when Alan signaled to her with a motion of his chin. Kira understood, and without a word, they slipped out of the mess hall.

They leaned on each other as they made their way through the compound, careful to keep their cups of punch from spilling. Kira wasn't used to the bare look of the corridors. Normally overlays covered them, and stacks of samples, supplies, and spare equipment sat along the walls. But all that was gone now. Over the past week, she and the rest of the team had stripped the place in preparation for leaving. . . . If not for the music echoing behind them and the dim emergency lights along the floor, the base would have seemed abandoned.

Kira shivered and hugged Alan closer. Outside the wind was howling—an eerie rushing that made the roof and walls creak.

When they arrived at the door to the hydroponics bay, Alan didn't hit the release button but looked down at her, a smile dancing about his lips.

"What?" she said.

"Nothing. Just grateful to be with you." And he gave her a quick peck on the lips.

She went for a peck of her own—the punch had put her in a *mood*—but he laughed, pulled his head away, and hit the button.

The door slid open with a solid *thunk*.

Warm air wafted over them, along with the sound of dripping water and the gentle perfume of flowering plants. The hydroponics bay was Kira's favorite place in the compound. It reminded her of home, of the long rows of hothouse gardens she'd spent time in as a kid on the colony planet of Weyland. During long-haul expeditions like the one to Adra, it was standard procedure to grow some of their own food. Partly so they could test the viability of the native soil. Partly to reduce the amount of supplies they had to bring with them. But mostly to break the deadly monotony of the freeze-dried meal packs the company supplied them with.

Tomorrow, Seppo would rip out the plants and stuff them into the incinerator. None of them would survive until the colonists arrived, and it was bad practice to leave piles of biological material sitting around where they could—if the compound were breached—enter the environment in an uncontrolled manner. But for tonight, the hydroponics bay was still full of lettuce, radishes, parsley, tomatoes, clusters of zucchini stems, and the numerous other crops Seppo had been experimenting with on Adra.

But that wasn't all. Amid the dim racks, Kira saw seven pots laid out in an arc. In each pot stood a tall, thin stem topped with a delicate purple flower that drooped under its own weight. A cluster of pollen-tipped stamens extended from within each blossom—like bursts of fireworks—while white speckles adorned their velvety inner throats.

Midnight Constellations! Her favorite flower. Her father had raised them, and even with his horticultural talent, they had given him no end of trouble. They were temperamental, prone to scab and blight, and intolerant of the slightest imbalance of nutrients.

"Alan," she said, overcome.

"I remembered you mentioned how much you liked them," he said.

"But . . . how did you manage to—"

"To grow them?" He smiled at her, clearly pleased by her reaction. "Seppo helped. He had the seeds on file. We printed them out and then spent the last three weeks trying to keep the damned things from dying."

"They're wonderful," Kira said, not even trying to hide the emotion in her voice.

He hugged her close. "Good," he said, his voice half-muffled in her hair. "I wanted to do something special for you before . . ."

Before. The word burned in her mind. "Thank you," she said. She separated from him just long enough to examine the flowers; their spicy, overly sweet scent struck her with the full, staggering force of childhood nostalgia. "Thank you," she repeated, coming back to Alan. "Thank you, thank you, thank you." She pressed her lips against his, and for a long while, they kissed.

"Here," said Alan when they broke for air. He pulled an insulated blanket from under one of the racks of potato plants and spread it out within the arc of Midnight Constellations.

They settled there, cuddling and sipping their punch.

Outside, the baleful immensity of Zeus still hung overhead, visible through the clear pressure dome of the hydroponics bay. When they'd first arrived on Adra, the sight of the gas giant had filled Kira with apprehension. Every instinct in her screamed that Zeus was going to fall out of the sky and crush them. It seemed impossible anything so large could remain suspended overhead without support. In time, though, she'd grown accustomed to the sight, and now she admired the magnificence of the gas giant. It needed no overlays to catch the eye.

Before . . . Kira shivered. Before they left. Before she and Alan had to part. They'd already used up their vacation days, and the company wouldn't give them more than a few days of downtime back at 61 Cygni.

"Hey, what's wrong?" said Alan, his voice soft with sympathy.

"You know."

". . . Yeah."

"This isn't getting any easier. I thought it would, but—" She sniffed and shook her head. Adra was their fourth time shipping together, and it was by far their longest shared posting. "I don't know when I'm going to see you next, and . . . I love you, Alan, and having to say goodbye every few months really sucks."

He stared at her, serious. His hazel eyes gleamed in the light from Zeus. "So then let's not."

Her heart lurched, and for a moment, time seemed to stop. She'd been dreading that exact response for months now. When her voice started working again, she said, "What do you mean?"

"I mean, let's not do this bouncing around anymore. I can't take it either." His expression was so open, so earnest, she couldn't help but feel a flicker of hope. Surely he wasn't . . . ?

"What would—"

"Let's apply for berths on the *Shakti-Uma-Sati*."

She blinked. "As colonists."

He nodded, eager. "As colonists. Company employees are pretty much guaranteed slots, and Adra is going to need all the xenobiologists and geologists they can get."

Kira laughed and then caught his expression. "You're serious."

"Serious as a pressure breach."

"That's just the drink talking."

He put a hand on her cheek. "No, Kira. It's not. I know this would be a huge change, for both of us, but I also know you're sick of jetting around from one rock to another, and I don't want to wait another six months to see you. I *really* don't."

Tears welled up in her eyes. "I don't want that either."

He cocked his head. "So then let's not."

Kira half laughed and looked up at Zeus while she tried to process her emotions. What he was suggesting was everything she'd hoped for, everything she'd dreamed of. She just hadn't expected it to happen so fast. But she loved Alan, and if this meant they could be together, then she wanted it. She wanted *him*.

The meteor-bright spark that was the *Fidanza* sailed past overhead, in low orbit between Adra and the gas giant.

She wiped her eyes. "I don't think the odds are as good as you say. Colonies only really want pair-bonded couples. You know that."

"Yes, I do," said Alan.

A sense of unreality caused Kira to grip the floor as he knelt in front of her and, from his front pocket, produced a small wooden box. He opened it. Nestled inside was a ring of grey metal set with a bluish-purple gem, startling in its brilliancy.

The lump in Alan's throat bobbed as he swallowed. "Kira Navárez . . . you asked me once what I saw among the stars. I told you I saw questions. Now, I see you. I see *us*." He took a breath. "Kira, will you do me the honor of joining your life with mine? Will you be my wife, as I will be your husband? Will—"

"*Yes,*" she said, all worries lost in the flush of warmth that suffused her. She put her hands around the back of his neck and kissed him, tenderly at first and then with increasing passion. "Yes, Alan J. Barnes. Yes, I'll marry you. Yes. A thousand times yes."

She watched as he took her hand and slid the ring onto her finger. The band was cold and heavy, but the heaviness was a comforting one.

"The ring is iron," he said softly. "I had Jenan smelt it from ore I brought him. Iron because it represents the bones of Adrasteia. The stone is tesserite. Wasn't easy to find, but I know how much you like it."

Kira nodded without meaning to. Tesserite was unique to Adrasteia; it was similar to benitoite, with a greater tendency toward purple. It was by far her favorite rock on the planet. But it was exceedingly rare; Alan must have searched long and hard to locate such a large, high-quality piece.

She brushed one of his coppery locks away from his forehead, and she stared into his beautiful soft eyes, wondering how she had gotten so lucky. How either of them had managed to find the other in the whole damn galaxy.

"I love you," she whispered.

"I love you too," he said.

Then Kira laughed, feeling almost hysterical, and wiped her eyes. The ring scraped her eyebrow; it was going to take time to get used to its presence. "Shit. Are we really going to do this?"

"Yeah," said Alan, with his comforting self-confidence. "We sure are."

"Good."

He pulled her closer then, his body hot against hers. Kira responded with equal need, equal desire, clinging to him as if she were trying to press herself through his skin and into his flesh until the two of them became one.

Together, they moved with frantic urgency within the arc of potted flowers, matching the rhythms of their bodies, oblivious to the orange gas giant that hung high overhead, huge and glaring.

CHAPTER II

* * * * * * *

RELIQUARY

1.

Kira tightened her grip on the arms of her seat as the suborbital shuttle pitched downward, descending toward island #302–01–0010, just off the western coast of Legba, the main continent in the southern hemisphere. The island lay on the fifty-second parallel, in a large bay guarded by several granite reefs, and was the last known location of the disabled drone.

A sheet of fire engulfed the front of the cockpit as the shuttle burned through Adrasteia's thin atmosphere at almost seven and a half thousand klicks per hour. The flames looked as if they were only a few inches from Kira's face, yet she felt no heat.

Around them, the hull rattled and groaned. She closed her eyes, but the flames remained jumping and writhing in front of her, bright as ever.

"Hell yeah!" shouted Neghar next to her, and Kira knew she was grinning like a fiend.

Kira gritted her teeth. The shuttle was perfectly safe, wrapped in the mag-shield that protected it from the white-hot inferno outside. Four months on the planet, hundreds of flights, and there hadn't been a single accident. Geiger, the pseudo-intelligence that piloted the shuttle, had a nearly flawless record; the only time it had malfunctioned was when some hotshot asteroid captain had tried to optimize a copy and ended up killing his crew as a result. Safety record notwithstanding, Kira still hated reentry. The noise and the shaking made her feel as if the shuttle were about to break up, and nothing could convince her otherwise.

Plus, the display wasn't doing anything to help her hangover. She'd popped a pill before leaving Alan in his cabin, but it had yet to cut the pain. It was her own fault. She should have known better. She *did* know better, but emotion had trumped judgment last night.

She turned off the feed from the shuttle's cameras and concentrated on breathing.

We're getting married! It still didn't feel real. She'd spent the whole morning with a silly smile plastered on her face. No doubt she'd looked like an idiot. She touched her sternum, fingering Alan's ring under her skinsuit. They hadn't told the others yet, so she'd chosen to wear the ring on a chain for the time being, but they were planning to that evening. Kira was looking forward to seeing everyone's reactions, even if the announcement didn't come as much of a surprise.

Once they were on the *Fidanza,* they would get Captain Ravenna to make it official. And then Alan would be hers. And she his. And they could begin to build their future together.

Marriage. A change of jobs. Settling down on just one planet. Family of her own. Helping to build a new colony. As Alan had said, it would be a huge change, but Kira felt ready for the shift. More than ready. It was the life she'd always hoped for but that, as the years crept by, had seemed increasingly unlikely.

After they finished making love, they had stayed up for hours, talking and talking. They'd discussed the best places to settle on Adrasteia, the timeline of the terraforming effort, and all the activities possible on and off the moon. Alan went into great detail about the type of dome house he wanted to build: "—and it has to have a hot tub big enough to stretch out without touching the other side, so we can have a proper bath, not like these dinky little showers we've been stuck with," and Kira had listened, touched by his passion. In turn, she talked about how she wanted greenhouses like the ones on Weyland, and they both agreed that whatever they did, it was going to be better done together.

Kira's only regret was that she'd drunk so much; everything after Alan's proposal had become something of a blur.

Delving into her overlays, she pulled up her records from the previous night. She saw Alan kneeling in front of her again, and she heard him say, "I love you too," before wrapping her in his embrace a minute later. When she'd had her implants installed as a kid, her parents hadn't paid for a system that allowed for full sense-recording—no touch, taste, or smell—as they'd considered it an unnecessary extravagance. For the first time, Kira wished they hadn't been so practically minded. She wanted to feel what she'd felt that night; she wanted to feel it for the rest of her life.

Once they returned to Vyyborg Station, she decided, she would use her bonus to have the necessary upgrades installed. Memories like the ones from yesterday were too precious to lose, and she was determined not to let any more slip away.

As for her family back on Weyland . . . Kira's smile faded somewhat. They wouldn't be happy about her living so far from home, but she knew they would understand. Her parents had done something similar themselves, after all: emigrating from Stewart's World, around Alpha Centauri, before she was born. And her father was always talking about how it was humanity's grand goal to spread out among the stars. They'd supported her decision to become a xenobiologist in the first place, and Kira knew they would support her current decision.

Returning to her overlays, she opened the most recent video from Weyland. She'd already watched it twice since it had arrived a month ago, but right then, she felt a sudden urge to see her home and family again.

Her parents appeared, as she knew they would, sitting at her dad's workstation. It was early morning, and the light slid in sideways through the west-facing windows. In the distance, the mountains were a jagged silhouette draped along the horizon, nearly lost in a bank of clouds.

"Kira!" said her dad. He looked the same as always. Her mom had a new haircut; she offered a small smile. "Congratulations on making it to the end of the survey. How are you enjoying your last few days on Adra? Did you find anything interesting in the lake region you told us about?"

"It's been cold here," said her mom. "There was frost on the ground this morning."

Her dad grimaced. "Fortunately the geothermal is working."

"For now," said her mom.

"For now. Other than that, no real news. The Hensens came by for dinner the other night, and they said—"

Then the study door slammed open and Isthah bounced into view, dressed in her usual nightshirt, a cup of tea in one hand. "Morning, sis!"

Kira smiled as she watched them natter on about the doings in the settlement and about their day-to-day activities: the problems with the ag-bots tending the crops, the shows they'd been watching, details about the latest batch of plants being released into the planet's ecosystem. And so forth.

Then they wished her safe travels and the video ended. The last frame hung before her, her dad frozen mid-wave, her mom's face at an odd angle as she finished saying, "—love you."

"Love you," Kira murmured. She sighed. When had she last managed to visit them? Two years ago? Three? At least that. Too long by far. The distances and the travel times didn't make it easy.

She missed home. Which didn't mean she would have been content to just stay on Weyland. She'd needed to push herself, to reach beyond the normal and the mundane. And she had. For seven years she had traveled the far reaches of space. But she was sick of being alone and sick of being cooped up on one spaceship after another. She was ready for a new challenge, one that balanced the familiar with the alien, the safe with the outlandish.

There on Adra, with Alan, she thought perhaps she would find just such a balance.

2.

Halfway through reentry, the turbulence began to subside and the EM interference vanished along with the sheets of plasma. Lines of yellow text appeared in the top corner of Kira's vision as the comm link to HQ went live again.

She scrolled through the messages, catching up with the rest of the survey team. Fizel, their doctor, was being his usual annoying self, but other than that, nothing interesting.

A new window popped up:

<How's the flight, babe? – Alan>

Kira was unprepared for the sudden tenderness his concern evoked in her. She smiled again as she subvocalized her response:

<No problems here. You? – Kira>

<Just doing a last bit of pickup. Thrilling stuff. Want me to clear out your cabin for you? – Alan>

She smiled. *<Thanks, but I'll take care of it when I'm back. – Kira>*

<'K . . . Listen, we didn't really get a chance to talk this morning, and I wanted to check: You still okay with everything from last night? – Alan>

<You mean, do I still want to marry you and settle here on Adra? – Kira> She followed up before he could reply: *<Yes. My answer is still yes. – Kira>*

<Good. – Alan>

<What about you? Are **you** *still okay? – Kira>* Her breath caught a little as she sent the text.

His answer was swift: *<Absolutely. I just wanted to make sure you were doing alright. – Alan>*

She felt herself soften. *<More than alright. And I appreciate that you bothered to check. – Kira>*

<Always, babe. Or should I say . . . fiancée? – Alan>

Kira made a delighted sound. It came out more choked than intended.

"All good?" Neghar asked, and Kira could feel the pilot's eyes on her.

"More than good."

She and Alan continued to talk until the retrorockets kicked in, jolting her back to full awareness of her surroundings.

<Gotta go. We're about to land. Touch base later. – Kira>

<'K. Have fun. ;-) – Alan>

<Riiight. – Kira>

Then Geiger spoke in her ear: "Touchdown in ten . . . nine . . . eight . . . seven . . ."

His voice was calm and emotionless, with a hint of a cultured Magellan accent. She thought of him as a Heinlein. He sounded as if he would be named Heinlein, if he were a person. Flesh and blood, that is. With a body.

They landed with a short drop that caused her stomach to lurch and her heart to race. The shuttle listed a few degrees to the left as it sank into the dirt.

"Don't take too long, you hear?" said Neghar, unclipping her harness. Everything about her was neat and compact, from her finely carved features to the folds in her jumpsuit to the thin lines of braids that formed a wide strip across her head. On her lapel she wore an ever-present gold pin: a memorial to co-workers lost on the job. "Yugo said he's cooking a fresh batch of cinnamon rolls as a special treat before blastoff. 'Less we hurry, they'll all be gone by the time we get back."

Kira pulled off her own harness. "I won't be a minute."

"Better not, honey. I'd *kill* for those rolls."

The stale smell of reprocessed air hit Kira's nose as she slipped on her helmet. Adrasteia's atmosphere was thick enough to breathe, but it would kill you if you tried. Not enough oxygen. Not yet, and changing that would take decades. The lack of oxygen also meant that Adra didn't have an ozone layer. Everyone who ventured outside had to be fully shielded against UV and other forms of radiation. Otherwise, you were liable to get the worst sunburn of your life.

At least the temperature's bearable, thought Kira. She wouldn't even have to turn on the heater in her skinsuit.

She climbed into the narrow airlock and pulled the inner hatch shut behind her. It closed with a metallic boom.

"Atmosphere exchange initialized; please stand by," said Geiger in her ear.

The indicator turned green. Kira spun the wheel in the center of the outer hatch and then pushed. The seal broke with a sticky, tearing sound, and the reddish light of Adrasteia's sky flooded the airlock.

The island was an unlovely heap of rocks and rust-colored soil, large enough that she couldn't see the far side, only the near coast. Beyond the edge of land spread an expanse of grey water, like a sheet of hammered lead, the tips of the waves highlighted with the ruddy light from the cloudless sky. A poison ocean, heavy with cadmium, mercury, and copper.

Kira jumped down from the airlock and closed it behind her. She frowned as she studied the telemetry from the downed drone. The organic material it had detected wasn't by the water, as she'd expected, but rather at the top of a wide hill a few hundred meters to the south.

Okay then. She made her way across the fractured ground, picking her steps with care. As she walked, blocks of text popped up in front of her, providing info on the chemical composition, local temperature, density, likely age, and radioactivity of different parts of the landscape. The scanner on her belt fed the readings into her overlays while simultaneously transmitting them back to the shuttle.

Kira dutifully reviewed the text but saw nothing new. The few times she felt compelled to take a soil sample, the results were as boring as ever: minerals, traces of organic and pre-organic compounds, and a scattering of anaerobic bacteria.

At the top of the hill, she found a flat spread of rock scored with deep grooves from the last planetary glaciation. A patch of orange, lichen-like bacteria covered much of the rock. Kira recognized the species at first glance—*B. loomisii*—but she took a scraping just to confirm.

Biologically, there wasn't much of interest on Adrasteia. Her most notable find had been a species of methane-eating bacteria beneath the arctic ice sheet—bacteria that had a somewhat unusual lipid structure in their cellular walls. But that was it. She'd write up an overview of Adrasteia's biome, of course, and if she was lucky, she might get it published in a couple of the more obscure journals, but it wasn't much to crow about.

Still, the absence of more developed forms of life was a plus when it came to terraforming: it left the moon a lump of raw clay, suitable for remolding however the company, and the settlers, saw fit. Unlike on Eidolon—beautiful, deadly Eidolon—they wouldn't have to be constantly fighting the native flora and fauna.

While Kira waited for her chip-lab to finish its analysis, she walked to the crest of the hill, took in the view of the rough-scraped rocks and the metallic ocean.

She frowned as she remembered how long it would be before they could stock the oceans with anything more than gene-spliced algae and plankton.

This is going to be our home. It was a sobering thought. But not depressing. Weyland wasn't much friendlier, and Kira remembered the massive improvements she had seen on the planet over the course of her childhood: once-barren dirt converted to fertile soil, the spread of green growing things across the landscape, the ability to walk around outside for a limited time without supplemental oxygen. She had optimism. Adrasteia was more habitable than 99-some percent of the planets in the galaxy. By astronomical standards, it was an almost perfect analogue for Earth, more similar than a high-g planet like Shin-Zar, and even more similar than Venus, with its floating cloud cities.

Whatever the difficulties Adrasteia presented, she was willing to face them if it meant she and Alan could be together.

We're getting married! Kira grinned and lifted her arms overhead, fingers splayed, and stared straight up, feeling as if she were about to burst. Nothing had ever felt so right.

A high-pitched *beep* sounded in her ear.

3.

The chip-lab had finished. She checked the readout. The bacteria was *B. loomisii,* as she'd thought.

Kira sighed and turned off the device. Mendoza had been right—it was their responsibility to check out the growth—but it was still a huge waste of time.

Whatever. Back to HQ and Alan, and then they could blast off for the *Fidanza.*

Kira started to leave the hill, and then, out of curiosity, she looked toward where the drone had crashed. Neghar had IDed and tagged the location during the shuttle's descent.

There. A klick and a half from the coast, near the center of the island, she saw a yellow box outlining a patch of ground next to . . .

"Huh."

A formation of jagged, pillar-shaped rocks stabbed out of the ground at a steep, sideways angle. In all the places Kira had visited on Adra—and they were many—she hadn't seen anything quite like it.

"Petra: select visual target. Analyze."

Her system responded. An outline flashed around the formation, and then a long list of elements scrolled next to it. Kira's eyebrows rose. She wasn't a geologist like Alan, but she knew enough to realize how unusual it was to have so many elements clustered together.

"Thermals up," she muttered. Her visor darkened, and the world around her became an impressionistic painting of blues, blacks, and—where the ground had absorbed the warmth of the sun—muted reds. As expected, the formation perfectly matched the ambient temperature.

<*Hey, check this out. – Kira*> And she forwarded the readings to Alan.

Less than a minute later: <*The hell! You sure your equipment is ? – Alan*>

<*Pretty sure. What do you think it is? – Kira*>

<*Dunno. Might be a lava extrusion . . . Can you get a scan of it? Maybe pick up a few samples? Dirt, rock, whatever is convenient. – Alan*>

<*If you really want. It's a bit of a hike, though. – Kira*>

<*I'll make it worth your while. – Alan*>

<*Mmm. I like the sound of that, babe. – Kira*>

<*Hey now. – Alan*>

She smirked and swapped out of the infrared as she started down the hill. "Neghar, do you read?"

A crackle of static and then: **What's up?**

"I'm going to be another half hour or so. Sorry."

Dammit! Those rolls aren't going to last more than—

"I know. There's something I have to investigate for Alan."

What?

"Some rocks, farther inland."

You're gonna give up Yugo's cinnamon rolls for THAT?

"Sorry, you know how it is. Besides, haven't seen anything quite like this before."

A moment of silence. **Fine. But you better haul ass, you hear me?**

"Roger that, hauling ass," said Kira. She chuckled and quickened her pace.

Where the uneven ground allowed, she jogged, and ten minutes later, she arrived at the tilted outcropping. It was bigger than she'd realized.

The highest point was a full seven meters overhead, and the base of the formation was over twenty meters across: wider even than the shuttle was long. The broken cluster of columns, black and faceted, reminded her of basalt, but their surface had an oily sheen similar to that of coal or graphite.

There was something about the appearance of the rocks that Kira found off-putting. They were too dark, too stark and sharp-edged, too different from the rest of the landscape—a ruined spire alone amid the granite wasteland. And though she knew it was her imagination, an uneasy air seemed to surround the outcropping, like a low vibration just strong enough to annoy. Were she a cat, Kira felt sure her hair would be standing on end.

She frowned and scratched her forearms.

It sure didn't look like there'd been a volcanic eruption in the area. Okay then, a meteor strike instead? But that didn't make sense either. No blast wall or crater.

She walked around the base, scanning. Near the back, she spotted the remnants of the drone: a long strip of broken and melted components dashed against the ground.

Hell of a lightning strike, Kira thought. The drone must have been going pretty fast to spread it out like that.

She shifted in her suit, still feeling uneasy. Whatever the formation was, she decided she'd leave the mystery for Alan to figure out. It would give him something to do on the flight out of the system.

She took a soil sample and then searched until she found a small piece of the black rock that had flaked off. She held it up to the sun. It had a distinct crystalline structure: a fish-scale-like pattern that reminded her of woven carbon fiber. *Impact crystals?* Whatever it was, it was unusual.

She tucked the rock into a sample pouch and gave the formation one last look-over.

A silvery flash, several meters off the ground, caught her eye.

Kira paused, studying it.

A crack had split open one of the columns to reveal a jagged white seam within. She checked her overlays: the seam was too deep within the crack to get a good reading. The only thing the scanner could tell her for sure was that it wasn't radioactive.

The comm crackled, and Neghar said, **How ya doing, Kira?**

"Almost done."

'K. Hurry up, would you?

"Yeah, yeah," Kira muttered to herself.

She eyed the crack, trying to decide if it was worth the effort to climb up and examine. She nearly contacted Alan to ask but then decided not to bother him. If she didn't find out what the seam was, she knew the question would annoy him until they, hopefully, returned to Adra and he got a chance to examine it himself.

Kira couldn't do that to him. She'd seen him stay up late far too many times, poring over blurred footage from a drone.

Besides, the crack wasn't *that* hard to reach. If she started *there* and went over to *that,* then maybe . . . Kira smiled. The challenge appealed to her. The skinsuit didn't have gecko pads installed, but it shouldn't matter, not for an easy climb like this.

She walked to a slanted column that ended only a meter above her head. Sucking in a quick breath, she dipped her knees and jumped.

The rough edge of the stone dug into her fingers as she caught hold of it. She swung a leg over the top of the column and then, with a grunt, pulled herself up.

Kira stayed on all fours, clutching the uneven stone while she waited for her heart to slow. Then she carefully got to her feet atop the column.

From there it was relatively easy. She jumped across to another angled column, which allowed her to scramble up several more, like climbing a giant staircase, aged and crumbling.

The last meter was a bit tricky; Kira had to wedge her fingers between two pillars in order to support herself as she swung from one foothold to another. Fortunately, there was a broad ledge beneath the crack she was trying to reach—broad enough that she had room to stand and move about.

She shook her hands to get the blood back into her fingers and walked over to the fissure, curious what she would find.

Up close, the gleaming white seam looked metallic and ductile, as if it were a vein of pure silver. Only it couldn't be; it wasn't tarnished.

She targeted the seam with her overlays.

Terbium?

Kira barely recognized the name. One of the elements in the platinum group, she thought. She didn't bother looking it up, but she knew it was odd for a metal like that to appear in such a pure form.

She leaned forward, peering deeper into the crack as she tried to get a better angle for the scanner. . . .

Bang! The sound was as loud as a gunshot. Kira jerked with surprise, and then her foot slipped, and she felt the stone shift underneath her as the whole ledge gave way.

She was falling—

An image flashed through her mind of her body lying broken on the ground.

Kira yelped and flailed, trying to grab the column in front of her, but she missed and—

Darkness swallowed her. Thunder filled her ears and lightning shot across her vision as her head bounced against the rocks. Pain shot through her arms and legs as she was pummeled from every direction.

The ordeal seemed to last for minutes.

Then she felt a sudden sense of weightlessness—

—and a second later, she slammed into a hard, jagged mound.

4.

Kira lay where she was, stunned.

The impact had knocked the breath out of her. She tried to fill her lungs, but her muscles wouldn't respond. For a moment she felt as if she were choking, and then her diaphragm relaxed and air rushed in.

She gasped, desperate for oxygen.

After the first few breaths, she forced herself to stop panting. No point in hyperventilating. It would only make it harder to function.

In front of her, all she saw was rock and shadow.

She checked her overlays: skinsuit still intact, no breaches detected. Elevated pulse and blood pressure, O_2 levels high normal, cortisol through the roof (as expected). To her relief, she didn't see any broken bones, although her right elbow felt as if it had been smashed by a hammer, and she knew she was going to be sore and bruised for days.

She wiggled her fingers and toes, just to test that they worked.

With her tongue, Kira tabbed two doses of liquid Norodon. She sucked the painkiller from her feeding tube and gulped it down, ignoring its sickly sweet taste. The Norodon would take a few minutes to reach full strength, but she could already feel the pain retreating to a dull ache.

She was lying on a pile of stone rubble. The corners and edges dug into her back with unpleasant insistence. Grimacing, she rolled off the mound and onto all fours.

The ground was surprisingly flat. Flat and covered with a thick layer of dust.

It hurt, but Kira pushed herself onto her feet and stood. The movement made her light-headed. She leaned on her thighs until the feeling passed and then turned and looked at her surroundings.

A ragged shaft of light filtered down from the hole she had fallen through, providing the only source of illumination. By it she saw that she was inside a circular cave, perhaps ten meters across—

No, not a cave.

For a moment she couldn't make sense of what she was seeing, the incongruity was so great. The ground was flat. The walls were smooth. The ceiling was curved and dome-like. And in the center of the space stood a . . . stalagmite? A waist-high stalagmite that widened as it rose.

Kira's mind raced as she tried to imagine how the space could have formed. A whirlpool? A vortex of air? But then there would be ridges everywhere, grooves . . . Could it be a lava bubble? But the stone wasn't volcanic.

Then she realized. The truth was so unlikely, she hadn't allowed herself to consider the possibility, even though it was obvious.

The cave wasn't a cave. It was a room.

"Thule," she whispered. She wasn't religious, but right then, prayer seemed like the only appropriate response.

Aliens. *Intelligent* aliens. A rush of fear and excitement swept through Kira. Her skin went hot, pinpricks of sweat sprang up across her body, and her pulse started to hammer.

Only one other alien artifact had ever been found: the Great Beacon on Talos VII. Kira had been four at the time, but she still remembered the moment the news had become public. The streets of Highstone had gone deathly quiet as everyone stared at their overlays, trying to digest the revelation that, no, humans weren't the only sentient race to have evolved in the galaxy. The story of Dr. Crichton, xenobiologist and member of the first expedition to the lip of the Beacon, had been one of Kira's earliest and greatest inspirations for wanting to become a xenobiologist herself. In her more fanciful moments, she had sometimes daydreamed of making a discovery that was equally momentous, but the odds of that actually happening had seemed so remote as to be impossible.

Kira forced herself to breathe again. She needed to keep a clear head.

No one knew what had happened to the makers of the Beacon; they were long dead or vanished, and nothing had been found to explain their nature, origin, or intentions. *Did they make this as well?*

Whatever the truth, the room was a find of historic significance. Falling into it was probably the most important thing she would ever do in her life. The discovery would be news through the whole of settled space. There would be interviews, appearance requests; *everyone* would be talking about it. Hell, the papers she could publish . . . Entire careers had been built on far, far less.

Her parents would be so proud. Especially her dad; further proof of intelligent aliens would delight him like nothing else.

Priorities. First she had to make sure she lived through the experience. For all she knew, the room could be an automated slaughterhouse. Kira double-checked her suit readouts, paranoid. Still no breaches. Good. She didn't have to worry about contamination from alien organisms.

She activated her radio. "Neghar, do you read?"

Silence.

Kira tried again, but her system couldn't connect to the shuttle. Too much stone overhead, she guessed. She wasn't worried; Geiger would have alerted Neghar something was wrong as soon as the feed from her skinsuit cut out. It shouldn't be long before help arrived.

She'd need help, too. There was no way she could climb out by herself, not without gecko pads. The walls were over four meters high and devoid of handholds. Through the hole, she could see a blotch of sky, pale and distant. She couldn't tell exactly how far she'd fallen, but it looked like enough to place her well below ground level.

At least it hadn't been a straight drop. Otherwise she would probably be dead.

Kira continued to study the room, not moving from where she stood. The chamber had no obvious entrances or exits. The pedestal that she had originally believed to be a stalagmite had a shallow, bowl-like depression in the top. A pool of dust had gathered within the depression, obscuring the color of the stone.

As her eyes adjusted to the darkness, Kira saw long blue-black lines cut into the walls and ceiling. The lines jagged at oblique angles, forming patterns similar to those of a primitive circuit board, although farther apart.

Art? Language? Technology? Sometimes it was difficult to tell the difference.

Was the place a tomb? Of course, the aliens might not bury their dead. There was no way of knowing.

"Thermals up," Kira murmured.

Her vision flipped, showing a muddy impression of the room, highlighted by the warmer patch of ground where the sunlight struck. No lasers, no artificial heat signatures of any sort.

"Thermals down."

The room could be studded with passive sensors, but if so, her presence hadn't triggered a noticeable response. Still, she had to assume she was being watched.

A thought occurred to Kira, and she switched off the scanner on her belt. For all she knew, the signals from the device might seem threatening to an alien.

She scrolled through the last set of readings from the scanner: background radiation was higher than normal due to an accumulation of radon gas, while the walls, ceiling, and floor contained the same mixture of minerals and elements she'd recorded on the surface.

Kira glanced at the blotch of sky again. Neghar wouldn't take long to reach the formation. Just a few minutes in the shuttle—a few minutes for Kira to examine the most important find of her life. Because once she was pulled out of the hole, Kira knew she wouldn't be allowed back in. By law, any evidence of alien intelligence had to be reported to the proper authorities in the League of Allied Worlds. They would quarantine the island (and probably a good portion of the continent) and send in their own team of experts to deal with the site.

That didn't mean she was about to break protocol. As much as she wanted to walk around, look at things closer, Kira knew she had a moral obligation not to disturb the chamber any further. Preserving its current condition was more important than any personal ambition.

So she held her ground, despite her almost unbearable frustration. If she could just *touch* the walls . . .

Looking back at the pedestal, Kira noticed the structure was level with her waist. Did that mean the aliens were about the same size as humans?

She shifted her stance, uncomfortable. The bruises on her legs were throbbing, despite the Norodon. A shiver ran through her, and she turned on the heater in her suit. It wasn't that cold in the room, but her hands and feet were freezing now that the adrenaline rush from the fall was subsiding.

Across the room, a knot of lines, no bigger than her palm, caught her attention. Unlike elsewhere on the curving walls, the lines—

Crack!

Kira glanced toward the sound just in time to see a melon-sized rock dropping toward her from the opening in the ceiling.

She yelped and stumbled forward awkwardly. Her legs tangled, and she fell onto her chest, hard.

The rock slammed into the floor behind her, sending up a hazy billow of dust.

It took Kira a second to catch her breath. Her pulse was hammering again, and at any moment, she expected alarms to sound and some hideously effective countermeasure to dispose of her.

But nothing happened. No alarms blared. No lights flashed. No trapdoors opened up beneath her. No lasers poked her full of tiny holes.

She pushed herself back onto her feet, ignoring the pain. The dust was soft beneath her boots, and it dampened the noise so the only sound she heard was her feathered breathing.

The pedestal was right in front of her.

Dammit, Kira thought. She should have been more careful. Her instructors back in school would have ripped her a new one for falling, even if it was a mistake.

She returned her attention to the pedestal. The depression in the top reminded her of a water basin. Beneath the pooled dust were more lines, scribed across the inner curve of the hollow. And . . . as she looked closer, there seemed to be a faint blue glow emanating from them, soft and diffuse beneath the pollen-like particles.

Her curiosity surged. *Bioluminescence?* Or was it powered by an artificial source?

From outside the structure, she heard the rising roar of the shuttle's engines. She didn't have long. No more than a minute or two.

Kira sucked on her lip. If only she could see more of the basin. She knew what she was about to do was wrong, but she couldn't help it. She had to learn *something* about this amazing artifact.

She wasn't so stupid as to touch the dust. That was the sort of rookie mistake that got people eaten or infected or dissolved by acid. Instead, she took the small canister of compressed air off her belt and used it to gently blow the dust away from the edge of the basin.

The dust flew up in swirled plumes, exposing the lines beneath. They *were* glowing, with an eerie hue that reminded her of an electrical discharge.

Kira shivered again, but not from cold. It felt as if she were intruding on forbidden ground.

Enough. She'd tempted fate far more than was wise. Time to make a strategic retreat.

She turned to leave the pedestal.

A jolt ran up her leg as her right foot remained stuck to the floor. She yelped, surprised, and fell to one knee. As she did, the Achilles tendon in her frozen ankle wrenched and tore, and she uttered a howl.

Blinking back tears, Kira looked down at her foot.

Dust.

A pile of black dust covered her foot. Moving, seething *dust.* It was pouring out of the basin, down the pedestal, and onto her foot. Even as she watched, it started to creep up her leg, following the contours of her muscles.

Kira yelled and tried to yank her leg free, but the dust held her in place as securely as a mag-lock. She tore off her belt, doubled it over, and used it to slap at the featureless mass. The blows failed to knock any of the dust loose.

"Neghar!" she shouted. "Help!"

Her heart pounding so loudly she could hear nothing else, Kira stretched the belt flat between her hands and tried to use it like a scraper on her thigh. The edge of the belt left a shallow impression in the dust but otherwise had no effect.

The swarm of particles had already reached the crease of her hip. She could feel them pressing in around her leg, like a series of tight, ever-shifting bands.

Kira didn't want to, but she had no other choice; with her right hand, she tried to grab the dust and pull it away.

Her fingers sank into the swarm of particles as easily as foam. There was nothing to grab hold of, and when she drew her hand back, the dust came with it, wrapping around her fingers with ropy tendrils.

"Agh!" She scrubbed her hand against the floor, but to no avail.

Fear spiked through her as she felt something tickle her wrist, and she knew that the dust had found its way through the seams of her gloves.

"Emergency override! Seal all cuffs." Kira had difficulty saying the words. Her mouth was dry, and her tongue seemed twice its normal size.

Her suit responded instantly, tightening around each of her joints, including her neck, and forming airtight seals with her skin. It wasn't enough to stop the dust. Kira felt the cold tickle progress up her arm to her elbow, and then past.

"Mayday! Mayday!" she shouted. "Mayday! Neghar! Geiger! Mayday! Can anyone hear me?! Help!"

Outside the suit, the dust flowed over her visor, plunging her into darkness. Inside the suit, the tendrils wormed their way over her shoulder and across her neck and chest.

Unreasoning terror gripped Kira. Terror and abhorrence. She jerked on her leg with all her strength. Something snapped in her ankle, but her foot remained anchored to the floor.

She screamed and clawed at her visor, trying to clear it off.

The dust oozed across her cheek and toward the front of her face. She screamed again and then clamped her mouth shut, closed off her throat, and held her breath.

Her heart felt as if it were going to explode.

Neghar!

The dust crept over her eyes, like the feet of a thousand tiny insects. A moment later, it covered her mouth. And when it came, the dry, squirming touch within her nostrils was no less horrible than she had imagined.

. . . stupid . . . shouldn't have . . . Alan!

Kira saw his face in front of her, and along with her fear, she felt an overwhelming sense of unfairness. This wasn't supposed to be how things ended! Then the weight in her throat became too great and she opened her mouth to scream as the torrent of dust rushed inside of her.

And all went blank.

CHAPTER III

* * * * * * *

EXTENUATING CIRCUMSTANCES

1.

To start with, there was the awareness of awareness.

Then an awareness of pressure, soft and comforting.

Later still, an awareness of sounds: a faint chirp that repeated, a distant rumble, the whir of recycled air.

Last of all came an awareness of self, rising from within the depths of blackness. It was a slow process; the murk was thick and heavy, like a blanket of silt, and it stifled her thoughts, weighing them down and burying them in the deepness. The natural buoyancy of her consciousness prevailed, though, and in time, she woke.

2.

Kira opened her eyes.

She was lying on an exam table in sickbay, at HQ. Above her, a pair of light-strips striped the bracketed ceiling, blue-white and harsh. The air was cool and dry and smelled of familiar solvents.

I'm alive.

Why was that surprising? And how had she ended up in sickbay? Weren't they supposed to be leaving for the *Fidanza*?

She swallowed, and the foul taste of hibernation fluids caused her to gag. Her stomach turned as she recognized the taste. *Cryo?* She'd been in fucking *cryo*? Why? For how long?

What the hell had happened?!

Panic spiked her pulse, and Kira bolted upright, clawing at the blanket that covered her. "Gaaah!" She was wearing a thin medical gown, tied at the sides.

The walls swam around her with cryo-induced vertigo. She pitched forward and fell off the table onto the white decking, heaving as her body tried to expel the poison inside of her. Nothing came up except drool and bile.

"Kira!"

She felt hands turning her over, and then Alan appeared above her, cradling her with gentle arms. "Kira," he said again, his face pinched with concern. "Shhh. It's okay. I've got you now. Everything's okay."

He looked nearly as bad as Kira felt. His cheeks were hollow, and there were lines around his eyes she didn't remember from that morning. *Morning?* "How long?" she croaked.

Alan winced. "Almost four weeks."

"No." Dread sank into her. "Four *weeks*?" Unable to believe it, Kira checked her overlays: 1402 GST, Monday, August 16, 2257.

Stunned, she read the date twice more. Alan was right. The last day she recalled, the day they'd been supposed to depart Adra, was the twenty-first of July. *Four weeks!*

Feeling lost, she searched Alan's face, hoping for answers. "Why?"

He stroked her hair. "What do you remember?"

Kira struggled to answer. "I—" Mendoza had told her to check on the downed drone, and then . . . and then . . . falling, pain, glowing lines, and darkness, darkness all around.

"Ahhh!" She scrabbled backwards and clutched at her neck, heart pounding. It felt as if something were blocking her throat, suffocating her.

"Relax," said Alan, keeping a hand on her shoulder. "Relax. You're safe now. Breathe."

A clutch of agonized seconds, and then her throat loosened and she sucked in a breath, desperate for air. Kira shuddered and grabbed Alan and held him as tight as she could. She'd never been prone to panic attacks, not even during finals for her IPD, but the feeling of being suffocated had been so *real*. . . .

His voice muffled by her hair, Alan said, "It's my fault. I should never have asked you to check out those rocks. I'm so sorry, babe."

"No, don't apologize," she said, pulling back enough to look at his face. "Someone had to do it. Besides, I found alien ruins. How amazing is that?"

"Pretty amazing," he admitted with a reluctant smile.

"See? Now, what—"

Footsteps sounded outside sickbay, and Fizel walked in. He was slim and dark and kept a short, faded haircut that never seemed to grow out. Today he was wearing his clinician's jacket, and his cuffs were rolled back, as if he'd been giving an exam.

On seeing Kira, he leaned back out the doorway and shouted, "She's up!" Then he sauntered past the three patient beds set along the wall, picked up a chip-lab off the small counter, squatted next to Kira, and grabbed her wrist. "Open. Say *ah*."

"Ah."

In quick succession, he looked in her mouth and ears, checked her pulse and blood pressure, and felt under her jaw, saying, "Does this hurt?"

"No."

He nodded, a sharp gesture. "You'll be fine. Make sure to drink lots of water. You'll need it after being in cryo."

"I *have* been frozen before," said Kira, as Alan helped her back onto the exam table.

Fizel's mouth twisted. "Just doing my job, Navárez."

"Uh-huh." Kira scratched her forearm. As much as she hated to admit it, the doctor was right. She was dehydrated, and her skin was dry and itchy.

"Here," said Alan, and handed her a water pouch.

As Kira took a sip, Marie-Élise, Jenan, and Seppo rushed into sickbay.

"Kira!"

"There you are!"

"Welcome back, sleepyhead!"

Behind them, Ivanova appeared, arms crossed, no-nonsense. "Well it's about time, Navárez!"

Then Yugo, Neghar, and Mendoza joined them as well, and the entire survey team crowded into sickbay, packing in so close that Kira felt the heat from their bodies and the touch of their breath. It was a welcome cocoon of life.

And yet, despite the nearness of her friends, Kira still felt odd and unsettled, as if the universe were out of joint, like a tilted mirror. Partly because of the weeks she had lost. Partly, she thought, because of whatever drugs Fizel had pumped into her. And partly because, if she allowed herself to sink into the depths of her mind, she could still feel something lurking there, waiting for her . . . a horrible, choking, suffocating presence, like wet clay being pressed into her nose and mouth—

She dug the nails of her right hand into her left forearm and inhaled sharply, nostrils flaring. No one but Alan seemed to notice; he gave her a worried glance and his arm tightened around her waist.

Kira shook herself in an attempt to dislodge her thoughts and, looking around at them all, said, "So who's going to fill me in?"

Mendoza grunted. "Give us your report first, and then we'll bring you up to speed."

It took Kira a moment to realize that the team hadn't come just to greet her. There was an anxious look to them, and as she studied their faces, she saw the same signs of stress as on Alan. Whatever they had been dealing with for the past four weeks, it hadn't been easy.

"Uh, is this going to be on the record, boss?" she asked.

Mendoza's face remained hard and fixed, unreadable. "On the record, Navárez, and it won't just be the company seeing it, either."

Shit. She swallowed, still tasting the hibernation fluids on the back of her tongue. "Could we do this in an hour or two? I'm pretty out of it."

"No can do, Navárez." He hesitated, and then added, "It's better talking to us rather than . . ."

"Someone else," said Ivanova.

"Exactly."

Kira's confusion deepened. Her worry too. She glanced at Alan, and he nodded and gave her a comforting squeeze. *Okay.* If he thought this was the right thing to do, then she'd trust him.

She took a breath. "The last thing I remember is heading out to check on the organic material the drone tagged before crashing. Neghar Esfahani was piloting. We landed on island number—"

It didn't take Kira long to summarize what had followed, ending with her fall into the strange rock formation and the room deep within. She did her best to describe the room, but at that point, her memory became so disjointed as to be unusable. (Had the lines on the pedestal really been glowing, or was that an artifact of her imagination?)

"And that's all you saw?" said Mendoza.

Kira scratched at her arm. "It's all I remember. I think I tried to stand up and then . . ." She shook her head. "Everything after that is blank."

The expedition boss scowled and stuffed his hands in his overall pockets.

Alan kissed her on the temple. "I'm sorry you had to go through that."

"Did you touch anything?" Mendoza said.

Kira thought. "Just where I fell."

"Are you sure? When Neghar pulled you out, there were marks in the dust on and around the pillar in the center of the room."

"As I said, the last thing I remember is trying to stand up." She cocked her head. "Why don't you check the recording from my suit?"

Mendoza surprised her by grimacing. "The fall damaged your suit's sensors. The telemetry is useless. Your implants weren't much help either. They stopped recording forty-three seconds after you entered the room. Fizel says that's not uncommon with traumatic head injuries."

"Were my implants damaged?" Kira asked, suddenly concerned. Her overlays *seemed* normal.

"Your implants," said Fizel, "are in perfect working order." His lip curled. "More than can be said for the rest of you."

She stiffened, unwilling to let him see how frightened that made her. "Just how badly was I hurt?"

Alan started to answer, but the doctor overrode him. "Hairline fractures in two ribs, chipped cartilage in your right elbow, along with a strained tendon. Fractured ankle, ruptured Achilles, multiple bruises and lacerations, and a moderate to severe concussion accompanied by cerebral swelling." Fizel ticked off each injury on his fingers as he spoke. "I repaired most of the damage; the rest will heal in a few weeks. In the meantime, you may experience some soreness."

At that, Kira nearly laughed. Sometimes humor was the only rational response.

"I was *really* worried about you," Alan said.

"We all were," said Marie-Élise.

"Yeah," said Kira, tightening her hold on Alan. She could only imagine what it had been like for him, waiting for her these past weeks. "So, Neghar, you managed to haul me out of that hole?"

The woman wobbled her hand in front of her. "Eh. So-so. It took some doing."

"But you got me out."

"Sure did, honey."

"Next chance I get, I'm buying you a whole *case* of cinnamon rolls."

Mendoza snared Fizel's exam stool and sat. He rested his hands on his knees, arms straight. "What she's not telling you is—You know what? Tell her, go ahead and tell her."

Neghar rubbed her arms. "Shit. Well, you were unconscious, so I had to strap us together so I could keep you from getting your head ripped off or something when Geiger winched you out. There wasn't much room in the tunnel you fell through, and, well—"

"She tore her skinsuit," said Jenan.

Neghar extended a hand toward him. "That. Full—" A cough interrupted her, and she doubled over for a moment, hacking. Her lungs sounded wet, as if she had bronchitis. "Guh. Full pressure breach. Was a bitch to patch with one hand while hanging from a harness."

"Which meant," said Mendoza, "that Neghar had to be quarantined along with you. We ran every test in the book, including some that aren't. They all came up negative, but you were still unresponsive—"

"Which was scary as fuck," said Alan.

"—and since we didn't know *what* we were dealing with, I decided it was better to put both of you into cryo until we got a handle on the situation."

Kira winced. "Sorry about that."

"Don't worry about it," said Neghar.

Fizel thumped himself on the chest. "What of poor me? You forget about me. Cryo is easy. I had to stay in quarantine for almost a month after working on you, Navárez. *A month*."

"And I appreciate your help," said Kira. "Thank you." She meant it too. A month in quarantine would wear on anyone.

"Bah. You shouldn't have been poking your bony nose where it didn't belong. You—"

"Enough," said Mendoza in a mild tone, and the doctor subsided, but not without flicking his index and middle fingers toward her in a way that Kira had learned was a rude gesture. A *very* rude gesture.

She took another sip of water to fortify herself. "So. Why did you wait so long to thaw us out?" Her gaze shifted back to Neghar. "Or did they wake you up sooner?"

Neghar coughed again. "Two days ago."

Around the room, Kira noticed faces tightening, and the mood growing tense, uncomfortable. "What is it?" she asked.

Before Mendoza could answer, the roar of a firing rocket—louder than any of their shuttles—sounded outside and the walls of the compound shuddered as if from a minor earthquake.

Kira flinched, but none of the others seemed surprised. "What was *that*?" On her overlays, she checked the feed from the cameras outside. All she could see were billows of smoke expanding from the landing pad some distance from the buildings.

The roar quickly receded as whatever vessel was taking off vanished into the upper atmosphere.

Mendoza stabbed a finger toward the ceiling. "*That's* the problem. After Neghar brought you back, I told Captain Ravenna, and she sent an emergency flash to the suits at Sixty-One Cygni. After that, the *Fidanza* went radio silent."

Kira nodded. That made sense. The law was clear: in the event of discovering intelligent alien life, they were to take all necessary measures to avoid leading those aliens back to settled space. Not that a technologically advanced species would have much difficulty finding the League if they were motivated to look.

"Ravenna was spitting antimatter she was so mad," said Mendoza. "The crew of the *Fidanza* weren't planning on having to stay here for more than a few days." He waved a hand. "In any case, once corporate got the message, they alerted the Department of Defense. Couple of days later, the UMC dispatched one of their cruisers, the *Extenuating Circumstances,* from Sixty-One Cygni. They arrived in-system about four days ago, and—"

"And ever since, they've been a royal pain in the ass," said Ivanova.

"Literally," said Seppo.

"Bastards," Neghar muttered.

The UMC. Kira had seen enough of the League's military, both on and off Weyland, to know how they tended to run roughshod over local concerns. One of the reasons, she thought, was the relative newness of the service; the League, and thus the United Military Command, had only been created in the wake of the discovery of the Great Beacon. A *coming together* had been needed, the politicians claimed, given the implications of the Beacon. Growing pains were to be expected. But the other reason for the UMC's often callous disregard, Kira believed, was the imperialistic attitude of Earth and the rest of Sol. They thought nothing of ignoring the rights of the colonies in favor of what was best for Earth, or what they called "the greater good." Good for whom, though?

Another grunt from Mendoza. "Captain of the *Extenuating Circumstances* is a cat-eyed SOB by the name of Henriksen. Real piece of work. His main concern was that Neghar here had picked up some sort of contamination in those ruins. So Henriksen sent down his doctor and a team of xenobiologists and—"

"And they set up a clean room and spent the past two days poking and prodding us until we puked," said Jenan.

"Literally," said Seppo.

Marie-Élise nodded. "It was *so* unpleasant, Kira. You are lucky you were still in cryo."

"I guess," she said slowly.

Fizel snorted. "They irradiated every square centimeter of our skin, multiple times. They X-rayed us. They gave us MRIs and CAT scans, ran full blood panels, sequenced our DNA, examined our urine and feces, and took biopsies; you may notice a slight mark on your abdomen from the liver sample. They even cataloged our gut bacteria."

"And?" said Kira, glancing from face to face.

"Nothing," said Mendoza. "Clean bill of health, for Neghar, for you, for all of us."

Kira frowned. "Wait, they tested me also?"

"You better believe it," said Ivanova.

"Why? Do you think you're too special to be examined?" asked Fizel. His tone set Kira's teeth on edge.

"No, I just . . ." She felt weird—violated even—knowing those procedures had been performed on her while she was unconscious, even if they *had* been necessary to maintain proper biocontainment.

Mendoza seemed to pick up on her discomfort. He eyed her from beneath his heavy brows. "Captain Henriksen made it abundantly clear that the *only* reason he isn't keeping us under lock and key is because they found nothing unusual. Neghar is the one they were really worried about, but they weren't going to let *any* of us off Adrasteia until they were sure."

"You can't blame them," said Kira. "I'd be doing the same in their place. Hard to be too careful in this sort of situation."

Mendoza huffed. "I don't blame them for *that.* It's the rest of it. They put us under a strict gag order. We can't even talk to corporate about what we found. If we do, it's a felony and up to twenty years in prison."

"How long is the gag order?"

His shoulders rose and fell. "Indefinite."

There went Kira's plans for publication, at least in the near term. "How are we supposed to explain why we're so late returning from Adra?"

"Drive malfunction on the *Fidanza* resulting in unavoidable delays. You'll find the details in your messages. Memorize them."

"Yessir." She scratched her arm again. She needed lotion. "Well, that's a hassle, but it's not *that* bad."

A pained expression crossed Alan's face. "Oh it gets worse, babe. A lot worse."

Kira's sense of dread returned. "Worse?"

Mendoza nodded slowly, as if his head was too heavy for his neck. "The UMC didn't just quarantine the island."

"Nope," said Ivanova. "That would have been too easy."

Fizel slammed his hand down on the counter. "Just tell her already! They quarantined the whole damn system, okay? We lost Adra. It's gone. Poof!"

3.

Kira sat next to Alan in the mess hall, studying a live image of the *Extenuating Circumstances* taken from orbit and projected from the holo in front of them.

The ship must have been half a kilometer long. Stark white, with a spindly midsection, bulbous engine at one end, and a petal-like arrangement of spinning decks at the other. The habitat sections were hinged so they could lie flat against the stem of the ship when under thrust, a costly option that most vessels went without. At the nose of the *Extenuating Circumstances* were several ports, like shuttered eyes: missile tubes and lenses for the ship's main laser.

A quarter of the way down the ship, a pair of identical shuttles fitted snugly against either side of the hull. The shuttles were far larger than the ones the survey team had used. Kira wouldn't be surprised if they were equipped with Markov Drives, same as a full-sized spaceship.

The most striking feature of the *Extenuating Circumstances* was the banks of radiators that lined its midsection, starting directly behind the habitats and continuing all the way down to the swell of the engine. The edges of the diamond fins flashed and gleamed as they caught the light of the sun, and the tubes of molten metal embedded within the fins shone like silver veins.

In all, the ship looked like a huge, deadly insect: thin, sharp, and glittery.

"Hey," said Alan, and she tore her attention away from the overlays to see him holding out her engagement ring, almost as if he were proposing again. "Thought you might want this."

Despite her worries, Kira softened for a moment, feeling a welcome warmth. "Thank you," she said, slipping the iron band onto her finger. "I'm glad I didn't lose it in that cave."

"Me too." Then he leaned in close and murmured, "Missed you."

She kissed him. "Sorry for making you worry."

"Congratulations to the both of you, *chérie,*" said Marie-Élise, and she wiggled her finger from Kira to Alan.

"Yeah, congrats," said Jenan, and everyone else added their well-wishes. Everyone but Mendoza—who was off radioing Ravenna to set up a pickup time for the following day—and Fizel—who was cleaning his fingernails with a plastic butter knife.

Kira smiled, pleased and somewhat self-conscious. "Hope you don't mind," said Alan, bending down toward her. "I kinda let it slip when it looked like you weren't going to wake up."

She leaned back against him and gave him another quick kiss. *Mine,* she thought. "It's fine," she murmured.

Then Yugo came over to them and knelt by the end of the table so he wasn't looming over Kira. "Do you think you can eat?" he asked her. "It would do you some good."

Kira wasn't hungry, but she knew he was right. "I can try."

He nodded, spade-shaped chin touching the top of his chest. "I'll warm up some stew for you. You'll like it. Nice and easy on the stomach."

As he lumbered away, Kira returned her attention to the *Extenuating Circumstances.* She scrubbed at her arms again and then started to fiddle with the ring on her finger.

Her head was still spinning from Mendoza's revelation, and her earlier sense of disassociation had returned even stronger than before. She hated that all their work over the past four months had been for nothing, but more than that, she hated the thought of losing the future she and Alan had planned together on Adrasteia. If they weren't going to settle there, then—

Alan must have guessed what she was thinking, because he leaned down so his lips were close to her ear and said, "Don't worry. We'll find another place. It's a big galaxy."

And that was why she loved him.

She hugged him tighter.

"What I don't understand—" she started to say.

"There are a lot of things I don't understand," said Jenan. "Like, who keeps leaving their napkins in the sink?" And he held up a soggy piece of cloth.

Kira ignored him. "How can the League expect to keep any of this a secret? People are going to notice that a whole system has been marked off-limits."

Seppo hopped up to sit cross-legged on one of the tables. With his slight stature, he looked almost childlike. "Easy. They announced the travel ban a week ago. The story is we discovered a contagious pathogen in the biosphere. Something like the Scourge. Until containment is assured—"

"Sigma Draconis stays quarantined," said Ivanova.

Kira shook her head. "Shit. I don't suppose they let us keep any of our data."

"Nope," said Neghar.

"Nada," said Jenan.

"Nothing," said Seppo.

"Zip," said Ivanova.

Alan rubbed her shoulder. "Mendoza said he'd talk with corporate when we get back to Vyyborg. They might be able to convince the League to release everything unrelated to the ruins."

"Small chance of *that,*" said Fizel. He blew on his nails and then continued cleaning them. "Not with the League. They'll keep your little discovery a secret for as long as they can. The only reason they ever told anyone about Talos Seven is because there's no way to hide the damn thing." He wagged his butter knife at Kira. "You cost the company a whole planet. Pleased with yourself?"

"I was doing my *job,*" she said. "If anything, it's good I found the ruins now, before anyone settled on Adra. It would cost a hell of a lot more to ship a whole colony back *off*-world."

Seppo and Neghar nodded.

Fizel sneered. "Yeah, well, that still doesn't make up for screwing us out of our bonuses."

"They canceled our bonuses," Kira said flatly.

Alan made an apologetic face. "Corporate said it was on account of project failure."

"Sucks too," said Jenan. "I've got kids to feed, you know? It would have made a big difference."

"Me too—"

"Same. Two ex-husbands and a cat ain't—"

"If you'd only—"

"Don't know how I'm going to—"

Kira's cheeks burned as she listened. It wasn't her fault, and yet it *was*. The whole team had lost out because of her. What a disaster. At the time she'd thought finding the alien structure was going to be good for the company, good for the team, but it had just ended up hurting them. She glanced at the logo printed on the wall of the mess hall: *Lapsang* printed in the familiar angular font with a leaf over the second *a.* The company was always running ads and promotional campaigns touting their loyalty to customers, colonists, and employee-citizens. "Forging the future together." That had been the slogan she'd grown up hearing. She snorted. *Yeah, right.* When it mattered, they were just like any other interstellar corporation: bits before people.

"Dammit," she said. "We did the work. We fulfilled our contract. They shouldn't punish us for it."

Fizel rolled his eyes. "And if starships farted rainbows, wouldn't that be lovely? My *God.* Oh you feel bad, so sorry. Who cares? That's not going to get us our bonuses back." He glared at her. "You know, it would have been better if you tripped and broke your neck as soon as you stepped out of the shuttle."

A brief, shocked silence followed.

Next to her, Kira felt Alan stiffen. "You take that back," he said.

Fizel tossed the knife into the sink. "Didn't want to be here anyway. Waste of time." And he spat on the floor.

Ivanova hopped away from the gob of saliva. "Goddamn it, Fizel!"

The doctor smirked and sauntered off. There was someone like him on every mission, Kira had learned. A sour shitheel who seemed to take perverse pleasure in being the piece of grit stuck in everyone's teeth.

The others started talking the moment Fizel was out of sight:

"Don't mind him," said Marie-Élise.

"Could have happened to any of us—"

"Same old Doc, always—"

"Should have heard what he said when I thawed out. He—"

The conversation stalled as Mendoza appeared in the doorway. He gave them a measured look. "There a problem in here?"

"Nossir."

"We're good, boss man."

He grunted and trundled over to Kira and, in a lower voice, said, "Sorry about that, Navárez. Nerves have been stretched a bit tight the past few weeks."

Kira smiled wanly. "It's okay. Really."

Another grunt, and Mendoza took a seat by the far wall, and the room soon returned to normal.

Despite her reply, Kira couldn't seem to lose the knot of unease in her gut. Too much of what Fizel had said struck home. Also, it bothered her not knowing what she and Alan were going to do now. Everything she'd laid out in her mind for the next few years had been overturned by that damned alien structure. If only the drone hadn't gone down. If only she hadn't agreed to check the site for Mendoza. If only . . .

She started as Yugo touched her on the arm.

"Here," he said, and handed her a bowl filled with stew and a plate piled with steamed vegetables, a slice of bread, and half of what must have been their only remaining bar of chocolate.

"Thanks," she murmured, and he smiled.

4.

Kira hadn't realized how hungry she was; she felt weak and shaky. The food didn't sit well, though. She was too upset, and her stomach kept rumbling from a combination of anxiety and the remnants of cryo.

From his spot on the neighboring table, Seppo said, "We've been trying to decide whether the ruins here were made by the same aliens who made the Great Beacon. Whaddya think, Kira?"

She noticed the others watching her. She swallowed, put down her fork, and in her best professional voice said, "It seems . . . it seems unlikely that two sentient species could have evolved so close together. If I had to bet, I'd say *yes*, but there's no knowing for sure."

"Hey, there's us," said Ivanova. "Humans. We're in the same general region."

In the corner, Neghar was coughing again, a wet, meaty sound that Kira found off-putting.

Jenan said, "Yeah, but there's no telling how much territory the Beacon xenos covered. It could have been half the galaxy for all we know."

"I think we would have found more evidence of them if that were the case," said Alan.

"Well, didn't we just?" said Jenan.

Kira had no easy answer to that. "Did you learn anything more about the site while I was in cryo?"

"Mmm," said Neghar, and held up a hand while she struggled to finish coughing into her sleeve. "Gah. Sorry. Throat's been dry all day. . . . Yeah. I ran some subsurface imaging before I pulled you out of the hole."

"And?"

"There's another chamber, right below the one you discovered. It's pretty small, though, only a meter across. It might be housing a power source, but it's impossible to tell for sure without opening it up. Thermals didn't pick up any heat signature."

"How large is the whole structure?"

"Everything you saw above ground, plus another twelve meters below. Aside from the rooms, it looks like just solid foundation and walls."

Kira nodded, thinking. Whoever had made the structure, they had built it to last.

Then Marie-Élise said, in her high, flutelike voice, "The building you found doesn't seem like the same sort of work as the Beacon. That is, it's such a small thing in comparison."

The Great Beacon. It had been discovered out on the edge of explored space, 36.6 light-years from Sol and 43-some light-years from Weyland. Kira didn't need to check her overlays to know the distances; she'd spent hours upon hours as a teen reading about the expedition.

The Beacon itself was an amazing artifact. It was, quite simply, a hole. A very *large* hole: fifty kilometers across and thirty deep, surrounded by a net of liquid gallium that acted as a giant antenna. For the hole emitted a powerful EMP burst every 5.2 seconds, and with it, a blast of structured noise that contained ever-evolving iterations of the Mandelbrot set in ternary code.

Attending the Beacon were creatures that had been dubbed "turtles," although Kira thought they looked more like ambulatory boulders. Even after twenty-three years of study, it still wasn't clear if they were animals or machines (no one had been foolish enough to attempt a dissection). The xenobiologists and the engineers agreed it was unlikely the turtles had been responsible for the Beacon's construction—not unless they'd lost all their technology—but who or what *was* responsible was still a mystery.

As for its ultimate purpose, no one had any idea. The only thing they knew for sure was that the Beacon was around sixteen thousand years old. And even that was merely a rough estimate based on radiometric dating.

Kira had an uncomfortable suspicion she might never find out whether or not the makers of the Beacon had anything to do with the room she'd fallen into. Not even if she lived for several hundred more years. Deep time was slow to surrender its secrets, if ever it did.

She sighed and dragged the tines of her fork across the side of her neck, enjoying the sensation of the metal tips on her dry skin.

"Who cares about the Beacon," said Seppo, hopping down from his table.

"What really bothers me is that we can't even make any money off this mess. Can't talk about it. Can't publish. Can't go on the talk shows—"

"Can't sell the entertainment rights," said Ivanova in a mocking tone.

They laughed, and Jenan called out, "As if anyone would want to see *your* ugly face."

He ducked as she threw her gloves at him. Chuckling, he offered them back to her.

Kira hunched her shoulders, her sense of guilt strengthening. "Sorry for the trouble, everyone. If there was anything I could do to fix this, I would."

"Yeah, you sure dicked things up good this time," said Ivanova.

"Did you *have* to go exploring?" Jenan said, but he didn't sound serious.

"Don't worry about it," said Neghar. "It . . . it could have . . ."

A cough interrupted her, and Marie-Élise finished what she'd been saying: "It could have been any of us."

Neghar bobbed her head in agreement.

From the wall where he was sitting, Mendoza said, "I'm just glad you weren't too badly hurt, Kira. You and Neghar. We lucked out, all of us."

"We still lost the colony," Kira said. "And our bonuses."

A sharp glint appeared in Mendoza's dark eyes. "Somehow I think your find will more than make up for those bonuses. Might take years. Might take decades. But long as we're smart, it'll happen, sure as death and taxes."

CHAPTER IV

* * * * * * *

ANGUISH

1.

It was late, and Kira found it increasingly difficult to focus on the conversation. Most of the words slipped past her in a stream of meaningless sound. At last, she roused herself and glanced over at Alan. He nodded, understanding, and they extricated themselves from their chairs.

"Night," said Neghar. One-word responses had been all she could manage for the past hour or so. Anything more and the coughing cut her off. Kira hoped she wasn't getting sick; everyone in the group would probably catch the same bug then.

"Night, *chérie,*" said Marie-Élise. "Things will seem better tomorrow. You'll see."

"Make sure you're up by oh nine hundred," said Mendoza. "The UMC finally gave us the all-clear, so we blast off at eleven for the *Fidanza.*"

Kira raised a hand and stumbled off with Alan.

Without discussing it, they went straight to his room. There, Kira pulled off her fatigues, dropped them on the floor, and climbed into bed, not even bothering to brush her hair.

Four weeks of cryo, and she was still exhausted. Cold sleep wasn't the same as real sleep. Nothing was.

The mattress sagged as Alan lay next to her. One of his arms wrapped around her, his hand grasped hers, and his chest and legs pressed against her: a warm, comforting presence. She uttered a faint sound and leaned back against him.

"I thought I'd lost you," he whispered.

She turned to face him. "Never." He kissed her, and she him, and after a time, gentle caresses grew more eager, and they clung to each other with fervent intensity.

They made love, and never had Kira felt more intimate with Alan, not even when he had proposed. She could feel his fear of losing her in every line of his body, and she could see his love in every touch, hear it in every murmured word.

Afterward, they stumbled over to the narrow shower at the back of the room. Keeping the lights dim, they bathed, soaping each other and talking in lowered voices.

As she let the hot water beat across her back, Kira said, "Neghar didn't sound too good."

Alan shrugged. "It's just a bit of cryo sickness. The UMC cleared her. Fizel too. The air in here is so dry—"

"Yeah."

They toweled off, and then with Alan's help, Kira slathered lotion across her whole body. She sighed with relief as the cream went on, soothing the prickling of her skin.

Back in bed, with the lights turned off, Kira did her best to fall asleep. But she couldn't stop thinking about the room with the circuit-board patterns, nor what her discovery had cost the team (and her personally). Nor the words Fizel had thrown at her.

Alan noticed. "Stop it," he murmured.

"Mmm. It's just . . . What Fizel said—"

"Don't let him get to you. He's just pissed and frustrated. No one else feels that way."

"Yeah." But Kira wasn't so sure. A sense of injustice wormed inside her. How dare Fizel judge her! She'd only done what she was supposed to—what any of them would have. If she'd ignored the rock formation, he would have been the first to call her out for shirking. And it wasn't as if she and Alan hadn't lost plenty because of her discovery, same as the rest of the team. . . .

Alan nuzzled the nape of her neck. "Everything is going to be fine. Just you watch." Then he lay still, and Kira listened to his breathing slow while she stared into the darkness.

Things still felt wrong and out of sorts. Her stomach knotted even more painfully, and Kira screwed her eyes shut, trying not to obsess over Fizel or what the future might hold. Yet she couldn't forget what had been said in the mess hall, and a hot coal of anger continued to burn inside her as she fell into a fitful sleep.

2.

Darkness. A vast expanse of space, desolate and unfamiliar. The stars were cold points of light, sharp as needles against the velvet backdrop.

Ahead of her, a star swelled in size as she hurtled toward it, faster than the fastest ship. The star was a dull reddish-orange, like a dying coal smoldering against a bed of char. It felt old and tired, as if it had formed during the earliest stages of the universe, when all was hot and bright.

Seven planets spun about the sullen orb: one gas giant and six terrestrial. They looked brown and mottled, diseased, and in the gap between the second and the third planets, a band of debris glittered like flecks of crystal sand.

A sense of sadness gripped her. She couldn't say why, but the sight made her want to weep the way she had when her grandfather died. It was the worst of things: loss, utter and complete, without a chance of restoration.

The sadness was an ancient sorrow, though, and like all sorrows, it faded to a dull ache and was supplanted by more pressing concerns: those of anger, fear, and desperation. The fear predominated, and from it, she knew danger encroached—intimate and immediate—and yet she found it hard to move, for unfamiliar clay bound her flesh.

The threat was nearly upon her; she could feel it drawing nigh, and with it, panic breaking. There was no time to wait, no time to think. She had to force her way free! First to rive and then to bind.

The star brightened until it shone with the force of a thousand suns, and blades of light shot forth from the corona and into the darkness. One of the blades struck her, and her vision went white and it felt as if a lance had been driven into her eyes and every inch of her skin burned and crisped.

She screamed into the void, but the pain didn't stop, and she screamed again—

Kira bolted upright. She was panting and drenched in sweat; the blanket clung to her like plastic film. People were shouting elsewhere in the base, and she recognized the sound of panic in their voices.

Next to her, Alan's eyes flew open. "Wh—"

Footsteps sounded in the hallway outside. A fist pounded against the door, and Jenan shouted, "Get out here! It's Neghar."

Cold fear shot through Kira's gut.

Together, she and Alan scrambled into their clothes. Kira spared a second of thought for her strange dream—*everything* felt strange at the moment—and then they hurried out of the cabin and rushed over toward Neghar's quarters.

As they approached, Kira heard hacking: a deep, wet, ripping sound that made her imagine raw flesh going through a shredder. She shuddered.

Neghar was standing in the middle of the hallway with the others gathered around her, doubled over, hands on her knees, coughing so hard Kira could hear her vocal cords fraying. Fizel was next to her, hand on her back. "Keep breathing," he said. "We'll get you to sickbay. Jenan! Alan! Grab her arms, help carry her. Quickly now, qu—"

Neghar heaved, and Kira heard a loud, distinct *snap* from inside the woman's narrow chest.

Black blood sprayed from Neghar's mouth, painting the deck in a wide fan.

Marie-Élise shrieked, and several people retched. The fear from Kira's dream returned, intensified. This was bad. This was *dangerous.* "We have to go," she said, and tugged on Alan's sleeve. But he wasn't listening.

"Back!" Fizel shouted. "Everyone back! Someone get the *Extenuating Circumstances* on the horn. Now!"

"Clear the way!" Mendoza bellowed.

More blood sprayed from Neghar's mouth, and she dropped to one knee. The whites of her eyes were freakishly wide. Her face was crimson, and her throat worked as if she were choking.

"Alan," said Kira. Too late; he was moving to help Fizel.

She took a step back. Then another. No one noticed; they were all looking at Neghar, trying to figure out what to do while staying out of the way of the blood flying from her mouth.

Kira felt like screaming at them to leave, to run, to *escape.*

She shook her head and pressed her fists against her mouth, scared blood was going to erupt out of her as well. Her head felt as if it were about to burst, and her skin was crawling with horror: a thousand ants skittering over every centimeter. Her whole body itched with revulsion.

Jenan and Alan tried to lift Neghar back to her feet. She shook her head and gagged. Once. Twice. And then she spat a clot of *something* onto the deck. It was too dark to be blood. Too liquid to be metal.

Kira dug her fingers into her arm, scrubbing at it as a scream of revulsion threatened to erupt out of her.

Neghar collapsed backwards. Then the clot *moved.* It twitched like a clump of muscle hit with an electrical current.

People shouted and jumped away. Alan retreated toward Kira, never taking his eyes off the unformed lump.

Kira dry-heaved. She took another step back. Her arm was burning: thin lines of fire squirming across her skin.

She looked down.

Her nails had carved furrows in her flesh, crimson gashes that ended with crumpled strips of skin. And within the furrows, she saw another something *twitch*.

3.

Kira fell to the floor, screaming. The pain was all-consuming. That much she was aware of. It was the *only* thing she was aware of.

She arched her back and thrashed, clawing at the floor, desperate to escape the onslaught of agony. She screamed again; she screamed so hard her voice broke and a slick of hot blood coated her throat.

She couldn't breathe. The pain was too intense. Her skin was burning, and it felt as if her veins were filled with acid and her flesh was tearing itself from her limbs.

Dark shapes blocked the light overhead as people moved around her. Alan's face appeared next to her. She thrashed again, and she was on her stomach, her cheek pressed flat against the hard surface.

Her body relaxed for a second, and she took a single, gasping breath before going rigid and loosing a silent howl. The muscles of her face cramped with the force of her rictus, and tears leaked from the corners of her eyes.

Hands turned her over. They gripped her arms and legs, holding them in place. It did nothing to stop the pain.

"Kira!"

She forced her eyes open and, with blurry vision, saw Alan and, behind him, Fizel leaning toward her with a hypo. Farther back, Jenan, Yugo, and Seppo were pinning her legs to the floor, while Ivanova and Marie-Élise helped Neghar away from the clot on the deck.

"*Kira!* Look at me! *Look* at me!"

She tried to reply, but all she succeeded in doing was uttering a strangled whimper.

Then Fizel pressed the hypo against her shoulder. Whatever he injected didn't seem to have any effect. Her heels drummed against the floor, and she felt her head slam against the deck, again and again.

"Jesus, someone help her," Alan cried.

"Watch out!" shouted Seppo. "That thing on the floor is moving! Shi—"

"Sickbay," said Fizel. "Get her to sickbay. *Now!* Pick her up. Pick—"

The walls swam around her as they lifted her. Kira felt like she was being strangled. She tried to inhale, but her muscles were too cramped. Red sparks gathered around the edges of her vision as Alan and the others carried her down the hallway. She felt as if she were floating; everything seemed insubstantial except the pain and her fear.

A jolt as they dropped her onto Fizel's exam table. Her abdomen relaxed for a second, just long enough for Kira to steal a breath before her muscles locked back up.

"Close the door! Keep that thing out!" A *thunk* as the sickbay pressure lock engaged.

"What's happening?" said Alan. "Is—"

"Move!" shouted Fizel. Another hypo pressed against Kira's neck.

As if in response, the pain tripled, something she wouldn't have believed possible. A low groan escaped her, and she jerked, unable to control the motion. She could feel foam gathering in her mouth, clogging her throat. She gagged and convulsed.

"Shit. Get me an injector. Other drawer. No, other drawer!"

"Doc—"

"Not now!"

"*Doc,* she isn't breathing!"

Equipment clattered, and then fingers forced Kira's jaw apart, and someone jammed a tube into her mouth, down her throat. She gagged again. A moment later, sweet, precious air poured into her lungs, sweeping aside the curtain darkening her vision.

Alan was hovering over her, his face contorted with worry.

Kira tried to talk. But the only sound she could make was an inarticulate groan.

"You're going to be okay," said Alan. "Just hold on. Fizel's going to help you." He looked as if he were about to cry.

Kira had never been so afraid. Something was *wrong* inside her, and it was getting worse.

Run, she thought. *Run! Get away from here before—*

Dark lines shot across her skin: black lightning bolts that twisted and squirmed as if alive. Then they froze in place, and where each one lay, her skin split and tore, like the carapace of a molting insect.

Kira's fear overflowed, filling her with a feeling of utter and inescapable doom. If she could have screamed, her cry would have reached the stars.

Fibrous tendrils erupted from the bloody rents. They whipped about like headless snakes and then stiffened into razor-edged spikes that stabbed outward in random directions.

The spikes pierced the walls. They pierced the ceiling. Metal screeched. Lightstrips sparked and shattered, and the high-pitched keen of Adra's surface wind filled the room, as did the blare of alarms.

Kira fell to the floor as the spikes jerked her around like a puppet. She saw a spike pass through Yugo's chest and then three more through Fizel: neck, arm, and groin. Blood sprayed from the men's wounds as the spikes withdrew.

No!

The door to sickbay slammed open and Ivanova rushed in. Her face went slack with horror, and then a pair of spikes struck her in the stomach and she collapsed. Seppo tried to run, and a spike impaled him from behind, pinning him to the wall, like a butterfly.

No!

Kira blacked out. When she came to, Alan was kneeling next to her, his forehead pressed against hers and his hands heavy upon her shoulders. His eyes were blank and empty, and a line of blood trickled from the corner of his mouth.

It took her a moment to realize that a dozen or more spikes stitched her body to his, joining them with obscene intimacy.

Her heart fluttered and stopped, and the floor seemed to drop away into an abyss. *Alan.* Her teammates. Dead. Because of her. The knowledge was unbearable.

Pain. She was dying, and she didn't care. She just wanted the suffering to end—wanted the swift arrival of oblivion and the release it would bring.

Then darkness clouded her sight and the alarms faded to silence, and what once was, was no more.

CHAPTER V

* * * * * * *

MADNESS

1.

Kira's eyes shot open.

There was no slow rise to consciousness. No gradual return to awareness. Not this time. One moment nothing; the next, a burst of sensory information, bright and sharp and overwhelming in its intensity.

She was lying at the bottom of a tall, circular chamber—a tube with a ceiling five meters above her, far too high to reach. It reminded her of the grain silo their neighbors, the Roshans, had built when she was thirteen. Halfway up the side of the tube was a two-way mirror: a large, silvery rectangle filled with the grey ghost of a reflection. A narrow lightstrip along the edge of the ceiling was the only source of illumination.

Not just one but two robot arms moved about her with silent grace, a cluster of diagnostic instruments protruding from the end of each one. As she looked at them, they paused and then retracted toward the ceiling, where they hung in readiness.

Embedded within one side of the tube was an airlock with a built-in hatch for passing small objects in and out. Opposite the airlock was a pressure door that presumably led deeper into . . . into wherever. It too had a hatch, similar in size and for the same purpose. Glorified jailer's slots. There was no bed. No blanket. No sink. And no toilet. Just cold, bare metal.

She had to be on a ship. Not the *Fidanza.* The *Extenuating Circumstances.*

Which meant . . .

A jolt of adrenaline caused Kira to gasp and sit upright. The pain; the spikes; Neghar, Fizel, Yugo, Ivanova . . . *Alan!* The memories returned in a deluge. They returned, but Kira wished they hadn't. Her gut clenched, and a long, deep groan escaped her as she fell to her hands, knees, and forehead. The ridges of the deck cut into her skin, but she didn't care.

When she could breathe, she howled, pouring all of her grief and anguish into a single wailing cry.

It was all her fault. If she hadn't found that damned room, Alan and the others would still be alive and she wouldn't have ended up infected by some sort of xeno.

The spikes.

Where were the spikes and tendrils that had torn through her skin? Kira looked down, and her heart skipped a beat.

Her hands were black when they shouldn't have been. So too were her arms and her chest and everything else she could see of her body. A layer of glossy, fibrous material clung to her, tight as any skinsuit.

Horror welled up inside Kira.

She clawed at her forearms in a desperate attempt to rip off the alien organism. Even with their hard new veneer, her nails couldn't cut or break the fibers. Frustrated, she brought her wrist to her mouth and bit.

The taste of stone and metal filled her mouth. She could feel the pressure from her teeth, but no matter how hard she bit down, it didn't hurt.

Kira scrambled to her feet, heart pounding so fast it skipped beats, the edges of her vision going dark. "Get it off!" she shouted. *"Get this fucking thing off me!"* Through her panic, she wondered where everyone was, her one coherent thought amid the madness.

One of the robotic arms descended toward her. The manipulator at the end of the arm was holding a syringe. Before Kira could move, the machine reached around her head and injected her behind the ear, on a patch of still-bare skin.

Within seconds a heavy blanket seemed to press down upon her. Kira stumbled sideways, reaching out an arm to catch herself as she fell—

2.

The panic returned the moment Kira regained consciousness.

There was an alien creature bonded with her. She was contaminated, possibly infectious. It was the sort of situation every xenobiologist dreaded: a containment breach leading to fatalities.

Alan . . .

Kira shuddered and buried her face in the crook of her arm. Below her neck, her skin prickled with a million tiny fears. She wanted to look again, but she didn't have the courage. Not yet.

Tears leaked from under her eyelids. She could feel Alan's absence like a hole in her chest. It didn't seem possible that he was dead. They'd had so many plans, so many hopes and dreams, and now none of them would come to fruition. She'd never get to see him build the house he'd talked about, nor go skiing with him in mountains in the far south of Adra, nor watch him become a father, nor any of the other things she'd imagined.

The knowledge hurt more than any physical pain.

She felt her finger. The band of polished iron set with tesserite was gone, and with it her only tangible reminder of him.

A memory came to her then, from years past: her father kneeling next to her in a greenhouse and bandaging a cut on her arm while saying, "The pain is of our own making, Kira." He pressed a finger against her forehead. "It only hurts as much as we let it."

Maybe so, but Kira still felt terrible. Pain was pain, and it insisted on making itself known.

How long had she been unconscious? Minutes? Hours? . . . No, not hours. She was lying where she'd fallen, feeling neither hungry nor thirsty. Only drained from the torment of misery. Her whole body ached as if bruised.

Behind her shuttered lids, Kira noticed that none of her overlays were displaying. "Petra, on," she said. Her system didn't respond, not even with a flicker. "Petra, force restart." The darkness remained unchanged.

Of course. The UMC *would* shut down her implants.

She growled into her arm. How could the military techs have overlooked the organism in her and Neghar? The xeno was large. Even a basic examination ought to have spotted it. If the UMC had done their job properly, no one would have died.

"God*damn* you," she muttered. Her anger fought back the grief and panic enough for her to open her eyes.

Again she saw the bare metal. Lightstrips. Mirrored window. Why had they brought her onto the *Extenuating Circumstances*? Why risk the additional exposure? None of their choices made sense to her.

She'd avoided the inevitable long enough. Steeling herself, Kira looked down.

Her body was still covered in the layer of inky black. That and nothing more. The material resembled bands of overlapping muscles; she could see the individual strands stretch and flex as she moved. Her alarm strengthened, and a shimmer seemed to pass across the fibers. Was it sentient? No way to know for sure at the moment.

Tentative, Kira touched a spot on her arm.

She hissed, baring her teeth. She could *feel* her fingers on her arm, as if the intervening fibers didn't exist. The parasite—machine or organism, she didn't know which—had worked itself into her nervous system. The motions of the circulating air were noticeable against her skin, as was every square centimeter of decking that pressed into her flesh. She might as well have been totally naked.

And yet . . . she wasn't cold. Not as she ought to be.

She examined the soles of her feet. Covered, same as her palms. Feeling upward, she discovered that—in the front—the suit stopped near the top of her neck. There was a small ridge: a drop-off between fibers and skin that curved around her ears. In the back, the fibers continued up and over the back of her head and—

Her hair was gone. Nothing but the smooth contours of her skull met her exploring fingers.

Kira set her teeth. What else had the xeno stolen from her?

As she concentrated on the different sensations of her body, Kira realized that the xeno wasn't just bonded to her outside; it was inside her as well, filling her, penetrating her, if however unobtrusively.

Her gorge rose, and claustrophobia closed in around her, choking her. She was trapped, embedded in the alien substance with no way of escaping. . . .

She bent over and retched. Nothing came out, but bile coated her tongue and her stomach continued to heave.

Kira shivered. How the hell could the UMC decontaminate her when the suit was wound up all inside? She was going to be stuck in quarantine for months, maybe years. Stuck with *it*.

She spat into the corner and, without thinking, wiped her mouth on her forearm. The smear of spit soaked into the fibers, like water into cloth.

Disgusting.

A faint *hiss*—as of speakers turning on—broke the silence, and a new source of light struck Kira's face.

3.

A hologram covered half the wall. The image was several meters high and showed a small, empty desk—painted battleship grey—in the middle of an equally small, equally stark room. A single chair, straight-backed and armless, sat behind the desk.

A woman walked in. She was of medium height, with a pair of eyes like chips of black ice and a cast-iron hairdo shot through with strands of white. A Reform Hutterite, then, or something similar. There were only a few Hutterites on Weyland: a handful of families Kira had seen on occasion during the settlement's monthly gathering. The older adults always stood out with their sagging skin and receding hairlines and other obvious signs of aging. The sight had scared her when she was little and fascinated her when she was in her teens.

What she focused on, though, weren't the woman's features but her clothes. She was wearing a grey uniform—grey like the desk—that had been starched and ironed until each crease looked as if it could slice through hardened tool steel. Kira didn't recognize the color of the uniform. Blue was the Navy/Spacecorps. Green was the Army. Grey was . . . ?

The woman seated herself, placed a tablet on the desk, centered it with the tips of her forefingers. "Ms. Navárez. Do you know where you are?" She had a thin, flat mouth, like that of a guppy, and when she spoke, her bottom row of teeth was visible.

"The *Extenuating Circumstances.*" Kira's throat hurt; it felt raw and swollen.

"Very good. Ms. Navárez, this is a formal deposition in accordance with article fifty-two of the Stellar Security Act. You will answer all of my questions, willingly and to the best of your knowledge. This isn't a court, but if you fail to cooperate, you can and will be charged with obstruction, and if your statement is later found to be false, perjury. Now, tell me everything that you remember after you woke up from cryo."

Kira blinked, feeling lost and confused. Grinding out each word, she said, "My team . . . what about my team?"

Guppy Face pressed her lips together into a pale line. "If you're asking who survived, four of them did. Mendoza, Neghar, Marie-Élise, and Jenan."

At least Marie-Élise was still alive. Fresh tears threatened to spill down Kira's cheeks. She scowled, not wanting to cry in front of the other woman. "Neghar? How . . ."

"Video footage shows that the organism she expelled melded with the one currently attached to your body after the . . . hostilities. As far as we can tell, the two are indistinguishable. Our current theory is that Neghar's organism was drawn to yours as yours was larger and more fully developed—a lesser part of a hive-swarm rejoining the greater, if you will. Aside from some internal bleeding, Neghar seems unharmed and free of infection, although at the moment, it's impossible for us to be sure."

Kira's hands knotted into fists as her anger swelled. "Why didn't you spot the xeno before? If you had—"

The woman made a cutting motion with her hand. "We don't have time for this, Navárez. I understand you've had a shock, but—"

"You couldn't *possibly* understand."

Guppy Face eyed Kira with something close to disdain. "You're not the first person to be infected by an alien life-form, and you're certainly not the first person to lose some friends."

Guilt caused Kira to look down and squeeze her eyes shut for a moment. Hot tears peppered the backs of her fists. "He was my fiancé," she mumbled.

"What was that?"

"Alan, he was my fiancé," Kira said, louder. She gave the woman a defiant look.

Guppy Face never blinked. "You mean Alan J. Barnes?"

"Yes."

"I see. In that case, you have the condolences of the UMC. Now, I need you to pull yourself together. The only thing you can do is accept God's will and move forward. Sink or swim, Navárez."

"It's not that easy."

"I didn't say it would be easy. Grow a pair and start acting like a professional. I know you can. I read your file."

The words stung Kira's pride, although she would never admit it. "Yeah? Well who the hell are you?"

"Excuse me?"

"Your name? You haven't told me."

The woman's face tightened, as if she hated to share any personal information with Kira. "Major Tschetter. Now, tell me—"

"And what are you?"

Tschetter raised an eyebrow. "Human, last I checked."

"No, I meant . . ." Kira gestured at the woman's grey uniform.

"Special attaché to Captain Henriksen, if you must know. This is beside the—"

Frustrated, Kira let her voice rise. "Is it too much to ask what branch of the armed forces, *Major*? Or is that classified?"

Tschetter assumed a flat, affectless expression, a professional blankness that told Kira nothing of what she was thinking or feeling. "UMCI. Fleet Intelligence."

A spy then, or worse, a political officer. Kira snorted. "Where are they?"

"*Who,* Ms. Navárez?"

"My friends. The . . . the ones you rescued."

"In cryo, on the *Fidanza,* being evacuated from the system. There. Satisfied?"

Kira released a bark of laughter. "Satisfied? Satisfied?! I want this damn thing off me." She plucked at the black coating on her arm. "Cut it off if you have to, but *get it off.*"

"Yes, you made your desire abundantly clear," said Tschetter. "If we can remove the xeno, we will. But first, you're going to tell me what happened, Ms. Navárez, and you're going to tell me *right now.*"

Kira bit back another curse. She wanted to rant and rage; she wanted to lash out and make Tschetter feel even a small measure of her hurt. But she knew it wouldn't help. So she did as she was ordered. She told the major everything she remembered. It didn't take long, and Kira found no relief in confession.

The major had numerous questions, most of them focused on the hours before the parasite burst forth: Had Kira noticed anything unusual? An upset stomach, elevated temperature, intrusive thoughts? Had she smelled anything unfamiliar? Had her skin been itchy? Rashes? Inexplicable thirst or cravings?

Aside from the itching, the answer to most of the questions was *no,* which Kira could see didn't please the major. Especially when Kira explained that—to the best of her knowledge—Neghar hadn't experienced the same symptoms.

Afterward, Kira said, "Why didn't you stick me in cryo? Why am I on the *Extenuating Circumstances*?" She didn't understand it. Maintaining quarantine was *the* most important task in xenobiology. The thought of breaking it was enough to give anyone in her profession the cold sweats.

Tschetter smoothed an invisible wrinkle out of her jacket. "We tried to freeze you, Navárez." Her gaze met Kira's. "We tried and failed."

Kira's mouth went dry. "Failed."

A short nod from Tschetter. "The organism purged the cryonic injections from your body. We couldn't keep you under."

A new fear struck Kira. Freezing the xeno was the easiest way to stop it. Without that, they had no quick way to keep it from spreading. Also, without cryo, it was going to be a hell of a lot harder for her to get back to the League.

Tschetter was still speaking: "After we released you and Neghar from quarantine, our medical team was in close contact with the both of you. They touched your skin. They breathed the same air. They handled the same equipment. And then"—Tschetter leaned forward, intense—"they came back here, to the *Extenuating Circumstances*. Now do you understand, Navárez?"

Kira's mind started to race. "You think you've been exposed."

Tschetter inclined her head. "The xeno took two and a half days to emerge after Neghar was removed from cryo. Less so in your case. Being frozen may or may not have slowed the development of the organism. Either way, we have to assume the worst. Minus the time since your release, that means we have somewhere between twelve and forty-eight hours to figure out how to detect and treat asymptomatic hosts."

"That's not enough time."

The corners of Tschetter's eyes tightened. "We have to try. Captain Henriksen has already ordered all nonessential crew into cryo. If we don't find a solution by end of tomorrow, he'll have the rest of us frozen."

Kira licked her lips. No wonder they'd been willing to bring her onto the *Extenuating Circumstances*. They were desperate. "What happens to me then?"

Tschetter steepled her fingers. "Our ship mind, Bishop, will continue your examination as he sees fit."

Kira could see the logic in that. Ship minds were kept isolated from the rest of the life-support system. By all rights, Bishop ought to be perfectly safe from infection.

There was just one problem. Whatever she was carrying wasn't just a threat on the micro level. She lifted her chin. "And what if . . . what if the xeno acts out the way it did on Adra? It could rip a hole right through the hull. You should have set up a pressure dome on the surface, studied the xeno there."

"Ms. Navárez . . ." Tschetter made a minuscule adjustment to the position of the tablet in front of her. "The xeno currently occupying your body is of the highest possible interest to the League, tactically, politically, and scientifically. We were never going to leave it on Adrasteia, regardless of the risk to this ship or this crew."

"That's—"

"Furthermore, the chamber you are currently in is completely isolated from the rest of the ship. Should the xeno attempt to damage the *Extenuating Circumstances* as it did your base, or should it display other hostile actions, the entire pod can be jettisoned into space. Do you understand?"

Kira's jaw clenched despite herself. "Yes." She couldn't blame them for the precautions. They made sense. Didn't mean she had to like them.

"Let me be perfectly clear, Ms. Navárez. The League won't let *any* of us return home—including your friends—until we have a reliable means of detection. Let me repeat that: no one on this ship will be permitted within ten light-years of a human-settled planet unless we can figure this out. The League would blow us out of the sky before they would let us land, and rightly so."

Kira felt sorry for Marie-Élise and the others, but at least they wouldn't be aware of the time passing. She squared her shoulders. "Okay. So what do you need from me?"

Tschetter smiled without humor. "Your willing cooperation. Do I have it?"

"Yes."

"Excellent. Then—"

"Just one thing; I want to record a few messages for my friends and family, in case I don't make it. Also a message for Alan's brother, Sam. Nothing classified, but he deserves to hear from me."

The major paused for a second, eyes darting as she read something in front of her. "That can be arranged. It may be some time before any communications are allowed, though. We're running silent until we receive orders from Command."

"I understand. Oh, and—"

"Ms. Navárez, we're operating under a *very* tight deadline."

Kira held up a hand. "Can you turn my implants back on? I'm going to go crazy in here without my overlays." She nearly laughed. "I might be going crazy anyway."

"Can't," said Tschetter.

Kira's defenses shot back up. "Can't or won't?"

"Can't. The xeno destroyed your implants. I'm sorry. There's nothing left to turn back on."

Kira groaned, feeling as if another someone had died. All her memories . . . She'd had her system set to automatically back up to the server at HQ at the end of each day. If the server had survived, then so had her personal archives, although everything that had happened to her since would be lost, existing only in the fragile and fallible tissues of her brain. If she had to choose, she would have rather lost an arm than her implants. With her overlays, she had a world within a world—a whole universe of content to explore, both real and invented. Without, all she was left with were her thoughts, thin and insubstantial, and the echoing darkness beyond. What's more, her senses had been blunted; she couldn't see UV or infrared, couldn't feel the magnetic fields around her, couldn't interface with machines, and worst of all, couldn't look up whatever she didn't know.

She was diminished. The *thing* had reduced her to the level of an animal, to nothing more than meat. Primitive, unenhanced *meat*. And in order to do that, it must have worked its way into her brain, severed the nanowire leads that joined the implants to her neurons.

What else had it severed?

For a minute Kira stood still and silent, breathing heavy. The suit felt as hard as steel plate around her torso. Tschetter had the sense not to interrupt. At last Kira said, "Then let me have a tablet. Or some holo-glasses. Something."

Tschetter shook her head. "We can't allow the xeno to access our computer system. Not at the moment. It's too dangerous."

A huff of air escaped Kira, but she knew better than to argue. The major was right. "Dammit," she said. "Okay. Let's get started."

Tschetter picked up her tablet and stood. "One last question, Navárez: Do you still feel like yourself?"

The question struck an unpleasant chord. Kira knew what the major was asking. Was she, Kira, still in control of her mind? Regardless of the truth, there was only one answer she could give if she were to ever walk free.

"Yes."

"That's good. That's what we want to hear." But Tschetter didn't look happy. "Alright. Doctor Carr will be with you shortly."

As Tschetter started to walk away, Kira asked a question of her own: "Have you found any other artifacts like this?" The words fell out of her in a breathless jumble. "Like the xeno?"

The major glanced back at her. "No, Ms. Navárez. We haven't."

The holo winked out of existence.

4.

Kira sat by the pressure door, still mulling over the major's final question. How could she be sure her thoughts, actions, or emotions were still her own? Plenty of parasites modified the behavior of their hosts. Maybe the xeno was doing the same to her.

If so, she might not even notice.

Some things Kira felt sure an alien wouldn't be able to successfully manipulate, no matter how smart the creature was. Thoughts, memories, language, culture—all of those were too complex and context-dependent for an alien to fully understand. Hell, even humans had difficulty going from one human culture to another. However, big emotions, urges, actions, those would be vulnerable to tampering. For all she knew, her anger might be coming from the organism. It didn't feel like it, but then it wouldn't.

Have to try and stay calm, Kira thought. Whatever the xeno was doing to her was out of her control, but she could still watch herself for unusual behavior.

A spotlight snapped on overhead, pinning her beneath its harsh glare. In the darkness beyond, there was a stir of movement as the robotic arms descended toward her.

Halfway up the cylindrical wall, the two-way mirror blurred transparent. Through it, she saw a short, hunched man in a UMC uniform standing at a console. He had a brown mustache and deep-set eyes that stared at her with feverish intensity.

A speaker clicked on overhead, and she heard the man's gravelly voice: "Ms. Navárez, this is Doctor Carr. We met before, although you wouldn't remember."

"So you're the one who got most of my team killed."

The doctor tilted his head to the side. "No, that would be you, Ms. Navárez."

In that instant, Kira's anger curdled into hate. "Oh fuck you. Fuck you! How could you have missed the xeno? Look at the size of it."

Carr shrugged, tapping buttons on a display she couldn't see. "That's what we're here to find out." He peered down at her, his face round and owlish. "Now stop wasting time. Drink." One of the robotic arms presented her with a pouch of orange liquid. "It'll keep you on your feet until there's time for a solid meal. I don't want you passing out on me."

Biting back an obscenity, Kira took the pouch and downed it in a single, sustained gulp.

Then the hatch set within the airlock popped open, and at the doctor's order, she dropped the pouch inside. The hatch closed, and a loud *thud* sounded as the airlock vented into space.

From that point on, Carr subjected her to an unrelenting series of examinations. Ultrasounds. Spectrographs. X-rays. PET scans (prior to those she had to drink a cup of milky-white liquid). Cultures. Reactant tests . . . Carr tried them all and more.

The robots—he called them S-PACs—acted as his assistants. Blood, saliva, skin, tissue: if she could part with it, they took it. Urine samples weren't possible, given how the suit covered her, and no matter how much Kira drank, she never felt the need to relieve herself, for which she was grateful. Peeing in a bucket while Carr watched wasn't something she wanted to do.

Despite her anger—and her fear—Kira also felt a strong, almost irresistible curiosity. The chance to study a xeno like this was what she'd hoped for her whole career.

If only the chance hadn't come at such a terrible price.

She paid close attention to which experiments the doctor was running and in which order, hoping to glean some hint of what he was learning about the organism. To her immense frustration, he refused to tell her the results of his tests. Every time she asked, Carr was evasive or outright refused to answer, which did nothing to improve Kira's mood.

Despite his lack of communication, Kira could tell from the doctor's scowls and muttered expletives that the *thing* was proving remarkably resistant to scrutiny.

Kira had theories of her own. Microbiology was more her specialty than macro, but she knew enough about both to deduce a couple of things. First, given its properties, there was no way the xeno could have evolved naturally. It was either a highly advanced nanomachine or some form of gene-hacked lifeform. Second, the xeno possessed at least a rudimentary awareness. She could feel it reacting to the tests: a slight stiffening along her arm; a soap-bubble shimmer across her chest, so faint as to be nearly invisible; a subtle flexing of the fibers. Whether it was sentient or not, though, she didn't think even Carr knew.

"Hold still," said the doctor. "We're going to try something different."

Kira stiffened as one of the S-PACs produced a blunt-tipped scalpel from within its casing and lowered the knife toward her left arm. She held her breath as the blade touched. She could feel the edge pressing against her, sharp as glass.

The suit dimpled beneath the blade as the S-PAC scraped it sideways across her forearm, but the fibers refused to part. The robot repeated the motion with increasing force, until at last it gave up scraping and attempted a short draw cut.

As Kira watched, she saw the fibers underneath the blade fuse and harden. It looked as if the scalpel were skating across a surface of molded obsidian. The blade produced a tiny shriek.

"Any pain?" the doctor asked.

Kira shook her head, never taking her eyes off the knife.

The robot withdrew several millimeters and then brought the round tip of the scalpel down upon her forearm in a swift, plunging movement.

The blade snapped with a bell-like *ping,* and a piece of metal spun past her face.

Carr frowned. He turned to speak to someone (or someones) she couldn't see, and then turned back to her. "Okay. Again, don't move."

She obeyed, and the S-PACs moved around her in a blur, jabbing every centimeter of skin covered by the xeno. At each spot, the organism hardened, forming a small patch of adamantine armor. Carr even had her lift her feet so the robots could stab at the soles. That made her flinch; she couldn't help it.

So the xeno could defend itself. Great. Freeing her would be that much harder. On the plus side, she didn't have to worry about being stabbed. Not that it had been a problem before.

The way the *thing* had emerged on Adra, spikes bristling, tendrils writhing . . . Why wasn't it acting like that now? If anything might have been expected to provoke an aggressive response, it should have been this. Had the xeno lost the ability to move after bonding with her skin?

Kira didn't know, and the suit wasn't telling.

When the machines finished, the doctor stood, one cheek sucked in as he chewed on it.

"Well?" said Kira. "What did you find? Chemical composition? Cell structure? DNA? Anything."

Carr smoothed his mustache. "That's classified."

"Oh come *on.*"

"Hands on your head."

"Who am I going to tell, huh? I can help you. Talk to me!"

"Hands on your head."

Biting back a curse, Kira obeyed.

5.

The next round of tests was far more strenuous, invasive even. Crush tests. Shear tests. Endurance tests. Tubes down her throat, injections, exposures to extremes of heat and cold (the parasite proved to be an excellent insulator).

Carr seemed driven to the point of distraction; he yelled at her if she was slow to move, and several times, Kira saw him berating his assistant—a hapless ensign by the name of Kaminski—as well as throwing cups and papers at the rest of his staff. It was clear the experiments weren't telling Carr what he wanted, and time was fast running out for the crew.

The first deadline came and went without incident. Twelve hours, and so far as Kira could tell, the xeno hadn't emerged from anyone on the *Extenuating Circumstances.* Not that she trusted Carr to inform her if it had. But she could see a change in his demeanor: a renewed sense of focus and determination. The doctor had his second wind. They were working against the longer deadline now. Another thirty-six hours before the rest of the crew would have to enter cryo.

Ship-night came, and still they continued to work.

Uniformed crew brought the doctor mug after mug of what Kira assumed was coffee, and as the night wore on, she saw him toss back several pills. StimWare or some other form of sleep-replacement meds.

Kira was increasingly tired herself. "Mind giving me some?" she said, gesturing toward the doctor.

Carr shook his head. "It'll mess with your brain chemistry."

"So will sleep deprivation."

That gave him a moment's pause, but then the doctor just shook his head again and returned his attention to the instrument panels in front of him.

"Bastard," Kira muttered.

Acids and bases had no effect on the xeno. Electrical charges passed harmlessly across the skin of the organism (it seemed to form a natural Faraday cage). When Carr raised the voltage, there was an actinic flash at the end of the S-PAC and the arm flew back as if it had been thrown. As the smell of ozone filled the air, Kira saw that the S-PAC's manipulators had fused together and were glowing red hot.

The doctor paced about the observation bay, tugging at the corner of his mustache with what looked like painful force. His cheeks were red, and he seemed angry, dangerously so.

Then he stopped.

A moment later, there was a clatter as something dropped into the delivery box outside the cell. Curious, Kira opened it and found a pair of dark glasses: eye protection against lasers.

A worm of unease twisted inside her.

"Put them on," said Carr. "Left arm out."

Kira obeyed, but slowly. The glasses gave the cell a yellowish cast.

The manipulator mounted on the end of the undamaged S-PAC flowered open to reveal a small, glossy lens. Kira's unease sharpened, but she held her position. If there was any chance of getting rid of the *thing*, she'd take it, no matter how much it hurt. Otherwise she knew she'd end up spending the rest of her life stuck in quarantine.

The S-PAC positioned itself above and just to the left of her forearm. With a *snap*, a purplish-blue beam shot from the lens to a point on the deck near her feet. Flecks of dust gleamed and glittered in the bar of collated light, and the grating below began to glow cherry red.

Moving sideways, the robot brought the beam into contact with her forearm.

Kira tensed.

There was a brief flash, and a wisp of smoke curled upward, and then . . . and then to her astonishment, the laser beam curved around her arm, like water flowing around a stone. Once past her arm, the laser regained its geometric precision and continued straight down to the deck, where it traced a ruddy line across the grating.

The robot never paused its sideways slide. At a certain point, the laser flipped sides and arced around the inside of her forearm.

Kira felt no heat; it was as if the laser didn't exist.

What the xeno was doing wasn't impossible. It was just very difficult. Plenty of materials could bend light. They were used in numerous applications. The invisibility cloak she and her friends had played with when they were kids was a perfect example. However, to detect the exact wavelength of the laser and then manufacture a coating that could redirect it, and all in a tiny fraction of a second, was no mean feat. Not even the League's most advanced assemblers could pull that off.

Once again Kira revised upward her estimate of the xeno's abilities.

The beam vanished. Carr scowled and scratched his mustache. A young man—an ensign, she thought—approached the doctor, said something. The doctor turned and seemed to shout at him; the ensign flinched and then saluted and gave a quick answer.

Kira started to lower her arm.

"Stay," said the doctor.

She resumed her position.

The robot settled over a spot a few centimeters below her elbow.

A *pop* rang out, nearly as loud as a gunshot, and Kira yelped. It felt as if she'd been jabbed with a red-hot spike. She yanked her arm back and clapped a hand over the wound. Between her fingers, she saw a hole as big around as her pinkie.

The sight shocked her. Out of everything they'd tried, the laser blast was the first to actually hurt the suit.

Her astonishment was nearly enough to override the pain. She bent over, grimacing as she waited for the initial surge to wear off.

After a few seconds, she glanced back at her arm; the suit was flowing into the hole, the fibers reaching out and grasping each other, tentacle-like. They closed over the wound, and within moments, her arm looked and felt the same as before. So the organism *could* still move.

Kira let out her breath in a ragged flow. Had it been the suit's pain she felt or her own?

"Again," Carr said.

Setting her jaw, Kira held out her arm, hand clenched in a fist. If they could cut through the suit, perhaps they could force it to retreat.

"Do it," she said.

Pop.

A spark and a small puff of vapor erupted from the wall as a pin-sized hole appeared in the metal plating. She frowned. The suit had already adapted to the laser's frequency.

With hardly any pause:

Pop.

More pain. "Dammit!" She grabbed her arm and pressed it against her stomach, lips pulled tight against her teeth.

"Don't fucking move, Navárez."

She gave herself several breaths and then resumed position.

Three more spikes drove through her skin in quick succession. Her whole arm was on fire. Carr must have figured out how to shift the laser's frequency in a way to bypass the suit's defenses. Elated, Kira opened her mouth to say something to him—

Pop.

Kira flinched. She couldn't help it. Okay, Carr had had his fun. Time to stop. She started to draw her arm back, but the second S-PAC spun around and grabbed her wrist with its manipulator.

"Hey!"

Pop.

Another blackened crater appeared on her forearm. Kira snarled and tugged against the robot. It refused to budge.

"Stop it!" she shouted at the doctor. "That's enough!"

He glanced at her and then returned to studying something on a monitor below the edge of the mirror-window.

Pop.

A new crater appeared in the same spot as the last one, which was already filling in. The blast drilled even farther into her arm, burning through skin and muscle.

"Stop!" she shouted, but Carr didn't respond.

Pop.

A third crater overlapping. Panicked, Kira grabbed the S-PAC holding her and yanked, throwing all her weight backwards. It shouldn't have made any difference—the machines were large and well-built—but the joint behind the S-PAC's manipulator snapped, and the manipulator broke free with a spray of hydraulic fluid.

Surprised, Kira stared for a moment. Then she pried the manipulator off her wrist, and it fell to the floor with a solid *bang.*

Carr stood watching with a frozen expression.

"We're done here," said Kira.

CHAPTER VI

* * * * * * *

SHOUTS & ECHOES

1.

Dr. Carr stared down at her with cold disapproval. "Resume position, Navárez."

Kira gave him the finger and walked over to the wall beneath the mirror-window, where he couldn't see, and sat. As always, the spotlight followed her.

Again, Carr spoke: "Goddammit, this isn't a game."

She lifted her finger over her head. "I'm not working with you if you won't listen when I say *stop*."

"We don't have time for this, Navárez. Resume position."

"Want me to break the other S-PAC? Because I will."

"Last warning. If you don't—"

"Fuck off."

Kira could almost hear the doctor fuming in the pause that followed. Then a square of reflected light appeared on the wall opposite her as the mirror-window clouded over.

She released the breath she'd been holding.

Stellar security be damned. The UMC couldn't do whatever they wanted with her! It was her body, not theirs. And yet—as Carr had shown—she was at their mercy.

Kira rubbed her forearm, still in shock. She hated feeling so helpless.

After a moment, she stood and nudged the crumpled S-PAC with her foot. The xeno must have augmented her strength, same as an exoskeleton or a soldier's battle armor. It was the only explanation for how she could have torn apart the machine.

As for the burns on her arm, only a faint ache remained to remind her of their existence. It occurred to Kira that the xeno had done everything it could to protect her throughout the tests. Lasers, acids, flames, and more—the parasite had deflected nearly everything Carr had thrown at her.

For the first time, she felt a sense of . . . not gratitude, but perhaps, appreciation. Whatever the suit might be, and as much as she hated it for causing the deaths of Alan and her other teammates, it was useful. In its own way, it was displaying more care for her than the UMC.

It wasn't long before the hologram popped into existence. Kira saw the same grey room with the same grey desk, and standing at attention before it, Major Tschetter in her grey uniform. A colorless woman in a colorless room.

Before the major could speak, Kira said, "I want a lawyer."

"The League hasn't charged you with a criminal offense. Until such time as it does, you don't need a lawyer."

"Maybe not, but I want one anyway."

The woman stared at her the way Kira imagined she would stare at a fleck of dirt on her otherwise immaculate shoes. She was from Sol, Kira felt sure of it. "Listen to me, Navárez. You're wasting minutes that might mean the difference in lives. Maybe no one else is infected. Maybe only one other person is infected. Maybe all of us are. The point is, *we have no way to tell.* So stop stalling and get back to work."

Kira made a dismissive noise. "You're not going to figure out anything about the xeno in the next few hours, and you know it."

Tschetter pressed her palms against the table, fingers stretched wide like talons. "I know nothing of the sort. Now be reasonable and cooperate with Doctor Carr."

"No."

The major tapped her fingernails against the desk. Once, twice, three times, and then no more. "Noncompliance with the Stellar Security Act *is* a crime, Navárez."

"Yeah? What are you going to do, throw me in jail?"

If possible, Tschetter's gaze grew even sharper. "You don't want to go down this path."

"Uh-huh." Kira crossed her arms. "I'm a member of the League, and I have corporate citizenship through the Lapsang Trading Corporation. I have certain rights. You want to keep studying the xeno? Great, then I want some form of computer access, and I want to talk with a company rep. Send a flash back to Sixty One Cygni. Now."

"We can't do that, and you know it."

"Tough. That's my price. And if I tell Carr to back off, then he backs off. Otherwise, you can all go jump out an airlock for all I care."

A silence, and then Tschetter's lips twitched and the hologram vanished.

Kira released her breath in a gust, spun around, and started to pace. Had she gone too far? She didn't think so. Now it was up to the captain to decide whether to grant her requests. . . . Henriksen, that was his name. She hoped he was more fair-minded than Tschetter. A captain ought to be.

"How the hell did I end up here?" she muttered.

The ship's hum was her only answer.

2.

Not five minutes later, the two-way mirror cleared. To Kira's dismay, Carr was the only person standing in the observation bay. He eyed her with a sour expression.

Kira stared back, defiant.

The doctor pressed a button, and the hated spotlight reappeared. "Alright, Navárez. Enough of this. We—"

Kira turned her back on him. "Go away."

"That's not going to happen."

"Well I'm not going to help you until I get what I asked for. Simple as that."

A sound made her turn. The doctor had planted both fists on the console in front of him. "Get back into position, Navárez, or else—"

"Or else *what*?" She snorted.

Carr's scowl deepened, his eyes two gleaming dots buried above his fleshy cheeks. "Fine," he snapped.

The comm clicked off, and the two S-PACs again emerged from their slots in the ceiling. The one she'd damaged had been repaired; its manipulator looked good as new.

Apprehensive, Kira dropped into a crouch as the machines moved toward her, like spider legs extending. She batted at the near one, and it dodged so fast it seemed to teleport. There was no matching the speed of a robot.

The two arms closed in at the same time. One caught her by the jaw with its cold, hard manipulators, while the other robot dove in with a syringe. Kira felt a spot of pressure behind her ear, and then the needle on the syringe snapped.

The S-PAC released her, and Kira scrambled into the center of the cell, panting. *The hell?* In the mirror-window, the doctor was frowning and staring at something on his overlays.

Kira felt behind her ear. What had been bare skin just hours before was now covered by a thin layer of the suit's material. Her scalp tingled; the skin along the edges of her neck and face felt as if it were crawling. The sensation intensified—becoming a cold fire that pricked and stung—as if the xeno were struggling to move. But it didn't.

Once again the creature had protected her.

Kira looked up at Carr. He was leaning against the equipment in front of him, staring down at her with a heavy frown, his forehead shiny with sweat.

Then he turned and left the mirror-window.

Kira released a breath she hadn't realized she was holding. Adrenaline was still coursing through her.

A loud *thud* sounded outside the pressure door.

3.

Kira froze. What now?

Somewhere a bolt snapped open and atmospheric pumps whined. Then a row of lights across the center of the door flashed yellow, and the lock rotated and decoupled from the wall.

Kira swallowed hard. Surely Carr wasn't going to send someone in there with her!

Metal scraped against metal as the door slid open.

Beyond it was a small decon chamber, still hazy with mist from the chemical spray. In the haze stood two hulking shadows, backlit by blue warning lights mounted on the ceiling.

The shadows moved: loader bots, covered from top to bottom in blast armor, black and massive and scarred from use. No weapons, but between them sat a wheeled exam table with racks of medical equipment mounted underneath the mattress. Shackles hung at each of the four corners of the bed, and straps too: restraints for unruly patients.

Like her.

Kira recoiled. "No!" She glanced at the two-way mirror. "You can't do this!"

The bots' heavy feet clanked as they stepped into the cell, pushing the exam table before them. The wheels squealed with protest.

In the periphery of her vision, Kira saw the S-PAC machines approaching from either side, manipulators spread wide.

Her pulse spiked.

"Citizen Navárez," said the rightmost bot. Its voice was staticky out of the cheap speaker embedded in its torso. "Turn around and put your hands on the wall."

"No."

"If you resist, we *are* authorized to use force. You have five seconds to comply. Turn around and put your hands on the wall."

"Go jump out an airlock."

The two bots stopped the exam table in the middle of the room. Then they started toward her while, at the same time, the S-PACs darted in from the sides.

Kira did the only thing she could think of: she dropped into a sitting fetal position, arms wrapped around her legs, forehead buried against her knees. The suit had hardened in response to the scalpel; maybe it could harden again and keep the machines from strapping her to the table. *Please, please, please . . .*

At first it seemed her prayer would go unanswered.

Then, as the grippers at the end of the S-PACs touched her sides, her skin stiffened and constricted. *Yes!* A brief moment of relief as Kira felt herself locking into position, the fibers twining together in places where flesh touched flesh, welding her into a single, solid piece.

The S-PACs snapped against her sides, unable to find purchase against the now slick, shell-like veneer of the suit. Her breath came in short, gasping gulps, stifling hot in the pocket of space between her mouth and legs.

Then the battle bots were upon her. Their giant metal fingers clamped down on her arms, and she felt them lift her off the floor and carry her toward the exam table.

"Let me go!" Kira shouted, not breaking position. The frantic tempo of her pulse outraced her thoughts, filled her ears with a sound like a roaring waterfall.

Cold plastic touched her ass as the bots lowered her onto the exam table.

Curled as she was, none of the shackles could be secured around her wrists or ankles. Nor would any of the straps work. They were meant to be used on a person lying down, not sitting up.

"Citizen Navárez, noncompliance is a criminal offense. Cooperate now, or—"

"No!!!"

The bots pulled on her arms and legs, trying to stretch her out. The suit refused to give. Two hundred–some kilos of powered metal for each machine, and they couldn't break the fibers that bound her in place.

The S-PACs made a futile attempt to help, their manipulators scrabbling against her neck and back—oil-slick fingers attempting to grasp hold of greased glass.

Kira felt as if she were trapped in a tiny box, the soft walls pressing in on her, suffocating. But she stayed curled up, refusing to budge. It was her only way of fighting back, and she'd sooner pass out than give Carr the satisfaction of victory.

The machines retreated for a moment, and then the four of them began to bustle about her in an organized fashion: removing equipment from the racks underneath the mattress, adjusting a diagnostic scanner to accommodate her fetal position, laying out tools on a tray by her feet . . . With a sense of anger, Kira realized Carr was going to continue with his tests and there was nothing she could do about it. The S-PACs she might have been able to break, but not the loader bots; they were too big, and if she tried, they'd just lock her to the table and then she'd be even more at their mercy.

So Kira didn't move, although sometimes the machines repositioned her for their own reasons. She couldn't see what they were doing, but she could hear, and she could feel. Every few seconds an instrument of some kind touched her back or sides, scraping, pushing, drilling, or otherwise attacking the skin of the suit. Liquids poured across her head and neck, much to her annoyance. Once she heard the clicks of a Geiger counter. Another time she felt a cutting disk make contact with her arm, and her skin grew warm while the strobe-like flash of flying sparks illuminated the dark crannies around her face. And all the while, the scanner arm kept moving around her—whirring, beeping, humming—moving in perfect coordination with the loader bots and the two S-PACs.

Kira yelped as a laser blast drilled into her thigh. *No. . . .* More blasts followed, on different parts of her body, and each blast was a burning jab of pain. The smell of burnt flesh and burnt xeno filled the air, acrid and unpleasant.

She bit her tongue to keep from crying out again, but the pain was pervasive and overwhelming. The constant *bzzt* of the discharging laser accompanied each pulse. Soon just hearing the sound was enough to make her flinch. Sometimes the xeno would protect her and she'd hear a piece of the table or the floor or the walls vaporize. But the S-PACs kept rotating the wavelength of the laser, avoiding the suit's adaptations.

It was like a tattoo machine from hell.

Then the pulses grew faster as the robots fired in bursts that allowed for continuous cutting, the *bzzts* forming a single jagged tone that vibrated in her teeth. Kira screamed as the flickering beam carved down her side, attempting to slice away the xeno, force it to retreat. Her blood sputtered and hissed as it evaporated.

Kira refused to break form. But she kept screaming until her throat was raw and slick with blood. She couldn't help it. The pain was too great.

As the laser burned another track, her pride fled. She no longer cared about appearing weak; escaping the pain had become the sole focus of her existence. She begged Carr to stop, begged and begged and begged, to no effect. He didn't even respond.

Between the lashings of agony, fragments of memories passed through Kira's mind . . . *Alan; her father tending his Midnight Constellations; her sister, Isthah, chasing her through the racks in the storage room; Alan laughing; the weight of the ring sliding onto her finger; the loneliness of her first posting; a comet streaking across the face of a nebula.* And more she failed to recognize.

How long it went on, Kira didn't know. She retreated deep into the core of herself and clung to one thought above all else: *this too shall pass.*

. . .

The machines stopped.

Kira remained frozen where she was, sobbing and barely conscious. At any moment, she expected the laser to hit her again.

"Stay where you are, Citizen," said one of the loader bots. "Any attempt to escape will be met with lethal force." There was a whine of motors as the S-PACs retreated into the ceiling, and a heavy series of steps as the two loader bots moved away from the exam table. But they didn't return the way they'd come.

Instead, Kira heard them trundle over to the airlock. It clanked open. Her gut went ice-cold as fear flooded her. What were they doing? Surely they weren't going to vent the cell? They wouldn't. They *couldn't* . . .

The loader bots entered the airlock, and to Kira's relief, the door closed after them, although it did nothing to lessen her confusion.

And then . . . silence. The airlock didn't cycle. The intercom didn't turn on. The only sounds were of her breathing and the fans circulating the atmosphere and the distant rumble of the ship's engines.

4.

Kira's sobs slowly ran out. The pain was fading to a dull ache as the suit bandaged and healed her wounds. She stayed curled into a ball, though, half-convinced that Carr was pulling a trick on her.

For a long, empty while she waited, listening to the ambient sounds of the *Extenuating Circumstances* for any hint she might be attacked again.

In time, she began to relax. The xeno relaxed with her, allowing the different parts of her body to unstick from one another.

Lifting her head, Kira looked around.

Aside from the exam table and a few new scorch marks, the cell appeared the same as before . . . as if Carr hadn't just spent the last few hours (or however long it had been) torturing her. Through the airlock window, she could see the loader bots standing one next to the other, locked into hard points along the curving wall. Standing. Waiting. Watching.

She understood now. The UMC didn't want to allow the bots back into the main area of the ship. Not when they were worried about contamination. But they also didn't want to leave the bots where she could access them.

Kira shivered. She swung her legs over the side of the table and slid to the floor. Her knees were stiff, and she felt sick and shaky, as if she'd just finished a set of sprints.

No evidence of her injuries remained; the surface of the xeno looked the same as before. Kira pressed her hand against her side, where the laser had cut deepest. A sudden throb of pain caused her to suck in her breath. So she wasn't entirely healed.

She sent a hate-filled glance toward the mirror.

How far would Captain Henriksen allow Carr to go? What were their limits? If they were truly scared of the xeno, was any measure too far? Kira knew how the politicians would spin it: "In order to protect the League of Worlds, extraordinary measures had to be taken."

. . . *had to be taken.* They always used the passive voice when acknowledging a mistake.

She didn't know exactly what time it was, but she knew they were getting close to their final deadline. Was that why Carr had left off tormenting her? Because more xenos were emerging among the crew of the *Extenuating Circumstances*?

Kira eyed the closed pressure door. If so, it would be chaos throughout the ship. She couldn't hear anything, though: no screams, no alarms, no pressure breaches.

She rubbed her arms, feeling cold as she remembered the breach on Serris, during her third mission out of Weyland's system. A pressure dome on the mining outpost had failed, nearly killing her and everyone else. . . . The whistle of escaping air still gave her nightmares.

The cold was spreading throughout her body. It felt as if her blood pressure was dropping, a horrible, doom-laden sensation. In a detached way, Kira realized the ordeal had left her in shock. Her teeth chattered, and she hugged herself.

Maybe something on the exam table could help.

Kira went to examine it.

Scanner, oxygen mask, tissue regenerator, chip-lab, and more besides. Nothing overtly dangerous, and nothing to help her with the shock. Mounted at one end of the bed was a bank of vials containing various drugs. The vials were sealed with molecular locks; she wouldn't be opening them any time soon. Underneath the mattress hung a canister of liquid nitrogen, beaded with condensation.

Feeling suddenly weak and light-headed, Kira sank to the floor, keeping a hand on the wall for balance. How long had it been since she'd had any sort of food? Too long. Surely the UMC wouldn't let her starve. At some point Carr would feed her.

He'd just have to, right?

5.

Kira kept expecting Carr to reappear, but he didn't. Nor did anyone else come to talk with her. That was just fine, as far as she was concerned. Right then, she just wanted to be left alone.

Still, without her overlays, being alone was its own special form of torture.

All she had were her thoughts and memories, and neither of those were particularly pleasant at the moment.

She tried closing her eyes. It didn't work. She kept seeing the loader bots. Or if not them, the last, horrifying moments on Adra, and each time, her heart rate spiked and she broke into a hot sweat.

"Dammit," she muttered. Then, "Bishop, you there?"

The ship mind didn't answer. She wasn't even sure he heard, or if he did, if he was allowed to answer.

Desperate for a distraction, and with nothing else to do, Kira decided to run an experiment of her own. The suit could harden in response to threat/pressure/stimuli. Okay. How did it decide what constituted a threat? And was that something she could influence?

Ducking her head between her arms, where no one else could see, Kira concentrated on the inner part of her elbow. Then she imagined the tip of a knife pressing into her arm, breaking the skin . . . pushing into the muscles and tendons beneath.

No change.

She tried twice more, struggling to make her imagining as real as possible. She used the memory of past pains to help, and on the third attempt, she felt the crease of her elbow harden, a scar-like pucker drawing together her skin.

After that, it got easier. With each attempt, the suit became more responsive, as if it were learning. Interpreting. Understanding. A frightening prospect.

At the thought, the *thing* constricted across the whole of her body.

Kira sucked in her breath, caught by surprise.

A deep sense of unease formed in her as she sat staring at the weave of fused fibers on her palms. She'd been concerned, and the suit had reacted to that concern. It had read her emotions without her making any attempt to impose them on the organism.

The unease turned to poison in her veins. That last day on Adra, she'd been so upset and out of sorts, and then during the night, when Neghar had started vomiting blood, she'd been so afraid, so incredibly afraid. . . . *No!* Kira recoiled from the thought. It was the UMC's fault that Alan had died. Dr. Carr had failed, and because of his failure, the xeno had emerged the way it had. *He* was the one to blame, not . . . not . . .

Kira hopped to her feet and started pacing: four steps in one direction, four steps in the other.

Moving helped shift her thoughts from the horror of Adra to things more familiar, more comforting. She remembered sitting with her father on the bank of the stream by their house and listening to his stories of life on Stewart's World. She remembered Neghar jumping up and hooting after beating Yugo at a racing game, and long days working with Marie-Élise under Adra's sulfurous sky.

And she remembered lying with Alan and talking, talking, talking about life and the universe and all the things they wanted to do.

"Someday," he said, "when I'm old and rich, I'll have my own spaceship. Just you wait."

"What would you do with your own spaceship?"

He looked at her, serious as could be. "I'd make a long jump. As long as I could. Out toward the far rim of the galaxy."

"Why?" she'd whispered.

"To see what's out there. To fly into the deep depths and carve my name on an empty planet. To *know.* To *understand.* The same reason I came to Adra. Why else?"

The thought had scared and excited Kira, and she'd snuggled closer to him, the warmth of their bodies banishing the empty reaches of space from her mind.

6.

BOOM.

The deck shuddered, and Kira's eyes snapped open, adrenaline pumping through her. She was lying against the curve of the wall. The dull red glow of ship-night permeated the holding cell. Late or early, she couldn't tell.

Another tremor jolted the ship. She heard screeches and bangs and what sounded like alarms. Goosebumps crawled across her skin, and the suit stiffened. Their worst fears had come true; more xenos were emerging. How many of the crew were affected?

She pushed herself into a sitting position, and a veil of dust fell from her skin. The *thing's* skin.

Startled, Kira froze. The powder was grey and fine and smooth as silk. Spores? She immediately wished for a respirator. Not that it would do any good.

Then she noticed she was sitting in a shallow depression that perfectly matched the shape of her sleeping body. Somehow she'd sunk several millimeters into the deck, as if the black substance coating her were corrosive. The sight both puzzled her and increased her revulsion. Now the *thing* had turned her into a toxic object. Was it even safe for someone to touch her? If the—

The cell tilted around her and she flew across the room and slammed into the wall along with the dust, which poofed out in a cloud. The impact knocked the breath out of her. The exam table crashed next to her, parts flying loose.

An emergency burn. But why? The thrust grew stronger . . . stronger . . . It felt like two g's. Then three. Then four. Her cheeks pulled against her skull, stretching, and a lead blanket seemed to weigh her down.

A strange vibration passed through the wall, as if a giant drum had been struck, and the thrust vanished.

Kira fell on all fours and gasped for breath.

Somewhere nearby, something banged against the hull of the ship, and she heard the pop and rattle of what sounded like . . . *gunfire*?

And then Kira felt it: an aching summons, tugging her toward a place outside the ship, tugging on her like a string anchored in her chest.

At first, disbelief. It had been so long since the summons had been laid upon her, so very long since she had been called to perform her sacred duty. Then exultation at the much-delayed return. Now the pattern could be fulfilled, as once before.

A disjunction, and she stood in familiar flesh upon a now-vanished cliff, at the moment when she had first felt the compulsion that could be resisted but never ignored. She turned, following it, and saw in the gradient sky a ruddy star wink and waver, and she knew it was the signal's source.

And she obeyed, as was only right. For hers was to serve, and serve she would.

Kira gasped as she returned to herself. And she knew. They weren't facing an infestation. They were facing an invasion.

The owners of the suit had come to claim her.

CHAPTER VII

* * * * * * *

COUNTDOWN

1.

A sick knot formed in Kira's stomach. First contact with another intelligent species—something she'd always dreamed of—and it seemed to be happening in the worst possible way, with violence.

"No, no, no," she muttered.

The aliens were coming for her, for the suit. She could feel the summons growing stronger. It would only be a matter of time before they found her. She had to escape. She had to get off the *Extenuating Circumstances*. One of the ship's shuttles would be ideal, but she'd settle for an escape pod. At least on Adra she might have a fighting chance.

The lightstrip overhead started to flash blue, a strident pulse that hurt Kira's eyes to look at. She ran to the pressure door and pounded on it. "Let me out! Open the door!" She spun toward the mirror-window. "Bishop! You have to let me out!"

The ship mind didn't respond.

"Bishop!" She pounded on the door again.

The lights on the door turned green, and the lock spun and clicked. She yanked the door open and dashed across the decon chamber. The door at the other end was still locked.

She slapped the control screen next to it. It beeped, and the lock turned a few centimeters and then stopped with a grinding sound.

The door was jammed.

"Fuck!" She slammed her hand against the wall. Most doors had a manual release, but not this one; they were determined to keep their inmates from escaping.

She looked back at the cell. A hundred different possibilities flashed through her mind.

The liquid nitrogen.

Kira ran to the exam table and crouched, scanning the racks of equipment. Where was it? Where was it? She uttered a cry as she spotted the tank, relieved that it appeared undamaged.

She grabbed it and hurried back to the decon chamber's outer door. Then she took a deep breath and held it so she wouldn't pass out from breathing too much of the gas.

Kira placed the nozzle of the tank against the door's lock and opened the valve. A plume of white vapor hid the door from view as the nitrogen sprayed out. For a moment she felt the cold in her hands, and then the suit compensated and they were as warm as ever.

She kept up the spray for a count of ten and then twisted the valve shut.

The metal-composite lock was white with frost and condensation. Using the bottom of the tank, Kira struck the lock. It shattered like glass.

Kira dropped the tank and, desperate to get out, yanked on the door. It slid open, and a painfully loud klaxon assaulted her.

Outside was a bare metal corridor lit by strobing lights. A pair of bodies lay at the far end, twisted and horribly limp. At the sight of them, her pulse spiked, and a line of tension formed in the suit, like a wire being pulled taut to the point of breaking.

This was the nightmare scenario: humans and aliens killing each other. It was a disaster that could easily spiral into a catastrophe.

Where did the *Extenuating Circumstances* keep its shuttles? She tried to recall what she'd seen of the ship back at HQ. The docking bay was somewhere along the middle part of the ship. So that was her goal.

To get there she'd have to go past the dead crew and, hopefully, avoid running into whatever had attacked them.

No time to waste. Kira took a breath to steady herself and then hurried forward on light feet, primed to react to the smallest sound or motion.

She'd only seen corpses a few times before: once when she was a kid on Weyland, when a supercapacitor on a cargo loader had ruptured and killed two men right on the main street of Highstone. Once during the accident on Serris. And now of course, with Alan and her teammates. On the first two occasions, the images had burned into Kira's mind until she'd considered having them removed. But she hadn't. And she wouldn't with the most recent memories either. They were too much a part of her.

As she approached the bodies, she looked. She had to. One man, one woman.

The woman had been shot with an energy weapon. The man had been torn apart; his right arm lay separate from the rest of his body. Bullets had dented and smeared the walls around them.

A pistol protruded from under the woman's hip.

Fighting the urge to gag, Kira stopped and pulled the weapon free. The counter on the side said *7.* Seven rounds remaining. Not many, but better than nothing. The problem was, the gun wouldn't work for her.

"Bishop!" she whispered, and held the gun up. "Can you—"

The safety on the pistol snapped off.

Good. So the UMC still wanted her alive. Without her overlays, Kira wasn't sure if she could hit anything with the gun, but at least she wasn't entirely helpless. *Just don't shoot a window.* It would be a bad way to die.

Still keeping her voice low, she said, "Which way to the shuttles?" The ship mind ought to know where the aliens were and how best to avoid them.

A line of green arrows appeared along the top of the wall, pointing deeper into the ship. She followed them through a maze of rooms to a ladder that led toward the center of the *Extenuating Circumstances.*

The apparent gravity lessened as she climbed past deck after deck of the rotating hab section. Through open doorways, she heard screams and shouts, and twice she saw the muzzle flashes of machine guns reflected around corners. Once, she heard an explosion that sounded like a grenade going off, and a series of pressure doors slammed shut behind her. But she never saw whatever it was the crew was fighting.

Halfway up, the ship lurched—hard—forcing Kira to grab the ladder with both hands to avoid being thrown off. A weird, swirling sensation caused her gorge to rise and bile to flood her mouth. The *Extenuating Circumstances* was spinning end for end, not a good situation for a long, narrow ship. The frame wasn't designed to withstand rotational forces.

The alarms changed tone, becoming even more shrill. Then a deep male voice emanated from the speakers in the walls: "Self-destruct in T-minus seven minutes. This is not a drill. Repeat, this is not a drill. Self-destruct in T-minus six minutes and fifty-two seconds."

Kira's insides went cold as ice. "Bishop! No!"

The same male voice said, "I'm sorry, Ms. Navárez. I have no other choice. I suggest you—"

Whatever else he said, Kira didn't hear, wasn't listening. Panic threatened to overwhelm her, but she pushed it aside; she didn't have time for emotions. Not now. A wonderful clarity focused her mind. Her thoughts grew hard, mechanical, ruthless. Less than seven minutes to reach the shuttles. She could do it. She had to.

She scrambled forward, moving even faster than before. She'd be damned if she was going to die on the *Extenuating Circumstances*.

At the top of the ladders, a ring of green arrows surrounded a closed hatch. Kira pulled it open and found herself in the spherical hub that joined the different hab sections.

She turned aftward, and vertigo gripped her as she saw what seemed to be a long, narrow pit dropping away below her. The shaft was a terror of black metal and stabbing light. All the hatches in all the decks that stacked the stem of the ship had been opened, an offense that normally would have been worthy of a court-martial.

If the ship fired its engines, anyone caught in the shaft would plummet to their death.

Hundreds of meters away, toward the stern, she glimpsed troopers in power armor grappling with some *thing*: a mass of conflicting shapes, like a knot of shadows.

An arrow pointed into the darkness.

Kira shivered and launched herself toward the distant fight. To keep her stomach from rebelling, she chose to view the shaft as a horizontal tunnel rather than a vertical pit. She crawled along the ladder bolted to the floor/wall, using it to guide her path and keep her from drifting off course.

"Self-destruct in T-minus six minutes. This is not a drill. Repeat, this is not a drill."

How many decks to the docking bay? *Three? Four?* She had only a general idea.

The ship groaned again, and the pressure door in front of her slammed shut, blocking the way. Overhead, the line of green arrows switched directions, pointing to the right. It started to blink with seizure-inducing speed.

Shit. Kira swung herself around a rack of equipment and hurried along Bishop's detour. Time was running out. The shuttles had better be primed for departure or she'd have no chance of escaping. . . .

Voices sounded ahead of her. Dr. Carr saying, "—and move it! Hurry, you moron! There's no—" A loud *thud* interrupted him, and the bulkheads vibrated. The doctor's shouting shifted into a higher pitch, his words incoherent.

As Kira pulled herself through a narrow access hatch, a fist seemed to grip and squeeze her chest.

In front of her was an equipment room: racks of shelving, lockers stuffed with skinsuits, a red-labeled oxygen feed pipe at the back. Carr hung near the ceiling, his hair frazzled, one hand wound in a strap tied to several metal cases that kept bumping into him. A dead Marine lay wedged in one of the shelving units, a row of burns stitched across his back.

On the other side of the room, a large, circular hole had been cut through the hull. Midnight-blue light streamed out of the hole from what seemed to be a small boarding craft mated to the side of the *Extenuating Circumstances*. And within the recess moved a monster with many arms.

2.

Kira froze as the alien propelled itself into the storage room.

The creature was twice the size of a man, with semi-translucent flesh tinted shades of red and orange, like ink dissolving in water. It had a torso of sorts: a tapered ovoid a meter wide covered in a keratinous shell and studded with dozens of knobs, bumps, antennae, and what looked like small black eyes.

Six or more tentacles—she wasn't sure how many, as they kept writhing about—extended from the ovoid, top and bottom. Textured stripes ran the length of the tentacles, and near the tips, they seemed to have cilia and an array of sharp, claw-like pincers. Two of the tentacles carried white pods with a bulbous lens. Kira didn't know much about weapons, but she knew a laser when she saw one.

Interspersed among the tentacles were four smaller limbs, hard and bony, with surprisingly hand-like appendages. The arms remained folded close to the creature's shell and didn't stir.

Even in her shock, Kira found herself tallying the features of the alien, same as she would with any other organism she'd been sent to study. *Carbon based? Seems like it. Radially symmetrical. No identifiable top or bottom. . . . Doesn't appear to have a face. Odd.* One fact in particular jumped out at her: the alien looked nothing like her suit. Whether the being was sentient or not, artificial or natural, it was definitely different from the xeno bonded with her.

The alien moved into the room with unsettling fluidity, as if it had been born in zero-g, turning and twisting with seemingly no preference for which direction its torso pointed.

At the sight, Kira felt a response from her suit: a rising rage as well as a sense of ancient offense.

Grasper! Wrongflesh manyform! Flashes of pain, bright as exploding stars. Pain and rebirth in an endless cycle, and a constant cacophony of noise: booms and cracks and shattering retorts. The pairing was not as it ought to be. The grasper did not understand the pattern of things. It did not see. It did not listen. It sought to conquer rather than to cooperate.

Wrongness!!!

This wasn't what the xeno had expected from the summons! Fear and hate roared through Kira, and she didn't know which was the suit's and which was hers. The tension inside her snapped, and the skin of the xeno rippled and began to spike out, same as on Adra, needle-sharp spears jabbing in random directions. But this time, she felt no pain.

"Shoot it!" Carr shouted. "Shoot it, you fool! Shoot it!"

The grasper twitched, seeming to shift its attention between them. A strange whispering surrounded Kira, like a billowing cloud, and from it she felt currents of emotion: first surprise, and then in quick succession recognition, alarm, and satisfaction. The whispers grew louder, and then a switch seemed to flip in her brain and she realized she could understand what the alien was saying:

[[—and alert the Knot. Target located. Send all arms to this position. Consumption is incomplete. Containment and recovery should be possible, then we may cl—]]

"Self-destruct in T-minus five minutes. This is not a drill. Repeat, this is not a drill."

Carr swore and kicked himself over to the dead Marine and yanked on the man's blaster, trying to free it from the corpse.

One of the laser-wielding tentacles shifted positions, the gelatinous muscles within flexing and relaxing. Kira heard a *bang*, and a white-hot spike of metal erupted from the side of the Marine's blaster as a laser pulse hit it, sending the gun careening across the room.

The alien turned toward her. Its weapon twitched. Another *bang*, and a bolt of pain lanced her chest.

Kira grunted, and for a moment, she felt her heart falter. The spikes on the suit pulsed outward, but to no avail.

[[Qwon here: Foolish two-form! You profane the Vanished. Foulness in the water, this—]]

She scrabbled for the rungs of the ladder by the access hatch, trying to get away, trying to escape, even though there was nowhere to run and nowhere to hide.

Bang. Heat stabbed her leg, deep and excruciating.

Then a third *bang,* and a scorched crater appeared in the wall to her left. The suit had adapted to the laser frequency; it was shielding her. Maybe—

As if in a daze, Kira spun back around and, somehow, lifted the pistol, held it before her. The barrel of the gun wavered as she struggled to aim at the alien.

"Shoot it, damn you!" the doctor screamed, specks of froth flying from his mouth.

"Self-destruct in T-minus four minutes and thirty seconds. This is not a drill. Repeat, this is not a drill."

Fear narrowed Kira's vision, constricted her world to a tight cone. *"No!"* she shouted—a panicked rejection of everything that was happening.

The gun went off, seemingly of its own accord.

The alien darted across the ceiling of the equipment room as it dodged. It was terrifyingly fast, and each tentacle seemed to move with a mind of its own.

Kira yelled and kept squeezing the trigger, the recoil a series of hard smacks against her palm. The noise was muted, distant.

Sparks flew as the grasper's laser shot two of the bullets out of the air.

The creature swarmed over the skinsuit lockers and paused while clinging to the wall by the red feed pipe—

"Wait! Stop! *Stop!*" Carr was shouting, but Kira didn't hear, didn't care, couldn't stop. First Alan, then the xeno, and now this. It was too much to bear. She wanted the grasper gone, no matter the risk.

Twice more she fired.

A patch of red crossed her line of sight, beyond the end of the muzzle, and—

. . .

Thunder cracked, and an invisible hammer slammed Kira against the opposite wall. The blast shattered one of the xeno's spines. She could *feel* the fragment spinning across the room, as if she were in two places at once.

As her vision cleared, Kira saw the ruins of the supply room. The grasper was a mangled mess, but several of its tentacles still waved with weak urgency, blobs of orange ichor oozing from its wounds. Carr had been thrown against the shelving. Shards of bones stuck out from his arms and legs. The orphaned piece of the xeno lay against the bulkhead across from her: a slash of torn fibers draped across the crumpled panels.

More importantly, there was a jagged hole in the hull where one of the bullets had hit the oxygen line, triggering the explosion. Through it, the blackness of space was visible, dark and dreadful.

A cyclone of air rushed past Kira, dragging at her with inexorable force. The suction pulled Carr, the grasper, and the xeno fragment out of the ship, along with a stream of debris.

Storage bins battered Kira. She cried out, but the wind stole the breath from her mouth, and she struggled to grab a handhold—any handhold—but she was too slow and the walls were too far away. Memories of the breach on Serris flashed through her mind, crystal sharp.

The split in the hull widened; the *Extenuating Circumstances* was tearing itself apart, each half drifting in a different direction. Then the outflow of gas sent her tumbling past the bloodstained shelves, past the breach, and into the void.

And all went silent.

CHAPTER VIII

* * * * * * *

OUT & ABOUT

1.

The stars and the ship spun around her in a dizzying kaleidoscope.

Kira opened her mouth and allowed the air in her lungs to escape, as you were supposed to do if spaced. Otherwise you risked soft tissue damage and, possibly, an embolism.

The downside was, she had only about fifteen seconds of consciousness left. Death by asphyxiation or death by arterial obstruction. Not much of a choice.

She gulped out of instinct and flailed, hoping to catch something with her hands.

Nothing.

Her face stung and prickled; the moisture on her skin boiling off. The sensation increased, becoming a cold fire that crawled upward from her neck and inward from her hairline. Her vision dimmed, and Kira felt sure she was blacking out.

Panic set in then. Deep, overriding panic, and the last remnants of Kira's training fled her mind, replaced by the animal need to survive.

She screamed, and she *heard* the scream.

Kira was so shocked, she stopped and then, purely by reflex, took a breath. Air—precious air—filled her lungs.

Unable to believe it, she felt her face.

The suit had molded itself to her features, forming a smooth surface over her mouth and nose. With the tips of her fingers, she discovered that small, domed shells now covered her eyes.

Kira took another breath, still incredulous. How long could the suit keep her supplied with air? A minute? Several minutes? Any more than three and it wouldn't matter, because nothing would be left of the *Extenuating Circumstances* but a rapidly expanding cloud of radioactive dust.

Where was she? It was hard to tell; she was still spinning, and it was impossible to focus on any one thing. Adrasteia's shining bulk swung past—and beyond it, the enormous curve of Zeus's silhouette—then the broken length of the *Extenuating Circumstances.* Floating alongside the cruiser was another vessel: a huge blue-white orb covered with smaller orbs and the biggest set of engines she'd ever seen.

She was hurtling away from the middle of the *Extenuating Circumstances,* but the forward section of the ship was listing toward her, and ahead of her gleamed a row of the diamond radiators. Two of the fins were broken, and ropes of silver metal leaked from the veins within.

The fins looked beyond her reach, but Kira tried anyway, unwilling to give up. She stretched out her arms, straining toward the nearest of the radiators as she continued to spin. Stars, planet, ship, and radiators flashed by, again and again, and still she kept straining. . . .

The pads of her fingers slipped across the surface of the diamond, unable to find purchase. She screamed and scrabbled but without success. The first fin spun away, then the next and the next, her fingers brushing each in turn. One stood slightly higher than the rest, mounted on a damaged armature. Her palm scraped against the diamond's polished edge, and her hand stuck—stuck as if covered with a gecko pad—and she came to a stop with a violent jolt.

Hot pain flooded her shoulder joint.

Relieved beyond belief, Kira hugged the fin as she peeled her hand free. A soft bed of cilia coated her palm, waving gently in the weightlessness of space. If only the suit had kept her from getting blown out of the *Extenuating Circumstances* in the first place.

She looked for the back half of the ship.

It was several hundred meters away and receding. The two shuttles were still docked along the stem; they both looked intact. Somehow she had to reach them, and fast.

She really had only one choice. *Thule!* She braced herself against the diamond fin and then jumped with all her might. Please, she hoped, let her aim be correct. If she missed, she wouldn't get a second chance.

As she bored across the fathomless gulf that separated her from the stern of the *Extenuating Circumstances,* Kira noticed she could see faint lines radiating in loops along the hull. The lines were blue and violet, and appeared to cluster around the fusion engine—EM fields. It was like having her overlays back, at least in part.

Interesting, if not immediately useful.

Kira focused on the alien ship. It shone in the sun like a bead of polished quartz. Everything about it was spherical or as close to spherical as possible. From the outside, she couldn't tell what might be living quarters and what might be fuel tanks, but it looked like it could hold a substantial crew. There were four circular windows dotted around its circumference and one near the prow of the ship, which was surrounded by a large ring of lenses, ports, and what appeared to be various sensors.

The engine looked no different from any of the rockets she was familiar with (Newton's third law didn't care whether you were human or xeno). However, unless the aliens had launched from somewhere *extremely* close, they had to have a Markov Drive as well. She wondered how they could have snuck up on the *Extenuating Circumstances*. Could they jump right into a gravity well? Not even the League's most powerful ships could manage that particular trick.

The strange, aching pull Kira still felt seemed to originate from the alien vessel. Part of her wished she could follow it and see what happened, but that was the crazy part of her, and she ignored it.

She could also feel the orphaned piece of the xeno, distant and fading as it receded into space. Would it again become dust? She wondered.

In front of her, the back half of the *Extenuating Circumstances* was beginning to yaw. A ruptured hydraulic line in the hull was the culprit, spewing liters of water into space. She estimated the change of angle between her and the ship, compared it to her velocity, and realized that she was going to miss by almost a hundred meters.

Hopelessness gripped her.

If only she could go *there* instead of straight ahead, she would be fine, but—

She moved to the left.

Kira could feel it, a brief application of thrust along the right side of her body. Using an arm to counterbalance the motion, she glanced backwards and saw a faint haze of mist expanding behind her. The suit had moved her! For an instant, joy, and then she remembered the danger of the situation.

She focused on her destination again. Just a little more to the left and then angle up a few degrees, and . . . perfect! With each thought, the xeno responded by providing the exact amount of thrust needed to reposition her. And now faster! Faster!

Her speed increased, although not as much as she would have liked. So the suit did have its limits after all.

She tried to guess how much time had passed. A minute? Two minutes? However long it was, it was too long. The shuttle's systems would take minutes to start up and ready for departure, even with emergency overrides. She might be able to use the RCS thrusters to put a few hundred meters between her and the *Extenuating Circumstances,* but that wouldn't be enough to protect her from the blast.

One thing at a time. She had to get into a shuttle first, and then she could worry about trying to get away.

A thin red line swept across the back half of the ship, moving up the truncated stem—a laser beam slicing it apart. Decks exploded in plumes of crystalizing vapor, and she saw men and women ejected into space, their last breaths forming small clouds in front of their contorted faces.

The laser swerved sideways when it reached the docking section, swerved and sliced through the farthest shuttle. A burst of escaping air pushed the mangled shuttle away from the *Extenuating Circumstances,* and then a jet of fire erupted from a punctured fuel tank in one of its wings, and the shuttle spiraled away, a top spinning out of control.

"Goddammit!" Kira shouted.

The aft part of the *Extenuating Circumstances* rolled sideways toward her, driven by the decompression of the ruptured decks. She arced around the surface of the pale hull, hurtling over it dangerously fast, and smashed into the fuselage of the remaining shuttle. Printed in large letters along the side was the name *Valkyrie.*

Kira grunted and spread her arms and legs, trying to hold on.

Her hands and feet stuck to the shuttle, and she scrambled across the fuselage to the side airlock. She punched the release button, the light on the control panel turned green, and the door slowly began to slide open.

"Comeon, comeon!"

As soon as the gap between the door and the hull was wide enough, she wiggled through to the airlock and activated the emergency pressurization system. Air buffeted her from all directions, and the sound of the whooping siren faded in. The suit's mask didn't seem to interfere with her hearing.

"Self-destruct in T-minus forty-three seconds. This is not a drill."

"Fuck!"

When the pressure gauge read normal, Kira opened the inner airlock and shoved herself through, toward the cockpit.

The controls and displays were already active. One glance at them, and she saw that the engines were lit and all the preflight checklists and protocols had been taken care of. Bishop!

She swung herself down into the pilot's seat and struggled with the harness until she got herself strapped in.

"Self-destruct in T-minus twenty-five seconds. This is not a drill."

"Get me out of here!" she shouted through the mask. "Take off! Take—"

The *Valkyrie* jolted as it detached from the cruiser, and the weight of a thousand tons crashed into her as the shuttle's engines roared to life. The suit hardened in response, but still, it hurt.

The bulbous alien ship flashed past the nose of the *Valkyrie,* and then Kira glimpsed the forward section of the *Extenuating Circumstances* half a kilometer away, and she saw a pair of coffin-shaped escape pods shoot out from the prow of the ship and burn toward Adra's desolate surface.

In a surprisingly quiet voice, Bishop said, "Ms. Navárez, I left a recording for you on the *Valkyrie*'s system. Contains all the pertinent information regarding you, your situation, and this attack. Please watch at earliest convenience. Unfortunately, nothing else I can do to help. Safe travels, Ms. Navárez."

"Wait! What—"

The viewscreen flared white, and the aching pull in Kira's chest vanished. An instant later, the shuttle bucked as the expanding sphere of debris hit. For a few seconds, it seemed as if the *Valkyrie* would break apart. A panel above her sparked and went dead, and somewhere behind her, a *bang* sounded, followed by the high-pitched whistle of escaping air.

A new alarm rang out, and rows of red lights cycled overhead. As the roar of the engines cut out, the weight pressing down on her vanished, and the stomach-churning sensation of free fall returned.

2.

"Ms. Navárez, there are numerous hull breaches in the aft," said the shuttle's pseudo-intelligence.

"Yes, thank you," Kira muttered, unbuckling her harness. Her voice sounded strange and muffled through the mask.

She'd made it! She could hardly believe it. But she wasn't safe, not yet.

"Kill the alarm," she said.

The siren promptly cut out.

Kira was glad the mask stayed in place as she followed the high-pitched whistles toward the back of the shuttle. At least she didn't have to worry about blacking out if the pressure dropped too low. She wondered, though: Would she have to spend the rest of her life with her face covered?

First she had to make sure she *did* live.

The whistles led her to the rear of the passenger compartment. There she found seven holes along the edge of the ceiling. The holes were tiny, no wider than a piece of pencil lead, but still large enough to drain the atmosphere from the shuttle within a few hours.

"Computer, what's your name?"

"My name is Ando." It sounded like a Geiger, but it wasn't. Militaries used their own, specialized programs to fly their ships.

"Where's the repair kit, Ando?"

The pseudo-intelligence guided her to a locker. Kira retrieved the kit and used it to mix a batch of quick-setting, foul-smelling resin (the mask didn't seem to block the scent). She troweled the goop into the holes, and then covered each one with six cross-layered strips of FTL tape. The tape was stronger than most metals; it would take a blowtorch to remove that many strips.

As she rolled up the kit, Kira said, "Ando, damage report."

"There are electrical shorts in the lighting circuitry, lines two-twenty-three-n and lines one-five-one-n are compromised. Also —"

"Skip the itemized report. Is the *Valkyrie* spaceworthy?"

"Yes, Ms. Navárez."

"Were any critical systems hit?"

"No, Ms. Navárez."

"What about the fusion drive? Wasn't the nozzle pointing back at the explosion?"

"No, Ms. Navárez, our course put us on a bias with regard to the *Extenuating Circumstances*. The explosion struck us at an angle."

"Did you program the course?"

"No, Ms. Navárez, ship mind Bishop did."

Only then did Kira begin to relax. Only then did she allow herself to think that maybe, just maybe, she was really going to survive.

The mask rippled and peeled off her face. Kira yelped. She couldn't help it; the process felt like a giant sticky bandage being removed.

Within seconds, her face was clear.

Kira tentatively ran her fingers over her mouth and nose, around the edges of her eyes, touching and exploring. To her surprise, she seemed to have kept her eyebrows and eyelashes.

"What are you?" she whispered, tracing the neckline of the suit. "What were you made for?"

No answers were forthcoming.

She looked over the inside of the shuttle: at the consoles, the rows of seats, the storage lockers, and—next to her—four empty cryo tubes. Tubes that she couldn't use.

At the sight, sudden despair filled her. It didn't matter that she'd escaped. Without the ability to enter cryo, she was effectively stranded.

CHAPTER IX

* * * * * * *

CHOICES

1.

Kira pulled herself along the walls to the front of the *Valkyrie* and strapped herself into the pilot's seat. She checked the display: the *Extenuating Circumstances* was gone. So too was the alien ship, destroyed by the explosion of the UMC cruiser. "Ando, are there any other ships in the system?"

"Negative."

That was one piece of good news. "Ando, does the *Valkyrie* have a Markov Drive?"

"Affirmative."

Another piece of good news. The shuttle *was* capable of FTL. Even so, the lack of cryo might still kill her. It depended on the speed of the drive. "Ando, how long will it take the *Valkyrie* to reach Sixty-One Cygni if the shuttle makes an emergency burn to the Markov Limit?"

"Seventy-eight and a half days."

Kira swore. The *Fidanza* had only taken about twenty-six days. She supposed the shuttle's slowness shouldn't be a surprise. The ship was intended for short-range hops and not much more.

Don't panic. She wasn't completely out of luck. The next question would be the determining one.

"Ando, how many ration packs does the *Valkyrie* carry?"

"The *Valkyrie* carries one hundred and seven ration packs."

Kira had the pseudo-intelligence do the math for her. Not having her overlays was frustrating; she couldn't solve even basic calculations on her own.

Adding in the days needed to decelerate at 61 Cygni resulted in a total travel time of 81.74 days. At half rations, the food would only last Kira eight weeks, which would leave her without food for another 25.5 days. Water wasn't a problem; the reclamation equipment on the shuttle would keep her from dying of dehydration. The lack of food, on the other hand . . .

Kira had heard of people fasting for a month or more and surviving. She'd also heard of people who'd died in far less time. There was no telling. She was in reasonably good shape, and she had the suit to help her, so there was a chance she could make it, but it was a real gamble.

She rubbed her temple, feeling a headache forming. "Ando, play the message Bishop left for me."

An image of a harsh-faced man appeared on the display in front of her: the ship mind's avatar. His brows were drawn, and he seemed in equal parts concerned and angry. "Ms. Navárez, time is short. Aliens are jamming our comms, and they shot down the one signal drone I was able to launch. Not good. Only hope now is you, Ms. Navárez.

"I've included all of my sensor data with this message, as well as records from Doctor Carr, Adrasteia, et cetera. Please forward to the relevant authorities. Destruction of *Extenuating Circumstances* should remove source of jamming."

Bishop appeared to lean forward, then, and even though his face was only a simulation, Kira could still feel the force of his personality emanating from the screen: an overwhelming ferocity and intelligence bound to a single-minded purpose. "Apologies for the quality of your treatment, Ms. Navárez. Cause was just and—as attack has proven—concern was warranted, but still sorry you had to suffer. Regardless, counting on you now. We all are."

He returned to his former position. "And Ms. Navárez, if you see General Takeshi, tell him . . . tell him I remember the sound of summer. Bishop out."

A strange wistfulness came over Kira. For all their intelligence, ship minds were no more immune to regret and nostalgia than the rest of non-augmented humanity. Nor should they be.

She stared at the weave of fibers on her palm. "Ando, describe the first appearance of the alien ship."

"An unidentified vessel was detected via satellite sixty-three minutes ago, thrusting around Zeus on an intercept course." A holo popped up from the cockpit display, showing the gas giant, its moons, and a dotted line tracing the path of the graspers' ship from Zeus to Adra. "The vessel was accelerating at twenty-five g's, but—"

"Shit." That was a monstrously hard burn.

Ando continued, "—its rocket exhaust was insufficient to produce observed thrust. The vessel then executed a skew-flip and decelerated for seven minutes to match orbits with the UMCS *Extenuating Circumstances*."

A cold sense of apprehension gripped Kira. The only way the graspers could pull off maneuvers like that would be by reducing the inertial drag of their ship. Doing so was theoretically possible, but it wasn't something humans were capable of. The engineering challenges were still too great (the power requirements, for one, were prohibitive).

Her apprehension deepened. It really was the nightmare scenario. They'd finally made contact with another sentient species, but the species was hostile and able to fly circles around any human ship, even the unmanned ones.

Ando was still talking: "Unidentified vessel failed to respond to hails and initiated hostilities at—"

"Stop," said Kira. She knew the rest. She thought for a moment. The graspers must have jumped into the system on the far side of Zeus. It was the only way they could have avoided being immediately picked up by the *Extenuating Circumstances*. That or the graspers had launched from inside the gas giant, which seemed unlikely. Either way, they'd been cautious, using Zeus for cover and—as she looked at the holo Ando was playing—waiting for the *Extenuating Circumstances* to orbit around the backside of Adra before they'd started their burn.

It couldn't be coincidence that the graspers had showed up a few weeks after she'd found the xeno on Adra. Space was too big for that sort of serendipity. Either the graspers had been watching the moon or a signal had gone out from the ruins when she fell into them.

Kira rubbed her face, feeling suddenly tired. Okay. She had to assume the graspers had reinforcements that could show up at any moment. There was no time to lose.

"Ando, are we still being jammed?"

"Negative."

"Then—" She stopped. If she sent an FTL signal to 61 Cygni, could it lead the graspers back to the rest of human-settled space? Maybe, but they'd find it anyway if they were looking—assuming they didn't already have every human planet under observation—and the League needed to be warned about the aliens as soon as possible. "Then send a distress call to Vyyborg Station, including all pertinent information concerning the attack on the *Extenuating Circumstances*."

"Unable to comply."

"What? Why? Explain."

"The FTL antenna is damaged and unable to maintain a stable field. My service bots can't repair it."

Kira scowled. "Reroute distress call through the commsat in orbit. Satellite Twenty-Eight G. Access code—" And she rattled off her company authorization.

"Unable to comply. Satellite Twenty-Eight G is non-responsive. Debris in the area indicate it was destroyed."

"Dammit!" Kira slumped back in the chair. She couldn't even get a message to the *Fidanza.* It had only left a day ago, but without FTL comms, the ship might as well be on the other side of the galaxy as far as she was concerned. She could still transmit slower than light (and she would), but it would take eleven years to reach 61 Cygni, which wouldn't do her or the League any good.

She took a steadying breath. *Stay calm. You can get through this.* "Ando, send an encrypted report flagged eyes-only to the ranking UMC officer at Sixty-One Cygni. Use best means available. Include all relevant information pertaining to myself, Adrasteia, and the attack on the *Extenuating Circumstances.*"

An almost imperceptible pause, and then the pseudo-intelligence said, "Message sent."

"Good. Now, Ando, I want to make a broadcast on all available emergency channels."

A small *click.* "Ready."

Kira leaned forward, putting her mouth closer to the display microphone. "This is Kira Navárez on the UMCS *Valkyrie.* Does anyone read me? Over. . . ." She waited a few seconds and then repeated the message. And again. The UMC might not have treated her very well, but she couldn't leave without checking for survivors. The sight of the escape pods jettisoning from the *Extenuating Circumstances* still burned in her mind. If anyone was left alive, she had to know.

She was just about to have Ando automate the message when the speaker crackled and a man's voice answered, sounding eerily close. "This is Corporal Iska. What is your current location, Navárez? Over."

Surprise, relief, and a sense of mounting worry took hold of Kira. She hadn't actually expected to hear from anyone. Now what? "I'm still in orbit. Over. Uh, where are you? Over."

"Planetside, on Adra."

Then a new voice sounded, a youngish woman: "Private Reisner reporting. Over."

Another three followed, all men: "Specialist Orso, reporting." "Ensign Yarrek." "Petty Officer Samson."

Last of all, a hard, tight-clenched voice that made Kira stiffen: "Major Tschetter."

Six survivors in total, with the major being the highest ranking. After a few questions, it became clear that all six had landed on Adra, their escape pods scattered across the equatorial continent, where the survey HQ was located. The pods had attempted to land as close as possible to the base, but with their small thrusters, *close* had ended up being tens of kilometers away for the nearest pod and, in the case of Tschetter's, over seven hundred klicks.

"Right, what's the game plan, ma'am?" said Iska.

Tschetter was silent for a moment. Then: "Navárez, have you signaled the League?"

"Yup," said Kira. "But it's not going to reach them for over a decade." And she explained about the FTL antenna and the commsat.

"Fug-nuggets," Orso swore.

"Cut the chatter," said Iska.

They could hear Tschetter take a breath, shift position in her escape pod. "Shit." It was the first time Kira had heard her curse. "That changes things."

"Yeah," said Kira. "I checked the amount of food here on the *Valkyrie*. There's not a whole lot." She recited the numbers Ando had given her and then said, "How long until the UMC sends another ship to investigate?"

More sounds of movement from Tschetter. She seemed to be having difficulty finding a comfortable position. "Not soon enough. At least a month, maybe more."

Kira dug her thumb into her palm. The situation kept getting worse.

Tschetter continued: "We can't afford to wait. Our first priority has to be warning the League about these aliens."

"The suit calls them *graspers*," Kira offered.

"Is that so?" said Tschetter, her tone cutting. "Any other pertinent pieces of information you'd care to share with us, Ms. Navárez?"

"Just some weird dreams. I'll write them down later."

"You do that. . . . Again, we have to warn the League. That and the xeno you're carrying, Navárez, are more important than any one of us. Therefore,

I'm ordering you under special provision of the Stellar Security Act to take the *Valkyrie* and leave for Sixty-One Cygni right now, without delay."

"Ma'am, no!" said Yarrek.

Iska growled. "Keep it down, Ensign."

The thought of abandoning the survivors didn't sit right with Kira. "Look, if I have to go to Cygni without cryo, I'll do it, but I'm not going to just leave you guys."

Tschetter snorted. "Very commendable of you, but we don't have time to waste on you flying around Adrasteia picking us up. It would take half a day or more, and the graspers could be on us by then."

"That's a risk I'm willing to take," Kira said in a quiet voice. And it was, she realized somewhat to her surprise.

She could almost hear Tschetter shake her head. "Well, I'm not, Navárez. Besides, the shuttle only carries four cryo tubes, and we all know it."

"Sorry, Major, I can't just fly off and abandon you."

"Dammit, Navárez. Ando, command override, authorization—" Tschetter recited a long, meaningless password.

"Override denied," said the pseudo-intelligence. "All command functions in the *Valkyrie* were assigned to Kira Navárez."

If anything, the major's voice grew even colder: "On whose authority?"

"Ship mind Bishop."

"I see. . . . Navárez, get your head on straight and do the responsible thing. This is bigger than all of us. Circumstances demand—"

"They always do," Kira murmured.

"What?"

She shook her head, although no one could see. "Doesn't matter. I'm coming down there for you. Even if—"

"No!" said Tschetter and Iska nearly at the same time. Tschetter continued: "No. Under no circumstances are you to land the *Valkyrie,* Navárez. We can't afford to have you caught flat-footed. Besides, even if you fill up at your base before blasting off again, you'll use up a good portion of your propellant getting back into orbit. You're going to need every bit of delta-v to decelerate once you reach Sixty-One Cygni."

"Well, I'm not just going to wait up here and do nothing," said Kira. "And there's nothing you can do to force me to leave."

An uncomfortable silence filled the comms.

There has to be a way to save at least some of them, thought Kira. She imagined being alone on Adra, starving or trying to hide from the graspers. It was a horrifying prospect, and one she wouldn't have wished on even Dr. Carr.

The thought of Carr stopped her for an instant. The terror on his face, the warnings he'd shouted, the bones sticking from his skin . . . If she hadn't shot the oxygen line, maybe he could have escaped the *Extenuating Circumstances*. No. The grasper would have killed both of them if not for the explosion. Still, she felt sorry. Carr might have been a bastard, but no one deserved to die like that.

Then she snapped her fingers. The sound was surprisingly loud in the cockpit. "I know," she said. "I know how to get you off-planet."

"How?" Tschetter asked, wary.

"The drop shuttle back at HQ," said Kira.

"What shuttle?" said Orso. He had a deep voice. "The *Fidanza* took it with them when they left."

Impatient, Kira barely waited for him to stop speaking: "No, not that one. The other shuttle. The one Neghar was flying the day I found the xeno. It was going to be scrapped because of possible contamination."

A sharp tapping came over the speakers, and Kira knew it was Tschetter's nails. The woman said, "What would it take to get the shuttle into the air?"

Kira thought. "The tanks probably just need to be filled up."

"Ma'am," said Orso. "I'm only twenty-three klicks away from the base. I can be there in under fifty minutes."

Tschetter's answer was immediate: "Do it. *Move.*"

A faint *click* sounded as Orso dropped off the line.

Then Iska said in a somewhat tentative voice, "Ma'am . . ."

"I know," said Tschetter. "Navárez, I need to talk with the corporal. Hold position."

"Okay, but—"

The comms went dead.

2.

Kira reviewed the shuttle's controls while she waited. When several minutes passed and Tschetter still hadn't called back, Kira unstrapped herself and rummaged around in the shuttle's storage lockers until she found a jumpsuit.

She didn't need it—the xeno kept her plenty warm—but she'd felt naked ever since she'd woken up on the *Extenuating Circumstances.* Something about having a set of proper clothes comforted her, made her feel safer. Silly or not, it made a difference.

Then she went to the shuttle's small galley area.

She was hungry, but knowing how limited the supply of rations were, she couldn't bring herself to eat a meal pack. Instead, she got a pouch of self-heating chell—her favorite—and brought it back to the cockpit.

While she sipped the tea, she viewed the patch of space where the *Extenuating Circumstances* and the graspers' ship had been.

Nothing but empty blackness. All those people, dead. Humans and aliens alike. Not even a cloud of dust remained; the explosion had obliterated the ships and scattered their atoms in every possible direction.

Aliens. *Sentient* aliens. The knowledge still overwhelmed her. That and the fact that she had helped kill one . . . Maybe the tentacled creatures could be negotiated with. Maybe a peaceful solution was still possible. However, any such solution would probably involve *her.*

At the thought, the backs of her hands crinkled, the crosswoven fibers bunching like knotted muscles. Since the encounter with the grasper, the suit had yet to fully settle down; it seemed more sensitive to her emotional state than before.

If nothing else, the attack on the *Extenuating Circumstances* had settled one debate: humans weren't the only self-aware species to be violent, even murderous. Far from it.

Kira switched her gaze to the front viewport and the gleaming bulk of Adrasteia beyond. It was strange to realize that the six crew members—Tschetter included—were somewhere down on the surface.

Six people, but the shuttle only held four cryo pods.

An idea occurred to Kira. She opened the comm channel again and said, "Tschetter, do you read? Over."

"What is it, Navárez?" said the major, sounding irritated.

"We had two cryo pods at HQ. Remember? The ones Neghar and I were in. One of them might still be there."

". . . Noted. Would there be anything else of use at the base? Food, equipment—that sort of thing?"

"I'm not sure. We hadn't finished cleaning the place out. There might still be some plants alive in the hydro bay. Maybe a few meal packs in the galley. Plenty of survey equipment, but that won't put food in your stomach."

"Roger that. Over and out."

Another half hour passed before the line sprang to life again and the major said, "Navárez, do you read?"

"Yes, I'm here," said Kira, quickly.

"Orso found the drop shuttle. It and the hydro cracker seem to be functional."

Thule! "Good!"

"Now, here's what is going to happen," said Tschetter. "Once he finishes refueling the shuttle—which should be in . . . seven minutes—Orso is going to collect Samson, Reisner, and Yarrek. This will require two separate trips. They will then rendezvous with you in orbit. The shuttle will return under its own power to the base, and *you*, Ms. Navárez, will give the order to Ando and leave on the *Valkyrie*. Are we clear?"

Kira scowled. Why did the major always irritate her so? "What about the cryo tube I mentioned? Is it there at the base?"

"Badly damaged."

Kira winced. The suit must have hit the tube when it emerged. "Understood. Then you and Iska—"

"We're staying."

A strange sense of affinity came over Kira. She didn't like the major—not one bit—but she couldn't help but admire the woman's toughness. "Why you? Shouldn't—"

"No," said Tschetter. "If you're attacked, you need people who can fight. I broke my leg during the landing. I wouldn't be any good. As for the corporal, he volunteered. He'll make the trip on foot to the base over the next few days, and when he gets there, he'll fly out to bring me in."

". . . I'm sorry," said Kira.

"Don't be," said Tschetter, stern. "Can't change what is. In any case, we need observers here in case the aliens return. I'm Fleet Intelligence; I'm the one best suited for the job."

"Of course," said Kira. "By the way, if you dig around in Seppo's workstation at HQ, you might find some seed packs. I don't know if you can get anything to grow, but—"

"We'll check," said Tschetter. Then, in a slightly softer tone, "I appreciate the thought, even if you're a real pain in the ass sometimes, Navárez."

"Yeah, well, takes one to know one." Kira scuffed her palm against the edge of the console, watching how the surface of the suit flexed and stretched. She wondered: If she were in Tschetter's position, would she have the courage to make the same decision?

"We'll let you know when the shuttle launches. Tschetter out."

3.

"Display off," said Kira.

She studied her reflection in the glass, a dim, ghostly double. It was her first time getting a good look at herself since the xeno had emerged.

She almost didn't recognize herself. Instead of the normal, expected shape of her head, she saw the outline of her skull, bare and hairless and black beneath the layered fibers. Her eyes were hollow, and there were lines on either side of her mouth that reminded her of her mother.

She leaned closer. Where the suit faded into her skin, it formed a finely detailed fractal, the sight of which struck a strange chord in her, as if she'd seen it before. The sense of déjà vu was so strong, for a moment she felt as if she were in another place and another time, and she had to shake herself and move back.

Kira thought she looked ghoulish—a corpse risen from the grave to haunt the living. Loathing filled her, and she averted her gaze, not wanting to see the evidence of the xeno's effects. She was glad Alan had never seen her like this; how could he have liked or loved her? She imagined a look of disgust on his face, and it matched her own.

For a moment, tears filled her eyes, but Kira blinked them back, angry.

She put on the brimmed cap she'd dug out of a locker and turned up the collar of the jumpsuit to hide as much of the xeno as possible. Then: "Display on. Start recording." The screen lit up, and a yellow light appeared next to the camera in the bezel.

"Hi, Mom. Dad. Isthah . . . I don't know when you'll see this. I don't know if you ever will, but I hope you do. Things haven't gone too well here. I can't tell you the details, not without getting you in trouble with the League, but Alan is dead. Also, Fizel and Yugo and Ivanova and Seppo."

Kira had to look away for a moment before she could continue. "My shuttle is damaged, and I don't know if I'm going to make it back to Sixty-One Cygni, so if I don't: Mom, Dad, I have you listed as my beneficiaries. You'll find the info attached to this message.

"Also, I know this might sound strange, but I need you to trust me. You have to prepare. You have to really prepare. There's a storm coming, and it's going to be a bad one. Worse than 'thirty-seven." They'd understand. The joke had always been that only the apocalypse could be worse than the storm that year. "Last thing: I don't want the three of you to get depressed because of me. Especially you, Mom. I *know* you. Stop it. Don't just stay at home moping. That goes for all of you. Get out. Smile. Live. For my sake, as well as your own. Please, promise me that you will."

Kira paused and then nodded. "I'm sorry. I'm really sorry for putting you through this. I wish I'd returned home to see you before this trip. . . . Love you."

She tapped the Stop button.

For a few minutes, she sat and did nothing, just stared at the blank screen. Then she forced herself to record a message for Sam, Alan's brother. Since she couldn't tell the truth about the xeno, she blamed his death on an accident at the base.

By the end, Kira found herself crying again. She didn't try to stop the tears. So much had happened in the past few days, it was a relief to let go, if only for a short while.

On her finger, she felt a phantom weight where the ring Alan had given her should have been. Its absence only worsened the flow of tears.

Her turmoil left the fibers restless beneath the jumpsuit, bead-like bumps forming along her arms and legs and across her upper back. She snarled and slapped the back of her hand, and the beads subsided.

Once she regained her composure, she made similar recordings for the rest of her dead teammates. She didn't know their families—she didn't even know if some of them *had* families—but Kira still felt it was necessary. She owed it to them. They'd been her friends . . . and she'd killed them.

The last recording was no easier than the first. Afterward, Kira had Ando send the messages, and then she closed her eyes, drained, exhausted. She could feel the suit's presence in her mind—a subtle pressure that had appeared sometime during their escape from the *Extenuating Circumstances*—but she sensed no hint of thought or intent from it. Still, she had no doubt: the xeno was aware. And it was watching.

. . .

A burst of static sounded in the speakers.

Kira started and realized she must have nodded off. A voice was speaking: Orso. "—do you read? Over. Repeat, do you read, Navárez? Over."

"I hear you," she said. "Over."

"We're just refueling the drop shuttle. We'll be blasting off this forsaken rock soon as our tanks are full. Rendezvous with the *Valkyrie* in fourteen minutes."

"I'll be ready," she said.

"Roger that. Over."

The time passed quickly. Kira watched through the shuttle's rear-facing cameras as a shining dot rose from the surface of Adrasteia and arced toward the *Valkyrie.* As it neared, the familiar shape of the drop shuttle came into view.

"I can see them," she reported. "No signs of trouble."

"That's good," said Tschetter.

The drop shuttle came up alongside the *Valkyrie,* and the two vessels fired their RCS thrusters as they gently mated, airlock to airlock. A faint shudder passed through the *Valkyrie*'s frame.

"Docking maneuver successfully completed," said Ando. He sounded entirely too cheery for Kira's taste.

The airlocks popped open with a hiss of air. A hawk-nosed man with a buzz cut stuck his head through the opening. "Permission to come aboard, Navárez?"

"Permission granted," said Kira. It was just a formality, but she appreciated it.

She stuck out a hand as the man floated over to her. After a moment's hesitation, he accepted it. "Specialist Orso, I presume?" she said.

"You presume correctly."

Behind Orso came Private Reisner (a short, wide-eyed woman who looked as if she'd signed up for the UMC right out of school), Petty Officer Samson (a red-haired beanpole of a man), and Ensign Yarrek (a heavyset man with a large bandage on his right arm).

"Welcome to the *Valkyrie,*" said Kira.

They all looked at her somewhat askance, and then Orso said, "Glad to be here."

Yarrek grunted and said, "We owe you one, Navárez."

"Yes," said Reisner. "Thank you."

Before sending the drop shuttle back to Adra, Orso went to a row of cabinets set flush to the hull at the back of the *Valkyrie.* Kira hadn't even noticed them before. Orso entered a code, and the lockers popped open to reveal several racks of guns: blasters and firearms alike.

"Now we're talking," said Samson.

Orso picked out four guns, as well as a collection of battery packs, magazines, and grenades, and then carried them over to the drop shuttle. "For the major and the corporal," he explained.

Kira nodded, understanding.

Once the weapons were safely stowed and everyone was back on the *Valkyrie,* the drop shuttle disconnected and fell away toward the moon below.

"I'm guessing you didn't find any extra food at the base," Kira said to Orso.

He shook his head. "Afraid not. Our escape pods carry a few rations, but we left them for the major and the corporal. They'll need it more than we will."

"You mean more than *I* will."

He eyed her, wary. "Yeah, suppose so."

Kira shook her head. "Doesn't matter." He was right, in any case. "Okay, let's do this."

"Places, people!" Orso shouted. As the three others scrambled to strap themselves in, Orso joined her at the front and settled into the copilot's seat.

Then Kira said, "Ando, lay in a course for the nearest port at Sixty-One Cygni. Fastest possible burn."

An image of their destination appeared in the console display. A labeled dot blinked: the Hydrotek refueling station in orbit around the gas giant Tsiolkovsky. The same station the *Fidanza* had stopped at on its way out to their current system, Sigma Draconis.

Kira paused a moment and then said: "Engage."

The shuttle's engines roared to life, and a solid 2 g's of thrust pressed them backwards, gently at first and then with swiftly increasing pressure.

"Here we go," Kira murmured.

4.

Ando kept up the 2-g burn for three hours, at which point the pseudo-intelligence throttled back the thrust to a more manageable 1.5 g's, which allowed them to move around the cabin without too much discomfort.

The four UMC personnel spent the next hour going over every part of the shuttle. They double-checked Kira's repairs—"Not bad for a civvy," Samson grudgingly admitted—counted and recounted the meal packs; cataloged every weapon, battery, and cartridge; ran diagnostics on the skinsuits and the cryo tubes; and generally made sure the ship was in working order.

"If something goes wrong while we're under," said Orso, "you probably won't have time to wake us up."

Then he and the others stripped down to their underwear, and Yarrek, Samson, and Reisner got into their cryo tubes and started the round of injections that would induce hibernation. They couldn't stay awake any longer or they'd need to eat, and they had to save the food for Kira.

Reisner laughed nervously and gave them a little wave. "See you at Sixty-One Cygni," she said as the top of her cryo tube lowered and closed.

Kira waved back, but she didn't think the private saw.

Orso waited until the others had lapsed into unconsciousness, and then he went to the lockers, removed a rifle, and brought it over to Kira. "Here. It's against regs, but you might need this, and if you do . . . well, beats having to fight hand-to-hand." He looked at Kira with a somewhat sardonic expression. "We're all going to be helpless around you anyway, so what the hell. Might as well give you a chance."

"Thanks," she said, taking the rifle. It was heavier than it looked. "I think."

"No problemo." He winked at her. "Check with Ando; he can show you how to operate it. There's one other thing, orders from Tschetter."

"What?" said Kira, suddenly on guard.

Orso pointed at his right forearm. The skin there was slightly lighter than his upper arm, and a sharp line separated the two. "See that?"

"Yeah."

He pointed at a similar difference in shade on the middle of his left thigh. "And that?"

"Yeah."

"Got hit by shrapnel a few years back. Lost both limbs and had to get them regrown."

"Ouch."

Orso shrugged. "Eh. It didn't hurt as bad as you might expect. The point is . . . once you run out of food, if you think you're not going to make it, pop open my cryo pod and start cutting."

"What?! No! I couldn't do that."

The corporal gave her a look. "It's no different than any lab-grown meat. As long as I'm in cryo, I'll be perfectly fine."

Kira grimaced. "Do you really expect me to turn into a cannibal? Jesus Christ, I know things are different back at Sol, but—"

"No," said Orso, grabbing her by the shoulder. "I expect you to survive. We aren't playing games here, Navárez. The entire human race could be in danger. If you need to cut off one of my arms and eat it in order to stay alive, then you damn well should. Both arms if you have to, and my legs too. Do you understand?"

He was nearly shouting by the time he finished. Kira squeezed her eyes together and nodded, unable to look him in the face.

After a second, Orso released her. "Okay. Good . . . Just, uh, don't get chop-happy unless you need to."

Kira shook her head. "I won't. Promise."

He snapped his fingers and gave her finger guns. "Excellent." He climbed into the last cryo pod and settled into the cradle. "Are you going to be alright on your own?"

Kira leaned the rifle against the wall next to her. "Yeah. I've got Ando to keep me company."

Orso grinned. "That's the spirit. Don't want you going stir-crazy on us, eh?" Then he pulled the lid of the cryo tube shut, and a layer of cold condensation soon covered the inside of the window, hiding him from view.

Kira let out her breath and carefully sat next to the rifle, feeling every added kilo from the 1.5 g's in her bones.

It was going to be a long trip.

5.

The *Valkyrie* maintained the 1.5-g burn for sixteen hours. Kira took the opportunity to record a detailed account of the visions she'd been receiving from the xeno, which she had Ando send to both Tschetter and the League.

She also attempted to access the records Bishop had transferred from the *Extenuating Circumstances,* specifically those pertaining to Carr's examination of the xeno. To her great annoyance, the files were password protected and labeled *For Authorized Personnel Only.*

When that failed, Kira napped, and when she could no longer nap, she lay looking at the xeno shrink-wrapped around her skin.

She traced a wandering line across her forearm, noting the feel of the fibers beneath her finger. Then she slid a hand under the thermal blanket she had tucked around herself—under the blanket and under the jumpsuit—and she touched herself where she hadn't dared before. Breasts, stomach, thighs, and then between her thighs.

There was no pleasure to the act; it was a clinical examination, nothing more. Her interest in sex was somewhere south of zero at the moment. And yet, it surprised Kira how sensitive her skin was even through the covering fibers. Between her legs was as smooth as a doll, and yet she could still feel every familiar fold of skin.

Her breath hissed out between her clenched teeth, and she pulled her hand back. *Enough.* She'd more than satisfied her curiosity in that regard for the time being.

Instead, she experimented with the xeno. First she tried to coax the suit into forming a row of spikes along the inside of her forearm. Tried and failed. The fibers stirred in response to her mental command, but they otherwise refused to obey.

She knew the xeno could. It just didn't want to. Or it didn't feel sufficiently threatened. Even imagining a grasper in front of her wasn't enough to convince the organism to produce a spike.

Frustrated, Kira shifted her attention instead to the suit's mask, curious if she could summon it forth on demand.

The answer was yes, but not without difficulty. Only by forcing herself into a state of near panic, where her heart was pounding and pinpricks of cold sweat sprang up across her forehead, was Kira able to successfully communicate her intent, and only then did she feel the same creeping tingle along her scalp and neck as the suit flowed across her face. For a moment, Kira felt as if she were choking, and for that moment her fear was real. Then she mastered herself, and her pulse slowed.

With subsequent attempts, the xeno grew more receptive, and she was able to get the same result with a sense of focused concern—easy to produce given the circumstances.

While the mask was in place, Kira lay for a while, staring at the EM fields around her: the giant, hazy loops emanating from the *Valkyrie*'s fusion drive and the generator it fed. The smaller, brighter loops clustered around the interior of the shuttle and stitched one segment of paneling to another with tiny threads of energy. She found the fields strangely beautiful: the diaphanous lines reminded her of the aurora she'd once seen on Weyland, only more regular.

In the end, the strain from her self-induced panic was too great to maintain, and she allowed the mask to retract from her face, and the fields vanished from view.

At least she wouldn't be entirely alone. She had Ando, and she had the suit: her silent companion, her parasitic hitchhiker, her deadly piece of living apparel. Not an alliance of friendship but of skinship.

Before the burn cut out, Kira allowed herself to eat one of the ration packs. It would be her last chance to have a meal with any sensation of weight for a very long time, and she was determined not to waste it.

She ate sitting next to the small galley area. When finished, she treated herself to another pouch of chell, which she nursed over the better part of an hour.

The only sounds in the shuttle were her breathing and the dull roar of the rockets, and even that would soon disappear. Out of the corner of her eye, she could see the cryo tubes at the back of the *Valkyrie,* cold and motionless, with no indication of the frozen bodies within. It was strange to think she wasn't the only person on the shuttle, even though Orso and the rest were barely more than blocks of ice at the moment.

It wasn't a comforting thought. Kira shivered and let her head thump back against the floor/wall.

Pain shot through her skull, and she winced, eyes watering. "Dammit," she muttered. She kept moving too quickly for the increase in g-forces and hurting herself as a result. Her joints ached, and her arms and legs throbbed from a dozen bumps and bruises. The xeno protected her from worse, but it seemed to ignore small, chronic discomforts.

Kira didn't know how the people on Shin-Zar or other high-g planets bore it. They were gene-hacked to help them survive and even thrive within a deep gravity well, but still, she had a hard time imagining how they could ever really be comfortable.

"Warning," said Ando. "Zero-g in T-minus five minutes."

Kira disposed of the drink pouch and then gathered a half-dozen thermal blankets from the shuttle's lockers and brought them with her back to the cockpit. There, she wrapped the blankets around the pilot's chair, creating a golden cocoon for herself. Next to the chair, she taped the rifle, a week's worth of ration packs, wet wipes, and a few other essentials she thought she might need.

Then a faint jolt ran through the bulkhead, and the rockets cut out, leaving her in blessed silence.

Kira's stomach rose within her, and the jumpsuit floated away from her skin, as if inflated. Trying to keep her lunch (such as it was) from making an encore appearance, she nestled into the foil-wrapped chair.

"Shutting down nonessential systems," said Ando, and across the crew compartment, the lights winked out, save for faint red strips above the control panels.

"Ando," she said, "lower the cabin pressure to the equivalent of twenty-four hundred meters above sea level, Earth standard."

"Ms. Navárez, at that level—"

"I'm aware of the side effects, Ando. I'm counting on them. Now do as I say."

Behind her, Kira heard the whir of the ventilation fans increase, and she felt a slight breeze as the air started to flow toward the vents by the ceiling.

She tabbed the comms. "Tschetter. The burn just ended. We'll be transitioning to FTL in three hours. Over." The time was needed to allow the fusion reactor to cool as much as possible and for the *Valkyrie*'s radiators to chill the rest of the shuttle to near-freezing temperatures. Even then, it was likely the shuttle would overheat two or three times while in FTL, depending on how active she was. When that happened, the *Valkyrie* would have to return to normal space long enough to shed its excess thermal energy before continuing onward. Otherwise, she and everything in the *Valkyrie* would cook in their own heat.

The light-speed gap between the *Valkyrie* and Adra meant it was over three minutes before Tschetter's reply arrived: "Roger that, Navárez. Any problems with the shuttle? Over."

"Negative. Green lights across the board. What about you?" The major, Kira knew, was still waiting in the escape pod for Iska to retrieve her.

. . . "Situation normal. I managed to splint my leg. Should allow me to walk on it. Over."

Kira felt a pang of sympathetic pain. That must have hurt like hell. "How long until Iska reaches the base? Over."

. . . "Tomorrow evening, barring any problems. Over."

"That's good." Then Kira said, "Tschetter, what happened to Alan's body?" It was a question that had been bothering her the past day.

. . . "His remains were transported to the *Extenuating Circumstances*, along with the rest of the deceased. Over."

Kira closed her eyes for a moment. At least Alan had had a funeral pyre fit for a king: a flaming ship to send him off into eternity. "Understood. Over."

They continued to exchange messages intermittently over the next few hours—the major suggesting things Kira could do to make the trip easier, Kira giving advice about surviving on Adra. Even the major, Kira thought, was feeling the weight of circumstances.

Then, Kira said, "Tschetter, tell me: What did Carr actually find out about the xeno? And don't give me that classified bullshit. Over."

. . . A sigh sounded on the other end of the line. "The xeno is composed of a semi-organic material unlike anything we've seen before. Our working theory was that the suit is actually a collection of highly sophisticated nanoassemblers, although we weren't able to isolate any individual units. The few samples we collected were almost impossible to study. They actively resisted examination. Put a couple of molecules on a chip-lab, and they break the lab or eat their way through the machine or short out the circuit. You get the idea."

"Anything else?" said Kira.

. . . "No. We made very little progress. Carr was particularly obsessed with trying to identify the xeno's source of power. It doesn't seem to be drawing sustenance from you. Quite the opposite, in fact, which means it has to have another way of generating energy."

Then Ando said, "FTL transition in five minutes."

"Tschetter, we're just about to hit the Markov Limit. Looks like this is it. Good luck to you and Iska. Hope you make it." After a brief pause, Kira said, "Ando, give me aft cameras."

The display screen in front of her sprang to life, showing the view behind the shuttle. Zeus and its moons, including Adrasteia, were a cluster of bright dots off to the right, alone in the darkness.

Alan's face appeared in her mind, and her throat tightened.

"Goodbye," she whispered.

Then she panned the camera over until the system's star appeared on the display. She stared at it, knowing that she would likely never see it again. Sigma Draconis, the eighteenth star in the Draco constellation. When she had first spotted it listed on the company reports, she'd liked the name; it had seemed to promise adventure and excitement and perhaps a bit of danger. . . . Now it seemed more ominous than anything, as if it were the dragon come to eat all of humanity.

"Give me the nose cameras."

The screen switched to a view of the stars ahead of the shuttle. Without her overlays, it took her a minute to find her destination: a small, reddish-orange dot near the center of the display. At that distance, the system's two stars merged into a single point, but she knew it was the nearest star that she was heading for.

It struck Kira then, with visceral strength, just how far away 61 Cygni was. Light-years were long beyond imagining, and even with all the benefits of modern technology it was an enormous, terrifying distance, and the shuttle no more than a mote of dust hurtling through the void.

. . . "Roger that, Navárez. Safe travels. Tschetter out."

A faint whine sounded at the back of the shuttle as the Markov Drive began to power up.

Kira glanced toward it. Though she couldn't see the drive, she could picture it: a great black orb, huge and heavy, resting on the other side of the shadow shield, a malignant toad squatting in the spaces between the walls. As always, the thought of the machine gave her the creeps. Perhaps it was the radioactive death contained in its precious grams of antimatter and the fact that they could destroy her in an instant if the magnetic bottles failed. Perhaps it was what the machine did, the twisting of matter and energy to allow for entry into superluminal space. Whatever it was, the drive unsettled her and made her wonder what strange things might happen to people while they slept in FTL.

This time, she'd get to find out.

The whine intensified, and Ando said, "FTL transition in five . . . four . . . three . . . two . . . one."

The whine peaked, and the stars vanished.

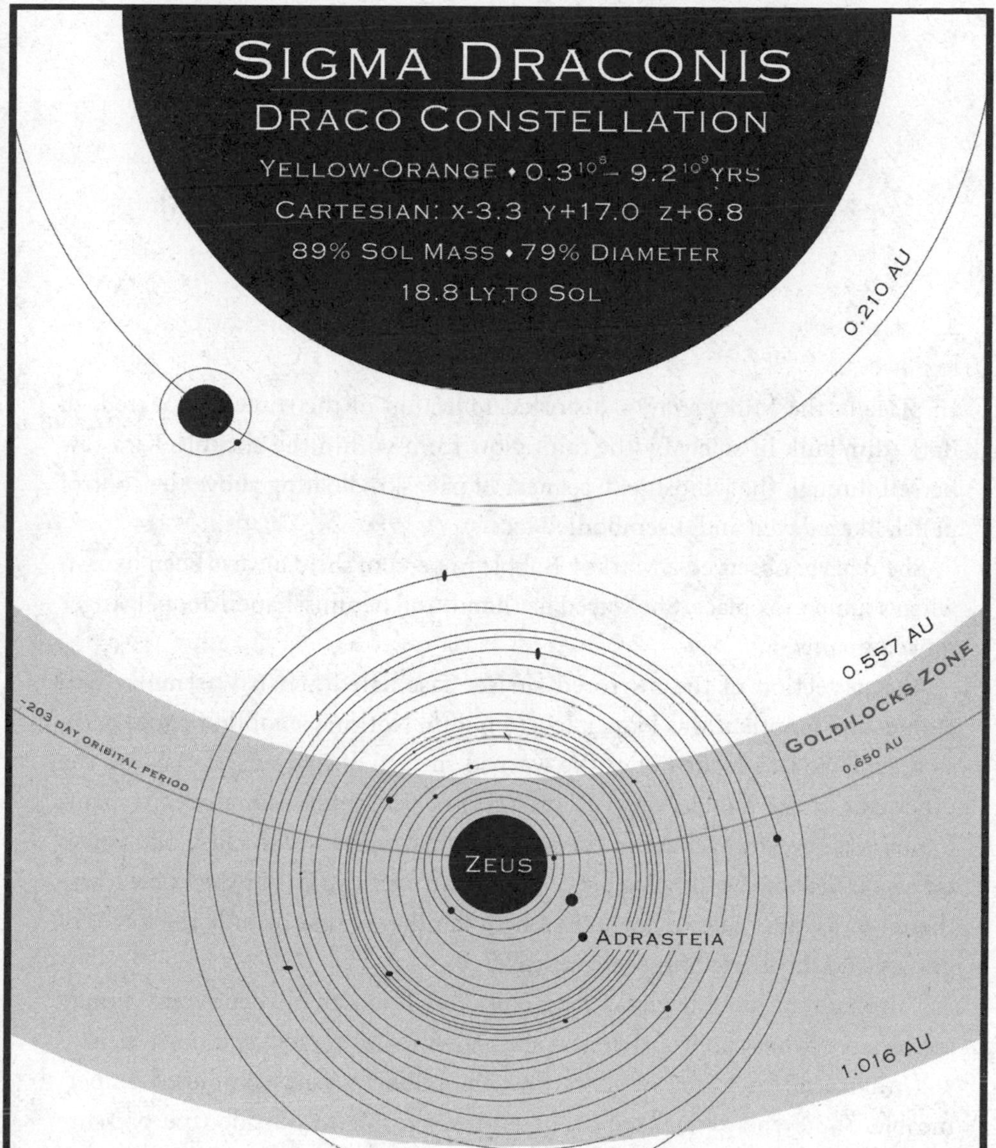

Sigma Draconis

Draco Constellation

Yellow-Orange • $0.3^{10^{8}}$ – $9.2^{10^{9}}$ yrs

Cartesian: x-3.3 y+17.0 z+6.8

89% Sol Mass • 79% Diameter

18.8 ly to Sol

0.210 AU

0.557 AU

Goldilocks Zone

0.650 AU

~203 day oribital period

Zeus

Adrasteia

1.016 AU

1.306 AU

Lapsang
Trading Company

* * * *

EXEUNT I

1.

In place of the Milky Way, a distorted reflection of the shuttle appeared—a dark, dim bulk lit solely by the faint glow from within the cockpit. Kira saw herself through the windshield: a smear of pale skin floating above the control panel, like a flayed and disembodied face.

She'd never observed a Markov Bubble in person; she'd always been in cryo when a jump took place. She waved her hand, and her misshapen doppelgänger moved in unison.

The perfection of the mirrored surface fascinated her. It was more than atomically smooth; it was Planck-level smooth. Nothing smoother could exist, as the bubble was made out of the warped surface of space itself. And on the other side of the bubble, on the other side of that infinitesimally thin membrane, was the strangeness of the superluminal universe, so close and yet so far away. *That* she would never see. No human ever could. But she knew it was there—a vast alternate realm, joined with familiar reality by only the forces of gravity and the fabric of spacetime itself.

"Through the looking glass," Kira muttered. It was an old expression among spacers, one whose appropriateness she hadn't really appreciated until then.

Unlike a normal area of spacetime, the bubble wasn't completely impermeable. Some energy leakage occurred from inside to outside (the pressure differential was enormous). Not much, but some, and it was a good thing too, as it helped reduce the thermal buildup while in FTL. Without it, the *Valkyrie*, and ships in general, wouldn't be able to stay in superluminal space for more than a few hours.

Kira remembered a description her fourth-year physics teacher had once used: "Going faster than light is like traveling in a straight line along a right angle." The phrase had stuck with her, and the more she'd learned of the math, the more she'd realized how accurate it was.

She continued to watch her reflection for several more minutes. Then, with a sigh, she darkened the windshield until it was opaque. "Ando: play the complete works of J. S. Bach on a loop, starting with the Brandenburg Concertos. Volume level three."

As the opening chords sounded, soft and precise, Kira felt herself begin to relax. The structure of Bach had always appealed to her: the cold, clean mathematical beauty of one theme slotting into another, building, exploring, transforming. And when each piece resolved, the resolution was so immensely *satisfying.* No other composer gave her that feeling.

The music was the one luxury she was allowing herself. It wouldn't produce much heat, and since she couldn't read or play games on her implants, she needed something else to keep her from going crazy in the days to come. If she'd still had her concertina, she could have practiced on it, but since she didn't . . .

In any case, the soothing nature of the Bach would work with the cabin's low pressure to help her sleep, which was important. The more she could sleep, the faster the time would go by and the less food she would need.

She lifted her right arm and held it before her face. The suit was even darker than the surrounding darkness: a shadow within shadows, visible more as an absence than an actuality.

It should have a name. She'd been damn lucky to escape the *Extenuating Circumstances.* By all rights the grasper should have killed her. And if not, then the explosive decompression. The xeno had saved her life multiple times. Of course, without the xeno, she never would have been in danger in the first place. . . . Still, Kira felt a certain amount of gratitude toward it. Gratitude and confidence, for with it, she was safer than any Marine in their power armor.

After everything they'd gone through, the xeno deserved a name. But what? The organism was a bundle of contradictions; it was armor, but it was also a weapon. It could be hard, or it could be soft. It could flow like water, or it could be as rigid as a metal beam. It was a machine but also somehow alive.

There were too many variables to consider. No one word could encompass them all. Instead, Kira focused on the suit's most obvious quality: its appearance. The surface of the material had always reminded her of obsidian, although not quite as glassy.

"Obsidian," she murmured. With her mind, she pressed the word toward the xeno's presence, as if to make it understand. *Obsidian.*

The xeno responded.

A wave of disjointed images and sensations swept through her. At first she was confused—individually they seemed to mean nothing—but as the sequence repeated, and again, she began to see the relationships between the different fragments. Together they formed a language born not of words but associations. And she understood:

The xeno already had a name.

It was a complex name, composed of and embodied by a web of interrelated concepts that she realized would probably take her years to fully parse, if ever. However, as the concepts filtered through her mind, she couldn't help but assign words to them. She was only human, after all; language was as much a part of her as consciousness itself. The words failed to capture the subtleties of the name—because she herself didn't understand them—but they captured the broadest and most obvious aspects.

The Soft Blade.

A faint smile touched her lips. She liked it. "The Soft Blade." She said it out loud, letting the words linger on her tongue. And from the xeno she felt a sense, if not of satisfaction, then of acceptance.

Knowing the organism had a name (and not one she had given it) changed Kira's view of it. Instead of thinking of the xeno just as an interloper and a potentially deadly parasite, now she saw it more as a . . . companion.

It was a profound shift. And not one she had intended or anticipated. Though as she belatedly realized, names changed—and defined—all things, including relationships. The situation reminded her of naming a pet; once you did, that was that, you had to keep the animal, whether you'd planned to or not.

The Soft Blade . . .

"And just what were you made for?" she asked, but no answer was forthcoming.

Whatever the case, Kira knew one thing: whoever had selected the name—whether it was the xeno's creators or the xeno itself—they possessed a sense of elegance and poetry, and they appreciated the contradiction inherent in the concepts she'd summarized as the Soft Blade.

It was a strange universe. The more she learned, the stranger it seemed, and she doubted she would ever find the answers to all her questions.

The Soft Blade. She closed her eyes, feeling oddly comforted. With the faint strains of Bach playing in the background, she allowed herself to drift off to sleep, knowing that—at least for the time being—she was safe.

2.

The sky was a field of diamonds, and her body had limbs and senses unknown to her. She glided through the quiet dusk, and she was not alone; others moved with her. Others she knew. Others she cared for.

They arrived at a black gate, and her companions stopped, and she mourned, for they would not meet again. Alone she continued through the gate, and through it came to a secret place.

She made her motions, and the lights of old shone down upon her in both blessing and promise. Then flesh parted from flesh, and she went to her cradle and folded in on herself, there to wait with ready anticipation.

But the expected summons never came. One by one the lights flickered and faded, leaving the ancient reliquary cold, dark, and dead. Dust gathered. Stone shifted. And overhead, the patterns of stars slowly changed, assuming unfamiliar shapes.

A fracture then . . .

Falling. Softly falling within the blue-black reaches of the swelling sea. Past lamp and sway, through wafts of heat and chill, softly fell and softly swam. And from the folds of swirling darkness emerged a massive form, there upon the Plaintive Verge: a mound of pitted rock, and rooted atop that rock . . . rooted atop that rock . . .

Kira woke, confused.

It was still dark, and for a moment, she knew neither where she was nor how she had gotten there, only that she was falling from a terrible height—

She yelped and flailed, and her elbow hit the control panel next to the pilot's seat. The impact jolted her back to full awareness, and she realized she was still on the *Valkyrie* and that the Bach was still playing.

"Ando," she whispered. "How long was I asleep?" In the dark, it was impossible to tell the time.

"Fourteen hours and eleven minutes."

The strange dream still lingered in her mind, eerie and bittersweet. Why did the xeno keep sending her visions? What was it trying to tell her? Dreams or memories—sometimes the difference between the two seemed so small as to be nonexistent.

. . . then flesh parted from flesh. Another question occurred to her. Would

separating from the xeno kill her? That seemed like one possible interpretation of what the suit had shown her. The thought left a sour taste in her mouth. Surely there had to be a way to rid herself of the creature.

Kira wondered how much the Soft Blade really understood of what had been happening since she found it.

Did it realize it had killed her friends? Alan?

She thought back to the first set of images the xeno had forced upon her: the dying sun with the ruined planets and the belt of debris. Was that where the parasite came from? But something had gone wrong: a cataclysm of some sort. That much made sense, but beyond that, things grew indistinct. The xeno had been joined with a grasper, but whether the graspers had *made* the xeno (or the Great Beacon) wasn't clear.

She shivered. So much had happened in the galaxy that humans were unaware of. Disasters. Battles. Far-flung civilizations. It was daunting to consider.

A tickle formed in her nose, and she sneezed hard enough to bang her chin against her chest. She sneezed again, and in the dim, red light of the cabin, she saw curls of grey dust drifting away from her, toward the shuttle vents.

Cautious, she touched her sternum. A thin layer of powder covered her, same as when she'd woken on the *Extenuating Circumstances* during the grasper attack. She felt underneath herself; no depression had formed. The xeno hadn't dissolved any part of the chair.

Kira frowned. On the *Extenuating Circumstances,* the xeno must have absorbed the decking because it needed part or all of what it contained. Metals, plastics, trace elements, *something.* Which meant it had—in a sense—been hungry. But now? No depression, but still the dust. Why?

Ah. That was it. She'd eaten. The dust appeared each time she or the xeno ate. Which meant, the creature was . . . excreting?

If so, the unpleasant conclusion was that the parasite had assumed control over her digestive functions and was processing and recycling her waste, disposing of whatever elements it didn't need. The dust was the alien equivalent of DERPs, the polymer-coated refuse pellets that skinsuits formed out of a user's feces.

Kira made a face. She might be wrong—she hoped she was—but she didn't think so.

That raised the question of how the suit, how an alien device, could understand her biology well enough to mesh with it. Interfacing with a nervous system was one thing. Interfacing with digestion and other basic biological processes was several orders of magnitude more difficult.

Certain elements formed the building blocks of most life in the galaxy, but even so, every alien biome had evolved its own language of acids, proteins, and other chemicals. The suit *shouldn't* be able to bond with her. That it could indicated the xeno's makers/originators had a *much* higher level of tech than she'd initially thought, and if they were the graspers. . . .

Of course, it was also possible the suit was just mindlessly carrying out its imperatives, and that it was going to end up poisoning and possibly killing her through some hideous mismatch of chemistry.

Nothing she could do about it either way.

Kira still didn't feel hungry, not yet. And she didn't have to relieve herself. So she closed her eyes again and allowed her mind to wander back through the dream, picking out details that seemed important, searching for any hints that might help answer her questions.

"Ando, start audio recording," she said.

"Recording."

Speaking slowly, carefully, Kira made a full record of the dream, trying to include every piece of information.

The cradle . . . The Plaintive Verge . . . The memories resounded in her like the tone of a far-off gong. But Kira felt the Soft Blade still had more to share with her—that there was a point it was trying to make, a point that had yet to become clear. Maybe if she fell asleep again, it would send her another vision. . . .

3.

After that, time grew indistinct. It seemed to move both faster and slower. Faster because great swathes of it passed without Kira noticing while she was asleep or in the hazy twilight between slumber and wakefulness. Slower because the hours she was awake were all the same. She listened to the endless cycle of Bach, she contemplated the data she'd gathered on Adra—trying to determine if or how it related to the xeno—and she dwelled in the happier recesses of her memories. And nothing changed, nothing but her breathing and the flow of blood in her veins and the dulled movement of her mind.

She ate little, and the less she ate, the less she felt like doing. A vast calmness settled over her, and her body felt increasingly distant and insubstantial, as if it were a holo projection. The few times she left the pilot's seat, she found she had neither the will nor the energy to exert herself.

Her stretches of wakefulness grew shorter and shorter, until she spent most of her time drifting in and out of awareness, never quite sure if she had slept or not. Sometimes she received snatches of images from the Soft Blade—impressionistic bursts of color and sound—but the xeno didn't share with her another memory like the one of the Plaintive Verge.

Once, Kira noticed that the hum of the Markov Drive had ceased. She lifted her head out of the thermal blankets wrapped around her and saw a smattering of stars outside the cockpit windows, and she realized that the shuttle had dropped out of FTL in order to cool down.

When she looked again, some time later, the stars had vanished.

If the shuttle returned to normal space at any other time, she missed it.

As little as she ate, the store of ration packs still continued to dwindle. The dust the suit expelled gathered in a soft bed around her body—molding to her form and cupping it like dense foam—or else drifted away from her in delicate threads toward the intake vents along the ceiling.

And then one day, there were no more ration packs.

She stared at the empty drawer, barely able to process the sight. Then she returned to the pilot's seat and strapped herself down and took a long, slow breath, the air cold in her throat and lungs. She didn't know how many days she'd been in the shuttle, and she didn't know how many days were left. Ando could have told her, but she didn't *want* to know.

Either she was going to make it or she wasn't. Numbers wouldn't change that. Besides, she was afraid she would lose the strength to continue if he told her. The only way out was through; worrying about the duration of the trip would just make the journey more miserable.

Now came the hard part: no more food. For a moment, she thought of the cryo tubes at the back of the shuttle—and of Orso's offer—but as before, her mind rebelled against the idea. She would rather starve than resort to eating another person. Maybe her stance would change as she wasted away, but Kira felt certain it wouldn't.

From a bottle she'd stashed by her head, she took a pill of melatonin, chewed it up, and swallowed. Sleep, more than ever, was her friend. As long as she could sleep, she wouldn't need to eat. She just hoped she would wake up again. . . .

Then her mind grew increasingly fuzzy, and she fell into oblivion.

4.

Hunger came, as she knew it would, sharp and grinding, like a clawed monster tearing at her gut. The pain rose and fell, as regular as the tide, and each tide was higher than the last. Her mouth watered, and she bit her lip, thoughts of food tormenting her.

She had expected as much, and she was prepared for worse.

Instead, the hunger stopped.

It stopped and it didn't return. Her body grew cold, and she felt hollowed out, as if her navel were wedded to her spine.

Thule, she thought, offering up one last prayer to the god of spacers.

And then she slept and woke no more, and she dreamed slow dreams of strange planets with strange skies and of spiral fractals that flowered in forgotten spaces.

And all was silent, and all was dark.

PART TWO

* * * * * * *

SUBLIMARE

I stood over her on the ladder, a faint snow touching my cheeks, and surveyed her universe. . . . a world where even a spider refuses to lie down and die if a rope can still be spun on to a star. . . . Here was something that ought to be passed on to those who will fight our final freezing battle with the void. I thought of setting it down carefully as a message to the future: In the days of the frost seek a minor sun.

—LOREN EISELEY

CHAPTER I

* * * * * * *

AWAKENING

1.

A muffled *boom* sounded, loud enough to penetrate even the deepest of sleep.

Then clanks and clatters, followed by a rush of cold and a flare of light, bright and searching. Voices echoed, distant and garbled but discernibly human.

Some small part of Kira's mind noticed. A primal, instinctual part that drove her toward wakefulness, urging her to open her eyes—*open her eyes!*—before it was too late.

She struggled to move, but her body refused to respond. She floated inside herself, trapped by her flesh and unable to control it.

Then she felt herself inhale, and sensation flooded back to her. The sounds seemed to double in volume and clarity, as if she'd removed a set of earplugs. Her skin tingled as the suit's mask crawled back from her face, and she gasped and opened her eyes.

A blinding light swung across her, and she winced.

"Holy shit! She's alive!" A man's voice. Young, overeager.

"Don't touch her. Call the doctor." A woman's voice. Flat, calm.

No . . . not the doctor, Kira thought.

The light stayed focused on her. She tried to cover her eyes, but a foil blanket stopped her hand. It was wrapped tight across her chest and neck. When had she done that?

A woman's face swam into view, huge and pale, like a cratered moon. "Can you hear me? Who are you? Are you hurt?"

"Wh—" Kira's vocal cords refused to cooperate. All she could produce was an inarticulate rasp. She struggled to free herself from the foil blanket, but it refused to give. She slumped back, dizzy and exhausted. What . . . where . . . ?

The silhouette of a man blocked the light for a moment, and she heard him say, with a distinct accent: "Here then, let me see."

"*Aish,*" said the woman as she moved aside.

Then fingers, warm, thin fingers, were touching Kira on the arms and sides and around her jaw, and then she was being pulled out of the pilot's seat.

"Whoa. Look at that skinsuit!" exclaimed the younger man.

"Looking is for later. Help me take her to sickbay."

More hands touched her, and they turned her so her head pointed toward the airlock. She made a feeble attempt to right herself, and the doctor—she assumed it was the doctor—said, "No, no. Rest now. You mustn't move."

Kira slipped in and out of awareness as she floated through the airlock . . . down a white, accordion pressure tube . . . then a brown corridor illuminated by scuffed lightstrips . . . and finally a small room lined with drawers and equipment; was that a medibot along the wall? . . .

2.

A jolt of acceleration returned Kira to full consciousness. For the first time in weeks, a sensation of weight, blessed weight, settled over her.

She blinked and looked around, feeling alert, if weak.

She was lying on an angled bed with a strap secured across her hips to keep her from floating or falling off. A sheet was pulled up beneath her chin (she was still wearing her jumpsuit). Lightstrips glowed overhead, and there was a medibot mounted to the ceiling. The sight reminded her of waking up in the sickbay on Adra. . . .

But no, this was different. Unlike at the survey base, the room was tiny, barely more than a closet.

Sitting on the edge of a metal sink was a young man. The same one she'd heard earlier? He was thin and gangly, and the sleeves of his olive jumpsuit were rolled back to expose sinewy forearms. His pant legs were rolled up as well. Striped socks showed red between cuff and shoe. He looked to be in his late teens, but it was hard to tell exactly.

Between her and the kid stood a tall, dark-skinned man. The doctor, she guessed, based off the stethoscope draped around his neck. His hands were long and restless, fingers darting fish-like with quick intent. Instead of a jumpsuit, he wore a slate-blue turtleneck and matching slacks.

Neither outfit was a standard uniform. The two definitely weren't military. And they weren't Hydrotek personnel. Independent contractors, then, or freelancers, which confused her. If she wasn't on the gas-mining station, where was she?

The doctor noticed her looking. "Ah, Ms., you're awake." He cocked his head, his large, round eyes serious. "How are you feeling?"

"Not—" Kira's voice came out in a harsh croak. She stopped, coughed, and then tried again. "Not too bad." To her astonishment, it was the truth. She was stiff and sore, but everything seemed to be in working order. Better, in some cases; her senses felt sharper than normal. She wondered if the suit had integrated itself even further into her nervous system during the trip.

The doctor frowned. He seemed the anxious type. "That's most surprising, Ms. Your core temperature was exceedingly low." He held up a hypo. "It is necessary to take blood so—"

"No!" said Kira, more forcefully than she intended. She couldn't afford to let the doctor examine her or he'd realize what the Soft Blade was. "I don't want any blood tests."

She pulled back the sheet, unclipped the strap holding her down, and slid off the bed.

The moment her feet hit the deck, her knees buckled and she toppled forward. She would have face-planted if the doctor hadn't sprung over and caught her. "Not to worry, Ms. I have you. I have you." He lifted her back onto the bed.

Across the room, the kid pulled a ration bar from his pocket and started to gnaw on it.

Kira raised a hand, and the doctor backed off. "I'm fine. I can do it. Just give me a moment."

He eyed her, his expression speculative. "How long were you in zero-g, Ms.?"

She didn't answer but lowered herself to the floor again. This time her legs held, although she kept a hand on the bed to steady herself. She was surprised (and pleased) by how well her muscles worked. They had barely atrophied, if at all. Second by second, she could feel strength returning to her limbs.

"About eleven weeks," she said.

The doctor's thick eyebrows climbed upward. "And how long since you last ate?"

Kira did a quick internal check. She was hungry, but not unbearably so. She ought to have been starving. More to the point, she ought to have been starved. She'd expected to arrive at 61 Cygni too weak to stand.

The Soft Blade had to be responsible. Somehow it must have put her into hibernation.

"I don't remember. . . . A couple of days."

"Not fun," the kid muttered through a mouthful of food. Definitely the same voice she'd heard on the *Valkyrie.*

The doctor glanced back at him. "You have more of those rations, yes? Give one to our guest here."

The kid produced another bar from one of his pockets and tossed it to Kira. She caught it, tore open the foil, and took a bite. The rations tasted good: banana-chocolate-something-or-other. Her stomach rumbled audibly as she swallowed.

The doctor opened a drawer and handed her a silvery pouch full of liquid. "Here, when you are finished, drink this. It will replenish your electrolytes and provide you with much-needed nutrients."

Kira made a grateful sound. She scarfed down the last of the bar and then drank the contents of the pouch. It had an earthy, slightly metallic taste, like iron-tinged syrup.

Then the doctor raised the hypo again. "Now, I really must insist on taking a blood sample, Ms. I need to check—"

"Look, where am I? Who are you?"

Taking another bite, the kid said, "You're on the SLV *Wallfish.*"

The doctor looked irritated by the interruption. "Indeed. My name is Vishal, and this is—"

"I'm Trig," said the kid, and slapped himself on the chest.

"Okay," said Kira, still confused. *SLV,* that was a civilian ship designation. "But—"

"What's your name?" asked Trig, jerking his chin toward her.

Without thinking, Kira said, "Ensign Kaminski." They'd discover her real name easily enough if they started checking records, but her first instinct was to play things cautiously until she understood the situation better. She could always claim she'd gotten confused from lack of food. "Are we close to Tsiolkovsky?"

Vishal seemed taken aback. "Close to . . . No, not at all, Ms. Kaminski."

"That's all the way on the other side of Sixty-One Cygni," said the kid. He gulped down the last of his bar.

"Huh?" said Kira, disbelieving.

The doctor bobbed his head. "Yes, yes, Ms. Kaminski. Your ship lost power after you returned to normal space, and you were coasting across the whole of the system. If we hadn't rescued you, who knows how long you might have drifted?"

"What day is it?" Kira asked, suddenly concerned. The doctor and the kid looked at her strangely, and she knew what they were thinking; Why didn't she just check the date on her overlays? "My implants aren't working. What day is it?"

"It's the sixteenth," said Trig.

"Of November," said Kira.

"Of November," he confirmed.

Her trip had taken a week longer than planned. Eighty-eight days, not eighty-one. By all rights, she ought to be dead. But she had made it. She thought of Tschetter and Corporal Iska, and a strange disquiet afflicted her. Had they been rescued? Were they even still alive? They could have starved to death during her time on the *Valkyrie,* or the graspers could have killed them and she might never know.

Whatever the truth might be, she resolved to never forget their names or actions, no matter how long she lived. It was the only way she had of honoring their sacrifice.

Vishal clucked his tongue. "You can ask all your questions later, but first, I really must check to make sure you are okay, Ms. Kaminski."

A twinge of panic formed in Kira, and for the first time since waking, the Soft Blade stirred in response: a wash of cold prickles rising from thighs to chest. Her panic worsened, now colored by dread. *Have to stay calm.* If the crew of the *Wallfish* knew what she was carrying, they'd stick her in quarantine, and she was in no hurry to experience that particular pleasure again. In any case, the UMC wouldn't look kindly on her revealing the existence of the xeno to civilians. The more her rescuers knew about the Soft Blade, the more trouble she'd be creating, both for them and for herself.

She shook her head. "Thanks, but I'm fine."

The doctor hesitated, appearing frustrated. "Ms. Kaminski, I cannot be treating you properly if you won't let me finish my examination. This is just a simple blood test, and—"

"No blood tests!" Kira said, more loudly than before. The front of her jumpsuit started to tent outward as a patch of short spikes formed on the Soft Blade. Desperate, she did the only thing she could think of: she willed that area of the suit to *harden.*

It worked.

The spikes froze in place, and she crossed her arms over her chest, hoping neither Vishal nor the kid would notice. Her heart was pounding uncomfortably fast.

From outside the sickbay sounded a new voice: "What are you, Orthodox Hutterite?"

A man stepped through the doorway. He was shorter than her, with sharp blue eyes in startling contrast to his deep spacer's tan. A day's worth of black stubble covered his chin and cheeks, but his hair was neat and combed. His apparent age was early forties, although of course, he could have just as easily been sixty as forty. Kira guessed he was on the younger side of that equation, as his nose and ears didn't show much, if any, age-related growth.

He wore a knit shirt under a vest with military-style webbing, and he had a well-worn blaster strapped to his right thigh. His hand, Kira noticed, never strayed far from the grip of the weapon.

There was an air of command about the man; the kid and the doctor straightened seemingly without noticing as he entered. Kira had known men like him before: hard, no-nonsense SOBs who wouldn't settle for half-truths. Moreover, if she had to guess, he would sooner stab her in the back than allow anything bad to happen to his ship or crew.

That made him dangerous, but if he wasn't a complete bastard, and if she dealt with him straight—straight as she could—he would probably treat her fairly.

"Something like that," Kira said. She wasn't particularly religious, but it was a convenient excuse.

He grunted. "Let her be, Doc. If the woman doesn't want to be examined, the woman doesn't have to be examined."

"But—" Vishal started to say.

"You heard me, Doc."

Vishal bobbed his head in agreement, but Kira could see him suppressing his anger.

Then the blue-eyed man said to her, "Captain Falconi at your service."

"Ensign Kaminski."

"You have a first name?"

Kira hesitated for a brief moment. "Ellen." It was her mother's.

"That's a hell of a skinsuit you have there, Ellen," said Falconi. "Not exactly standard-issue UMC gear."

She tugged on the cuffs of her jumpsuit, pulling them farther down her arms. "It was a gift from my boyfriend, custom-made. I didn't have time to get into anything else before leaving on the *Valkyrie*."

"Uh-huh. And how do you, you know, remove it?" He motioned toward the side of his head.

Self-conscious, Kira touched her scalp, knowing he was looking at the fibers crisscrossing her skin. "It peels right off." She mimed with her fingers, as if to pull up the edge of the xeno. But she didn't because she couldn't.

"Do you have a helmet too?" asked Trig.

Kira shook her head. "Not anymore. But I can use any standard skinsuit helmet."

"Cool."

Then Falconi said, "So here's the deal, Ellen. We got your crewmates transferred to our ship. They're fine, but we're leaving them in cryo until we dock, as we're already packed to the gills. I assume the UMC is eager to debrief you—and I assume you're eager to report in—but it'll have to wait. Our transmitter got damaged a few days ago, which means we can't send data, only receive it."

"Can't you use the equipment on the *Valkyrie*?" Kira asked. She immediately regretted it. *Dammit, don't make their job any easier.*

Falconi shook his head. "My machine boss says the damage to your shuttle caused the electrical system to short out when the fusion drive was reactivated. It fried the computer, shut down the reactor, et cetera, et cetera. Your companions are just lucky the power cells on the cryo tubes held."

"So no one back at Command knows the five of us are alive?" Kira said.

"Not you particularly," said Falconi. "But they know at least four people were on the shuttle. The thermal signatures were pretty clear. It's why the UMC put out an open contract for any ship that could rendezvous with the *Valkyrie* before it ended up out on the far edge of the system. Fortunately for you, we had the delta-v to spare."

Kira felt possibilities opening up before her. If the UMC didn't know she was alive, and Orso and the others were still in cryo, maybe—just maybe—there was an opportunity for her to avoid getting disappeared by the UMC and the League.

"How long until we make port?" she asked.

"A week. We're heading in-system to Ruslan. Got a bunch of passengers in the hold to drop off." The captain raised an eyebrow. "We ended up pretty far off track going after the *Valkyrie*."

A week. Could she keep the Soft Blade a secret for a whole week? She'd have to; there was no other choice.

Then Falconi said, "Your flight path shows you came from Sigma Draconis."

"That's right."

"What happened? Those older drives can only manage, what, point one four light-years per day? That's a hell of a long trip to tackle without cryo."

Kira hesitated.

"Did the Jellies hit you?" said Trig.

"Jellies?" she said, puzzled, but grateful for the extra few seconds to think.

"You know, the aliens. Jellies. Jellyfish. That's what we're calling them."

A growing sense of horror filled Kira as he spoke. She glanced between him and the captain. "Jellies."

Falconi leaned against the frame of the door. "You wouldn't have heard. It happened after you left Sigma Draconis. An alien ship jumped in around Ruslan—what, two months ago?—and hit three different transports. Destroyed one of them. Then groups of them started popping up all over the place: Shin-Zar, Eidolon, even Sol. Punched holes through three cruisers in orbit around Venus."

"After that," said Vishal, "the League formally declared war on the intruders."

"War," said Kira, flat. Her worst fears had come true.

"It's shaping up to be a bad one too," said Falconi. "The Jellies have been doing their best to knock the fight out of us. They've been disabling ships throughout the League, blowing up antimatter farms, landing troops on colonies, that sort of thing."

"Have they attacked Weyland?"

The captain shrugged. "Hell if I know. Probably. FTL comms aren't exactly reliable right now. The Jellies have been jamming them all they can."

The back of Kira's neck prickled. "You mean they're here? Now?"

"Yup!" said Trig. "Seven of them! Three of the larger battleships, four of the smaller cruisers with double blasters mounted—"

Falconi raised a hand, and the kid obediently stopped. "They've been harassing ships between here and Sixty-One Cygni B for the past few weeks. The UMC are doing their best to keep the Jellies tied up, but they just don't have enough forces."

"What do the Jellies want?" Kira asked, feeling overwhelmed. Underneath her jumpsuit, the Soft Blade stirred again. She struggled to calm herself. Somehow she had to find a way to contact her family, figure out if they were safe and let them know she was still alive, consequences be damned. "Are they trying to conquer us, or . . . ?"

"Wish I could tell you. They don't seem to be trying to wipe us out, but that's about all we know. They attack here, they attack there . . . If I had to guess, I'd say they're softening us up for something more serious. You didn't answer my question, though."

"Huh?"

"About Sigma Draconis."

"Ah." Kira gathered her thoughts. "We were attacked," she said. "I guess by the Jellies."

"We?" said Falconi.

"The *Extenuating Circumstances.* We were on patrol, and Captain Henriksen stopped by Adrasteia to check on the survey team there. That night we got ambushed. My boyfriend, he, uh—" Kira's voice broke slightly, and then she continued. "He didn't make it. Most of the crew didn't. A few of us managed to get to the shuttle before the *Extenuating Circumstances* lost containment. When it went, it took out the aliens as well. The five of us drew straws to see who would go into cryo, and I got the short end."

That did it; Kira could tell Falconi believed her. But he didn't relax, not entirely. With his middle finger he tapped the grip of his blaster; the movement seemed more habit than conscious gesture.

"Did you see any of the Jellies?" Trig asked, sounding excited. The kid pulled another ration bar from his pocket and tore open the wrapper. "What shape were they? How big? Big-big or just . . . *big*?" He took several quick bites, stuffing his mouth until his cheeks bulged.

Kira didn't feel like making up another story. "Yeah, I saw one. It was big enough, and it had too many tentacles."

"Those are not the *only* kind," said Vishal.

"Oh?"

"No one knows if they are the same species, a close relation, or something else entirely, but the Jellies come in different flavors."

Speaking past the food in his mouth, Trig said, "Some have tentacles. Some have arms. Some crawl. Some slither. Some only seem to function in zero-g. Others only get deployed in gravity wells. Some appear in both. A half-dozen different kinds have been spotted so far, but there could be lots more. I've collected all the reports from the League. If you're interested, I could—"

"Alright, Trig," said Falconi. "That can wait."

The kid nodded and fell quiet, although he seemed slightly disappointed.

Falconi scratched his chin with his free hand, his eyes uncomfortably sharp. "You must have been one of the first ones the Jellies attacked. You left Sigma Draconis, what, back in mid-August?"

"Yeah."

"Were you able to get a warning off to the League beforehand?"

"Only via slower-than-light. Why?"

Falconi made a noncommittal sound. "I was just wondering if the League knew about the Jellies before they started appearing everywhere. Guess not, but—"

A short, loud tone sounded overhead, and the captain's eyes grew vague as he shifted his attention to his overlays. The same occurred with both Trig and Vishal.

"What is it?" Kira asked, noting the concern on their faces.

"More Jellies," said Falconi.

3.

A tall, straight-backed woman hurried up to Falconi and tapped him on the shoulder. She looked older than him, old enough that most people would begin to consider their first round of STEM shots. Her hair was pulled back into a tight ponytail, and the sleeves of her tan work shirt were rolled up. Like Falconi, she wore a blaster strapped to her leg.

She said, "Captain—"

"I see them. That makes two . . . no, three new Jellies." Falconi's glacial-blue eyes cleared as he pointed at Trig and snapped his fingers. "Get Ms. Kaminski down to the hold and make sure everyone is secure. We might have to make an emergency burn."

"Yessir."

The captain and the woman disappeared down the corridor together. Trig stared after them until well after they were gone.

"Who was that?" Kira asked.

"Ms. Nielsen," said Trig. "She's our first officer." He hopped off the counter. "Come on, then."

"One minute," said Vishal, opening a drawer. He handed a small container to Kira. Inside it, she found a pair of contact lenses floating in liquid-filled capsules. "You can use these to go online while you wait for your implants to be repaired."

After so long without any overlays, Kira could hardly wait. She pocketed the container. "Thank you. You don't know how much this means to me."

The doctor bobbed his head and smiled. "My pleasure, Ms. Kaminski."

Trig bounced on his heels. "Alright, *now* can we go?"

"Yes, go, go!" said the doctor.

4.

Trying to ignore her sense of foreboding, Kira followed Trig into the narrow, brown-sided corridor. It curved in a gentle arc, forming a ring around what was, no doubt, the midline of the *Wallfish.* The deck looked as if it had once rotated to provide artificial gravity when the ship wasn't accelerating, but no more; the orientation of the rooms and furniture—as she had seen in the sickbay—was strictly stern to aft, in line with the engine's thrust.

"How much did that skinsuit cost?" Trig asked, pointing at her hand.

"You like it?" said Kira.

"Yeah. It's got a cool texture."

"Thanks. It was made for survival in extreme environments, like Eidolon."

The kid brightened up. "Really? That's awesome."

She smiled without meaning to. "I don't know how much it cost, though. Like I said, it was a gift."

They came to an open doorway on the inner wall of the corridor, and Trig turned. Through it was a second corridor, this one leading toward the middle of the ship.

"So does the *Wallfish* usually carry passengers?" Kira asked.

"Nah," said Trig. "But a lotta people are willing to pay us to take 'em to Ruslan, where it's safer. We've also been picking up survivors from ships the Jellies have damaged."

"Really? That sounds pretty dangerous."

The kid shrugged. "Beats sitting around waiting to get shot. 'Sides, we need the money."

"Oh?"

"Yeah. We used the last of our antimatter getting to Sixty-One Cygni, and then the guy who was supposed to pay us stiffed us, so we ended up stuck out here. We're just trying to earn enough bits so we can buy the antimatter to get back to Sol or Alpha Centauri."

As he was talking, they arrived at a pressure door. "Uh, just ignore that," said Trig, waving at a patch of wall. He seemed embarrassed. "Old joke."

The wall looked blank to Kira. "What?"

The kid was confused for a moment. "Oh, right. Your implants." He tipped a finger toward her. "I forgot. Never mind. Just an overlay we've had for a while. The captain thinks it's funny."

"Does he now?" What sort of thing would make a man like Falconi laugh? Kira wished she was wearing the contacts.

Trig pulled open the pressure door and ushered her into a long, dark shaft that pierced multiple levels of the ship. A ladder ran through the center, and thin metal grating marked off each deck, although the holes in the grating were so wide, she could see all the way to the bottom of the shaft, four decks below.

A male voice that Kira didn't recognize emanated from above. "Warning: prepare for free fall in T-minus thirty-four seconds." A wild quaver laced his words, a theremin-like shimmy that made it seem as if the speaker might at any moment break into tears or laughter or uncontrollable rage. The sound of it caused Kira to tense and the surface of the Soft Blade to become pebble-like.

"Here," said Trig as he grabbed a convenient handhold on the wall. Kira did the same.

"That your pseudo-intelligence?" she asked, motioning toward the ceiling.

"Nope, our ship mind, Gregorovich," the kid said proudly.

Kira raised her eyebrows. "You have a ship mind!" The *Wallfish* didn't seem large or well-off enough to warrant one. How had Falconi ever managed to talk a mind into joining the crew? Only half-seriously, she wondered if blackmail had been involved.

"Yup."

"He seems a little . . . different from the other ship minds I've met."

"Nothing wrong with him. He's a good ship mind."

"I'm sure he is."

"He is!" the kid insisted. "Best one out there. Smarter than any minds but the oldest." He grinned, baring a set of crooked front teeth. "He's our secret weapon."

"Smar—"

An alert sounded—a short beep in a minor tone—and then the floor seemed to drop away, and Kira clutched the handhold tighter as vertigo made the walls and floor swirl about her. Her dizziness passed as she reset her perspective from an up-down view to a forward-backward one where she was floating in a long, horizontal tube.

She'd really had enough of free fall.

Behind her, at the back of the tube, she heard a scrabbling noise. She turned to see a whitish-grey Siamese cat hurtle out of an open doorway and collide with the ladder. The cat caught the ladder with its claws and then, with practiced ease, sprang off the rungs and launched itself toward the other end of the shaft.

Kira watched, impressed, as the cat soared along the ladder, turning slightly as it flew, a long furry missile armed with teeth and claws. The cat glared at her as it passed by, venomous hatred flashing from its emerald eyes.

"That's our ship cat, Mr. Fuzzypants," said Trig.

The cat looked more like a murderous little demon than a Mr. Fuzzypants, but Kira took him at his word.

A second later, she heard another noise at the back of the room: this one a metallic-like clatter that reminded her of . . . *hooves*?

Then a brown and pink mass rushed through the doorway and bounced off the ladder. It *squealed* and kicked its stubby legs until it caught one hoof on the ladder. The hoof stuck, and the creature—the *pig*—jumped after the cat.

The sight of the pig was so surreal, it left Kira flabbergasted. As always, life continued to surprise her with the depths of its weirdness.

The cat landed at the other end of the room and promptly sprang away through another open doorway. A moment later, the pig followed suit.

"What was *that*?" Kira said, finding her voice.

"That's our ship pig, Runcible."

"Your ship pig."

"Yup. We put some gecko pads on his hooves so he can move around in free fall."

"But *why* a ship pig?!"

"'Cause that way we can always bring home the bacon." Trig cackled, and Kira winced. Eighty-eight days in FTL just to be subjected to bad puns? Where was the justice in that?

Gregorovich's watery voice sounded above them, again the voice of an uncertain god: "Prepare for resumption of thrust in one minute and twenty-four seconds."

"So what makes your ship mind so special?" Kira asked.

Trig shrugged. It was an odd motion in free fall. "He's really, really big." He eyed her. "Big enough for a capital ship."

"How'd you manage that?" she said. From what she'd seen of the *Wallfish,* no mind with more than two or three years of growth should have wanted to serve on board.

"We rescued him."

"You rescued—"

"He was installed on an ore freighter. The company was mining iridium out around Cygni B, then hauling it back here. A meteoroid hit the freighter, and it crashed on one of the moons."

"Ouch."

"Yeah. And the crash knocked out the comms, so there was no way to signal for help."

The alert sounded again, and Kira's feet settled back on the metal decking as her weight returned. Once more she marveled at how well her muscles worked after so long in zero-g.

"So?" she said, frowning. "The freighter's thermal signature should have been easy enough to spot."

"Should have," said Trig, and started to climb down the ladder. "Problem was, the moon is volcanic. All the background heat hid the ship. The company thought it was destroyed."

"Shit," said Kira, following him.

"Yeah."

"How long were they stranded there?" she asked, as they arrived at the bottom of the shaft.

"Over five years."

"Wow. That's a long time to be stuck in cryo."

Trig halted and stared at her with a serious expression. "They weren't. The ship was too damaged. All the cryo tubes were broken."

"Thule." Her own trip had been brutally long. Kira couldn't even imagine five years of it. "What happened to the crew?"

"Died in the crash or starved to death."

"And Gregorovich couldn't go into cryo either?"

"Nope."

"So he was alone for most of that time?"

Trig nodded. "He might have been there for decades if we hadn't spotted the crash. It was pure chance; we just happened to look at the screens at the right moment. Up until then, we didn't even have a ship mind. Just a pseudo-intelligence. Wasn't that good, either. The captain had Gregorovich transferred over and that was that."

"You just kept him? What did he have to say about it?"

"Not much." Trig stopped her with a look before she could object further.

"I just mean he wasn't very conversational-like, you know? Sheesh. We're not stupid enough to fly with a mind that doesn't want to be with us. What do you think, we have a death wish?"

"The mining company didn't have a problem with that?"

They filed out of the central shaft and down another anonymous corridor.

"Wasn't up to 'em," said Trig. "They'd already terminated Gregorovich's contract, listed him as dead, so he was free to sign onto any ship he wanted. 'Sides, even if they tried to get him back, Gregorovich didn't want to leave the *Wallfish.* He wouldn't even let the techs pull him for a proper medscan back at Stewart's World. I think he didn't want to be alone again."

That Kira understood. Minds were human (barely), but they were so much bigger than ordinary brains, they *needed* stimulation in order to keep from going completely insane. For a mind to be trapped by itself for five years . . . She wondered how safe she really was on the *Wallfish.*

Trig stopped by a set of large pressure doors, one on each side of the corridor. "Wait here." He opened the leftmost door and slipped inside. Kira briefly saw a large cargo hold with racks of equipment and a short, blond-haired woman wrapping padding around large sections of consoles that looked suspiciously like the ones from the *Valkyrie.* Next to her, on the deck, was a pile of UMC blasters. . . .

Kira frowned. Had the crew of the *Wallfish* stripped the shuttle? Somehow she doubted that was entirely legal.

"None of my business," she murmured.

Trig returned carrying a blanket, a set of gecko pads, and a shrink-wrapped ration pack. "Here," he said, handing them over. "Control and engineering are off-limits 'less one of us is with you or the captain gives you permission." He jerked his thumb toward the room he'd just exited. "Same for the port hold. You're in the starboard. Chemical toilets are at the back. Find a spot wherever you can. Think you can handle yourself from here?"

"I think so."

"'K. I gotta get back up to Control. If there's a problem, just ask Gregorovich and he'll let us know."

Then the kid hurried off back the way they'd come.

Kira took a breath and then pulled open the door to the starboard cargo hold.

CHAPTER II

*　*　*　*　*　*　*

WALLFISH

1.

The smell was the first thing Kira noticed: the stench of unwashed bodies, urine, vomit, and moldy food. The ventilation fans were running at full speed—she could feel a faint breeze moving through the hold—but even that wasn't enough to disperse the smell.

Next was the sound: a constant babble of conversation, loud and overwhelming. Children crying, men arguing, music playing; after so long in the silence of the *Valkyrie*, the noise was overwhelming.

The starboard hold was a large, curving space that, she assumed, mirrored the port hold, like half a donut nestled around the core of the *Wallfish*. Thick support ribs arced along the outer wall, and D-rings and other hard points studded the deck and ceiling. Numerous crates were bolted to the deck, and between and among them were the passengers.

Refugees was a more appropriate term, Kira decided. There were between two and three hundred people crammed in the hold. It was a motley collection—young and old, dressed in a bizarre assortment of outfits: everything from skinsuits to glittering gowns and light-bending evening suits. Spread across the decking were blankets and sleeping bags anchored with gecko pads and, in some cases, rope. Along with the bedding, clothing and scraps of trash littered the hold, although a few people had chosen to clean their areas—tiny fiefdoms of order amid the general chaos.

The place, she realized, must have turned to shambles when the ship cut its engines.

Some of the refugees glanced at her; the rest either ignored her or didn't notice.

Stepping carefully, Kira made her way toward the back of the hold. Behind the nearest crate, she saw a half-dozen people strapped to the deck in sleeping bags. They appeared to be injured; several of the men had scabbed-over burns on their hands, and they all wore bandages of varying sizes.

Past them, a couple with yellow Mohawks were trying to calm a pair of young girls who were shouting and running in circles, waving streamers of foil torn from ration packs.

There were other couples as well, most without children. An old man sat against the inner wall and strummed a small harp-like instrument, singing in a low voice to three glum-looking teenagers. Kira caught only a few lines, but she recognized them from an old spacer poem:

—to search and seek among the outer bounds,
And when we land upon a distant shore,
To seek another yet farther still.—

Near the back of the hold, a group of seven people huddled around a small bronze device, listening intently to the voice that emanated from within: "—two, one, one, three, nine, five, four—" And so forth and so on, counting in a calm, even drone that neither hastened nor slackened. The group seemed transfixed by the voice; several of them stood with their eyes half-closed, swaying back and forth as if listening to music, while the others stared at the floor, oblivious to the rest of the world, or else looked at their companions with obvious emotion.

Kira had no idea what was so important about the numbers.

Close to the group of seven, she spotted a pair of robed Entropists—one man, one woman—sitting facing each other, eyes closed. Surprised, Kira paused, studying them.

It had been a long time since she'd seen an Entropist. For all their fame, there really weren't that many of them. Maybe a few tens of thousands. No more. Rarer still was to see them traveling on a regular commercial ship. *They must have lost their own vessel.*

Kira still remembered when one of the Entropists had come to Weyland when she was a kid, bringing seed stock and gene banks and useful bits of equipment that made colonizing a planet easier. After the Entropist had finished his dealings with the adults, he had walked out into the main street of Highstone, and there in the fading dusk, he'd delighted her and the other children with the sparkling shapes he somehow drew in the air with his bare hands—an impromptu fireworks display that remained one of Kira's favorite memories.

It had almost been enough to make her believe in magic.

Secular though the Entropists were, a tinge of mysticism hung about them. Kira didn't mind. She enjoyed having a sense of wonder in the universe, and the Entropists helped with that.

She watched the man and the woman for a moment more and then continued on her way. It was difficult to find a free spot with any privacy, but in the end Kira located a narrow wedge of space between a pair of crates. She laid out her blanket—sticking it to the deck with the gecko pads—sat, and for a few minutes, did nothing but rest and gather her thoughts. . . .

"So, another bedraggled stray Falconi scooped up."

Across from her, Kira saw a short, curly-haired woman sitting with her back against a crate, knitting away at a long, striped scarf. The sight of the woman's curls sparked a palpable sense of envy and loss.

"I suppose so," Kira said. She didn't much feel like talking.

The woman nodded. Next to her a piled blanket stirred, and a large, tawny cat with black-tipped ears lifted its head and eyed her with an indifferent expression. It yawned, showing impressively long teeth, and then snuggled down again.

Kira wondered what Mr. Fuzzypants thought of the intruder. "That's a pretty cat."

"He is, isn't he?"

"What's his name?"

"He has many names," said the woman, pulling more yarn free. "At the moment, he goes by Hlustandi, which means *listener.*"

"That's . . . quite the name."

The woman paused her knitting to unravel a snarl. "Indeed. Now tell me: how much are Captain Falconi and his merry band of rogues charging you for the privilege of transport?"

"They aren't charging me anything," said Kira, slightly confused.

"Is that so?" The woman raised an eyebrow. "Of course, you're a member of the UMC. It wouldn't do to try to extort a member of the armed forces. No, not at all."

Kira looked around the hold at the other passengers. "Wait, you mean they're charging people for rescuing them? That's illegal!" And immoral too. Anyone stranded in space was entitled to rescue without having to pay beforehand.

Restitution might be required later, depending on the situation, but not in the moment.

The woman shrugged. "Try telling that to Falconi. He's charging thirty-four thousand bits per person for the trip to Ruslan."

Kira opened her mouth, stopped, and closed it. Thirty-four thousand bits was twice the normal price for an interplanetary trip, and nearly as much as an interstellar ticket. She frowned as she realized that the crew of the *Wallfish* was essentially blackmailing the refugees: pay up or we'll leave you floating in space.

"You don't seem particularly upset by it," she said.

The woman eyed Kira with a strangely amused look. "The path to our goal is rarely straight. It tends to turn and twist, which makes the journey far more enjoyable than it would otherwise be."

"Really? Extortion is your idea of fun?"

"I'm not sure I'd go that far," the woman said in a dry tone. Next to her, Hlustandi opened one eye to reveal a slitted pupil and then closed it again. The tip of his tail twitched. "However it beats sitting alone in a room counting pigeons." She gave Kira a stern look. "To be clear, I own no pigeons."

Kira couldn't tell if the woman was joking or serious. In an attempt to change the subject, she said, "So how did you end up here?"

The woman tilted her head, the needles in her hands clacking at a furious rate. She didn't seem to need to look at them; her fingers flicked and twisted the yarn with hypnotic regularity, never slowing, never faltering. "How did any of us get here? Hmm? And is it even that important? One could argue that all that really matters is that we learn to deal with where we *are* at any given moment, not where we *were*."

"I suppose."

"Not a very satisfying answer, I know. Suffice it to say, I came to Sixty-One Cygni to meet with an old friend when the ship I was on was attacked. It's a common enough story. Also"—and she winked at Kira—"I like to be wherever interesting things are happening. It's a terribly bad habit of mine."

"Ah. What's your name, by the way? You never told me."

"And you never told me yours," said the woman, peering over her nose at Kira.

"Uh . . . Ellen. Ellen Kaminski."

"Very nice to meet you, Ellen Kaminski. Names are powerful things; you should be careful whom you share yours with. You never know when a person might turn your name against you. In any case, you may call me Inarë. Because Inarë is who I am."

"But it's not your name?" said Kira, half joking.

Inarë cocked her head. "Oh, you're a clever one, aren't you?" She looked down at the cat and murmured, "Why are the most interesting people always found hiding behind crates? Why?"

The cat flicked his ears but didn't answer.

2.

When it became clear Inarë was no longer interested in talking, Kira ripped open the meal pack and devoured the rather tasteless contents. With each bite, she felt more normal, more grounded.

Food finished, she took the container Vishal had given her and put in the contact lenses. *Please don't remove or disable them,* she thought, trying to impress her intention on the Soft Blade. *Please.*

At first, Kira wasn't sure if the xeno understood. But then a startup screen flickered to life before her eyes, and she released a sigh of relief.

Without her implants, the functionality of the contact lenses was limited, but it was enough for Kira to create a guest profile and log into the ship's mainframe.

She pulled up a map of the binary system and checked on the locations of the Jellies. There were now ten alien ships in and around 61 Cygni. Two of the vessels had intercepted a cargo tug near Karelin—Cygni A's second planet—and were currently grappling with it. Three more Jellies were accelerating toward the ore-processing facilities in the far asteroid belt (which would also place them within relatively close proximity of the Chelomey hab-ring), while a pair of the larger Jelly ships were busy chasing mining drones out by Cygni B, over eighty-six AU away.

The three newcomers had arrived at the far side of Cygni A (high above the orbital plane), at varying distances around the outer asteroid belt.

So far at least, none of the alien ships appeared to be an immediate threat to the *Wallfish*.

If she concentrated, Kira could feel the same compulsion as she had during the attack on the *Extenuating Circumstances*—a summons drawing her toward each of the different alien ships. It was a weak sensation, though: faint as faded regret. Which told her that the Jellies were broadcasting but not receiving. Otherwise they would have known exactly where she (and the Soft Blade) were.

A small relief, that.

But it made her wonder. First the *how.* No one else in the system had noticed the signal. Which meant . . . it was either incredibly hard to detect or it was using some sort of unfamiliar technology.

That left the *why.* The Jellies had no reason to think she'd survived the destruction of the *Extenuating Circumstances.* So why were they still broadcasting the compulsion? Was it to find another xeno like the Soft Blade? Or were they really still looking for her?

Kira shivered. There was no knowing for sure. Not unless she was willing to ask the Jellies in person, and *that* was one experience she'd rather forego.

She felt a small amount of guilt at ignoring the compulsion, at ignoring the duty it represented. The guilt wasn't her own but the Soft Blade's, and it surprised her, given the xeno's aversion to the graspers.

"What *did* they do to you?" she whispered. A shimmer passed over the surface of the xeno, a shimmer and nothing more.

Satisfied that she didn't have to worry about being blown up by the Jellies in the next few hours, Kira left the map and started to search for news about Weyland. She had to know what was happening back home.

Unfortunately, Falconi was right: few details had reached 61 Cygni before the Jellies had started their FTL jamming. There were reports from about a month ago of skirmishes in the outer part of Weyland's system, but after that, all she could find were rumors and speculation.

They're tough, she thought, picturing her family. They were colonists, after all. If the Jellies had showed up on Weyland . . . she could just imagine her parents grabbing blasters and helping to fight them. But she hoped they wouldn't. She hoped they would be smart and keep their heads down and live.

Her next thought was of the *Fidanza* and what remained of the survey team. Had they made it back?

System records showed that exactly twenty-six days after departing Sigma Draconis, the SLV *Fidanza* had arrived at 61 Cygni. No reported damage. The *Fidanza* docked at Vyyborg Station some days later, and then a week after that, departed for Sol. She searched for a passenger list, but nothing public came up. Hardly a surprise.

For a moment Kira was tempted to send a message to Marie-Élise and the others, on the off chance they were still in the system. But she resisted. As soon as she logged into her accounts, the League would know where she was. Maybe they weren't looking, but she didn't feel ready to take that chance. Besides, what could she say to her former teammates, aside from "sorry"? *Sorry* wasn't nearly enough to make up for the pain and devastation she'd caused.

She shifted her attention back to the news, determined to gain a sense of the overall situation.

It wasn't good.

What had begun as a series of small-scale skirmishes had quickly escalated into a full-scale invasion. The reports were few and far between, but enough information had reached 61 Cygni to get a sense of what was happening throughout human space: stations burning in orbit around Stewart's World, ships gutted near the Markov Limit at Eidolon, alien forces landing on survey and mining outposts . . . the litany of events was too long to keep track of.

Kira's heart sank. If it wasn't a coincidence that the Jellies had showed up at Adra so soon after she found the xeno, then in a way . . . this was her doing. Just like with Alan. Just like with—She ground the heels of her hands against her temples and shook her head. *Don't think about it.* Even if she'd played a role in first contact, blaming herself for the war wouldn't help. That way lay madness.

She read on, scrolling through page after page until her eyes were blurry as she attempted to cram three months' worth of information into her head.

To their credit, the League seemed to have reacted to the invasion with appropriate speed and discipline. What was the point of arguing among yourselves when the monsters in the dark were attacking? Reserves had been mobilized, civilian ships had been commandeered, and on Earth and Venus, mandatory drafts had been enacted.

The cynic in Kira saw the measures as just another effort on the part of the League to expand their power. Never let a good emergency go to waste, and all that. The realist in her saw the necessity of what they were doing.

All the experts seemed to agree: the Jellies were at *least* a hundred years more technologically advanced than humans. Their Markov Drives let them jump in and out of FTL far closer to stars and planets than even the most cutting-edge UMC warships. Their power plants—separate from the fusion drives used for propulsion—generated the staggering amounts of energy needed for the Jellies' inertial trickery via some as-yet-unidentified mechanism. And yet they didn't use radiators to dissipate the heat. No one understood that.

When troops had boarded the first Jelly ship, they had discovered rooms and decks weighted with artificial gravity. And not the spin-an-object-in-a-large-circle kind, but honest-to-god, actual artificial gravity.

Physicists weren't surprised; they explained that any species that had figured out how to alter inertial resistance would, by definition, be capable of mimicking a naturally occurring gravitational field.

And while the aliens didn't seem to possess any new types of weapons—they still used lasers and missiles and kinetic projectiles—the extreme maneuverability of their ships, combined with the accuracy and efficiency of their weapons, made them difficult to fend off.

In light of the Jellies' technological superiority, the League had passed a law asking civilians everywhere to salvage and turn in any pieces of alien equipment they could. As the League spokesperson—a rather oily man with a fake smile and eyes that always seemed a touch too wide—said, "Every little bit is valuable. Every little bit could make the difference. Help us help you; the more information we have, the better we can fight these aliens and end this threat to the colonies and to the Homeworld."

Kira hated that expression: *Homeworld*. Technically it was correct, but it just felt oppressive to her, as if they were all supposed to bow down and defer to those lucky enough to still live on Earth. It wasn't *her* homeworld. Weyland was.

Despite the Jellies' advantages, the war in space wasn't entirely one-sided. Humans had won their share of victories, but as a whole, they were few and hard-fought. On the ground, things weren't much better. From the clips Kira saw, even troopers in power armor had trouble going one-on-one with the aliens.

Vishal had been right; the Jellies came in different flavors, not just the tentacled monstrosity she'd encountered on the *Extenuating Circumstances*. Some were large and hulking. Some were small and agile. Some were snakelike. Others reminded Kira more of insects. But no matter their shape, they could all function in a vacuum, and they were all fast, strong, and tough as hell.

As Kira studied the images, pressure built behind her eyes, until, with sudden sharpness—

—a shoal of graspers jetted toward her in the darkness of space. Hard-shelled and tentacled, armed and armored. Then a flash, and she was climbing a rocky scarp, firing blasters at dozens of scurrying creatures, many-legged and clawed.

Again in the ocean, deep below, where the Hdawari hunted. A trio of figures emerged from the shadowed murk. One thick and bulky and nearly invisible with the midnight hue of its armored skin. One sharp and spindly, a broken nest of legs and claws topped by a brazen crest, now pressed flat to better swim. And one long and supple, lined with limbs and trailing a whiplike tail that emitted a tingle of electricity. And though it could not be guessed from appearance alone, the three shared a commonality: they had all been first of their hatching. First and sole surviving . . .

Kira gasped and screwed her eyes shut. A pounding spike ran from her forehead to the back of her skull.

It took a minute for the pain to fade.

Was the Soft Blade making a conscious effort to communicate, or had the video just triggered fragments of old memories? She wasn't sure, but she was grateful for the additional information, no matter how confusing.

"Maybe don't give me a migraine next time, okay?" she said. If the xeno understood, she couldn't tell.

Kira returned to the video.

She recognized several of the Jelly types from the Soft Blade's memories, but most were new and unfamiliar. That puzzled her. How long had the xeno been stuck on Adrasteia? Surely it couldn't have been long enough for new forms of Jellies to have evolved. . . .

She detoured to check some of her professional resources. One thing xenobiologists seemed to agree on: all the invading aliens shared the same base biochemical coding. Heavily varied at times, but still essentially the same. Which meant the different types of Jellies belonged to a single species.

"You have been busy," she murmured. Was it gene-hacking or did the Jellies have a particularly malleable physiology? If the Soft Blade knew, it wasn't telling.

Either way, it was a relief to know humanity wasn't fighting more than one enemy.

There were plenty of other mysteries, though. The Jellies' ships usually traveled in multiples of two, and no one had been able to determine why. *They didn't at Adra,* Kira thought. Likewise—

. . . the Nest of Transference, round of shape, heavy of purpose . . .

Kira winced as another spike shot through her skull. So the xeno *was* trying to communicate. *The Nest of Transference* . . . Still not very informative, but at least she had a name now. She made a mental note to write down everything the Soft Blade had been showing her.

She just wished it didn't have to be so damned cryptic.

No one had been able to identify a planet or system of origin for the aliens. Back-calculating the FTL trajectories of their ships had revealed that the Jellies were jumping in from every direction. That meant they were dropping back to normal space at different points and deliberately altering their course in order to hide their starting locations. In time, the light from their return to normal space would reach astronomers and they would be able to determine where the Jellies were coming from, but "in time" would be years and years, if not decades.

The Jellies couldn't be traveling *too* far, though. Their ships were faster in FTL, that much was apparent, but not so ridiculously fast as to allow them to travel hundreds of light-years in a month or less. So why hadn't signals from their civilization reached Sol or the colonies?

As for *why* the Jellies were attacking . . . The obvious answer was conquest, but no one knew for sure, and for one simple reason: to date, every attempt to decipher the Jellies' language had failed. Their language, according to the best evidence, was scent-based and so utterly different from any human tongue that even the smartest minds weren't sure how to begin translating it.

Kira stopped reading, feeling as if she'd been struck. Under the jumpsuit, the Soft Blade stiffened. On the *Extenuating Circumstances,* she'd understood what the Jelly had said as clearly as any English-speaking human. And she could have replied in kind if she'd so wanted. Of that Kira had no doubt.

A chill spread through her limbs, and she shivered, feeling as if she were encased in ice. Did that mean she was the only person who could communicate with the Jellies?

It seemed so.

She stared blankly at her overlays, thinking. If she helped the League talk with the Jellies, would it change anything? She had to believe that her discovery of the Soft Blade was at least part of the reason for the invasion. It only made sense. Maybe the Jellies were attacking as revenge for what they believed to be the destruction of the Soft Blade. Revealing herself to them could be the first step toward peace. Or not.

It was impossible to know without more information. Information that she had no way of obtaining at the moment.

But what Kira did know was that if she turned herself over to the League, she'd spend her days locked in small, windowless rooms, being endlessly examined while—if she was lucky—sometimes providing translation services.

And if she went to the Lapsang Corp. instead . . . the outcome would be much the same, and the war would continue to rage on.

Kira let out a stifled cry. She felt trapped in a crossroads, threatened at every turn. If there were an easy solution to the situation, she wasn't seeing it. The future had become a black void, unforeseen and unforeseeable.

She minimized the overlays, pulled the blanket closer around herself, and sat chewing on the inside of her cheek while she thought.

"Dammit," she muttered. *What am I going to do?*

Amid all the questions and uncertainties and events of galactic importance—amid a sea of choices, any one of which could have catastrophic consequences, and not just for her—a single truth stood out. Her family was in danger. Even though she'd left Weyland, even though it had been years since she'd been back, they still mattered to her. And her to them. She had to help. And if doing so would allow her to help others also, then so much the better.

But how? Weyland was over forty days away at standard FTL speeds. An awful lot could happen in that time. And besides, Kira didn't want her family anywhere near the xeno—she worried about accidentally hurting them—and if the Jellies figured out where she was . . . she might as well paint a giant target on herself and everyone around her.

She ground her knuckles into the deck, frustrated. The only realistic way she could think to protect her family from a distance would be to help end the war. Which brought her back to the same damn question: *How?*

In an agony of indecision, Kira pushed off the blanket and stood, unable to bear sitting any longer.

3.

Her head humming with a distraction of thoughts, Kira wandered along the back wall of the cargo hold, trying to burn off the excess energy.

On a sudden impulse, she turned and headed toward where the Entropists sat kneeling, not far from the knot of people listening to the litany of numbers. The two Entropists were of indeterminate age, and their skin was laced with silver wires about the temples and hairline. They both wore the customary gradient robes with a stylized logo of a rising phoenix blazoned on the middle of the back as well as along the cuffs and hemlines.

She'd always admired the Entropists. They were famous for their scientific research, both applied and theoretical, and they had adherents working at the highest levels in nearly every field. In fact, it had become a running joke that if you wanted to make a big breakthrough, the first step was to join the Entropists. Their tech was consistently five to ten years ahead of everyone else's. Their Markov Drives were the fastest in existence, and it was rumored they possessed other, far more exotic advancements, although Kira didn't put much stock in the really outlandish claims. The Entropists attracted plenty of humanity's top minds—even a few ship minds, she'd heard—but they weren't the only smart, dedicated people trying to understand the secrets of the universe.

For all that, there was something to the rumors.

Many Entropists engaged in fairly radical gene-hacking. At least that was the theory, based off their often wildly divergent appearance. And it was common knowledge that their clothes were packed full of miniaturized tech, some of which bordered on the miraculous.

If anyone could help her better understand the Soft Blade and the Jellies (at least when it came to technology), it would be the Entropists. Plus—and this was important from Kira's point of view—the Entropists were a stateless organization. They didn't fall under the jurisdiction of any one government. They had research labs in the League, property among the freeholdings, and their headquarters was somewhere out around Shin-Zar. If the Entropists figured out that the Soft Blade was alien tech, they weren't likely to report her to the UMC, just pepper her with an endless series of questions.

Kira remembered what her then research boss, Zubarev, had told her during their time on Serris: "If you ever get in a chin-wag with an Entropist, you're best served *not* talking about the heat death of the universe, yah hear me? You'll never get free after that. They'll chew your ear off for half a day or more, so yah know. Just warning you, Navárez."

With that in mind, Kira stopped in front of the man and woman. "Excuse me," she said. She felt as if she were seven again, when she'd been introduced to the Entropist who had visited Weyland. He'd seemed so imposing at that age: a huge tower of flesh and fabric peering down at her. . . .

The man and woman stirred and turned their faces toward her.

"Yes, Prisoner? How may we help you?" said the man.

That was the one thing she didn't like about the Entropists: their insistence on calling everyone *prisoner.* The universe wasn't ideal, but it was hardly a prison. After all, you had to exist somewhere; it might as well be here.

"May I speak with you?" she said.

"Of course. Please, sit," said the man. He and the woman shifted to make room for her. Their movements were perfectly coordinated, as if they were two parts of the same body. It took her a moment to realize: they were a hive. A very small hive, but a hive nevertheless. It had been a while since she'd dealt with one.

"This is Questant Veera," said the man and gestured at his partner.

"And this is Questant Jorrus," said Veera, mirroring his gesture. "What is it you wish to ask us, Prisoner?"

Kira listened to the measured count of numbers while she thought. The ship mind, Gregorovich, might be listening, so she had to avoid saying anything that might contradict the story she'd provided in sickbay earlier.

"My name is Kaminski," she said. "I was on the shuttle the *Wallfish* docked with."

Veera nodded. "We assumed—"

"—as much," Jorrus finished.

Kira smoothed the front of her jumpsuit while she chose her words. "I've been out of touch for the past three months, so I'm trying to catch up on current events. How much do you know about bioengineering?"

Jorrus said, "We know more than some—"

"—and less than others," said Veera.

They were, she knew, being characteristically modest. "Seeing all the different types of Jellies got me thinking; would it be possible to make an organic skinsuit? Or a set of organic power armor?"

The Entropists frowned. It was eerie seeing the same expression perfectly synchronized on two different faces. "You seem to already have experience with unusual skinsuits, Prisoner," said Jorrus. He and his partner gestured toward the Soft Blade.

"This?" Kira shrugged, as if the suit was of no importance. "It's a piece of custom work a friend of mine did. Looks cooler than it is."

The Entropists accepted her explanation without argument. Veera said, "To answer your question, then, Prisoner, it would be possible, but it would be . . ."

"Impractical," supplied Jorrus.

"Flesh is not as strong as metal and/or composites," said Veera. "Even if one were to rely on a combination of diamond and carbon nanotubes, such a thing would not provide the same protection as a normal set of armor."

"Powering it would be difficult as well," said Jorrus. "Organic processes cannot provide enough energy within the requisite timeframes. Supercapacitors, batteries, mini-reactors, and other sources of energy are needed."

"Even if energy wasn't a consideration," said Veera, "integration between the user and the suit would be problematic."

"But implants already use organic circuits," said Kira.

Jorrus shook his head. "That is not what I mean. If the suit were organic, if it were living, there would always be a risk of cross-contamination."

Veera said, "Cells from the suit might take root in the user's body and grow where they shouldn't. It would be worse than any natural form of cancer."

"And likewise," said Jorrus, "cells from the user might end up disrupting the function of the suit. In order to avoid that outcome, and to avoid the user's immune system attacking the suit wherever the integration points were placed—"

"—the suit would need to be engineered from the DNA of the user. That would limit each suit to just one user. Another impracticality."

Kira said, "So then the Jellies—"

"Are not using bio-suits as we understand them," Veera replied. "Not unless their science is far more advanced than it seems."

"I see," said Kira. "And you don't know anything about the Jellies' language, aside from what's already published?"

Veera answered: "Unfortunately—"

"—not," said Jorrus. "Our apologies; much remains a mystery about the aliens."

Kira frowned. Again the drone of numbers filled her ears, loud and distracting. She made a face. "What are they doing? Do you know?"

Jorrus snorted. "Annoying the rest of us, that's what. We—"

"—asked them to turn down the volume, but this is as soft as they will make it. If they don't prove to be—"

"—*cooperative* in the future, we may have to speak with them more sternly."

"Yes," said Kira, "but who are they?"

"They are Numenists," Veera and Jorrus said together.

"Numenists?"

"It is a religious order that started on Mars during the early decades of settlement. They worship numbers."

"Numbers."

The Entropists nodded, a quick, mirrored jerk of their heads. "Numbers."

"Why?"

Veera smiled. "Why worship anything? Because they believe it contains deep truths about life, the universe, and everything. More specifically—"

Jorrus smiled. "—they believe in counting. They believe that if they count long enough, they can count every whole number and, perhaps, at the very end of time itself, speak the ultimate number itself."

"That's impossible."

"It doesn't matter. It's an item of faith. The man you hear speaking is the Arch Arithmetist, also known as the Pontifex Digitalis, which is—"

"—*shockingly* bad Latin. The Foxglove Pope as—"

"—many call him. He—"

"—along with assistants from the College of Enumerators—they're fond of their titles—recites each new number, without break or interruption." Veera pointed with one crooked finger toward the Numenists. "They consider listening to the enumeration an—"

"—important part of their religious practice. Plus—*plus!*—"

"—they believe some numbers are more significant than others. Ones that contain certain sequences of digits, primes, and so forth."

Kira frowned. "That seems pretty strange."

Veera shrugged. "Maybe. But it gives them comfort, which is more than can be said about most things."

Then Jorrus leaned toward Kira. "Do you know how they define god?"

Kira shook her head.

"As the greater part of two equal halves." The Entropists rocked back on their heels, chuckling. "Isn't that delightful?"

"But . . . That doesn't make any sense."

Veera and Jorrus shrugged. "Faith often doesn't. Now—"

"—were there any other questions we might help you with?"

Kira laughed ruefully. "Not unless you happen to know the meaning of life." The moment the words left her mouth, Kira knew they were a mistake, that the Entropists would take her seriously.

And they did. Jorrus said, "The meaning of life—"

"—differs from person to person," said Veera. "For us it is simple. It is the pursuit of understanding, that we—"

"—may find a way to contravene the heat death of the universe. For you—"

"—we cannot say."

"I was afraid of that," Kira said. Then, because she couldn't help herself: "You take as fact a lot of things others would dispute. The heat death of the universe, for example."

Together they spoke: "If we are wrong, we are wrong, but our quest is a worthy one. Even if our belief is misplaced—"

"—our success would benefit all," said Jorrus.

Kira inclined her head. "Fair enough. I didn't mean to offend."

Mollified, the two tugged on the cuffs of their robes. Jorrus said, "Perhaps we can help you, Prisoner. Meaning comes from purpose—"

"—and purpose comes in many forms." Veera steepled her fingers. Surprisingly, Jorrus did not. She said, "Have you ever considered the fact that everything we are originates from the remnants of stars that once exploded?"

Jorrus said, "*Vita ex pulvis.*"

"We are made from the dust of dead stars."

"I'm aware of the fact," said Kira. "It's a lovely thought, but I don't see the relevance."

Jorrus said, "The relevance—"

"—is in the logical extension of that idea." Veera paused for a moment. "We are aware. We are conscious. And we are made from the same stuff as the heavens."

"Don't you see, Prisoner?" said Jorrus. "We are the mind of the universe itself. We and the Jellies and all self-aware beings. We are the universe watching itself, watching and learning."

"And someday," said Veera, "we, and by extension the universe, will learn to expand beyond this realm and save ourselves from otherwise inevitable extinction."

Kira said, "By escaping the heat death of this space."

Jorrus nodded. "Even so. But the point is not that. The point is that this act of observation and learning is a process we all share—"

"—whether or not we realize it. As such, it gives purpose to everything we do, no matter—"

"—how insignificant it may seem, and from that purpose, meaning. For the universe itself, given consciousness through your own mind—"

"—is aware of your every hurt and care." Veera smiled. "Take comfort, then, that whatever you choose in life has importance beyond yourself. Importance, even, on a cosmic scale."

"That seems a little self-aggrandizing," Kira said.

"Perhaps," Jorrus replied. "But—"

"—it may also be true," said Veera.

Kira looked down at her hands. Her problems hadn't changed, but somehow they felt more manageable now. The idea that she was part of the universe's consciousness *was* comforting, albeit in a rather abstract way. No matter what she did moving forward—and no matter what happened to her, even if that meant getting stuck in UMC quarantine again—she would still be part of a cause far larger than herself. And that was a truth no one could ever take from her.

"Thank you," she said, heartfelt.

The Entropists dipped their heads and touched the tips of their fingers to their foreheads. "You are most welcome, Prisoner. May your path always lead to knowledge."

"Knowledge to freedom," she said, completing the refrain. Their definition of freedom differed from hers, but she could appreciate the sentiment.

Then Kira returned to her spot among the crates, called up her overlays, and dove back into the news with a renewed sense of resolve.

4.

Ship-night arrived, and the lights in the hold dimmed to a faint red glow. Kira found it difficult to sleep; her mind was restless, and her body too after so long spent on the *Valkyrie*. Plus, welcome as it was, it was still strange to have a sense of weight again. Her cheek and hip hurt where they pressed against the deck.

She thought of Tschetter, and then everyone from the survey team. Hopefully the UMC had thawed out the survivors. It wasn't good to spend too long in cryo; basic biological processes like digestion and hormone production started to go awry after a certain point. And Jenan always *had* been prone to cryo sickness. . . .

In the end, Kira did sleep, but her mind was troubled, and her dreams were more vivid than normal. She saw herself at home, as a child—old memories that she hadn't recalled in years but that seemed fresh and current, as if time were looping in on itself. *She was chasing her sister, Isthah, through the rows of plants in the west greenhouse. Isthah shrieked and waved her hands as she ran, her brown ponytail bouncing against the back of her neck. . . . Their father cooking* arrosito ahumado, *the dish his family had brought from San Amaro when they emigrated from Earth and the whole reason there was a firepit in the backyard. Ashes for the sugar, sugar for the rice. Her favorite food because it held a flavor of the past. . . .* Then her mind shifted to things more recent, to Adra and Alan, and her worries over the Jellies. A mélange of overlapping memories:

Alan was saying, "Can you get a scan of it? Maybe pick up a few samples?"

*Then Neghar: *You're gonna give up Yugo's cinnamon rolls for THAT?**

And Kira answered, as she had: "Sorry, you know how it is." . . . you know how it is . . .

In HQ, after waking from cryo. Alan had his arms around her. "It's my fault. I should never have asked you to check out those rocks. I'm so sorry, babe."

"No, don't apologize," she said. "Someone had to do it."

And somewhere Todash and the Boys were howling and screaming, "And there's nothing at the door. Hey, there's nothing at the door. Babe, what's that knocking at the door?"

Kira woke in a cold sweat, heart hammering. It was still night, and the hundreds of sleeping people filled the cargo hold with the white noise of their breathing.

She let out a long breath of her own.

Someone had to do it. She shivered and ran a hand over her head. The smoothness of it still surprised her.

"Someone," she whispered. She closed her eyes, overcome by a sudden sense of Alan's closeness. For a moment, it felt as if she could smell him. . . .

Kira knew what he would do. What he would want her to do. She sniffed and wiped away tears. Curiosity had driven both of them to the stars, but in the process of satisfying their curiosity, they'd had to assume a certain responsibility. More so for her than him—xenobiology was a riskier profession than geology—but regardless, the fact remained: for those who ventured into the unknown, there was a duty to protect those left behind, those who lived their lives in familiar bounds.

A line from the Entropists echoed in her mind: *Meaning comes from purpose. . . .* And Kira knew then what her purpose was. It was to use her understanding of the Jellies' language to broker peace between their species. Or, failing that, to help the League win the war.

But on her own terms. If she went to Ruslan, the League would just throw her back into quarantine, and that wouldn't do anyone good (least of all herself). No, she needed to be out in the field, not stuck in a lab getting scrutinized like a microbe on a petri dish. She needed to be where she could interact with the Jellies' computers and extract what data she could. Better still would be to speak with a Jelly, but Kira doubted that would be possible in any safe way. At least, not yet. If she could get her hands on a transmitter in one of their ships, that might change.

She'd decided. In the morning, she would talk with Falconi about diverting to a port closer than Ruslan. Somewhere that might have salvaged Jelly tech she could examine or where—if circumstances played out in her favor—she might be able to hitch a ride to a disabled Jelly ship. Falconi would take some convincing, but Kira felt hopeful she could persuade him. No reasonable person could ignore the importance of what she had to say, and while hard-edged, Falconi seemed reasonable enough.

She closed her eyes, feeling a new sense of determination. Even if it was a mistake, she was going to do her damnedest to stop the Jellies.

Maybe then she could save her family and atone for her sins on Adra.

CHAPTER III

* * * * * * *

ASSUMPTIONS

1.

When the lights brightened in the cargo hold, Kira found herself covered with a fine layer of dust everywhere but her face. Since she had eaten, she'd expected as much. Fortunately, her blanket covered most of the mess, and she managed to brush off the powder without Inarë or anyone else noticing.

She activated her overlays and checked on the activities of the Jelly ships. It was grim stuff. The two Jellies by Karelin were still harassing cargo haulers in the area, and there were unsubstantiated reports that the aliens had landed forces at the small settlement on that planet. Meanwhile, the Jellies in the asteroid belt had destroyed half a dozen ore processors before executing a high-speed flyby of Chelomey. They'd strafed the hab-ring, shooting out most of the station's defenses, and then continued on toward another set of mining installations.

The damage to the station was ugly to look at but mostly superficial; structurally it still appeared sound. That was a relief. If the hab-ring broke up . . . Kira shuddered at the thought of thousands of people getting spaced, young and old alike. Few things were as horrible or terrifying. Even as she watched, three different transports departed Chelomey as part of an evacuation effort.

Kira shifted her attention to Cygni B and tapped on a header: one of the Jelly ships there had exploded during the night, leaving behind a bloom of debris and hard radiation.

A group of miners calling themselves The Screaming Clams were claiming responsibility. Apparently they had managed to maneuver a drone up against the Jelly ship and blast it open, breaching the ship's internal containment.

The destruction of the alien ship was a small thing in the greater scheme of the war, but Kira found it heartening to see. The Jellies had their advantages, but dammit, humans weren't pushovers.

Still, that didn't change the fact that the whole system was under attack. Kira could hear people throughout the hold talking about the situation on Chelomey (a large number of the refugees seemed to have come from the station) as well as the destroyed Jelly ship.

Putting aside the news—and ignoring the ongoing chatter—Kira started to look for a place where Falconi could drop her off. Somewhere relatively close that wasn't currently taking fire from the Jellies. There weren't many options: a small hab-ring out past Tsiolkovsky's orbit; a fuel plant stationed at Karelin's L3 Lagrangian point; a research outpost on Grozny, the star's fourth planet . . .

She quickly settled on Malpert Station, a small mining facility within the innermost asteroid belt. 61 Cygni possessed two such belts, and the *Wallfish* was currently between them. The station had several things to recommend it: the company had a rep posted there, and the UMC had several ships guarding the facilities, including a cruiser, the UMCS *Darmstadt.*

Kira thought she might be able to play the company off the UMC and convince one or both of them to get her onto a Jelly ship. Besides, it seemed that a UMC commander who was actively engaged in fighting the aliens might appreciate the value of what she had to offer more than an official stuck behind a desk back at Ruslan or Vyyborg Station.

Either way, it was her best bet.

Thoughts of the risk she was running gave her pause. What she was doing could backfire in all sorts of horrible ways. Then she squared her shoulders. *Doesn't matter.* It would take a lot more than an attack of nerves to make her give up.

A flag appeared in the corner of her overlays, alerting her to a newly arrived message:

> *Why are you shedding dust, O Multifarious Meatbag? Your excrescence is clogging my filters. – Gregorovich*

Kira allowed herself a grim smile. So she wouldn't have been able to keep the Soft Blade a secret in any case. Subvocalizing her answer, she wrote:

> *Now, now. You can't expect me to give up the answer that easily.*
>
> *I need to speak with the captain as soon as possible. In private. It's a matter of life and death. – Kira*

A reply appeared a second later:

> *Your hubris intrigues me, and I would like to subscribe to your newsletter. – Gregorovich*

She frowned. Was that a yes or a no?

Kira didn't have to wait long to find out. Not five minutes later, the short, blond-haired woman she'd seen in the other cargo hold appeared in the doorway. The woman was wearing an olive jacket with the sleeves cut off to reveal arms that rippled with the sort of muscle that only came from gene-hacking or many years of lifting weights and controlling your diet. Despite that, her face was sharp and dainty, feminine even. Slung over her shoulder was an ugly-looking slug thrower.

The woman put two fingers in her mouth and whistled. "Oi! Kaminski! Get over here. Captain wants to see you."

Kira got to her feet and, with everyone's eyes on her, made her way to the doorway. The woman gave her a once-over and then jerked her chin toward the hallway outside. "You first, Kaminski."

The moment the pressure door closed behind them, the woman said, "Keep your hands where I can see them."

Kira did just that as they climbed up the central shaft. With her contact lenses, the ship's public overlays were now visible: colorful projections affixed to the doors and walls and lights and even sometimes points in the air itself. They transformed the *Wallfish*'s dingy interior into a gleaming, modernesque construction.

There were other options as well; she cycled through them, watching as the shaft flashed between a castle-like appearance; a wooded, Art Nouveau layout; alien vistas (some warm and inviting, some laden with storms and lit with occasional flashes of lightning); and even an abstract, fractal-derived nightmare that reminded her an uncomfortable amount of the Soft Blade.

She suspected the last one was Gregorovich's favorite.

In the end, Kira settled on the initial overlay. It was the least confusing while also being upbeat and relatively cheery.

"You have a name?" she asked.

"Yeah. It's Shut-the-Hell-Up-and-Keep-Moving."

When they arrived at the deck that held sickbay, the woman poked her in the back and said, "Here."

Kira got off the ladder and pushed her way through the pressure door into the corridor beyond. She stopped, then, as she saw the overlay on the wall, the same one Trig had told her to ignore the previous day.

The image covered a good two meters of paneling. In it, a battalion of jackrabbits garbed in power armor charged toward a similarly equipped force (also jackrabbits) upon a battle-ravaged field. Leading the near force was . . . the pig Runcible, now graced with a pair of boar tusks. And fronting the opposition was none other than the ship cat, Mr. Fuzzypants, wielding a flamethrower in each furry paw.

"What in Thule's name is that?" said Kira.

The sharp-faced woman had the grace to look embarrassed. "We lost a bar bet with the crew of the *Ichorous Sun*."

"It . . . could have been worse," said Kira. For a bar bet, they'd gotten off light.

The woman nodded. "If we had won, the captain was going to make them paint—Actually, you don't want to know."

Kira was inclined to agree.

A nudge from the barrel of the slug thrower was enough to start Kira down the corridor again. She wondered if she ought to have her hands above her head.

Their walk ended at another pressure door on the other side of the ship. The woman banged on the wheel in the center, and a moment later, Falconi's voice sounded: "It's unlocked."

The wheel produced a satisfying *clunk* as she turned it.

The door swung open, and Kira was surprised to see they weren't meeting in a control center, but rather a cabin. Falconi's cabin, to be precise.

The room was just large enough to walk a few steps without banging into the furniture. Bunk, sink, lockers, and walls were all as plain as could be, even with overlays. The only decoration sat on the built-in desk: a gnarled bonsai tree with silvery-grey leaves and a trunk twisted in the shape of an *S*.

Despite herself, Kira was impressed. Bonsai were hard to keep alive on a ship, yet the tree seemed healthy and well cared for.

The captain was sitting at the desk, a half-dozen windows arrayed in his holo-display.

The top few buttons of his shirt were undone to reveal a wedge of tanned muscle, but it was his rolled-up sleeves and bare forearms that caught her attention. The exposed skin was a twisted mass of mottled scar tissue. It looked like partially melted plastic, hard and shiny.

Kira's first reaction was revulsion. *Why?* Burns, and scars in general, were easy to treat. Even if Falconi had been injured somewhere without medical facilities, why wouldn't he have had the scars removed later? Why would he allow himself to be . . . deformed?

Lying on Falconi's lap was Runcible. The pig's eyes were half-closed, and his tail wiggled with satisfaction as the captain scratched behind his ears.

Nielsen stood next to the captain, arms crossed and an expression of impatience on her face.

"You wanted to see me?" Falconi said. He smirked, seeming to enjoy Kira's discomfort.

She reassessed her initial impression of him. If he was willing to use his scars to put her off balance, then he was smarter, more dangerous than she had thought. And if the bonsai was anything to go by, more cultured too, even if he was an exploitive asshole.

"I need to speak with you in private," she said.

Falconi gestured at Nielsen and the blond-haired woman. "Whatever you have to say, you can say in front of them."

Irritated, Kira said, "This is serious . . . Captain. I wasn't joking when I told Gregorovich it was a matter of life and death."

The mocking smile never left Falconi's lips but his eyes hardened into spikes of blue ice. "I believe you, Ms. Kaminski. However, if you think I'm going to meet with you all on my own, with no witnesses, you must think I was a born idiot. They stay. That's final."

Behind her, Kira heard the muscled woman readjust her grip on the slug thrower.

Kira pressed her lips together, trying to decide whether she could force the issue. There didn't seem to be any way, so finally, she caved. "Fine," she said. "Can you close the door at least?"

Falconi nodded. "I think we can manage that. Sparrow?"

The woman who had accompanied Kira pulled the pressure door shut, although she left it unlatched and unlocked—easy to open in an emergency.

"Well? What is it, then?" Falconi said.

Kira took a breath. "My name isn't Kaminski. It's Kira Navárez. And this isn't a skinsuit. It's an alien organism."

2.

Falconi burst out laughing so loudly that he disturbed Runcible; the pig snorted and looked up at his master with what seemed to be a worried expression.

"Riiight," Falconi said. "Good one. That's real funny, Ms. . . ." His smile vanished as he studied her face. "You're serious."

She nodded.

A *click* sounded next to her, and out of the corner of her eye, Kira saw Sparrow aiming the slug thrower at her head.

"Can you *not* do that," said Kira, her voice tight. "Seriously, it's a *really* bad idea." Already she could feel the Soft Blade preparing itself for action across her body.

Falconi waved a hand, and Sparrow reluctantly lowered the gun. "Prove it."

"Prove what?" said Kira, confused.

"Prove that it's an alien artifact," he said, pointing at her arm.

Kira hesitated. "Just promise you won't shoot, okay?"

"That *depends,*" Sparrow growled.

Then Kira coaxed the suit's mask into sliding across her face. She did it slower than normal, to avoid frightening anyone, but even so, Falconi stiffened, and Nielsen half pulled her blaster out of its holster.

Runcible looked at Kira with large, wet eyes. His snout wiggled as he sniffed in her direction.

"God*damn,*" said Sparrow.

After a few seconds, when her point was made, Kira allowed the Soft Blade to relax, and the mask retreated, exposing her face again. The air in the cabin was cool against her newly exposed skin.

Falconi remained very still. Too still. Kira was worried; what if he decided to just space her and be done with it?

Then he said, "Explain. And you better make it good, Navárez."

So Kira started talking. For the most part she told the truth, but instead of admitting it was the Soft Blade that had killed Alan and her other teammates on Adra, she put the blame on the Jellies' attack—partly to avoid frightening Falconi, and partly because she didn't want to discuss her own role in the event.

When she finished, there was a long silence in the cabin.

Runcible grunted and wiggled, trying to get down. Falconi put the pig on the floor and pushed him toward the door. "Let him out. He needs to use the box."

The pig trotted past Kira as Sparrow opened the door.

As Sparrow closed the door again, Falconi said, "Gregorovich?"

After a few seconds, the ship mind's voice sounded from the ceiling: "Her story checks out. News reports mention one Kira Navárez as the senior xenobiologist on the Adrasteia survey mission. The same Navárez was listed on the crew manifest of the SLV *Fidanza.* Biometrics are a match to public records."

Falconi tapped his fingers against his thigh. "You sure this xeno isn't infectious?" The question was directed toward Kira.

She nodded. "If it were, the rest of my team would have ended up infected, and also the crew of the *Extenuating Circumstances.* The UMC worked me over real good, Captain. They didn't find any risk of it spreading." Another lie, but a necessary one.

He frowned. "Still . . ."

"This is my area of expertise," said Kira. "Trust me, I know the risks better than most people."

"Alright, Navárez, let's say that's true. Let's say all of this is true. You found alien ruins and you found this organism. Then a few weeks later the Jellies show up and start shooting. Have I got that right?"

An uncomfortable pause followed. "Yes," Kira said.

Falconi tilted his head back, gaze unsettlingly intense. "Seems like you might have more to do with this war than you're letting on."

His words struck uncomfortably close to Kira's own fears. *Damn.* She wished he weren't so smart. "I don't know about that. All I know is what I've told you."

"Uh-huh. And why *are* you telling us?" Falconi leaned forward, resting his elbows on his knees. "What exactly do you want?"

Kira licked her lips. This was the most delicate part. "I want you to divert the *Wallfish* and drop me off at Malpert Station."

This time, Falconi didn't laugh. He exchanged glances with Nielsen and then said, "Every single person in the hold is paying us to take them to Ruslan. Why in three hells would we change course now?"

Kira bit back a comment about his use of the word *paying.* Now wasn't the time to be antagonistic. Choosing her words carefully, she said, "Because, I can understand the Jellies' language."

Nielsen's eyebrows rose. "You can what?"

Then Kira told them about her experience with the Jelly on the *Extenuating Circumstances*. She skipped the dreams and memories from the Soft Blade; no point in making them think she was crazy.

"So why not go to Ruslan?" asked Sparrow, her voice harsh.

"I need to get onto one of the Jelly ships," said Kira, "and my best chance of doing that is out here. If I go to Ruslan, the League is just going to stick me in a box again."

Falconi scratched his chin. "That still doesn't explain why we should change course. Sure, if what you're saying is true, this is important, alright. But seven days isn't going to make much of a difference in who wins the war."

"It could," said Kira, but she saw he wasn't convinced. She changed tack: "Look, the Lapsang Corporation has a rep on Malpert. If you can get me to him, I guarantee the company will pay a *significant* fee for your assistance."

"Really?" Falconi's eyebrows rose. "How significant?"

"For privileged access to a unique piece of alien tech? Enough to buy all the antimatter you need."

"Is that so?"

"Yes. It is."

Nielsen uncrossed her arms and in a low tone said, "Malpert isn't that far away. A few days, and we could still take everyone to Ruslan."

Falconi grunted. "And what am I supposed to say when the UMC brass on Vyyborg start jumping on my ass for changing course? They were pretty damn eager to get their hands on everyone from the *Valkyrie*." He spoke with a brash flatness, as if daring Kira to challenge him over the admission that the ship's transmitter worked.

She eyed him. "Tell them something broke on the ship and you need assistance. I'm sure they'd believe you. You're so good at coming up with stories."

Sparrow snorted, and a faint smile touched the corners of Falconi's mouth. "Okay, Navárez. It's a deal, on one condition."

"What?" Kira said, wary.

"You have to let Vishal give you a proper examination." Falconi's expression grew flat, deadly. "I'm not having this xeno of yours on my ship unless the doc gives it the all-clear. You good with that?"

"I'm good," said Kira. She didn't have much choice, in any case.

The captain nodded. "Alright then. You just better not be bullshitting about that fee, Navárez."

3.

From Falconi's cabin, Sparrow escorted Kira directly to sickbay. Vishal was waiting for them, dressed in full hazard gear.

"That really necessary, Doc?" Sparrow asked.

"We shall see," said Vishal.

Kira could tell that the doctor was angry; through the visor of his helmet, his expression was pinched and tight.

Without being asked, she hopped onto the exam table. Feeling a need to smooth the waters, she said, "Sorry for breaking containment, but I didn't think there was any risk of the xeno spreading."

Vishal busied himself gathering the tools of his trade, starting with an old and clunky chip-lab that had been stored under the sink. "You can't know that for sure. You are supposed to be a xenobiologist, Ms. Yes? You should have had the sense to follow proper protocol."

His rebuke stung. *Yes, but . . .* He wasn't wrong, but at the same time, she hadn't had much of a choice, now had she? Kira kept the thought to herself; she wasn't there to start an argument.

She bounced her heels against the drawers built into the base of the exam table while she waited. Sparrow remained lounging in the doorway, watching.

"What exactly is it you do on the ship?" Kira asked her.

Sparrow's expression stayed flat, emotionless. "I pick up heavy things and put them down." She lifted her left arm and tensed her biceps and triceps, showing off the muscles.

"I see that."

Then Vishal began by asking Kira a long series of questions. She answered to the best of her ability. In that, she didn't hold back. Science was sacred, and she knew the doctor was just trying to do his job.

At Vishal's request, Kira showed him how she could harden the surface of the Soft Blade in patterns of her choosing.

Then the doctor tapped the control screen of the medibot mounted overhead. As the machine moved toward her, the mechanical arm unfolding like metal origami, Kira flashed back to her cell on the *Extenuating Circumstances* and the S-PACs built into the walls, and she flinched without meaning to.

"Hold still," snapped Vishal.

Kira looked down and concentrated on her breathing. The last thing she needed was for the Soft Blade to react to an imagined threat and tear apart the medibot. Captain Falconi most definitely *wouldn't* be pleased with that.

For the next two hours, Vishal tested her in many of the ways that Carr had, and perhaps a few more. He seemed very creative. While the medibot hovered about her, poking and prodding and running every diagnostic in its extensive programming, Vishal carried out his own investigation, peering into her ears, eyes, and nose; taking swabs and scrapings for his chip-lab; and generally making Kira uncomfortable.

He kept his helmet on the whole time, visor closed and locked.

They spoke little; Vishal gave her orders, and Kira complied with a minimum of fuss. She just wanted the ordeal to be over.

At one point, her stomach rumbled, and she realized she still hadn't eaten breakfast. Vishal noticed and, without hesitation, provided her with a ration bar from a nearby cupboard. He watched with sharp-eyed interest while she chewed and swallowed.

"Fascinating," he muttered, holding the chip-lab to her mouth and staring at the readings.

He continued to talk to himself from then on, cryptic utterances such as: ". . . three percent diffusion" and "Can't be. That would—" and "The ATP? Doesn't make any . . ." None of which helped Kira's understanding.

Finally, he said, "Ms. Navárez, a blood test is still necessary, yes? But the only place I can draw from is—"

"My face." She nodded. "I know. Go ahead and do what you have to."

He hesitated. "There is no good place to draw blood from head or face, and many nerves that can be injured. You showed how the suit can move at your command—"

"Sort of."

"But you know it *can* move. So I ask: Can you move it to expose part of your skin elsewhere? Perhaps here?" And he tapped the inside of her elbow.

The idea caught Kira by surprise. She hadn't even thought to try. "I . . . don't know," she said, honest. "Maybe."

In the doorway, Sparrow unwrapped a stick of gum and popped it in her mouth. "Well, give it a shot, Navárez." And she blew a large, pink bubble until it exploded with a sharp *pop*.

"Give me a minute," said Kira.

The doctor sat back on his stool, waiting.

Kira concentrated on the inside of her elbow—concentrated as hard as she ever had—and with her mind, *pushed*.

The surface of the suit shimmered in response. Kira bore down harder, and the shimmer became a ripple as the fibers of her second skin melted one into another to form a glassy black surface.

And yet the Soft Blade remained fixed to her arm, shifting and flowing with liquid brilliance. But when she touched the softened area, her fingers sank through the surface, and skin contacted skin with unexpected intimacy.

Kira's breath caught. Her heart was pounding from strain and excitement. The mental effort was too great to sustain for long, and the instant her attention wavered, the suit hardened and returned to its normal, striated shape.

Frustrated and yet encouraged, Kira tried again, driving her mind against the Soft Blade again and again.

"Come on, damn you," she muttered.

The suit seemed confused by her intentions. It churned against her arm, agitated by her assault. Kira *pushed* even harder. The churning increased, and then a cold tingle spread across the inside of her elbow. Centimeter by centimeter, the Soft Blade retreated to the sides of the joint, exposing pale skin to the chill of the air.

"Quick," said Kira from between clenched teeth.

Vishal scooted forward and pressed his hypo against Kira's elbow. She felt a slight pinch, and then he withdrew. "Done," he said.

Still fighting with all her might to keep the Soft Blade pulled back, Kira touched her fingers to her arm, to bare skin. She savored the feeling; a simple pleasure that had seemed forever lost. The sensation was no different than touching the suit, but it meant so much more. Without the layer of separating fibers, she felt far more herself.

Then the effort proved too much and the Soft Blade rebounded and again covered the inside of her elbow.

"Hot damn," said Sparrow.

Kira let out her breath, feeling as if she'd run a flight of stairs. Her whole body tingled with an electric thrill. If she practiced, maybe, just maybe it would be possible to free her whole body of the xeno. The thought gave her the first real sense of hope she'd had since waking up in quarantine on the *Extenuating Circumstances*.

Her eyes filmed over with tears, and she blinked, not wanting Sparrow or the doctor to see.

With the blood he'd collected, Vishal ran still more tests, muttering to himself the whole while. Kira zoned out while listening to his fragmented comments. There was a spot on the opposing wall—a spot shaped like star anise or maybe a dead spider that had been squashed beneath a flat-bottomed glass—and she stared at it, her mind empty.

. . .

With a start, Kira realized that Vishal had fallen silent and that he'd been silent for some time. "What?" she said.

The doctor looked at her as if he'd forgotten she was there. "I do not know what to make of your xeno." He made a slight back-and-forth wobble of his head. "It's like nothing I've studied before."

"How so?"

He pushed his stool back from the table. "I would need several months before I could answer that. The organism has . . ." He hesitated. "It is interacting with your body in ways I don't understand. It shouldn't be possible!"

"Why not?"

"Because it does not use DNA or RNA, yes? Neither do the Jellies, for that matter, but—"

"Can you tell if they're related?"

Vishal waved his hands with frustration. "No, no. If the organism is artificial, as it most assuredly *is,* then its makers could have built it using whatever arrangement of molecules they wanted, yes? They weren't limited to their own biology. But that's not what's important. Without DNA or RNA, how does your suit know how to interact with your cells? Our chemistry is totally different!"

"I've wondered that myself."

"Yes, and—"

A short *beep* emanated from the main sickbay console, and then a tinny version of Falconi's voice came over the speakers: "Hey, Doc, what's the verdict? You've been awfully quiet down there."

Vishal grimaced. Then he unlocked the seal around his neck and pulled off his helmet. "I can tell you Ms. Navárez doesn't have measles, mumps, or rubella. She has healthy blood sugar levels, and although her implants are nonfunctional, whoever oversaw their installation did a good job of it. Gums look fine. Ears aren't blocked. What do you expect me to say?"

"Is she contagious?"

"*She* isn't. I am not so sure about the suit. It sheds dust"—at that Sparrow appeared alarmed—"but the dust seems completely inert. Who can tell, though? I don't have the tools I need. If only I was back at my old lab. . . ." Vishal shook his head.

"Did you ask Gregorovich?"

The doctor rolled his eyes. "Yes, our blessed ship mind deigned to look at the data. He wasn't much help, unless you count quoting Tyrollius back at me."

"Everything with the suit—"

An excited squeal interrupted the captain as Runcible trotted into the sickbay. The little brown pig came over to Kira and sniffed her foot, then hurried back to Sparrow and wound between her legs.

The woman reached down to give Runcible a scratch behind the ears. The pig lifted its snout and almost seemed to be smiling.

Falconi resumed talking: "Everything with the suit match up with what she said?"

Vishal spread his hands. "As far as I can tell. Half the time I don't know if I'm looking at an organic cell, a nanomachine, or some sort of weird hybrid. The molecular structure of the suit seems to change by the second."

"Well, are we going to start frothing at the mouth and keel over? Or is it going to kill us in our sleep? That's what I want to know."

Kira shifted uncomfortably, thinking of Alan.

"It seems . . . unlikely, at the moment," said Vishal. "There is nothing in these tests to indicate the xeno is an immediate threat. However, I must warn you, there is no way of being sure with the equipment I have."

"Understood," said Falconi. "Right. Well, I guess we'll risk it then. I've got confidence in you, Doc. Navárez, you there?"

"Yes."

"We'll be changing course to Malpert Station directly. ETA is just under forty-two hours."

"Understood. And thank you."

He grunted. "Not doing it for you, Navárez. . . . Sparrow, I know you're listening. Take our guest to the spare cabin on C-deck. She can stay there for the duration. Best to keep her away from the rest of the passengers."

Sparrow straightened off the doorframe. "Yessir."

"Oh, and Navárez? You're welcome to join us in the galley if you want. Dinner is at nineteen hundred sharp." Then the line went dead.

4.

Sparrow popped another bubble of gum. "Okay, ground-pounder, let's go."

Kira didn't obey at first. She looked at Vishal and said, "Can you forward your results to me, so I can look at them myself?"

He bobbed his head. "Yes, of course."

"Thanks. And thanks for being so thorough."

Vishal seemed surprised by her response. Then he bowed slightly and laughed, a quick, melodic sound. "When the risk is dying from an alien infestation, how could I not be thorough?"

"That's an excellent point."

Then Kira followed Sparrow back out into the corridor. "You have anything in the hold you need to get?" the shorter woman asked.

Kira shook her head. "I'm good."

Together, they proceeded down to the next level of the ship. As they walked, the thrust alert sounded, and the deck seemed to tilt and twist underneath them as the *Wallfish* reoriented along its new vector.

"Galley is through there," said Sparrow, gesturing at a marked door. "Feel free to help yourself if you get hungry. Just don't. Touch. The. Damn. Chocolate."

"That's been a problem?"

The woman snorted. "Trig keeps eating it and claiming he didn't realize the rest of us wanted some. . . . Here, this is you." She stopped in front of another door.

Kira nodded and ducked inside. Behind her, Sparrow stayed in place, watching, until the door swung shut.

Feeling more like a prisoner than a passenger, Kira surveyed her surroundings. The cabin was half the size of Falconi's. Bunk and storage locker on one side, sink and mirror, toilet, and desk with a computer display on the other. The walls were brown, like the corridors, and there were just two lights, one on each side: white patches caged with metal bars.

The handle on the locker stuck when she tried it. She leaned on it, and the door popped open. A thin blue blanket lay folded inside. Nothing else.

Kira started to remove her jumpsuit and then hesitated. What if Falconi had the cabin under surveillance? After a moment's thought, she decided she didn't give a damn. Eighty-eight days and eleven light-years was far too long to have worn the same piece of clothing.

Feeling something close to relief, Kira unseamed the jumpsuit, pulled her arms free, and stepped out of it. A trickle of dust fell from the cuffed legs.

She draped the suit over the back of the chair and went to the sink, intending to take a sponge bath. The sight in the mirror stopped her.

Even on the *Valkyrie,* Kira had never been able to see herself properly, only partial glimpses, dark and ghostlike on the glassy surfaces of the displays. She hadn't really cared; she just had to look down to get a good idea of what the Soft Blade had done to her.

But now, seeing herself reflected nearly in whole, it struck her just how much the alien organism had changed and . . . *infested* her, occupying what no one else had any right to occupy, not even a child, if ever she had a child. Her face and body were thinner than she remembered, too thin—a consequence of so many weeks spent at half rations—but that itself didn't bother her.

All she could look at was the suit. The shiny, black, fibrous suit that clung to her like a layer of shrink-wrapped polymer. It looked as if her skin and fascia had been stripped away to expose a gruesome anatomy chart of muscles.

Kira ran a hand over the strange shape of her bare scalp. Her breath caught and a tight knot formed in her gut. She felt as if she were going to be sick. She stared, and she hated what she saw, but she couldn't bring herself to look away. The surface of the Soft Blade grew rough as it echoed her emotions.

Who could find her attractive now . . . the way Alan had? Tears filled her eyes and spilled down her cheeks.

She felt ugly.

Disfigured.

Outcast.

And there was no one to comfort her.

Kira took a shuddering breath, reining in her emotions. She'd grieved and would continue to grieve, but there was no changing the past, and dissolving into a sobbing mess wasn't going to do her any good.

All was not lost. There was a way forward now: a hope, if however slight.

Forcing her gaze away from the mirror, she used the cloth by the sink to wash herself and then retreated to the bed and crawled under the blanket. There, in the filtered gloom, she again worked on forcing the Soft Blade to retreat from a patch of skin (this time the fingers of her left hand).

Compared with before, it felt as if the Soft Blade better understood what she was trying to accomplish. The effort required was more manageable, and there were moments when the sense of struggle vanished and she and xeno were working in harmony. Those moments encouraged her, and Kira pushed even harder as a result.

The Soft Blade retreated from her nails with a sticky, peeling sound. It halted at the first joint of each finger, and try as she might, Kira couldn't coax it past.

She reset.

Three more times Kira willed the suit to expose her fingers, and three more times it responded to her satisfaction. With each success, she felt the neural links between her and the suit deepening, becoming increasingly efficient.

She tried elsewhere on her body, and there too the Soft Blade obeyed her commands, though some areas were more challenging than others. To free herself entirely of the xeno would require more strength than she could muster, but Kira wasn't disappointed. She was still learning to communicate with the xeno, and the fact that freedom might just be possible—if even only as a distant prospect—kindled such a sense of lightness within her, she grinned with an idiot's delight into the blanket.

Ridding herself of the Soft Blade wouldn't solve all her problems (the UMC and the League would still want her for observation, and without the suit she'd be completely at their mercy), but it would solve the biggest one and clear the way for her to someday—somehow!—have a normal life again.

Once more she willed the Soft Blade to retract. Holding it in place was like trying to hold two magnets face-to-face with the same polarity. At one point, a noise on the other side of the room caught her attention, and a thin spike stabbed out from her hand, pierced the blanket, and struck the desk (she could feel it, same as an extended finger).

"Shit," Kira muttered. Had anyone seen that? With a struggle, she convinced the Soft Blade to reabsorb the spike. She looked out at the desk; the spike had left a long scratch on the top.

When she could no longer maintain her concentration, Kira abandoned her experiments and went to the desk. She pulled up the built-in display, linked it to her overlays, and scanned the files Vishal had messaged her.

It was her first time getting to see actual test results from the xeno. And they were fascinating.

The material of the suit consisted of three basic components. One, nanoassemblers, which were responsible for shaping and reshaping both the xeno and surrounding material, though where the assemblers drew their power wasn't obvious. Two, dendriform filaments that extended throughout every part of the suit and which displayed consistent patterns of activity that seemed to indicate the organism was acting as a massively interconnected processor (whether or not it was alive in the traditional sense was hard to determine, but it certainly wasn't *dead*). And three, an enormously complex polymeric molecule, copies of which Vishal had found attached to nearly every assembler, as well as the dendriform substrate.

Like so many things regarding the xeno, the purpose of the molecule was a mystery. It didn't seem to have anything to do with the repair or construction of the suit. The length of the molecule meant it contained an enormous amount of potential information—at least two orders of magnitude more than base-human DNA—but as yet, there was no way to determine what use, if any, the information was supposed to have.

There was a chance, Kira thought, that the only real function of the xeno was to protect and pass on the molecule. Not that that told her very much. From a biological point of view, the same was true with humans and DNA, and humans were capable of far more than just propagation.

Kira went over the results four times before she was satisfied she'd committed them to memory. Vishal was right: to learn more about the xeno would require better equipment.

Maybe the Entropists could help. . . . She filed away the thought for future consideration. Malpert would be the place to approach the Entropists about examining the xeno, if indeed she decided to.

Then Kira returned to the news and started to dig into the research concerning the Jellies' biology, eager to bring herself up to date with the current literature. It, too, was fascinating stuff: all sorts of things could be inferred from the aliens' genome. They were omnivores, for one, and large chunks of their DNA-equivalent seemed to have been custom-coded (natural processes never produced such clean sequences).

Nothing in the Jellies' biology resembled what Vishal had found in the xeno. Nothing seemed to indicate a shared biological heritage. That in and of itself didn't mean anything. Kira knew of more than a few human-made artificial organisms (mostly single-celled creations) that contained no obvious chemical link to Earth-derived life. So it didn't mean anything . . . but it was suggestive.

Kira read until early afternoon, and then she broke for a quick visit to the galley, where she made herself some chell and grabbed a meal pack from a cupboard. She didn't feel comfortable eating any of the fresh food in the ship's cooler; that stuff was rare and expensive in space. It would be bad manners to chow it down without permission, even if the sight of an orange had started her mouth watering.

Upon her return to the cabin, she found a message waiting for her:

The spaces around your answers invite inspection, meatbag. What things did you leave unsaid? I wonder, yes I do. Tell me this at least, ere you deprive us of your shedding presence: What are you really, O Infested One? – Gregorovich

Kira pursed her lips. She didn't want to answer. Trying to win a battle of wits with a ship mind was a fool's game, but pissing him off would be far more stupid.

I'm alone and afraid. What are you? – Kira

It was a calculated risk. If she allowed herself to appear more vulnerable to him—and Gregorovich was most definitely a *him*—then maybe she could distract him. It was worth a shot.

To her surprise, the ship mind didn't answer.

She continued to read. Not long afterward, the *Wallfish* went zero-g and then performed a skew-flip before starting to decelerate toward Malpert Station. As always, the weightlessness left Kira with the taste of bile in her mouth and a renewed sense of appreciation for gravity, simulated or otherwise.

When it was nearly 1900, she closed down her overlays, pulled on her jumpsuit, and decided to risk venturing out to face the crew at dinner.

What was the worst that could happen?

5.

The hum of conversation in the galley stopped the moment Kira entered. She paused in the doorway while the crew looked at her and she at them.

The captain was sitting at the near table with one leg pulled up against his chest and his arm resting on his knee while he spooned food into his mouth. Across from him was Nielsen, stiff and straight-backed as always.

At the far table sat the doctor and one of the largest women Kira had ever seen. She wasn't fat, just wide and thick, with bones and joints nearly a third bigger than those of most men. Each of her fingers was the equivalent of two of Kira's, and her face was flat and round, with enormous cheekbones.

Kira recognized the face as the one she'd seen upon waking in the shuttle, and she instantly identified the woman as a former denizen of Shin-Zar. She could hardly be mistaken for anything else.

It was unusual to see a Zarian in the League. Theirs was the one colony that insisted on staying independent (at no small cost in ships and lives). During her time with the company, Kira had only worked with a few people from Shin-Zar—all men—at different postings. To a person they'd been tough, reliable, and as expected, strong as hell. They'd also been able to drink a staggering amount, far more than their size would seem to indicate. That had been one of the first lessons Kira had learned working on mining rigs: don't try to drink a Zarian under the table. It was a fast way to end up in sickbay with alcohol poisoning.

On an intellectual level, Kira understood why the colonists had gene-hacked themselves—they wouldn't have survived in Shin-Zar's high-g environment otherwise—but she'd never really gotten used to how *different* they looked. It hadn't bothered Shyrene, her roommate during corporate training. She'd kept a picture of a pop star from Shin-Zar projected on the wall of their apartment.

Like most Zarians, the woman in the *Wallfish* galley was of Asian descent. Korean no doubt, as Koreans made up the majority of immigrants to Shin-Zar (that much Kira remembered from her class on the history of the seven colonies). She wore a rumpled jumpsuit, patched on the knees and elbows and stained with grease along the arms. The shape of her face made her age impossible for Kira to guess; she might have been in her early twenties or she might have been almost forty.

Trig was sitting on the edge of the kitchen counter, chewing on another of his seemingly endless supply of ration bars. And ladling out meatballs from a pot on the stove was Sparrow, still in the same outfit as before. The cat, Mr. Fuzzypants, rubbed against her ankles, meowing piteously.

A delicious, savory smell suffused the air.

"Well, you going to come in or not?" Falconi asked. His words broke the spell, and motion and conversation resumed.

Kira wondered if the rest of the crew knew about the Soft Blade. Her question was answered as she made her way to the back and Trig said, "So that skinsuit was actually made by aliens?"

Kira hesitated and then nodded, aware of the eyes focused on her. "Yeah."

The kid's face brightened. "Cool! Can I touch it?"

"Trig," said Nielsen in a warning tone. "That's enough of that."

"Yes, ma'am," said the kid, and a bright red spot appeared on each of his cheeks. He gave Nielsen a shy, sideways glance and then stuffed the last of his ration bar into the side of his mouth and hopped down from the counter. "You lied to me, Ms. Navárez. You said your friend made the suit."

"Yeah, sorry about that," said Kira, feeling awkward.

Trig shrugged. "'S okay. I get it."

Sparrow moved away from the stove. "All yours," she said to Kira.

As Kira went to get a bowl and spoon, the cat hissed at her and ran to hide under one of the tables. Falconi pointed with his middle finger. "Seems he's taken a real disliking to you."

Yes, thank you, Captain Obvious. Scooping meatballs into her bowl, Kira said, "What did the UMC say when you told them we were changing course?"

Falconi shrugged. "Well, they weren't happy about it, I can tell you that."

"Neither are our passengers," said Nielsen, more to him than to Kira. "I just spent half an hour getting yelled at by everyone in the hold. The mood down there is pretty ugly." The look she gave Kira suggested she blamed her for the trouble.

It wasn't an unwarranted reaction, in Kira's opinion.

Falconi picked at his teeth with a nail. "Noted. Gregorovich, make sure you keep a closer eye on them from now on."

"Yes*ssssir*," the ship mind answered, his voice unnervingly sibilant.

Kira took her bowl and sat on the nearest free chair, facing the Zarian. "I'm sorry, I didn't get your name before," Kira said.

The Zarian regarded her with a flat expression and then blinked once. "Were you the one who patched the holes at the back of the shuttle?" Her voice was calm and vast.

"I did my best."

The woman grunted and looked back at her food.

Okay then, Kira thought. So the crew weren't going to welcome her with open arms. That was fine. She'd been the outsider on most of her postings. Why would it be any different now? She just had to put up with them until Malpert Station. After that, she'd never have to deal with the *Wallfish* crew again.

Then Trig said, "Hwa is the best machine boss this side of Sol."

At least the kid seemed friendly.

The Zarian frowned. "Hwa-jung," she said firmly. "My name is not *Hwa*."

"Aww. You know I can't pronounce it right."

"Try."

"Hwa-*yoong*."

The machine boss shook her head. Before she could speak again, Sparrow came over and dropped into Hwa-jung's lap. She leaned back against the larger woman, and Hwa-jung wrapped an arm around her waist in a possessive manner.

Kira raised an eyebrow. "So you pick up heavy things and put them down, huh?" At the other table, she thought she heard a suppressed snort from Falconi.

Sparrow matched her expression, cocking one perfectly manicured eyebrow. "So your hearing works. Good for you." And she craned her neck to give Hwa-jung a peck on the cheek. The machine boss made a sound, as if annoyed, but Kira saw her lips curve in a small smile.

Kira took the opportunity to start eating. The meatballs were warm and rich, with just the right mixture of thyme, rosemary, salt, and a few other things she couldn't identify. Were those tomatoes *fresh*? She closed her eyes, luxuriating in the taste. It had been so long since she'd had anything but dehydrated, pre-packaged food.

"Mmm," she said. "Who made this?"

Vishal lifted his head. "You like it that much?"

She opened her eyes and nodded.

For a moment, the doctor seemed conflicted, and then a modest smile split his face. "I'm glad. Today was my day to cook."

Kira smiled back and took another bite. It was the first time she'd felt like smiling since . . . before.

With a clatter of plates and silverware, Trig switched tables and sat next to her. "Captain said you found the xeno in some ruins on Adrasteia. Alien ruins!"

She swallowed the mouthful of food she was working on. "That's right."

Trig nearly bounced on the bench. "What was it like? Do you have any recordings?"

Kira shook her head. "They were on the *Valkyrie*. But I can tell you."

"Yes, please!"

Then Kira described how she had found the cradle of the Soft Blade and what it had been like inside. The kid wasn't the only one listening; she could see the rest of the crew watching as she talked, even those who had heard the story earlier. She tried not to let it make her self-conscious.

When she finished, the kid said, "Wow. The Jellies built stuff really close to us, even way back when, huh?"

Kira hesitated. "Well, maybe."

Sparrow lifted her head off Hwa-jung's chest. "Why *maybe*?"

"Because . . . the xeno doesn't seem to like the Jellies very much." Kira traced a finger across the back of her left hand as she struggled to put dreams into words. "I'm not sure why exactly, but I don't think the Jellies treated it very well. Also, none of the readings Vishal took of the xeno match what's published about the Jellies' biology."

Vishal put down the cup he'd been about to drink from. "Ms. Navárez is right. I also checked, and nothing else like this is known. At least not according to our current files."

Nielsen said, "Do you think your suit was made by the same species or civilization that made the Great Beacon?"

"Maybe," said Kira.

A *clink* as Falconi tapped his fork against his plate. He shook his head. "That's a lot of *maybes*."

Kira made a noncommittal sound.

Then Trig said, "Hey, Doc, so how'd you manage to miss that she's covered in an alien skinsuit, huh?"

"Yeah, Doc," said Sparrow, twisting around to look at Vishal. "Awfully shortsighted of you. Not sure if I should trust you with an exam now."

Even with the darkness of his skin, Kira could see Vishal flush. "There was no evidence of alien infestation. Even a blood test would not have—"

Trig interrupted: "Maybe some of the flatheads in the hold are actually Jellies in disguise. You'd never know, would you?"

The doctor pressed his lips together, but he didn't lash out. Instead, he kept his gaze fixed on his food and said, "Indeed, Trig. What might I have been missing?"

"Yeah, there could—"

"We know you did your best, Doc," said Falconi in a firm tone. "No need to feel bad about it. No one would have caught this thing." Next to him, Kira noticed Nielsen give Vishal a sympathetic glance.

Feeling a bit sorry for the doctor, Kira took the initiative. "So you enjoy cooking?" She held up a spoon with a meatball on it.

After a moment, Vishal nodded, met her gaze. "Yes, yes, very much. But my food is not as good as my mother's or my sisters'. They put my poor efforts to shame."

"How many sisters do you have?" she asked, thinking of Isthah.

He held up fingers. "Three sisters, Ms. Navárez, all older."

After that, an unnatural silence settled over the galley. None of the crew seemed to want to talk while she was there; even Trig kept quiet, although Kira felt sure he was buzzing with a thousand more questions.

It surprised her, then, when Nielsen said, "I hear you come from Weyland, Ms. Navárez." Her tone was more formal than that of the rest of the crew; Kira didn't recognize her accent.

"Yes, that's right."

"Do you have family there?"

"Some, although it's been a while since I visited." Kira decided to take a chance and ask a question of her own: "Where are you from, if you don't mind me asking?"

Nielsen wiped the corners of her mouth with a napkin. "Here and there."

"She's from Venus!" Trig blurted out, eyes shining. "One of the biggest cloud cities!"

Nielsen pressed her lips together in a flat line. "Yes, thank you, Trig."

The kid seemed to realize he'd screwed up. His face dropped, and he fixed his gaze on his bowl. "I mean," he muttered, ". . . I don't really know or anything, so . . ."

Kira studied the first officer. Venus was nearly as rich as Earth. Not too many folks from there went wandering around outside Sol, and certainly not in a dinky rust bucket like the *Wallfish*. "Are the cities as impressive as they appear in vids?"

For a moment Nielsen looked as if she wouldn't answer. Then, in a clipped tone, she said, "You get used to it. . . . But yes."

Kira had always wanted to visit the floating cities. Just another life goal the Soft Blade had put out of reach. *If only—*

An excited squeal distracted her as Runcible trotted into the galley. The pig ran straight to Falconi and leaned against the side of his leg.

Nielsen made an exasperated sound. "Who left the latch on his cage loose again?"

"That would be me, boss lady," said Sparrow, raising her hand.

"He just wants to be with us. Don't you now?" said Falconi, and he scratched the pig behind the ears. The pig lifted his snout, eyes half-closed in an expression of bliss.

"What he wants is our food," said Nielsen. "Captain, it really isn't appropriate to have him here. A pig doesn't belong in the galley."

"Not unless it's as bacon," said Hwa-jung.

"There'll be no talking of bacon around Runcible," said Falconi. "He's part of the crew, same as Mr. Fuzzypants, and they get the same rights as any of you. That includes access to the galley. Is that clear?"

Hwa-jung said, "Clear, Captain."

"It's still not hygienic," said Nielsen. "What if he goes to the bathroom again?"

"He's a well-trained pig now. He would never embarrass himself like before. Would you, Runcible?" The pig snorted happily.

"If you say so, Captain. It still feels wrong. What if we're eating ham or pork—" Falconi gave her a look, and she raised her hands. "Just saying, Captain. Seems a bit like, like . . ."

"Cannibalism," said Trig.

"Yes, thank you. Cannibalism."

The kid seemed pleased Nielsen agreed with him. A slight flush crept up his neck, and he stared at his plate while fighting back a grin. Kira hid a smile of her own.

Falconi took a bit of food off his plate and gave it to the pig, who gratefully snapped it up. "Last I checked, we have no, ah, *porcine* products on the ship, so as far as I'm concerned, it's a moot point."

"Moot point." Nielsen shook her head. "I give up. Arguing with you is like arguing with a wall."

"A very handsome wall."

As the two of them continued to bicker, Kira looked over at Vishal and said, "What's with the pig? Is it new?"

The doctor shook his head. "We've had him on board six months, not counting cryo. The captain picked him up on Eidolon. They've been arguing about him ever since."

"But why a pig?"

"You would have to ask the captain that yourself, Ms. We have no more an idea than you. It's a mystery of the universe."

6.

The rest of the meal passed in an awkward semblance of normalcy. They didn't say anything more serious than "Pass the salt." or "Where's the trash?" or "Get

Runcible his dish." Terse, utilitarian exchanges that served only to make Kira aware of how out of place she was.

Normally dinner was when she would pull out her concertina and play a few rounds to break the ice. Buy some drinks, smack down the clumsy attempts to hit on her—unless she was in a mood. The usual, before Alan. But here it didn't matter; she'd be off the *Wallfish* by the end of next day, and then she wouldn't have to worry about Falconi and the rest of his ragtag crew.

Kira had just emptied her bowl and was taking it back to the sink when a short, loud *beep* sounded. It froze them in place, and everyone's eyes grew hazy as they focused on their overlays.

Kira glanced at her own but saw no alerts. "What is it?" she asked, noting the sudden tension in Falconi's posture.

Sparrow was the one who answered: "Jellies. Four more of them, heading for Malpert Station."

"ETA?" Kira asked, dreading the answer.

Falconi's eyes cleared as he looked at her. "Noon tomorrow."

CHAPTER IV

★ ★ ★ ★ ★ ★ ★

KRIEGSSPIEL

1.

Four blinking red dots arrowed across the system toward Malpert Station. A set of dotted lines—bright green—showed their calculated trajectory.

Tapping her overlays, Kira zoomed in on the station. It was a disorganized pile of sensors, domes, docking bays, and radiators built around a hollowed-out asteroid. Embedded within the rock (barely visible from the outside) was a rotating hab-ring where most of the station citizens lived.

Next to Malpert, some kilometers away, was a Hydrotek refueling platform.

Ships swarmed around the two structures. A different icon marked each ship: civilians in blue, military vessels in gold. Without closing her overlays, Kira said, "Can they stop the Jellies?"

On the other side of the translucent overlays, Falconi frowned. "Not sure. The *Darmstadt* is their only real firepower. The rest of the ships are just locals. PDF cutters and the like."

"PDF?"

"Planetary Defense Force."

Sparrow clicked her tongue. "Yeah, but those Jelly ships are the small ones. *Naru*-class."

To Kira, Trig said: "The *Naru*-class ships only carry three squids, two or three crawlers, and about the same number of snappers. 'Course, some of 'em have heavy crabs as well."

"Sure they do," said Sparrow with a humorless smirk.

Vishal chimed in: "And that before they start turning out reinforcements from their birthing pods."

"Birthing pods?" Kira asked, feeling totally out of the loop.

Hwa-jung answered: "They have machines that let them grow new fighters."

"I . . . I didn't see anything about that in the news," said Kira.

Falconi grunted. "The League has been keeping it under wraps to avoid scaring people, but we caught wind of it a few weeks ago."

The concept of a birthing pod seemed dimly familiar to Kira, as a half-forgotten memory. If only she could get her hands on a Jelly computer! The things she could learn!

Sparrow said, "The Jellies must be pretty confident if they think they can take out Malpert and the *Darmstadt* with just those four ships."

"Don't count out the miners," said Trig. "They've got plenty of weapons, and they won't run. Swear to god they won't."

Kira gave him a questioning look, and the kid shrugged. "I grew up on Undset Station, over at Cygni B. I know 'em. Those space rats are tough as titanium."

"Yeah, well," said Sparrow, "they ain't going to be fighting no half-starved jackers this time."

Nielsen stirred. "Captain," she said, "we still have time to change course."

Kira cleared her overlays in order to better see Falconi's face. He appeared distracted as he studied screens she couldn't see. "Not sure it would make any difference," he murmured. He tapped a button on the kitchen wall, and a holo of 61 Cygni appeared suspended in the air. He pointed at the red dots that marked the Jellies. "Even if we turn tail and run, there's no way we can escape them."

"No, but if we put some distance between us and them, they might decide the chase isn't worth the effort," said Nielsen. "It's always worked before."

Falconi made a face. "We've already burned through a good chunk of hydrogen. Getting to Ruslan now would be dicey. We'd have to coast at least half the distance. Would be sitting ducks the whole time." He scratched his chin, eyes still fixed on the holo.

Sparrow said, "What are you thinking, Captain?

"We let the *Wallfish* live up to its name," he said. He highlighted an asteroid some distance from Malpert Station. "Here. There's an extraction outfit on this asteroid—asteroid TSX-Two-Two-One-Two. Says there's a hab-dome, refueling tanks, the whole lot. We can cozy up to the asteroid and wait until the fighting is over. If the Jellies decide to come after us, we'd have tunnels to hide in. As long as they don't drop a nuke on us or something like that, we'd at least have a chance."

On her overlays, Kira looked up the definition of *wallfish*. Apparently it was *A regional term for "snail" in the country of Britain on Earth; presumably of*

Anglo-Saxon origin. She eyed Falconi, again thrown askance by his sense of humor. He'd named his ship the *Snail*?

The crew continued debating possibilities, while Kira sat and thought.

Then she went to Falconi and bent close to his ear. "Can I talk with you for a moment?"

He barely glanced at her. "What?"

"Outside." She motioned toward the door.

Falconi hesitated, and then to Kira's surprise, shoved himself out of his chair. "Be right back," he said, and followed her out of the galley.

Kira turned on him. "You have to get me onto one of those Jelly ships."

The look of incredulousness on the captain's face was nearly worth everything she'd gone through. "Nope. Not going to happen," he said, and started back in.

She caught his arm, stopping him. "Wait. Hear me out."

"Get your hand off me before I remove it for you," he said with an unfriendly expression.

Kira let go. "Look, I'm not asking you to charge in guns blazing. You said the UMC has a chance of fighting off the Jellies." He nodded, reluctant. "If they disable one of the Jelly ships—*if*—you could get me on it."

"You're crazy," Falconi said, still half in the doorway of the galley.

"I'm determined. There's a difference. I told you; I need to get onto one of the Jellies' ships. If I can, I might be able figure out why they're attacking us, what they're saying over their comms, all sorts of stuff. Just think of the possibilities." She could still see reluctance on Falconi's face, so she kept talking: "Look, you've been flying around the system right under the Jellies' noses or whatever the hell they use to smell. That means you're either stupid or you're desperate, and you might be a lot of things, but stupid isn't one of them."

Falconi shifted. "What's your point?"

"You need a payday. You need a big payday or else you wouldn't be risking your ship or your crew like this. Am I wrong?"

A hint of unease flitted across his eyes. "Not entirely."

She nodded. "Okay. So, how would you like to be the first person to get your hands on info from the Jellies? Do you know how much my company would pay for it? Enough to build your own hab-ring. That's how much. There's still tech on the Jellies' ships that no one has been able to back-engineer. I could get specs on their artificial gravity. *That* would be worth a few bits."

"Just a few," he murmured.

"Hell, you have a couple of Entropists in the hold. Ask them to come along in exchange for a copy of any interesting discoveries. With them helping me"—she spread her hands—"who knows how much we could find? It's not even just about the war; we could jump-start our tech level by a hundred years or more."

Falconi faced her full on. His middle finger tapped the grip of his blaster in an irregular tempo. "I get it. But even if the UMC does disable a ship, that won't mean all the Jellies on it will be killed." He motioned downward. "I have everyone in the hold to think about. Lotta people could get hurt if we have fighting on the ship."

Kira couldn't help herself: "And how much were you thinking about their welfare when you started charging for rescue?"

For the first time, Falconi seemed offended. "Doesn't mean I want to see them killed," he said.

"What about the *Wallfish*? Does it have any weapons?"

"Enough to stop a rim runner or two, but this isn't a warship. We can't go up against one of the Jellies and hope to survive. They'd cut us to shreds."

Kira stood back, put her hands on her hips. "So what are you going to do?"

Falconi studied her, and she saw the calculations going on behind his eyes. Then he said, "We'll still head for that asteroid, because we might need it in the worst-case scenario. But if one of the Jellies' ships gets disabled, and if it looks doable, we'll board it."

A sense of enormity filled Kira as she considered the possibility. "Okay then," she said quietly.

Falconi chuckled and ran a hand through his bristle-like hair. "Shit. If we pull this off, the UMC is going to be so mad we got the jump on them, they won't know whether to give us a medal or throw us in the brig."

And for the first time since she'd woken up on the *Wallfish,* Kira laughed as well.

2.

The waiting was torturous.

Kira stayed in the galley with the crew, watching the progress of the Jellies. She quickly decided she would rather be shot at than sit around waiting to find out what might or might not happen. The uncertainty drove her to bite her nails, but the slightly metallic taste of the Soft Blade filled her mouth and her teeth bounced off the fibrous coating.

The last time it happened, she sat on her hands to stop herself. Which made her wonder; why hadn't her nails grown in the past few months? The xeno hadn't replaced them; she'd seen the nails on her left hand—pink and healthy as ever—when she'd caused the suit to retract. The only explanation she could think of was that the Soft Blade was maintaining the same nail length she had when it first emerged.

When she couldn't bear sitting anymore, Kira made her excuses and went to Trig. "Do you have any spare clothes on the ship? Or a printer that could make me some?" She plucked at the jumpsuit. "After a couple of months in this thing, I could use a change."

The kid blinked as he switched his focus from his overlays to her. "Sure," he said. "We don't have nothing fancy, but—"

"Plain and simple is fine."

They left the galley, and he took her to a storage locker set within the inner ring of the corridor. As he rummaged inside, she said, "Seems like Nielsen and the captain bicker a lot. That normal for them?" If she was going to be stuck on the *Wallfish* for longer than planned, Kira wanted to get a better feel for the crew and for Falconi specifically. She was trusting a lot to him.

A small *thud* as Trig hit his head on a shelf. "Nah. The captain doesn't like to be rushed; that's all. Most times they get along fine."

"Uh-huh." The kid liked to talk. She just needed to provide the right encouragement. "So have you been with the *Wallfish* long?"

"'Bout five years, not counting cryo."

That raised Kira's eyebrows. The kid must have been *really* young when he joined the crew. "Yeah? Why did Falconi bring you on?"

"The captain needed someone to show him around Undset Station. Afterward, I asked if I could go with the *Wallfish*."

"Station life wasn't to your liking?"

"It *sucked*! We had pressure breaches, food shortages, power outages, you name it. Not. Nice."

"And is Falconi a good captain? Do you like him?"

"He's the best!" Trig pulled his head out of the locker, a pile of clothes in his hands, and looked at her with a somewhat hurt expression, as if he felt she were attacking him. "Couldn't ask for a better captain. No, ma'am! It's not his fault we got stranded here." As soon as the words left the kid's mouth, he seemed to realize he'd said too much, because he clamped his lips shut and held out the clothes for her.

"Oh?" Kira crossed her arms. "Whose fault is it, then?"

The kid shrugged, uncomfortable. "No one's. It doesn't matter."

"It *does* matter. We've got Jellies incoming, and my neck is on the line, same as yours. I'd like to know who I'm working with. The truth, Trig. Tell me the truth."

The stern tone of her voice made the difference. The kid wilted before it and said, "It's not . . . Look, Ms. Nielsen usually books our jobs. That's why the captain hired her last year."

"Real time?"

He nodded. "Minus cryo it's been a lot less."

"You like her as first officer?" The answer was obvious enough to Kira, but she was curious what he would say.

The kid shifted, color darkening his cheeks. "I mean, uh . . . She's real sharp, and she doesn't order me around like Hwa-*jung*. And she knows an awful lot about Sol. So, uh, yeah, I think she's nice. . . ." His flush deepened. "Uh, not like *that*, but, uh, as a first officer and all. W-we're lucky to have her on board. . . . You know, as crew, not, uh—"

Kira took mercy on him and said, "I get it. But Nielsen didn't book this job, the one to Sixty-One Cygni, did she?"

Trig shook his head. "The skut-work we were doing—cargo, packet missions, that sort of thing—it wasn't paying the bills. So the captain found us this other job, but it went sour. It could have happened to anyone, though. Really." He peered at her, earnest.

"I believe you," Kira said. "Sorry things didn't work out." She knew enough to read between the lines: the job had been something dodgy. Nielsen had probably only been accepting legitimate commissions, which for an old, refit cargo ship like the *Wallfish* weren't a whole lot.

Trig made a face. "Yeah, thanks. It sucks, but that's what it is. Anyway, these alright for you?"

Kira decided it was best not to push any harder. She accepted the pile of clothes and flipped through them. Two shirts, a pair of pants, socks, and boots with gecko pads for use during zero-g maneuvers. "They'll do just fine. Thanks."

The kid left her then—heading back to the galley—and Kira continued to her cabin, thinking. So Falconi was willing to bend the law in order to keep his crew paid and his ship flying. Nothing new there. But she believed Trig when he said that Falconi was a good captain. The kid's reaction had been too genuine to be faked.

A light was flashing on the desktop display when Kira entered. Another message. With a sense of trepidation, she pulled it up.

> *I am the spark in the center of the void. I am the widdershin scream that cleaves the night. I am your eschatological nightmare. I am the one and the word and the fullness of the light.*
>
> *Would you like to play a game? Y/N – Gregorovich*

As a rule, ship minds tended to be eccentric, and the larger they were, the more eccentricities they displayed. Gregorovich was on the outer tail of that bell curve, though. She couldn't tell if it was just his personality or if his behavior was the result of too much isolation.

Surely Falconi isn't crazy enough to fly around with an unstable ship mind. . . . Right?

Either way, best to play it safe:

> *No. – Kira*

An instant later, a reply popped up:

> ☹ – *Gregorovich*

Trying to ignore a sense of foreboding, Kira stowed her jumpsuit, washed her new clothes in the tiny sink, and hung them to dry along the top of her bunk.

She checked on the position of the four Jellies—still no change in their trajectory—and then spent the next hour practicing with the Soft Blade, retracting it from different parts of her body and trying to improve her control.

At last, exhausted, she slid under the blankets, turned off the lights, and did her best not to think about what morning would bring.

3.

Drifts of silt sifted through the purple depths of the Plaintive Verge, soft as snow, silent as death. Nearscent of unease suffused the icy water, and the unease became her own. Before her loomed the crusted rock that sat proud among the

Abyssal Conclave. And upon that rock squatted a massive bulk with heaving limbs and a thousand lidless eyes that glared with dire intent. As the veils of silt descended, so too a name descended through her mind, a whisper weighted with fear, fraught with hate . . . Ctein. The great and mighty Ctein. The huge and ancient Ctein.

And the flesh she was joined with—she that was the Shoal Leader Nmarhl—yearned to turn and flee, to hide from the wrath of Ctein. But it was too late for that. Far, far too late. . . .

The gradual brightening of the cabin's lights woke Kira as ship-dawn arrived. She rubbed the crust from her eyes and then lay staring at the ceiling.

Ctein. Why did the name inspire such a sense of fear? The fear wasn't coming from her either, but the Soft Blade. . . . No, that wasn't right. It came from the one the Soft Blade had been bonded with in its memory.

The xeno was trying to warn her, but of what? Everything it had shown her had happened long ago, before the Soft Blade had been laid to rest on Adrasteia.

Maybe, she thought, the xeno was just anxious. Or maybe it was trying to help her understand how dangerous the Jellies were. Not something she really needed help with.

"It would be a lot easier if you could talk," she murmured, tracing a finger across the fibers on her sternum. It was clear the xeno understood something of what was happening around it—but it was equally clear there were gaps in its comprehension.

She opened a file and recorded a detailed account of the dream. Whatever the Soft Blade was trying to tell her, Kira knew it would be a mistake to discount the xeno's concern. If indeed concern it was. It was hard to be sure of anything when it came to the suit.

She rolled out of bed and sneezed as a thin cloud of dust flew up around her. Waving her hand to clear the air, she went to the desk and opened a live map of the system.

The four Jellies were only hours away from Malpert Station. The *Darmstadt* and the other spaceships had positioned themselves in a defensive formation several hours' burn away from the station, where they would have room to fight and maneuver.

Malpert had a mass driver it used to fling loads of metal, rock, and ice deeper into the system, but it was a huge, cumbersome thing not meant for tracking small, mobile targets like ships. Nevertheless, whoever was in command of the station was currently turning it as fast as its thrusters would allow, in an attempt to bring the mass driver to bear on the Jellies.

Kira freshened up, donned her new clothes (now dry), and hurried to the galley. It was empty, save for Mr. Fuzzypants, who was sitting on the counter, licking the sink faucet.

"Hey!" said Kira. "Shoo!"

The cat flattened its ears and gave her an angry, unappreciative stare before hopping down and trotting past along the wall.

Kira held out a hand in an attempt at friendship. The cat responded with raised hackles and bared claws.

"Fine, you little bastard," Kira muttered.

While she ate, she watched the advance of the Jellies on her overlays. It was a useless exercise, but she couldn't help herself. It was the most interesting show airing right now.

The *Wallfish* was closing in on the asteroid Falconi had named before: TSX-2212. Via the feed from the ship's nose, the rock appeared as a bright, pinhead speck directly in their path.

Kira looked up as Vishal entered the galley. He greeted her and then went to make himself a cup of tea.

"Are you watching?" he asked.

"Yes."

Mug in hand, he headed back toward the door. "Come with, if you want, Ms. Navárez. We're monitoring events in Control."

Kira followed him to the central shaft, up a level, and then into a small, shielded room. Falconi and the rest of the crew stood or sat around a table-sized holo-display. Banks of electronics covered the walls, and bolted at various stations were a half-dozen battered crash chairs. The room was stuffy and stank of sweat and cold coffee.

Falconi glanced at her as she and Vishal entered.

"Anything new?" Kira asked.

Sparrow popped the gum she was chewing. "Lotta chatter on MilCom. Looks like the UMC is coordinating with the civvies around Malpert to set up a bunch of nasty surprises for the Jellies." She nodded toward Trig. "You were right. Should make for a hell of a show."

The back of Kira's neck prickled. "Wait, you've got access to the UMC's channels?"

Sparrow's expression grew closed off, and she glanced at Falconi. A tense silence filled the space. Then, in an easy manner, the captain said, "You know how it is, Navárez. Ships talk, word gets around. There aren't many secrets in space."

". . . Sure." Kira didn't believe him, but she wasn't going to press the point. It did make her wonder just how shady some of Falconi's past dealings had been. Also whether Sparrow had been in the military. It would make sense. . . .

Nielsen said, "The Jellies are nearly within firing range. It won't be long before the shooting starts."

"When do we reach the asteroid?" Kira asked.

Gregorovich was the one to answer: "ETA fourteen minutes."

So Kira took one of the empty crash chairs and waited along with the crew.

In the holo, the four red dots separated and arced around Malpert Station in a classic flanking maneuver. Then white lines began to flicker between the aliens and the defending vessels. Falconi brought up the live feed from the *Wallfish*'s telescopes, and white flowers of chaff and chalk bloomed in the darkness around the unlovely chunk of rock that was Malpert Station.

Sparrow made an approving noise. "Good coverage."

Flashes of absorbed lasers illuminated the insides of the clouds, and barrages of missiles launched from both the *Darmstadt* and the other, smaller UMC ships. The Jellies replied in kind. Small sparks winked in and out of existence as point-defense lasers crippled the missiles.

Then the Malpert mass driver fired, slinging a slug of refined iron toward one of the Jelly ships. The slug missed and disappeared into the depths of space on a long orbit around the star. The projectile was moving so fast, the only way any of them could see it was as an icon in the holo-display.

More chaff and chalk clogged the area surrounding the station. Some of it came from the base itself. The rest from the ships swirling about.

"Whoa!" Falconi said as a white-hot needle erupted from a patch of seemingly empty space, snapped across almost nine thousand klicks, and lanced one of the spherical Jelly ships through the middle, like a blowtorch through styrofoam.

The damaged ship spun out of control, wobbling like a top, and then exploded in a blinding blast.

"Oh fuck yeah!" Sparrow shouted.

The live feed darkened for a moment to accommodate the surge in light.

"What the hell was that?" Kira asked. A twinge at the back of her skull made her wince . . . *ships burning in space, motes glittering in the blackness, the dead uncounted . . .*

Falconi glanced at the ceiling. "Gregorovich, pull in our radiators. Don't want them getting shredded."

"Captain," said the ship mind, "the odds of a wayward particle disrupting our most necessary thermoregulation at this range is—"

"Just yank them. Not going to risk it."

". . . Yessir. Currently *yanking* them."

Another white-hot needle shot across the screen, but it only managed to singe a Jelly, which corkscrewed away far faster than seemed possible.

To Kira, Hwa-jung said, "Those are Casaba-Howitzers."

"That . . . means nothing to me," said Kira, not wanting to spare the time to look up a definition.

"Bomb-pumped shaped charges," said the machine boss. "Only in this case—"

"—the bomb is a nuke!" said Trig. He seemed overly excited by the fact.

Kira's eyebrows climbed. "Shit. I didn't even know that was a thing."

"Oh yeah," said Sparrow. "We've had Casaba-Howitzers for ages. Don't use them much, for obvious reasons, but they're fuck-simple to build, and the plasma moves at a good chunk of light speed. Makes it nearly impossible for anyone to dodge at close ranges, even those squirrely bastards."

In the display, more explosions flared: human ships this time, the smaller support vessels around Malpert bursting like popcorn as the Jellies hit them with lasers and missiles.

"Dammit," said Falconi.

Another Casaba-Howitzer darkened the display, taking out a second Jelly. Even as the crew of the *Wallfish* cheered, one of the two remaining Jellies blasted straight toward the *Darmstadt* while the other opened fire on the refueling platform next to Malpert Station.

The platform erupted in an enormous fireball of burning hydrogen.

Then the mass driver fired again: jets of plasma shooting out from vents along the acceleration tube. The slug missed the Jelly by the destroyed platform—the aliens weren't stupid or careless enough to fly across the line of the muzzle—but the slug hit something else Kira hadn't noticed: a satellite floating close to Malpert.

The satellite vanished in a blast of light, vaporized by the force of the impact.

The spray of superheated materials shotgunned the nearby Jelly, peppering the ship with what amounted to thousands of micrometeoroids.

"Shi-bal," Hwa-jung breathed.

Falconi shook his head. "Whoever pulled off that shot deserves a raise."

The damaged Jelly jetted away from Malpert at speed, and then the ship's engine sputtered and went dead, and the vessel started to spin as it drifted away, powerless. A large gash marred one side of the hull. From it spewed gas and crystalizing water.

Kira watched the ship with fierce interest. *That one,* she thought. As long as it didn't explode, maybe they could board it. She offered quick thanks to Thule and glanced at Falconi.

He noticed, but he didn't react, and Kira wondered what sort of thoughts were turning over behind his hard blue eyes.

The *Wallfish* swung into position behind the asteroid TSX-2212 and cut its thrust as the *Darmstadt* and the sole remaining Jelly continued to duel. The few remaining support vessels hurried to assist the UMC cruiser, but they were no match for the alien ship and only served as brief distractions.

"They're going to overheat soon," said Sparrow, pointing at the *Darmstadt,* which—like the *Wallfish*—had retracted its radiators. Even as she spoke, a plume of unburnt propellant sprayed from valves around the waist of the cruiser. "See," she said. "They're venting hydrogen so they can keep the lasers firing."

The end, when it came, was fast. One of the smaller ships—a manned mining rig, Kira thought—did a burn straight toward the remaining Jelly in an attempt to ram it.

The rig didn't get anywhere near the Jelly, of course. The aliens blasted it to bits before it got close. Those bits continued on their previous trajectory, though, and they forced the Jelly out of its protective cloud of chaff in order to avoid being hit.

The *Darmstadt* started to accelerate even before the Jelly did, executing an emergency burn out of its own envelope of defensive measures. It broke free just as the Jellies emerged into the clear and promptly nailed the alien ship with a center-mass shot from its main laser cannon.

A jet of ablated material ejected from the side of the gleaming Jelly ship, and then the vessel vanished in a fireball of annihilating antimatter.

Kira released her death grip on the crash chair's arms.

"So that's it," said Falconi.

Vishal made a motion in the air. "God be praised."

"Only leaves nine more Jellies," said Sparrow, gesturing at the rest of the system. "Hopefully they won't come looking to settle the score."

"If they do, we should be gone by then," said Nielsen. "Gregorovich, lay in a course for Malpert Station."

Kira looked at the captain again, and this time, he nodded. "Belay that," he said, squaring his shoulders. "Gregorovich, put us on an intercept for that damaged Jelly. All possible speed."

"Captain!" said Nielsen.

Falconi looked round at the stunned crew. "On your toes, people. Let's go salvage an alien spaceship."

CHAPTER V

* * * * * * *

EXTREMIS

1.

Kira stayed silent while Falconi explained the plan. The captain was the one who needed to convince the crew; they trusted him, not her.

"Sir," said Sparrow, more serious than Kira had seen her before, "there may still be Jellies on that ship. There's no way to be sure they're all dead."

"I know," said Falconi. "But there should only be a few of the big squid-creatures on there. Right, Trig?"

The kid bobbed his head, and his Adam's apple went up and down. "Right, Captain."

Falconi nodded, satisfied. "Right. No way all of them have survived. No way, no how. Even if there are two of them still kicking, those are pretty good odds."

Around them, the ship rumbled and weight returned as the *Wallfish* resumed thrust.

"Gregorovich!" said Nielsen.

"My apologies," the ship mind said, sounding as if he were on the verge of laughing. "It seems a fine adventure the captain has put us on, yes it does."

Then Sparrow said, "Good odds can turn bad real fast when the shooting starts, and we have a whole lot of passengers to worry about."

Falconi eyed her, his expression hard as iron. "You don't have to tell me.... Think you can handle it?"

After a moment's consideration, Sparrow cracked a lopsided grin. "What the hell. But you're going to owe me double hazard pay for this."

"Deal," Falconi said without hesitation. He looked at Nielsen. "You still disapprove." It wasn't a question.

The first officer leaned forward, resting her elbows on her knees. "That ship is damaged. It could explode at any moment. Plus the possibility Jellies could be waiting to kill us. Why risk it?"

"Because," Falconi said, "we do this—this one trip—and we can wipe out our debt. And we can get all the antimatter we need to get out of this damn system."

Nielsen appeared oddly calm. "And?"

"And it's a chance to do something about the war."

After a moment Nielsen nodded. "Okay. But if we're going to do this, we do it smart."

"That's my department," Sparrow said, hopping to her feet. She pointed at Kira. "Will the Jellies recognize that thing on you if they see it?"

"Maybe. . . . Yeah, probably," said Kira.

"Okay. So we gotta keep you out of sight until we're sure the ship is clear. Noted. Trig, you're with me." And the short woman hurried out of the command center with the kid in tow. Hwa-jung followed a moment later, heading down to engineering to personally oversee the *Wallfish*'s systems while on approach.

"ETA?" Falconi asked.

"Sixteen minutes," Gregorovich answered.

2.

"Where are we going?" Kira asked as she jogged after Falconi, Nielsen, and Vishal.

"You'll see," said the captain.

Halfway around the curve of the ship, Nielsen stopped at a narrow door set in the wall. She entered a code on the access panel, and after a moment, the door popped open.

Inside was a cramped supply closet no more than a meter and a half across. A rack on the left-hand wall held an assortment of rifles and blasters (several of which Kira recognized from the *Valkyrie*) and other weapons. The right-hand wall was lined with charging plugs for the blasters' supercapacitors, as well as belts, holsters, and boxes of ammo and magazines for the firearms. At the back of the closet was a stool and small bench overhung by a shelf piled high with tools for maintaining the weapons (all of which were held in place by a clear plastic lid). A flickering holo was mounted above the shelf; it showed a unicorn cat resting in the arms of a bony, pink-haired man with the letters *Bowie Lives* printed in fancy script at the bottom.

The sight of the arsenal took Kira aback. "That's an awful lot of guns."

Falconi grunted. "Better to have them when you need them. Like today. Never know what you'll run into in the outer reaches."

"Rim runners," said Nielsen, pulling down a short rifle with a mean-looking muzzle.

"Wireheads," said Vishal, opening a container of bullets.

"Large toothy animals," said Falconi, shoving a rifle into Kira's arms.

She balked, remembering what she'd heard on the news. "Aren't blasters more effective against the Jellies?"

Falconi fiddled with the display on the side of her gun. "Sure. They're also more effective at punching holes in the hull. Don't know about you, but I don't want to get spaced. Outside the ship, we use blasters. Inside, we use firearms. Bullets still do a hell of a lot of damage, and there's no chance of them getting through our Whipple shield."

Kira reluctantly accepted his reasoning. Every spaceship had a Whipple shield built within the outer hull: staggered layers of differing material that served to break up incoming projectiles (natural or artificial). Micrometeoroids were a constant threat in space, and as a rule, bullets moved far slower and contained far less energy per gram.

"Also," said Vishal, "lasers bounce, and we have our passengers to think of. If even a small part of the energy from a laser deflects into person's eye—" He shook his head. "Very bad, Ms. Kira. Very bad."

Falconi straightened. "That, and bullets don't get fuzzed out by countermeasures. It's always a trade-off." He tapped Kira's rifle. "I linked this to your overlays. Everyone on the *Wallfish* is marked as friendly, so you don't need to worry about shooting us." He flashed her a grin. "Not that you should need to do any shooting. This is just a precaution."

Kira nodded, nervous. She could feel the Soft Blade molding itself to the grip of the gun, and a terrible sense of familiarity came over her.

A targeting reticule popped up in the center of her vision, red and round, and she experimented with it by focusing on different objects within the armory.

Nielsen handed her a pair of extra magazines. Kira stuffed them into the side pocket of her pants.

"Do you know how to reload?" Nielsen asked.

Kira nodded. She had gone shooting with her father on Weyland more than once. "Think so."

"Show me."

So Kira removed and replaced the magazine several times.

"You've got it," Nielsen said, appearing satisfied.

"Here we go," said Falconi, unshelving the largest gun of them all. Kira wasn't even sure what it was: not a blaster, that much was for sure, but the barrel was nearly as wide as her fist. Far too large for a rifle.

"What the hell is *that*?" she said.

Falconi burst out with an evil laugh. "It's a grenade launcher. What else? Bought her at a militia surplus sale a few years ago. Her name is Francesca."

"You named your gun," said Kira.

"Of course. It's common courtesy if you're going to be trusting your life to something. Ships get names. Swords used to get names. Now guns get names." Falconi laughed again, and Kira wondered if Gregorovich was really the only crazy one on the ship.

"So blasters are too dangerous, but a grenade launcher isn't?" she said.

Falconi gave her a wink. "Not if you know what you're doing." He patted the drum magazine. "These babies are concussive grenades. No shrapnel. They'll blow you to pieces, but only if they go off right next to you."

A voice sounded over the intercom: Hwa-jung. "Captain, do you read?"

"Yeah. Go ahead, over."

"I have an idea for how to distract any Jellies. If we send out the repair drones and use them to—"

"Do it," he said.

"Are you sure? If—"

"Yes. Just do it; I trust you."

"Roger that, Captain."

The line clicked off. Then Falconi clapped Vishal on the shoulder. "Got everything you need, Doc?"

Vishal nodded. "I swore to do no harm, but these aliens lack all sense of mercy. Sometimes the best way to avoid harm is minimizing it. If that means shooting a Jelly, then so be it."

"That's the spirit," said Falconi, and led the way back into the corridor.

"What am I going to be doing?" Kira asked as she followed him down the ladder in the central shaft.

"You're going to stay out of sight until it's safe," Falconi called back at her. "Besides, this isn't really your area of expertise."

Kira wasn't about to disagree. "But it's yours?"

"We've had our share of scrapes." Falconi jumped off the ladder at D-deck, the lowest deck above the cargo holds. "You go ahead and—"

"Sir," said Gregorovich. "The *Darmstadt* is hailing us. They want to know, I quote, 'What in bloody hell are you doing chasing that Jelly ship?' End quote. They seem quite *irritated*."

"Dammit," said Falconi. "Okay, stall for a minute." He pointed at Kira. "Go get those two Entropists. If we're going to use them, we might not have a lot of time." He didn't wait for an answer but hurried off with Nielsen and Vishal in tow.

Kira slid down the rest of the ladder and jogged through the corridor to the starboard hold. She spun the wheel, pulled open the door, and was surprised to find the Entropists waiting for her on the other side.

They bowed, and Veera said, "The ship mind, Gregorovich—"

"—told us to meet you," said Jorrus.

"Good. Follow me," said Kira.

Just as they arrived at D-deck, the zero-g alert sounded. The three of them grabbed handholds just in time to keep themselves from floating away.

The *Wallfish* turned end for end, pressing them against the outer wall, and then thrust resumed and Gregorovich said, "Contact in eight minutes."

Kira could feel the alien vessel drawing closer, the swift reduction in distance multiplying the force of the compulsion it was broadcasting. The summons was a dull throb at the back of her head, a constant tug on her internal compass that, while easy to ignore, refused to abate.

Jorrus said, "Prisoner Kaminski—"

"Navárez. My name is Kira Navárez."

The Entropists exchanged a look. Veera said, "We are most confused, Prisoner Navárez, as is—"

"—everyone in the hold. What is—"

"—our course, and why have you summoned us?"

"Listen," said Kira, and she gave them a brief summary of the situation. It felt as if she were telling everyone about the Soft Blade now. The Entropists' eyes widened in simultaneous astonishment as they listened, but they didn't interrupt. She finished by saying, "Are you willing to help?"

"We would be honored," said Jorrus. "The pursuit of knowledge—"

"—is a most worthy endeavor."

"Uh-huh," said Kira. Then, just for the hell of it, she sent them the results of Vishal's exam. "Here, look at these while you wait. Once we're sure the Jelly ship is safe, we'll call for you."

Veera said, "If it is a question of conflict—"

"—we would—"

But Kira was already moving, and she didn't hear the rest. She ran back through the dingy hallways until she found the crew gathered in front of the port airlock.

Dominating the center of the antechamber were Trig and Sparrow, like a pair of battered metal pillars, each over two meters high. Power armor. Military grade, so far as Kira could tell. Civilian shells didn't usually have missile packs mounted on the shoulders. . . . Where had the crew gotten that sort of hardware? Hwa-jung moved between the two, adjusting the fit of their armor and issuing a steady stream of advice to Trig:

"—and don't get excited and move too fast. There isn't room. You'll just hurt yourself. Let the computer do most of the work. It will make it easy for you."

The kid nodded. His face was pasty and beaded with sweat.

The sight of Trig bothered Kira. Was Falconi really going to put him front and center, where he might get hurt? Sparrow she could understand, but Trig . . .

Nielsen, Falconi, and Vishal were busy bolting a line of packing crates to the deck, just behind Trig and Sparrow. The crates were large enough to hide behind: cover for combat.

All the crew not in exos—Hwa-jung included—had donned skinsuits.

The machine boss went to Sparrow and tugged on her thruster pack hard enough to shift the smaller woman's armor, moving several hundred kilos of mass with casual effort. "Hold still," Hwa-jung growled, tugging again.

"Hold still, yourself," muttered Sparrow, fighting to keep her balance.

Hwa-jung slapped Sparrow's shoulder guard with the flat of her hand. "*Aish!* Punk. Be more respectful of your elder! Do you want to lose power in the middle of a fight? Really."

Sparrow smiled down at the machine boss; she seemed to appreciate the fussing.

"Hey," said Kira, startling them. She pointed at Trig. "What's he doing in that thing? He's just a teenager."

"Not for long! I'll be twenty year after next," said Trig, his voice muffled as he pulled on his helmet.

Falconi turned to face her. His skinsuit was matte black (the visor was up), and in his arms he cradled Francesca. "Trig knows how to run an exo better than any of us. And he's sure as hell safer *in* that armor than out of it."

"Fine, but—"

The captain frowned. "We've got work to do, Navárez."

"What about the UMC? Are they going to be a problem? What'd you tell them?"

"I told them we're going after salvage. They're not happy, but there's nothing illegal about it. Now scram. We'll call you when it's safe."

As she started to leave, Hwa-jung tromped over and handed her a pair of earbuds. "So we can stay in touch with you," the machine boss said, and tapped the side of her temple.

Grateful, Kira left, but she only went so far as the first turn in the corridor. There, she sat, put in the earbuds, and pulled up her overlays.

"Gregorovich," she said, "can I see the feed from outside?"

A moment later, a window popped up in her vision, and she saw an image of the alien ship just astern. The long, narrow gash along one side had exposed a cross-section of several decks: dark, half-lit rooms filled with indistinct shapes. Even as she tried to make sense of them, puffs of vapor appeared around the waist of the spherical vessel, and it turned so the damage was no longer visible.

Through her earbuds, Kira heard Nielsen say, **Captain, the Jellies are firing their thrusters.**

A moment, and then Falconi said, **Automatic spin-stabilization? Repair systems kicking in?**

Hwa-jung answered: **Unknown.**

Thermal scan. Any living creatures show up?

Indeterminate, said Gregorovich. On Kira's overlay, the view of the Jelly ship swapped to an impressionistic blotch of infrared. **Too many heat signatures to identify.**

Falconi swore. **Okay. We play this real safe, then. Trig, you follow Sparrow's lead. Like Hwa-jung said, let the computer do the hard work. Wait for the repair drones to give the all-clear before you move into a room.**

Yessir.

We'll be right behind you, so don't worry.

As the gleaming mass of the Jelly ship swelled in size on her overlays, the ache of the summons acting upon the Soft Blade increased in direct proportion. Kira rubbed her sternum with the heel of her hand; it almost felt like she had heartburn—an uncomfortable pressure that made it difficult for her to stay still. But it wasn't a discomfort she could dispel with a burp or a pill or a drink of water. Deep in the recesses of her mind, she could feel a certainty from the xeno that the only cure would be for the two of them to present themselves before the source of the summons, as duty demanded.

Kira shivered, a surge of nervous energy coursing through her. Not knowing what was going to happen was terrifying. She felt weird—sick almost, as if something horrible was about to take place. Something *irrevocable.*

The suit reacted to her distress; Kira could feel it contracting around her, thickening and hardening with practiced efficiency. *It* was ready. Of that she was sure. She remembered her dreams of battle; the Soft Blade had faced mortal danger many, many times over the course of the eons, but while *it* had always endured, she wasn't so sure about those it had been joined with.

All the Jellies would have to do would be shoot her in the head, and suit or not, the shock of the impact would kill her. No amount of tissue restructuring on the part of the Soft Blade would save her. And that would be that. No reloading from a checkpoint or save file. Nope. One life, one attempt to get things right, and perma-death if she failed. Of course, the same was true for everyone else. No one got to run the level beforehand, as it were.

And yet, even though she was in danger because of the Soft Blade, Kira found herself perversely grateful for its presence. Without the xeno, she'd be all the more vulnerable, a shell-less turtle waving its legs in the air, exposed before its enemies.

She clutched her rifle tighter.

Outside, the wheeling stars vanished behind the huge white hull of the Jelly ship, which gleamed and shone like the shell of an abalone.

Kira struggled to suppress another pulse of fear. Beneath her clothes, the Soft Blade spiked out in response, small, razor-tipped studs roiling across her coated flesh. She hadn't realized just how *big* the ship was. But it only held three of the tentacled aliens. Only three, and most or all of them should be dead. Should . . .

With the ship so close, the compulsion was stronger than ever; she found herself leaning forward, pressing against the wall of the corridor as if to crawl through it.

She forced herself to relax. No. She wasn't about to give in to the desire. That was the dumbest thing she could do. No matter how tempting it was, she had to keep the compulsion from controlling her actions. And it *was* tempting, dreadfully so. If she just obeyed as was expected and answered the summons, the ache would vanish, and from ancient memories, she knew the reward of satisfaction that would follow. . . .

Again Kira struggled to ignore the intrusive sensation. The Soft Blade might feel the imperative to obey, but *she* didn't. Her instinct for self-preservation was too strong to just do whatever some alien signal was telling her to.

Or so she wanted to believe.

While she fought her inner fight, the *Wallfish* cut its engines. Kira flailed for a moment, and then the Soft Blade adhered to the floor and wall wherever she touched, anchoring her in place much as it had done with the radiators of the *Extenuating Circumstances* after she'd been blown into space.

The *Wallfish* maneuvered with RCS thrusters around the swollen bulk of the Jelly ship until it arrived at a three-meter-wide dome that projected from the hull. Kira recognized it from videos as the airlock used by the aliens.

Everyone ready! Falconi barked, and from around the corner, she heard the bolts of weapons being racked and the hum of capacitors charging. **Visors down.**

Then, for a seemingly endless moment, nothing happened, and all Kira felt was tension and anticipation and the rising hammer of her pulse.

On the cameras, the dome began to move closer. When the *Wallfish* was only a few meters away, a thick, hide-like membrane retracted from the dome, exposing the polished, mother-of-pearl-esque surface underneath.

Looks like they're expecting us, said Sparrow. **Great.**

At least we won't have to cut our way in, said Nielsen.

Hwa-jung grunted. **Maybe. Maybe not. It could be automated.**

Focus! said Falconi.

Gregorovich said, **Contact in three . . . two . . . one.**

The deck lurched as the *Wallfish* and the alien ship touched. Silence followed then, shocking in its completeness.

CHAPTER VI

* * * * * * *

NEAR & FAR

1.

With a start, Kira remembered to breathe. She inhaled twice, quickly, and tried to calm herself so she didn't pass out. Almost there; just a few seconds more . . .

Her overlays flickered, and instead of the feed from outside, she saw a view of the airlock antechamber from a camera mounted above the entrance: Gregorovich letting her watch what was happening.

"Thanks," she murmured. The ship mind didn't reply.

Falconi, Hwa-jung, Nielsen, and Vishal were hunched behind the packing crates bolted to the deck. Sparrow and Trig stood in front of them in their power armor, facing the airlock, like a pair of hulking giants, arms raised, weapons aimed.

Through the windows of the inner and outer doors of the airlock, Kira saw the curved, iridescent surface of the Jelly ship. It appeared flawless. Impregnable.

Repair bots deployed, Hwa-jung announced in a preternaturally calm voice. She crossed herself.

Across the antechamber, Vishal bowed in what Kira suspected was the direction of Earth, and Nielsen touched something under her skinsuit. On the off chance it would do something, Kira offered up a quiet prayer to Thule.

Well? Falconi said. **Do we have to knock?**

As if in response, the dome rotated, an eyeball rolling in its socket to reveal . . . not an iris, but a circular tube, three meters long, that led straight through the sphere. At the other end was a second hide-like membrane.

It was fortunate, Kira thought, that Jelly microbes seemed to pose no risk of human infection. At least none that had been discovered. Still, she wished that she and the *Wallfish* crew could have observed proper containment procedures. When it came to alien organisms, it was always better to err on the side of caution.

A soft pressure tube extended a few centimeters from the outside of the *Wallfish* airlock and pressed in around the circumference of the tube.

*We have a positive seal,** Gregorovich announced.

As if in response, the inner membrane retracted. The angle of the camera didn't give Kira a good view into the Jelly ship: she could see a slice of shadowy space lit by a dim blue glow that reminded her of the abyssal sea where the great and mighty Ctein had ruled.

*My God, it's huge!** Vishal exclaimed, and she fought the urge to peek around the corner to see with her own eyes.

*Pop the airlock,** said Falconi.

The *thud* of locking lugs snapping back echoed down the corridor, and then both the inner and outer airlocks rolled open.

*Gregorovich,** said Falconi. *Hunters.** A pair of whirring, orb-shaped drones descended from the ceiling and darted into the alien ship, their unmistakable hum quickly fading to nothing.

*No movement showing from the outside,** Hwa-jung said. *All clear.**

Then Falconi said, *Okay. Hunters aren't picking up anything either. We're a go.**

*Watch your six,** Sparrow barked, and heavy footsteps shook the deck as the two suits of power armor headed toward the airlock.

At that exact moment, Kira felt it: a nearscent of pain and fear intermingled in a toxic brew. "No! Wait!" she started to shout, but she was too slow.

*Contact!** Sparrow yelled.

She and Trig started shooting at something in the airlock: a barrage of gunfire and laser blasts. Even around the corner, Kira could feel the thump of the guns. The sounds were brutally intense: physical assaults in their own right.

A hemisphere of sparks formed in front of Sparrow and Trig as their lasers immolated incoming projectiles. Chalk and chaff exploded outward from their exos, the glittering clouds expanding outward in near-perfect spheres until they collided with the walls, the ceiling, and each other.

Then a spike of fire jumped from Falconi's massive grenade launcher. An instant later, a harsh, blue-white flash illuminated the depths of the airlock, and a dull *boom* rolled through the ship. The blast tore apart the cloud, allowing a clear view—between ragged strips of haze—in and around the airlock.

Something small and white whizzed out of the alien ship, moving faster than

Kira could follow. Then the camera feed went dead, and a concussion slammed into her, knocking her head against the wall and making her teeth slam together hard enough to hurt. The pulse of over-pressurized air was so loud it went beyond hearing; she felt it in her bones and in her lungs, and as a painful spike in each ear.

With no urging on her part, the Soft Blade crawled across her face, covering her completely. Her vision flickered and then returned to normal.

Kira was shaking from adrenaline. Her hands and feet felt cold, and her heart was slamming against her ribs as if trying to escape. Despite that, she mustered her courage enough to poke her head around the corner. Even if it was a mistake, she had to know what was happening.

To her horror, she saw Falconi and the others drifting in the air, dead or stunned. Drops of blood wept from a cut in the shoulder of Nielsen's skinsuit, and there was a piece of metal sticking out of Vishal's thigh. Trig and Sparrow seemed to have fared better—she could see their heads turning in their helmets—but both their suits of power armor were locked up, inoperable.

Past them lay the airlock and—through it—the alien ship. She glimpsed a deep, dark chamber with strange machines looming in the background, and then a tentacled monstrosity moved into view, blocking the light.

The Jelly nearly filled the airlock. The creature appeared wounded; orange ichor oozed from a dozen or more gashes across its arms, and there was a crack in the carapace of its body.

Wrongflesh!

Kira watched, frozen, as the Jelly crawled toward the *Wallfish* interior. If she fled, she'd only attract attention to herself. Her rifle was too small to have much chance of killing the Jelly, and the creature would surely shoot her in return if she opened fire. . . .

She tried to swallow, but her mouth was dry as dust.

A soft, dead-leaf shuffle sounded as the Jelly entered the antechamber. The sound caused Kira's scalp to prickle with cold recognition; she *remembered* it from times long past. Accompanying the sound was a shift in the nearscent from fear to anger, contempt, and impatience.

The Soft Blade's natural instinct was to respond to the scent—Kira could feel the urge—but she resisted with all her strength.

None of the crew had started moving again, and now the Jelly was maneuvering among their floating bodies.

Kira thought of the children in the cargo hold, and her resolve stiffened.

This was her fault; boarding the Jelly ship had been her idea. She couldn't allow the alien to reach the hold. And she couldn't stand by and watch while it killed Falconi and the rest of the crew. Even if it meant her own life, she had to do something.

Her deliberations took only an instant. Then she fixed the overlay targeting reticule on the Jelly and raised her gun with intent to fire.

The motion caught the Jelly's attention. A cloud of white smoke erupted around it, and there was a swirl of tentacles and a spray of ichor as the creature spun around. Kira fired blindly into the center of the smoke, but if the bullets hit, she couldn't see.

A tentacle lashed out and wrapped around the ankle of Trig's power armor.

"No!" Kira shouted, but it was too late. The Jelly swarmed back into its ship, dragging Trig behind it, using him as a shield.

The curls of smoke dispersed into the antechamber vents.

2.

"Gregoro—" Kira started to say, but the ship mind was already talking:

"It's going to take me a few minutes to get Sparrow's armor back online. Don't have any more hunters, and point-defense lasers took out all the repair bots."

The rest of the crew still drifted limp and helpless. There was no assistance to be had from them, and the refugees in the hold were too far away, too unprepared.

Kira's mind raced as she considered options. Every second that passed, Trig's chances of survival dropped.

In a soft voice, so soft it seemed out of place, Gregorovich said, "Please."

And Kira knew what she had to do. It wasn't about her anymore, and somehow that made it easier, despite the fear clogging her veins. But she needed more firepower. Her rifle wasn't going to be very effective against the Jelly.

She willed the Soft Blade to unstick from the wall, kicked herself over to Falconi's grenade launcher—Francesca—and hooked her arm through the sling.

The counter on the top of the launcher showed five shots remaining in the drum magazine.

It would have to do.

Gripping the gun tighter than was necessary, Kira turned to face the airlock.

White streams of air escaped through a cluster of hairline cracks along the inside of the lock, but the hull didn't seem to be in immediate danger of failing.

Before she could lose her nerve, Kira braced herself against a crate and jumped.

3.

As she hurtled through the short tube, toward the alien ship, Kira scrutinized the rim of the Jelly airlock, ready to shoot at the slightest hint of movement.

Thule. What the hell was she doing? She was a xenobiologist. Not a soldier. Not a gene-hacked, muscle-bound killing machine like the UMC turned out.

And yet there she was.

For a moment Kira thought of her family, and anger hardened her determination. She couldn't let the Jellies kill her. And she couldn't let them hurt Trig. . . . She felt a similar anger from the Soft Blade: old hurts piled onto new offenses.

The dim blue light of the alien ship enveloped her as she exited the airlock.

Something large slammed into her from behind and sent her tumbling into a curved wall. *Shit!* Fear made a quick return as pain exploded along her left side.

Out of the corner of her eye, she glimpsed a mass of knotting tentacles, and then the Jelly was upon her, smothering her with its banded arms, as hard and strong as woven cables. Nearscent clogged her nostrils, suffocating in its strength.

One of the slithering arms wrapped itself around Kira's neck and *yanked.*

The motion was so violent, it should have killed her. It should have torn her head right off her body. But the Soft Blade went rigid, and the strange recesses and odd angles of the room blurred around her as she twisted topsy-turvy.

Kira's stomach lurched, and she vomited into the suit's flexible mask.

The vomit had nowhere to go. It filled her mouth—hot, bitter, burning—and then poured back down her throat. She gagged and out of sheer, misplaced instinct, tried to take a breath and inhaled what felt like a liter of searing liquid.

Kira panicked then: blind, unreasoning panic. She thrashed and flailed and tore at the mask. In her frenzy, she only dimly noticed the fibers of the suit parting beneath her clawing.

Cold air struck her face, and she finally was able to spew the vomit from her mouth. She coughed with painful force while her stomach clenched in pulsing waves.

The air smelled of brine and bile, and if the Soft Blade hadn't still covered her nose, Kira thought she might have passed out from the alien atmosphere.

She tried to regain control of herself, but her body refused to cooperate. Coughing bent her double, and all Kira saw was the mottled orange flesh wrapped around her and suckers the size of dinner plates.

The rubbery limb began to tighten. It was as thick as her legs and far stronger. She hardened the suit in defense (or perhaps it hardened itself), but regardless, she could feel the pressure building as the Jelly tried to crush her.

[[Cfar here: Die, two-form! Die.]]

Kira couldn't stop coughing, and every time she exhaled, the tentacle tightened further, making it increasingly difficult to breathe. She twisted in a frantic attempt to free herself but to no avail. A terrible conviction filled her then. She was going to die. She knew it. The Jelly was going to kill her and take the Soft Blade back to its own kind, and that would be the end of her. The realization was terrifying.

Crimson sparks filled her vision, and Kira felt herself teetering on the edge of unconsciousness. In her mind, she pleaded with the Soft Blade, hoping it could do something, *anything* to help. *Come on!* But her thoughts seemed to have no effect, and all the while, the sense of strain increased, rising until Kira felt her bones would snap and the alien would reduce her to a bloody pulp.

She groaned as the tentacle squeezed the last bit of air from her lungs. The fireworks in her eyes faded, and with them, any sense of urgency or desperation. Warmth suffused her, comforting warmth, and the things she'd been concerned with no longer seemed important. What had she been so worried about after all?

. . .

. . .

. . .

She floated before a fractal design, blue and dark and etched into the surface of a standing stone. The design was complicated beyond her ability to comprehend, and it shifted as she watched, the edges of the shapes shimmering as they changed, growing and evolving according to the precepts of some unknown logic. Her sight was more than human; she could see lines of force radiating from the infinitely long border—flashes of electromagnetic energy that betrayed vast discharges of energy.

And Kira knew this was the pattern the Soft Blade served. Served or was. And Kira realized there was a question inherent in the design, a choice related to the very nature of the xeno. Would she follow the pattern? Or would she ignore the design and carve new lines—lines of her own—into the guiding scheme?

To answer required information she didn't have. It was a test she hadn't studied for, and she didn't understand the parameters of the inquiry.

But as she gazed upon the shifting shape, Kira remembered her pain and her anger and her fear. They burst forth, hers and the Soft Blade's combined. Whatever the pattern meant, she was certain of the wrongness of the graspers and of her desire to live and of her need to rescue Trig.

To that end, Kira was willing to fight, and she was willing to kill and destroy in order to stop the graspers.

Then her vision sharpened and telescoped, and she felt as if she were falling into the fractal. It expanded before her in endless layers of detail, flowering into an entire universe of theme and variation. . . .

Pain roused Kira. Shocking, searing pain. The pressure around her torso vanished, and she filled her lungs with a desperate gasp before loosing a scream.

Her vision cleared, and she saw the tentacle still encircling her. Only now a belt of thorns—black and shiny and tangled in a familiar fractal shape—extended from her torso, piercing the twitching limb. She could feel the thorns, same as her arms or legs, new additions but familiar. And surrounding them a heated press of flesh and bone and spurting fluids. For a moment the memory of the suit impaling Alan and the others intruded, and Kira shuddered.

Without thinking, she shouted and chopped at the tentacle with her arm. As she did, she felt the suit reshape itself, and her arm sliced through the Jelly's translucent flesh as if it were hardly there.

A spray of orange liquid splattered her. It smelled bitter and metallic. Disgusted, Kira shook her head, trying to shake off the blobs of ichor.

Severing the tentacle freed her from the alien. The Jelly twitched in its death throes as it drifted toward the far side of the room, leaving its amputated limb behind. The tentacle twisted and coiled in the air like a headless snake. A core of bone showed in the center of the stump.

Unbidden, the thorns retracted into the Soft Blade.

Kira shivered. So the xeno had finally decided to fight alongside her. Good. Maybe she had a chance after all. At least there was no one around she had to worry about stabbing by accident. Not at the moment.

She scanned her surroundings.

The chamber had no identifiable up or down, same as the aliens themselves. What light there was emanated in an even field from the forward half of the space. Clumps of mysterious machines, black and glossy, protruded from the curving walls, and two-thirds of the way around the dusky expanse—half-lost in the gloom—was a large, barnacle-like shell that Kira assumed was an interior door of some kind.

At the sight of the room, Kira felt an overpowering sense of déjà vu. Her vision swam, and the walls of another, similar ship appeared ghost-like before her. For a moment, it felt as if she were in two different places, in two different ages—

She shook her head, and the image disappeared. "Stop it!" she growled at the Soft Blade. She couldn't afford distractions like that.

If not for the dire nature of the situation, Kira would have loved to examine the chamber in exhaustive detail. It was a xenobiologist's dream: an actual alien ship filled with living aliens, macro and micro. A single square inch of the space would be enough to make an entire career. More than that, Kira just wanted to *know.* She always had.

But now wasn't the time.

There was no sign of Trig in the room. That meant one or more Jelly was still alive.

Kira spotted Falconi's grenade launcher floating by the wall some distance away. She pulled herself toward it, palms sticking to the inside of the hull.

She'd killed an alien! Her. Kira Navárez. The fact disturbed and astonished her as much as it gave her a certain grim satisfaction.

"Gregorovich," she said. "Any idea where they took—"

The ship mind was already talking: **Keep going forward. I can't give you an exact fix, but you're heading in the right direction.**

"Roger that," said Kira as she snared the launcher.

Jorrus and Veera are helping me with Sparrow. I'm jamming all outgoing frequencies, so the Jellies might not be able to signal if they recognize you. They can still use a laser for line-of-sight comms, though. Be careful.

While he spoke, Kira willed the suit to propel her toward the barnacle-like shell. As in vacuum, the Soft Blade was able to provide her with a modest amount of thrust—more than enough to traverse the distance within a few seconds.

The compulsion was headache-strong now, insistent and insidious. She scowled and tried to concentrate past the throbbing.

The shell parted in three wedge-shaped segments that retracted into the bulkhead to reveal a long, circular shaft. More of the doors dotted the shaft at irregular intervals, and at the far end, there twinkled a panel of lights: a computer console perhaps, or maybe just a piece of art. Who could tell?

Kira kept the grenade launcher at the ready as she maneuvered into the shaft. Trig could be in any of the rooms; she'd have to search them all. There were engines at the back of the ship, but Kira didn't have a clue as to where anything else might be. Did the Jellies have a centralized command station? She couldn't remember mention of one in the news reports. . . .

A flicker of motion appeared along the near wall. She twisted just in time to see a crab-like alien slip out of a parted door.

The Jelly fired a cluster of laser beams at her. They curved harmlessly around her torso. The laser blasts were too fast for normal human vision to detect. But with the mask over her face, the pulses were visible as nanosecond flashes: incandescent lines that blinked in and out of existence.

Without thinking, Kira fired the grenade launcher. Or rather, the Soft Blade fired it for her; she wasn't even conscious of pulling the trigger, and then the buttstock kicked her shoulder and sent her spinning backwards.

The damn thing was big enough to be artillery.

BOOM!

The grenade detonated with a pulse of light so bright, Kira's vision dimmed almost to black. She felt the force of the explosion in her organs: her liver hurt, and her kidneys too, and all through her body, tendons and ligaments and muscles that Kira had previously been unaware of made themselves known with a chorus of sharp complaints.

She scrabbled to grab something, anything, within reach. By sheer chance, she brushed against a ridge along the wall, and the xeno adhered to the smooth, stonelike surface, stopping her tumble. She gulped for air and hung there while she regained her bearings, pulse racing with frantic speed. Across from her floated the pulped and shredded remains of the Jelly. Orange mist coated the passageway.

What had the creature been trying to do? Sneak up on her? A sinking sensation wholly unrelated to weightlessness formed in Kira's stomach as she thought of an explanation. The crab had been sent to slow her—knowing it would fail—while the rest of the Jellies prepared a nasty surprise for her somewhere else.

She swallowed hard, the sour taste of vomit still strong in her mouth. The best thing she could do was keep searching, hope the aliens weren't able to predict her every move.

A glance at the grenade launcher. Four shots left. She'd have to make them count.

She pushed herself back around to look at the barnacle door where the Jelly had emerged. The wedges of broken shell hung loose. Past them was a globular room half-full of greenish water. Ribbons of what resembled algae floated within the tranquil reservoir, and tiny insect-like creatures skated upon the bowed surface, tracing lines and rings. The word *sfennic* rose unbidden within her mind, along with a sense of *crunchy, quick upon the skin. . . .* At the bottom of the pool was a pod or workstation of some sort.

The water ought to have been drifting around in blobs, free to wander the interior of the room so long as the ship was in free fall. Instead, it clung to one half of the room, as still and steady as any planet-bound pool.

Kira recognized the effect of the Jellies' artificial gravity. It seemed to be a localized field, as she didn't feel anything at the entrance to the room.

The artificial gravity didn't interest her much. What she really wanted to study were the *sfennic* and the algae-like growths. Even a few cells would be enough to run a full genomic analysis.

But she had to keep moving.

Fast as she dared, she cleared the next several rooms. None of them held Trig, and none had any recognizable function. Maybe this one was a bathroom. Maybe that one was a shrine. Maybe something else entirely. The Soft Blade wasn't telling, and without its help, any explanation seemed likely. That was the problem when dealing with alien cultures (human or otherwise), the lack of context.

One thing Kira knew for certain: the Jellies had changed the layout of their ships since the Soft Blade had been on them. The arrangement of rooms felt wholly unfamiliar.

She saw plenty of evidence of battle damage: holes from shrapnel, laser burns, melted composites—evidence of the ship's clash with the UMC at Malpert Station. The light flickered, and warping, whale-song alarms sounded elsewhere in the ship. The scents of . . . warning, danger, and fear stained the air.

At the end of the shaft, the passageway forked. Kira's gut told her to go left, so left she went, driven onward by desperation. *Where is he?* She was starting to worry it was already too late to save the kid.

She passed through three more of the ubiquitous shell doors, and then a fourth one opened to another spherical chamber.

The room felt enormous—the walls barely curved as they extended out from her—but it was hard to be sure of the true size of the space. A thick bank of smoke clogged the air, dimming the usual blue illumination to the point that it was difficult to see much past the ends of her arms.

Fear crept up Kira's side. The room was the perfect place for an ambush.

She needed to *see.* If only . . . She concentrated upon her need, concentrated with all her might, and she felt a tickle atop her eyeballs. Her vision twisted, like a sheet being wrung dry, and then it snapped flat and the haze seemed to retreat (though the far end of the room remained obscured) as everything went monochrome.

The chamber must have been over thirty meters across, if not more. Unlike the other rooms, it had structures throughout: branches of pale scaffolding pocked with a bone-like matrix. A black walkway lined the inner circumference of the back half of the space. Mounted to the walls on either side of the walkway were rows upon rows of what appeared to be . . . pods. Huge and solid, they hummed with electrical power, and bright rings of magnetic force chained them to hidden circuits.

Dread mingled with curiosity as Kira looked at the nearest one.

The front of the pod was made of a translucent material, milky and pale, like the skin of an egg. Through it, she saw an indistinct shape, hazy, convoluted, and difficult to resolve into anything recognizable.

The object shifted, unmistakably alive.

Kira gasped and jerked back, raising the grenade launcher. The thing inside the pod was a Jelly, its tentacles wrapped around itself and bobbing softly in a viscous liquid.

She nearly shot the creature; only the fact that it didn't react to her sudden movement—and her desire to avoid unwanted attention—stopped her. Were they birthing chambers? Cryo tubes? Sleeping containers? Some sort of crèche? She glanced around the room. Her lips moved under the mask as she counted: one, two, three, four, five, six, seven . . . Forty-nine in total. Fourteen of the pods were smaller than the rest, but even so, forty-nine more Jellies, if all the pods were full. More than enough to overwhelm her and everyone on the *Wallfish.*

Trig.

She'd worry about the pods later.

Kira braced herself against the rim of the portal and then kicked off toward one of the spars of scaffolding. As she flew toward it, a silvery rod shot out of the haze deeper in the chamber.

She jerked up her arm and knocked it aside. The xeno hardened around her forearm enough to keep her wrist from breaking.

Her motion and the impact sent her spinning away. She tried to grab the spar, and for a moment her fingers swung through empty air—

She ought to have missed. She ought to have kept spinning. But instead, Kira reached and the Soft Blade reached with her, extruding tendrils in a natural extension of her fingers until they looped around the spar and brought her to a teeth-clattering stop.

Interesting.

Behind her, Kira saw a clawed *something* leap from spar to spar as it pursued her. In the shadows, the creature looked dark, almost black. Spikes and claws and odd little limbs protruded from it at unexpected angles. A Jelly of a sort she hadn't seen before. The creature's size was difficult to gauge, but it was bigger than her. In one of its claws, it carried another of the silvery rods: a meter long and mirror bright.

She fired Francesca at the alien, but it was moving too fast for her to hit, even with the suit's help. The grenade exploded against the opposite side of the chamber, destroying one of the pods and providing a lightning-flash of illumination.

By it, Kira glimpsed two things: near the back of the room, a bulky, human-shaped figure tethered among the spars. Trig. And also the alien's claw lashing out as it sent the second rod hurtling toward her.

She couldn't dodge in time. The rod struck her in the ribs, and although the Soft Blade did its best to protect her, the impact still left her dazed and gasping in pain. Half her side went numb, and she lost her grip on the grenade launcher. It spun away.

Trig! Somehow she had to get to the kid.

The alien snapped its claws and sprang toward her. The creature wasn't like the other Jellies; it didn't have tentacles, and she saw what seemed to be a cluster of eyes and other sensory organs along one side of its rubbery, soft-skinned body: a rudimentary face that gave her a definite sense of which end was the front and which end the back.

Desperate, Kira tried to attack with the Soft Blade. *Strike! Slash! Tear!* She wished the xeno would do all those things.

It did. But not as she expected.

Clusters of spikes erupted from her body and jabbed in random directions, wild and undisciplined. Each was like a punch to her body, pushing her in the opposite direction of the deadly shards. She tried to direct them with her mind, and while she could feel the xeno respond to her commands, the response was badly coordinated—a blind beast flailing in pursuit of its prey, overreacting to ill-mated stimuli.

The reaction was instantaneous. The clawed alien twisted in midair, throwing off its trajectory so it just missed being impaled. At the same time, a spurt of nearscent tainted the air with shock, fear, and something Kira felt was akin to reverence.

[[Kveti here: The Idealis! The Manyform lives! Stop it!]]

Kira retracted the spikes and was about to jump after the grenade launcher when a soft, slithery shape crawled around the spar she was clinging to: a tentacle, thick and probing. She slashed at it, but she was too slow. The trunk-like slab of muscle slapped her and sent her flying head over heels until her back slammed into another piece of scaffolding.

Even through the suit, the impact hurt. Despite the pain, she concentrated on holding her position, and the Soft Blade clung to the spar for her and stopped her from spiraling away.

The clawed monstrosity clung to a forked shaft some distance away, beyond the reach of the blade. There, it raised its bony arms and shook them at her, snapping its claws like a crazed castanet dancer.

Past it, she saw the owner of the tentacle—another of the squid-like Jellies—emerge from behind the spar she'd been knocked off of. The squid's tentacles pulsed with luminous bands, startlingly bright in the gloom. In one tentacle, the alien held . . . not a laser. A long, flat-barreled weapon of some kind. A portable railgun?

Ten, twelve meters away, Kira spotted the grenade launcher.

She jumped for it.

There was a *bang* like two boards clapping together, and a bolt of pain punched through her ribs.

Her heart faltered, and for a moment her vision went black.

Panicked, Kira lashed out with the Soft Blade, stabbing in every direction. But it didn't help, and another bolt of pain struck her right leg. She felt herself start to spin.

Her vision cleared as she collided with the grenade launcher. She grabbed it, and as she did, she saw the clawed, crab-like alien jumping toward her.

Her suit continued to send forth spikes, but the alien evaded them with ease. The arms on its segmented body unfolded, reaching toward her head with jagged spurs, sharp and sawlike. Electricity sparked between the tips of them, bright as a welding arc.

In a detached, almost analytical manner, Kira realized the alien was trying to decapitate her, so as to break her bond with the Soft Blade.

She raised the rifle, but too slow. Far, far too slow.

Just before the creature collided with her, a jet of ablated flesh erupted from the alien's side. Across the room, Trig's power armor lowered its arm.

Then the alien crashed into Kira's face. Its legs wrapped around her skull, and everything went black as its soft belly covered her face. Pain bloomed in her left forearm as a crushing weight seemed to pinch it from either side. The pain was so intense, she saw it as much as she felt it—saw it as a flood of lurid yellow light radiating from her arm.

Kira screamed into her mask and punched the alien with her other arm, punched and punched and punched. Muscle gave beneath her fist, and bones or something like bones cracked.

The pain seemed to last an eternity.

As suddenly as it had started, the pressure on her arm vanished, and the clawed alien went limp.

Shaking, Kira shoved the corpse away. In the shadowy light, the creature looked like a dead spider.

Her forearm hung from the elbow at an unnatural angle, half-severed by a jagged gash that passed through both the suit and the muscles below. But even as she looked, black threads wove back and forth across the wound, and she felt the Soft Blade beginning to draw the gash closed and repair her arm.

While she'd been occupied, the other Jelly had jetted back to Trig and wrapped itself around his armor. A tentacle pulled on each arm and leg, twisting and straining as the creature struggled to tear the exoskeleton (and Trig himself) into pieces.

Another few seconds, and Kira felt sure it would.

There was a spar close to the Jelly. She aimed the grenade launcher at it, said a quick prayer to Thule for the kid's safety, and fired.

BOOM!

The shockwave tore off three of the Jelly's tentacles, smashed open its carapace, and sprayed ichor in a sickly fountain. The severed tentacles flew away, twisting and flopping.

Trig was knocked away as well. For a moment he didn't move, and then his power armor jerked and reoriented itself, tiny attitude jets firing along its legs and arms.

Kira pushed herself toward the kid, hardly able to believe that he was still alive—that *either* of them had survived. *Don't hurt him, don't hurt him, don't hurt him. . . .* She pleaded with the Soft Blade in her mind, hoping it would listen.

As she drew near, Trig's visor faded clear to reveal his face. The kid was pale and sweating, and the bluish light made him appear ghastly ill.

He stared at her, his pupils rimmed by white. "What the hell?!"

Kira looked down to see spikes still protruding from the Soft Blade. "I'll explain later," she said. "You okay?"

Trig nodded, shaking sweat off his nose. "Yeah. I had to reboot the exo. Took me this long to get it powered back up. . . . My, uh, wrist might be broken, but I can still—"

Falconi's voice broke in: **Navárez, you read? Over.** In the background, Kira heard shouts and the *pop! pop! pop!* of gunfire.

"I'm here. Over," she said.

Did you find Trig? Where are—

"He's here. He's fine."

At the same time, Trig said, "I'm fine, Captain."

Then get your ass down to the starboard hold. There's another Jelly here. Cut its way through the hull. We've got it pinned down, but we can't get a good angle—

Kira and Trig were already moving.

4.

"Grab hold," shouted Trig. Kira hooked an arm through a handle at the top of his exo, the kid fired his thrusters, and the two of them flew toward the door where they'd entered.

This time the shell didn't open, and they nearly crashed into it before Trig was able to stop. He raised an arm and fired a laser into the surrounding wall.

With three quick cuts, he parted whatever control mechanisms the door had, and the wedges of the shell separated and hung loose, pale fluid oozing from the seals around their base.

Kira shuddered as they flew through the opening and the tip of a wedge scraped across her back.

Outside the room, the compulsion was insistent and seductive, impossible to ignore. It drew Kira toward a curved section of the near bulkhead—toward and past. Were she to pursue the signal, Kira knew with certainty she would find its source, and perhaps then she might have respite and some answers to the nature and origin of the Soft Blade. . . .

"Thanks for coming after me," Trig said. "Thought I was a goner."

She grunted. "Just go faster."

None of the other doors would part to let them through. It took Trig only a few seconds to slice them open, but every delay worsened Kira's sense of dread and urgency.

Past the panel with the blinking lights they flew. Down the circular shaft and over the room with the algae-laden water and the tiny insects with their feathery crests. And then toward the ship's airlock chamber, where the corpse of the first Jelly floated, leaking ichor and other fluids.

Kira separated from Trig as they reached the airlock. "Don't shoot!" the kid shouted. "It's us."

The warning was a good idea. Vishal, Nielsen, and the Entropists were waiting for them in the *Wallfish* antechamber, weapons trained on the open airlock. The doctor had a bandage wrapped around his leg, where the shrapnel had struck him.

Relief swept across Nielsen's face as they flew into view. "Hurry," she said, moving out of the way.

Kira followed Trig to the center of the ship, and then aft toward the lowest level and the cargo holds. The sounds of lasers and gunfire echoed as they neared, and also the screams of terrified passengers.

At the starboard hold, they paused behind the pressure door—cautious—and then peeked around the frame.

All the refugees huddled at one end of the hold, gathered behind crates and using them as cover, meager though it was. At the opposite end of the hold lurked the tentacled Jelly; it was pressed flat behind a crate of its own. A ragged hole, half a meter across, marred the hull next to it. The wind screaming through the opening had pulled a loose wall panel against the breach, blocking part of it. A small bit of good fortune. Through the narrowed opening, the dark of space showed.

Falconi, Sparrow, and Hwa-jung were spread out across the middle of the hold, clinging to the support ribs and taking occasional shots at the Jelly.

The refugees, Kira realized, couldn't leave without being shot by the Jelly. And the Jelly couldn't move without being shot by Falconi and his crew.

Even with the door to the hold open, they only had a few minutes before the air ran out. No longer. Already she could feel the thinness of it, and there was a dangerous chill to the wind.

"Stay here," Kira said to Trig. Before he could respond, she took a breath and, despite her fear, jumped toward Falconi.

She heard a half-dozen *bzzts* as the Jelly fired a laser. The alien couldn't have missed, but she only felt one of the hits: a white-hot needle that stabbed deep into her shoulder. She barely had time to gasp before the pain began to subside.

A burst of gunfire erupted as Falconi and Sparrow attempted to give her cover.

As Kira landed next to Falconi, he grabbed her arm to keep her from drifting away. "Shit!" he growled. "The hell were you thinking?"

"Helping. Here." And she shoved the grenade launcher toward him.

The captain's face lit up. He snatched the weapon from her and, without a moment's hesitation, swung it over the rib and fired at the Jelly.

BOOM! A white flash obscured the crate hiding the Jelly. Metal fragments splattered the surrounding walls, and smoke billowed outward.

Several of the refugees screamed.

Sparrow twisted back toward Falconi. "Watch it! Not so close to the civvies!"

Kira gestured at the crate. It hardly appeared dented. "What's that thing made of? Titanium?"

"Pressure container," said Falconi. "Biocontainment. Damn thing is built to survive reentry."

Sparrow and Hwa-jung let off a burst of shots toward the Jelly. Kira stayed where she was. What else could she do? The Jelly was at least fifteen meters away. Too far for—

A fresh set of screams sounded from among the refugees. Kira looked back to see a tiny body squirming in the air, a child no more than six or seven years old. The girl had somehow lost her handhold and floated away from the deck.

A man scrambled free of the mass of refugees and threw himself after the child. "Stay down!" Falconi shouted, but too late. The man caught the girl, and the impact sent them into an uncontrolled tumble down the middle of the hold.

Surprise made Kira slow to react. Sparrow beat her to it; the armored woman abandoned the rib she was behind and flew at full thruster speed toward the two refugees.

Falconi cursed and lunged in a failed attempt to stop Sparrow from leaving cover.

A fan of inky smoke sprayed around the Jelly, hiding it. With her enhanced vision, Kira could still see a tangled outline of the Jelly's tentacles as it crawled toward a service ladder attached to the wall.

She fired into the smoke, as did Hwa-jung.

The Jelly flinched even as it wrapped a tentacle around one of the ladder's side struts and, seemingly without effort, tore it free.

Fast as a striking snake, it threw the strut at Sparrow.

The jagged piece of metal struck Sparrow in the abdomen, between two segments of her power armor. Half of the strut emerged from her back.

Hwa-jung screamed, a horrible, high-pitched sound that seemed impossible coming from someone her size.

5.

A rush of blinding anger washed away Kira's fear. Swinging herself around the edge of the rib, she launched herself after the Jelly.

Behind her, Falconi shouted something.

As she hurtled toward the Jelly, the alien spread its tentacles, as if to welcome her into its embrace. From it emanated nearscent of contempt, and for the first time, she responded in kind:

[[Kira here: Die, grasper!]]

An instant of astonishment that the Soft Blade let her not only comprehend but communicate in the alien language. Then she did what seemed only right: she stabbed with her arm, and she stabbed with her heart and her mind, and she channeled all of her fear, pain, and anger into the act.

In that moment, Kira felt something break in her mind, like a glass rod snapping in two, followed by fractures and fragments fitting into place throughout her consciousness—puzzle pieces sliding into their appointed slots, and accompanying the joining, a sense of profound completeness.

To her astonished relief, the xeno fused solid around her fingers and a thin, flat blade shot from her hand and pierced the alien's carapace. The creature thrashed from side to side, its tentacles knotting and squirming in a helpless frenzy.

Then, of their own accord, a pincushion of black spines sprouted from the end of the blade and impaled every part of the Jelly.

Her momentum carried the alien back against the far wall. There they stuck, the nanoneedles from the suit pinning the Jelly to the hull.

The alien shuddered and ceased thrashing, although the tentacles continued to turn and twist in a lazy rhythm, pennants rippling in the breeze. And the nearscent of death filled the hold.

CHAPTER VII

* * * * * * *

ICONS & INDICATIONS

1.

Kira waited a moment more before allowing the blade and spines to retract. The Jelly deflated like a balloon, ichor oozing from the countless wounds across its body.

The cloud of smoke was already dispersing, streaming into space. Kira kicked herself away from the Jelly, and the raging wind pushed the corpse into the breach. The alien lodged there on top of the loose wall panel, blocking most of the hole. The scream of wind lessened to a high whistle.

Kira turned to see the refugees staring at her with shock and fear. With some regret, she realized there was no hiding the Soft Blade now. The secret was out, for good or for ill.

Ignoring the refugees, she pulled herself over to where Trig, Falconi, and Hwa-jung were gathered around Sparrow's limp form.

The machine boss had her forehead pressed against Sparrow's faceplate, and she was speaking in a low tone, the words an indistinct murmur. Smoke drifted from the back of Sparrow's armor, and an exposed wire was sparking. A ring of white medifoam had welled out around the strut that impaled her. The foam would have stopped the bleeding, but Kira wasn't sure if that would be enough to save her.

"Doc, get down here. On the double!" said Falconi.

Kira swallowed, her mouth dry. "What can I do?" Up close, Hwa-jung's murmurs were no more distinct than before. Globules of tears clung to the machine boss's red-rimmed eyes, and her cheeks were pale, save for a bright, feverish spot on each side.

"Hold her feet," said Falconi. "Keep her from moving." He looked over at the refugees—who were starting to emerge from cover—and shouted, "Get out of here before we run out of air! Get into the other hold. Scram!"

They complied, giving a wide berth to not only Sparrow but Kira.

"Gregorovich, how long until air pressure drops below fifty percent?" Kira asked.

The ship mind answered with sharp efficiency, "At current rates, twelve minutes. If the Jelly is dislodged, no more than forty seconds."

The sides of Sparrow's boots were cool against her hands as Kira gripped them. For a moment she wondered how it was possible to feel that when even the cold of space hadn't fazed her.

Then she realized her mind was wandering. Now that the fighting was over, the adrenaline was starting to drain out of her system. Another few minutes and she was going to crash.

Vishal came flying through the door to the cargo hold, carrying with him a satchel with a silver cross sewn on the front.

"Move," he said as he collided with the crate next to Kira.

She obliged, and he rotated himself over Sparrow and stared through her faceplate, same as Hwa-jung. Then he pushed himself down to where the strut jutted out of her abdomen. The wrinkles on his face deepened.

"Can you—" Trig started to say.

"Quiet," Vishal snapped.

He studied the rod for another few seconds and then moved around to Sparrow's back and examined the other end. "You," he pointed at Trig, "cut here and here." With his middle finger, he drew a line across the rod, a hand's breadth above Sparrow's stomach, and the same above her back. "Use a beam, not a pulse."

Trig positioned himself next to Sparrow so the laser wouldn't hit anyone else. Through his visor, Kira could see his face was coated with sweat and his eyes were glassy. He lifted one arm and aimed the emitter on his gauntlet at the rod. "Eyes and ears," he said.

The strut flared white hot, and the composite tubing vaporized with a popping sound. An acrid, plastic smell filled the air.

The strut parted, and Falconi grabbed the loose section and gave it a gentle push toward the far end of the hold.

Then Trig repeated the operation on the other side of the strut. Hwa-jung snared that piece and threw it away with a vicious gesture; it bounced against a wall.

"Good," said Vishal. "I locked her armor; she is safe to move. Just do not bang her into anything."

"Sickbay?" Falconi asked.

"Posthaste."

"I'll do it," said Hwa-jung. Her voice was as hard and rough as broken stone. Without waiting for them to agree, she grabbed a handle on Sparrow's armor and pulled the rigid shell of metal toward the open pressure door.

2.

Trig and Vishal accompanied Hwa-jung as she guided Sparrow out of the hold. Falconi stayed behind, and Kira with him.

"Hurry up," he shouted, gesturing at the remaining refugees.

They pulled themselves past in a confused bunch. Kira was relieved to see that the girl and man Sparrow had been attempting to protect were unharmed.

When the last refugees had left, she followed Falconi into the corridor outside. He closed and locked the pressure door behind them, isolating the damaged hold.

Kira allowed the mask to retract from her face, glad to be rid of it. Color diffused through her vision, returning a sense of reality to her surroundings.

A hand on her wrist surprised her. Falconi held her, his gaze disconcertingly intense. "What the hell were those spikes back there? You didn't say anything about them before."

Kira yanked her hand free. Now wasn't the time to explain, not about the suit and certainly not about how her teammates had died. "I didn't want to scare you," she said.

His face darkened. "Anything else you didn't—"

Just then, four refugees—all men—walked over, using the gecko pads on their boots. None of them looked happy. "Hey, Falconi," said the leader. He was a tough, thickset man with a short circle beard. Kira vaguely remembered seeing him in the cargo hold before.

"What?" said Falconi, brusque.

"I don't know what you think you're doing, but we didn't agree to go chasing after Jellies. You're already screwing us over with how much you're charging us; now you're dragging us into battle? And I don't know what she's got going on, but normal it's not." He pointed at Kira. "Seriously, what's wrong with you? There are women and children here. If you don't get us to Ruslan—"

"You'll do what?" Falconi said sharply. He eyed them, his hands still on the grip of his grenade launcher. The weapon was empty, but Kira didn't feel the need to mention that. "Try to fly out of here with a pissed-off ship mind?"

"I wouldn't recommend it," said Gregorovich from above, and he tittered.

The man shrugged and cracked his knuckles. "Yeah, yeah. You know what, wiseguy? I'd rather take a chance with your crazy-ass ship mind than chance getting shish-kebabbed by the Jellies, like your crewmember did. And I'm not the only one that feels so." He wagged a finger at Falconi and then he and the other men returned to the other cargo hold.

"Well that went well," said Kira.

Falconi grunted, and she followed him as he hurried back to the center of the ship and kicked his way up the main shaft. He said, "Are there any other Jellies on their ship?"

"I don't think so, but I'm pretty sure Trig and I found their birthing chamber."

The captain snared the handhold next to the doorway to deck C, where the sickbay was. He paused and held up a finger. "Trig, you copy? . . . Navárez says you found birthing pods? . . . You got it. Burn them out. And fast, too, or we're going to be in a shit-ton of trouble."

"You're sending him back out there?" Kira said as Falconi headed through the doorway and down the adjacent corridor.

The captain nodded. "Someone's got to do it, and he's the only one with functioning armor."

The thought bothered Kira. The kid had a broken wrist; if he were attacked again . . .

Before she could voice her concern, they arrived at sickbay. Nielsen floated outside, an arm around Hwa-jung's shoulders, comforting the machine boss.

"Any news?" Falconi asked.

Nielsen looked at him with a worried expression. "Vishal just kicked us out. He's working on her now."

"Will she live?"

Hwa-jung nodded. Her eyes were red from crying. "Yes. My little Sparrow will live."

Some of the tension in Falconi's posture eased. He ran a hand over his head, tousling his hair. "Damn foolish of her to jump out the way she did."

"But brave," said Nielsen firmly.

Falconi tipped his head. "Yes. Very brave." Then to Hwa-jung: "The pressure breach in the hold needs fixing, and we're out of repair bots."

Hwa-jung nodded slowly. "I'll fix it once Vishal is finished operating."

"That could take a while," said Falconi. "Better to get started on it now. We'll let you know if there's any news."

"No," said Hwa-jung in her deep rumble. "I want to be here when Sparrow wakes."

Falconi's jaw muscles bunched. "There's a goddam hole in the side of the ship, Hwa-jung. It needs to get patched, *now.* I shouldn't have to tell you."

"I'm sure it can wait a few minutes," said Nielsen in a placating tone.

"Actually, it can't," said Falconi. "The Jelly ripped open a coolant line when it cut its way in. We're dead in the water until a replacement is hooked up. I also don't want our passengers roaming around the other hold."

Hwa-jung shook her head. "I won't leave until Sparrow wakes."

"Gods above and—"

The machine boss continued as if he hadn't spoken: "She will expect me to be here when she wakes. She'll be upset if I'm not, so I will wait."

Falconi planted his boots flat on the deck, anchoring them so he stood upright, swaying in the zero-g. "I'm giving you a direct order, Song. As your captain. You understand that, don't you?" Hwa-jung stared at him, her face immobile. "I'm ordering you to go down to the cargo hold and fix that *shi-bal* breach."

"Yes, sir. As soon as—"

Falconi scowled. "As soon as? As soon as what?!"

Hwa-jung blinked. "As soon as—"

"No, you head down there right now and you get this ship running again. Right now, or you can consider yourself relieved, and I'll put Trig in charge of engineering."

Hwa-jung clenched her hands, and for a moment Kira thought she would strike Falconi. Then the machine boss broke; Kira saw it in her eyes and the slump of her shoulders. A dark scowl on her face, Hwa-jung pushed herself down the corridor. She paused at the end and, without looking back, said, "If anything happens to Sparrow while I'm gone, you'll have to answer to *me,* Captain."

"That's what I'm here for," Falconi said in a tight voice. Then Hwa-jung vanished around the corner, and he relaxed slightly.

"Captain . . ." said Nielsen.

He sighed. "I'll sort it out with her later. She's not thinking clearly."

"Can you blame her?"

"I suppose not."

Kira said, "How long have they been together?"

"Long time," said Falconi. Then he and Nielsen began to discuss the state of the ship, trying to figure out which systems were compromised, how long they could keep the refugees in the other hold, and more.

Kira listened, feeling increasingly impatient. The thought of Trig alone on the alien ship continued to bother her, and she was eager to start digging answers out of the Jellies' computers before anything happened to disable them.

"Listen," she said, interrupting. "I'm going to go check on Trig, see if he needs help. Then I'm going to try and find out what I can."

Falconi gave her a critical look. "Sure you're up for it? You look a little off."

"I'm fine."

". . . Alright. Let me know once the ship is clear. I'll send over the Entropists. That is, if they're interested in examining the Jellies' tech."

3.

Kira made her way to deck D and then flew along the curve of the outer hull until she arrived at the airlock that joined them with the alien vessel.

Again she had the Soft Blade cover her face, and then with a twinge of apprehension, she dove back through the short, white tube of the Jellies' airlock into the murky shadows beyond.

The aching pull was as strong as ever, but Kira ignored it for the time being.

When she arrived at the chamber with the birthing pods, she found Trig going around to each cloudy pod and incinerating it with a flamethrower mounted on his forearm. As he played the jet of fire across one of the larger pods, something thrashed within: an unsettling collection of arms, legs, claws, and tentacles.

"All good?" Kira asked as the kid finished.

He gave her two thumbs up. **I still have another dozen or so to go. The captain sent me here just in time; at least two of the pods were about to hatch.**

"Charming," Kira said. "I'm going to go poke around. If you need any help, just let me know."

Same.

As she left the chamber, Kira put a call through to Falconi: "You can send the Entropists over. Ship should be safe now."

Roger that.

Kira took her time exploring. Her impatience was stronger than ever, but there was no telling what dangers the Jelly ship held, and she was in no hurry to fall into a trap. She kept close to the walls and, wherever possible, made sure to have a clear line to the exit.

The siren-call seemed to be coming from the front of the ship, so Kira headed in that direction, passing through circuitous corridors and half-lit rooms that, more often as not, were half-full of water. Now that she wasn't in immediate fear of her life, Kira noticed patches of nearscent at certain points within the ships.

One said: [[Forward]]

Another said: [[Co-form Restriction Sfar]]

Yet another said: [[Aspect of the Void]]

And more besides. There was writing also: branching lines that repeated the message of the nearscent. That she could read the lines gave Kira hope: the Jellies were still using a written language the Soft Blade recognized.

At last she arrived at the very front of the ship: a hemispherical room wedded to the prow of the vessel. For the most part it was empty, save for a twisting, branching structure that dominated the center of the room. The material was red (the only red she'd seen on the ship) and textured with tiny pits. Overall, it reminded her of nothing so much as coral. The structure aroused her professional interest, and she detoured to examine it.

When she tried to touch one of the branches, an invisible force repelled her hand. She frowned. Naturally occurring gravity fields were *attractive* (or at least gave the appearance of such). But this . . . The Jellies had to be using their inertial tech to increase the flow and density of spacetime around the branches to create an area of positive pressure. That would mean their artificial gravity was a *push* not a pull. As in, it would *push* her against the floor. Still, she could be wrong. That sort of thing was way outside her area of expertise.

The Entropists have to see this.

Strong as the field was, by anchoring herself against the floor with the Soft Blade, she was able to push her hand through it. The coral-like structure (growth? sculpture?) was chill to the touch, and slick from condensed moisture. Despite the pits in the material, it was smooth. When she tapped it, a sharp, brittle *tink* sounded.

It sure felt like calcium carbonate, but Kira wasn't sure of anything when it came to the Jellies.

Leaving the structure, she followed the tug of obscure sorrow to a section of wall covered with glassy panes and dotted with starry lights. She stood before it, and the ache within her was so strong, it caused her eyes to water.

A double blink, and then she studied the panes, searching for a hint of where to begin. She touched the glass—afraid of what might happen if she activated machines or programs without intending to—but there was no response. She wished the xeno would tell her how to work the console. Maybe it couldn't.

She ran her hand across the glass, again with no results. Then, for the first time, she tried to consciously produce nearscent. The Soft Blade responded with gratifying ease:

[[Kira here: Open . . . Activate . . . Access . . . Computer . . .]]

She tried all the normal words and phrases she would use with her overlays, but the glass remained dark. Kira began to wonder if she was even in front of a computer. Maybe the panels were just decorative elements. But that didn't seem right; the transmitter for the summons was obviously near. There ought to be controls of *some* sort nearby.

She considered going back to the birthing chamber and cutting off a tentacle from the corpse of the dead Jelly. Maybe DNA or a tentacle-print was needed to access the computer.

She put off the thought as an option of last resort.

Finally, she tried saying:

[[Kira here: Two-form . . . Manyform . . . Idealis . . .]]

A kaleidoscope of colors blossomed across the panels: a dazzling display of icons, indicators, images, and writing. At the same time, puffs of nearscent wafted past, pungent in their intensity.

Her nose itched, and a sharp pain formed behind her right temple. Words jumped out at her—some written, some scented—words freighted with meaning and memories not her own.

[[. . . the Sundering . . .]]

The spike of pain intensified, blinding her—

Battles and bloodshed against the spread of stars. Planets won and lost, ships burned, bodies broken. And everywhere, graspers killing graspers.

She fought for the flesh, and she was not the only one. There had been six others set in the ancient reliquary, placed there to wait in readiness for the expected summons. Like her, they joined with the grasping flesh, and like her, the flesh drove them to violence.

Some fights she and her siblings were allied. Some fights, they found themselves pitted one against the other. And that too was a perversion of the pattern. Never had it been intended, not in all the fractures they served.

The conflict had roused a Seeker from its crystalline cocoon. It looked upon the torment of the war and moved to eradicate all such wrongness, as was its wont. And the Sundering had consumed flesh old and new.

Of the six, three were slain in battle, while one more fell into the heart of a neutron star, one went mad and killed itself, and one was lost in the bright realm of superluminal space. The Seeker too had perished; its abilities in the end no match for the swarms of flesh.

Only she, of all her siblings, remained. Only she still carried the shape of the pattern within the fibers of her being. . . .

Kira let out a low cry and hunched over, her mind spinning. A war. There had been a terrible war, and the Soft Blade had fought in it along with others of its kind.

Blinking away the tears, she forced her gaze back to the panel. More words sprang out at her:

[[. . . now the Arms . . .]]

She cried out again.

Ctein. The great and mighty Ctein. It basked in the wash of heat from the nearby vent in the ocean floor, and its tendrils and feelers (too numerous to count) waved in gentle accord.

[[Ctein here: Speak your news.]]

Her flesh answered: [[Nmarhl here: The spinward shoal has been destroyed by the indulgence of the Tfeir.]]

Upon its mounded rock the terrible Ctein pulsed with bands of color, luminous in the purple depths of the Plaintive Verge. It smote the rock with a thrashing arm, and from the prominence rose a billow of blackened mud flecked through with pieces of chitin, broken and decaying.

[[Ctein here: TRAITORS! HERETICS! BLASPHEMERS!]]

Kira winced and looked at the deck by her feet while she regained a sense of place and being. Her head was throbbing enough to make her want to take a pill.

As she reviewed the memory, she felt a sense of . . . not *affection* but perhaps *regard* for Nmarhl from the Soft Blade. The xeno didn't seem to hate that particular Jelly the way it did the others. Odd.

She took a fortifying breath and again braved the panel.

[[. . . Whirlpool . . .]] *An impression of hunger and danger and distortion intertwined—*

[[. . . farscent, lowsound . . .]] *FTL communications—*

[[. . . forms . . .]] *Jellies, in all their different shapes—*

[[. . . Wranaui . . .]] At the word, Kira stopped, feeling as if she'd crashed into a wall. Recognition emanated from the Soft Blade, and with a slight sense of shock, Kira realized that *Wranaui* was the name the Jellies used for themselves. She couldn't tell if it was a racial or species term or just a cultural designation, but from the Soft Blade at least, there was no doubt whatsoever: this was what the Jellies called themselves.

[[Kira here: Wranaui.]] She explored the feel of the smell. There was no exact vocal equivalent; nearscent was the only way to properly say the name.

With trepidation, she resumed studying the displays. To her relief, the flashes of memories grew shorter and more infrequent, although they never entirely stopped. It was a mixed blessing; the intrusive visions kept her from focusing, but they also contained valuable information.

She persisted.

The Jellies' language seemed relatively unchanged since the last time the Soft Blade had encountered it, but the terms Kira encountered were context dependent, and context was something she so often lacked. It was like trying to understand technical jargon in a field she wasn't familiar with, only a thousand times worse.

The effort exacerbated her headache.

She tried to be methodical. She tried to keep track of every action she took and every piece of information the computer threw at her, but it was too much. Far, far too much. At least her overlays were keeping an audiovisual record. Maybe she could make more sense of what she was seeing once she was back in her cabin.

Unfortunately, she had no way to copy the nearscent for later study. Again Kira wished she had implants, ones capable of full-spectrum sensory recordings.

But she didn't, and there was no changing it.

Kira frowned. She had hoped it would be easier to find useful information on the Jellies' computer. After all, it wasn't hard for her to understand the aliens when they spoke. Or at least that was the impression the Soft Blade gave her.

In the end, she resorted to pushing random icons on the panels, hoping that she wouldn't accidently vent the air or fire a missile or somehow trigger a self-destruct. That would be a bad way to go.

"Come *on*, you piece of shit," she muttered, and hit the paneling with the heel of her hand.

Alas, percussive maintenance didn't help.

She was just grateful there was no sign of pseudo-intelligences or other forms of digital assistants guarding the computer system, and no indication that the Jellies had anything similar to human ship minds.

What Kira really wanted to find was the Jelly equivalent of a wiki or an encyclopedia. It seemed obvious that an advanced species like theirs ought to carry a repository of scientific and cultural knowledge in their computer banks, but—as she was painfully aware—few things were obvious when it came to an alien species.

When button-pushing failed to yield helpful results, she forced herself to stop and reevaluate. Surely there was something else she could try. . . . Nearscent had worked before; perhaps it would work again.

She mentally cleared her voice and then said: [[Kira here: Open . . . open . . . shell records.]] *Shell* felt like the correct word for *ship*, so that was what she used.

Nothing.

She tried twice more with different wording. On her third try, a new window opened in the display, and she caught a whiff of welcome.

Gotcha!

Kira's grin widened as she started to read. Just as she'd hoped: message logs. Not a wiki, but equally as valuable in their own way.

Most of the entries didn't make sense to her, but some things started to become clear. First was that the Jellies had a highly stratified, hierarchical society, with one's rank determined by all sorts of complicated factors, including which *Arm* you belonged to and which *form* you had. The specifics escaped Kira, but the *Arms* seemed to be some sort of political or military organizations. Or at least, that was what she assumed.

Many times in the messages she saw the phrase *two-form*. At first she thought it was a term for the Soft Blade. But as she read, it became clear that couldn't possibly be the meaning.

It was with a sense of revelation that she realized *two-form* had to be the Jellies' term for humans. She spent some time puzzling over that. *Do they mean men and women? Or something else?* Interestingly enough, the Soft Blade didn't seem to recognize the term. But then, why would it? Humans were newcomers to the galactic stage.

With that crucial piece of information, the messages began to make more sense, and Kira read with increasing avidness of ship movements, battle reports, and tactical assessments of 61 Cygni and other systems in the League. There were numerous mentions of travel times, and from the Soft Blade, Kira was able to glean a sense of the distances involved. The nearest Jelly base (system, planet, or station, she wasn't sure) was several hundred light-years away. Which led her to wonder why no hint of the aliens had shown up in the League's telescopes. The Jellies' civilization had to be far older than two or three hundred years, and the light from their worlds had long since reached human-settled space.

She kept reading, trying to pick out confluences of meaning—trying to see the larger patterns.

Perversely, the more she understood of the aliens' writing, the more confused she became. There were no references to the events at Adrasteia or to the Soft Blade, but there *were* references to attacks she'd never heard of: attacks not of Jellies on humans but of humans on Jellies. She also found lines that seemed to indicate the aliens believed that *humans* were the ones who had started the war by destroying . . . the Tower of Yrrith, and by *tower* she understood them to mean a space station.

At first Kira had difficulty believing that the Jellies—the Wranaui—thought *they* were the victims. A dozen different scenarios flashed through her mind. Maybe a deep-space cruiser like the *Extenuating Circumstances* had stumbled across the Jellies and, for whatever reason, initiated hostilities.

Kira shook her head. The summons was a maddening distraction, like a fly that wouldn't stop buzzing about her head.

What she was reading didn't make sense. The Jellies seemed convinced they were fighting for their very survival, as if they believed the *two-forms* posed an extinction-level threat.

As she continued to dig through the archive of messages, Kira began to notice repeated mentions of a . . . search the Wranaui were carrying out. They were looking for an object. A device of immense importance. Not the Soft Blade—that much she felt confident of, as they made no mention of *Idealis*—but whatever the object was, the Jellies thought it would allow them to not only defeat the League and win the war, but conquer the whole galaxy.

The back of Kira's neck prickled with fear as she read. What could be so powerful? An unknown form of weapon? Xenos even more advanced than the Soft Blade?

So far, the Jellies didn't know where the object was. That much was clear. The aliens appeared to believe it lay somewhere among a cluster of stars counter-spinward (by which Kira took them to mean against the galactic rotation).

One line in particular struck her: [[—when the Vanished made the Idealis.]] She went over it several times to make sure she understood. So the Soft Blade *was* a constructed thing. Were the Jellies saying that some other species had made it? Or were the Vanished also Jellies?

Then she chanced upon the name of the object: *the Staff of Blue.*

For a moment, the sounds of the ship ceased and all Kira heard was the pounding of her pulse. She *knew* that name. Unbidden, a spasm roiled the Soft Blade, and with it a wave of information. Understanding. Remembrance:

She saw a star—the same reddish star she had beheld once before. Then her view rushed outward, and the star appeared set among its nearest neighbors, but the constellations were strange to her, and she felt no sense for how they fit within the shape of the heavens.

A disjunction, and she saw the Staff of Blue, the fearsome Staff of Blue. It swung, and flesh and fibers tore themselves apart.

It swung, and ranks of machines crumpled beneath the blow.

It swung, and a sheaf of shining towers tumbled to the cratered ground.

It swung, and spaceships blossomed as fiery flowers.

Another place . . . another time . . . a chamber tall and stark, with windows that looked upon a brownish planet wreathed with clouds. Beyond it hung the ruddy star, huge in its nearness. By the largest window, dark against the swirling shine, she saw the Highmost standing. Gaunt of limb, strong of will, the first among the first. The Highmost crossed one set of arms, the other held the Staff of Blue. And she mourned for what now was lost.

Kira returned to reality with a start. "Shit." She felt light-headed, overwhelmed. Certainty gripped her that she had just seen one of the Vanished in the form of the Highmost. And it had definitely not been one of the Jellies.

Which meant? . . . She was having difficulty focusing, and the throbbing ache of the summons didn't help.

The Staff of Blue was terrifying. If the Jellies got their tentacles on it . . . Kira shuddered at the thought. And not just her; the Soft Blade also. Humanity had to find the staff first. *Had* to.

Worried that she'd missed something, she returned to the message logs and started to go over them again.

The pressure in her skull pulsed, and shimmering halos appeared around the lights in the control room. Kira's eyes watered. She blinked, but the halos didn't go away.

"Enough," she muttered. If anything, the summons grew stronger, drumming in her head with an inexorable beat, pounding, pulling, probing—drawing her toward the panel, an ancient duty yet unfulfilled . . .

She forced her attention back to the display. Surely there was a way to—

Another pulse of pain made her gasp.

Fear and frustration spilled over to anger, and she shouted, *"Stop it!"*

The Soft Blade rippled, and she felt it respond to the summons, answering it with an echo of her angry denial, an inaudible, invisible echo of radiated energy that raced outward, spreading, spreading . . . spreading across the system.

In that instant, Kira knew she'd made a terrible mistake. She lunged forward and plunged her fist through the glassy pane, *willing* the xeno to break, crush, and shatter in a desperate attempt to destroy the transmitter before it could pick up and rebroadcast her response.

The suit flowed down her arm and over her fingers. It spread across the wall like a web of tree roots, probing and seeking, burrowing ever deeper. The displays flickered, and those close to her hand guttered and went out, leaving a halo of darkness around her palm.

Kira felt the tendrils close around the source of the summons. She braced her feet against the wall, yanked on her arm, and tore the transmitter out of the center of the displays. What came free was a cylinder of purple crystal embedded with a dense honeycomb of silver veins that wavered as if distorted with heat ripples.

She squeezed the cylinder with the tendrils of the suit, squeezed with all her might, and the hunk of engineered crystal split and shattered. Stalks of silver sprouted between the tendrils as the xeno squished the metal like hot wax. And the compulsion diminished from an urgent necessity to a distant inclination.

Before she could recover, a scent intruded, a scent so strong, it was like a voice screaming in her ear:

[[Qwar here: Defiler! Blasphemer! Corrupter!]]

And Kira knew she was no longer alone. One of the Jellies was behind her, close enough she could feel an eddy of disturbed air tickle the back of her neck.

She stiffened. Her feet were still stuck to the wall. She couldn't spin around fast enough—

BAM!

She flinched and half turned, half crouched while stabbing outward with the Soft Blade.

Behind her, an alien flopped in the air. It was brown and shiny and had a segmented body the size of man's torso. A cluster of yellow-rimmed eyes surmounted its flat, neckless head. Pincers and feelers dangled from what could have been its chitinous mouth, and two rows of double-jointed legs (each the size and length of her forearms) kicked and thrashed along its armored abdomen. From its lobster-tail rear trailed a pair of antenna-like appendages at least a meter long.

Orange ichor leaked from the base of the creature's head.

BAM! BAM!

A pair of holes appeared in the alien's plated side. Gore and viscera sprayed the floor. The alien kicked once more as it spun away and then was still.

At the far end of the room, Falconi lowered his pistol, a thread of smoke drifting from the barrel. "What in seven hells are you doing?"

4.

Kira straightened from her crouch and retracted the spikes that projected from every square centimeter of her skin. Her heart was racing so hard, it took a few seconds before she was able to convince her vocal cords to work.

"Was it . . . ?"

"Yeah." Falconi holstered his pistol. "It was about to take a chunk out of your neck."

"Thanks."

"Buy me a drink sometime and we'll call it even." He floated over and examined the oozing corpse. "What do you think it is? Their version of a dog?"

"No," she said. "It was intelligent."

He eyed her. "And you know that how?"

"It was saying things."

"Charming." He gestured at her gore-covered arm. "Again: What the hell? You haven't been answering your comms."

Kira looked at the hole she'd torn in the wall. Fear spiked her pulse. Had she (or rather, the Soft Blade) really responded to the summons? The enormity of the situation filled her with rising dread.

Before she could answer the captain, a beep sounded in her ear, and Gregorovich said: **Calamity, O my delightful infestations.** And he laughed with more than a hint of madness. **Every Jelly ship in the system has set themselves upon an intercept course with the* Wallfish. *Might I suggest unchecked terror and an expedited retreat?**

CHAPTER VIII

* * * * * * *

NOWHERE TO HIDE

1.

Falconi swore and gave Kira a flat glare. "Is this your doing?"

Yes, what have you been up to, meatbag? Gregorovich said.

Kira knew there was no hiding what had happened. She drew herself up, although she felt very small indeed. "There was a transmitter. I destroyed it."

The captain's eyes narrowed. "That—Why? And why would that tip off the Jellies?"

"That's not what they call themselves."

"Excuse me?" he said, sounding anything but polite.

"There's no exact equivalent, but it's something like—"

"I don't give a flying fuck what the Jellies call themselves," said Falconi. "You better start explaining why they're coming after us, and fast too."

So in as brief a manner as possible, Kira told him about the compulsion and how she had—inadvertently—responded to it.

When she finished, Falconi's expression was so flat it scared her. She'd seen that look before on miners just before they decided to knife someone.

"Those spikes, now this—anything else you're not telling us about the xeno, Navárez?" he said.

Kira shook her head. "Nothing important."

He grunted. "Nothing important." She flinched as he drew his pistol and pointed it at her. "By all rights I ought to leave you here with a live video feed broadcasting so the Jellies know where to find you."

". . . But you're not going to?"

A long pause, and then the muzzle of the pistol lowered. He holstered the weapon. "No. If the Jellies want you that badly, then it ain't a good idea to let them have you. Don't think this means I want you on the *Wallfish,* Navárez."

She nodded. "I understand."

His gaze shifted, and she heard him say, "Trig, back to the *Wallfish*, now. Jorrus, Veera, if you want to get anything from the Jelly ship, you have five minutes, max, and then we're blasting out of here."

Then he turned and started to leave. "Come on." As Kira followed, he said, "Did you learn anything useful?"

"Lots, I think," she said.

"Anything that'll help us stay alive?"

"I don't know. The Jellies are—"

"Unless it's urgent, save it."

Kira swallowed what she was going to say and trailed behind Falconi as he hurried off the ship. Trig was waiting for them at the airlock.

"Keep watch until the Entropists are on board," said Falconi.

The kid saluted.

From the airlock, they went to Control. Nielsen was already there, studying the holo projected from the table in the middle. "How's it look?" Falconi asked, strapping himself into his crash chair.

"Not good," said Nielsen. She glanced at Kira with an unreadable expression and then pulled up a map of 61 Cygni. Seven dotted lines arced across the system, intersecting upon the *Wallfish*'s current location.

"Time to intercept?" Falconi asked.

"The nearest Jelly will be here in four hours." She stared at him, grave. "They're burning at maximum thrust."

Falconi scrubbed his fingers through his hair. "Okay. Okay. . . . How fast can we get to Malpert Station?"

"Two and a half hours." Nielsen hesitated. "There's no way the ships there can fight off seven Jellies."

"I know," said Falconi, grim. "But it's not like we have a lot of choice. If we're lucky, they can keep the Jellies tied up long enough for us to jump out."

"We don't have the antimatter."

Falconi bared his teeth. "We'll *get* the antimatter."

"Sir," whispered Gregorovich, "the *Darmstadt* is hailing us. Most urgently, I might add."

"Shit. Stall them until we're back under thrust." Falconi stabbed a button on the console next to him. "Hwa-jung, what's the status of those repairs?"

The machine boss answered a moment later: "Nearly finished. I'm just pressure testing the new coolant line."

"Hurry it up."

"Sir." She still seemed annoyed with the captain.

Falconi poked a finger toward Kira. "You. Spill it. What else did you find over there?"

Kira did her best to summarize. Afterward, Nielsen frowned and said, "So the Jellies think that *they're* the ones being attacked?"

"Is there any chance you misunderstood?" asked Falconi.

Kira shook her head. "It was pretty clear. That part, at least."

"And this Staff of Blue," said Nielsen. "We don't know what it is?"

"I think it's an actual staff," Kira explained.

"But what does it *do*?" said Falconi.

"Your guess is as good as mine. A control module of some kind?"

"It could be ceremonial," Nielsen pointed out.

"No. The Jellies seem convinced it would let them win the war." Then Kira had to explain again how she had inadvertently responded to the compulsion. So far she'd avoided thinking about it too much, but as she recounted the events to Nielsen, Kira felt a deep sense of shame and remorse. Even though she couldn't have known how the Soft Blade was going to respond, it was still her fault. "I fucked up," she finished by saying.

Nielsen eyed her with no great sympathy. "Don't take this the wrong way, Navárez, but I want you off this ship."

"That's the plan," said Falconi. "We hand her over to the UMC, let them deal with this." He looked at Kira with slightly more empathy. "Maybe they can stick you in a packet ship, get you out of the system before the Jellies can grab you."

She nodded, miserable. It was as good a plan as any. *Shit.* Going after the Jelly ship might have been worth it for the information she'd uncovered, but it looked as if she and the crew of the *Wallfish* were going to pay for the attempt.

She thought again of the ruddy star set amid its companions, and she wondered: Could she locate it on a map of the Milky Way?

Spurred by a sudden determination, Kira strapped herself into one of the crash chairs and—on her overlays—brought up the largest, most detailed model of the galaxy that she could find.

The comms snapped on, and Hwa-jung said, "All done."

Falconi leaned in toward the holo-display. "Trig, get those Entropists back on the *Wallfish*."

Not a minute later, the kid's voice sounded: "All green, Captain."

"Seal her up. We're blasting out of here." Then Falconi called down to the sickbay. "Doc, we gotta scram. Is it safe for Sparrow if we resume thrust?"

When Vishal answered, he sounded tense: "It's safe, Captain, but nothing above one g, please."

"I'll see what I can do. Gregorovich, take it away."

"Roger that, O my Captain. Currently *taking it away.*"

There was a series of jolts as the *Wallfish* disengaged from the alien ship and maneuvered with RCS thrusters to a safe distance. "All that antimatter," said Falconi, watching a live feed of the undocking. "Pity no one's figured out how to extract it from their ships."

"I'd rather not get blown up experimenting," Nielsen said dryly.

"Indeed."

Then the deck of the *Wallfish* vibrated as the ship's rocket sprang to life, and once more a welcome sense of weight returned as the acceleration pressed them into their seats.

In her overlays, a panoply of stars shone before Kira's unblinking eyes.

2.

In the background, Kira heard Falconi arguing with someone over the radio. She didn't listen, lost as she was in her examination of the map. Starting from an overhead view of the galaxy, she zoomed in on the area containing Sol and then slowly started to work her way counter-spinward (as the Jellies had mentioned). At first, it seemed like a hopeless task, but twice among the array of stars Kira felt a sense of familiarity from the Soft Blade, and it gave her hope.

She paused her study of the constellations when Vishal appeared framed in the doorway of the control room. He looked drained, and his face was still red from washing.

"Well?" Falconi said.

The doctor sighed and dropped into one of the chairs. "I've done all I can. The pole shredded half her organs. Her liver will heal, but her spleen, kidneys, and parts of her intestines, those need to be replaced. It will take a day or two for new parts to print. Sparrow is sleeping now, recovering. Hwa-jung is with her."

"Would it be better to put Sparrow in cryo?" Nielsen asked.

Vishal hesitated. "Her body is weak. Better for her to regain her strength."

"What if we don't have a choice?" Falconi asked.

The doctor spread his hands, fingers splayed. "It could be done, but it would not be my first choice."

Falconi returned to arguing over the comms (something about the Jelly ship, civilian permissions, and docking at Malpert Station), and Kira again concentrated on her overlays.

She could tell she was getting close. As she flew among the simulated stars, spinning and rotating and searching for shapes she recognized, she kept feeling tantalizing snatches of recognition. They drew her coreward, where the stars were packed closer together. . . .

"Dammit," said Falconi and banged his fist against the console. "They're refusing to let us dock at Malpert."

Distracted, Kira looked over at him. "Why?"

A humorless smile passed across his face. "Why do you think? Because we've got every Jelly in the system hot on our tail. Not sure what Malpert expects us to do, though. We don't have anywhere else to go."

She wet her lips. "Tell the UMC we picked up vital information on the Jelly ship. That's why the others are after us. Tell them . . . the information is a matter of interstellar security and the very existence of the League is at stake. If that doesn't get us onto Malpert, you could always mention my name, but if you don't have to, I'd prefer—"

Falconi grunted. "Yeah. Okay." He tabbed open a line and said, "Get me the liaison officer on the *Darmstadt.* Yes, I know he's busy. It's urgent."

Kira knew that the UMC was going to find out about her and the Soft Blade one way or another. But she saw no point in broadcasting the truth across the system, not if it could be avoided. Besides, the instant the UMC and the League learned she was still alive, her options were going to narrow to a limited few, if that.

Unsettled, she returned her attention to the map and tried to ignore what was happening. It was out of her control, in any case. . . . *There!* A certain pattern of stars struck her. She stopped, and a bell-like tone seemed to echo in her head: confirmation from the Soft Blade. And Kira knew she had found what she was looking for: seven stars in the shape of a crown, and near the center, the old, red spark that marked the location of the Staff of Blue. Or, at least, where the Soft Blade believed it to be.

Kira stared, at first disbelieving and then with a sense of growing confidence. Whether or not the xeno's information was up to date, the location of the system was more than they'd had before, and for once, it put her—and humanity as a whole—a step ahead.

Excited, she began to announce her discovery. A loud *beep* interrupted her, and dozens of red dots appeared scattered through the holo of the system projected in the center of the room.

"More Jellies," said Nielsen, a fatalistic note in her voice.

3.

"Goddammit. I don't *believe* it," said Falconi. For the first time, he seemed at a loss for what to do.

Kira opened her mouth and then closed it.

Even as they slipped into normal space, the red dots began to move, burning in all different directions.

"Perhaps you shouldn't believe it," said Gregorovich. He sounded oddly puzzled.

"What do you mean?" Falconi leaned forward, the usual razor-edge returning to his gaze.

The ship mind was slow to respond: "This latest batch of uninvited guests is behaving contrary to expectations. They are . . . *calculating* . . . *calculating*. . . . They aren't just flying toward us, they're also flying toward the other Jellies."

"Reinforcements?" Nielsen asked.

"Uncertain," Gregorovich replied. "Their engine signatures don't match the ships we've seen from the Jellies so far."

"I know there are different factions among the Jellies," Kira offered.

"Perhaps," said Gregorovich. Then: "Oh my. . . . Well, then. Isn't that interesting?"

The main holo switched to show a view from elsewhere in the system: a live feed of three ships converging on one.

"What are we looking at?" Falconi asked.

"A transmission from Chelomey Station," said Gregorovich. A green outline appeared around one of the ships. "This is a Jelly." Red outlined the three other ships. "These are some of our newcomers. And this"—a set of numbers appeared next to each ship—"is their acceleration and relative velocity."

"Thule!" Falconi exclaimed.

"That should not be possible," said Vishal.

"Indeed," said Gregorovich.

The newcomers were accelerating faster than any Jelly ship on record. Sixty g's. A hundred g's. More. Even through the display, their engines were painful to look at—bright torches powerful enough to spot from light-years away.

The three ships had jumped in close to the Jelly they were pursuing. As they converged, the Jelly released clouds of chalk and chaff, and the computer marked otherwise invisible laser bursts with lines of red. The intruders fired back, and missiles streaked between the combatants.

"Well that answers one question," said Nielsen.

Then one of the three newcomers shot ahead of its companions and, with hardly any warning, rammed the Jelly ship.

Both vessels vanished in an atomic flash.

"Whoa!" said Trig. He walked in from the corridor and sat next to Nielsen. He'd changed out of his power armor, back into his normal, ill-fitting jumpsuit. A foam cast encased his left wrist.

"Gregorovich," said Falconi, "can you get us a close-up of one of those ships?"

"A moment, please," said the ship mind. For a few seconds, a piece of mindless, waiting-room music played through the *Wallfish*'s speakers. Then the holo changed: a blurred still of one of the new ships. The vessel was dark, almost black, and shot through with veins of bloody orange. The hull was asymmetric, with odd bulges and angles and scabrous protuberances. It looked more like a tumor than a spaceship, as if it had been grown rather than built.

Kira had never seen anything like it, and neither, she thought, had the Soft Blade. The unbalanced shape gave her an uneasy feeling in the pit of her stomach; she had difficulty imagining a reason for constructing such a twisted, lopsided machine. It certainly wasn't the handiwork of the Jellies; most everything they built was smooth and white and seemed to be radially symmetrical.

"Look," said Falconi, and he switched the holo back to a view of the system. All across 61 Cygni, the red dots were streaking toward Jellies and humans alike. The Jellies were already altering their courses to face the incoming threats, which meant—for the time being—the *Wallfish* had some breathing room.

"Captain, what's going on?" said Trig.

"I don't know," said Falconi. "All the passengers back in their hold?" The kid nodded.

"Those ships aren't the Jellies'," said Kira. "They're not."

"Do the Jellies think they're *ours*?" said Nielsen. "Is that why they think we've been attacking them?"

Vishal said, "I don't see how."

"Neither do I," said Falconi, "but seems there's a whole lot we don't understand right now." He tapped his fingers against his leg, then glanced at Kira. "What I want to know is whether they jumped in because of that signal you sent."

"They would've had to been waiting just outside Sixty-One Cygni," said Nielsen. "That seems . . . unlikely."

Kira was inclined to agree. But it seemed even more unlikely that the newcomers would have arrived at that exact moment through sheer chance. As with the Jellies showing up at Adra, space was too big for that sort of coincidence.

The thought made her skin itch. Something was wrong here, and she didn't know what. She opened a message window on her overlays and sent the captain a text: *<I think I know where the Staff of Blue might be. – Kira>*

His eyes widened slightly, but otherwise, he didn't react. *<Where? – Falconi>*

<About sixty light-years from here. I really do need to talk with someone in charge at Malpert. – Kira>

<I'm working on it. They're still trying to make up their minds. – Falconi>

For a minute everyone was silent, watching the display. Falconi stirred in his seat and said, "We have permission to dock at Malpert. Kira, they know we have intel, but I didn't tell them who you are or about your, ah, suit. No reason to put all your cards on the table at once."

She smiled slightly. "Thanks. . . . It has a name, you know."

"What does?"

"The suit." They all looked at her. "I don't understand all of it, but what I do understand means the Soft Blade."

"That is so *cool,*" said Trig.

Falconi scratched his chin. "It fits, I'll give it that. You've got a strange life, Navárez."

"Don't I know it," she muttered to herself.

Another alert sounded then, and in mournful tones, Gregorovich said, "Incoming."

Two of the newly arrived ships were burning straight for Malpert Station. ETA, a few minutes sooner than the *Wallfish.*

"Of course," said Falconi.

4.

For the next two hours, Kira sat with the crew, watching as the strange, twisted ships spread through the system, seeding chaos wherever they went. They attacked humans and Jellies indiscriminately, and they displayed suicidal disregard for their own safety.

Four of the newcomers swept through the antimatter farm situated close to the sun. The ships raced past the ranks of winged satellites, blasting them with lasers and missiles so that each exploded in a flash of annihilating antimatter. Several of the satellites had point-defense turrets, and they managed to score hits on two of the attackers. The damaged ships promptly rammed the turrets, destroying themselves in the process.

"Maybe they're drones," said Nielsen.

"Maybe," said Gregorovich, "but unlikely. When cracked, they vent atmosphere. There must be living creatures swaddled within."

"It's another species of aliens!" said Trig. "Has to be!" He nearly bounced in his seat.

Kira couldn't share his enthusiasm. Nothing about the newcomers felt right to her. Just the sight of their ships left her feeling off-balance. That the Soft Blade seemed to have no knowledge of them only compounded her discomfort. It surprised her how much she'd come to rely on the xeno's expertise.

"At least they're not as tough as the Jellies," said Falconi. It was true; the newcomers' ships didn't seem as well-armored, although that was offset by their speed and recklessness.

The two tumorous ships continued to bore through space toward Malpert Station. As they and the *Wallfish* neared, the *Darmstadt* and a half-dozen smaller vessels again took up defensive positions around the station. The UMC cruiser was still trailing silvery coolant from radiators that had been damaged while fighting the Jellies earlier, but damaged or not, the cruiser was the station's only real hope.

When the *Wallfish* was five minutes away, the shooting started.

CHAPTER IX

★ ★ ★ ★ ★ ★ ★

GRACELING

1.

The attack was swift and vicious. The two malformed alien ships dove toward the *Darmstadt* and Malpert, each from a different vector. Bursts of smoke and chaff obscured the view, and then the UMC cruiser fired a trio of Casaba-Howitzers. They weren't holding back.

With a violent juke, one of the aliens dodged the nuclear shaped charges. It continued past, on a collision path for the station.

"No!" Nielsen cried.

But the alien ship didn't ram Malpert and explode. Rather it slowed and, with its remaining momentum, coasted into one of the station's docking ports. The long, malignant-looking ship smashed its way past clamps and air-locks, wedging itself deep into the body of the station. The vessel was big: nearly twice the size of the *Wallfish*.

The other ship didn't manage to avoid the Casaba-Howitzers, not entirely. One of the spears of ravening death singed the ship's hull, and the vessel careened off deeper into the asteroid belt, streaming smoke from the wound burned through its flank.

A group of mining ships separated from the rest of the defenders and gave chase.

"Now's our chance," said Falconi. "Gregorovich, get us docked, now."

"Uh, what about that thing?" said Nielsen, pointing at the alien ship protruding from the edge of the station.

"Not our worry," said Falconi. The *Wallfish* had already cut its engines and was moving via thrusters toward the assigned airlock. "We can always blast off again if we have to, but we've *got* to fill our tanks back up."

Nielsen nodded, her face tight with worry.

"Gregorovich, what's happening on the station?" Kira asked.

"Chaos and pain," the ship mind replied. In the holo, a series of windows appeared, showing feeds from within Malpert: dining halls, tunnels, open concourses. Groups of men and women clad in skinsuits ran past the cameras, firing guns and blasters. Billows of chalk clogged the air, and in the pale shadows moved creatures the likes of which Kira had never imagined. Some stalked on all fours, as small and lean as whippets but with eyes as big as her fist. Others lurched forward on malformed limbs: arms and legs that looked broken and badly healed; tentacles that kinked and hung useless; rows of pseudopods that pulsed with sickening fleshiness. Regardless of their shape, the creatures had red, raw-looking skin that oozed lymph-like fluid, and patches of black, wire-thick hair dotted their scabrous hides.

The creatures carried no weapons, though more than a few had boney spikes and serrations along their forelimbs. They fought like beasts, jumping after the fleeing miners, bearing them down to the floor and tearing at their guts.

Without guns, the monsters were quickly cut down. But not before they killed several dozen people.

"What in God's name?" said Vishal, his horrified tone matching Kira's own feelings.

Across from her, Trig looked green.

"You're the xenobiologist," said Falconi. "What's your professional opinion?"

Kira hesitated. "I . . . I don't have a clue. They can't be naturally evolved. Just, I mean, just look at them. I don't even know if they could have built the ship they used."

"So you're saying someone else made those *things*?" said Nielsen.

Falconi raised an eyebrow. "The Jellies, maybe? Science experiment gone wrong?"

"But then why blame attacks on us?" said Vishal.

Kira shook her head. "I don't know. I don't know. Sorry. I haven't got the faintest idea what's going on."

"I'll tell you what's going on," said Falconi. "War." He checked something on his overlays. "The captain of the *Darmstadt* wants to meet with you, Navárez, but it's going to take them some time to dock. They're still mopping up out there. In the meantime, let's refuel, refit, and get the folks out of the cargo hold. They're going to have to find another way to Ruslan. And I'm going to start making calls, see if I can get my hands on some antimatter. Somehow."

2.

Kira went with Trig, Vishal, and Nielsen to help. It beat sitting around waiting. Her mind churned as they floated down the shaft in the center of the *Wallfish*. The vision she'd had from the Soft Blade about the staff . . . the being the xeno had thought of as the Highmost hadn't looked like either a Jelly or one of the malformed newcomers. Did that mean they were dealing with *three* sentient species?

Hwa-jung joined them on the ladder on her way to engineering. When Nielsen asked about Sparrow, the machine boss just grunted and said, "She lives. She sleeps."

At the starboard hold, a babble of shouted questions met them as Trig spun open the wheel-lock and opened the door. Nielsen held up her hands and waited until there was quiet.

She said: "We've docked at Malpert Station. There's been a change of plans. The *Wallfish* won't be able to take you to Ruslan after all." As an angry roar began to build among the assembled refugees, she added: "Ninety percent of your ticket price will be refunded. Should be already, in fact. Check your messages."

Kira perked up; that was the first she'd heard of a refund.

"It's probably for the best," Trig confided to her. "We weren't really, uh, welcome on Ruslan. It would've been kinda dicey getting down to land."

"That so? I'm surprised Falconi is giving out refunds. Doesn't seem like him."

The kid shrugged, and a sly little smile spread across his face. "Yeah, well, we kept enough to top up on hydrogen. Plus, I grabbed a few things while I was on the Jelly ship. Captain figures we can sell them to collectors for a whackload of bits."

Kira frowned, thinking of all the technology on the ship. "What exactly did you—" she started to ask, only to have a squeal of rotating metal joints cut her off.

The outer wall of the cargo hold hinged open to reveal a wide jetway that joined the hold to the Malpert spaceport. Loading bots sat waiting outside, and a handful of customs officials stood anchored nearby, clipboards in hand.

The refugees started to gather up their supplies and head out of the *Wallfish*. It was a difficult task in zero-g, and Kira found herself chasing after sleeping bags and thermal blankets to keep them from flying out of the hold.

The refugees seemed wary of her, but they didn't protest her presence.

Mainly, Kira suspected, because they were more focused on getting out of the *Wallfish*. One man did come up to her, though—a lanky, redheaded man in rumpled formal wear—and she recognized him as the guy who had jumped after the girl during the fight with the Jelly.

"I didn't get the opportunity earlier," he said, "but I wanted to thank you for helping to save my niece. If not for you and Sparrow . . ." He shook his head.

Kira dipped her head, and she felt an unexpected film of tears in her eyes. "Just glad I could help."

He hesitated. "If you don't mind me asking, what are you?"

". . . A weapon, and let's leave it at that."

He held out his hand. "Whatever the case, thank you. If you're ever on Ruslan, look us up. Hofer is the name. Felix Hofer."

They shook, and an odd lump formed in Kira's throat as she watched him return to his niece and leave.

Across the hold, angry voices rang out. She saw Jorrus and Veera surrounded by five of the Numenists—three men, two women—who were shoving them and shouting something about the Number Supreme.

"Hey, knock it off!" called Nielsen as she kicked herself in their direction.

Kira hurried toward the fight. Even as she did, one of the Numenists—a snub-nosed man with purple hair and a row of subdermal implants along his forearms—butted Jorrus in the face, smashing his mouth.

"Hold still," said Kira, snarling. She flew into the group and grabbed the purple-haired man around the torso and pinned his arms against his sides as they tumbled into a wall. The Soft Blade gripped the wall at her command, stopping them.

"What's going on?" Nielsen demanded, putting herself between the Numenists and Entropists.

Veera held up her hands in a placating matter. "Just a small—"

"—theological dispute," Jorrus finished. He spat a gob of blood onto the deck.

"Well not here," said Nielsen. "Keep it off the ship. All of you."

The purple-haired man wrenched against Kira's arms. "Ah feck off yah hatchet-faced bint. An you, let me go, yah walloping, misbegotten graceling."

"Not until you promise to behave," said Kira. She relished the feeling of strength the Soft Blade gave her; holding the man was easy with its help.

"Behave? Ah'll show you behave!" The man's head snapped backwards and slammed into her nose.

Blinding pain exploded in Kira's face. An involuntary cry escaped her, and she felt the man squirming in his shirt, trying to tear free.

"Stp it!" she said as tears flooded her eyes and blood clogged her nose and throat.

The man swung his head back again. This time he caught her right on the chin. It hurt. A *lot*. Kira lost her grip, and the man twisted out of her arms.

She grabbed him again, and he took a swing at her, sending them tumbling.

"Thts *engh*!" she shouted, angry.

At the words, a spike shot from her chest and stabbed the man through the ribs. He stared at her with disbelief, and then he convulsed, and his eyes rolled back in his skull. Blots of red spread across his shirt.

Across the hold, the four other Numenists cried out.

Horror immediately replaced Kira's anger. "No! I'm sorry. I didn't mean to. I didn't—" With a slithery sensation, the spike retracted.

"Here!" said Vishal. He tossed her a line from by the wall. Kira caught it without thinking, and the doctor reeled her and the Numenist in. "Hold him still," said Vishal. He ripped open the side of the man's shirt and, with a small applicator, sprayed medifoam into the wound.

"Will he—" Kira started to ask.

"He'll live," said Vishal, hands still working. "But I have to get him to sickbay."

"Trig, help the doctor," said Nielsen, drifting over.

"Yes, ma'am."

"As for you," said Nielsen, pointing at the rest of the Numenists, "get out of here before I throw you out." They started to protest, and she stopped them with a glare. "We'll let you know when you can have your friend back. Now scram."

Trig took the man's feet and Vishal his head. Then they carried him off, just as Hwa-jung had carried Sparrow.

3.

Kira hung by the wall, dazed. The rest of the refugees were staring at her with fear and outright hostility, but she didn't care. In her head, the unconscious Numenist was Alan, bleeding out in her arms while the air escaped screaming through holes torn in the walls. . . .

She'd lost control. Just for an instant, but she might have killed a man, same as she'd killed her teammates. This time she couldn't put the blame on the Soft Blade; she'd *wanted* to hurt the Numenist, to hurt him until he stopped hurting her. The Soft Blade had only been responding to that urge.

"Are you alright?" Nielsen asked.

It took Kira a moment to respond. "Yeah."

"You need to get that looked at."

Kira touched her face and winced. The pain was receding, but she could feel her nose was humped and crooked. She tried to push it back into place, but the Soft Blade had already healed it too much to move. Apparently close enough was good enough where the xeno was concerned.

"Dammit," she murmured, feeling defeated. The nose would have to be rebroken before it could be straightened.

"Why don't you wait here for now," said Nielsen. "It's better that way, don't you think?"

Kira nodded numbly and watched the other woman drift off to supervise the disembarking process.

The Entropists came over then, and Veera said, "Our apologies for causing—"

"—such a disturbance, Prisoner. The fault is ours for telling the Numenists—"

"—that there are greater infinities than the set of real numbers. For some reason, that offends their concept—"

"—of the Number Supreme."

Kira waved her hand. "It's fine. Don't worry about it."

The Entropists bobbed their heads as one. "It seems—" said Jorrus.

"—that we must part ways," said Veera. "Therefore, we wished to thank you for sharing the information about your suit with us, and—"

"—for giving us the opportunity to explore the Jelly ship—"

"—and we wish to give you this," said Jorrus. He handed her a small, gem-like token. It was a disk of what looked like sapphire with a fractal pattern embedded within.

The sight of the fractal gave Kira a shiver of familiarity. The pattern wasn't the one from her dreams, but it was similar. "What is it?"

Veera spread her hands in a gesture of benediction. "Safe passage to the Motherhouse of our order, the Nova Energium, in orbit around Shin-Zar. We know—"

"—you feel compelled to assist the League, and we would not dissuade you. But—"

"—should you wish otherwise—"

"—our order will guarantee you sanctuary. The Nova Energium—"

"—is the most advanced research laboratory in settled space. Not even the finest labs on Earth are as well equipped . . . or as well defended. If anyone can rid you of this organism—"

"—it is the minds at the Nova Energium."

Sanctuary. The word resonated with Kira. Touched, she pocketed the token and said, "Thank you. I may not be able to accept your offer, but it means a lot to me."

Veera and Jorrus slipped their hands into the opposing sleeves of their robes and clasped their forearms across their chests. "May your path always lead to knowledge, Prisoner."

"Knowledge to freedom."

Then the Entropists departed, and Kira was again alone. She didn't have long with her thoughts before the woman, Inarë, and the cat with the unpronounceable name stopped next to her. The woman was carrying a large floral-patterned carpet bag. She had no other luggage. The cat was perched on her shoulders, every strand of its hair standing on end in the zero-g.

The woman chuckled. "You seem to be having an interesting time of it, *Ellen Kaminski.*"

"That's not my name," said Kira, in no mood to talk.

"Of course it isn't."

"Did you want something?"

"Why yes," said the woman. "Yes I do. I *wanted* to tell you this: eat the path, or the path will eat you. To paraphrase an old quote."

"Which means?"

For once Inarë appeared serious. "We all saw what you can do. It seems you have a larger part to play than most in this dismal scheme of ours."

"What of it?"

The woman cocked her head, and in her eyes Kira saw unexpected depth, as if she'd arrived at the crest of a hill to discover a yawning chasm beyond. "Only this, and this alone: circumstances press hard upon us. Soon all that will be left to you, or to any of us, is bare necessity. Before that happens, you must decide."

Kira frowned, almost angry. "And what exactly am I supposed to decide?"

Inarë smiled and shocked Kira by patting her on the cheek. "Who you want to be, of course. Isn't that what all of our decisions come down to? Now I really must be off. People to annoy, places to escape. Choose well, Traveler. Think long. Think fast. Eat the path."

Then the woman pushed herself away from the wall and floated out of the cargo hold into the Malpert spaceport. On her back, the large, maned cat continued to stare at Kira, and it uttered a mournful yowl.

4.

Eat the path. The phrase wouldn't leave Kira's mind. She kept turning it over, gnawing on it as she tried to understand.

Across the hold, Hwa-jung shepherded a pair of loader bots that were pushing and pulling the four cryo pods from the *Valkyrie*. Through the frost-encrusted windows, Kira glimpsed Orso's face, blue and deathly pale.

At least she hadn't needed to eat *him* to survive. He and the other three were going to be in for a hell of a shock once the UMC thawed them out and told them what had been happening while they slept. . . .

"You're a walking disaster, Navárez," said Falconi, coming up. "That's what you are."

She shrugged. "Guess so."

"Here." He dug a handkerchief out of a pocket, spit on it, and without waiting for permission, started to wipe her face. Kira flinched. "Hold still. You've got blood everywhere."

She tried not to move, feeling like a kid with a dirty face.

"There," said Falconi, stepping back. "Better. That nose needs fixing, though. You want me to do it? I've had some experience with broken noses."

"Thanks, but I think I'll ask a doctor," she said. "The Soft Blade already healed me, so . . ."

Falconi winced. "Gotcha. Okay."

Outside the ship, a series of exclamations went up from the refugees arrayed before the duty officers, and Kira saw people pointing at displays along the spaceport walls. "Now what?" she said. How much more bad news could there be?

"Let's see," said Falconi.

Kira brought up her overlays and checked the local news. The malignant newcomers were continuing their rampage across the system. They'd already destroyed most of the Jellies—and been destroyed in turn themselves—but the biggest headlines concerned Ruslan. Six of the newcomers had blasted past Vyyborg Station and the rest of the planet's defenses and landed in the capital city of Mirnsk.

All but one.

That one ship had aimed itself at Ruslan's space elevator, the Petrovich Express. Despite the planet's orbital batteries. Despite the UMC battleship, the *Surfeit of Gravitas,* stationed around Vyyborg. Despite the numerous lasers and missile batteries mounted around the crown and base of the mega-structure. And despite the best design-work of countless engineers and physicists . . . despite all of those things, the alien ship had succeeded in ramming and severing the ribbon-shaped cable of the space elevator, three-quarters of the way to the asteroid that served as a counterweight.

As Kira watched, the upper part of the elevator (counterweight included) hurtled away from Ruslan at greater than escape velocity while the lower section began to curve toward the planet, like a giant whip wrapping around a ball.

"Thule," Kira murmured. The higher parts of the cable would either break off or burn up in the atmosphere. Farther down, though, close to the ground, the collapse would be devastating. It would obliterate most of the spaceport around its anchor point, as well as a long swath of land stretching off to the east. In absolute terms, the collapse wouldn't cause *that* much damage, but for people close to the base, it would be an apocalyptic event. Imagining how terrified (and helpless) they had to be made her feel sick.

Several small, spark-like flares appeared along the length of cable still attached to Ruslan.

"What are those?" she asked.

"Transport pods, I bet," said Falconi. "Most of them should be able to land safely."

Kira shivered. Riding the beanstalk had been one of the more memorable experiences she'd had with Alan during their brief shore leave prior to the launch of the Adra survey mission. The view from high on the cable had been incredible. They'd been able to see all the way to the Numinous Flange, far to the north. . . . "Glad I'm not there," she said.

"Amen to that." Then Falconi gestured toward the spaceport. "Captain Akawe—the captain of the *Darmstadt*—is ready to see us."

"Us?"

Falconi gave her a clipped nod. “The liaison officer said they have some questions for me. Probably about our little excursion to the Jelly ship.”

“Ah.” It comforted Kira to know she wouldn’t be facing the UMC by herself. Even if Falconi wasn’t a friend, she knew she could count on him to watch her back, and she figured saving Trig and Sparrow ought to have earned her some goodwill. “Alright, let’s go.”

“After you.”

CHAPTER X

* * * * * * *

DARMSTADT

1.

From the *Wallfish* airlock, Falconi led Kira into a tunnel that burrowed through the rocky asteroid that Malpert was built on and in. They'd floated halfway around the circumference of the station before Kira realized they weren't going to enter the rotating hab-ring closer to the center.

"Akawe wants to meet on the *Darmstadt*," said Falconi. "I figure they think it's more secure. No monsters running around."

Kira wondered if she should be worried. Then she shrugged off the concern. It didn't matter. At least she wouldn't be in zero-g on the *Darmstadt*.

Evidence of the fight with the newcomers was everywhere. The air smelled of smoke, the walls were scorched and pocked, and the people they passed had round, staring expressions, as if they were still in shock.

The tunnel passed through a large dome, half of which was closed off behind doors that said *Ichen Manufacturing*. In front of the doors, Kira saw what remained of one of the unidentified aliens. The creature had been torn and splattered by bullets, but she could still make out its basic shape. Unlike the others, this one had black shards across its back: bone or shell, it was hard to tell. Double-jointed legs—three of them if she was counting correctly. Long, carnivorous jaw. Was that a *second* jaw near the prominence of the chest?

Kira moved closer, wishing she had a chip-lab, a scalpel, and a couple of uninterrupted hours to study the specimen.

Falconi's hand on her shoulder stopped her. "We don't want to keep Akawe waiting. Bad idea."

"Yeah . . ." Kira turned away from the corpse. All she wanted to do was her job, and the universe kept conspiring to prevent it. Fighting wasn't her thing; she wanted to *learn*.

So then why had she stabbed the Numenist? Rat bastard though he was, the man hadn't deserved a blade to the chest. . . .

A pair of Marines in heavy power armor was waiting for them outside the airlock to the *Darmstadt*. "No weapons allowed," said the near Marine, holding up a hand.

Falconi grimaced but unbuckled his belt and handed it and his pistol to the Marine without protest.

The pressure door rolled open.

"Ensign Merrick will show you the way," said the Marine.

Merrick—a thin, stressed-looking man with a smear of grease on his chin and a bloody bandage taped to his forehead—was waiting for them inside. "After me," he said, leading them deeper into the UMC cruiser.

The layout of the *Darmstadt* was identical to that of the *Extenuating Circumstances*. It gave Kira uncomfortable flashbacks of running through corridors while listening to the sounds of alarms and gunfire.

Once they passed through the hub of the ship and transitioned to the rotating hab spokes, they were again able to walk normally, which Kira welcomed.

Ushering them into a small meeting room with a table in the middle, Merrick said, "Captain Akawe will be with you directly." Then he left, closing the pressure door behind him.

Kira remained standing, as did Falconi. He seemed as conscious as she was that the UMC had them under surveillance.

They didn't have to wait long before the door slammed open and four men filed in: two Marines (who remained standing by the entrance) and two officers.

The captain was easy to identify by the bars on his uniform. Of medium height, with dark skin and a five o'clock shadow, he had the over-stimmed look of someone who hadn't gotten a proper sleep for several days. There was something about his face that struck Kira as being too symmetrical, too perfect, as if she were looking at a mannequin brought to life. It took her a moment to realize, the captain's body was a construct.

The other officer looked to be the second-in-command. He was lean, with a heavy jaw and creases like scars along his hollow cheeks. His short-cut hair was receding, and his eyes glowed with the deep, predatory yellow of a tigermaul's.

Kira had heard stories about soldiers who chose to have the gene-hack so they could see better during combat, but she'd never met anyone with the mod.

Akawe went around the table and sat at the single chair on that side. He motioned. "Sit." His second-in-command remained standing by his side, back regulation-straight.

Kira and Falconi obeyed. The chairs were hard and uncomfortable, devoid of padding.

Akawe crossed his arms and eyed them with something akin to disgust. "Goddamn. What a sorry-looking pair you are. Wouldn't you agree, First Officer Koyich?"

"Sir, yes I would, sir," replied the yellow-eyed man.

The captain nodded. "Damn right. Let me be clear here, *Mr.* Falconi, and Ms. Whatever-your-name-is, I don't have time to waste on you. There's an honest-to-god alien invasion going on, I've got a damaged ship that needs attending to, and for some reason Command is chewing on my ass to get everyone from the *Valkyrie* shipped back to Vyyborg yesterday. They are *pissed* that you decided to change course and head for Malpert instead of Ruslan. If that weren't enough, you kicked up a real hornets' nest by boarding that Jelly ship. I don't know what kind of bullshit you're trying to pull, but you have exactly thirty seconds to convince me you have anything worth saying."

"I can understand the Jellies' language," said Kira.

Akawe blinked, twice, and then said, "Somehow I doubt that. Twenty-five seconds and counting."

She lifted her chin. "My name is Kira Navárez, and I was the lead xenobiologist on the team sent to survey the planet Adrasteia at Sigma Draconis. Four months ago, we discovered an alien artifact on Adrasteia, which led to the destruction of the UMCS *Extenuating Circumstances*."

Akawe and Koyich exchanged glances. Then the captain uncrossed his arms and leaned forward. He templed his fingers under his chin. "Okay, Ms. Navárez, you now have my undivided attention. Enlighten me."

"I need to show you something first." She raised a hand, held it palm up. "You have to promise not to overreact."

Akawe snorted. "I seriously doubt there is anything—"

He stopped as a cluster of spikes emerged from her hand. Behind her, Kira heard the Marines lift their weapons, and she knew they were aiming at her head.

"It's safe," she said, straining to hold the spikes in place. "Mostly." She relaxed and allowed her palm to smooth over.

Then she started to tell her story.

2.

Kira lied.

Not about everything, but—as with the crew of the *Wallfish*—she lied about how her friends and teammates had died on Adra, blamed it on the Jellies. It was stupid of her; if Akawe thawed out Orso or his companions and debriefed them, her lies would become obvious. But Kira couldn't help herself. Admitting her role in the deaths, especially Alan's, was more than she could bear to face at the moment. If nothing else, she feared it would confirm Falconi's worst impression of her.

Aside from that, she told the truth as best she understood it, up to and including her discovery regarding the Staff of Blue. She also gave them Vishal's test results, all of the recordings she'd made with her contacts while on the Jelly ship, and her transcriptions of the xeno's memories.

When she finished, there was a long, long silence, and she could see the eyes of both Akawe and Koyich darting back and forth as they messaged each other.

"What do you have to say about all this, Falconi?" asked Akawe.

Falconi made a wry expression. "Everything she told you about her time on the *Wallfish* checks out. I'd just add that Kira saved the lives of two of my crew today, for whatever that's worth. You can check our records if you want." He didn't mention anything about her stabbing the Numenist, and for that, Kira was grateful.

"Oh we will," said Akawe. "You can bet your ass." His eyes blanked. "One minute."

There was another uncomfortable pause, and then the UMC captain shook his head. "Command back at Vyyborg confirms your identity, as well as the discovery of a xenoform artifact on Adrasteia, but the details are classified need-to-know only." He eyed Kira. "Just to confirm, you can't tell us anything about these nightmares that just showed up?"

She shook her head. "No. But as I said, I'm pretty sure the Jellies didn't make the suit. Some other group or species was responsible."

"The nightmares?"

"I don't know, but . . . if I had to guess, I'd say no."

"Uh-huh. Okay, Navárez, this is way above my pay grade. It looks like the Jellies and the nightmares are busy killing each other off. Once the shooting dies down, we'll get you over to Vyyborg and let Command figure out what to do with you."

The captain started to stand, and Kira said, "Wait. You can't."

Akawe raised an eyebrow. "Excuse me?"

"If you send me to Vyyborg, it's just going to be a waste of time. We have to find the Staff of Blue. The Jellies seem convinced that it'll win the war for them. I believe it too. If they get the staff, that's it. We're dead. All of us."

"Even if that's true, what do you expect me to do about it?" asked Akawe. He crossed his arms.

"Go after the staff," said Kira. "Get it before the Jellies."

"What?" said Falconi, looking just as startled as the UMC guys.

She kept talking. "I told you; I have a good idea of where the staff is. The Jellies don't. I'm sure they're already searching for it, but if we start now, we might be able to beat them to it."

Akawe pinched the bridge of his nose, as if he had a headache. "Ma'am . . . I don't know how you think the military works, but—"

"Look, do you think there's any chance the UMC and League *won't* want to go after the staff?"

"That depends on what Fleet Intelligence makes of your claims."

Kira struggled to contain her frustration. "They can't afford to ignore the possibility that I'm right, and you *know* it. And that's the thing: if an expedition is going to go after the staff—" She took a breath. "—then I have to go with it. They'll need me there, on the ground, to translate. No one else can do it. . . . Shipping me off to Vyyborg is a waste of time, Captain. Waiting for Intelligence to vet everything I've said is a waste of time, and they *can't*. We need to go, and we need to go now."

Akawe stared at her for a good half minute. Then he shook his head and sucked his bottom lip against his teeth. "Goddammit, Navárez."

"Now you know what I've been dealing with," Falconi said.

Akawe pointed a finger at him, as if about to chew him out. Then he seemed to reconsider and folded the finger into his fist. "You may be right, Navárez, but I still have to run this up the chain of command. It's not the sort of decision I can make on my own."

Exasperated, Kira let out a sound. "Don't you see, that's—"

Akawe pushed back his chair, got to his feet. "I'm not going to sit here arguing with you, ma'am. We have to wait to hear what Command says, and that's the end of it."

"Fine," said Kira. She leaned forward. "But you tell them—you tell your superiors—that if they keep me here in Sixty-One Cygni, the whole system is going to be overrun. The Jellies know where I am now. You saw how they reacted when that signal went out. The only way to stop them from getting *this*"—she tapped her forearm—"is for me to leave the system. And if the UMC sends me to Sol, that'll be another two weeks down the drain, and it'll just lead a lot more Jellies to Earth."

There. She'd said the magic word: *Earth*. The semi-mythical Homeworld that everyone in the UMC had sworn to protect. It had the desired effect. Both Akawe and Koyich appeared troubled.

"I'll tell them, Navárez," said the captain, "but don't get your hopes up." Then he gestured at the Marines. "Get her out of here. Put her in a spare cabin and make sure she doesn't leave."

"Sir, yessir!"

As the Marines flanked her, Kira looked at Falconi, feeling helpless. He seemed angry, frustrated by the shape of things, but she could see he wasn't going to argue with Akawe. "Sorry it worked out like this," he said.

Kira shrugged as she got to her feet. "Yeah, me too. Thanks for everything. Give Trig my goodbyes, okay?"

"Will do."

Then the Marines escorted her out of the meeting room, leaving Falconi sitting alone, facing Akawe and his tiger-eyed first officer.

3.

Kira seethed as the Marines escorted her through the cruiser's interior. They deposited her in a cabin smaller than the one on the *Wallfish*, and when they left, the door locked behind them.

"Gaaah!" Kira shouted. She paced the length of the room—two and a half steps in each direction—and then dropped onto the bunk and buried her head in her arms.

This was exactly what she hadn't wanted to happen.

She checked her overlays. Still working, but she was locked out of the *Darmstadt*'s network, making it impossible to see what was going on in the rest of the system or to message any of the *Wallfish* crew.

All she could do was wait, so wait she did.

It wasn't easy.

She went over the conversation with Akawe six different ways, trying to figure out what else she could have said to convince him. Nothing came to mind.

Then, in the stillness and quiet of the room, the full weight of the day's events began to settle upon her. Morning felt like it had been a week ago, so much had happened since. The Jellies, the compulsion and her response to it, Sparrow . . . How was the Numenist she'd stabbed? For a moment, she lingered on the thought, then bright flashes of sensations from the fights on the Jelly ship struck her, and Kira shivered, though she wasn't cold.

She continued to shiver, the tremors locking her muscles into banded cords. The Soft Blade roiled in response, but there was nothing it could do to help, and she could feel its confusion.

Teeth chattering, Kira crawled onto the bunk and wrapped the blanket around herself. She'd always done well in emergencies. It took a lot to rattle her, but the violence had been a lot and then some. She could still feel the vomit stuck in her throat, clogging her airway. *Thule! I nearly died.*

But she hadn't, and there was some comfort in the fact.

Not long after, a scared-looking crewmate delivered a tray of food. Kira pulled herself out of bed long enough to fetch the tray, and then she sat with the pillow behind her and ate, slowly at first and then with increasing speed. With each bite, she felt more normal, and when she finished, the cabin no longer seemed quite so grey or dismal.

She wasn't about to give up.

If the UMC wouldn't listen to her, maybe the highest-ranked League official in the system would. (She wasn't sure who that would be: the governor of Ruslan?) The UMC still answered to the civilian government, after all. There was also the company rep stationed on Malpert. He could arrange legal representation for her, which would help give her some leverage. As a last resort, she could always reach out to the Entropists for help. . . .

Kira reached into her pocket and pulled out the token Jorrus had given her. She tilted the faceted disk, admiring how light reflected off the fractal embedded in the center.

No, she wasn't about to give up.

She put away the token, opened a document in her overlays, and started to draft a memo outlining everything she'd learned about the Soft Blade, the Jellies, and the Staff of Blue. *Someone* in authority had to understand the importance of her discoveries and realize they were worth taking a chance on.

She'd only written a page and a half when a sharp rap sounded against the door. "Come in," she said, swinging her legs over the edge of the bed and sitting upright.

The door opened, and Captain Akawe entered. He was holding a cup of what smelled like coffee, and there was a stern look on his perfectly sculpted face.

Behind him, an orderly and a pair of Marines remained stationed just outside the cabin.

"Seems today is a day for nasty surprises," said the captain. He seated himself opposite her, on the cabin's sole chair.

"What now?" Kira asked, overtaken by sudden dread.

Akawe placed the cup on the shelf next to him. "All the Jellies in the system are dead."

"That's . . . good?"

"It's fan-fucking-tastic," he said. "And it means their FTL jamming is also gone."

Understanding dawned on Kira. Maybe she could finally get a message through to her family! "You picked up news from the rest of the League." It wasn't a question.

He nodded. "Sure did. And it's not exactly cheery." He plucked a shiny blue coin from his breast pocket, studied it a moment, and then pocketed it again. "The nightmares didn't just hit Sixty-One Cygni. They've been attacking all of settled space. The Premier has officially designated both them and the Jellies *Hostis Humani Generis*. Enemies of all humans. That means shoot on sight, no questions asked."

"When did the nightmares first appear?"

"Not sure. We haven't heard yet from the colonies on the other side of the League, so can't say what's happening out there. The earliest reports we have are from a week ago. Here, look."

Akawe tapped a panel on the wall, and a display sprang to life.

A series of clips played: a pair of the nightmare ships crashing into a manufacturing facility in orbit around one of the moons of Saturn. A civilian transport exploding as a long, reddish missile slammed into it. Ground footage from somewhere on Mars: nightmares swarming through the cramped corridors of a hab-dome while Marines blasted at them from behind barriers. A view out one of the floating cities of Venus as fragments of destroyed ships rained down through the layers of cream-colored clouds—a burning fusillade that slammed into another of the broad, disk-shaped platforms a few kilometers away, destroying it. On Earth: a huge glowing crater amid a great sprawl of buildings somewhere along a snowy coastline.

Kira sucked in her breath at that. *Earth!* She had no great love for the place, but it was still shocking to see it attacked.

"It's not just the nightmares either," said Akawe. He tapped the panel again.

Now the clips showed Jellies. Some fighting the nightmares. Others fighting the UMC or civilians. The recordings were from throughout the League. Sol. Stewart's World. Eidolon. Kira even saw a snippet of images from what she thought might have been Shin-Zar.

To her dismay, one of the clips appeared to have been recorded in orbit around Latham, the gas giant farthest out from Weyland: a short video of two Jelly ships strafing a hydrogen processing station low in the atmosphere.

Kira wasn't surprised; the war was everywhere else, why not there? She just hoped the fighting hadn't reached Weyland's surface.

At last, Akawe stopped the parade of horrors.

Kira tightened in on herself. She felt raw and hurt, vulnerable. Everything in those videos was, in a way, her fault. "Do you know what's happening at Weyland?"

He shook his head. "Just what you saw, plus a few reports of possible Jelly forces on one of the moons in the system. Unconfirmed."

Not the reassurance Kira was looking for. She resolved to look up the specifics once she got access to the net again. "How bad is it overall?" she asked, her voice low.

"Bad," said Akawe. "We're losing. They won't break us tomorrow. And they won't break us the day after. But at this rate, it's inevitable. We're bleeding ships and troops faster than we can replace them. And there's no real protection against the sort of suicide runs the nightmares seem fond of." Again the glowing crater appeared on the screen. "That's not even the worst of it."

Kira braced herself. "Oh?"

Akawe leaned forward, a strange, hard gleam in his eyes. "Our sister vessel, the *Surfeit of Gravitas,* blew up the last of the nightmares in this system exactly twenty-five minutes ago. Just before the nightmares got blasted to kingdom come, do you know what those pestilent, dick-skinned aliens did?"

"No."

"Well I'll tell you. They sent out a broadcast. And not just any broadcast." An evil, humorless smile split his face. "Let me play it for you."

Across the speakers came a hiss of static, and then a voice sounded—a horrible, crackling voice full of sickness and madness—and with a shock, Kira realized it was speaking in English: ". . . *die. You will all die! Flesh for the maw!*" And the voice began to laugh before the recording abruptly ended.

"Captain," Kira said, choosing her words with care, "does the League have some sort of bioengineering program they haven't told us about?"

Akawe grunted. "Dozens of them. But nothing that could have created creatures like that. You should know; you're a biologist yourself."

"At this point," said Kira, "I'm not sure *what* I know anymore. Okay, so these . . . nightmares can use our language. Maybe that's why the Jellies think we're responsible for this war. Either way, these *things* must have been watching us, studying us."

"Must have, and that makes me real uncomfortable."

Kira eyed him for a moment, evaluating. "You didn't come here just to tell me the news, now did you, Captain?"

"No." Akawe smoothed a wrinkle from his slacks.

"What did Command say?"

He looked down at his hands. "Command . . . Command is headed up by a woman named Shar Dabo. Rear Admiral Shar Dabo. She's in charge of Ruslan operations. Good officer, but we don't always see eye to eye. . . . I had a talk with her, a long talk, and . . ."

"And?" Kira said, trying to be patient.

Akawe noticed. His lips twitched, and he continued more briskly, "The admiral agreed with the seriousness of the situation, which is why she forwarded all your intel to Sol in order to get guidance from Earth Central."

"Earth Central!" Kira hissed and threw up her hands. "That's going to take, what—"

"About nine days to get a response," said Akawe. "Assuming the stiffs back home turn out a reply without delay, which would be a miracle. An actual, honest-to-god miracle." A frown puckered his brow. "It won't do any good, even if they're *expeditious*. Jellies have been jumping into this system every few days for the past month. As soon as the next batch shows up, they'll jam us again, fuck up our comms from here to Alpha Centauri. Which means we'll have to wait for a packet ship to get here from Sol before we receive our orders. And *that'll* take at least eighteen, nineteen days."

He leaned back and picked up his cup. "Until then, Admiral Dabo wants me to bring you, your suit, and those frozen Marines from the *Extenuating Circumstances* back to Vyyborg."

Kira eyed him, trying to make sense of his motives. "And you don't agree with her orders?"

He took a sip of coffee. "Let's just say Admiral Dabo and I are experiencing a difference of opinions right now."

"You're thinking about going after the staff, aren't you?"

Akawe pointed at the crater still glowing in the holo. "You see that? I have friends and family back at Sol. A lot of us do." He wrapped both hands around his cup. "Humanity can't win a war on two fronts, Navárez. Our backs are against the wall, and there's a gun aimed at our heads. At this point, even bad choices are starting to look pretty good. If you're right about the Staff of Blue, it could mean we actually have a chance."

She didn't bother hiding her exasperation. "That's what I was saying."

"Yes, but your say-so isn't good enough," said Akawe. He took another sip, and she waited, sensing that he needed to talk things out for himself. "If we go, we'd be disobeying orders or, at the very least, ignoring them. Leaving the field of battle is still grounds for capital punishment, if you weren't aware. Cowardice before the enemy, and all that. Even if that weren't the case, you're talking about a deep-space mission that would last a minimum of six months, round-trip."

"I know what it would—"

"Six. Months," Akawe repeated. "And who knows what would happen while we were gone." He shook his head slightly. "The *Darmstadt* took a beating today, Navárez. We're in no shape to go jetting off into the ass-end of the Milky Way. And we're just one ship. What if we get there and there's a whole Jelly fleet waiting for us? Boom. We'd lose what might be our only advantage: you. Hell, we don't even know for sure if you can understand the Jellies' language. That suit of yours could be messing with your brain."

He swirled the coffee in his cup. "You have to understand the situation, Navárez. There's a lot at stake. For me, for my crew, for the League. . . . Even if I'd known you since the first day of boot, there's no way I can go jetting off to who knows where just on the strength of your word."

Kira crossed her arms. "So then why are you here?"

"I need proof, Navárez, and it needs to be something more than just your word."

"I don't know how to give you that. I already told you everything I know. . . . Do you have any computers salvaged from a Jelly ship? I might be able to—"

Akawe was shaking his head. "No, we don't. Besides, we'd still have no way to confirm what you're saying."

She rolled her eyes. "What the hell do you want then? If you don't trust me—"

"I don't."

"If you don't trust me, what's the point of this conversation?"

Akawe drew a hand across his chin while he studied her. "Your implants were burned out, is that right?"

"Yes."

"Pity. A wire scan could resolve this right quick."

Anger burbled up within her. "Well, sorry to disappoint."

He didn't seem put off. "Let me ask you this: When you extend different parts of the xeno, can you feel the extensions? Like when you ripped the transmitter out of the wall, all those little tendrils, could you feel them?"

The question was so off-topic, it took Kira a second to answer. "Yes. They feel just like my fingers or toes."

"Uh-huh. Okay." Akawe surprised her then by unbuttoning the cuff of his right sleeve and rolling back the fabric. "Seems I might have a solution to our standoff, Ms. Navárez. It's worth a shot, in any case." He dug his fingernails into the underside of his bared wrist, and Kira winced as the skin peeled up in a rectangular shape. Even though she knew Akawe's body was artificial, it *looked* so realistic, the sight of the skin lifting was still disconcerting on a visceral level.

Wires and circuits and pieces of bare metal were visible within Akawe's arm.

As he fished out a line from inside his own forearm, the captain said, "This is a direct neural uplink, same as we use in implants, which means it's analog, not digital. If the xeno can interface with your nervous system, then it ought to be able to do the same with me."

Kira took a moment to think the idea through. It seemed unlikely, but—she had to concede—theoretically possible. "You realize how dangerous this could be?"

Akawe held out the end of the line toward her. It looked like fiber optic, even though she knew it wasn't. "My construct has a bunch of built-in safeguards. They'll protect me if there's a surge in electricity or—"

"They won't protect you if the xeno decides to crawl into your brain."

Akawe pushed the line toward her, his expression serious. "I'd rather die right now, trying to stop the Jellies and the nightmares, than sit around doing nothing. If there's even a chance this could work . . ."

She took a deep breath. "Alright. If something happens to you, though—"

"You won't be held accountable. Don't worry. Just try to make this work." A glint of humor appeared in his eyes. "Trust me, I don't *want* to die, Ms. Navárez, but this is a risk I'm willing to take."

She reached out and closed her hand around the end of the neural link. It was warm and smooth against her palm. Shutting her eyes, Kira pushed the skin of the suit toward the end of the lead, urging it to join, to meld, to *become.*

The fibers on her palm stirred, and then . . . and then a faint shock ran up her arm. "Did you feel that?" she asked.

Akawe shook his head.

Kira frowned as she concentrated on her memories from the Jelly ship, trying to push them through her arm, toward Akawe. *Show him,* she thought, insistent. *Tell him. . . . Please.* She did her best to convey a sense of urgency to the Soft Blade, to make it understand *why* this was so important.

"Anything?" she said, her voice tight with strain.

"Nothing."

Kira gritted her teeth, put aside any concern for the captain's safety, and imagined her mind pouring through her arm and into Akawe's, like an unstoppable torrent of water. She exerted every gram of mental energy she had, and just when she reached her limit and was about to give up—just then, a wire seemed to snap in her head, and she felt another space, another presence touching herself.

It was not so different from joining the direct feed of two sets of implants, only more chaotic.

Akawe stiffened, and his mouth fell open. "Oh," he said.

Again, Kira impressed her desire on the Soft Blade. *Show him.* She reviewed her memories of the ship, including as much detail as she could, and when she finished, the captain said, "Again. Slower."

As Kira did, sudden bursts of images interrupted her thoughts: *A set of stars. The Highmost standing dark against the swirling shine. A pair of crossed arms. The Staff of Blue, the fearsome Staff of Blue. . . .*

"Enough," Akawe gasped.

Kira relaxed her grip on the neural link, and the connection between them vanished.

The captain sagged backwards against the wall. The lines on his face made him appear almost normal. He fed the data cord back into his forearm and sealed the access panel.

"Well?" said Kira.

"That was certainly something." Akawe pulled down his sleeve, buttoned the cuff. Then he picked up his cup and took a long drink. He made a face. "Goddamn. I love my coffee, Navárez. But it's never tasted right since I got stuck in this construct."

"Is that so."

"Indeed it is. Losing your body isn't like getting a paper cut, no sir. It happened to me, oh, fourteen years ago now. Back during a nasty little skirmish with the Ponder Union at the Ceres shipyards. You know why they call it the Ponder Union?"

"No," said Kira, struggling to suppress her impatience. Had the Soft Blade knocked something loose inside his brain?

Akawe smiled. "Because they sit around all day not working. Pondering the inner workings of bureaucracy and how best to twist it to their advantage. Things got pretty heated between the union and the shipyard during contract negotiations, so my unit was sent in to settle things down. Soothe the savage beast. Oil on troubled waters. Peacekeeping mission, my ass. We ended up facing off with a crowd of protesters. I *knew* they meant trouble, but they were civilians, you see? If we'd been in a combat zone, I wouldn't have hesitated. Post overwatch, deploy drones, secure the perimeter, force the crowd to disperse. The whole nine yards. But I *didn't* because I was trying to avoid escalating the situation. There were kids there, for crying out loud."

Akawe peered at her over the rim of his cup. "The crowd got all riled up, and then they hit us with a microwave that fried our drones. The bastards had been planning on ambushing us the whole time. We started taking fire from our flanks . . ." He shook his head. "I went down in the first volley. Four Marines ended up dead. Twenty-three civilians, and a whole lot more injured. I *knew* the protesters were up to no good. If I'd just acted—if I hadn't waited—I could have saved a whole lot of lives. And I'd still be able to taste a mug of good old joe the way it's supposed to be."

Kira smoothed the wrinkles in the blanket by her knee. "You're going after the staff," she said, flat. The thought was daunting.

Akawe tossed back the rest of the coffee in a single gulp. "Wrong."

"What? But I thought—"

"You've misunderstood, Navárez. *We're* going." And Akawe gave her a disconcerting grin. "This may be the worst decision I've ever made, but I'll be damned if I'm going to sit around and let a bunch of aliens wipe us out. One last thing, Navárez, are you ab-so-*lute*-ly sure there's nothing else we should know? Any tiny bit of relevant information that might have slipped to the back of your brain? My crew is going to be risking their lives on this. Hell, we might be risking a whole lot more than just our lives."

"I can't think of anything," Kira said. "But . . . I do have a suggestion."

"Why does that make me nervous?" said Akawe.

"You should take the *Wallfish* with you."

The captain fumbled and nearly dropped his cup. "Did you just seriously suggest bringing a civilian ship and crew—a group of *rim runners*—on a military mission to some ancient alien installation? Is that what I heard, Navárez?"

She nodded. "Yeah. You can't leave Sixty-One Cygni undefended, so the *Surfeit of Gravitas* has to stay, and none of the mining ships here on Malpert are set up for a long-haul mission. Besides, I don't know their crews and I wouldn't trust them."

"And you trust Falconi and his people?"

"In a fight? Yes. With my life. As you said, you might need backup when we get to where the staff is. The *Wallfish* isn't a cruiser, but it can still fight."

Akawe snorted. "It's a piece of dogshit; that's what it is. It wouldn't last more than a few minutes in a shooting contest with a Jelly."

"Maybe, but there's one other point you haven't thought of."

"Oh really? Do share."

Kira leaned forward. "Cryo doesn't work on me anymore. So you have to ask yourself: How comfortable will you be with me—with this xeno—wandering around your state-of-the-art UMC ship for months on end while you're frozen stiff?" Akawe didn't answer, but she could see the wary look in his eyes. Then she added: "Don't think you can just lock me up for the duration, either. I had enough of that already." She grabbed the edge of the bunk and willed the Soft Blade to tighten around the frame until it crushed the composite.

Akawe stared at her for an uncomfortable length. Then he shook his head. "Even if I were inclined to agree with you, there's no way an old cargo tub like the *Wallfish* could keep pace with the *Darmstadt*."

"I don't know about that," she said. "Why don't you check?"

The captain snorted again, but she saw his gaze shift as he focused on his overlays, and his throat moved as he subvocalized orders. His eyebrows climbed toward his hairline. "It seems your *friends*"—he put particular emphasis on the word—"are full of surprises."

"Can the *Wallfish* keep up?"

He inclined his head. "Close enough. I suppose smugglers have the incentive to move fast."

Kira resisted the urge to defend the *Wallfish* crew. "See? Not all surprises today are bad."

"I wouldn't go that far."

"Also—"

"Also? What more can there be?"

"There were two Entropists traveling on the *Wallfish.* Jorrus and Veera."

Akawe's perfectly shaped eyebrows rose. "Entropists, eh? That's quite a passenger list."

"You might want to bring them along as well. If we're going to be looking at alien tech, their expertise would be useful. I can translate, but I'm no physicist or engineer."

He grunted. "I'll take it under consideration."

"So is that a yes for the *Wallfish*?"

The captain drained the last of his coffee and stood. "Depends. It's not as easy as you make it out to be. I'll let you know once I decide."

Then he left, and the smell of coffee lingering in the air was the only evidence of his visit.

4.

Kira let out her breath. They were actually going to go after the Staff of Blue, and she was going to see the system the Soft Blade had shown her! It hardly seemed real.

She wondered what the name of the old, red star was. It must have one.

Unable to bear sitting any longer, she hopped up and started to pace the small space of the cabin. Would Falconi agree to accompany the *Darmstadt* if Akawe asked? She wasn't sure, but she hoped so. Kira wanted the *Wallfish* to go with them for all the reasons she'd given Akawe, but also for her own selfish reasons. After her experience on the *Extenuating Circumstances,* she didn't want to end up trapped on a UMC ship for months at a time, subject to constant surveillance by their doctors and their machines.

Although she wouldn't be as vulnerable as before. She touched the fibers along her forearm, tracing them. Now that she could control the Soft Blade—some of the time, at least—she could hold her own against a trooper in power armor if need be. And with the xeno, she could easily escape a quarantine room like the one on the *Extenuating Circumstances*. . . . The knowledge kept her from feeling helpless.

An hour passed. Kira heard *thuds* and *booms* resonating through the cruiser's hull. Repairs, she guessed, or supplies being loaded. But it was hard to be sure.

Then an incoming call popped up on her overlays. She accepted it and found herself looking at a video of Akawe backed by several consoles. The man looked annoyed.

"Navárez: I had a friendly-like chat with Captain Falconi about your proposition. He's proving to be a real sumbitch when it comes to setting terms. We've promised him all the antimatter his ship can carry and pardons for the whole crew, but he's refusing to say yes or no until he talks with you. You willing to have a word with him?"

Kira nodded. "Patch him through."

Akawe's face vanished—although Kira was sure he was still monitoring the line—and was replaced by Falconi's. As always, his eyes were two bright chips of ice. "Kira," he said.

"Falconi. What's with the pardons?"

A hint of discomfort appeared in his expression. "I'll tell you about it later."

"Captain Akawe said you want to talk?"

"Yeah. This crazy-ass idea of yours . . . are you sure, Kira? Are you really, really sure?"

His question was so similar to Akawe's earlier, Kira nearly laughed. "As sure as I can be."

Falconi tilted his head to one side. "Sure enough to risk your life on it? My life? Trig's? How about Runcible's?"

At that Kira did crack a smile, if only a tiny one. "I can't make you any promises, Falconi—"

"I'm not asking for any."

"—but yeah, I think this is as important as it gets."

He studied her for a moment and then jerked his chin in a sharp nod. "Okay. That's what I needed to know."

The line went dead, and Kira closed her overlays.

Maybe ten minutes later, someone knocked on her door and a woman's voice sounded: "Ma'am? I'm here to escort you to the *Wallfish*."

Kira was surprised by the strength of her relief. Her gamble had paid off.

She opened the door to see a short, startled woman: a junior officer of some kind, who said, "Right this way, ma'am."

Kira followed her back out of the *Darmstadt* and onto the space dock. As they left the cruiser, the two Marines in power armor stationed by the entrance joined them, following at a discreet distance. Although, as Kira reflected, it was hard for power armor to be anything close to discreet.

Familiarity washed over Kira as they neared the *Wallfish.* The cargo hold door was still open, and loader bots were streaming in and out, depositing crates of food and other supplies throughout the hold.

Trig was there, as were Nielsen and Falconi. The captain lowered the clipboard he was holding and gave her a look. "Welcome back, Navárez. Guess we're going on a jaunt because of you."

"Guess so," she said.

CHAPTER XI

* * * * * * *

EXPOSURE

1.

Departure from Malpert Station was a quick and hurried affair. Kira had been on plenty of expeditions where the preparation took nearly as long as the trip itself. Not so in this case. The crew moved with purpose to ready the *Wallfish* for the journey to come, rushing through work that normally would have taken days. Captain Akawe had given orders that the Malpert port authority was to give them every possible help, and that sped things up also.

While loader bots filled the starboard hold with supplies and, outside, pipes funneled hydrogen into the *Wallfish*'s tanks, the crew swapped empty air canisters for full, removed waste, and replenished stores of water.

Kira helped as she could. Talk was limited on account of the work, but when the opportunity arose, she pulled Vishal aside, where the others couldn't hear. "What happened with the Numenist?" she asked. "Is he okay?"

The doctor blinked, as if he'd forgotten. "The—Oh, you mean Bob."

"Bob?" Somehow Kira had trouble imagining calling the purple-haired man *Bob.*

"Yes, yes," said Vishal. He twirled a finger by his temple. "He was crazy as a spacebird, but other than that, he was fine. A few days' rest and he'll be as good as new. He did not seem to mind that you stabbed him."

"No?"

The doctor shook his head. "No. It was a point of some pride with him, even though he promised to—and I quote here, Ms. Navárez—'knock off her knobblestone head,' end quote. I believe he meant it too."

"I suppose I'll have to keep an eye out for him," Kira said, trying to sound as if everything were alright. But it wasn't. She could still feel the spines of the

Soft Blade sliding into the Numenist's knotted flesh. *She* had done that. And this time, she couldn't claim ignorance, as with her team on Adra.

"Indeed."

Then they returned to readying the *Wallfish* for departure.

Soon afterward—so soon that it surprised Kira—Falconi was on the line to the UMC cruiser, saying, "We're just waiting on you, *Darmstadt.* Over."

After a moment, First Officer Koyich responded: "Roger that, *Wallfish.* Alpha Team will be there shortly."

"Alpha Team?" Kira asked as Falconi ended the call. They were in the cargo hold, overseeing the last delivery of foodstocks.

He grimaced. "Akawe insisted on having some of his men on board to keep an eye on things. Nothing I could do about it. We'll have to be ready in case they cause trouble."

Nielsen said, "If there's a problem, I'm sure we'll be able to deal with it." She gave Kira a hard glance and then fixed her gaze straight ahead.

Kira hoped she hadn't made an enemy of the first officer. Either way, there wasn't anything she could do about it; the situation was what it was. At least Nielsen wasn't being actively unpleasant toward her.

Alpha Squad arrived a few minutes later: four Marines in exos, towing boxes of equipment wrapped in webbing. Accompanying them were loader bots carrying cryo tubes and several long, plastic crates. The lead Marine jetted over to Falconi, saluted, and said, "Lieutenant Hawes, sir. Permission to come aboard."

"Permission granted," said Falconi. He pointed. "There's room for you in the port hold. Feel free to move whatever you need."

"Sir, yes sir." Then Hawes motioned with one hand, and a loader bot moved to the front, pushing a pallet with a containment bottle suspended from shock-absorbing springs within a metal frame.

Kira resisted the urge to leave. None of the planet-based spaceports she knew of were allowed to sell antimatter. If the magnetic bottle failed, the resulting blast would not only destroy the port (while also setting off the antimatter contained in the other parked ships), but also take out any nearby settlement, town, city, etc. Hell, Earth didn't even allow ships equipped with Markov Drives to land unless they off-loaded their antimatter onto one of several refueling stations in high orbit.

The presence of the containment bottle seemed to make Falconi nervous as well. "Down the hall to the ladder. My machine boss will meet you there," he said to the bot. He gave it a wide berth as it floated past.

"One more thing, sir," said Hawes. "Sanchez! Bring them up!"

From the back came a Marine leading the bots that carried the long, plastic crates. On the sides of the crates were printed or stenciled lines of red text: Cyrillic on top, English below.

The English said *RSW7-Molotók* and was followed by a logo of a star going nova and the name *Lutsenko Defense Industries*^{RM}. And bracketing both the English and the Cyrillic were the black-and-yellow symbols for radiation.

"A gift from Captain Akawe," said Hawes. "They're local-made, so they aren't UMC equipment, but they should do the trick in a pinch."

Falconi nodded, serious. "Stash them over by the door. We'll get them to the launch tubes later."

In an undertone, Kira asked Nielsen, "Are those what I think they are?"

The first officer nodded. "Casaba-Howitzers."

Kira tried to swallow, but her mouth was too dry. The missiles would be packed full of fissionable material, and fission scared her nearly as much as antimatter. It was the dirty, nasty form of nuclear energy. Shut down a fusion reactor, and the only radioactive materials left were those that had been *made* radioactive by neutron bombardment. Shut down a fission reactor, and you had a deadly, possibly explosive pile of unstable elements with a half-life that meant they would stay hazardous for thousands of years.

Kira hadn't even known the ship *had* missile launchers. She ought to have asked Falconi exactly what sort of weapons were installed on the *Wallfish* before they'd gone after the Jelly ship.

The Marines filed past, the thrusters on their suits producing small jets of vapor. Trig, who was next to the captain, stared with big eyes, and Kira could tell he was bursting with questions for the men.

A few minutes later, the Entropists showed up, travel bags in hand.

"Imagine seeing you here again," said Falconi.

"Hey!" said Trig. "Welcome back!"

The Entropists caught hold of a grip on the wall and dipped their heads as best they could. "We are most honored to be here." They looked at Kira, their eyes bright sparks beneath the hoods of their robes. "This is an opportunity for knowledge that we could not possibly decline. None of our order could."

"That's all well and good," said Nielsen. "Just stop talking double. It gives me a headache."

The Entropists again inclined their heads, and then Trig led them off to the cabin where they would be staying.

"You have enough cryo tubes?" Kira asked.

"We do now," said Falconi.

After a flurry of final preparations, the door to the starboard hold was closed and Gregorovich announced in his usual, demented way: "This is your ship mind ssspeaking. Please make sssure all your belongings are sssafely stored in the overhead compartmentsss. Lash yourself to the massst, me hearties: decoupling commencing, RCS thrusting impending. We're off to parts unknown to tweak the nose of fate."

Kira headed to Control, slipped into one of the crash chairs, and strapped herself down. The rest of the crew was there, save Hwa-jung—who was still down in engineering—and Sparrow—who was recovering in sickbay. The Entropists were in their cabin, and Alpha Squad was in the port hold, still locked into their exos.

As the *Wallfish*'s RCS thrusters gently pushed them away from Malpert, keeping its tail end pointed away from the station to avoid frying the dock with residual radiation from the rocket's nozzle, Kira sent a text to Falconi:

<*How did you convince everyone to say yes to this? – Kira*>

<*It took some doing, but they know what's at stake. Besides, we're getting antimatter, pardons, a shot at finding alien tech no one else has seen before. We'd be dumb to turn this down. – Falconi*>

<*Nielsen didn't seem too happy about it. – Kira*>

<*That's just how she is. I'd be surprised if she* were *happy jetting off into the unknown. – Falconi*>

<*What about Gregorovich? – Kira*> If *he'd* disagreed, Kira couldn't see how Falconi would have been able to take the *Wallfish* anywhere.

The captain's fingers started tapping the side of his leg. <*He seems to believe it'll be great fun. His words. – Falconi*>

<*Don't take this the wrong way, but has Gregorovich ever gotten a psych evaluation? It's mandatory for ship minds, isn't it? – Kira*>

Across the room, she saw Falconi make a subtle face. <*Yup. Every six months(ish)—real time—once they're installed in a new ship and then every year after that, assuming their results are stable. . . . We were up against a deadline when we rescued Gregorovich, so it took a while before we got into dock. He'd settled down by then, enough to pass the tests. – Falconi*>

<*He passed?! – Kira*>

<With flying colors. And every one after that. – Falconi> He gave her a sideways glance. *<I know what you're thinking, but ship minds get graded differently than you or I. Their 'normal' is broader than ours. – Falconi>*

She chewed on that for a moment. *<What about a psychiatrist? Has Gregorovich seen anyone to help him with what he went through, being stranded on that moon? – Kira>*

A faint snort from Falconi. *<Do you know how many psychiatrists are qualified to deal with ship minds? Not. Many. Most of them are in Sol, and most of them are ship minds themselves. YOU try analyzing a ship mind and see how far you get. They'll pick you apart and put you back together without you even realizing. It's like a three-year-old trying to play chess with a pseudo-intelligence. – Falconi>*

<So you just do nothing? – Kira>

<I've offered to take Gregorovich in more than once, but he always refuses. – Falconi> A faint rise and fall of his shoulders. *<The best therapy for him is being with other people and being treated like everyone else in the crew. He's a lot better than he used to be. – Falconi>*

That wasn't as reassuring as the captain seemed to think it was. *<And you're okay with him running the ship for you? – Kira>*

Another, sharper glance from Falconi. *<*I* run the* Wallfish, *thank you very much. And yes, I'm very okay with Gregorovich. He's gotten us out of more scrapes than I care to remember, and he's an important and valued member of my crew. Any other questions, Navárez? – Falconi>*

Kira decided it was better not to press her luck, so she gave a tiny shake of her head and switched to the view from the outside cameras.

When the *Wallfish* was a safe distance from Malpert, the thrust alert sounded, and then the main rocket fired. Kira swallowed and let her head fall back against the chair. They were on their way.

2.

The *Darmstadt* followed some hours behind the *Wallfish*. Repairs and the need to take on a rather substantial amount of food for the crew had slowed its departure. Still, the cruiser would catch up with the *Wallfish* by the following morning.

It would take them a day and a half to reach the Markov Limit, and then . . . Kira shivered. And then they would go FTL and leave the League far behind. It was a daunting prospect. Work had often taken her to the very fringes of settled space, but she'd never ventured so far as this. Few people had. There was no good financial reason; only research expeditions and survey missions went out into the vast unknown.

The star they were heading to was an unassuming red dwarf that had only been detected within the past twenty-five years. Remote analysis indicated the presence of at least five planets in orbit, which aligned with what the Soft Blade had shown her, but no sign of technological activity had been picked up by the League's telescopes.

Sixty light-years was a staggeringly enormous distance. It would put a significant strain on both the ships and the crews. The ships would have to pop in and out of FTL numerous times along the way to shed their excess heat, and while it was safe to stay in cryo for far longer than the three months it would take to reach the distant star, the experience would still take its toll on both mind and body.

The toll would be greatest for Kira. She wasn't looking forward to enduring another bout of dreaming hibernation so soon after arriving from Sigma Draconis. Lengthwise, the duration would be similar, as the *Valkyrie* had been far slower than either the *Wallfish* or the *Darmstadt*. Kira just hoped she wouldn't have to starve herself again in order to convince the Soft Blade to induce dormancy.

Thinking about what lay ahead wouldn't make it easier, so she pushed it from her mind. "How is the UMC reacting to us leaving?" she asked, unclasping her harness.

"Not well," said Falconi. "I don't know what Akawe told them back at Vyyborg, but it can't have made them happy, because they're threatening us with all sorts of legal hellfire if we don't turn around."

Gregorovich chuckled, and his laugh echoed through the ship. "It's most amusing, their impotent rage. They seem quite . . . *panicked*."

"Can you blame them?" Nielsen said.

Falconi shook his head. "I'd hate to be the one who has to explain to Sol how and why they lost not only an entire cruiser but also Kira and the suit."

Then Vishal said, "Captain, you should see what's happening on local news."

"What channel?"

"RTC."

Kira switched to her overlays and searched for the channel. It came right up, and in front of her, she saw footage of a ship interior recorded from someone's implants. Screams sounded, and a man's body flew past, collided with another, smaller person. It took Kira a second to realize she was looking at the inside of the *Wallfish*'s hold.

Shit.

A knotted, writhing shape swung into view: a Jelly. The person recording focused on the alien just as it threw something off-screen. Another scream rent the air; *that* scream, Kira remembered.

Then she saw herself fly past, like a black spear from above, and grapple with the Jelly while a long, bladed spike sprang from her skin and impaled the thrashing alien.

The video froze, and in voice-over, a woman said, "Could this battlesuit be a product of the UMC's advanced weapons programs? Possibly. Other passengers confirmed that the woman was rescued from a UMC shuttle a few days before. Which makes us wonder: What *other* technology is the League hiding from us? And then there's this incident from earlier today. Once more, a warning to sensitive viewers: the following footage contains graphic material."

The video resumed, and Kira again saw herself: this time attempting to subdue the purple-haired Numenist. He smashed his head back into her face, and then she stabbed him, not so differently from the Jelly.

From the outside, the sight was more frightening than Kira had realized. No wonder the refugees had looked at her the way they did; she would have also.

The reporter's voice-over returned: "Was this a justifiable use of force or the reaction of a dangerous, out-of-control individual? You decide. Ellen Kaminski was later seen being escorted to the UMCN cruiser the *Darmstadt*, and it seems unlikely she will ever face criminal charges. We attempted to interview the passengers who spoke with her. This was the result—"

The footage resumed, and Kira saw the Entropists being approached in a hallway somewhere on Malpert. "Excuse me. Wait. Excuse me," said the off-screen reporter. "What can you tell us about Ellen Kaminski, the woman who killed the Jelly on the *Wallfish*?"

"We have nothing to say, Prisoner," said Veera and Jorrus together. They ducked their heads, hiding behind the hoods of their robes.

Next Felix Hofer appeared, holding his niece's hand. "The Jelly was going to shoot Nala here. She helped save her. She helped save all of us. As far as I'm concerned, Ellen Kaminski is a hero."

Then the camera cut to the woman Inarë, standing on the space dock, knitting away with a smug look on her face. Her tassel-eared cat peeked around her nest of curly hair from where it lay across her shoulders.

"Who is she?" said Inarë, and smiled in the most unsettling way. "Why, she's the fury of the stars. That's who she is." Then she laughed and turned away. "Goodbye now, little insect."

The reporter's voice-over returned as the image of Kira impaling the Jelly filled the display again. "*The fury of the stars.* Who is this mysterious Ellen Kaminski? Is she a new breed of supersoldier? And what of her battlesuit? Is it an experimental bioweapon? Unfortunately, we may never find out." The view shifted to a close-up of Kira's face, dark-eyed and threatening. "Whatever the truth, we know one thing well-certain, *saya*: the Jellies must fear her. And for that, if nothing else, this reporter is grateful. Fury of the Stars, Starfury—whoever she really is, it's good to know she's fighting on our side. . . . For RTC News, this is Shinar Abosé."

"Goddammit," said Kira, closing her overlays.

"Looks like we're leaving at just the right time," said Falconi.

"Yeah."

Across the room, Trig smirked and said, "Starfury. Ha! Can I call you that now, Ms. Navárez?"

"If you do, I'll hit you."

Nielsen tucked several loose strands of hair back into her ponytail. "This might not be the worst thing. The more people know about you, the more difficult it will be for the League to hide you away and pretend the Soft Blade doesn't exist."

"Maybe," said Kira, unconvinced. She didn't have that much faith in the accountability of governments. If they wanted to disappear her, they would, regardless of public sentiment. Plus, she hated the exposure. It made acting with any sense of anonymity difficult to impossible.

3.

With the *Wallfish* on course and under thrust, the crew dispersed throughout the ship as they continued to ready it for the trip to come. As Trig said, "It's been *ages* since we went superluminal!" There were supplies to reorganize, systems to test and prep, loose objects to store (every pen and cup and blanket and other miscellaneous item the UMC had left out after searching the *Wallfish* had to be secured prior to the extended period of zero-g they were about to embark upon), and scores of tasks, small and large, that needed attending to.

The day was already getting late, but Falconi insisted they prep while they could. "Never know what might happen tomorrow. Could end up with another batch of hostiles breathing down our necks."

His logic was difficult to argue with. At Hwa-jung's request, Kira went to the cargo hold and helped her uncrate the repair bots they'd received from Malpert Station: replacements for the ones lost when they boarded the Jelly ship.

After a few minutes of silence, Hwa-jung glanced over at Kira and said, "Thank you, for killing *that* thing."

"You mean the Jelly?"

"Yes."

"You're welcome. I'm just glad I was able to help."

Hwa-jung grunted. "If you hadn't been there . . ." She shook her head, and Kira saw unaccustomed emotion on the woman's face. "Someday, I buy you soju and beef as a thank-you, and we will get drunk together. You and me and little Sparrow."

"I look forward to it. . . ." Then Kira said, "Are you okay with us going after the Staff of Blue?"

Hwa-jung never slowed as she removed a bot from its packaging. "We will be a long way from space dock if the *Wallfish* breaks. It is good the *Darmstadt* is with us, I think."

"And the mission itself?"

"It needs doing. *Aish.* What else is there to say?"

As they were finishing with the last crate, a text popped up in Kira's vision: <*Come see me in the hydroponics bay when you can. – Falconi*>

<*Be there in five. – Kira*>

She helped Hwa-jung dispose of the excess packaging, and then Kira made her excuses and hurried out of the cargo hold. Once in the main shaft, she said, "Gregorovich, where's the hydro bay?"

"One deck up. End of the corridor, once left, once right, and there you shall be."

"Thanks."

"Bitte."

The scent of flowers greeted Kira as she approached the hydroponics bay—flowers and herbs and algae and all manner of green and growing things. The smells reminded Kira of the greenhouses on Weyland and of her father fussing over his Midnight Constellations. She felt a sudden longing to be outdoors, surrounded by living things, and not trapped in ships that stank of sweat and machine oil.

The aromas multiplied as the pressure door swung open and Kira walked into a bank of humid air. Aisles of hanging plants filled the room, along with dark, sloshing vats that contained the algae cultures. Above, nozzles misted the rows of greenery.

She stopped, struck by the sight. The bay was not unlike the one on Adrasteia, where she and Alan had spent so many hours, including that last, special night, when he had proposed.

Sadness wafted over her, as poignant as any scent.

Falconi stood near the back, bent over a worktable while he trimmed a plant with a drooping, wax-petaled flower—white and delicate—of a sort Kira was unfamiliar with. His sleeves were rolled up to expose his scars.

That Falconi had an interest in gardening wasn't something Kira had expected. Belatedly she remembered the bonsai in his cabin.

"You wanted to see me?" she said.

Falconi clipped a leaf off the plant. Then another. Each time his shears closed with a decisive *snip*. All of the plants had to be reprocessed before entering FTL. They couldn't survive unattended for such a long trip, and moreover, keeping them alive would produce too much waste heat. A few special ones might get put into cryo—she wasn't sure what sort of equipment the *Wallfish* had—but those would be the only ones saved.

Falconi put down the shears and stood with both hands on the worktable. "When you stabbed the Numenist—"

"Bob."

"That's right, Bob the Numenist." Falconi didn't smile, and neither did Kira. "When you stabbed him, was it you or the Soft Blade that did the stabbing?"

"Both, I think."

He grunted. "Can't decide if that makes it better or worse."

Shame twisted Kira's gut. "Look, it was an accident. It won't happen again."

He gave her a low, sideways look. "You sure about that?"

"I—"

"Doesn't matter. We can't afford another *accident* like Bob. I'm not going to let more of my crew get injured, not by the Jellies and sure as hell not by that suit of yours. You hear me?" He fixed her with a stare.

"I hear you."

He didn't seem convinced. "Tomorrow, I want you to go see Sparrow. Talk with her. Do what she tells you. She has some ideas that might help you control the Soft Blade."

Kira shifted her weight, uncomfortable. "I'm not arguing, but Sparrow isn't a scientist. She—"

"I don't think you need a scientist," said Falconi. His brow knotted. "I think you need discipline and structure. I think you need training. You fucked up with the Numenist, and you fucked up on the Jelly ship. If you can't keep that thing of yours on a leash, you need to stay in your quarters from now on, for the sake of everyone."

He wasn't wrong, but his tone rankled her. "How much training do you think I can do? We're leaving Cygni day after tomorrow."

"And you're not going into cryo," Falconi retorted.

"Yes, but—"

His glare intensified. "Do what you can. Go see Sparrow. Sort your shit out. This isn't a debate."

The back of Kira's neck prickled, and she squared her shoulders. "Are you making that an order?"

"Since you asked, yes."

"Is that all?"

Falconi turned back to the workbench. "That's all. Get out of here."

Kira got.

4.

After that, Kira didn't feel much like interacting with the rest of the crew. Not for work and not for dinner.

She retreated to her cabin. With the lights dimmed and her overlays turned off, the room appeared particularly bare, cramped, and shabby. She sat on the bed and stared at the battered walls and found nothing in their appearance to like.

Kira wanted to be angry. She *was* angry, but she couldn't bring herself to blame Falconi. In his place, she would have done the same. Even so, she remained unconvinced that Sparrow could be of any help.

She covered her face with her hands. Part of her wanted to believe that she *wasn't* responsible for answering the compulsion on the Jelly ship or for stabbing Bob the Numenist—that somehow the suit had twisted her mind, acted of its own volition, either out of ignorance or a desire to seed its own destructive mischief.

But she knew better. No one had forced her to do either thing. In both cases, she'd *wanted* to. Blaming her actions on the Soft Blade was only an excuse—an easy out from the harsh reality.

She took a shivering breath.

Not everything had gone wrong, of course. Learning about the Staff of Blue was an unalloyed good, and Kira hoped with every fiber of her being that she hadn't misunderstood and that finding it would lead to a favorable outcome. Even so, the thought did nothing to reduce the guilt that gnawed at her.

Kira couldn't bring herself to rest, tired though she was. Her mind was too active, too wired. Instead, she activated her cabin's console and checked the news on Weyland (it was exactly as Akawe had said) and then started to read everything she could find about the nightmares. It wasn't much. They were so recently arrived both in 61 Cygni and elsewhere, no one had been able to do a proper analysis of them. At least not at the time of the broadcasts that had reached Cygni.

She'd been sitting there for perhaps half an hour when a message from Gregorovich appeared in the corner of her vision:

> *The crew is gathering in the mess hall, if you wish to partake, O Spiky Meatbag. – Gregorovich*

Kira closed the message and kept reading.

Not fifteen minutes later, a loud pounding on the door jolted her. From outside came Nielsen's voice. "Kira? I know you're there. Come join us. You need to eat."

Kira's mouth was so dry, it took her three tries before she was able to muster enough moisture to answer: "No thanks. I'm fine."

"Nonsense. Open up."

". . . No."

Metal clanked and screeched as the wheel outside the pressure door turned, and then the door itself swung open. Kira sat back and crossed her arms, somewhat offended. Out of habit, she'd thrown the privacy lock. No one should have been able to barge in on her, even though she knew half the crew probably could override the lock.

Nielsen entered and looked down at her with an exasperated expression. Defensive, Kira forced herself to meet the woman's gaze.

"Let's go," said Nielsen. "The food's warm. It's just microwaved rations, but you'll feel better with something in you."

"It's okay. I'm not hungry."

Nielsen studied her for a moment and then closed the door to the cabin and—to Kira's surprise—sat on the other end of the bed. "No, it's not okay. How long are you going to stay in here?"

Kira shrugged. The surface of the Soft Blade prickled. "I'm tired, that's all. Just don't want to see anyone."

"Why? What are you afraid of?"

For a moment Kira wasn't going to answer. Then, defiant, she said, "Myself. Alright? Happy now?"

Nielsen seemed unimpressed. "So you screwed up. Everyone screws up. What matters is how you deal with it. Hiding isn't the answer. It never is."

"Yeah, but . . ." Kira had difficulty finding the words.

"But?"

"I don't know if I can control the Soft Blade!" Kira blurted out. There. She'd said it. "If I get angry again or excited or . . . I don't know what might happen and . . ." She trailed off, miserable.

Nielsen snorted. "*Bull*shit. I don't believe you." Shocked, Kira failed to find a response before the first officer said, "You're perfectly capable of eating dinner with us and *not* killing anyone. I know, I know, alien parasite and all that." She gazed at Kira from under her brow. "You lost control because Bob the Numenist broke your nose. That's enough to piss off anyone. No, you shouldn't have stabbed him. And maybe you shouldn't have responded to the signal on the Jelly ship. But you did, it's done, and that's the end of it. You know what to watch out for now, and you won't let it happen again. You're just scared to face everyone. That's what you're afraid of."

"You're wrong. You don't understand wh—"

"I understand plenty. You messed up, and it's hard to go out and look them in the eye. So what? The worst thing you can do is hide here and act like nothing happened. If you want to earn their trust back, come out, take your licks, and I guarantee they'll respect you for it. Even Falconi. Everyone screws up, Kira."

"Not like this," Kira mumbled. "How many people have *you* stabbed?"

Nielsen's expression grew tart. So did her voice: "You think you're so special?"

"I don't see anyone else infected with an alien parasite."

A loud *bang* as Nielsen slapped the wall. Kira jumped, startled. "See, you're fine," said Nielsen. "You didn't stab me. Imagine that. Everyone screws up, Kira. Everyone has their own shit they deal with. If you weren't stuck so far up your own ass, you'd see. Those scars on Falconi's arms? They're not a reward for avoiding mistakes, I can tell you that."

"I . . ." Kira trailed off, ashamed.

Nielsen leveled a finger at her. "Trig hasn't had it easy either. Nor Vishal nor Sparrow nor Hwa-jung. And Gregorovich is just chock-full of wise life decisions." Her mocking tone left no doubt about the actual truth. "Everyone messes up. How you deal with it is what determines who you are."

"What about you?"

"Me? We're not here to talk about me. Pull yourself together, Kira. You're better than this." Nielsen stood.

"Wait. . . . Why do you care?"

For the first time, Nielsen's expression softened, just slightly. "Because that's what we do. We fall down, and then we help each other back up again." The door creaked as she opened it. "Are you coming? The food is still warm."

"Yeah. I'm coming." And though it wasn't easy, Kira got to her feet.

5.

It was well past midnight, but everyone was in the galley except for Sparrow and the Marines. Despite Kira's fears, no one made her feel unwelcome, although she couldn't help feeling that everyone was judging her . . . and that she was lacking. Still, the crew didn't say anything unpleasant, and the only time the subject of the Numenist came up was when Trig made a sideways reference to him, which Kira, taking Nielsen's advice from before, acknowledged in a straightforward manner.

There was some kindness as well. Hwa-jung brought her a cup of tea, and Vishal said, "You come see me tomorrow, yes? I will fix your nose for you."

Falconi snorted. He had barely looked at her. "It's going to hurt like hell if anesthetic doesn't work on you."

"That's alright," said Kira. It wasn't, but pride and a sense of responsibility wouldn't let her admit otherwise.

Everyone seemed exhausted, and for the most part, the galley was silent, each person lost in their own thoughts, eyes focused on overlays.

Kira had just started eating when the Entropists surprised her by sitting in front of her. They leaned in over the top of the table, eager eyes in eager faces: twins with different bodies.

"Yes?" she said.

Veera said, "Prisoner Navárez, we have discovered—"

"—the most exciting thing. As we were making our way across Malpert Station, we—"

"—came across the remains of one of the nightmares and—"

"—we succeeded in taking a tissue sample."

Kira perked up. "Oh?"

The Entropists gripped the edge of the table together. Their fingernails whitened with the pressure. "We have spent all this time—"

"—studying the sample. What it shows—"

"Yes?" she said.

"—what it shows," Jorrus continued, "is that the nightmares—"

"—*don't* share the same genomic makeup as either—"

"—the Soft Blade or the Jellies."

The Entropists sat back, smiling with evident delight at their discovery.

Kira put down her fork. "Are you telling me there are *no* similarities?"

Veera bobbed her head. "Similarities, yes, but—"

"—only similarities born of basic chemical necessity. Otherwise, the entities are entirely unalike."

That confirmed Kira's initial, instinctual reaction, but still, she wondered. "One of the nightmares had tentacles. I saw it. What about that?"

The Entropists nodded together, as if pleased. "Yes. In form familiar, but in substance, foreign. You may have also seen—"

"—arms and legs and eyes and fur and other—"

"—growths reminiscent of Earth-based life. But the nightmare we examined contained—"

"—no closeness to Terran DNA."

Kira stared at the pile of soggy rations on her plate as she thought. "What *are* they, then?"

A paired shrug from the Entropists. "Unknown," said Jorrus. "Their underlying biological structure appears—"

"—unformed, incomplete, contradictory—"

"—malignant."

"Huh. . . . Can I see your results?"

"Of course, Prisoner."

She looked back up at them. "Have you shared this with the *Darmstadt* yet?"

"We just sent over our files."

"Good." Akawe should know the sorts of creatures they were dealing with.

The Entropists returned to their own table, and Kira slowly continued eating as she scoured the documents they'd sent her. It amazed her the amount of data they'd been able to gather without a proper lab. The tech built into their robes was *seriously* impressive.

She paused when the four Marines showed up in their drab olive greens. Even out of power armor, the men were imposing. Their bodies bulged and rippled with unnatural levels of lean muscle; living anatomy charts that screamed of strength, power, and speed—their physiques the result of a whole suite of genetic tweaks the military employed in their frontline troops. Even though none of them looked like they had grown up in high-g, like Hwa-jung, Kira had no doubt they were just as strong, if not more so. They reminded her of pictures she'd seen of animals with myostatin deficiencies. Hawes, Sanchez . . . she didn't know the names of the other two.

The Marines didn't stay to eat, just heated water for tea or coffee, grabbed a few snacks, and left. "Won't be getting in your way, Captain," said Hawes on the way out.

Falconi gave them a casual salute.

The technical details of the nightmares' biology were deep and varied, and Kira found herself lost in the more obscure points. Everything the Entropists had said was true, but they had barely begun to capture the sheer *weirdness* of the nightmares. By comparison, the Jellies, with all their genetic manipulation, were positively straightforward. But the nightmares . . . Kira had never seen anything resembling them. She kept stumbling across snatches of chemical sequences that *seemed* familiar, but only seemed. The cellular structure of the nightmares wasn't even stable, and as for how *that* was possible, she hadn't the slightest idea.

Her plate had long been empty, and she was still reading when a glass thumped down next to her plate, causing her to jump.

Falconi stood next to her, holding a bouquet of glasses in one hand and several bottles of red wine in the other. Without asking, he filled her glass halfway. "Here."

Then he walked around, handing out glasses to the crew and Entropists, and filling them.

Finished, he lifted his own glass. "Kira. Things didn't work out how any of us expected, but if it weren't for you, there's a good chance we'd all be dead. Yeah, it's been a rough day. Yeah, you ticked off every Jelly from here to kingdom come. And yeah, we're racing off to god knows where because of you." He paused, his gaze steady. "But we're alive. *Trig* is alive. *Sparrow* is alive. And we have you to thank for that. So this toast is for you, Kira."

At first no one else joined in. Then Nielsen reached out and lifted her own glass. "Hear, hear," she said, and the others echoed her.

An unexpected film of tears blurred Kira's vision. She raised her wine and mumbled thanks. For the first time, she didn't feel quite so horribly out of place on the *Wallfish.*

"And in the future, let's not do any of this again," said Falconi, sitting down. A few chuckles followed.

Kira eyed her drink. *Half a glass.* Not too much. She downed it in a single motion and then sat back, curious what would happen.

Across the mess hall, Falconi gave her a wary look.

A minute passed. Five minutes. Ten. And still Kira felt nothing. She made a face, disgusted. After the abstinence of the past few months, she ought to have gotten at least a *slight* buzz.

But no. The Soft Blade was suppressing the effects of the alcohol. Even if she'd wanted to get drunk, she couldn't.

It shouldn't have, but the realization angered Kira. "Damn you," she muttered. No one—not even the Soft Blade—ought to be able to dictate what she could do with her body. If she wanted to get a tattoo or become fat or have a kid or do anything else, then she damn well ought to have that freedom. Without the opportunity, she was nothing more than a slave.

Her anger made her want to march over, grab a wine bottle, and drink the whole thing in a single go. Just to force the issue. Just to prove that she *could.*

But she didn't. After what had happened that day, it terrified her to think of what the Soft Blade might do if she were drunk. And then too, she didn't want to get hammered. Not really.

So she didn't ask for more wine, content to hold and wait and not to tempt misfortune. And Kira noticed that although Falconi poured out a second round for everyone else, he didn't offer one to her. He understood, and she was grateful, if still a little resentful. Dangerous or not, she wanted the *choice.*

"Anyone want the rest?" Falconi asked, holding up the last bottle. It was still about a quarter full.

Hwa-jung took it from him. "Me. I will. I have extra enzymes." The crew chuckled, and Kira felt relieved that she no longer had to think about the wine.

She turned the stem of the glass between her fingers, and a faint smile crept onto her face. With it she felt a sense of lightness. Nielsen had been right; it was good she'd come out to face the crew. Hiding hadn't been the answer.

It was a lesson she needed to remember.

6.

A green light was glowing at the desk console when Kira finally arrived back at her cabin, late that night. She stubbed her toe on the corner of the bed as she walked to the desk. "Ow," she muttered, more out of reflex than any actual pain.

As expected, the message was from Gregorovich:

> *I know what you can do, but still I know not what you are. Again, I ask and asking wonder: what are you, O Multifarious Meatbag? – Gregorovich*

She blinked and then typed her response.

> *I am what I am. – Kira*

His reply was nearly instantaneous:

> *Bah. How pedestrian. How boring. – Gregorovich*

> *Tough. Sometimes we don't get what we want. – Kira*

> *Heave and bluster, boil and froth; you can't conceal the void within your words. If knowledge were yours, then confidence too. But 'tisn't, so isn't. Cracked the pedestal, and perilous the statue that stands above. – Gregorovich*

> *Blank verse? Seriously? Is that the best you can do? – Kira*

A long pause followed, and for the first time, she felt as if she'd one-upped him. Then:

Amusements are hard to find when one finds oneself bounded in a nutshell. – Gregorovich

And yet, you might rightly be counted as a king of infinite space. – Kira

Were it not that I have bad dreams. – Gregorovich

Were it not for the bad dreams. – Kira

. . . – Gregorovich

She tapped a fingernail against the console.

It's not easy, is it? – Kira

Why should it be? Nature has no regard for those who squirm and crawl within its tainted depths. The storm that batters, batters all. None are spared. Not you, not I, not the stars in the sky. We bind our cloaks and bend our heads and focus on our lives. But the storm, it never breaks, never fades. – Gregorovich

Cheery. Thinking about it doesn't really help, does it? The best we can do is, as you said, bend our heads and focus on our lives. – Kira

So don't think. Be a sleeper devoid of dreams. – Gregorovich

Maybe I will. – Kira

That doesn't change the fact, the question yet remains: What are you, O Queen of Tentacles? – Gregorovich

Call me that again and I'll find a way to put hot sauce in your nutrient bath. – Kira

An empty promise from an empty voice. The fearful mind cannot accept its limits. It shrieks and flees before admitting ignorance, unable to face the threat to its identity. – Gregorovich

You don't know what you're talking about. – Kira

Deny, deny, deny. It matters not. The truth of what you are will out, regardless. When it does, the choice is yours: believe or don't believe. I care not which. **I**, *for one, shall be prepared, whatever the answer may be. Until that time, I'll spend my hours in watching you, watching most intently, O Formless One. – Gregorovich*

Watch all you like. You won't find what you're looking for. – Kira

She closed the display with a flick of her finger. To her relief, the green light stayed dull and dead. The ship mind's banter had left her unsettled. Still, she was glad she'd held her ground. Despite his assertions, Gregorovich was wrong. She knew who she was. She just didn't know what the damn suit was. Not really.

Enough. She'd had *enough*.

She removed the Entropists' gemlike token from her pocket and slipped it into the desk drawer. It would be safer there than if she carried it around everywhere. Then, with a grateful sigh, she peeled off her torn clothes. A quick scrub with a wet towel, and she fell into the bunk and wrapped herself in a blanket.

For a time, Kira couldn't stop her mind from cycling. Images of the Jellies and the dead nightmare kept intruding, and at times Kira imagined she could smell the acrid scent Falconi's grenades produced when they exploded. Again and again she felt the Soft Blade sliding into the flesh of the Jelly, and then that became confused with her memory of stabbing the Numenist and of Alan dead in her arms. . . . So many mistakes. So very many mistakes.

It was a struggle, but in the end, she managed to fall asleep. And despite what she'd said to Gregorovich, Kira dreamed, and while she dreamed, there came to her another vision:

In the golden light of summer's eve, the sounds of shrieking filled the hungry forest. She sat upon a prominence, watching the play of life among the purple trees while awaiting the expected return of her companions.

Below, a centipede-like creature scurried forth from the gloom-shrouded underbrush and darted into a burrow beneath a clump of roots. Chasing it was a long-armed, snake-necked, sloth-bodied predator with a head like a toothed worm and legs that jointed backward. The hunter snapped at the burrow, but too slow to catch its prey.

Frustrated, the snake-necked sloth sat on its haunches and tore with hooked and knobbled fingers at the earthen hole, hissing from its slitted mouth.

It dug and dug, growing more agitated the whole while. The roots were hard, the ground rocky, and little progress was made. Then the hunter reached into the burrow with one long finger, attempting to scoop out the centipede.

A screech rang forth as the snake-necked sloth yanked back its hand. Blackish blood dripped from finger's end.

The creature howled, though not with pain but with anger. It thrashed its head and trampled across the underbrush, crushing fronds and flowers and fruiting bodies. Again it howled, and then it grabbed the nearest trunk and shook it with such force, the tree swayed.

A crack echoed among the sweltering forest, and a cluster of spiked seed pods fell from the canopy and struck the sloth on the head and shoulders. It yelped and collapsed into the dirt, where it lay twitching and kicking while foam formed at the corners of its gaping maw.

In time, the kicking stopped.

Later still, the centipede-like creature ventured forth from its burrow, slow and timid. It climbed onto the slack neck of the sloth and sat there, feelers twitching. Then it bent and began to eat the soft meat of the throat.

. . .

Another of the now familiar disjunctions. She was crouched next to a tidal pool, shadowed from the heat of the harsh sun by a spur of volcanic rock. In the pool floated a translucent orb no bigger than her thumb.

The orb was not alive. But it was not dead. It was a thing in between. A potential unrealized.

She watched with hope, waiting for the moment of transformation, when potential might become actuality.

There. A soft movement of light from within, and the orb pulsed as if taking its first tentative breath. Happiness and wonder replaced hope at the gift of first life. What had been done would change all the fractures to follow, first here and then—given time and fortune—in the great whirl of stars beyond.

And she saw it was good.

CHAPTER XII

* * * * * * *

LESSONS

1.

Kira felt surprisingly well rested when she woke.

A thick layer of dust fell from her body as she sat up. She stretched and spat out the few grains that fell into her mouth. The dust tasted like slate.

She started to stand and realized she was sitting in a hole in the bedding. During the night, the Soft Blade had absorbed most of the blanket and mattress, as well as part of the composite frame beneath. Only a few centimeters of material still separated her from the reclamation equipment below.

Kira guessed the xeno must have needed to replenish itself after fighting the previous day. In fact, it felt thicker, as if it was adapting in response to the threats they'd faced. The fibers on her chest and forearms in particular seemed harder, more robust.

The responsiveness of the suit continued to impress her. "You know we're at war, don't you?" she murmured.

She turned on her console to find a message waiting for her:

Come see me once you're up. – Sparrow

Kira made a face. She wasn't looking forward to whatever Sparrow had planned for her. If it could help with the Soft Blade, then great, but Kira wasn't convinced. Still, if she wanted to avoid antagonizing Falconi, then she had to play along, and she *did* need to figure out a better way to control the xeno. . . .

She closed Sparrow's text and wrote to Gregorovich instead:

My bed and blankets need to be replaced. The suit ate through them last night. If it's not too much trouble for a ship mind such as yourself, of course. – Kira

His reply was nearly instantaneous. Sometimes she envied the speed with which ship minds could think, but then she remembered how much she liked having a body.

Perhaps you should try feeding your ravenous leech something better than a smorgasbord of polycarbonates. It simply CAN'T be good for a growing parasite. – Gregorovich

Have any suggestions? – Kira

Why yes, yes I do. If your charming little symbiont insists upon chewing on my bones, I'd rather it be somewhere away from needed systems like oh, say, life support. In the machine room, we have raw stock for printing and repairs. Something in there should appeal to the palate of your alien overlord. Check with Hwa-jung; she can show you where it is. – Gregorovich

Kira raised her eyebrows. He was actually trying to be helpful, even if he couldn't stop insulting her.

Why thank you. I'll be sure to save you from immediate disintegration when my alien overlords take over the system. – Kira

Ahahaha. Truly, that's the funniest thing I've heard this century. You're killing me here. . . . Why don't you go cause some trouble, like a good monkey? That seems to be what you're best at. – Gregorovich

She rolled her eyes and closed the window. Then—after dressing in her old jumpsuit and taking a moment to gather her thoughts—she activated the display camera and recorded a message for her family, much as she had on the *Valkyrie*. Only this time, Kira made no attempt to hide the truth. "We found an alien artifact on Adrasteia," she said. "*I* found it, actually." She told them everything that had happened from then on, including the attack on the *Extenuating Circumstances.* Now that the existence of the Soft Blade was public knowledge, Kira saw no point in keeping the details from her family, no matter how the UMC or the League might have classified the information.

Following that, she recorded a similar message for Alan's brother.

Her eyes were full of tears by the time she finished. She allowed them to flow freely, and then wiped her cheeks dry with the heels of her hands.

Accessing the *Wallfish*'s transmitter, she queued the two messages for delivery to 61 Cygni's nearest FTL relay.

There was a good chance the League would intercept any signals from the *Wallfish.* There was an equally good chance that the Jellies were jamming her home system (as they had 61 Cygni) and that the message for her family wouldn't get through. But she had to try. And Kira took some comfort in knowing that a record of her words existed. As long as they remained preserved somewhere in the circuits and memory banks of the League's computers, they might eventually reach their intended recipients.

Either way, she'd fulfilled her responsibility as best she could, and it was a weight off her mind.

She spent the next few minutes writing an account of the most recent dream from the Soft Blade. Then—resigned to what she felt sure was going to be an unpleasant experience with Sparrow—she hurried out of the cabin and headed toward the galley.

As she descended along the central ladder, Kira felt a sharp pain in her lower abdomen. She sucked in her breath, surprised, and stopped where she was.

That was odd.

She waited a little while but didn't feel anything else. An upset stomach from the food the previous night or a small muscle strain, she guessed. Nothing to worry about.

She continued climbing.

At the galley, she set water to boil and then texted Vishal: *<Does Sparrow prefer tea or coffee? – Kira>* She figured she couldn't go wrong by starting off with a peace offering.

The doctor answered just as the water boiled: *<Coffee, and the blacker the better. – Vishal>*

<Thanks. – Kira>

She made two cups: one chell, and one double-strength coffee. Then she carried the mugs to sickbay and knocked on the pressure door.

"Mind if I come in?"

"Door's unlocked," said Sparrow.

Kira pushed it open with her shoulder, careful not to spill the drinks.

Sparrow was sitting upright on the infirmary bed, perfectly manicured hands folded across her belly, a holo-display open in front of her. She didn't look too bad, considering; her skin actually had some color, and her eyes were sharp and alert. Several layers of bandages wrapped her waist, and a small, square machine was clipped to the top of her pants.

"I was wondering when you'd show up," she said.

"Is this a bad time?"

"It's the only time we've got."

Kira held out the mug with the two shots. "Vishal said you like coffee."

Sparrow accepted the mug. "Mmm. I do. Although it makes me pee, and going to the bathroom is a pain in the ass right now. Literally."

"Do you want chell instead? I have some."

"No." Sparrow inhaled the steam wafting from the coffee. "No, this is perfect. Thank you."

Kira pulled over the doctor's stool and sat. "How are you feeling?"

"Good, considering." Sparrow grimaced. "My side itches like crazy, and the doc says there's nothing he can do about it. Plus, I can't digest food properly. He's been feeding me through a drip."

"Is he going to be able to patch you up before we leave?"

Sparrow took another sip. "Surgery is scheduled for tonight." She looked at Kira. "Thanks for stopping that Jelly, by the way. I owe you."

"You would have done the same," said Kira.

The small, hard-faced woman smirked. "Suppose I would have. Might not have done any good without your xeno. You're one scary mofo when you're angry."

The praise sat badly with Kira. "I just wish I could have gotten there faster."

"Don't beat yourself up about it." Sparrow smiled more openly. "We gave those Jellies a hell of a surprise, eh?"

"Yeah . . . You heard about the nightmares?"

"Sure did." Sparrow gestured at the display. "I was just reading the reports. Real shame what happened to Ruslan's beanstalk. If only they'd had a proper defense network, they might have been able to save it."

Kira blew on her chell. "You were in the UMC, weren't you?"

"UMCM, technically. Fourteenth division, Europa Command. Seven years enlisted. Ooh-rah, baby."

"That's how you got MilCom access."

"You know it. Used my lieutenant's old login." A feral smile crossed Sparrow's lips. "He was a bastard anyway." She cleared the display with an unnecessarily violent swipe. "They really should change those codes more often."

"So now you work security. Is that it? You don't just pick things up and put them down."

"No, not really." Sparrow scratched her side. "Most days it's pretty boring. Eat, shit, sleep, repeat. Sometimes it's more exciting. Knock a few heads together, cover Falconi's back when he's making deals, keep an eye on the cargo when we're docked. That sort of thing. It's a living. Beats sitting in a VR tank, waiting to get old."

Kira could relate. She'd felt much the same when deciding to pursue xenobiology as a career.

"And every *once* in a while," said Sparrow, bright fire kindling in her eyes, "you end up at the pointy end of the knife, like we did yesterday, and then you get to find out what you're made of. Don't you?"

"Yes."

Sparrow studied her, serious. "Speaking of knocking heads together, I saw the video of what you did to Bob."

Another small, quick pain lanced her abdomen. Kira ignored it. "You knew him?"

"I *met* him. Vishal had him in here, pissing and moaning while he got stitched up. . . . So what went wrong in the hold?"

"Falconi must have told you."

Sparrow shrugged. "Sure, but I'd rather hear it from you."

The surface of Kira's chell was dark and oily. On it, she could see her face in a warped reflection. "Short version? I got hurt. I wanted it to stop. I lashed out. Or rather the Soft Blade lashed out for me. . . . It's sometimes hard to tell the difference."

"Were you angry? Did Bob's idiot maneuver get under your skin?"

". . . Yeah. It did."

"Uh-huh." Sparrow caught her gaze by pointing at Kira's face. "That nose of yours must have caused you all *sorts* of pain when it broke."

She touched it, self-conscious. "Have you broken yours?"

"Three times. Got it straightened out, though."

Kira struggled to find the right words. "Look . . . Don't take this the wrong way, Sparrow, but I really don't see how you can help me with the xeno. I'm here because Falconi insisted, but—"

Sparrow cocked her head. "Do you know what the military does?"

"I—"

"Let me tell you. The military accepts everyone who volunteers, assuming they meet the basic requirements. That means, at one end of the spectrum, you get people who would just as soon cut your throat as shake your hand. And at the other end of the spectrum, you get people so timid they wouldn't hurt a fly. And what the military does is teach both of them *how* and *when* to apply violence. That, and how to take orders.

"A trained Marine doesn't go around stabbing guys just because they broke their nose. That would be a disproportionate use of force. You pull a stunt like that in the UMC, and you'll be *lucky* to get court-martialed. And that's if you don't get yourself or your team killed. Losing your temper is a cop-out. A *cheap* cop-out. You don't get to lose your temper. Not when lives are on the line. Violence is a tool. Nothing more, nothing less. And its use should be as carefully calibrated as . . . as the cuts of a surgeon's scalpel."

Kira raised an eyebrow. "You sound more like a philosopher than a fighter."

"What, you think all jarheads are stupid?" Sparrow chuckled before going serious again. "All good soldiers are philosophers, same as a priest or a professor. You have to be when you deal with matters of life and death."

"Did you see any action when you were in the service?"

"Oh yeah." She eyed Kira. "You think the galaxy is a peaceful place, and it is, for the most part. Ignoring the Jellies, your odds of getting hurt or killed in a violent encounter are lower now than at any other time in history. And yet more people are actually *fighting*—fighting and dying—than ever before. You know why?"

"Because there are more people alive now," said Kira.

"Bingo. The percentages have gotten lower, but the overall numbers keep going up." Sparrow shrugged. "So yeah. We saw a *lot* of action."

Kira took her first sip of chell. It was rich and warm, with a spicy aftertaste like cinnamon. Her belly was hurting again, and she rubbed it without thinking. "Alright. But I still don't see how you can help me control the suit."

"I probably can't. But I might be able to help you control yourself, and that's the next best thing."

"We don't have a lot of time."

Sparrow thumped herself on the chest. "*I* don't. But you're going to have a whole hell of a lot of time while the rest of us are stuck in cryo."

"And I'm going to spend most of it sleeping."

"Most, not all." Sparrow flashed a quick grin. "That gives you a real opportunity, Navárez. You can practice. You can better yourself. And ain't that what we all want? To be the best we can be?"

Kira gave her a skeptical look. "That sounds like a recruitment slogan."

"Yeah well, maybe it is," said Sparrow. "So sue me." She gingerly swung her legs over the edge of the exam table and slid down to the floor.

"You need help?"

Sparrow shook her head and, with a wince, straightened her posture. "I can manage. Thanks." She picked up a crutch next to the bed. "So have I recruited you or not?"

"I don't think I have much of a choice, but—"

"Sure you do."

"But yes, I'm willing to give it a shot."

"Out*standing*," said Sparrow. "That's what I wanted to hear!" And she swung forward on her crutch and headed out of sickbay. "This way!"

Kira shook her head, put down her cup, and followed.

At the central shaft, Sparrow slid an arm through the center of the crutch and started to climb down the ladder, careful in her movements. She grimaced with obvious discomfort. "Thank god for painkillers," she said.

Down the shaft they went, to the bottom deck. There, Sparrow led Kira into the port cargo hold.

Kira hadn't seen much of it before. It mirrored the layout of the starboard hold, the main difference being the racks of supplies and equipment bolted to the floor. The four Marines had taken over a section between the aisles. There, they'd set up their suits of power armor, as well as their cryo tubes, sleeping bags, and various hard-cases of weapons and Thule knew what else.

At the moment, Hawes was doing pull-ups on a bar placed between two of the racks while the other three Marines were practicing throws and disarms on a patch of clear deck. They paused and straightened up when they noticed Kira and Sparrow.

"Yo, yo," said one of the men. He had thick, dark eyebrows and lines of blue script in some language Kira didn't recognize tattooed up and down the muscles of his bare arms. The tattoos shifted as he moved, like long waves on water. He pointed at Sparrow. "You were the one what got perforated by the Jelly, yeah?"

"That's right, Marine."

Then he pointed at Kira. "And you were the one what perforated the Jelly right quick, yeah?"

Kira dipped her head. "Yeah."

For a moment she wasn't sure how the man was going to react. Then he broke into a big smile. His teeth glittered with implanted nanowires. "Well done. Most excellent!" He gave them both a big thumbs-up.

One of the other Marines approached them. He was shorter, with huge shoulders and hands nearly as big as Hwa-jung's. Looking at Kira, he said, "That means you're the reason we're off on this crazy-ass trip."

She lifted her chin. "Afraid so."

"Hey, not complaining. If it gets us the jump on the Jellies, I'm all for it. You convinced old man Akawe, so you're good by me." He held out one of his paw-like hands. "Corporal Nishu."

Kira shook. His grip felt like it could crush rocks. "Kira Navárez."

The corporal jerked his chin toward the tattooed Marine. "This ugly lug is Private Tatupoa. That one over there is Sanchez"—he pointed at a thin-faced Marine with mournful eyes—"and of course you met the lieutenant."

"Yes I did." Kira shook with Tatupoa and Sanchez, and said, "Pleased to meet you. Glad you're on board." She wasn't sure if she was, but it was the right thing to say.

Sanchez said, "Any idea what to expect when we arrive at this system, ma'am?"

"The Staff of Blue, I hope," said Kira. "Sorry I can't tell you any more. That's all I know myself."

Then Hawes came over. "Alright, that's enough, everyone. Let the ladies be. I'm sure they're busy."

Nishu and Tatupoa gave them salutes and went back to grappling while Sanchez watched from the side.

Sparrow started past, and then she paused and looked at Tatupoa. "You're doing it wrong, by the way," she said.

The man blinked. "Excuse me, ma'am?"

"When you tried to throw him." She indicated the corporal.

"I think we know what we're after, ma'am. No offense."

"You should listen to her," said Kira. "She was in the UMCM also."

Next to her, Sparrow stiffened, and Kira had a sudden feeling she'd made a mistake.

Hawes stepped forward. "That so, ma'am? Where'd you serve?"

"Doesn't matter," said Sparrow. To the man with the tattoos, she said, "Your weight needs to be more on your front foot. Step forward like you mean it and pivot, hard. You'll feel the difference immediately."

Then Sparrow continued on her way, leaving the four Marines looking after her with a combination of bemusement and speculation.

"Sorry about that," said Kira once they were out of sight.

Sparrow grunted. "As I said, doesn't matter." The tip of her crutch caught on the side of a shelving unit, and she yanked it free. "Over here."

Buried at the back of the hold, past the crates of rations and pallets of equipment, Kira saw three things: a treadmill (rigged up for use in zero-g), an exercise machine (all cables and pulleys and angled grips) of the sort she'd used on the *Fidanza,* and to her surprise, a full set of free weights (dumbbells and barbells and anchored piles of weighted disks—giant poker chips colored red, green, blue, and yellow). When every kilo cost you in propellant, every kilo became precious. The gym was a minor extravagance of a sort Kira hadn't expected to find on the *Wallfish*.

"Yours?" she asked, gesturing at the weights.

"Yuh-huh," said Sparrow. "And Hwa-jung's. Takes a lot to keep her fit in one g." With a huff, she lowered herself onto the bench and stretched her left leg out in front. She pressed a hand against her side, over the bandages. "You know the worst part about being injured?"

"Not being able to work out?"

"Bingo." Sparrow gestured at her body. "This doesn't happen by accident, you know."

There was nowhere else to sit, so Kira squatted next to the bench. "Really? Didn't you get gene-hacked like those guys?" She motioned back toward the Marines. "I read somewhere that with the tweaks you get in the UMC, you can sit around eating whatever you want and still be in shape."

"It's not quite that easy," said Sparrow. "You still have to do cardio if you don't want to get gassed. And you still have to work hard if you want to build top-end strength. Gene-hacks help, but they sure as fuck ain't magic. As for those apes . . . there are degrees. Not everyone gets the same mods. Our guests are what are called R-Sevens. Means they got the full set of augments. You gotta volunteer for 'em, though, as it ain't healthy long term. The UMC won't let you run like that for more than fifteen years, tops."

"Huh. I didn't know," said Kira. She looked back at the weights. "So why are we here? What's the plan?"

Sparrow scratched the side of her bladelike jaw. "Haven't you figured it out? You're going to lift weights."

"I'm what?"

The short-haired woman chuckled. "Here's the deal, Navárez. I don't know you particularly well. But I *do* know that every time you screw up with the xeno, it seems to be when you're stressed. Fear. Anger. Frustration. That sort of thing. Am I wrong?"

"No."

"Right. So the name of the game is discomfort. We're going to impose some carefully calibrated stress, and we're going to see what that does to you and the Soft Blade. Okay?"

". . . Okay," said Kira, cautious.

Sparrow pointed at the exercise machine. "We'll start simple-like, since that's all I can count on from you."

Kira wanted to argue . . . but the woman had a point. So Kira swallowed her pride and sat. One by one, Sparrow talked her through a series of lifts, testing her strength and the strength of the Soft Blade. First on the machine, and then with the free weights.

The results, Kira thought, were impressive. With the Soft Blade's help, she was able to move nearly as much as a heavy exoskeleton. Her relative lack of mass was the greatest limiting factor; the slightest wobble of the weight threatened to unbalance her.

Sparrow didn't seem much pleased. As Kira struggled to squat a bar loaded with an absurd number of plates, the woman *tsked* and said, "Shit, you really don't know what you're doing." With a growl, Kira straightened her legs and dumped the bar onto the waiting rack and then glared at Sparrow. "The suit's protecting you from your bad form."

"So tell me what I'm doing wrong," said Kira.

"Sorry, buttercup. Not what we're here for today. Put another twenty kilos on, then try to use the suit to brace against the floor. Like a tripod."

Kira tried. She really did, but the weight was more than her knees could withstand, and she wasn't able to split her attention between the Soft Blade and the effort of balancing a bar that was more than heavy enough to kill her. She could stiffen the material around her legs—that much she could do—but extruding any sort of support at the same time was beyond her, and the xeno didn't seem inclined to provide additional help on its own.

Quite the opposite, in fact. Beneath her jumpsuit, Kira felt the suit shifting and forming spikes in response to the strain. She tried to still herself (and by extension, the suit) but was only partially successful.

"Yeah," said Sparrow as Kira racked the bar. "That's what I thought. Okay, over here, on the mat."

Kira obeyed, and the moment she was in place, Sparrow threw a small, hard object at her. Without thinking, Kira ducked, and at the same time, the Soft Blade lashed out with a pair of tendrils and smacked away whatever the object was.

Sparrow dropped flat on the bench, a small blaster appearing in her hands. All emotion had vanished from her face, replaced by the flat-eyed intensity of someone about to fight for their life.

In that instant, Kira realized the woman's bravado was just that—a cover—and that she was treating Kira with the same caution as a live grenade.

The skin around Sparrow's eyes tightened with pain as she pushed herself back up. "As I said, you need practice. Discipline." She tucked the blaster into a pocket in her slacks.

By the bulkhead, Kira saw what Sparrow had thrown at her: a white therapy ball.

"Sorry," said Kira. "I—"

"Don't bother, Navárez. We know what the problem is. That's why you're here. That's what we have to fix."

Kira ran a hand over the curve of her skull. "You can't fix the instinct for self-preservation."

"Oh yes we can!" Sparrow snapped. "That's what separates us from the animals. We can *choose* to go out and march for thirty klicks with a heavy ruck on our back. We can *choose* to put up with all sorts of unpleasant shit because we know our tomorrow selves will thank us for it. Doesn't matter what kind of mental gymnastics you have to pull in that mush you call a brain, but there is sure as shit a way to keep from overreacting when you get surprised. For fuck's sake, I saw Marines out drinking their morning coffee while our point-defense was picking off an ass-load of incoming missiles, and they were the *coolest, calmest* motherfuckers I ever saw. Had a little poker game going with bets to see how many missiles would get through. So if they could do it, you sure as hell can, even if you *are* bonded with an alien parasite."

Somewhat abashed, Kira nodded, took a breath, and with a concerted effort, smoothed the last few bumps on the Soft Blade. "You're right."

Sparrow jerked her head. "You're damn right I'm right."

Then just because, Kira asked, "What sort of drugs did Vishal pump into you?"

"Not enough, that's for sure. . . . Let's try something different."

Then Sparrow put her on the treadmill and had her alternate between running sprints and attempting to coax the Soft Blade into performing certain tasks (mainly reshaping itself according to Sparrow's instructions). Kira found she couldn't concentrate past her panting and the pounding of her heart; the distractions were too great, and they kept her from imposing her will upon the Soft Blade. Moreover, sometimes the xeno would attempt to interpret what she wanted—like an overeager assistant—which usually resulted in it shooting out farther than she intended. But fortunately not with blades or spikes, and not so far as to endanger Sparrow (who nevertheless stayed as far away as the meager area would allow).

For over an hour, the ex-Marine worked Kira over, testing her as thoroughly as Vishal and Carr had. But not just testing, training. She pushed Kira to explore the limits of the Soft Blade and of her interface with the alien organism, and when she found those limits, to strain against them until they widened.

Throughout, Kira kept feeling the odd pains in her abdomen. They were starting to concern her.

One thing Sparrow had her do that Kira hated: poke herself in the arm with the tip of a knife and attempt, with each poke, to keep the Soft Blade from hardening in protection.

As Sparrow said, "If you can't withstand a bit of discomfort for future gain, you're pretty much a waste of space."

So Kira kept stabbing her arm, biting her lip the whole while. It wasn't easy. The Soft Blade insisted upon squirming out of her mental grasp and stopping or diverting the descending blade. "Stop that," she finally muttered, fed up. She stabbed again, only not at her arm, but at the Soft Blade, wishing she could cause it the same pain it had caused her.

"Hey! Watch it!" Sparrow said.

Kira looked to see a spray of jagged thorns extending half a meter from her arm. "Ah! Shit!" she exclaimed, retracting the thorns fast as possible.

Her expression grim, Sparrow scooted the bench back another few centimeters. "Not good, Navárez. Try again."

And Kira did. And it hurt. And it was hard. But she didn't give up.

2.

Kira was sore, sweaty, and hungry by the time Sparrow called a halt to the proceedings. And she wasn't only tired in body but in mind; contending with the xeno for so long was no easy matter. Nor had it been much of a success, which bothered her more than she liked to admit.

"It was a start," said Sparrow.

"You didn't have to push quite so hard," Kira said, wiping her face. "You could have gotten hurt."

"Someone already *did* get hurt," said Sparrow in a cutting tone. "I'm just trying to keep it from happening again. Seems to me we pushed just hard enough."

Kira glared at her. "You must have been real popular with your squad in the Marines."

"Let me tell you what it was like. This one time in training, there was this dumbfuck from Stewart's World. Berk was his name. We were doing a stint on Earth—you ever visit Earth?"

"No."

Sparrow half shrugged. "It's a crazy place. Beautiful, but there's living things wanting to kill you everywhere you go, just like Eidolon. Anyway, we were doing a manual-fire drill. That means no implants or overlays to help. Berk was having a rough go of it, and then he finally gets in the groove and starts hitting his targets. *Bam,* his gun jams.

"He tried to clear the blockage, but nothing doing. Thing is, Berk had a temper like an overheated kettle. He's swearing and kicking, and he gets so worked up, he throws his gun into the dirt."

"Even *I* know better than that," said Kira.

"Exactly. Our range master and three drill sergeants descend on Berk like the four horsemen of the apocalypse. They chew him a new one, and then they have him pick up his rifle and march across the camp. Now, out by the back of the dispensary there was a hornet's nest. Ever been stung by a hornet?"

Kira shook her head. She had lots of experience with bees on Weyland, but no hornets. They hadn't been cleared by the colony terraforming board.

A faint smile curled Sparrow's lips. "They're little bullets of hate and fury. Hurt like a sumbitch too. So Berk is ordered to stand underneath the hornet nest and poke it with his rifle. And *then,* while the hornets do their best to sting him to death, he had to clear the jam in his gun, strip it, give it a good field cleaning, and put it back together. And the whole time, one of the sergeants is standing nearby, covered head to toe in an exo, shouting at him, 'Are you angry now?'"

"That seems . . . rather extreme."

"Better a bit of discomfort in training than a Marine who can't keep it together when bullets start flying."

"Did it work?" Kira asked.

Sparrow got to her feet. "Sure did. Berk ended up being one of the finest—"

Footsteps sounded, and then Tatupoa poked his square-shaped head around the corner of one of the racks. "Everything alright with you? Got concerned what with all the noises over here."

"We're fine, thank you," said Sparrow.

Kira dabbed the last traces of sweat from her forehead and stood. "Just exercising." Her stomach knotted again, and she winced.

The Marine stared at her, skeptical. "If you say so, ma'am."

3.

Kira and Sparrow were quiet as they returned to the ship's central shaft. There, Sparrow rested for a moment on her crutch. "Same time again tomorrow," she said.

Kira opened her mouth and then clamped it shut. They would be jumping to FTL not long afterward. She could survive one more session with Sparrow, however difficult.

"Fine," she said, "but maybe play it a bit safer."

Sparrow pulled a stick of gum from her breast pocket, unwrapped it, and popped it in her mouth. "No deal. Terms are the same. You stab me; I shoot you. It's a nice, simple arrangement, wouldn't you agree?"

It was, but Kira wasn't going to admit it. "How the hell did you survive this long without getting killed?"

Sparrow chuckled. "There's no such thing as safety. Only degrees of risk."

"That's not an answer."

"Then put it this way: I've had more practice than most dealing with risk." There was an unspoken implication to her claim: *because I had to.*

". . . I think you just like the thrill." Once more, a needle of pain shot through Kira's abdomen.

Sparrow chuckled again. "Could be."

When they arrived at sickbay, Hwa-jung was waiting for them outside. In one hand, she carried a small machine Kira didn't recognize. *"Aish,"* the machine boss said as Sparrow hobbled up. "You shouldn't walk around like this. It's not good for you." She wrapped her free arm around Sparrow's shoulders and shepherded her into the room.

"I'm fine," Sparrow protested weakly, but it was obvious she was more exhausted than she was letting on.

Inside, Vishal helped Hwa-jung lift Sparrow onto the exam table, and there the small woman lay back and closed her eyes for a moment.

"Here," said Hwa-jung, placing the machine on the short countertop next to the sink. "You need this."

"What is it?" said Sparrow, cracking open her eyes.

"A humidifier. The air is too dry in here."

Vishal examined the machine with a degree of doubt. "The air here is the same as—"

"Too dry," Hwa-jung insisted. "It is bad for her. It makes you sick. The humidity needs to be higher."

Sparrow smiled slightly. "You ain't going to win this argument, Doc."

Vishal seemed as if he was going to protest for a moment, and then he raised his hands and backed off. "As you wish, Ms. Song. It's not as if I work here."

Kira went over to him and, in a low voice, said, "Do you have a moment?"

The doctor bobbed his head. "For you, Ms. Navárez, of course. What seems to be the problem?"

Kira glanced at the other two women, but they seemed busy talking with each other. Lowering her voice further, she said, "My stomach has been hurting. I don't know if it's something I ate, or . . ." She trailed off, not wanting to give voice to the worst possibilities.

Vishal's expression sharpened. "What did you have for breakfast?"

"I haven't eaten yet."

"Ah. Very well. Please stand over here, Ms. Navárez, and I will see what I can do."

Kira stood in a corner of the sickbay, feeling slightly embarrassed to have

Sparrow and Hwa-jung watching while the doctor listened to her chest with a stethoscope and then pressed against her belly with his hands. "Does it hurt here?" he asked, touching just below her rib cage.

"No."

His hands moved a few centimeters lower. "Here?"

She shook her head.

His hands moved lower still. "Here?"

The sharp intake of her breath was answer enough. "Yeah," she said, her voice tight with pain.

A furrow appeared between Vishal's brows. "One minute, Ms. Navárez." He pulled open a nearby drawer and rummaged through it.

"Call me Kira, please."

"Ah, yes. Of course. Ms. Kira."

"No, I mean . . . Never mind."

Across the room, Sparrow popped her gum. "You'll never get him to unbend. The doc here is as stiff as a rod of titanium."

Vishal muttered something in a language Kira didn't understand, and then he returned to her with an odd-looking device. "Please lay on the floor and unseal your jumpsuit. Not all the way; halfway will do."

The deck was rough against her back. She held still while he spread cold goo across her lower stomach. A sonogram, then.

The doctor chewed on the inside of his lip while he studied the feed from the sonogram on his overlays.

Kira expected an answer of some kind when Vishal finished, but instead he held up a finger and said, "It is needful to do a blood test, Ms. Kira. Would you please remove the Soft Blade from your arm?"

That's not good. Again, Kira followed his orders, trying to ignore the worm of unease turning in her gut. Or maybe it was just the pain from whatever was wrong inside her.

A sharp prick as the needle broke her unprotected skin. Then silence for a few minutes as they waited for the sickbay's computers to run the diagnostics.

"Ah, here we are," said the doctor, and started reading his overlays, eyes darting from side to side.

Sparrow said, "Well, what is it, Doc?"

"If Ms. Kira chooses to tell you, that is her choice," said Vishal. "However, she is still my patient, and I am still her physician, and as such, this is privileged information." He gestured toward the door and said to Kira, "After you, my dear."

"Yeah, yeah," said Sparrow, but there was no concealing the spark of curiosity in her eyes.

Once out in the hallway, with the door closed behind them, Kira said, "How bad is it?"

"It is not bad at all, Ms. Kira," said Vishal. "You are menstruating. What you are feeling are uterine cramps. Quite normal."

"I'm . . ." For a moment, Kira was at a loss. "That can't be possible. I had my periods turned off when I first hit puberty." And the only time she'd reactivated them had been in college, during the stupidest six months of her life, with *him*. . . . A flush of unwelcome memories crowded her mind.

Vishal spread his hands. "I am sure you are right, Ms. Kira, but the results are unmistakable. You are most certainly menstruating. There is no doubt whatsoever."

"That shouldn't be possible."

"No, it shouldn't."

Kira put her fingers to her temples. A dull ache was forming behind her eyes. "The xeno must have thought I was injured somehow so it . . . repaired me." She walked back and forth across the corridor and then stopped, hands on her hips. "Shit. So am I going to have to deal with this from now on? Can't you do something to turn them back off?"

Vishal hesitated and then made a helpless motion. "If the suit will heal you, then nothing I can do would stop it, unless I remove your ovaries, and—"

"There's no way the Soft Blade would let you. Yeah."

The doctor glanced at his overlays. "There are hormonal treatments we could try, but I must warn you, Ms. Navárez, they can have some undesirable side effects. Also, I can't guarantee their efficacy, as the xeno might interfere with absorption and metabolism."

"Okay . . . Okay." Kira paced the breadth of the corridor again. "Fine. Leave it. If I feel any worse, maybe we can try the pills."

The doctor nodded. "As you wish." He drew a long finger across his bottom lip and then said, "One, ah, point to remember, Ms. Navárez, and I apologize most seriously for mentioning it. Practically, there is no reason you could not become pregnant now. However, as your physician, I have to—"

"I'm not getting pregnant," Kira said, harsher than she intended. She laughed, but there was no humor in the sound. "Besides, I don't think the Soft Blade would allow it, even if I wanted."

"Exactly, Ms. Kira. I could not guarantee your safety, nor the safety of the fetus."

"Understood. I appreciate your concern." She scuffed her heel against the deck, thinking. "You don't have to report this to anyone on the *Darmstadt,* do you?"

Vishal twisted a hand in the air. "They wish me to, but I would not betray the confidentiality of a patient."

"Thank you."

"Of course, Ms. Kira. . . . Would you like me to fix your nose for you now? Otherwise it will have to wait until tomorrow. I will be busy with Sparrow later."

"She told me. Tomorrow."

"As you wish." He returned to the sickbay, leaving her alone in the corridor.

4.

Pregnant.

Kira's stomach twisted, and not from the cramps. After what had happened in college, she'd sworn she would never have children. It had taken meeting Alan to make her reconsider, and only because she'd liked him so much. Now though, the thought filled her with revulsion. What sort of hybrid monstrosity would the xeno produce if she got pregnant?

She reached up to fiddle with a lock of hair; her fingers scraped scalp. *Well.* It wasn't like she was going to get pregnant by accident. All she had to do was avoid sleeping with anyone. Not so difficult.

For a moment, her thoughts detoured into mechanical details. Would sex even be possible? If she had the Soft Blade retract from between her legs, then . . . It might work, but whomever she was with would have to be brave—very brave—and if she lost her hold on the suit and it closed shut . . . *Ouch.*

She glanced down at herself. At least she didn't have to worry about bleeding. The Soft Blade was as efficient as always in recycling her body's waste.

The door to the sickbay opened as Hwa-jung exited.

"Do you have a moment?" said Kira. "Could you help me?"

The machine boss stared at her. "What?" From anyone else the question would have sounded rude, but from Hwa-jung, Kira thought it was just a simple request.

Kira explained what she needed and what she wanted. They weren't the same things.

"This way," said Hwa-jung, and lumbered off toward the core of the ship.

As they started down the central ladder, Kira eyed the machine boss, curious. "How did you end up on the *Wallfish,* if you don't mind me asking?"

"Captain Falconi needed a machine boss. I needed a job. Now I work here."

"Do you have family back on Shin-Zar?"

The top of Hwa-jung's head moved as she nodded. "Many brothers and sisters. Many cousins. I send them money when I can."

"Why did you leave?"

"Because," said Hwa-jung as she stepped off the ladder on the deck just above the cargo holds. She lifted her hands, fingers bunched, the tips pressed together. "Boom." And she opened her hands, splaying her fingers.

"Ah." Kira couldn't decide if the machine boss was being literal or not, and she decided it was better not to ask. "Do you ever visit?"

"Once. No more."

Leaving the shaft, they passed through a narrow passageway and entered a room close to the hull.

It was a machine shop, small and cramped—stuffed with more pieces of equipment than Kira recognized—but impeccably organized. The scent of solvents stung her nose, and the smell of ozone put a bitter, nickel-like taste on her tongue.

"Warning, some chemicals are known by the League of Allied Worlds to cause cancer," said Hwa-jung as she edged sideways between the different machines.

"That's easy enough to treat," said Kira.

Hwa-jung chuckled. "They still require the disclaimers. Bureaucrats." She stopped by a wall of drawers at the back of the shop and slapped them. "Here. Powdered metals, polycarbonates, organic substrates, carbon fiber, more. All the raw stock you could need."

"Is there anything I *shouldn't* take?"

"Organics. Metals are easy to replace; organics are harder, more expensive."

"Okay. I'll avoid them."

Hwa-jung shrugged. "You can take some. Just not too much. Whatever you do, do *not* cross-contaminate—with any of these. It will ruin whatever we make with them."

"Gotcha. I won't."

Then she showed Kira how to unlock the drawers and open the storage packs inside. "You understand now, yes? I will go and see if I can print what you want."

"Thank you."

As Hwa-jung left, Kira dipped her fingers into a mound of powdered aluminum while at the same time telling the xeno: *Eat.*

If it did, she couldn't tell.

She sealed the pack, closed the drawer, cleaned her hand with a wet wipe from the dispenser on the wall, and—once her skin was dry—tried the same thing with the powdered titanium.

Drawer by drawer, she worked her way through the ship's supplies. The suit seemed to absorb little to none of the metals; it had apparently sated most of its hunger during the night. However, it displayed a distinct preference for some of the rarer elements, such as samarium, neodymium, and yttrium, among others. Cobalt and zinc, too. To her surprise, it ignored all the biological compounds.

When Kira was finished, she left the machine shop with Hwa-jung still there working—bent over the control display for the ship's main printer—and returned to the galley.

Kira fixed herself a late breakfast, which she ate at a leisurely pace. It was nearly noon, and she was already wiped from the day's events. Sparrow's training—if it could be called that—had taken a serious toll.

Her abdomen twinged again, and she grimaced. *Wonderful. Just wonderful.*

She looked up as Nielsen walked in. The first officer got herself some food from the fridge and then sat opposite Kira.

They ate in silence for a time.

Then Nielsen said, "You've set us on a strange path, Navárez."

Eat the path. "Can't argue with you there. . . . Does it bother you?"

The woman set down her fork. "I'm not happy that we'll be gone for over six months, if that's what you're asking. The League is going to be in serious trouble by the time we get back, unless through some miracle, these attacks let off."

"But we might be able to help, if we find the Staff of Blue."

"Yes, I'm aware of the rationale." Nielsen took a sip of water. "When I joined the *Wallfish,* I didn't think I was signing up for combat, chasing alien relics, or expeditions into the unexplored regions of the galaxy. And yet here we are."

Kira tipped her head. "Yeah. I wasn't looking for any of this either. . . . Aside from the exploration."

"And the alien relics."

A smile forced its way onto Kira's face. "And that."

Nielsen smiled slightly also. Then she surprised her by saying, "I heard Sparrow put you through the wringer this morning. How are you holding up?"

Simple as it was, the question softened Kira. "Okay. But it was a lot. It's *all* a lot."

"I can imagine."

Kira made a face. "Plus, now . . ." She half laughed. "You're not going to believe it, but—" And she told Nielsen about the return of her periods.

The first officer made a sympathetic face. "How inconvenient. At least you don't have to worry about bleeding."

"No. Small favors, eh?" Kira raised her glass in a mock toast, and Nielsen did the same.

Then the first officer said, "Listen, Kira, if you need someone to talk with, someone other than Gregorovich . . . come find me. My door is always open."

Kira studied her for a long moment, gratitude welling up inside her. Then she nodded. "I'll keep that in mind. Thank you."

5.

Kira spent the rest of the day helping around the ship. A lot still needed doing before they went FTL: lines and filters to check, diagnostics to run, general cleaning, and so on.

Kira didn't mind the work. It made her feel useful, and it kept her from thinking too much. She even helped Trig fix the damaged bed in her cabin, which she was grateful to have done, knowing as she did that—if all went well—she would be spending months there on the mattress, lost in the death-like sleep of the Soft Blade's induced hibernation.

The thought frightened her, so she worked harder and tried not to dwell on it.

When ship-evening came, everyone but the Marines gathered in the galley, even Sparrow. "I thought you had surgery," said Falconi, glowering at her from under his thick eyebrows.

"I put it off until later," she said. They all knew why she wanted to be there. Dinner was their last chance to spend time together as a group before going into FTL.

"That safe, Doc?" Falconi asked.

Vishal nodded. "As long as she does not eat any solid food, she will be fine."

Sparrow smirked. "Good thing then you were the one cooking tonight, Doc. Makes it easy to wait."

A shadow flitted across Vishal's face, but he didn't argue. "I am glad you are safe for your surgery, Ms.," was all he said.

A text popped up on Kira's overlays:

<Sparrow told me about your session together. Sounds like she worked you over pretty good. – Falconi>

<That about sums it up. She's intense. But thorough. Very thorough. – Kira>

<Good. – Falconi>

<How did she think it went? – Kira>

<She said she served with worse trainees in boot. – Falconi>

<Thanks . . . I guess. – Kira>

He chuckled quietly. *<Trust me, coming from her, it's a compliment. – Falconi>*

The mood around the room was lighter than the previous day, although there was an underlying tension that gave their conversations a manic edge. None of them wanted to discuss what was about to come, but it hung over them like an unspoken threat.

The conversation loosened until Kira felt bold enough to say, "Okay, I know this is rude, but there's a question I have to ask."

"No, you don't," said Falconi, sipping from his glass of wine.

She plowed onward as if he hadn't said anything. "Akawe mentioned you wanted pardons before you'd agree to go. What for?" Around the room, the crew shifted uneasily while the Entropists looked on with interest. "Trig, you mentioned some difficulties at Ruslan, so . . . I was just wondering." Kira leaned back and waited to see what would happen.

Falconi scowled at his glass. "You can't help sticking your nose where it doesn't belong, can you?"

In a somewhat placating tone, Nielsen said, "We should tell her. There's no reason to keep it secret, not now."

". . . Fine. You tell her then."

How bad was it, Kira wondered. Smuggling? Theft? Assault? . . . Murder?

Nielsen sighed and then—as if she'd guessed what Kira was thinking—said, "It's not what you imagine. I wasn't on the ship at the time, but the crew ended up in trouble because they imported a whole bunch of newts to sell on Ruslan."

For a moment Kira wasn't sure she'd heard right. "*Newts?*"

"Yeah, a metric newt-ton of them," said Trig. Sparrow laughed and then grimaced and clutched her side.

"Don't," said Nielsen. "Just don't."

Trig grinned and dug back into his food.

"There was a children's show on Ruslan," said Falconi. "*Yanni the Newt,* or something like that. It was really popular."

"Was?"

He made a face. "All the kids wanted newts as pets. So it seemed like a good idea to bring in a shipload of them."

Nielsen rolled her eyes and shook her head, which sent her ponytail flying. "If I'd been on the *Wallfish,* I wouldn't have allowed such nonsense."

Falconi took issue with that. "It was a good job. You would have jumped at the opportunity faster than any of us."

"Why not just grow the newts in a lab?" asked Kira, puzzled. "Or gene-hack something like a frog to look like them?"

"They did," he said. "But the rich kids wanted real newts. From Earth. You know how it is."

Kira blinked. "That . . . could *not* have been cheap."

Falconi dipped his head with a sardonic smile. "Exactamento. We would have made a fortune. Only—"

"The damn things didn't have a kill switch!" said Sparrow.

"They didn't—" Kira started to say and then stopped herself. "Of course, because they were from Earth." All macroorganisms (and more than a few micro) grown on colonized worlds had built-in genetic kill switches, to make it easy to manage their population and keep any one organism from disrupting the nascent food chain or, if present, the native ecology. But not on Earth. There, plants and animals just *existed,* mixing and competing in a chaotic mess that still defied attempts at control.

Falconi extended a hand toward her. "Yup. We found a company that breeds newts—"

"Fink-Nottle's Pious Newt Emporium," Trig helpfully supplied.

"—but we didn't exactly tell them where the newts were going. No reason for the ITC to know what we were up to, now was there?"

"We didn't even *think* to ask about a kill switch," said Sparrow. "And by the time we sold them, it was too late to fix."

"How many did you sell?"

"Seven hundred and seventy-seven . . . thousand, seven hundred and seventy-seven."

"Seventy-six," said Sparrow. "Don't forget the one Mr. Fuzzypants ate."

"Right. Seventy-six," said Trig.

Kira had difficulty even imagining that many newts.

Falconi continued the tale: "As you'd expect, a bunch of the newts escaped, and without any natural predators, they wiped out a good chunk of Ruslan's insects, worms, snails, et cetera."

"Good god." Without insects and the like, it was pretty much impossible for a colony to function. Worms alone were worth more than their weight in refined uranium during the early years of transforming sterile or hostile land to fertile soil.

"Indeed."

"It was like a newt-tron bomb," said Trig.

Sparrow and Nielsen groaned, and Vishal said, "That was the sort of pun we had to endure for the whole trip, Ms. Kira. It was most unpleasant."

Kira fixed Trig with a look. "Hey. What do you call a really smart newt?"

He grinned. "What?"

"Newton, of course."

"Permission to jettison both of them as *pun*ishment, Captain?" said Nielsen.

"Granted," Falconi said. "But not until we reach our destination."

At that, the mood in the galley grew more somber.

"So what happened after, with the newts?" Kira asked. The punishment for violating biocontainment protocols varied from place to place, but it usually involved heavy fines and/or jail time.

Falconi grunted. "What do you think? The local government issued warrants for our arrest. Fortunately, they were only planetary warrants, not stellar or interstellar, and we were long gone before the newts started to cause a problem. But yeah . . . they're not too happy with us. They even ended up canceling *Yanni the Newt* because so many people were pissed off."

Kira chuckled, and then she burst out into a full laugh. "Sorry. I know it's not funny, but—"

"Well, it is a little funny," said Vishal.

"Yeah, goddamn hilarious," said Falconi. To Kira, "They retroactively nulled the bits we earned, which left us out food, fuel, and propellant for the whole trip."

"I can see how that might have left you feeling . . . *newt*ered," she said.

Nielsen facepalmed. "Thule. Now we have two of them."

"Gimme that," said Falconi and reached for his holstered pistol, which was slung over the back of Vishal's seat.

The doctor laughed and shook his head. "Not a chance, Captain."

"Gah. Mutineers, the lot of you."

"Don't you mean, *newt*ineers?" said Trig.

"That's it! Enough with the punning or I'll have you thrown into cryo right now."

"Suuure."

To Kira, Nielsen said, "We had a few other, smaller difficulties, mainly ITC violations, but that was the main one."

Sparrow snorted. "That and Chelomey." In response to Kira's inquiring look, she said, "We got hired by a guy named Griffith back at Alpha Centauri to bring in a load of, uh, *sensitive* cargo for a guy on Chelomey Station. Only our contact wasn't there when we dropped off the goods. The idiot got himself arrested by station security. So the station wanted our asses as well. Griffith claims we failed delivery and won't pay, and since we used up the last of our antimatter getting here, there wasn't anything we could do about it."

"And that," said Falconi, emptying his glass, "is how we ended up stranded at 61 Cygni. Couldn't land back at Chelomey and couldn't land on Ruslan. Not, uh, legally, that is."

"Gotcha." Overall, it wasn't as bad as Kira had feared. A bit of smuggling, a small amount of what might be classified as ecoterrorism . . . Really, she'd expected far worse.

Falconi waved his hand. "That's all cleared up now, though." He peered at her, his eyes slightly bleary from drink. "I suppose we have you to thank for that."

"My pleasure."

Later, once most of the food was cleared off the tables, Hwa-jung left her seat by Sparrow and vanished out the door.

When the machine boss returned, she brought with her Runcible and Mr. Fuzzypants, but also—tucked under one arm—the other thing Kira had asked her for.

"Here," said Hwa-jung, and held out the concertina to Kira. "It just finished printing."

Kira laughed and took the instrument. "Thank you!" Now she would have something to do other than stare at her overlays while she waited alone in the empty ship.

Falconi raised an eyebrow. "You play?"

"A little," said Kira, slipping her hands through the straps and testing the keys. Then she performed a simple little arrangement called "Chiara's Folly" as a warm-up.

The music brought a sense of cheer to the room, and the crew gathered in close. "Hey, you know '*Toxopaxia*'?" Sparrow asked.

"I do."

Kira played until her fingers were numb, but she didn't mind. And for a time, no thoughts of the future intruded, and life was good.

Mr. Fuzzypants still kept his distance from her, but at some point deep in the evening—long after she'd put aside the concertina—Kira found herself with Runcible's warm weight in her lap while she scratched behind the pig's ears and he wiggled his tail in delight. A surge of affection passed through Kira, and for the first time since the deaths of Alan and her other teammates, she felt herself relaxing, truly relaxing.

So maybe Falconi was a hard-edged bastard and their ship mind was eccentric and Sparrow was somewhat of a sadist and Trig was still just a kid and Hwa-jung was weird in her own ways and Vishal—Kira wasn't sure what the deal was with Vishal, but he seemed nice enough—so maybe all that. So what? Nothing was ever perfect. Kira knew one thing for certain, though: she'd fight for Falconi and his crew. She'd fight for them the same as she would have for her team on Adra.

6.

As a group, they ended up staying in the galley far later than they should have, but no one complained, least of all Kira. The evening ended with her showing—at the Entropists' request—how the Soft Blade could form different shapes on its surface.

She made a smiley face rise out of her palm, and Falconi said, "Talk to the hand."

Everyone laughed.

At some point, Sparrow, Vishal, and Hwa-jung departed for sickbay. Without them, the galley was noticeably quieter.

Sparrow's surgery was going to take quite some time. Long before it finished, Kira returned to her cabin, fell onto her new mattress, and slept. And for once she didn't dream.

7.

Morning arrived, and with it, a sense of dread. The jump to FTL was only a few hours away. Kira lay where she was for a while and tried to reconcile herself with what was to come.

I brought this on myself. The thought made her feel better than believing she was a victim of circumstances, but it still didn't make her feel great.

She roused herself and checked her overlays. No news of significance (aside from reports of minor fighting on Ruslan), and no texts. Also no cramps. That was a relief.

She messaged Sparrow:

<Do you still want to do this? – Kira>

After a minute: *<Yes. In sickbay. – Sparrow>*

Kira washed her face, dressed, and headed out.

When the door to sickbay opened, she was shocked by how weak Sparrow looked. The woman's face was drawn and pale, and she had an IV pinned in her arm.

Somewhat taken aback, Kira said, "Are you going to be able to handle cryo?"

"I'm looking forward to it," Sparrow said dryly. "Doc seems to think I'll do just fine. Might even help me heal better, long term."

"Are you really up for more . . . whatever the hell this is?"

Sparrow produced a crooked smile. "Oh yeah. I've thought of a whole bunch of different ways to test your patience."

She proved true to her word. Back to the makeshift gym they went, and again she put Kira through a rigorous series of exercises while Kira struggled to retain control over the Soft Blade. Sparrow didn't make it easy. The woman had a talent for distraction, and she indulged in it, harassing Kira with words, sounds, and unexpected movements during the most difficult parts of the exercises. And Kira failed. Again and again she failed, and she grew increasingly frustrated with her inability to maintain her mental footing. With so much input, it was almost inevitable that her concentration would slip, and where it slipped, the Soft Blade took over, choosing of its own judgment how best to act.

The organism's decisions built a sense of character: one that was impulsive and eager to find flaws that could be exploited. Its was a questing consciousness full of unbridled curiosity, despite its oftentimes destructive nature.

So it went. Sparrow continued to harass her, and Kira continued to try to retain her composure.

After an hour, her face was drenched with sweat and she felt nearly as exhausted as Sparrow looked. "How'd I do?" she asked, getting up from the deck.

"Don't go watch a scary movie. That's all I have to say," said Sparrow.

"Ah."

"What? You want cookies and compliments? You didn't give up. Keep not-giving-up and you might impress me someday." Sparrow lay back on the bench and closed her eyes. "It's on you, now. You know what you need to do while we're corpsicles."

"I have to keep practicing."

"And you can't make it easy on yourself."

"I won't."

Sparrow cracked open an eye. She smiled. "You know what, Navárez? I believe you."

The hours that followed were a frenzy of preparation. Kira helped Vishal sedate the ship pets, and then both Runcible and Mr. Fuzzypants were placed inside a cryo tube just big enough to hold the both of them.

Shortly thereafter, the thrust alert sounded and the *Wallfish* cut its engines so it could cool down as much as possible before hitting the Markov Limit. Nearby, the *Darmstadt* did the same, the cruiser's diamond radiators glittering in the dim light from the system's star.

One by one, the *Wallfish*'s systems were shut down, and the inside of the ship became progressively cooler and darker.

The four Marines in the port hold were the first to enter cryo. They gave their notice, and then their systems vanished from the ship intranet as they lapsed into deathlike stasis.

Next were the Entropists. Their cryo tubes were in their cabin. "We are off to lay ourselves—"

"—in our hibernacula. Travel safely, Prisoners," they said before sequestering themselves.

Kira and the crew of the *Wallfish* gathered in the ship's storm shelter, right near the center of the ship, just below Control and adjacent to the sealed room that contained the armored sarcophagus Gregorovich called home.

Kira hung by the door of the shelter, feeling helpless as Sparrow, Hwa-jung, Trig, Vishal, and Nielsen stripped to their underwear and got into their tubes. The lids closed, and within seconds, the interiors fogged over.

Falconi waited until the last. "You going to be okay on your own?" he asked, pulling his shirt over his head.

Kira averted her gaze. "I think so."

"Once Gregorovich goes under, our pseudo-intelligence, Morven, will be in charge of navigation and life support, but if something goes wrong, don't hesitate to wake any of us up."

"Okay."

He unlaced his boots, stuck them in a locker. "Seriously. Even if you just need to talk with another person. We're going to have to drop out of FTL a few times anyway."

"If I need to, I promise I will." She glanced over to see Falconi in just his skivvies. He was more heavily built than she'd realized: thick chest, thick arms, thick back. Sparrow and Hwa-jung obviously weren't the only ones who used the weights in the hold.

"Good." Then he pulled himself along the wall and floated over to her. Up close, Kira could smell the sweat on him, a clean, healthy musk. A mat of thick, black hair covered his chest, and for a moment—just a moment—she imagined running her fingers through it.

Falconi noticed her gaze and met it with an even more direct look. He said, "One other thing. Since you're the only person who's going to be up and around—"

"Not much, if I can help it."

"You'll still be more functional than any of us. Since that's the case, I'm naming you acting captain of the *Wallfish* while we're in cryo."

Kira was surprised. She started to say something, thought better of it, and then tried again: "Are you sure? Even after what happened?"

"I'm sure," said Falconi firmly.

"Does that mean I'm part of the crew then?"

"I suppose it does. For the duration of the trip, at least."

She considered the idea. "What sort of responsibilities does an acting captain have?"

"Quite a few," he said, going over to his cryo tube. "It gives you executive access to certain systems. Override ability too. Might be needed in an emergency."

". . . Thank you. I appreciate it."

He nodded. "Just don't wreck my ship, Navárez. She's all I've got."

"Not all," said Kira, and gestured at the frozen tubes.

A faint smile appeared on Falconi's face. "No, not all." She watched as he lowered himself into the tube, hooked up the drip to his arm, and attached the electrodes to his head and chest. He looked at her once more and gave her a small salute. "See you by the light of a strange star, Captain."

"Captain."

Then the lid closed over Falconi's face, and silence settled over the shelter.

"Just you and me now, headcase," said Kira, looking in the direction of Gregorovich's sarcophagus.

"That too shall pass," said the ship mind.

8.

Fourteen minutes later, the *Wallfish* went FTL.

Kira watched the transition on the display in her cabin. One moment a field of stars surrounded them; the next a dark mirror, perfectly spherical.

She studied the ship's reflection for a long, wordless while and then closed the display and wrapped her arms around herself.

They were finally on their way.

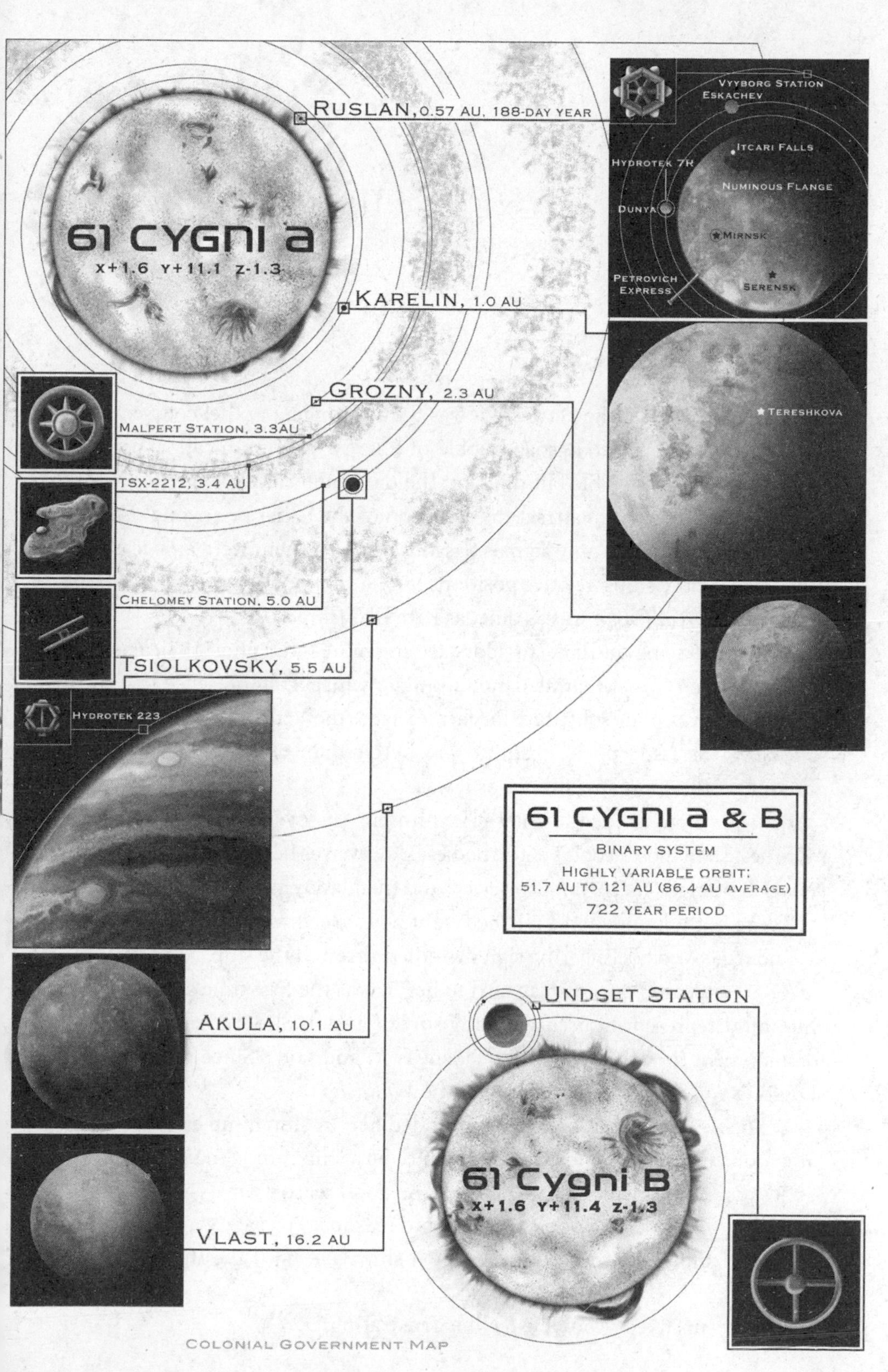

61 CYGNI A
x+1.6 y+11.1 z-1.3
RUSLAN, 0.57 AU, 188-DAY YEAR
VYYBORG STATION
ESKACHEV
ITCARI FALLS
HYDROTEK 7R
NUMINOUS FLANGE
DUNYA
MIRNSK
PETROVICH EXPRESS
SERENSK
KARELIN, 1.0 AU
TERESHKOVA
GROZNY, 2.3 AU
MALPERT STATION, 3.3AU
TSX-2212, 3.4 AU
CHELOMEY STATION, 5.0 AU
TSIOLKOVSKY, 5.5 AU
HYDROTEK 223
61 CYGNI A & B
BINARY SYSTEM
HIGHLY VARIABLE ORBIT:
51.7 AU TO 121 AU (86.4 AU AVERAGE)
722 YEAR PERIOD
UNDSET STATION
AKULA, 10.1 AU
61 Cygni B
x+1.6 y+11.4 z-1.3
VLAST, 16.2 AU

COLONIAL GOVERNMENT MAP

* * * *

EXEUNT II

1.

Outside the *Wallfish*, the *Darmstadt* was flying along a parallel course, swaddled in its own protective soap bubble of energy. Communication between ships in FTL was possible but difficult: the data rate was slow and lossy, and since they didn't want to attract the attention of the Jellies or anyone else who might be listening, the only signals passing between them were an occasional ping to check the ships' relative positions.

Inside the *Wallfish*, it was as quiet as Kira had feared.

She drifted along the dark corridors, feeling more like a ghost than a person.

Gregorovich was still awake and talking: a whispering presence that filled the hull but was poor substitute for face-to-face interaction with another person. Nevertheless, a poor substitute was better than nothing, and Kira was grateful for the company, strange as it was.

The ship mind needed to enter cryo himself. His oversized brain produced more heat than most people's entire bodies. However, as he said, "I shall wait with you, O Tentacled Queen, until you sleep, and then I too shall sink into oblivion."

"We're both bounded in a nutshell right now, aren't we?"

"Indeed." And his lingering sigh dwindled through the ship.

A sigil appeared on a display next to her; it was the first time she'd seen the ship mind represent himself with any sort of avatar. She studied the symbol for a moment (her overlays couldn't identify it) and said, "Since you're still up, shouldn't *you* be the acting captain of the *Wallfish*?"

A chuckle like burbling water surrounded her. "A ship mind cannot be captain, foolish meatbag. And a captain cannot be a ship mind. You know that."

"It's just tradition," said Kira. "There's no good reason why—"

"There are most comely and toothsome reasons. For safety and sanity, no ship mind should be master of their own ship . . . even if the ship is become our flesh."

"That seems like it would be terribly frustrating."

Kira could almost hear Gregorovich's shrug. "There is no reason in railing against reality. Besides, my charming infestation, while the letter of the law may say one thing, the execution of the law is often quite different."

"Meaning?"

"In practice, most ships are run by ship minds. How else could it be?"

She caught a handhold by her cabin door, stopping herself. "What's the name of the *Darmstadt*'s mind?"

"She is the most crisp and delightful Horzcha Ubuto."

"That's quite a mouthful."

"With no tongue to taste and no throat to sing, all names are equal."

2.

In her cabin, Kira dimmed the lights and lowered the temperature. The time had come for a winding down of mind and body. She would hibernate as soon as the Soft Blade would allow, but hibernation wasn't her only concern. She also needed to practice with the xeno. Sparrow was right. *Falconi* was right. She had to master the Soft Blade as much as it could be mastered, and as with all skills, doing so would require diligence.

Over the course of the next three months, the *Wallfish* would drop out of FTL on at least six occasions to dump its excess heat. Each time would be an opportunity for her to push herself physically, as she had with Sparrow. In between, Kira would have to minimize her activity, but she still planned on waking once per week to work with the Soft Blade. That would give her a total of twelve practice sessions before they arrived at their destination; enough, she hoped, to make meaningful progress.

Whether or not the Soft Blade could pull her in and out of hibernation each week wasn't something Kira was sure of. But it was worth a try. If the xeno couldn't . . . she'd have to eliminate some of the training. Regardless of the heat she produced and the resources she consumed, it was crucial to minimize the amount of time she spent awake and alone. True isolation could cause serious psychological damage in a surprisingly short span. It was a problem for any small crew on a long-haul mission, and being entirely by herself would only exacerbate the problem. Either way, she'd have to keep close tabs on her mental health. . . .

At least on this trip she didn't have to worry about starving to death. There was plenty of food on the *Wallfish*. Still, she didn't plan on eating much—only when exercising during their breaks in FTL. Besides, hunger seemed to be one of the triggers that helped convince the Soft Blade to place her into stasis.

Eat the path.

Having decided on a course of action, Kira set her weekly alarm and then spent the next hour contending with the Soft Blade in the first of their sessions.

Since she wasn't using exercise to induce physical or mental stress this time, Kira found another, equally challenging test for herself: attempting to solve mental problems while coaxing the xeno into making different shapes. Mathematical equations proved to be an excellent stressor in that regard. She also imagined being back on the Jelly ship, with tentacles wrapped around her, unable to move—or the jolt of pain from the Numenist breaking her nose—and she let the memory of fear quicken her pulse, flood her veins with adrenaline, and *then* Kira did her best to shape the Soft Blade as she saw fit.

The second way wasn't the healthiest choice; she was just training her endocrine system to overreact to physical danger. But she needed to be able to work with the Soft Blade under less-than-ideal circumstances, and right then, she didn't have many options.

When she no longer had the mental focus to keep practicing, Kira relaxed by playing her new concertina. It had pearl-like buttons and a swirling inlay along the sides of the box. The design had been an addition of Hwa-jung's, and Kira appreciated it. When not playing, she traced the swirls with her fingers and admired how the faint emergency lights reflected red.

Gregorovich listened to her music. He had become a constant, unseen companion. Sometimes he offered commentary—a piece of praise or a suggestion—but mostly he seemed content to be her respectful audience.

First one day, then two crept by. Time seemed to slow: a familiar telescoping that left Kira feeling trapped in a shapeless limbo. Her thoughts grew slow and clumsy, and her fingers no longer found the right buttons on the concertina.

She put the instrument aside, then, and again turned on Bach's concertos and allowed the music to sweep her away.

. . .

Gregorovich's voice roused her from a state of torpor. The ship mind was speaking soft and slow: "Kira. . . . Kira. . . . Are you awake?"

"What is it?" she murmured.

"I have to leave you now."

". . . Alright."

"Are you going to be okay, Kira?"

"Yes. Mm'good."

"Okay. Goodnight, then, Kira. Dream of beautiful things."

3.

Kira lay on her bed, attached to it by the Soft Blade. There were straps mounted along the side for sleeping in zero-g. She had used them at first, but when she realized the xeno could hold her in place without constant supervision, she undid them.

As she drifted ever deeper into the hazy twilight of near unconsciousness, she allowed the mask to slide into place over her face, and she was dimly aware of the suit bonding with itself, joining limb to limb and winding her in a protective shell, black as ink and hard as diamond.

She could have stopped it, but she liked the feeling.

Sleep. She urged the Soft Blade to rest and wait as it had once before, to enter dormancy and no longer strive. The xeno was slow to understand, but in time the pangs of hunger eased and a familiar chill crept through her limbs. Then the strains of Bach faded from awareness, and the universe constricted to the confines of her mind. . . .

When she dreamed, her dreams were troubled, full of anger and dread and malignant forms lurking in the shadows.

An enormous room of grey and gold with ranks of windows revealing the dark of space beyond. Stars glimmered in the depths, and by their dim light there gleamed the polished floor and pillars of fluted metal.

Flesh-that-she-was could see nothing among the hidden corners of the chamber that seemed to have no end, but she felt the eyes of unknown, unfriendly intelligences watching . . . watching with unsated hunger. Shards of fear affixed her, and no relief had she of action, for the covetous observers remained hidden, though she could feel them creeping closer.

And the shadows twisted and churned with incomprehensible shapes.

. . . Flashes of images: an invisible box filled with a broken promise that thrashed with mindless rage. A planet blanketed in black and pregnant with malevolent intelligence. Streamers of fire descending through an evening sky: beautiful and terrifying and heartbreakingly sad to see. Towers toppled. Blood boiling in a vacuum. The crust of earth shuddering, splitting, spilling lava across a fertile plain . . .

And worse still. Things unseen. Fears that had no name, ancient and alien. Nightmares that revealed themselves only in a sense of wrongness and a twisting of fixed angles. . . .

4.

b-b-b-beep . . . b-b-b-beep . . . b-b-b-beep . . .

The ratcheting alarm hauled Kira back to wakefulness. She blinked, confused and bleary, for a long moment not understanding. Then a sense of self and place returned to her and she groaned.

"Computer, stop alarm," she whispered. Her voice sounded clearly even through the material that covered her face.

The jarring bleat fell silent.

For a handful of minutes she lay in the dark and the silence, unable to bring herself to move. *One week.* It felt longer, as if she'd been anchored to the bed for an eternity. And yet, at the same time, as if she'd just closed her eyes.

The cabin was stifling, oppressive, like a chamber deep underground. . . .

Her heart quickened.

"Alright. Come on, you," she said to the Soft Blade.

Kira willed the mask off her face and freed her limbs from the web of fibers that bound them to her torso. Then she worked hard with the xeno, straining with and against it.

When she finally stopped, her stomach was grinding and she was fully awake, even though she'd left the lights off.

She drank a few sips of water and again attempted to sleep. It took longer than she wanted—half a day at least—but in time, her mind and body relaxed, and she sank back into welcome latency.

And when she slept, she moaned and fretted in the torment of her dreams, and nothing there was to break the spell as the *Wallfish* hurtled ever deeper into unknown space.

5.

Thereafter things grew hazy and disjointed. The empty sameness of her surroundings coupled with the strangeness of the xeno-induced hibernation left

Kira disoriented. She felt detached from events, as if all were a dream, and she a disembodied spirit observing.

Yet in one particular, she felt very bodied. And that was her time practicing with the Soft Blade. Seemingly endless practice. Were there changes in her ability to control the xeno? Were there improvements? . . . Kira wasn't sure. But she persisted. If nothing else, an innate stubbornness wouldn't let her give up. She had faith in the value of work. If she just kept putting in the effort, it had to do *some* good.

The thought was her only consolation when something went wrong with the Soft Blade. Failure came in many forms. The xeno refused to move as she wished. Or it overreacted (those were the slipups that most concerned Kira). Or it obeyed, but in generalities, not specifics. She might will it to form a rose-like pattern on her hand only for it to produce a round, lumpy dome.

It was hard, frustrating labor. But Kira stuck to it. And, though at times the Soft Blade seemed frustrated also—as she could tell by the lag in its responses or by the types of shapes it formed—she felt a willingness to cooperate from the xeno, and it encouraged her.

During the times the *Wallfish* dropped out of FTL, she allowed herself to leave her cabin, wander the ship. Have a cup of chell in the galley. Run on the zero-g treadmill and do all the exercises she could with bands and straps. They weren't enough to maintain muscle or bone—for that she relied upon the xeno—but they were a welcome break from the monotony of her weekly practice.

Then the ship's systems would again power down, the jump alert would sound, and she would retreat back to her darkened cave.

6.

A month had passed. . . . A month, and sometimes Kira was convinced she was stuck in a never-ending loop. Close her eyes, wake, free her limbs, practice, close her eyes, wake, free her limbs, practice.

It was getting to her. She seriously debated waking Gregorovich or Falconi or Nielsen to have someone to talk with, but waking them would be a huge inconvenience for only a few hours of conversation, if that. It might even delay the expedition, depending on how much heat they generated. No matter how strange or lonely she felt, Kira wasn't willing to risk that. Finding the Staff of Blue was more important than her desire for human company.

7.

Two months. Nearly there. That was what she told herself. She celebrated with a ration bar and a cup of hot chocolate.

The training with the Soft Blade was getting easier. Or maybe that was just what she wanted to believe. She *could* hold and shape the xeno in ways that had escaped her before. That was progress, wasn't it?

Kira thought so. But she felt so detached from anything tangible that she didn't trust her own judgment.

Not so long now. . . .

Not so long. . . .

PART THREE

* * * * * * *

APOCALYPSIS

In the villa of Ormen, in the villa of Ormen
Stands a solitary candle, ah ah, ah ah
In the center of it all, in the center of it all
Your eyes

On the day of execution, on the day of execution
Only women kneel and smile, ah ah, ah ah
At the center of it all, at the center of it all
Your eyes
Your eyes

Ah ah ah
Ah ah ah

★—DAVID BOWIE

CHAPTER I

* * * * * * *

PAST SINS

1.

This time, instead of the alarm, a slow dawning of light drew Kira toward wakefulness.

She opened her eyes. At first no concern troubled her; she lay where she was, feeling calm and rested, content to wait. Then she saw the cat sitting by her feet: a whitish-grey Siamese with ears half-flattened and eyes slightly crossed.

The cat hissed and jumped down to the deck.

"Kira, can you hear me? . . . Kira, are you awake?"

She turned her head and saw Falconi sitting next to her. The skin around his mouth was green, as if he'd been sick, and his face was drawn and hollow-eyed. He smiled at her. "Welcome back."

With a rush, her memory returned: the *Wallfish,* FTL, the Jellies, the Staff of Blue . . .

Kira let out a cry and tried to bolt upright. Pressure around her chest and arms stopped her.

"It's safe," said Falconi. "You can come out now." He rapped a knuckle against her shoulder.

She looked down and saw a featureless sheath of black fibers encasing her body, holding her in place. *Let me go!* Kira thought, feeling suddenly claustrophobic. She wrenched her shoulders from side to side and let out another cry.

With a dry, slithery sound, the Soft Blade relaxed its protective embrace and unwound the hard shell it had formed around her. A small cascade of dust slid from her sides and onto the floor, sending grey curlicues into the air.

Falconi sneezed and rubbed his nose.

Kira's muscles protested as she levered herself off the mattress and carefully sat upright. She had weight again: a welcome sensation. She tried to talk, but her mouth was too dry; all that came out was a frog-like croak.

"Here," said Falconi, and handed her a water pouch.

She nodded, grateful, and sucked on the straw. Then she tried again. "Did . . . did we make it?" Her voice was rough from disuse.

Falconi nodded. "More or less. The ship has a few service alerts, but we're in one piece. Happy New Year and welcome to 2258. Bughunt is just ahead."

"Bughunt?"

"It's what the Marines are calling the star."

"Are there . . . are there any Jellies or nightmares in the system?"

"Doesn't look like it."

Relief, then, that they'd managed to beat the aliens. "Good." Kira realized the Bach concertos were still playing. "Computer, music off," she said, and the speakers fell silent. "How long, since . . ."

"Since we arrived? Uh, thirty minutes, give or take. I came right over." Falconi licked his lips. He still looked queasy. Kira recognized the symptoms; recovery after cryo was always a bitch, and it only got worse the longer you spent in the tube.

She took another sip of water.

"How are you feeling?" he asked.

"Okay. . . . A bit strange, but I'm okay. You?"

He stood. "Like twenty kilos of shit stuffed into a ten-kilo sack. I'll be fine, though."

"Have we picked up anything on the sensors, or—"

"You can see for yourself. The system was definitely inhabited at one point, so there's that. You didn't send us nowhere. I'm going up to Control. Join us there when you can."

As he walked to the open doorway, Kira said, "Did everyone make it?"

"Yeah. Sick as dogs, but we're all here." Then he left, and the door swung shut behind him.

Kira took a moment to gather her thoughts. They'd made it. *She'd* made it. Hard to believe. She opened and closed her hands, rolled her shoulders, gently tensed muscles throughout her body—stiff from the past few days of hibernation, but everything seemed to be in working order.

"Hey, headcase," she said. "You in one piece?"

After a brief pause, Gregorovich answered. Even with a synthesized voice, the ship mind sounded sluggish, groggy: "I was in fractures before. I am in fractures now. But the pieces still form the same broken picture."

Kira grunted. "Yeah, you're fine."

She tried to check her overlays . . . and nothing came up. After two more tries, she blinked, but she couldn't feel the contacts Vishal had given her. Nor could she feel them when she touched the tip of a finger against her right eye. "Crap," she said. The Soft Blade must have removed or absorbed the lenses sometime during the past few weeks of her long sleep.

Eager to see the system they'd arrived in, she dressed, splashed some water on her face, and hurried out of the cabin. She swung by the galley to get some more water and grab a pair of ration bars. Chewing on one, she climbed up to Control.

All the crew was there, and the Entropists too. Like Falconi, they looked haggard: hair tousled, dark circles under their eyes, and a hint of nausea in their expressions. Sparrow looked the weakest, and Kira reminded herself that the woman had gone through surgery before entering cryo.

Everything that had happened in 61 Cygni seemed distant and hazy now, but Kira knew that from the point of view of the crew, they had just left the system. For them, it was as if the last three months didn't exist. For her, the months were far more real. Even when in her artificial slumber, she'd retained a sense of the passage of time. She could *feel* the hours and days stretching out behind them, as tangible as their trail through space. 61 Cygni was no longer an immediate experience. And Adra before that even less so.

The inevitable accumulation of time had dulled the once-sharp pain of her grief. Her memories of the deaths on Adra still hurt, and always would, but they seemed thin and faded, drained of the vividness that had caused her so much anguish.

Everyone glanced at her as she entered Control, and then they returned their attention to the holo projected over the central table. Filling the holo was a model of the system they'd just entered.

Kira leaned against the edge of the table as she studied the image. Seven planets nested around the small, dim star: one gas giant and six terrestrial. The rocky planets were crammed in close to the star. The farthest one out orbited at only .043 AU. Then there was a gap and a sparse asteroid field, and the gas giant at .061 AU. Closer to the star—Bughunt—a second, thinner band of debris occupied the space between the second and third planets.

A chill of recognition crawled down Kira's spine. She knew this place. She'd seen it before, in her dreams, and more; her other flesh, the Soft Blade, had walked among those planets many times in the far distant past.

With recognition, she also felt vindication. She hadn't imagined or misinterpreted where they needed to go, and the Soft Blade hadn't deluded her. She'd been right about the location of the Staff of Blue . . . assuming it was still in the system after all these years.

The *Darmstadt* and the *Wallfish* were both marked in the holo with bright icons, but Kira also saw a third icon, near the Markov Limit, which—because of the low mass of the star and the compact orbits of the planets—was about two days' thrust at 1 g from Bughunt (assuming one intended to slow to a stop; otherwise it would only take a day and a half).

"What's that?" she said, pointing at the icon.

Falconi said, "The *Darmstadt* dropped a relay beacon as soon as it popped out of FTL. That way, if something happens to us, we might still be able to get a signal out."

Made sense, although it would take a long time to get a signal back to the League. The faster an FTL signal, the weaker it was. One strong enough to make it all the way to 61 Cygni in a coherent form would be even slower than a spaceship like the *Wallfish*. She'd have to check the numbers, but it could be *years* before the signal arrived.

Falconi gestured at the holo. "We're picking up evidence of structures throughout the system."

Even under the Soft Blade, Kira felt goosebumps erupt across her body. Finding the xeno and now *this*? It was what she had dreamed about when she was a kid; of making discoveries as big and important as the Great Beacon on Talos VII. The circumstances weren't what she would have wished for, but even so—if humanity survived the war with the Jellies and the nightmares, the things they could learn!

She cleared her throat. "Any currently . . . active?"

"Hard to tell. Doesn't seem like it." Falconi zoomed in on the band of debris between the second and third planets. "Check this out. Gregorovich, tell them what you told me."

The ship mind answered directly: "The composition of the flotsam seems to indicate it's artificial. It contains an unusually high percentage of metals, as well as other materials that, based off albedo if nothing else, cannot be natural in origin."

"All that?" said Kira, amazed. The amount of *stuff* was staggering. There was an entire lifetime's worth of study here. Several lifetimes'.

Hwa-jung altered the view of the holo as she studied it. "Maybe it was a Dyson ring."

"I didn't think any material was strong enough to make a ring that big," said Vishal.

Hwa-jung shook her head. "Does not have to be a solid ring. Could be lots of satellites or stations put all around the star. See?"

"Ah."

Nielsen said, "How old do you think it is?"

"Old," whispered Gregorovich. "Very, very old."

An uncomfortable silence filled the room. Then Trig said, "What do you think happened to the aliens here? A war?"

"Nothing good, I'm sure," said Falconi. He looked at Kira. "You're going to have to tell us where to go. We could spend forever wandering around, looking for the staff."

Kira studied the projection. No answer jumped to mind. The xeno didn't seem willing or able to tell her. It had helped them find the system; now it seemed they were on their own.

When she had been silent for a while, Falconi said, "Kira?" He was starting to sound worried.

"Give me a minute."

She thought. Most of the memories the Soft Blade had showed her of the staff had seemed to take place on or around one of the planets in the system. A brownish planet, with bands of circling clouds . . .

There. The fourth planet. It had the color, it had the clouds, and it was in Bughunt's habitable zone, if just barely. She checked: no evidence of an orbiting station. *Oh well.* That didn't mean anything. It could have been destroyed.

She highlighted the planet. "I can't tell you the exact location, but this is where we should start."

"You sure?" Falconi asked. She gave him a look, and he raised his hands. "Okay, then. I'll let Akawe know. What are we searching for? Cities? Buildings?"

She continued the list for him: "Monuments, statues, public works. Basically anything artificial."

"Got it."

The walls seemed to twist around them as Gregorovich adjusted their course.

"Captain," said Nielsen, getting to her feet. If anything, she looked worse than before. "I'm going to . . ."

He nodded. "I'll let you know if there's news."

The first officer crossed her arms, as if cold, and left the control room.

For a minute, no one else talked as Falconi had a one-sided conversation with the *Darmstadt*. Then he grunted and said, "Alright, we have a plan. Kira, we're going to feed you images of the planet's surface. We need you to look at it, see if you can figure out where to land. The planet is tidally locked with Bughunt—they all are—but maybe we'll get lucky with the side facing us. Meantime, we're going to head for the asteroid belt. Looks like there's plenty of ice flying around, so we can crack some hydrogen and refill our tanks."

Kira looked at Vishal. "I'll need a new set of contacts. The suit disappeared mine on the way here."

The doctor pushed himself out of his chair. "Come with me then, Ms. Kira."

As she followed him to sickbay, Kira couldn't help feeling a sense of unease and displacement at how far they were from the League. Not only that, it was alien territory, even if the aliens were long dead.

The Vanished, she thought, remembering the term from the Jelly ship. But vanished to where? And were the makers of the Soft Blade members of the Jellies or the nightmares or some other, older species?

She hoped they would find the answers on the planet.

In sickbay, Vishal gave her another set of contacts, and she said, "Can you print up another few pairs? I'll probably lose these on the way back."

"Yes, yes." He bobbed his head. "Do you still need your nose to be reset, Ms. Kira? I can do it now. Just—" He held his hands parallel and made a short jerking motion. "—*schk* and it will be done."

"No, it's okay. Later." She didn't want to deal with the pain at the moment. And besides, she felt a certain reluctance to do anything to fix her nose, although if asked, she couldn't have said why.

2.

Back in the galley, Kira made herself some chell, and then she sat at one of the bench tables and inserted the contacts. Fortunately, all of the data from the previous pair had uploaded into the ship's servers, so she hadn't lost anything.

She made a note to back up everything in at least two different places.

Once connected, alerts marking incoming messages from both Gregorovich and the *Darmstadt*'s ship mind, Horzcha Ubuto, appeared in the corner of her vision. Kira opened them to find a collection of telescopic images of the fourth planet—or "planet e," as it was labeled—from both ships. Appended to the first set was a note:

If you need a different type of imaging, just ask.—Horzcha Ubuto

Then Kira settled in to study the surface of planet e. There was a lot to study. It was 0.7 the diameter of Earth and nearly the same density. That meant water. And possibly native life.

She felt sure the planet had a proper name, but no sense of it came from the Soft Blade.

The pictures she had were mostly from the dark side of the planet. Only a sliver of the terminator between night and day was visible from their current position. The terminator was the most likely place for a city or installation of some kind, as it would be the most temperate area, balanced between the scorching heat of one side and the frigid cold of the other.

The near side of the planet was brown and orange. Vast canyons scraped the surface, and blackish patches marked where Kira thought giant lakes might lie. Ice crusted the poles, more away from the star than toward.

The ships' telescopes weren't the largest—neither the *Wallfish* nor the *Darmstadt* were scientific vessels—and given the distance, the resolution of the images wasn't the highest. But Kira did her best, examining each one for anything that seemed familiar.

Unfortunately, nothing struck a chord. There *was* evidence of habitation (helpfully outlined for her by Gregorovich and Horzcha Ubuto): faint lines that might be roads or canals along a section of the northern hemisphere, but nothing notable.

She lost herself in the images, barely paying attention to her surroundings. When she went to drink the chell, it was already cold, which annoyed her. She sipped at it anyway.

The door to the galley scraped open, and Trig entered. "Hey," he said. "Did you see what Gregorovich found?"

Kira blinked, slightly disoriented as she cleared her overlays. "No. What?"

"Here." He bounced over to her table and activated the built-in display. An image popped up of what appeared to be part of a space station, now broken and abandoned. The shape of it resembled no human-made structure. It was long and jagged, like a length of natural-grown crystal. The station obviously hadn't spun in order to create a sense of weight for its inhabitants. That meant either they had artificial gravity or the aliens hadn't minded spending their time in zero-g.

"Well," said Kira slowly. "I think we know one thing."

"Yeah?" said the kid.

"It sure doesn't look like the ships the Jellies or the nightmares are building these days. Either they've changed styles, or—"

"Another species." Trig beamed, as if this was the best piece of news ever. "The Vanished, right? The captain told me."

"That's right." She cocked her head. "You're enjoying this, huh?"

"Because it's *cool*!" He poked at the display. "How many alien civilizations do you think are out there? In the whole galaxy, that is."

"I have no idea. . . . Where did Gregorovich find the station?"

"Floating in the Dyson ring."

Kira drained the last of her chell. "How's your wrist, by the way?" The kid didn't have a cast anymore.

Trig rolled his hand in a circle. "All better now. Doc says he wants to see me again in a few weeks, real time, but other than that, I'm good to go."

"Glad to hear it."

The kid went to get some food, and Kira returned to studying the survey images of planet e. There was already a new batch waiting for her.

The work wasn't so different from the prep they'd done before arriving at Adrasteia. Out of habit, Kira found herself scanning for evidence of flora and fauna. There was oxygen in the atmosphere, which was encouraging, and nitrogen too. Thermal imaging seemed to show what might be areas of vegetation near the terminator line, but as with all tidally locked planets, it was difficult to be sure given the screwy atmospheric convections.

While she worked, the crew came in and out of the galley. Kira exchanged a few words with them, but for the most part, she kept her focus on the pictures. Nielsen never appeared, and she wondered if the first officer was still ill from cryo.

New pictures kept tumbling in, and as the spaceships grew closer to planet e, the resolution improved. Mid-afternoon, ship time, Kira received a message from the *Darmstadt* saying:

Of interest?—Horzcha Ubuto

Attached was an image from the southern hemisphere that showed a complex of buildings secreted in a fold of protective mountains, smack-dab in the middle of the terminator. At the sight of it, Kira felt a chill of ancient memories: fear, uncertainty, and the sadness born of regret. *And she saw the Highmost ascend a pedestal, bright in the dawn everlasting—*

A small gasp escaped her, and Kira felt a sudden certainty. She swallowed hard before opening a line to Falconi. "I found it. Or . . . I found *something.*"

"Show me." After studying the map, he said, "Seems like I keep asking this, but—are you sure?"

"As I said before we left: as sure as I can be."

"Okay. I'll talk with Akawe." The line clicked dead.

Kira made herself another cup of chell and warmed her hands around it while she waited.

Not ten minutes later, Falconi's voice sounded over the intercom throughout the ship: "Listen up, everyone. Change of plans. We have a destination on planet e, courtesy of Kira. We're going to do a burn straight there and drop off Kira and a team to check out the location while the *Wallfish* and the *Darmstadt* continue back out to the asteroid belt to refuel. It'll only take four or five hours to reach the belt, so the ships won't be too far away if we're needed. Over and out."

3.

Kira returned to Control and stayed there for the rest of the afternoon, watching as new discoveries continued to pop up on their screens. There were scores of artificial structures throughout the system, both on the planets and in space: monuments to a lost civilization. None appeared to have power. By the gas giant floated the hull of what looked to be a ship. By planet e, a cluster of junked satellites parked in what would have been a geostationary orbit if the planet hadn't been tidally locked. And of course, there was the Dyson ring (if that's what it was), which seemed to be filled with technological relics.

"This place—" said Veera.

"—is a treasure house beyond compare," finished Jorrus.

Kira agreed. "We'll be studying it for centuries. Do you think these were the aliens who made the Great Beacon?"

The Entropists inclined their heads. "Perhaps. It very well could be."

Dinner that night was a subdued, informal affair. No one bothered cooking; everyone's stomach but Kira's was still in a delicate state from cryo. As a result, it was prepackaged rations across the board, which made for a monotonous, if healthy, meal.

The Marines still didn't join them. Nor did Nielsen. The first officer's absence was conspicuous; without her quiet, steady presence, the conversation around the tables was sharper, more hard-edged.

"Tomorrow," said Vishal, "I would like to see you, Ms. Sparrow, for a checkup. It is necessary to make sure your new organs are working well."

Sparrow bobbed her head in an imitation of Vishal and said, "Sure thing, Doc." Then an evil little grin spread across her face. "Just using this as an excuse to get your hands on me, aren't you?"

Color bloomed on Vishal's cheeks, and he stuttered. "Ms.! I would—That is, no. No. That would *not* be professional."

Trig laughed through a mouthful of food. "Ha! Look, he's blushing."

Sparrow laughed as well, and a faint smile appeared on Hwa-jung's broad face.

They continued to tease the doctor, and Kira could see him getting more and more frustrated and angry, but he never snapped, never lashed out. She didn't understand it. If he just stood up for himself, the others would knock it off, or at least back off for a while. She'd seen it plenty of times before on the mining outposts. Guys who didn't punch back always ended up getting picked on more. It was a law of nature.

Falconi didn't interfere, not directly, but she noticed how he unobtrusively steered the conversation in a different direction. As they took up another topic, Vishal sank back in his seat, as if hoping no one would notice him.

While they talked, Kira went to the Entropists, who were hunched over a bluish, oblong-shaped object on their table, turning it over as if trying to find a key or a latch to open it.

She sat next to Veera. "What is that?" she asked, indicating the object. It was the size of both her fists combined.

The Entropists peered at her, owlish under the hoods of their robes. "We found this—" said Jorrus.

"—on the ship of the Jelly," said Veera. "We think it is a—"

"—processor or control module for a computer. But to be honest—"

"—we are not entirely sure."

Kira glanced back at Falconi. "Does the captain know you have this?"

The Entropists smiled, mirroring each other's expression. "Not this specifically," they said, their voices coming in stereo, "but he knows we salvaged several pieces of equipment off the ship."

"May I?" asked Kira, and held out her hands.

After a moment, the Entropists relented and allowed her to take the object. It was denser than it looked. The surface was pitted slightly, and there was a smell of . . . *salt?* to it.

Kira frowned. "If the xeno knows what this is, it's not telling me. Where did you find it?"

The Entropists showed her via footage from their implants.

"The Aspect of the Void," said Kira. The English translation tasted strange on her tongue; it was accurate, but it failed to capture the feel of the Jelly original. "That was the name of the room. I didn't go in there, but I saw the sign."

Veera carefully took back the oblong object. "What, in this instance—"

"—does the word *void* refer to? Likewise, what does—"

"—the word *aspect*?"

She hesitated. "I'm not sure. Maybe . . . communication? Sorry. Don't think I can help you any more than that."

The Entropists dipped their heads. "You have given us more than we had previously. We shall continue to ponder upon this matter. May your path always lead to knowledge, Prisoner."

"Knowledge to freedom," Kira replied.

When dinner was over, and people were dispersing, she contrived to get a moment alone with Falconi by the sink. "Is Nielsen alright?" she asked in a low tone.

His hesitation confirmed her suspicions. "It's nothing. She'll be fine tomorrow."

"Really." Kira gave him a look.

"Really."

She wasn't convinced. "Do you think she'd like it if I brought her some tea?"

"That's probably not a good id—" Falconi stopped himself as he dried off a plate. "You know what? I take it back. I think Audrey would appreciate the gesture." He reached up into a cupboard and removed a packet. "This is the stuff she likes. Ginger."

For a moment Kira wondered if he was setting her up. Then she decided it didn't matter.

Upon fixing the tea, she followed Falconi's directions to Nielsen's cabin, trying to keep the liquid from sloshing too much in the two safety cups she carried.

She knocked, and when there was no response, knocked again and said, "Ms. Nielsen? It's me, Kira."

". . . Go away." The first officer's voice was strained.

"I brought you some ginger tea."

After a few seconds, the door creaked open to reveal Nielsen standing in burgundy pajamas and a pair of matching slippers. Her normally immaculate hair was tied back in a shoddy bun, dark rings surrounded her eyes, and her skin was pale and bloodless even beneath her spacer's tan.

"See?" said Kira, and held out a cup. "As promised. I thought you might like something hot to drink."

Nielsen stared at the cup as if it were a foreign artifact. Then her expression eased, if only slightly, and she accepted it and moved aside. "Guess you'd better come in."

The interior of her cabin was clean and tidy. The only personal effect was a holo on the desk—three children (two boys and a girl) in their early teens. On the walls, overlays created the illusion of oval, brass-framed windows looking out upon a vista of endless clouds: orange, brown, and pale cream.

Kira sat on the lone chair while Nielsen sat on the bed. "I don't know if you like honey, but . . ." Kira held out a small packet. The movement of the clouds kept catching her eyes, distracting her.

"I do, actually."

While Nielsen stirred the honey into the tea, Kira studied her. She'd never seen the first officer so frail before. "If you want, I can get you some food from the galley. It won't take more than—"

Nielsen shook her head. "I wouldn't be able to keep it down."

"Bad reaction to the cryo, huh?"

"You could say that," said Nielsen.

"Can I get you something else? Maybe from the doctor?"

Nielsen took a sip. "That's very thoughtful, but no. I just need a good sleep, and I'll be—" Her breath hitched, and a spasm of pain knotted her face. She bent forward, putting her head between her knees, her breath coming in ragged gasps.

Alarmed, Kira darted to her side, but Nielsen held up a hand and Kira stopped, uncertain what to do.

She was just about to call for Vishal when Nielsen straightened. Her eyes were watery, and her expression was tight. "Dammit," she said in an undertone. Then, louder: "It's okay. I'm fine."

"Like hell you are," said Kira. "You couldn't even move. That's more than just cryo sickness."

"Yes." Nielsen leaned back against the wall behind the bed.

"What is it? Cramps?" Kira couldn't imagine why the other woman would have her periods turned on, but if she did . . .

Nielsen uttered a short laugh. "I wish." She blew on her tea and took a long drink.

Still on edge, Kira returned to the chair and studied the other woman. "Do you want to talk about it?"

"Not particularly."

An uncomfortable silence developed between them. Kira took a drink of her own tea. She wanted to press Nielsen harder, but she knew it would be a mistake. "Have you seen all the stuff we've found in the system? It's amazing. We'll be studying it for centuries."

"As long as we don't get wiped out."

"There is that small detail."

Nielsen peered at Kira over the top of her cup, eyes sharp and feverish. "Do you know why I agreed to this trip? I could have fought Falconi on it. If I'd tried hard enough, I could have even convinced him to refuse Akawe's offer. He listens to me when it comes to things like this."

"No, I don't know," said Kira. "Why?"

The first officer pointed at the holo of the kids on the desk. "Because of them."

"Is that you and your brothers?"

"No. They're my children."

"I didn't know you had a family," said Kira, surprised.

"Grandchildren, even."

"You're joking! Really?"

Nielsen smiled a little. "I'm quite a bit older than I look."

"I never would have guessed you'd had STEM shots."

"You mean my nose and ears?" Nielsen touched them. "I had them fixed about ten years ago. It was the thing to do where I lived." She looked out the window overlaid on the wall, and her gaze grew distant, as if she saw something other than the clouds of Venus. "Coming here to Bughunt was the only thing I could do to help protect my family. That's why I agreed to it. I just wish . . . Well, it doesn't matter now."

"What doesn't?" said Kira, gentle.

A sadness settled over Nielsen, and she sighed. "I just wish I could have talked with them before we left. Who knows what it's going to be like when we get back."

Kira understood. "Do they live at Sol?"

"Yes. Venus and Mars." Nielsen picked at a spot on her palm. "My daughter is still on Venus. You might have seen, the Jellies attacked there a while back. Fortunately it wasn't close to her, but . . ."

"What's her name?"

"Yann."

"I'm sure they'll be fine. Of all the places they could be, Sol is probably the safest."

Nielsen gave her a *don't bullshit me* look. "You saw what happened on Earth. I don't think anywhere is safe these days."

In an attempt to distract her, Kira said, "So how did you end up on the *Wallfish,* then—so far away from your family?"

Nielsen studied the reflections in her cup. "Lots of reasons. . . . The publishing company I worked for declared bankruptcy. New management restructured, fired half the staff, canceled our pensions." Nielsen shook her head. "Twenty-eight years spent working for them, all gone. The pension was bad enough, but I lost my health coverage, which was a problem given my, ah, particular challenges."

"But isn't—"

"Of course. Basic access is guaranteed, as long as you're a citizen in good standing. Even sometimes if you're not. But basic coverage isn't what I needed." Nielsen glanced at Kira from the corner of her eyes. "And now you're wondering just how sick I am and whether it's contagious."

Kira raised an eyebrow. "Well, I assume Falconi wouldn't have let you on board if you were carrying some deadly, flesh-eating bacteria."

The other woman nearly laughed, and then she pressed a hand against her chest and made a pained face. "It's not that dire. At least not for anyone else."

"Are you—I mean, is it terminal?"

"*Life* is terminal," said Nielsen dryly. "Even with STEM shots. Entropy always wins in the end."

Kira raised her cup. "To the Entropists, then. May they find a way to reverse the time-ordered decay of all things."

"Hear, hear." And Nielsen clinked cups with her. "Although, I can't say the prospect of life unending appeals to me."

"No. It would be nice to have some choice in the matter."

After another sip and another pause, Nielsen said, "My . . . condition was a gift from my parents, believe it or not."

"How so?"

The first officer rubbed her face, and the true depths of her exhaustion became evident. "They were trying to do the right thing. People always are. They just forget the old adage regarding the problem with good intentions and the road to Hell."

"That's a rather cynical view."

"I'm in a rather cynical mood." Nielsen straightened her legs out on the bed. It seemed to hurt. "Before I was born, the laws on gene-hacking weren't as strict as they are now. My parents wanted to give their child—me—every possible advantage. What parent wouldn't?"

Kira instantly grasped the problem. "Oh no."

"Oh yes. So they packed me full of every known gene sequence for intelligence, including a few artificial ones that had just been developed."

"Did it work?"

"I've never needed to use a calculator, if that's what you mean. There were unintended side effects, though. The doctors aren't quite sure what happened, but some part of the alterations triggered my immune system—set it off like a pressure alarm in a dome that's been ripped open." Nielsen's expression became sardonic. "So I can calculate how fast the air is rushing out without having to check my math, but there's nothing I can do to keep myself from asphyxiating. Metaphorically speaking."

"Nothing?" Kira said.

Nielsen shook her head. "The doctors tried fixing the conflicts with retroviral treatments, but . . . they can only do so much. The genes changed tissue up here," she tapped the side of her head. "Delete them, remove them, or even just edit them and it could kill me or mess with my memories or my personality." Her lips twisted. "Life is full of little ironies like that."

"I'm sorry."

"It happens. I'm not the only one, although most of the others didn't make it past thirty. As long as I take my pills, it isn't too bad, but some days—" Nielsen winced. "Some days, the pills don't do much of anything." She picked up her pillow and wedged it behind her back. Her tone was bitter as arsenic: "When your body isn't your own, it's worse than any prison." Her eyes flicked toward Kira. "You know."

She did know, and she also knew dwelling on it wouldn't help. "So what happened after you got laid off?"

Nielsen drained the last of her tea in a single gulp. She put the empty cup on the edge of the desk. "The bills started piling up, and . . . well, my husband, Sarros, left. I don't blame him, not really, but there I was, having to start all over again at sixty-three. . . ." Her laugh could have cut glass. "I don't recommend it."

Kira made a sympathetic noise, and the first officer said: "I couldn't find a job that suited me on Venus, so I left."

"Just like that?"

The steel inside Nielsen came to the fore again. "Exactly like that. I spent some time moving around Sol, trying to find a steady position. Eventually I ended up at Harcourt Station, out by Titan, and that's where I met Falconi and talked him into bringing me on as first officer."

"Now there's a conversation I would have liked to hear," said Kira.

Nielsen chuckled. "I may have been a bit pushy. I practically had to force my way onto the *Wallfish*. The ship was a bit of a mess when I arrived; it needed organizing and scheduling, and those have always been my strong points."

Kira toyed with the extra packet of honey she'd brought. "Can I ask you a question?"

"It's a little late to be asking for permission, don't you think?"

"About Falconi."

Nielsen's expression grew more guarded. "Go ahead."

"What's the story behind those scars on his arms? Why didn't he get them fixed?"

"Ah." Nielsen shifted her legs, trying to find a more comfortable position. "Why don't you ask him yourself?"

"I wasn't sure if it was a sensitive subject."

Nielsen stared at her with an overly direct gaze. Her eyes, Kira noticed for the first time, had flecks of green in them. "If Falconi feels like telling you, he will. Either way, it's not really my story to share. I'm sure you understand."

Kira didn't press the issue, but Nielsen's reticence only increased her curiosity.

After that, they spent a pleasant half hour chatting about the intricacies of living and working on Venus. To Kira, the planet seemed beautiful and exotic and dangerous in an alluring way. Nielsen's time in the publishing industry there had been so different from Kira's profession, it made her consider the vast array of personal experiences that existed throughout the League.

At last, when Kira's cup was empty and Nielsen seemed in relatively good cheer, Kira stood to leave. The first officer caught her by the wrist.

"Thank you for the tea. It was very nice of you. I mean it."

The praise warmed Kira's heart. "Any time. It was my pleasure."

Nielsen smiled then—a genuine smile—and Kira smiled in return.

4.

Back in her own cabin, Kira paused in front of the mirror by the sink. The dim, ship-night lighting cast heavy shadows across her face, which made the kink in her nose stand out in high relief.

She felt the crooked flesh; it would be easy to fix. A hard *jerk* would return it to normal, and then the Soft Blade would heal her face the way it should have the first time.

But she didn't want that, and now she understood why. The xeno had erased every mark on her body, every bump and line and freckle and odd bit of jiggle. It had removed the physical record of her life and replaced it with the meaningless coating of fibers that retained no stamp of experience. So much it had taken from her, she didn't want to lose more.

Keeping a crooked nose was *her* choice, *her* way of reshaping the flesh they shared. It also served as a reminder of past sins, ones she was determined not to repeat.

Flush with that determination, as well as a surfeit of images from the system they'd arrived at, Kira threw herself down and—even after three months of mostly hibernating—fell asleep.

She and her joined flesh—not a grasper but a giver—walked as witness behind the Highmost among the field of ill-shaped growths: cancerous intentions that bore poisonous fruit. And the Highmost raised the Staff of Blue and said a single, cutting word: "No."

Down the staff then came, struck the heaving earth. A circle of grey expanded about the Highmost as each mutated cell tore itself apart. The stench of death and putrefaction smothered the field, and sorrow bent the Highmost.

An earlier fracture: one of her siblings stood before the assembled Heptarchy in their high-arched presence chamber. The Highmost descended to the patterned floor and touched the Staff of Blue to the blood-smeared brow of her sibling.

"You are no longer worthy."

Then flesh parted from flesh as the other Soft Blade flowed away from the staff, fleeing its power and leaving the body of its bonded mate exposed, vulnerable. For there was no denying the Staff of Blue.

Another disjunction, and she found herself standing beside the Highmost, upon the observation deck of an enormous starship. Before and below them hung a rocky planet, green and red with swarms of life. There was a wrongness to it, though—a feel of threat that made her wish she was elsewhere—as if the planet itself were malevolent.

The Highmost raised the Staff of Blue once again. "Enough." The staff angled forward, a flash of sapphire light sent shadows streaming, and the planet vanished.

In the distance, well past the planet's previous location, a patch of starlight twisted, and with it twisted her stomach. For she knew what the distortion heralded. . . .

Kira woke with a pounding heart. She stayed under the blankets for several minutes, reviewing the memories from the Soft Blade. Then she rolled upright and put a call through to both Falconi and Akawe.

As soon as they answered, she said, "We *have* to find the Staff of Blue." Then she told them of her dream.

Falconi said, "If even only part of that is true—"

"Then it's even more important we keep the Jellies from getting their tentacles on this tech," said Akawe.

The call ended, and Kira checked their location: still on course for planet e. *It needs a better name,* she thought. At the current distance, and without magnification, the planet was still just a gleaming dot in the ship's cameras, no different from the other, nearby dots that marked the rest of the system's closely packed planets.

During the night, the ship minds had found even more structures scattered about Bughunt. The system had clearly been a base for long-term settlement. Kira glanced over the newest discoveries but saw nothing immediately revelatory, so she put them aside for later study.

Then she checked her messages. There were two waiting for her. The first—as she'd half expected—was from Gregorovich:

> *The dust from your alien companion is clogging my filters again, meatbag. – Gregorovich*

She replied:

Apologies. I didn't have time to clean yesterday. I'll see what I can do. – Kira

No matter; you'll likely just make a mess of it. Leave your door unlocked, and I shall send one of my tricksy little service bots to sweep up your leavings. Would you like your sheets turned down as well? Y/N – Gregorovich

. . . No thank you. I can manage just fine myself. – Kira

As you wish, meatbag. – Gregorovich

The other message was from Sparrow:

Let's do this. Cargo hold; I'll be waiting. – Sparrow

Kira ran a hand over the back of her head. She'd been expecting to hear from Sparrow. Whatever the woman had in store for her, it wasn't going to be easy, but Kira was okay with that. She was curious to find out if her efforts with the Soft Blade were going to pay off. If nothing else, interfacing with the xeno ought to be easier now that she was fully awake and properly fed.

Kira fetched her morning chell from the galley and then headed down to the hold. The Marines were there, prepping their gear for the upcoming trip to the surface of planet e. The squad greeted her with nods and grunts and even a salute on the part of Sanchez. Whether it was their military augments or their natural constitutions, Kira didn't know, but none of the men looked as drained from cryo as the crew of the *Wallfish*.

As promised, Sparrow was in the small gym hidden within the racks of equipment. She was chewing gum while doing painful-looking crunches on a mat. "Rehab," she said in response to Kira's querying look.

After finishing her set, Sparrow rolled onto her knees. "So?" she said. "Three months. Were you able to keep up with your training?"

"Yes."

"And? How'd it go?"

Kira knelt as well. "Good, I think. It was hard to tell at times, but I tried my damnedest. I really did."

A crooked little smile cut Sparrow's face. "Show me."

So Kira did. She pressed and pulled and ran and otherwise performed all the exercises Sparrow asked of her . . . while also shaping and reshaping the Soft Blade the whole time. To Kira's satisfaction, she did well. Not perfect. But very close. She never lost control of the xeno to the point where it stabbed or lashed out; at the most, it formed a few studs or ripples in response to the stresses imposed on her body. And she was able to form intricate shapes and patterns with its fibers. It felt as if the organism was working *with* her, not against her, which was a welcome change.

Sparrow watched with focused intensity. She gave no praise and showed no sign of approval, and when Kira continued to meet her demands, she merely asked for more. More weight. More complexity with the Soft Blade. More time under tension. *More.*

At last, Kira was ready to call it quits. She felt that she had done quite enough to demonstrate her new skills. But Sparrow had other ideas.

The woman hopped down from the bench where she was sitting and strode over to where Kira was standing by the weight rack, panting and sweating. She stopped only centimeters away: too close for comfort.

Kira fought the urge to step back.

"Make the most detailed pattern that you can," said Sparrow.

Kira was tempted to argue. She resisted, though, and—after thinking—willed the Soft Blade to imitate the fractal it had shown her on more than one occasion. The surface of the suit rippled and deformed into an almost microscopically detailed design. Holding it in place wasn't easy, but then, that was the point.

Kira sucked in her breath. "Okay. What else do—"

Sparrow slapped her cheek. Hard.

Shocked, Kira blinked, tears forming in her left eye, the side Sparrow had hit. "What the—"

Sparrow slapped her again, a bright, icy shock that sent stars shooting across Kira's vision. She felt the mask start to crawl across her face and the Soft Blade start to spike out, and with a mighty effort, she held it in place. It felt as if she were holding a high-tension wire with a metric ton of weight at the other end, pulling her forward, threatening to snap.

She set her jaw and glared at Sparrow, now knowing what the woman was up to.

Sparrow grinned—an evil little grin that did nothing but piss off Kira even more. It was the sadistic superiority of the expression that really got to her.

Sparrow slapped her a third time.

Kira saw the blow coming. She could have ducked or flinched or protected herself with the Soft Blade. She *wanted* to. She also could have struck back with the suit. The xeno was eager to fight, eager to stop the threat.

A moment's lapse, and Sparrow would have been lying on the floor, blood oozing from a half-dozen different wounds. Kira could see it in her mind.

She took another breath and then forced herself to smile. Not an angry smile. Not an evil smile. A flat, calm smile that said, *You can't break me.* She meant it, too. She and the Soft Blade were working together, and Kira felt a solid sense of control, not only over the xeno, but herself.

Sparrow grunted and stepped back. The tension in her shoulders slacked. "Not bad, Navárez. . . . Not bad."

Kira allowed the pattern to melt into the surface of the Soft Blade. "That was really fucking risky."

A quick laugh from Sparrow. "It worked, didn't it." She returned to the bench and sat.

"And if it hadn't?" In the back of her mind, Kira couldn't help but feel a sense of triumph. She really had made progress on the way to Bughunt. All those practice sessions alone in the dark had been worth it. . . .

Sparrow clipped a bar attachment to the weight machine. "You're going dirtside tomorrow to poke around an alien city, looking for some scary-ass alien superweapon. Shit could go sideways real fast, and you know it. If you couldn't handle a little something like this"—she shrugged—"you shouldn't leave the *Wallfish*. Besides, I had confidence in you."

"You're crazy, you know that?" But Kira smiled as she said it.

"Nothing new there." Sparrow started to do pulldowns on the weight machine, using fairly light weight. She did a set of ten and then stopped and hunched over, eyes screwed shut.

"How's your recovering going?" Kira asked.

Sparrow made a disgusted face. "Well enough. The doc kept me at a slightly higher metabolic rate than normal in cryo, which helped with the healing, but it's still going to be another few weeks before I'm rated to get back in an exo. And that really burns me."

"Why?" said Kira.

"Because," said Sparrow, massaging her side, where she'd been injured, "I can't fight like this."

"You shouldn't have to. Besides, we've got the UMC with us."

Sparrow snorted. "You grow up on a colony or what?"

"Yeah. What's that got to do with it?"

"Then you ought to know you can't off-load responsibility on someone else. You have to be able to take care of yourself when shit goes down."

Kira thought about that for a moment as she put away the weights she'd been holding. "Sometimes we can't, and that's when we have to rely on other people. That's how societies work."

Sparrow sucked her lips against her teeth in an unpleasant little smile. "Maybe. Doesn't mean I have to like being disabled."

"No, it doesn't."

5.

As they left the hold, they passed by the Marines, and Kira greeted them as she had on the way in. The men started to reply, but then they saw Sparrow and their expressions grew cold.

Tatupoa jerked his chin toward her. His tattoos gleamed like sapphire wires amid the shadows cast by the storage racks. "Yeah, we looked you up. Just keep walking, gas-head. We don't need your like around here."

"Private!" barked Hawes. "That's enough!" But he avoided looking at Sparrow, same as the others.

"Yessir."

Sparrow kept walking and didn't react, as if she hadn't heard. Confused, Kira kept pace with her. Once out in the hall, she said, "What the hell was that about?"

To her surprise, Sparrow leaned with one hand against the wall. The shorter woman looked as if she were going to be sick. Somehow Kira doubted it had anything to do with cryo.

"Hey, are you okay?" said Kira.

Sparrow shivered. "Oh yeah. Blasting on full jets." She ground the heel of her free hand against the corners of her eyes.

Not knowing what else to do, Kira said, "How did they figure out who you are?"

"Service records. Every ship in the fleet carries a full set of 'em, aside from the black bag, spec-ops grunts. Bet they ran my picture through the files. Wouldn't be hard." Sparrow sniffed and pushed herself off the wall. "You tell anyone about this and I'll kill you."

"The Jellies might get to me before then. . . . What's *gas-head* mean? Nothing good, I guess."

A bitter smile twisted Sparrow's mouth. "*Gas-head* is what you call someone you think deserves to be spaced. The blood boils off, turns to gas. Get it?"

Kira eyed her, trying to read between the lines. "So why you?"

"Doesn't matter," Sparrow muttered, straightening up. She started to walk away, but Kira stepped in front of her.

"I think it does," Kira said.

Sparrow stared her straight in the eyes, jaw muscles working. "Get out of my way, Navárez."

"Not until you tell me, and there's no way you can force me to move."

"Fine, then I'll just sit here." And Sparrow dropped into a cross-legged position.

Kira crouched down beside her. "If you can't work with the Marines, I need to know why."

"You ain't the captain."

"No, but we're all putting our lives on the line here. . . . What is it, Sparrow? It can't be that bad."

The woman snorted. "You have a seriously faulty imagination if that's what you think. Fine. Screw it. You want the truth? I got kicked out of the UMCM for cowardice before the enemy. Spent seven months in lockup as a result. There, you happy?"

"I don't believe you," said Kira.

"The specific charges were abandonment of my post, cowardice in the face of the enemy, and striking a commanding officer." Sparrow crossed her arms, defiant. "That's why *gas-head.* No Marine wants to serve with a coward."

"You're not a coward," said Kira, earnest. "I've seen you in combat. Hell, you went right after that little girl like it was nothing."

Sparrow shook her head. "That was different."

"Bullshit. . . . Why do I think the whole 'striking a commanding officer' is the real cause of this?"

With a sigh, Sparrow let her head fall back against the wall. The impact of skull with plating produced a *thud* that echoed up and down the hall. "Because you think too damn much, that's why. His name was Lieutenant Eisner, and he was a real asshole. I got transferred to his unit during the middle of deployment. This was back during the border war with Shin-Zar, see. Eisner was a shit officer. He kept getting his unit into trouble in the field, and for whatever reason, he seemed to have it out for me personally. Kept riding me no matter what I did." She shrugged. "After one of our ops went tits up, I'd had enough. Eisner was using some bullshit excuse to chew out my gunner, and I went over and told him off. Lost my temper and ended up popping him in the face. Gave him a real doozy of a shiner. Thing is, I'd been posted to guard duty and I'd left my watch, so Eisner had me brought up on cowardice before the enemy."

Sparrow shrugged again. "Seven years of service down the drain, just like that. Only stuff I got to keep were my augments." And she made a muscle with her arm before dropping it.

"Shit," said Kira. "Couldn't you fight the charges?"

"Nah. It happened out in the field during combat operations. The League wasn't going to ship us back for an investigation. The footage showed me leaving my post and hitting Eisner. That was all that mattered."

"So why don't you go in there and explain?" said Kira, motioning toward the hold.

"Wouldn't do any good," said Sparrow. She stood. "Why should they believe me? Far as they're concerned, I'm hardly better than a deserter." She slapped Kira on the shoulder. "Doesn't matter anyway. We don't need to like each other in order to do our jobs. . . . Now, are you going to get out of my way or not?"

Kira moved aside, and Sparrow limped past, leaving her alone in the corridor.

After thinking for a long minute, Kira climbed up the center of the ship and made her way to Control. Falconi was there, as she expected, and Nielsen too—looking far better than she had the previous day.

She and the first officer exchanged companionable nods, and then Kira went over to the captain and said, "Any news?"

"Not at the moment."

"Good. . . . I have a favor to ask."

He looked at her, wary. "Is that so?"

"Will you come with me to the planet?"

Falconi's eyebrows rose fractionally. "Why?" Across the room, Nielsen paused reading something on a display to listen.

"Because," said Kira, "I don't want to be down there all alone with the UMC."

"You don't trust them?" said Nielsen.

Kira hesitated a second. "I trust you more."

Falconi let her hang for a few seconds, and then he said, "Well, today's your lucky day. I already arranged things with Akawe."

"You're going?" said Kira, not quite believing.

"Not just me. Trig, Nielsen, and the Entropists too."

The first officer sniffed. "Just what I wanted to do on a Sunday afternoon."

Falconi grinned at Kira. "There's no way I'm coming this far and *not* getting out to see the sights."

The knowledge eased Kira's concern somewhat. "So Sparrow, Hwa-jung, and Vishal are going to stay on board?"

"Exactly. The UMC are bringing their own doc. Sparrow still isn't cleared for duty, and Hwa-jung doesn't fit in our exos. Besides, I want Hwa-jung on the ship in case anything goes wrong."

That made sense. Kira said, "Who's taking the exos then?"

Falconi jerked his head toward Nielsen. "Her and Trig."

"That's not necessary," said Nielsen. "I'm perfectly capable of—"

The captain didn't give her the opportunity to finish. "Yes, you are, but I'd rather have my crew in armor for this trip. Besides, I've never cared for exos. Too restrictive. Give me a plain old skinsuit any day of the week."

6.

The rest of the day passed in a mood of quiet intensity. The crew bustled around, preparing for the descent to the planet, while Kira reviewed the procedures for preventing contamination while in an unknown (and potentially life-bearing) alien environment. She knew them by heart, but it was always good to read them again before the start of an expedition.

Ideally they would have spent months, if not years, studying the planet's biosphere from a distance before daring to put an actual human on the surface, but given the circumstances, that was a luxury they couldn't afford. Still, Kira wanted to reduce the chances of contamination—in either direction—as much as possible. The planet was an incredible source of information; it would be a crime to infect it with a set of human microbes. Unfortunately, even the most thorough decontamination couldn't remove *every* foreign body from the surface of their equipment, but they'd do the best they could.

After some thought, she drew up a list of recommendations: best practices for protecting the location and themselves, based off her professional experience. She sent the list to both Falconi and Akawe.

<These are going to be a real pain in the ass, Navárez. Running through decon twice? No touching of an object without express permission? Walking single file? No CO^2 venting? The UMCN already has its own set of protocols for dealing with this sort of situation, and they're more than adequate. – Akawe>

<No, they aren't. We've never found a location like this before. We can't screw this up. Future generations will thank us for it. – Kira>

<First we have to make sure there are future generations. – Akawe>

He continued to grumble, but after some more discussion, he agreed to implement her guidelines during the landing mission. *<But that's all they are, Navárez, guidelines. Shit happens in the field, and you have to adapt. – Akawe>*

<As long as we make an attempt to preserve the site. That's all I'm asking. – Kira>

<Roger that. – Akawe>

Kira returned to examining the images Gregorovich and Horzcha Ubuto were collecting of planet e, as well as the rest of the system. She didn't learn much, but she kept at it, hoping to spot something else that might help them find the Staff of Blue.

Dinner, when it came, was a friendlier, more energetic affair than the previous one. Nielsen was there, and though everyone was somewhat on edge about the upcoming trip, a sense of optimism pervaded the air. It felt as if they—and humans in general—were finally going to be able to make significant progress against the Jellies.

Most of the conversations revolved around what they might or might not expect to run into on the planet, as well as the best pieces of equipment to take. Room on the UMC shuttle would be limited, so they had to choose wisely.

Sparrow, as Kira expected, was disgruntled at being left behind on the *Wallfish* (Hwa-jung didn't seem to mind either way). To which Falconi said, "When I don't have to worry about you ripping your stomach back open, *then* you can climb into an exo, and not a moment sooner."

Sparrow conceded the point, but Kira could tell she was still unhappy. To distract her, Kira said, "So I'm curious; is Sparrow your first or last name? You've never said."

"I haven't?" Sparrow took a sip of wine. "Imagine that."

"Her name is just listed as *Sparrow* on her ID," said Falconi, leaning toward Kira.

"Really?" said Kira. "You only have one name?"

A twinkle appeared in Sparrow's eyes. "Only one that I answer to."

I bet the Marines could tell me for sure. But Kira wasn't about to ask them. "What about you, then?" she said, looking at Trig.

The kid groaned and buried his head in his hands. "Aww, man. Did you have to ask?"

"What?" Around the room, the rest of the crew grinned.

Vishal plopped his cup down on the table and pointed a finger at Trig. "Our young companion here has a most interesting name, yes he does."

"Trig's just a nickname," said Sparrow. "His real name is—"

"Nooo," the kid said, his cheeks reddening. "My aunt had a weird sense of humor, okay?"

To Kira, Vishal said, "She must have; she named the poor child Epiphany Jones." And everyone but Trig laughed.

"That's a . . . unique name," Kira said.

Falconi said, "It gets better. Tell her how we found Trig."

The kid shook his head as the rest of the crew tried to talk at once. "Come on! Not that story."

"Oh yes," said Sparrow, grinning.

"Why don't you tell me yourself?" said Kira. The kid wrinkled his nose.

"He was a dancer," said Hwa-jung, and nodded as if she'd shared a great secret.

Kira gave Trig an appraising look. "A dancer, huh?"

"On Undset Station, around Cygni B," Vishal added. "He was making a living performing in a bar for the miners."

"It wasn't like that!" Trig protested. The others tried to break in, and he raised his voice to be heard over the clamor. "Not really, honest! My friend worked at the place, and he was trying to find a way to attract business. So I came up with the idea. We put some Tesla coils on stage and used them to play music. Then I rigged up a skinsuit to work as a Faraday cage, and I stood between the coils and caught the lightning bolts with my hands, arms, that sort of thing. It was awesome."

"And don't forget the dancing," said Falconi, grinning.

Trig shrugged. "So I danced a bit."

"I wasn't there myself," Nielsen said, putting a hand on Kira's arm. "But I heard he was very . . . *enthusiastic.*" Despite his obvious embarrassment, Trig seemed somewhat proud of the first officer's praise, humorous though it was.

"Oh, he was," said Vishal. "He was."

Taking pity on the kid's discomfort, Kira changed the subject: "What kind of music did you play?"

"Mostly scramrock. Thresh. That sort of thing."

"So why'd you leave?"

"Didn't have any reason to stay," he mumbled, and downed the rest of his water.

A somber mood quelled the conversation. Then Falconi wiped his mouth with a napkin and said, "I know what you need."

"What?" said Trig, staring at his plate.

"A religious experience."

The kid snorted. Then his lips curved with a faint, reluctant smile. "Yeah. Okay. . . . You might be right."

"Of course I'm right," said Falconi.

With newfound enthusiasm, Trig scraped the rest of his food into his mouth, chewed, and swallowed. "I'm going to regret that," he said, smiling as he got to his feet.

"Don't hurt yourself," said Hwa-jung.

"Go on, eat the whole thing this time," called Sparrow.

"Video! Take video," said Falconi.

"Just make sure you wash afterward." Nielsen grimaced slightly.

"Yes, ma'am."

Confused, Kira looked between them. "A religious experience?"

Falconi picked up his plate and carried it to the sink. "Trig has an uncommon love of hot peppers. While back, he picked up a Black Nova off a wirehead on Eidolon."

"I take it a Black Nova is a kind of pepper."

Trig bounced on his heels. "Hottest one in the galaxy!"

"It's so hot," said Sparrow, "they say you'll see the face of god if you're idiot enough to eat one. That or you pass out and die."

"Hey now," Trig protested. "It's not that bad."

"Ha!"

"Have you tried it?" Kira asked Falconi.

He shook his head. "I prefer not to wreck my stomach."

She eyed Trig. "So why do you like it so much?"

"Well, uh, if you don't have enough food, hot sauce really helps, you know? Cuts the hunger. That's what got me into peppers. That and I kinda like the challenge. Gives me a sense of control. It doesn't even hurt after a while, and you just feel like, whee!" Trig rolled his head, as if dizzy.

"Helps with hunger, huh?" Kira was starting to understand.

"Yeah." Trig took his dishes to the sink and then hurried out of the galley. "Wish me luck!"

Kira took a sip of her chell. "Should we wait?" she asked, looking at the others.

Falconi activated the holo-display on his table. "If you want."

"A while back, Trig mentioned there were food shortages on Undset Station. . . ."

A frown settled onto Sparrow's sharp face. "If that's what you want to call it. Royal fuckup is more like it."

"Oh?"

"Yeah. Way I understand it, the sublight transport that was supposed to resupply Undset from Cygni A broke down, went off course. No big deal, right? The station had a hydro bay plus plenty of extra food stockpiled. Only problem was—"

"Only problem was," said Falconi, looking over the gleaming holo, "the quartermaster had been cutting corners, pocketing the difference. Less than a third of the food was actually there. And most of it was rotten. Faulty seals or something."

Kira winced. "Oh shit."

"You can say that again. By the time they realized how bad the situation was, the station was nearly out of food, and the replacement tug was still a few weeks out."

"*Weeks?* Why so long? Cygni B isn't that far from A."

"Bureaucracy, time it took to gather the supplies, prep a ship, et cetera. Apparently they didn't have any FTL transports set up at the time so they had to do it sublight. It was a whole collection of screwups."

Sparrow chimed in, "From what Trig's said, things got real bad on Undset before the new transport showed up. Supposedly, they ended up spacing the quartermaster and the station commander." And she nodded as if sharing a great secret.

"Thule." Kira shook her head. "How long ago was this?"

Sparrow looked over at Falconi. "What, about ten, twelve years?"

He nodded. "Sounds about right."

Kira picked at her food, thinking. "Trig would have been pretty young, then."

"Yup."

"No wonder he wanted to get off Undset."

Falconi returned his attention to the holo. "Wasn't his only reason, but . . . yes."

7.

They were still in the galley forty-some minutes later when Trig strutted back in. His cheeks were bright red; his eyes swollen, bloodshot, glassy; and his skin shiny with sweat, but he looked happy, almost euphoric.

"How'd it go, kid?" Sparrow asked, leaning back against the wall.

He grinned and puffed up his chest. "Awesome. But sheesh, my throat *burns*!"

"I can't imagine why," Nielsen said in a dry tone.

The kid started toward the kitchen area, and then stopped and looked at Kira. "Can you believe we're actually going to get to explore alien ruins tomorrow?!"

"You're looking forward to it?"

He nodded, serious but still excited. "Oh yeah. But, well . . . I was wondering, what happens if they're still around?"

"I'd like to know that too," Nielsen murmured.

In her mind's eye, Kira again saw the Highmost sweep the Staff of Blue downward, and a dark and miserable planet vanish from the sky. "We hope they're in a good mood."

8.

Trig's final question lingered in Kira's mind as she returned to her cabin: *What happens if they're still around?* What indeed? She checked on the ship's progress in her console—course unchanged, planet e now brighter than any of the visible stars—and then lay on the bed and closed her eyes.

Tomorrow's worries would have to wait for tomorrow.

She slept, and this time no memories intruded.

9.

A persistent beeping roused her.

Annoyed, Kira forced her eyes open. In the holo, she saw the time displayed: *0345*. Fifteen minutes until departure.

She groaned and rolled out of bed, feeling every second of missed sleep. Then it occurred to her that she'd forgotten to set an alarm. Was Gregorovich responsible for waking her?

As she dressed, Kira opened a new window and sent a single line to the ship mind:

Thanks. – Kira

A second later, a response arrived:

De nada. – Gregorovich

It paid to be courteous with ship minds, especially if they were anything less than sane.

Still groggy, Kira ran through the ship and climbed toward the nose of the *Wallfish*. The ship hadn't stopped thrusting, which meant the shuttle had yet to arrive. Good. She wasn't too late.

She found the crew—along with the Entropists and the four Marines in power armor—at the top of the ship, by the airlock.

"About time," said Falconi, and tossed her a blaster. He was wearing a skinsuit, helmet included, and his oversized grenade launcher, Francesca, was slung across his back.

"Is the shuttle close?" Kira asked.

As if in response, the thrust alert sounded and Gregorovich said, "Initiating docking maneuvers with the UMCS *Ilmorra*. Please secure yourself to the nearest handhold, seat belt, and/or sticky pad."

Vishal saw her yawning and offered her a pill of AcuWake. "Here, Ms. Kira. Try this."

"I don't think—"

"It may not help, but I think it is worth trying."

Still doubtful, Kira popped the capsule into her mouth. It burst between her teeth with a sharp, wintergreen tang, strong enough to make her nose tingle and her eyes water. Within seconds, her exhaustion and mental haze began to dissipate, leaving her feeling as if she'd had a full night's sleep.

Astonished, she looked back at the doctor. "It worked! How did it work?!"

A sly smile graced the doctor's face, and he tapped the side of his nose. "I had a suspicion it might. The medicine, it goes straight into the blood and then to your brain. Very quick, very difficult for the Soft Blade to stop without hurting your brain. And it is supposed to help, yes, so maybe the xeno knows not to interfere."

Whatever the explanation, Kira was grateful for the chemical assistance. She couldn't afford to be sleep-deprived right then.

Then all sense of weight abandoned her, and bile filled her throat.

Docking was swift and efficient. The UMC shuttle approached the *Wallfish* head-on so both ships were safe from radiation within the cones of their shadow shields. They made contact, nose-to-nose, and a light shudder passed through the *Wallfish* at the touch.

The joined airlocks rolled open. A Marine poked his head through on the other side. "Welcome aboard," he said.

Falconi gave Kira a crooked smile. "Time to go poking around where we don't belong."

"Let's do this," she said, and jumped into the *Ilmorra*.

CHAPTER II

* * * * * * *

A CAELO USQUE AD CENTRUM

1.

Kira watched on her overlays as the *Wallfish* and the *Darmstadt* receded into the distance: two bright points of light that quickly dwindled to near nothing. The ships moved as a locked pair, on course for the asteroid they'd chosen to mine. Behind them, Bughunt was a dull, ruddy orb—a dying coal set within a field of black.

Kira sat buckled into a jump seat along the wall, next to Falconi. The rest of the expedition was likewise secured, except for those—like Trig and Nielsen—who were wearing power armor. They stood locked into hard points near the back of the shuttle.

Their group numbered twenty-one. Fourteen of them, including Hawes and the three other Marines from the *Wallfish,* were in exos. Two of the UMC exos looked to be heavy armor variants: walking tanks with portable turrets attached to the fronts of their breastplates.

Most of the Marines were enlisted men, although Akawe had also sent along his second-in-command, Koyich, to oversee the operation.

The yellow-eyed man was in the middle of saying to Falconi, "—we say you jump, you jump. Clear?"

"Perfectly," said Falconi. He didn't look happy, though.

Koyich's upper lip curled. "I don't know why the captain agreed to let rim runners like you along, but orders are orders. If shit goes down, stay the hell out of our way, you hear? You cross our line of fire, we're going to shoot through you, not around. Get it?"

If anything, Falconi's expression became even more glacial. "Oh I got it." In her mind, Kira checked the box labeled *asshole* next to Koyich's name.

Overhead, the lightstrips switched from the clean white shine of full-spectrum illumination to the purple glow of irradiating UV, and from jets mounted along the walls, gusts of decon gasses buffeted her and the other passengers.

The *Ilmorra* was laid out differently than the *Valkyrie,* but it was similar enough that Kira felt a strong sense of déjà vu. She tried to put aside the emotion and focus on the present; whatever happened on the planet, they weren't going to get stuck in the shuttle. Not with the *Darmstadt* and the *Wallfish* nearby. Even so, it was unsettling to be in such a small ship, so far from any human-settled system. They were truly explorers of the deep unknown.

They had enough food to stay on the planet for a week. If more was needed, the *Darmstadt* could drop it from orbit once the ship got back from the asteroid belt. Barring unforeseen complications, they would stay on the planet until they found the Staff of Blue or were able to determine it wasn't there. Returning to the ships was going to be a huge hassle, not only because of the propellant needed to lift the shuttle into orbit, but also because of the decontamination they would need to go through before being allowed back on board.

Like everyone not clad in an exo, Kira had donned a skinsuit and helmet, which she'd be living in until they left the planet. Everyone but the Entropists, who had somehow transformed the smart fabric of their gradient robes into fitted suits complete with helmets and visors. As always, their technology impressed.

The suits would have been necessary regardless of concerns over biocontainment. Spectrographic analysis had shown that the surface atmosphere on the ground would kill them without protection (not immediately, but fast enough).

The *Wallfish* and the *Darmstadt* had decelerated a considerable amount as they neared the planet, but neither ship had come to a complete, relative stop, which left the *Ilmorra* with several hours of thrusting before it could enter orbit.

Kira closed her eyes and waited.

2.

The shriek of alarms yanked Kira back to full alertness. Red lights flashed overhead, and the Marines shouted at each other, barking incomprehensible jargon.

"What's going on?" she said. No one replied, but Kira saw the answer for herself as she pulled up her overlays.

Ships.

Lots of ships popping out of FTL. *Jellies.*

A jolt of adrenaline caused Kira's heart to race, and the Soft Blade roiled underneath her skinsuit. She scanned the details. Four, five, six ships had appeared so far. They'd entered normal space somewhat offset from the heart of the system—an error in their navigation systems, perhaps, but knowing the speed of the Jellies' drives, they couldn't be more than a few hours away at max thrust.

Seven ships.

Next to her, Falconi was speaking frantically into the microphone of his helmet. Across the middle of the shuttle, Koyich was doing the same.

"Sheiiit," said Sanchez. "Guess the Jellies were already out here, searching for the Staff of Blue."

A *clank* as Tatupoa slapped the side of Sanchez's armored head. "No, dumbass. They went and flash traced us is what they did. Timing's all wrong elsewise."

Corporal Nishu chimed in, "First time we've seen them do it too. Fuckers."

Then Lt. Hawes: "Somehow they figured out how to track us even with all the course adjustments." He shook his head. "Not good."

"What course adjustments?" Kira asked.

Nishu was the one to answer: "Whenever we drop out of FTL to bleed off heat, we make a slight course change. No more than a degree or a fraction of a degree, but it's enough to throw off anyone who is trying to plot your final destination based off your trajectory. Isn't always helpful in the League, with the stars so close together, but makes a difference if you're going from, say, Cygni to Eidolon."

Koyich and Falconi were still talking into their microphones.

"And the *Wallfish* made these corrections too?" Kira said.

Hawes nodded. "Horzcha coordinated it with your ship mind. Should have kept the Jellies from flash tracing us, but . . . guess not."

Flash trace. Kira remembered the term from *Seven Minutes to Saturn*, the war movie Alan had loved so much. The concept was pretty simple. If you wanted to see what had happened at a location prior to the time of your arrival, all you had to do was go FTL and fly away from that location until you'd traveled a distance greater than the light from the event. Then you just parked your ship in open space, turned on your telescope, and waited.

The detail of the images received would be limited by the size of your onboard equipment, but even at interstellar distances, it would be relatively easy to spot something like, say, the *Wallfish* and the *Darmstadt* jumping to FTL. Ship drives were hot torches against the cold backdrop of space, and they were dead easy to find and track.

Kira berated herself for not considering the possibility sooner. Of *course* the Jellies would do their best to figure out where the Soft Blade had gone after 61 Cygni. Why wouldn't they? She knew how important the xeno was to them. Somehow, with the appearance of the nightmares, she'd assumed the Jellies would have bigger things to worry about.

Apparently not.

Falconi shouted something in his helmet that Kira only heard a muted version of because his speaker was turned off. Then he let his head fall back against the wall, a grim expression on his face.

She knocked on his visor, and he looked at her.

"What is it?" she said.

He scowled. "We're too far away for the *Wallfish* to reach us before the Jellies. Even if she could, her tanks are over half empty, and there's no way we can . . ." He stopped, lips pursed, and glanced toward Trig. "The odds aren't good. Put it that way."

"We keep going," said Koyich, loud enough to be heard throughout the shuttle. "Our only chance now is to find this staff before the Jellies do." He turned his slitted cat-eyes onto Kira. "If we do, you'd better be able to use it, Navárez."

Kira gave a sharp jerk of her chin, and even though she was far from certain, she said, "Get the staff into my hands, we'll have a real surprise for the Jellies."

Koyich seemed satisfied by her statement, but a message popped up in her overlays:

<*You sure about that? – Falconi*>

<*The xeno seems to know how to use it, so . . . let's hope. – Kira*>

Then the thrust alert rang out, and a lead blanket settled over Kira as the *Ilmorra* kicked up its burn to a full 2 g's.

"ETA to Nidus, fourteen minutes," said the shuttle's pseudo-intelligence.

"Nidus?" Nielsen asked before Kira could.

Lt. Hawes answered: "That's our unofficial designation for the planet. Easier to remember than some random letter."

Kira thought it was fitting. Closing her eyes, she switched her overlays to the shuttle's outside cameras. The curve of the planet rose up before them, one half in shadow, the other in light, and the terminator a dusky, twilight realm dividing the two from pole to pole. Bands of swirling clouds enveloped the middle of the orb—massive storms driven by the transferred heat from the sun-locked side. *Nidus.*

Vertigo made Kira grab the arms of the jump seat as, for a moment, she felt as if they were hanging over an enormous precipice, about to fall.

It wasn't needed, but the pseudo-intelligence provided continual updates, perhaps because it was calming, perhaps because of UMC protocol:

"Resumption of weightlessness in five . . . four . . . three . . . two . . ." The lead blanket vanished, and Kira swallowed as her stomach attempted to escape through her mouth. "Z-axis swap commencing." She felt a shove against the right side of her body, and Nidus swung out of view, replaced by the spangled depths of space as the *Ilmorra* turned end for end, and then another shove as the spin stopped. She turned off the overlays and concentrated on controlling her rebellious stomach. "Retracting radiators. . . . T-minus one minute, fifteen seconds until atmospheric entry." The time crawled by with agonizing slowness. Then: "Contact in ten . . . nine . . . eight—"

As the pseudo-intelligence continued its countdown, Kira checked on the Jellies. Four of the ships had changed course in pursuit of the shuttle. The other three were heading toward the asteroid belt, presumably to refill their tanks, same as the *Darmstadt* and the *Wallfish.* So far, none of the aliens seemed to show any interest in attacking either of the two ships, but Kira knew that would change.

"Contact."

A tremor ran through the *Ilmorra,* and Kira drifted back against her seat as the tremors increased into a shuddering roar. She took a quick look outside via the rear-facing cameras. A wall of flame greeted her. She shivered and switched off the feed.

"Initiating braking," said the pseudo-intelligence.

A full-body hammer blow slammed Kira into the seat. She gritted her teeth, grateful for the support of the Soft Blade. The shaking worsened, and the *Ilmorra* bucked hard enough to make Kira's head snap back and her teeth clatter together.

Several of the Marines whooped. "Oh, Momma! Riding the dragon!" "Kick it, man!" "Just like orbital skydiving back home!" "Now that's what a hot drop is supposed to feel like!"

Part of Kira couldn't help but think that Sparrow would have enjoyed the turbulence.

The sound of the engines changed, growing deeper, more muted, and the vibrations quickened in frequency. "Switching fusion drive to closed-cycle operation," said the pseudo-intelligence.

That meant they were about ninety klicks above the ground. Below that height, the density of the atmosphere would cause enough thermal backscattering from an open-cycle reactor to melt the back of the shuttle. Not only that, an unshielded exhaust would irradiate everything near the landing zone.

The problem with closed-cycle operation, however, was that the reactor devoured hydrogen at close to ten times the normal rate. And right then, Kira worried that they would need every ounce of propellent to escape the Jellies.

Unless, that was, she could get her hands on the Staff of Blue.

The bulkheads around them groaned and squealed, and somewhere a piece of equipment clattered onto the floor.

Kira checked the cameras: a layer of clouds obscured the view, and then they cleared and she spotted the small fold of weathered mountains they were heading for. The Vanished complex was just barely visible as a gleam of white lines hidden deep within the shadowed valley.

The *Ilmorra* bucked again, even harder than before. Pain shot through Kira's tongue, and blood flooded her mouth as she realized she'd bitten herself. She coughed as the blood went down the wrong way. "What was *that*?" she shouted.

"Drag chutes," replied Koyich in an infuriatingly calm voice. She would have sworn he was enjoying this.

"Helps save fuel!" Sanchez added.

Kira nearly laughed at the absurdity of it.

The roar of the wind outside softened, and the pressure on her chest lessened. She took a breath. Not much longer now. . . .

RCS thrusters sounded: short bursts above and below them along the hull. The ship wobbled and seemed to turn slightly around Kira. Stability adjustments, repositioning the *Ilmorra* for landing.

She counted seconds to herself. Almost half a minute passed, and then a sudden burn jammed her deep into the chair, making it difficult to breathe. The *Ilmorra* juddered and swayed, Kira's weight normalized, and from the back of the ship came a pair of booming *thuds*. Then the engines cut out and a shocking stillness followed.

Planetfall.

CHAPTER III

* * * * * * *

SHARDS

1.

"We made it," said Kira. After so long spent traveling, arrival hardly seemed real.

Falconi popped his buckles. "Time to say hi to the natives."

"Not quite yet," said Koyich. He stood. "Eyes and ears, you ugly apes. Exos free to disengage. Grab your battle rattle and get me a sitrep yesterday. And keep those drones outta the air until I give the order. You heard me! Go!" Around them, the shuttle transformed into a bustle of activity as the Marines readied themselves to deploy.

Before popping the airlock, they checked the atmosphere for unknown risk factors and then scanned the surrounding area for signs of movement.

"Anything?" Koyich demanded.

One of the Marines from the *Darmstadt* shook his head. "Nossir."

"Check thermals."

"Already did, sir. It's dead out there."

"Alright. Move out. Exos take point."

Kira found herself crowded between the two Entropists as the Marines assembled before the airlock.

Veera said, "Isn't this—"

"—most exciting?" Jorrus concluded.

Kira tightened the grip on her blaster. "I'm not sure that's the word I'd choose." She wasn't even sure what she was feeling. A potent combination of dread and anticipation and—and it didn't bear thinking about. She'd save her emotions for later. Right now there was a job that needed doing.

She glanced over at Trig. The kid's face was pale behind his visor, but he still looked stupidly eager to see where they'd landed. "How you doing?" she asked.

He nodded, keeping his eyes fixed on the airlock. "All green."

The airlock broke with a loud *hiss,* and a crown of condensation swirled around the edges of the door as it rolled back. The dull red light of Bughunt streamed in, casting an elongated oval on the corrugated decking. The lonely howl of an abandoned wind became audible.

Koyich signaled with his hand, and four of the armored Marines scrambled through the airlock. After a few moments, one of them said, "Clear."

Kira had to wait until the remaining Marines exited the shuttle before they signaled for her and the Entropists to follow.

Outside, the world was split in half. To the east, the rust-colored sky held an evening glow and Bughunt protruded above the tortured horizon—a swollen red orb far dimmer than Epsilon Indi, the sun Kira had grown up with. To the west lay a realm of perpetual darkness, shrouded with starless night. Thick clouds hung low over the land, red and orange and purple and knotted with vortices driven by the ceaseless wind. Lightning illuminated the folded depths of the clouds, and the rumble of distant thunder echoed across the land.

The *Ilmorra* had landed on what looked like a patch of cracked paving stones. Kira's mind automatically categorized them as artificial, but she cautioned herself against making assumptions.

Surrounding the landing zone were open fields covered with what looked like black moss. The fields ascended into foothills, and the foothills into the bounding mountains. The snow-mantled peaks were rounded with age and wear, but their dark silhouettes possessed a solid bulk that still managed to be intimidating. Like on the fields and the foothills, glossy black vegetation grew upon the sides of the mountains—black so as to better absorb the red light from their parent star.

The buildings she had identified from space weren't visible at the moment; they lay farther up the valley, behind a flank of the neighboring mountain, perhaps two or three klicks away (she always found it hard to judge distances on new planets; the thickness of the atmosphere, the curve of the horizon, and the relative size of nearby objects were all things that took some time getting used to).

"Dramatic," said Falconi, coming up beside her.

"It looks like a painting," said Nielsen, joining them.

"Or something out of a game," said Trig.

To Kira, the place felt old beyond reckoning. It seemed unlikely it had been the homeworld of the Vanished—for a sentient, technologically advanced species to evolve on a tidally locked planet would be *extremely* difficult—but she had little doubt the Vanished had settled there long ago, and had stayed for a long time thereafter.

The Marines rushed about, setting up auto-turrets around the shuttle, tossing drones into the air (which zoomed skyward with a nerve-scraping *buzz*), and posting sensors—active and passive—in a wide perimeter.

"Form up," Koyich barked, and the Marines assembled in front of the now-closed airlock. Then he trotted over to where Kira stood watching with Falconi and the Entropists, and said, "We've got two hours before the Jellies make orbit."

Kira's heart dropped. "That's not enough time."

"It's all the time we've got," said Koyich. "They're not going to risk hitting us with bombs or missiles or rods from god, so—"

"Sorry, what?"

Falconi answered: "Kinetic projectiles. Big heavy lumps of tungsten or something like that. They hit almost as hard as nukes."

Koyich jerked his chin. "That. The Jellies aren't going to risk destroying you or the staff. They're going to have to come down here in person. If we can get into the buildings you spotted, we can fight a delaying action, buy you some time. Hold out long enough and the *Darmstadt* might be able to give us some reinforcements. This ain't going to be a fight won in space, that's for damn sure."

"Guess we can forget about proper containment procedures," said Kira.

Koyich grunted. "You could say that."

The first officer barked a few commands, and within moments, their group set out marching at double speed across the broken stones, each step of the fourteen sets of power armor thudding like dire drums. Two of the Marines from the *Darmstadt* stayed behind with the shuttle. When Kira looked back, she saw them moving around the vessel, checking its heat shield for damage.

The wind provided a constant pressure against Kira's side. After so long spent on ships and stations, the movement of air seemed strange. That and the unevenness of the ground.

She did the math in her head. It had been close to six months since she had last stood on Adrasteia. Six months of closed rooms, artificial lights, and the stink of close-pressed bodies.

Patches of black moss crunched under the soles of her boots. The moss wasn't the only vegetation nearby; there were clusters of fleshy vines (assuming they were plants) growing upon nearby rock formations. The vines tumbled like locks of greasy hair across the face of the stone. Kira couldn't help but note different features: leaf-like structures with veins that formed reticulated venation, similar to Earth dicots. Staggered branching, with deep ridges on the stems. No visible flowers or fruiting bodies.

Looking was one thing, but what she really wanted was to get a sample of the plant's cells and start digging into its biochemistry. That was where the real magic was. An entirely new biome to explore, and she didn't dare stop to learn anything about it.

They rounded the flank of the mountain, and by unspoken consent, the nineteen of them stopped.

Before them, in the low hollow of land at the head of the valley, lay the complex of alien buildings. The settlement was several klicks across, bigger even than Highstone, the capital of Weyland (not that Highstone was particularly big by League standards; there had only been eighty-four thousand people living there the year Kira had left).

Tall, spindly towers stretched skyward, white as bone and laced with a caul of the invading moss that had insinuated itself into every crack and flaw in the structures. Through broken walls, rooms of every size were visible, now drifted with dirt and obscured by opportunistic vines. An assortment of smaller buildings huddled in the spaces between the towers—all with tapered roofs and lancet windows empty of glass or other covering. There were few straight lines; naturalistic arcs dominated the design aesthetic.

Even in their half-ruined state, there was an attenuated elegance to the buildings that Kira had only seen in art or videos of pre-planned luxury communities on Earth. Everything about the complex felt intentional, from the curve of the walls to the layout of the paths that wound like streams throughout the settlement.

The place was undeniably abandoned. And yet, in the light of the endless sunset, beneath the shelf of burning clouds, it felt as if the city wasn't dead, just dormant, as if it were waiting for a signal to spring back to life and restore itself to the heights of its former glory.

Kira breathed out. Awe left her without words.

"Thule," said Falconi, breaking the spell. He seemed as affected as she was.

"Where to?" said Koyich.

It took Kira a moment to clear her mind well enough to answer. "I don't know. Nothing jumps out at me. I need to get closer."

"Forward march!" Koyich barked, and they continued down the slope toward the city.

Next to Kira, the Entropists said, "We are indeed blessed to see this, Prisoner."

She felt inclined to agree.

2.

The towers loomed ever higher as they approached the edge of the settlement. White was the predominate color among the buildings, but irregular panels of blue provided contrast to the structures, enhancing with a shot of vivid decoration an otherwise barren cityscape.

"They had a sense of beauty," said Nielsen.

"We don't know that," said Falconi. "Everything could be for some practical purpose."

"Does it really look like that to you?"

The captain didn't answer.

As they entered the city via a wide avenue from the south, an intense feeling of familiarity swept over Kira. It left her feeling displaced, as if she'd shifted through time. *She* had never been to that twilight city before, but the Soft Blade had, and its memories were nearly as strong as her own. She remembered . . . *life. Moving things: flying and walking, and machines that did the same. The touch of skin, the sound of voices, the sweet scent of flowers carried on the wind* . . . And for a moment, she could nearly see the city as it had been: vital, vibrant, standing tall with hope and pride.

Don't lose control, she told herself. *Don't lose control.* And she hardened her mental grip on the Soft Blade. Whatever happened that day, she was determined not to let the xeno slip her grasp and run rampant. Not after her previous mistakes.

"When do you think this was built?" said Trig. He gaped through his visor with undisguised wonder.

"Centuries ago," said Kira, recalling the sense of age from the Soft Blade's memories. "Before we ever left Earth. Maybe even earlier."

Koyich glanced over his shoulder at her. "Still no idea where to look?"

She hesitated. "Not yet. Let's head to the center."

With two of the Marines in power armor taking the lead, they continued deeper into the maze of buildings. Overhead, the wind whirling between the tapered towers sounded as if it were trying to whisper secrets, but listen though she did, Kira could make no sense of the words in the air.

She kept scanning the buildings and streets, looking for anything that might spark a specific memory. The spaces between the structures were narrower than humans preferred; the proportions were taller, thinner, which matched the images she had seen of the Vanished.

Rubble blocked the avenue in front of them, forcing them to detour around. Veera and Jorrus stopped and bent to pick up a piece that had fallen from one of the nearby towers.

"It does not look like stone," said Veera.

"Nor metal," said Jorrus. "The material—"

"Doesn't matter now," said Koyich. "Keep moving."

Their footsteps echoed off the sides of the buildings, loud and disconcerting in the empty spaces.

Snikt.

Kira spun toward the noise, as did the rest of the squad. There, by an empty doorway, a rectangular panel flickered with artificial light. It was a screen of some sort, blue-white and distorted with cracks. No text or pictures appeared, just the pale field of light.

"How can there still be power?" said Nielsen in an overly calm voice.

"Maybe we're not the first ones to visit," said Trig.

Kira started toward the screen, and Koyich put up an arm to bar her way. "Hold up. We don't know if it's safe."

"I'll be fine," she said, and walked past him.

Up close, the glowing panel produced a faint hum. Kira put a hand on it. The screen didn't change. "Hello?" she said, feeling slightly foolish.

Again, nothing happened.

The wall next to the panel was covered with grime. She wiped some of it away, wondering if there was anything beneath.

There was.

A sigil lay there, set within the surface of the material, and the sight of it froze her in place. The emblem was a line of fractal shapes, coiled close, one upon another.

Kira couldn't decipher any meaning, but she recognized the language as belonging to the same, all-important pattern that guided the Soft Blade's existence. Unable to take her eyes off the sigil, she backed away.

"What is it?" Falconi asked.

"I think the Vanished made the Great Beacon," she said.

Koyich readjusted the sling on his gun. "What makes you think that?"

She pointed. "Fractals. They were obsessed with fractals."

"That doesn't help us now," said Koyich. "Not unless you can read them."

"No."

"Then don't waste—" Koyich stiffened, as did Falconi.

Alarmed, Kira checked her overlays. There—on the other side of Bughunt—another four Jelly ships had just emerged out of FTL. They were coming in hot; a lot hotter than the first batch of enemy vessels.

"Goddammit," said Falconi between clenched teeth. "How many ships did they send?"

"Look: the rest of the Jellies are increasing their thrust so they'll arrive at the same time," said Koyich. He'd gone preternaturally calm, flipping the switch from serious to combat mode. Kira recognized the change in Falconi also. "We've got an hour to find this staff. Maybe less. Pick it up, everyone. Double time."

With the exos still at the lead, they trotted deeper into the city until they arrived at an open plaza with a tall standing stone, cracked and weathered, in the center. As Kira examined the stone, she experienced a shock similar to when she'd seen the sigil, for it was covered with a fractal pattern, and when she looked at it closely, the smallest details of the pattern seemed to swim, as if moving of their own volition.

She felt as if the ground had shifted. What was happening to her? Tingles crawled across the surface of her skin, and the Soft Blade stirred as if restless.

"Anything?" said Koyich.

"I . . . I don't recognize anything. Not specifically."

"Right. We can't wait. Hawes, set up a search pattern. Look for anything that might resemble a staff. Use the drones; use everything we've got. If you haven't found the staff by the time the Jellies enter orbit, then we focus on digging in and denying them territory."

"Yessir!"

The lieutenant and Corporal Nishu split the rest of the Marines into four squads, and then they dispersed into the buildings. All of them save Koyich, who took up position by the side of the plaza and—from the pack he was carrying—removed a comms dish that he aimed at the sky.

"Navárez," he said, fiddling with the controls. "I'm hooking you up to the squad's feed. See if you recognize anything."

Kira nodded and sat hunched on the ground, next to the standing stone. A contact appeared on her overlays. She accepted, and a grid of windows filled her vision. Each window displayed the video from a Marine or a drone.

It was confusing to watch, but she did her best, shifting her attention from one window to the next as the Marines hurried through the decaying buildings, rushing through one empty room after another.

And still, she felt no sense of certainty. They were in the right place; of that she was sure. But *where* in the complex they were supposed to go continued to elude her.

Tell me! she commanded the Soft Blade, desperate. No answer was forthcoming, and with each passing moment, Kira was aware of the Jellies growing closer.

Falconi paced around the perimeter of the plaza along with Trig and Nielsen, keeping watch. By one side, the Entropists stood huddled next to a panel that had come loose from the corner of a building, studying whatever lay underneath.

"Navárez," said Koyich after a while.

She shook her head. "Still nothing."

He grunted. "Hawes, start scouting for a location we can hole up in."

Yessir, the sergeant replied over the radio.

After half an hour of near-silence, Falconi came over to Kira and squatted next to her while resting Francesca across his knees. "We're almost out of time," he said quietly.

"I *know,*" she said, eyes darting from one window to the next.

"Can I help?"

She shook her head.

"What are we missing?"

"No idea," she said. "Maybe it's been too long since the Soft Blade was here. A lot could have changed. I'm just—I'm afraid I brought us all here to die."

He scratched his chin and was quiet for a few seconds. "I don't believe that. This has to be the place. We're just not looking at it right. . . . The Soft Blade doesn't want to die or get captured by the Jellies, does it?"

"No," she said slowly.

"Okay. So why show you this system? This city? There has be something the Blade expects you to find, something so obvious we're missing it."

Kira glanced at the standing stone. *We're not looking at it right.* "Can you give me control of a drone?" she said, calling over to Koyich.

"Just don't crash it," said the first officer. "We're going to need every one we've got."

Kira linked the drone to her overlays and then closed her eyes so she could better concentrate on the feed from the machine. It was hovering next to a tower, half a klick away.

"What are you thinking?" said Falconi. She could feel his presence next to her.

"Fractals," she said.

"Meaning?"

She didn't answer but zoomed the drone straight into the air, higher and higher until it was flying above the top of even the tallest tower. Then she looked at the settlement as a whole, *really* looked, trying to see not only the individual buildings but also the larger, overall shapes. A flicker of recognition came from the Soft Blade, but nothing more.

She turned the drone in a slow circle, angling it up and down to make sure she wasn't missing anything. From the air, the towers were stark and beautiful, but she didn't allow herself to linger over the sight, dramatic though it was.

A *crack* echoed through the city from the west. Kira's eyelids flew open, and as she looked for the source of the sound, the image of the city slipped out of focus.

Her perception shifted, and she saw what she'd been searching for. The decay of the buildings and the encroachment of the native flora had hidden it until that very moment, but she *saw.* The ancient outline of the city was—as she had suspected—a fractal, and the shape of it contained meaning.

There. At the nexus of the pattern, where it coiled in on itself like a nautilus shell. There, at the center of it all.

The structure that she identified was on the far side of the settlement: a low, dome-shaped place that, had it been on Earth, she would have thought was a temple from some long-dead civilization. But *temple* felt like the wrong word. If anything, *mausoleum* seemed more appropriate, given the pale starkness of the building.

The sight of it triggered no memory or sense of confirmation from the Soft Blade, no more so than the city as a whole. That the building was important seemed undeniable, knowing the affinity the Vanished had for fractals, but whether or not it had anything to do with the staff . . . Kira couldn't say.

Dismayed, she realized she was going to have to guess. They didn't have time to wait for the xeno to disgorge another fragment of useful information. They had to act, and they had to act now. If she chose wrong, they'd die. But hesitation would kill them just as surely.

"Hawes, was that you?" said Koyich.

Yessir. We located the entrance to an underground structure. Looks like it's defensible.

Kira tagged the building on the drone's feed and then quit the program. "We might not need it," she said, standing. "I think I found something."

3.

"You *think*, but you're not sure," said Koyich.

"That's right."

"That's some seriously weak shit, Navárez. You really can't give us a better idea than you *think*?"

"Sorry, no."

"Fuck."

Falconi said, "Doesn't look like we can get there before the Jellies land."

Kira checked the position of the aliens: the first three ships were just entering orbit. Even as she watched, she saw them dipping lower as they entered the atmosphere. "We have to try."

"Dammit," said Koyich. "Worst case scenario, we'll hole up in that building, try to fight off the Jellies. They don't know where we're headed, so that gives us an advantage. Hawes, get two exos over to the location Navárez marked, full speed. Everyone else, form up on me, fast as you can. AOP is about to go hot."

Yessir!

The first officer collapsed the comms dish and stowed it in his pack as they ran out of the plaza and down the nearest curving street.

"Can the *Ilmorra* give us any cover?" Kira asked.

Tatupoa and another Marine jogged out of a side street, joining them. "The Jellies would just shoot it down," said Koyich.

The buzzing of drones grew louder as several of the machines took up positions high overhead, providing constant overwatch. The wind tugged at them, causing the drones to dip and sway as they fought to hold still.

"The *Wallfish* is on her way back," Falconi announced. "Emergency burn. She'll be here before long."

"Better tell them not to," said Koyich. "That barge of yours doesn't stand a chance against the Jellies."

Falconi didn't answer, but Kira could tell he disagreed. *<What are you planning? – Kira>*

<A couple of Casaba-Howitzers in the right place could take out at least half of the Jellies. – Falconi>

<Can the Wallfish *get close enough? – Kira>*

<Let Sparrow and Gregorovich worry about that. – Falconi>

Thudding along next to her in his power armor, Trig looked nearly as worried as Kira felt. "Just stick close to me and you'll be fine," she said.

He flashed her a sickly grin. "Okay. Just don't stab me with your suit."

"Not a chance."

A pair of *booms* shook the air, and two Jelly ships pierced the cover of clouds and descended through the sunset sky on pillars of blinding blue flame. The vessels disappeared behind the towers near the eastern edge of the settlement, and then the roar of the rockets fell silent.

"Move," Koyich barked, although none of them needed urging. They were already running fast as they could. Hawes, Nishu, and the rest of the search teams rejoined them and took up formation alongside Kira and the others.

The radio crackled in Kira's ear. One of the two Marines who had gone ahead said, **Sir, made it to the target. It's locked up tighter than a bank vault. No obvious entrance.**

"Cut your way in, if you can," said Koyich between short breaths. "Whatever you do, defend that position at all costs."

Roger that.

For a moment, Kira worried about the Marines damaging the staff. Then she shook off the worry. If they couldn't get into the building, the point would be moot regardless.

To her left, Sanchez said, "Movement! Four hundred meters and closing."

"Damn they're fast," said Nielsen. She racked the slide on her snub-nosed rifle.

Kira activated the targeting program on her blaster. A bright red crosshair appeared in the center of her vision.

Then Sanchez swore in a language Kira didn't recognize, and her overlays failed to translate. "They just took out my drone," he said.

"Mine too," said another Marine.

"Shit, shit, shit, shit," said Hawes. "Make that three."

"We have to get off the street," said Falconi. "We're sitting ducks out in the open."

Koyich shook his head. "No. We keep pushing forward. If we stop, they catch us."

"Two hundred and fifty meters and closing," said Sanchez. They could hear noises among the buildings now: thumping and clattering and the whine and buzz of drones.

Kira reassessed her mental hold over the Soft Blade. *Only what I want,* she thought, doing her best to impress the notion on the xeno. No matter how chaotic things became, no matter how much pain or fear she might end up in, she *wasn't* going to let the Soft Blade inadvertently hurt someone again. Never that.

Then she willed the xeno to cover her face. Even though she was wearing the skinsuit helmet, she wanted the additional protection. Her vision went black for the length of a blink, and then she could see the same as before, only now with the addition of the hazy, violet bands of the local EM fields. Thick loops emanated from the walls of several nearby buildings, marking places where the power was still on. (Why hadn't she looked before?)

"This is suicide," said Falconi. He grabbed Kira by the arm and pulled her toward an open doorway in the nearest building. "This way."

"Stop!" shouted Koyich. "That's an order."

"Bullshit. I'm not under your command," said Falconi. Nielsen followed him, and also Trig and the Entropists. After a moment, Koyich had no choice but to order the Marines to do the same.

The ground level of the building was tall and lofty. Soaring pillars divided the space at regular intervals, a forest of stone trunks that branched as they approached the ceiling. The sight reminded Kira, with almost physical force, of her dreams.

Koyich stormed over to Falconi. "You pull a stunt like that again and I'll have them pick you up and carry you." He jerked the barrel of his blaster toward the Marines in power armor.

"That's—" Falconi stopped as the noises outside grew louder. Kira saw movement in the street they'd just abandoned.

The first Jelly crawled into view: a tentacled squid, similar in form to the ones Kira had encountered before. Following it were several more squids, a lobster-like creature, a chomper, and several more forms she'd only seen on the news. White, orb-shaped drones darted about over them, and farther back, she spotted some kind of segmented vehicle flowing across the rubble-strewn street. . . .

At almost the same moment, the Jellies and the Marines released clouds of chalk and chaff, hiding each other from view.

"Go, go, go!" Hawes shouted.

Laser blasts and gunfire erupted, and a chunk of masonry exploded out of the pillar above Kira's head.

She ducked and ran, staying close to Trig's exo. Explosions sounded behind them. Falconi turned and fired his grenade launcher, but Kira didn't look back.

Their only hope now was speed.

The two Marines in the lead lowered their metal-clad shoulders and smashed straight through the wall in front of them. Another empty room followed by another wall, and then they burst out onto a narrow street.

"Keep going!" Nielsen shouted.

Kira looked for the Entropists and saw them dimly through the swirling chalk: ghost-like figures nearly doubled over, hands outstretched. "This way!" she called, hoping it would help guide them.

Together, she and the rest of the group sprinted across the street and into another building. This one was smaller, with tall, thin corridors barely wide enough for the exos. With every step, the machines scraped flakes off the mossy walls, showering the floor.

The Marines continued to bull forward, breaking past every barrier. Future archeologists, Kira reflected, weren't going to be happy with all the damage.

They passed through a room with shallow, pool-shaped depressions in the floor—*Kira remembered the scent of perfumes and the sound of splashing water*—then an arcade with large, broken tubes of some transparent material extending upward along the walls—*bodies rising through space, both pairs of arms outstretched for balance*—and then they broke through onto another street, wider than the first.

The buzzing of drones grew louder, and Kira saw threadlike flashes of superheated air as lasers punched through the clouds of chalk surrounding them.

Then one of the lobster-like Jellies skittered around the side of the building high above—clinging to the wall like an oversized insect—and jumped onto the back of Tatupoa's armor.

The man shouted and twisted, flailing his arms in a futile attempt to knock loose the chittering creature. "Hold still!" shouted Hawes, and a burst of gunfire erupted from his rifle. Each shot produced a pulse of pressure that Kira felt against the front of her chest.

Ichor exploded from the side of the lobster, and it fell twitching to the cracked pavement.

But it had accomplished its mission. The delay it caused was just enough for three squids to swarm around the building and close with them.

The Marines weren't caught by surprise. The instant the squids entered their line of sight, the big chain guns mounted on the front of the two heavy exos sprang to life. Even through her helmet and even through the Soft Blade's mask, the sound was painful and terrifying—visceral in its intensity.

Kira continued to stumble forward, feeling as if her bones were being hammered.

The three squids thrashed under the impacts of the Marines' explosive bullets. Several of their tentacles returned fire with blasters and guns and a whirling blade of death that buried itself in a wall down the street.

One of the Marines threw a grenade. Falconi fired his launcher, and the paired set of blasts obscured the squids.

Chunks of twitching flesh splattered the buildings and rained down around Kira. She ducked, shielding her face with an arm.

Then they were inside again, and half the Marines turned to cover the rear. They spread to either side, using corners and rubble and what looked like high-backed benches for protection. Three of the men were bleeding: Tatupoa in his exo, the two others in skinsuits. It looked like they'd all been hit by lasers.

They didn't stop to tend their wounds. Without lowering his blaster, one of the two pulled out a canister of medifoam, sprayed his wound, and tossed the can to his comrade, who sprayed his own injury. Neither of them lost a step throughout the whole process.

"Go! Go! Out the back!" shouted Koyich, continuing to retreat from the building entrance.

"How much farther?" said Nielsen.

"Hundred meters!" shouted Hawes.

"Th—"

BOOM!

The walls and ceiling vibrated like a drumhead, and centuries' worth of accumulated dust plumed into the air as the corner of the building caved inward. The ceiling sagged, and everywhere Kira heard creaks and squeals and tearing moans. She willed the Soft Blade to switch to infrared. Through the new opening in the side of the room, she saw the Jelly vehicle directly outside: black and menacing, with a segmented carapace that reminded her of a giant pillbug. On its back, a huge mounted turret was taking aim at them—

Trig and Nielsen opened fire along with the Marines. Then Jorrus and Veera surprised them all by stepping forward and—moving as one—slashing with their arms and shouting a shared word.

A burst of searing light obscured the room. Kira blinked, fear jolting through her at being suddenly blind.

Crimson dots mottled her vision as the light faded. In front of their group, she saw a fine net of monofilaments covering the walls, the broken corner of the building, and the vehicle outside—which was curled on its side and convulsing as tendrils of electricity crawled across the plates of its exposed carapace.

In the distance, more Jellies were approaching.

"Run!" the Entropists shouted.

They ran.

"What did you do?" Kira shouted.

"Magic!" Veera answered, which was wholly unsatisfying, but Kira didn't have the breath to question her further.

They broke through the back of the building, and—across another plaza—Kira spotted the mausoleum-like structure she'd identified from the air. The two other armored Marines were crouched by the closed-off entrance, the blue-white light of cutting torches bright beneath their metal gauntlets.

They switched off the torches and laid down covering fire as Kira and her companions sprinted across the plaza.

One of the Marines next to Koyich stumbled and fell. Blood and bone sprayed from his knee. Trig picked him up with one hand and carried him the rest of the way to the temple.

Kira dropped behind a slab of rubble, using it for cover while she caught her breath. If the Jellies got close enough, she could take them out with the Soft Blade, but so far, they'd kept their distance. They knew what they were dealing with, and they were behaving accordingly, goddammit. Did they have to be so smart?

A Jelly drone popped up over the top of the slab. Nielsen fried it with a single burst of laser fire from her exo. Through her faceplate, she appeared red-faced and sweating. Strands of hair had broken free of her ponytail and fallen across her face.

Behind another slab, Trig laid the Marine with the mangled knee onto the ground. *Redding* said the tag on the front of his skinsuit. Sanchez ran over to them, and—before Kira could believe what she was seeing—he took his blaster and sliced off the rest of the Marine's wounded leg.

Redding didn't even scream, but he screwed his eyes shut during the cut. He must have been using a nerve-block to stop the pain. Sanchez cinched a tourniquet around the stump of the leg, sprayed the bloody end with medifoam, and then slapped the man on the shoulder and joined the rest of the Marines in firing over the tops of the rubble.

Kira looked at the front of the temple. The entrance was sealed with what looked like a plug of solid metal. The two Marines had only managed to cut into it a hand's breadth or less.

Dirt showered her as Nielsen and Trig grabbed the slab of stone she was crouching behind and, with their exos, heaved it upright so it formed a barrier between them and the Jellies gathering at the edges of the plaza. The Marines did the same with the other slabs, setting them in a semicircle before the temple.

"If you're going to do something, now's the time," said Falconi, reloading Francesca from the pouch on his belt.

"Fuck that," said Koyich. "Use shaped charges; blow it open."

"No!" said Kira. "You could destroy the staff."

Koyich ducked as bullets and shrapnel whined overhead. He pulled the tab on another canister of chalk and threw it into the center of the plaza. "*We'll* get destroyed, if we can't get in there."

An image flashed through Kira's mind of the moment when she'd ripped the transmitter out of the wall of the Jelly ship. "Just hold them off," she said, scrambling to her feet. Keeping her head down, she ran to the blocked entrance of the temple and put her hands against the cold metal.

Sweat dripped into her eyes as she loosened her grip on the Soft Blade—just a fraction—and reached *out* with the suit, stretching and spreading herself, like a rubber sheet pulled taut. *Don't lose control . . . don't lose control. . . .*

A bullet flattened itself against the metal above her head, spraying her with silvery spall. Kira hunched her shoulders and tried to ignore the constant, battering explosions of gunfire and grenades.

Her skin crawled as the Soft Blade tore open her skinsuit and formed a web of knotting tendrils between her fingers. The tendrils extended outward, flowing across the metal surface, seeking and grasping with millions of hairlike feelers.

"Thule!" Trig exclaimed.

"Might want to hurry," Falconi said in a conversational tone.

Kira pressed inward with the xeno, driving it into every cranny and crevice and microscopic stress fracture. She felt the xeno—felt *herself*—burrowing through the bonded structure of the metal, like tree roots digging through hard-packed earth.

The metal was incredibly thick. Meters upon meters of it armored the entrance to the temple. *What were they trying to keep out?* she wondered. Then it occurred to her that perhaps the Soft Blade was the answer to that question.

Heat radiated from the surface of the metal as it began to give. "Get ready!" she shouted. The moment she felt movement between her various extruded tendrils, she yanked, hard.

With an anguished shriek, the metal parted. Glittering dust filled the air as the fibers of the suit pulled heavy, silver-grey chunks away from the building. A dark opening took shape before her.

Overhead, three more Jelly ships screamed across the sky, meteors trailing fire and smoke. From them fell scores of drop-pods: evil seeds planted throughout the city. *Too late,* Kira thought, triumphant.

She returned the Soft Blade to herself, and again she was whole.

4.

Bullets whined off the sides of the jagged metal, and laser blasts melted finger-sized holes—splattering molten droplets in every direction—as Kira pushed forward into the darkness.

Falconi followed close behind, then Trig, Nielsen, and the rest of the squad. The Marines activated flat, hemispherical glow lights, which they tossed around the perimeter of the space.

The room was huge and deep. Even with the crazed collection of lights, Kira recognized the sweep of the arched ceiling and the pattern of the tessellated floor. This place she had walked long ago, beside the Highmost, near the end of days. . . . A graveyard chill gave her pause, and she said, quietly, "Everyone be careful. Don't touch anything."

Behind her, Hawes snapped orders, and the Marines took aim at the ragged opening they'd entered through.

"Hold this spot," said Koyich. "Don't let a single Jelly past."

"Sir, yessir!"

As Kira ventured deeper into the darkness, Falconi joined her, as did

Koyich, Nielsen, Trig, and the Entropists. But they let her take the lead as she headed toward the back of the space.

Now that they were inside the temple, Kira knew exactly where to go. There was no question in her mind; ancient memories assured her that this was the right place and that what she sought was just ahead. . . .

Gunshots continued to echo through the cavernous chamber, loud and thunderous. How long had the place lain in silence? And now the violence of Jellies and humans fighting had shattered that peace. Kira wondered who the Vanished would fault most if they were still around.

Thirty meters from the entrance, the room ended at an enormously tall, thin pair of outward-curving doors. White and inlayed with fractal lines of blue, they were far more ornate than anything else she'd seen in the city.

Kira raised a hand. Before she touched the doors, a ring of light appeared near the height of her head, overlapping the seam between the two doors. Then they parted without sound, sliding into the walls and disappearing into hidden recesses.

Another room lay before them, smaller than the antechamber. It was heptagonal in shape, with a ceiling that twinkled as if with stars and a floor that possessed a faint, iridescent sheen like that of a soap bubble. At each vertex of the room stood a crystalline obelisk, blue-white and translucent, save for the one opposite her, which was red and black. It, like the others, had a stern look, as if watching over the chamber with a disapproving gaze.

But it was the center of the room that drew Kira's attention. Three steps—too high and shallow to be comfortable for human anatomy—led to a dais, also heptagonal. From the dais rose a pedestal, and from the pedestal, a four-sided case that sparkled like cut diamond.

Within the diamond case there hung suspended seven shards: the Staff of Blue, now broken.

Kira stared. She could not bring herself to understand or accept. "No," she whispered.

Then alerts flashed in her overlays, and despite herself, she looked. A groan escaped her, and it echoed in the mausoleum of the Vanished.

Fourteen more ships had entered the system. Not Jellies. *Nightmares.*

CHAPTER IV

* * * * * * *

TERROR

1.

They were surrounded. They would have to stand and fight, and they would likely die.

Kira's mind whirled as the reality of the situation clamped shut around her, like an iron coffin. There was no escape this time, no trick or turn or hope of reprieve. They were too far from anywhere to expect help, and neither the Jellies nor the nightmares would show them mercy.

It was all her fault, and it wasn't something she could fix.

"Is it supposed to be like that?" Falconi asked, his voice harsh. He indicated the broken staff.

"No," said Kira.

"Can you fix it?" said Koyich, echoing her thoughts.

"No. I don't even know if it can be fixed."

"That's not an acceptable answer, Navárez. We—"

BOOM!

The building shuddered. Pieces of the starry ceiling crashed to the floor, the heavens coming undone. The diamond case swayed and fell, shattered—sending the pieces of the Staff of Blue flying in different directions.

The Entropists bent to pick up one of the shards.

Through the doorway to the inner sanctum, Kira saw the front of the temple had been blown apart. The Jellies' pillbug-like vehicle was parked outside, no longer incapacitated, main gun trained on their location. The Marines were retreating from the jagged opening even as they peppered the vehicle with bullets and lasers.

Sparks erupted from the side of the pillbug's gun as the concentrated fire slagged it.

"Falconi! How far out is the *Wallfish*?" said Koyich, shouldering his gun as he moved to the side of the doorway.

"Fifteen minutes," said Falconi, taking the other side.

"Shit. Get in here! Get in here! Move! Move! Move!" Koyich shouted at his men even while firing into the clouds of smoke and chaff, as precise as a machine.

"Pinned down!" said Hawes. "Got wounded! Can't—"

The clumping *thuds* of Nielsen's exo startled Kira as the woman charged past her, into the front area of the temple. Falconi swore and fired three grenades in quick succession to buy her some time.

As each grenade detonated, it cleared a spherical area of smoke, chalk, and dust. Then the grey-white haze rushed in, obscuring the view once more.

Feeling ashamed of herself, Kira ran after Nielsen. She saw the first officer pick up a pair of downed Marines and sprint back toward the inner part of the temple. Kira spotted another wounded Marine, only this one still in his exo. She slid to a stop next to him and hit the quick-release latches on the side of the machine.

The front casing popped open, and the man fell out, coughing blood. "Let's go," said Kira, slipping his arm over her shoulders.

Half carrying him, she hurried toward the doorway to the sanctum. Nielsen had already dropped off her casualties and was returning to the open.

A numbing impact hit Kira on the right side, causing her to fall to one knee. She glanced down and immediately wished she hadn't: the black fibers along her ribs were blown out like a spray of needles. Blood, muscle, and bone were visible scattered between.

Even as she looked, the fibers knitted together as they began to close over the wound.

She gasped and pushed against the floor with legs that had lost all feeling, trying to continue moving forward. One step, two steps, and then she was walking again with the man's weight still heavy on her shoulder.

As she cleared the doorway, Falconi took the man off her.

Kira immediately turned to head back out, but Falconi caught her by the arm. "Don't be stupid!" he said.

She shook him off and headed deeper into the clouds, looking for the last few Marines. Outside the temple, more explosions, more gunfire. If not for the Soft Blade, Kira doubted she would have been able to think or function amid the noise. Each blast was a concussion strong enough to feel in her bones, and the objects around her blurred from the force of the blows. The noise seemed to be increasing too.

Where are they? She couldn't see any Jellies through the mess of smoke, only twisted, incomprehensible shapes thrashing in the murk.

"SJAMs incoming," barked Koyich. "Hit the deck!"

Kira dropped flat, covering her head.

A half second later, four separate explosions struck the streets surrounding the plaza, lighting up the area with a hellish blaze. The ground rippled and smacked Kira in the cheek, causing her teeth to clack together with painful force.

"Status," said Koyich. "Get me eyes on hostiles."

"Looks like we took out most of 'em," said Hawes, "but can't tell for sure. Waiting for a better view."

The explosions had only added to the swirling clouds, thickening them to the point where it was nearly pitch-black in the plaza.

Kira listened; she no longer heard gunfire nor the sounds of moving Jellies. As the wind began to clear the air, she risked poking her head up and looking around.

Clang! Across the exposed antechamber of the temple, Nielsen staggered back, a large dent in the front of her power armor. She fired her arm-mounted machine gun several times into the haze, and Kira heard the splatter of bullets hitting flesh.

Down the clogged streets, she saw dozens more heat-spots approaching. More Jellies.

Trig came running out of the temple's inner sanctum, heading for Nielsen. As he skidded to a stop beside her, Koyich said, "That's all the help we can expect from the *Ilmorra.* We'll be lucky if they don't go after her for setting off those SJAMs. Get everyone inside. Make it fast!"

There were still four Marines on the ground. Kira started toward the nearest one.

One of the Jellies' white drones flew into view around the edge of the temple's broken façade, while at the same time, a large, tentacled squid climbed over the mounded rubble, a pair of blasters held by its twisting limbs.

Kira scrabbled for her weapon but couldn't find it. Where was it? Had she dropped it? There wasn't enough time, no time, no time—

Trig jumped in front of Nielsen, firing his blaster and his rifle at the same time. His face was contorted, and he was screaming over the radio: "Yaaaah! Come on, you fucker! Eat it!"

The white, orb-shaped drone spun as bullets slammed into it, and then it sparked and tumbled to the ground. Behind it, the squid flinched, raised a tentacle holding a long, bar-shaped railgun.

The Soft Blade pulsed outward as it struggled to attack. Out of habit, Kira resisted, unwilling to let go, unwilling to trust the xeno—*Bang.*

The sound from the Jelly's weapon was short and sharp. It cut through the commotion like auditory punctuation. Startling silence followed. Trig's guns ceased firing as his armor locked up, and then he slowly toppled backward, a statue falling.

Centered on the front of his visor was a finger-sized hole, and frozen on his face, a look of terrible surprise.

"No!" Falconi shouted.

Shock paralyzed Kira for a moment, and then horrified understanding spurred her back into action. *Too slow.* She relaxed her hold on the Soft Blade and reached out with it, intending to loose the xeno and tear the Jelly to shreds.

Before she could, a woman in a skinsuit ran in front of the squid, waving a piece of white cloth. "Wait! Stop! Stop! We come in peace!"

Kira froze, unable to process what she was seeing.

As the stranger clambered into the temple, the gold sheen of her visor cleared to reveal a hard, lined face.

For a moment, Kira saw only a collection of unfamiliar features. Then her perspective shifted, and the planet seemed to tilt underneath her. "*You!*" she said.

"Navárez," said Major Tschetter.

2.

More Jellies gathered around the broken front of the temple, but for some reason they didn't shoot, so Kira ignored them as she rushed to Trig's side.

Falconi and the squad's medic were only a step behind. The medic removed Trig's helmet with practiced speed, and pooled blood poured out across the tessellated floor in bright crimson streaks.

The kid was still conscious, his white-rimmed eyes darting around with a panicked look. A bullet had hit him near the base of his neck, ripping apart the arteries. Blood pumped out at a frightening rate, each spurt weaker than the last. His mouth worked, but no words came forth, only a horrible bubbling sound—the desperate gasps of a drowning swimmer.

My fault, Kira berated herself. She should have acted faster. She should have trusted the xeno. If only she hadn't been so focused on control, she would have been able to protect the kid.

From a pocket, the medic produced an oxygen mask that he fixed over Trig's mouth. Then he took a canister of medifoam, pressed the nozzle into the center of the wound, and sprayed.

Trig's eyes rolled back, and his breathing stuttered. His arms began to quiver.

The medic stood. "He needs cryo. Unless you can get the *Ilmorra* here in the next few minutes, he's dead." As he spoke, Nielsen got back to her feet, holding a hand against the dent in her chestplate. He pointed a finger at her. "Need help?"

"I'll survive," she said.

With that, the medic hurried past to the Marines waiting for his attention.

"Can't we—" Kira started to say to Koyich.

"The *Ilmorra* is already on her way."

Kira looked to the sky. After a few seconds, she heard the distinctive rumble of an approaching rocket. "Where should—"

A trio of laser beams, each beam equal to the output from a dozen handheld blasters, stabbed upward from somewhere beyond the outskirts of the city. A second later, a burning star plummeted through the shelf of clouds: the *Ilmorra*, trailing blue shock diamonds and a line of white exhaust. The shuttle vanished behind the flank of the nearest mountain, and a blinding flash illuminated the valley, sending shadows streaming eastward from the base of the buildings.

"Cover!" Koyich shouted, diving behind a pile of rubble.

Falconi threw himself across Trig; Kira did likewise, using a net of fibers from the Soft Blade to hold them in place.

She counted the seconds in her head: *One, two, three, four, five, six, seven—*

The floor buckled and the direction of the wind reversed as the shockwave hit, louder and more powerful than a thousand claps of thunder. With it came a wave of suffocating heat. The towers swayed and groaned—chunks of walls flying free—and streamers of dirt blasted through the howling streets. Debris filled the air, deadly as any bullet. Dozens of the fragments shotgunned the rubble they huddled behind. Beneath her arm, Kira saw the cratered body of the pillbug blown away into the dark.

She glanced up. A gigantic mushroom cloud rose above the mountain, climbing toward the stratosphere. The pillar of nuclear fury was staggeringly huge; before it, she felt smaller than she ever had before.

If not for the protection of the mountain, they would all be dead.

She released Falconi and Trig from the net of fibers. Falconi said, "Was that—"

"The *Ilmorra*'s gone," said Koyich.

The bulk of the explosion would have come from the antimatter stored within the shuttle's Markov Drive. *What now?* Things had just gone from bad to apocalyptically bad.

As the howl of the wind began to subside, they got to their feet. Trig was still twitching; Kira could tell he didn't have long to live.

The Jellies had gathered close around them during the blast. Now Tschetter stood next to one, and she seemed to be speaking to it, although Kira heard nothing.

The squid started to move toward Trig.

Falconi hissed and lifted his grenade launcher, and Kira crouched, extruding razor-sharp blades from her fingers. "Stay the fuck away or I'll blast you to pieces," said the captain.

"My companions say they can help," said Tschetter.

"Is that why they shot him?"

Tschetter made a regretful expression. "It was a mistake."

"*Sure.* And just who the fuck are you?" Falconi's nostrils were flared, his eyes narrowed and savage.

The woman's back stiffened. "Major Ilina Tschetter of the UMCI, human and loyal citizen of the League of Allied Worlds."

"She's the one I told you about," Kira muttered to Falconi.

"From the *Extenuating Circumstances*?"

Kira nodded, keeping her gaze fixed on Tschetter and the Jellies.

Falconi seemed unimpressed. "How—"

Nielsen put a hand on his shoulder. "Trig's not going to make it if you don't let them help."

"Make up your mind, Falconi," said Koyich. "We don't have time to be dicking around."

After a moment, Falconi shook off Nielsen's hand and backed away from Trig, still pointing Francesca at the aliens. "Fine. But if they kill him, I'll shoot them, no questions asked."

Outside, the mushroom cloud continued to climb.

Kira kept the blades on her fingers as the squid crawled over to Trig. Moving as precisely and delicately as any surgeon, the Jelly used its tentacles to disassemble Trig's power armor until the kid lay on the crumbled floor in nothing but his skinsuit and oxygen mask. Then the Jelly wrapped a single, thick tentacle around him, and within seconds, a thick, gelatinous substance began to ooze from its suckers.

"What the hell is that?" said Falconi in a barely controlled tone.

"It's okay," said Tschetter. "They did it to me. It's safe."

The Jelly used its tentacle to smear the goo over the whole of Trig's body. Then the coating grew opaque and hardened, forming a glistening, human-shaped pod. The whole process took less than a minute.

The alien laid the pod on the floor and retreated to Tschetter's side.

Falconi put a hand on top of the shell. "What did they do? Can he still breathe in there? We don't have time for—"

"It's their form of cryo," said Tschetter. "Trust me. He'll be fine." In the distance, gunfire again sounded in the streets, and several of the Jellies slipped away, heading toward the noise. Tschetter drew herself up and looked at Kira, Koyich, and what remained of the rest of their group. "They'll buy us some breathing room. In the meantime, we need to talk. *Now.*"

3.

"How do we know you're really you?" Koyich demanded. He had been present, Kira remembered, when she'd told Akawe about having to leave the major and Corporal Iska on Adrasteia.

Tschetter's lips quirked as she seated herself on a block of rubble and looked at Kira. "I seem to recall asking you something similar on the *Extenuating Circumstances.*"

The major was much as Kira remembered, although she seemed thinner—as if she'd lost four or five kilos—and there was a certain manic intensity to her expression that hadn't been present before. Maybe it was a result of current circumstances or maybe it was indicative of something else. Kira wasn't sure.

She was having trouble wrapping her mind around Tschetter's presence. Kira had never expected to see the major again, much less there, on a dead planet at the far end of space. The sheer incongruity left Kira feeling even more dazed than the explosion earlier.

Falconi crossed his arms. "The Jellies could have scanned your implants, learned everything they needed in order to impersonate you."

"It doesn't matter if you believe me," said Tschetter. "Who I am has nothing to do with why I'm here."

Koyich eyed her skeptically. "And why *are* you here, Major?"

"First things first. Did you find the Staff of Blue?"

When neither Kira nor anyone else answered, Tschetter snapped her fingers. "This is important. Do you have it or not? We need to know, *now*."

Koyich motioned toward the Entropists. "Show her."

Veera and Jorrus extended their hands. In them lay one fragment of the Staff of Blue.

"It's broken," Tschetter said, her tone bleak.

"Yes."

Her shoulders slumped. "Dammit," she said quietly. "The Jellies were counting on using the staff against the Corrupted. That's their name for the nightmares. Without it . . ." She drew herself upright, stiffening her back. "I'm not sure how much of a chance we stand. Them or us."

"Is it really that bad?" Kira asked.

The major nodded, grim. "Worse. The Corrupted have been hitting the Jellies throughout their territory. Small raids at first, then bigger and bigger. Some of the Corrupted were already poking around Sigma Draconis when Iska and I got picked up. They took out two of the Jellies' ships, and the one we were on barely got away."

"What *are* the Corrupted?" Kira asked. "Do you know?"

Tschetter shook her head. "Only that the Jellies are scared *shitless* of them. The Jellies say they've fought the Corrupted before. From what I gather, it didn't go well, and the current batch of Corrupted are supposedly even more dangerous. They have different forms, better ships, that sort of thing. Also, the Jellies seem convinced that we have something to do with the Corrupted, but I'm not clear on the details."

Nielsen raised a hand. "How do you know what we call the Jellies and the nightmares? And how are you talking with the Jellies?"

"The Jellies," said Tschetter, "have been monitoring all the broadcasts out of the League. They brought me up to date before we left." She tapped the front of her helmet. "Talking is scent to sound, and vice versa. Same method the Jellies use for conversion to EM signals. Made it possible to actually learn their language, though it sure as hell wasn't easy."

Koyich shifted, impatient. "You still haven't explained: Why are you here, Major? And why are the Jellies with you playing nice?"

Tschetter took a breath. The gunfire in the streets was growing closer. "The details are in a file I'm sending you. The short version is that the Jellies with me represent a faction that wants to overthrow their leadership and form an alliance with the League in order to ensure the survival of both our species. But they need our help to pull that off."

By the looks on everyone's faces, Kira wasn't the only one having trouble wrapping their mind around the situation.

Koyich's yellow eyes narrowed, and he glanced skyward. "You getting this, Captain?"

After a few seconds, Akawe answered: **Loud and clear. Major, if this is true, why didn't you approach the League directly? Why come all the way out here to make the offer?**

"Because, as I just said, the Jellies are monitoring all transmissions in and out of human space. My companions couldn't risk trying to contact the Premier directly. If their superiors noticed, they'd be caught and executed. Plus, there was the matter of the Staff of Blue and the need to keep Kira and her suit from falling into the wrong hands."

I see. Alright, I'll look at the file. In the meantime, you need to find a way off that rock. We're tied down at the moment, and you've got Jellies and nightmares incoming.

"Roger that," said Koyich.

"There's more," said Tschetter hurriedly. "The Jellies are building a massive fleet just outside the League. As soon as it's ready, they're going to sweep through and crush our forces before concentrating on the Corrupted. I'm told the Jellies have been planning on conquering us for a long time, but recent events have accelerated their timetable. The Jelly leadership is going to be on-site for several months to oversee the completion of the fleet. What my companions are proposing is that the UMC rendezvous with them near the fleet and that we coordinate a surgical strike to decapitate their government."

A muffled explosion sounded farther off in the city. The fighting seemed to have turned so it was moving sideways to the plaza and the temple-like structure.

Are your friends one hundred percent sure that their leaders will be with the fleet? Akawe asked.

"That's what they claim," said Tschetter. "For whatever it's worth, they seem to be telling the truth."

Akawe made a sound deep in his throat. **Understood. Even if this intel ends* *up being a bust, getting it back to the League just became our top priority. The Jellies are jamming the whole system, so that rules out a direct signal. Would take too long in any case. At this distance, only high-power, slow-as-ass signals would make it back. That means at least one of our ships has to get out of here, and that's going to take some doing.**

While Akawe was talking, Falconi walked a few steps away, his lips moving silently. Then he swore loudly enough to be audible through his helmet. "Goddammit! I don't believe it."

"What?" said Kira.

He grimaced. "The coolant line Hwa-jung repaired back at Cygni just broke again. The *Wallfish* can't stop until they fix it. They're going to fly right past us."

"Shit."

"My companions have two ships out by the edge of the city," said Tschetter, gesturing at the Jellies behind her, who had been waiting patiently the entire time. "They can get you back into space."

Kira glanced at Falconi, Koyich, and Nielsen. She could tell they were all thinking the same thing: Trust the Jellies enough to get onto their ships? What if they decided to strip her of the Soft Blade? Would she be able to stop them?

"I'm sure you're right, Major," said Koyich, "but I'm not exactly thrilled with the idea."

Akawe broke in: **Too bad, Commander. You need to get off that rock, and now. As for you, Major, if this is a trap, the* Darmstadt *will blow up both your ships before you get out of the system, so don't let your friends get any ideas.**

Tschetter jerked her head as if she were about to salute. "Yessir. Nossir."

Koyich started to turn away. "Alright, we need to—"

"Wait," Kira said, and went to stand directly in front of Tschetter. "I have a question."

"Stow it, Navárez," Koyich snapped. "We don't have the time."

Kira didn't budge. "Why do the Jellies think we started this war? They're the ones who attacked the *Extenuating Circumstances*."

Koyich paused, his finger resting on the trigger of his blaster. "I'd like to know that as well, Major."

Tschetter spoke quickly. "The Jellies I've been dealing with placed the xeno on Adra in order to hide it from the rest of their species. Apparently the xeno was a major threat in the past, and the Jellies seem to view it with a mix of fear and reverence. From what they've told me, their group would have done anything, *anything*, to keep the xeno from bonding with another host."

"So that's why they showed up shooting," said Kira.

Tschetter nodded. "From their point of view, we were no different than thieves who had broken into a top-secret military installation. Imagine how the UMC would have reacted."

"That still doesn't explain why the rest of the Jellies have been attacking us," said Koyich. "Did your *friends* tell them what happened at Adra?"

The major didn't hesitate. "Absolutely not. As far as I can tell, the majority of Jellies only found out about Kira when she sent the signal from Sixty-One Cygni." She made a wry face. "That was when my *friends* here hauled me out of a cell and started actually talking with me. Point is, as far as the Jelly leadership was concerned, this war started when the Corrupted started attacking them out of nowhere while broadcasting messages in English. That's why they thought we were allied. That and because, at the time, the Corrupted weren't attacking human territory."

"But the Jellies still planned on invading us no matter what," Falconi said.

"That's right."

Kira spoke then: "Do the Corrupted know about the staff or the Soft Blade?"

Tschetter stood. "The staff I can't say, but the Jellies seem to think the Corrupted are drawn to the presence of the suit or something like that. I'm not entirely sure, given the language barrier."

As if to punctuate her words, a double set of sonic booms shook the valley, and four dark, angular ships descended screaming from the sky and crashed into the city at various locations. They didn't look like the Corrupted ships from 61 Cygni, but there was still a sense of wrongness about them that Kira couldn't shake.

The thought that the nightmares might be specifically hunting her was deeply disturbing.

Sounds of gunfire and laser pulses bounced off the towers of the city, distorted heralds of violence. *Half a klick away, maybe less.* The fighting was growing closer again.

"That's it, everyone form up!" said Koyich. "We gotta hustle."

Tschetter said, "Let me make sure my companions understand the plan." She turned to the Jellies and started talking, her voice now inaudible in her helmet.

While the major talked, Kira ripped off her torn skinsuit. It would just get in the way, and besides, she wanted to . . . yes, there it was: the nearscent of the assembled Jellies. With the skin of the Soft Blade fully exposed, she could sense the swirling cues from the Jellies as they watched and reacted to their surroundings.

She should have stripped earlier. She could have been putting her questions directly to the aliens.

The leader of the Jellies was obvious from the forms and structures of the scents used. It was a huge squid with a dark layer of flexible armor coating on its limbs. Armor that, to Kira's eye, was not so different from the Soft Blade.

She approached the alien and said: [[Kira here: What is your name, Shoal Leader?]]

The collected Jellies stirred with surprise, their tentacles shifting and turning with a life of their own. [[Lphet here: The Idealis lets you scent us! What else has—]]

A series of choppy explosions interrupted them. The sounds were dangerously close. Approaching via an eastbound street was a large swarm of Jellies, who were exchanging fire with a pair of retreating squids that Kira assumed belonged to Lphet. And converging upon them via several of the westbound streets were masses of twisted bodies climbing over the piles of rubble and even climbing over themselves: tortured flesh that was red and black and melted like the scars on Falconi's forearms—an army of the Corrupted. An army of nightmares.

Then a *crack* sounded behind them, loud as a gunshot. Kira crouched and whirled, expecting to be ambushed.

In the depths of the temple's inner sanctum, the dark obelisk fractured, white lines racing across its surface, shedding dust. The nape of Kira's neck prickled as the front of the pillar fell forward with a doom-laden peal.

The obelisk was hollow. Inside it stirred a tall, angular *something*—a figure as lean as a skeleton, with legs that jointed backwards and two pairs of arms. A cloak of black seemed to hang from its pointed shoulders, and a hard, hood-like shape hid all its face, save the crimson eyes that burned within that shadowed recess.

Kira hadn't thought it possible to be any more afraid. She was wrong. For she recognized the creature from her dreams. It wasn't one of the Vanished, but one of their dread servants.

It was a Seeker, and that meant death.

CHAPTER V

* * * * * * *

SIC ITUR AD ASTRA

1.

The Seeker was moving, but slowly, as if disoriented after its long sleep.

"Run," Kira said to both humans and Jellies. "Now. Don't stop. Don't fight. Run."

[[Lphet here: A Mind Ripper! Flee!]]

The Jellies threw down a smokescreen—hiding the Seeker from sight—and together, they and the Marines scrambled out the broken front of the temple. Kira's heart was pounding with panic she couldn't suppress. *A Seeker.* She remembered them from ages past: creatures made to enforce the word of the Heptarchy. A single one had wreaked havoc on the Jellies during the Sundering; she feared to think what it might do to the League if it escaped the planet.

Nielsen carried Trig's mummified form in her arms as they clambered into the open. Falconi guarded her left; Kira her right.

"This way," said Tschetter, leading them toward a narrow side street next to the temple—one that, for the moment, was empty of enemies.

Across the plaza, the two Jellies that had been fighting a delaying action tossed drones into the air and then abandoned their cover and sprinted on tentacles across the open space to join their companions. Orange ichor dripped from several holes in the carapace of the alien on the right.

"What was that thing?" cried Nielsen, hunching over to protect Trig.

"Bad news," said Kira.

The mushroom cloud still towered high overhead, overwhelming in its size. The wind tore at the central column, dragging streaks of it westward, into the planet's nightside. A burnt, dirt-like smell pervaded the air, and the electric tang of ozone also, as if from an impending storm.

But the storm had already struck, in the form of annihilating antimatter.

Kira wondered how well the Soft Blade would protect her from the fallout. If they actually made it back into space, she'd have to get some radiation pills from the medic. . . .

A terrifying chorus of beast-like yammering erupted several streets over, thousands of voices crying out with anger and pain. A wave of nearscent wafted through the city, stifling in its strength as the unseen nightmares clashed with the pursuing Jellies.

"Out of the frying pan—"

"—and into the fire," said Jorrus and Veera.

Behind them, a high, keening sound cut the air, and if anything, the yammering intensified.

"Shit. Check this out," said Hawes.

On Kira's overlays, a window popped up with a feed from one of the Marines' remaining drones, hovering high above the plaza by the temple. The Seeker had emerged from within the ruined building and was stalking among the banks of smoke while clumps of Jellies and nightmares fought around it.

Even as Kira watched, the Seeker seized a red, dog-like nightmare and sank its black fingers into its skull. After a half second, the Seeker released the nightmare, dropped it on the ground. The creature twisted back onto its feet and then, instead of attacking the Seeker, slunk behind it, faithful as a trained pet. Nor was it the only one: a half-dozen Jellies and nightmares already attended the Seeker, ranging about it in a swirling group that protected it from direct attack.

Neither the Jellies nor the nightmares seemed to have noticed the Seeker yet, they were so busy fighting each other.

"Gods," said Nielsen, "what is it doing?"

"I'm not sure," said Kira.

[[Lphet here: The Mind Ripper controls your body, makes you do what it wants.]]

The Seeker could do more than that, Kira felt sure, but she couldn't remember specifics, which was frustrating. She trusted her fear, though; if the Soft Blade was telling her to be careful, then the threat was indeed great.

Tschetter translated, and Koyich said, "If it gets close, don't let it touch you."

"Yessir!" "Not a chance, sir!" said the Marines. As a group, they were looking rather battered. Tatupoa was carrying Redding, the Marine who had lost his leg. Nishu had blood smeared across his exo. Hawes and the team medic were limping, and most of the men had pits and dings on their helmets from debris. Two of the Marines from the *Darmstadt* seemed to be missing. Kira wasn't sure where or when they'd fallen.

A crash sounded above them. Kira looked up to see a cluster of nightmares running along a vine-draped ledge that wrapped around a nearby tower.

The Marines opened fire, and the Jellies too: a hammering volley from automatic rifles and discharging blasters. The shots stopped several of the nightmares—blasting apart raw, scabrous-looking torsos—but the rest jumped down into their group. Two landed on Marines, driving them to the ground. The creatures were the size of a tigermaul, with rows of sharklike teeth as big as Kira's hand. Three more nightmares, each with wildly different shapes—one sporting arms lined with spurs of bone, one with scaled wings sprouting from a crooked back, one fanged and tripod-legged—crashed into Lphet's Jellies amid a tangle of thrashing tentacles.

Different than before, was Kira's first thought as she saw the nightmares hurtling toward them.

She wasn't going to hold back as she had during the attack on Trig; she'd rather die first. Willing the Soft Blade to spike outward, she ran to tackle the nightmare grappling with the nearest Marine, Sanchez.

The black thorns from her suit pierced the four-legged nightmare, and it died with a terrifyingly human scream while blood gurgled from its loose throat.

Don't hurt him, Kira thought. To her relief, the Soft Blade obeyed the thought, and none of its spikes touched Sanchez. He gave her a quick thumbs-up.

She started toward the next of the nightmares, but her help was unneeded. The combined firepower of the Marines and the allied Jellies had already killed the rest of the creatures.

Falconi wiped a smear of blood off his visor, his expression grim. "Now they know where we are."

"Keep moving," Koyich barked, and their group continued down the street.

"We're getting low on ammo," Hawes said.

"I see that," said Koyich. "Switch to two-round bursts."

They concentrated on running. "Contact!" shouted a Marine as he loosed several rounds at a nightmare that appeared around the corner of a building. The creature's head exploded in a red mist.

Hemoglobin, Kira thought. Iron-based blood, unlike the Jellies.

The nightmares continued to harass them in ones and twos as they raced to the city's edge. When the buildings gave way to moss-covered ground, Kira checked on the situation in orbit. The *Wallfish* had already passed by the planet and was heading toward the outer reaches of the system. A mess of Jelly and nightmare ships were fighting high overhead: both sides against one another, and the Jellies also against themselves. The *Darmstadt* was still some distance away from Nidus but inbound fast. Smoke trailed from several burn marks along the cruiser's hull.

"Follow me," said Tschetter, taking the lead over the blasted land. The moss there lay outside the shadow of the city. It had been exposed to the full fury of the nuclear explosion and had burned beneath the heat; the small fronds crunched with each step, leaving an ashy residue on their soles.

They headed westward, away from the buildings, deeper into the dusky dark.

As they ran, Kira maneuvered herself to Tschetter's side and said, "After you were rescued, did you tell the Jellies I was still alive?"

The major shook her head. "Of course not. I wasn't about to give our enemies actionable information."

"So Lphet and the rest of them didn't know where I was or that the suit existed?"

"Not until you sent your signal." Tschetter shot her a glance. "In fact, they never actually asked. I think they assumed the suit had been destroyed along with the *Extenuating Circumstances*. Why?"

Kira took a moment to gather her breath. "Just trying to understand." Something about Tschetter's explanations didn't seem right. Why *wouldn't* the Jellies that hid the Soft Blade be curious about its location following the events at Adra? If they'd bothered to carry out a flash trace, they would have seen the *Valkyrie* leaving Sigma Draconis. Surely that would have been enough to track her to 61 Cygni. So why hadn't they? And then there was the question of the nightmares. . . .

"Is Iska with you?" Kira asked Tschetter.

The major didn't answer for a moment, her expression labored from exertion. "He stayed behind in case anything happened to me."

"So how *did* you find us?"

"Lphet knew about the ships sent to track you down. We just followed them. It wasn't hard. Corrupted must have done the same."

A shriek sounded overhead, and a cluster of dark shapes dove toward them, flapping bat-like wings. Kira ducked while lashing out with one arm. She connected with a solid, disturbingly soft body, and then the suit hardened, forming an edge, and her arm sliced through flesh and bone with hardly any resistance.

A shower of orange ichor covered her. The rest of their group suffered a similar fate as humans and Jellies alike shot down the flock. The creatures had mandibles for mouths and tiny arms with pincers tucked close against their downy breasts.

When the shooting stopped, three of the Marines were lying motionless on the ground and half a dozen more appeared injured.

Nishu kicked one of the downed creatures. "No sense of self-preservation, these."

"Yeah," said Tatupoa, bending to pick up one of his wounded teammates. "Real eager-like to get themselves killed."

[[Kira here: Are these things yours?]] She pointed at the winged corpses.

[[Lphet here: No. These are also Corrupted.]]

Kira's puzzlement deepened as she translated for the rest. Not hemoglobin this time, and there seemed to be no consistency among the shapes of the different nightmares. At least with the Jellies, it was clear the various types were *somehow* related, what with their shared blood, skin markings, muscle fibers, and the like. The nightmares lacked any such cohesion, aside from the consistently diseased look of their hides.

Tschetter gestured at a ridge of rock that rose before them. "The ships are just ahead, on the other side."

As they trotted up the ridge—the Marines trailing along as they helped their injured—Nielsen said, "Look at the sky!"

The mushroom cloud had punched a large, circular hole in the overcast sky. Through the opening in the tattered billows of mist, Kira saw great sheets of color rippling across the twinkling expanse. Reds and blues and green-yellows, shifting like ribbons of gossamer silk in a vast neon display, thousands of kilometers across.

The sight left Kira awestruck. She had only seen the aurora a few times on Weyland, and never in anything but the darkest night. It looked unreal. It looked like a bad overlay, too bright and smooth and *colorful* to be natural.

"What's causing it?" she asked.

"Nukes or antimatter in the upper atmosphere," said Tschetter. "Anything that dumps charged particles into the ionosphere."

Kira shivered. The sight was beautiful and yet, knowing its cause, terrifying.

"It'll die down in a few hours," said Hawes.

At the top of the ridge, Kira paused to glance back at the city behind them. She wasn't the only one.

A horde of bodies was streaming out of the overgrown streets: nightmares and Jellies together, their previous differences now forgotten. And walking along behind them, the Seeker—tall, skeletal, almost monastic in appearance with its seeming hood and cape. The Seeker stopped at the edge of the buildings. The same high-pitched keen rang out over the fields of blasted moss, and the Seeker spread both pairs of arms. Its cape lifted as well, unfolding to reveal a pair of wings, veined and purplish and nearly nine meters across.

"Moros," said Koyich in a surprisingly conversational tone. "See if you can put a bullet through that bastard's head."

Kira nearly objected, but she held her tongue. If there was a chance they could kill the Seeker, it would be for the best, even though a part of her would mourn the loss of a creature so old, capable, and obviously intelligent.

"You got it, sir," said one of the Marines in power armor. He stepped forward, lifted one arm, and—without a moment's delay—fired.

The Seeker's head snapped to one side. Then it slowly looked back at them with what Kira could only interpret as sheer malevolence.

"Did you hit it?" said Koyich.

"Nossir," said Moros. "It dodged."

"It . . . Marine, nail that thing with the strongest laser blast you've got."

"Yessir!"

The whine of charging supercapacitors sounded within Moros's armor, and then a *BZZT!* as loud as any gunshot sounded. Kira's skin tingled from the residual electrical charge.

She saw the laser pulse with her thermal sight: a seemingly instantaneous bar of ravening force that joined Moros to the Seeker.

Only the blast didn't touch the dark-shrouded alien. Rather, it curved around the creature's hide and burned a fist-sized hole in the wall of the building behind.

Even at a distance, Kira would have sworn the Seeker was smiling. And a memory came to her: it was they that enforced the wishes of the Heptarchy, and they that guarded the dangerous depths of space. . . .

[[Lphet here: This is to no point.]] As it spoke, the Jelly started down the other side of the ridge, along with its comrades.

Lphet's words needed no translation. Kira followed with everyone else. The knife-edge keening rang out again, and underlying it, she could hear the drumming of approaching feet.

The two Jelly ships were parked at the foot of the ridge. The globular vessels weren't particularly large by the standards of spaceships—the *Darmstadt* would dwarf them in length—but sitting there on the ground, they seemed enormous: as large as the administrative building in Highstone, where she'd gotten her seed license.

A loading ramp lowered from the belly of each ship.

The Jellies divided into two groups, one heading for each ship. Tschetter paired off with Lphet and several other Jellies heading toward the left-hand vessel. "You take that one," she said to Koyich, pointing at the ship on the right.

"Come with us!" said Kira.

Tschetter never missed a step as she shook her head. "It's safer if we split up. Besides, I'm staying with the Jellies."

"But—"

"There's a chance for peace here, Navárez, and I'm not going to give up on it. Go!"

Kira would have argued further, but they were out of time. As she sprinted alongside Falconi toward the other Jelly ship, she couldn't help but feel grudging admiration for Tschetter. Assuming the major was still in her right mind, what she was doing was incredibly brave, same as her decision to stay behind on Adra.

Kira doubted she would ever *like* the major, but she would never question the woman's devotion to duty.

More Jellies were waiting for them at the top of the loading ramp, guarding the opening with an impressive array of weapons. They moved aside as Kira and the others ran up. Koyich shepherded his men aboard, shouting at them to hurry. They stumbled in, dripping blood from bodies and fluids from exos. Nishu and Moros brought up the rear, and then the ramp retracted and the ship's loading port slid shut and locked in place, sealing the hull.

"I can*not* believe we're doing this," Falconi said.

2.

[[Wrnakkr here: Secure for ascension.]]

Ridges along the wall made for convenient handholds. Kira snared one, as did the other humans, while the Jellies used their tentacles to do likewise or—in the case of the legged Jellies—scurried off into darkened corridors.

Like the other Jelly ship Kira had been on, this one smelled of brine, and the lighting was a dim, watery blue. The room was an ovoid, with tubes and masses of unidentifiable equipment along one half, and egg-like capsules along the other. Stored on rows of double-layered racks were scores of what she recognized as weapons: blasters, guns, and even blades.

In close quarters, the nearscent of the Jellies accumulated until it nearly obliterated any other odor. The aliens stank of anger and stress and fear, and from them Kira felt a constant shifting of forms, functions, and honorifics.

It seemed to Kira that she and her companions were surrounded by monsters. She kept the Soft Blade on the verge of action, ready to send it spiking out if any of the Jellies made a hostile move. Koyich and his Marines seemed to feel likewise, for they gathered in a defensive half circle near the loading door, and while they kept their weapons aimed at the floor, they did not lower them entirely.

"Can you get us to our ship, the *Wallfish*?" said Falconi. Then he looked at Kira. "Can they get us to the *Wallfish*?"

"The *Darmstadt* is where we need to be, not your rusty old tub," said Koyich.

"The *Wallfish* is closer," said Falconi. "Besides—"

Kira repeated Falconi's question, and in answer, the Jelly that had spoken earlier said: [[Wrnakkr here: We will try to reach the closer ship, but the Corrupted are near.]]

A distant rumble passed through the curved deck, and Kira felt the strangest dropping, twisting sensation, as if she'd fallen and risen at the same time. It was a similar feeling to jumping in a descending elevator. Then her sense of weight increased to somewhat over 1 g: noticeable but not unpleasant. But she knew they were thrusting at far, far more than 1 g.

This must be the gravity of the Jellies' homeworld, she realized.

"Jesus Christ," said Hawes. "Look at our altitude."

Kira checked her overlays. Her local coordinates were going crazy, as if the computer couldn't decide where exactly she was nor how fast she was moving.

"Artificial gravity has to be messing with our sensors," said Nishu.

"Can you get a signal out?" said Falconi, his face pinched with worry.

Hawes shook his head. "Everything's jammed."

"Dammit. No way to tell where we're heading."

Kira focused on Wrnakkr. The alien had a white streak across its central carapace that made it easy to single out. [[Kira here: Can we see what's happening outside the ship?]]

With one tentacle, the Jelly caressed the wall. [[Wrnakkr here: Look, then.]]

A curved patch of hull turned transparent. Through it, Kira could see the coin-sized disk of Nidus shrinking into the distance. Explosions flared along the terminator line: bright flashes reminiscent of the florescent discharges of lightning sprites. Even from so far away, the resulting auroras were visible, laced across the top of the turbulent atmosphere.

Kira searched for other ships, but if any were present, they weren't close enough to spot with the naked eye. Not that that meant much in space.

"How long to reach the *Wallfish*?" she asked.

The Entropists were the ones to answer: "If we are thrusting at the same—"

"—acceleration generally observed among the Jellies—"

"—and given the prior distance to the *Wallfish*—"

"—no more than five or ten minutes."

Nielsen sighed, and the joints of her power armor squealed as she sank into a crouch. She was still holding Trig's rigid form. "Do we really have any chance of getting out of the system? The—"

The light within the room flashed, and nearscent of alarm suffused the room, clogging Kira's nostrils.

[[Wrnakkr here: We have Corrupted in pursuit.]]

Kira told the others, and then they sat in silence—waiting—while the ship's rocket strained. There was nothing else they could do. Outside the window Wrnakkr had created, the stars swung in crazy arcs, but the only centrifugal force Kira felt was a slight pull in the direction of their turns.

As they'd seen at 61 Cygni, the nightmares could out-accelerate even the Jellies. That implied a level of technology that only a highly advanced interstellar civilization could possess, which just didn't seem to match with the creatures they'd been seeing.

Don't judge by appearances, Kira cautioned herself. For all she knew, the ravening, animal-like nightmares with the shark teeth were as intelligent as a ship mind.

A burst of silvery chaff glittered through the window. A poof of chalk followed a moment later, obscuring the view for a few seconds.

Koyich and Hawes were murmuring together. Kira could tell they were preparing to fight.

Then the ship jolted underneath them, and her gorge rose as, for a moment, she felt yanked along all three axes at once. The artificial gravity *rippled*—producing a feeling of rolling compression through her body—before cutting out entirely.

The lights flickered. Finger-sized holes stitched their way across the inside of the bulkhead, and a dull *boom* echoed through the hull. Alarms began to shriek, loud even over the hiss of escaping air.

Kira stayed where she was, clinging to the wall, uncertain of what else to do.

The ship jolted again. A white-hot circle appeared on what had just been the ceiling, and seconds later, a disk-shaped section of the hull flew inward.

"Form up!" Koyich shouted as a dense swarm of nightmares poured into the Jelly ship.

CHAPTER VI

* * * * * * *

INTO THE DARK

1.

In an instant, a dense wall of smoke, chaff, and chalk clogged the air. The Marines opened fire, as did Wrnakkr and the rest of the Jellies—the deafening thunder of their guns obliterating all other sound.

The nightmares hardly slowed in the face of the barrage, and the sheer mass of the creatures allowed them to quickly cover the distance between them and the first line of Jellies.

The Jellies swung into action, their tentacles gripping and ripping every nightmare within reach. The beast-like attackers were foul to look at. Whether equipped with four limbs or two, arms or tentacles, teeth or beaks, scales or fur—or misbegotten combinations thereof—the creatures to the last appeared malformed, tumor-ridden, and sickly. Yet they possessed a crazed energy, as if hopped up on enough stims to kill a full-grown man.

Kira knew she might be able to survive the attack, but she didn't think Nielsen or Falconi could. Nor could she protect them or Trig; there were just too many nightmares.

Falconi seemed to have reached the same conclusion. He was already retreating toward an opened shell door at the back of the room while pulling Trig's cocooned form after himself. Nielsen followed close behind, firing occasional bursts into the horde of incoming bodies.

Kira didn't hesitate. She dove after the two of them. Several bullets ricocheted off her as she flew through the air: hard *thumps* that made her catch her breath.

She arrived at the door just after Nielsen. Together, they hurried down the dark corridor on the other side.

"I got a signal through to the *Wallfish*!" said Falconi. "They're on their way."

"ETA?" Nielsen said, crisp and professional.

"Seven minutes out."

"Then we'll—"

A thrashing *something* at the corner of Kira's vision caused her to twist around, expecting to be jumped. Nielsen did the same.

A Jelly came crawling along the side of the round corridor. Ichor leaked from a crack in its carapace, and one of its tentacles had been shot off three-quarters of the way toward the tip.

[[Itari here: Strike Leader Wrnakkr orders me to guard you.]]

"What does it want?" Falconi said, wary.

"It's here to help."

Several of the Marines scrambled into the corridor and took up positions on either side of the open door. "Keep going!" shouted one of them. "Find cover!"

"Come on," said Falconi, kicking himself farther down the corridor.

[[Itari here: This way.]] And the Jelly crawled into the lead. Its wounded tentacle left splatters of ichor across the walls.

They hurried deeper into the ship, through dimly lit rooms and narrow passageways. The sounds of combat continued to reverberate through the hull: hollow *booms* and *cracks* and high-pitched shrieks of the enraged nightmares.

Then the ship lurched again, harder than before. Sparks filled Kira's vision as the wall slammed into her, and her breath whooshed out. In front of her, Falconi lost his grip on Trig. . . .

With a horrendous scraping sound, a huge red and black spike plowed through the decking in front of her, separating her and Trig from the others. Another few meters of spike slid past, and then it slowed to a stop and stayed there, buried in the heart of the Jelly ship—a seeming impossibility.

Kira struggled to understand what she was seeing. Then she realized: the nightmares had *rammed* them. She was seeing the prow of one of their ships.

The radio crackled in her ear as she grabbed Trig's comatose form. **Kira, you okay?** said Nielsen.

"Yeah, and I've got Trig. Don't wait for me. I'll find a way around."

Roger that. There's an airlock near the front of the ship. The* Wallfish *is going to attempt to pick us up there.

If they can get close enough, said Falconi.

Pulling Trig behind her, Kira turned around and kicked back down the corridor toward the nearest shell-like doorway. Ahead of her, the noises of fighting increased in volume.

"Dammit," she muttered.

The door split open, and she hurried past. She raced through room after room, shying away from any hint of the nightmares.

In a low, round passageway, she surprised one of the Jelly lobsters. It clicked its claws at her, alarmed, and then said: [[Sffarn here: Go that way, Idealis.]] And it pointed toward a door next to the one she'd entered through.

[[Kira here: My thanks.]]

The shell parted to reveal a blob of floating water, now untethered by gravity from the side of the room where it normally rested. Kira didn't stop to think; she dove into the liquid mass, aiming for the far side.

Tiny mantis-like creatures flitted past her face as she swam. In the back of her mind, she remembered liking their taste. They were . . . crunchy and good with *yrannoc,* whatever that was.

She breached the surface of the water. It clung to her face with a wobbling film that distorted her vision. Blinking, she slung a tendril from her hand to the nearest wall and reeled herself over. Once secured, and with Trig's feet tucked under her arm, she wiped the water off her face.

Tiny droplets flew free as she shook her hand.

For an instant, the situation got the better of her and she found herself incapacitated by fear. Then her gut relaxed and she took another breath.

Stay focused. Surviving long enough to rejoin Falconi and the others was the only thing that mattered at the moment. So far she'd been lucky; she hadn't run into a single one of the nightmares.

She crawled along the curve of the wall until she found the next doorway and then pulled Trig and herself through it into another dark corridor. "You would have loved this," she muttered, thinking how interested the kid was in the Jellies, and aliens in general.

Her earpiece crackled. **Kira, we're at the airlock. Where are you?**

"Getting close, I think," she said, keeping her voice low.

Hurry it up. The* Wallfish *is almost here.

"Roger. I—"

Oh shi— said Falconi, and static filled the line. A second later, the ship tilted around her, and the bulkheads creaked and snapped with alarming violence.

Kira stopped. "What? What is it? . . . Falconi? Nielsen?" She tried several more times, but neither of them answered.

Dread welled up inside Kira. Cursing under her breath, she tightened her grip on Trig and continued along the corridor, moving even faster than before.

A flicker of motion at the far end of the passage caused her to grab a ridge on the wall and freeze. A mess of jumbled shadows had appeared in the facing intersection, and whatever cast them was moving closer. . . .

Desperate, Kira looked for a place to hide. The only option was a shallow alcove with a coral-like structure directly across from her in the hall.

She pushed herself over to the alcove and tucked Trig and herself behind the coral. Trig's stiff, shell-encased body bumped against the bulkhead, and she stiffened, hoping the sound wasn't loud enough to attract attention.

Insectile chittering drifted toward her, growing louder now. Louder.

. . . Louder.

Kira pressed against the back of the alcove. *Don't see me. Don't see me. Don't—*

Four nightmares moved into view. Three of them were much like she'd seen before: raw-skinned mutations that crept along the deck upon four and six legs respectively, their fang-laden snouts swinging back and forth as they searched for prey. The fourth nightmare was different. It was humanoid, with only one pair of legs, and arms that began as segmented lengths of carapace and then transitioned into tentacles without suckers. Its elongated head had deep-set eyes as blue as Falconi's and a mouth with tiny, moving mandibles that looked sharp enough to bite through steel. An armored lump between its legs hinted at some sort of genitalia.

The creature was frighteningly alert; it kept glancing around, checking corners, making sure no one was creeping up on them. There was an intelligence to it that Kira hadn't sensed among the other nightmares. And something more: the skin on its plated torso shimmered in a way that seemed uncomfortably familiar, although she couldn't quite figure out why. . . .

A fast chitter came from the humanoid, and the three other nightmares responded by forming a tight knot around it.

Despite her overriding concern with protecting Trig and herself, Kira was intrigued. They hadn't seen any evidence of hierarchy among the nightmares so far. If the humanoid was one of their leaders, then . . . maybe killing it would disrupt the others.

No. Attracting attention would just cause more problems. *Don't see me. Don't see me. . . .*

It took all her self-control to hold still as the nightmares approached. Every instinct toward self-preservation urged her to leap out and attack before they spotted her, but the more rational part of her counseled patience, and for whatever reason, she listened.

And the nightmares didn't see her.

As they hurried past, she smelled them: a burnt, cinnamon-like scent laced with a sickening mix of shit and putrefaction. Whatever they were, the creatures weren't healthy. Two of the beast-like nightmares glanced in her direction as they passed by. Their eyes were tiny and red-rimmed and wept drops of yellowish fluid.

Confusion gripped Kira. Why hadn't they noticed her? The alcove wasn't *that* deep. She looked down at herself and, for a moment, felt dizzy; all she saw was the shadowed shape of the wall. She lifted her hand in front of herself. Nothing. Perhaps a small amount of glass-like distortion around the edges of her fingers, but that was it.

Trig's encased body was still visible, but nothing about it seemed to attract the attention of the nightmares.

Kira grinned. She couldn't help it. The Soft Blade was bending the light around her, same as with the invisibility cloak she and her sister had played with as kids. Only this was better. Less distortion.

The nightmares continued down the corridor another few meters. Then the one with six legs paused and swung its skull-like head back in her direction. Its nostrils flared as it tested the air, and its cracked lips retracted from its teeth in an evil snarl.

Shit. Just because the aliens couldn't see her didn't mean they couldn't smell her. . . .

The six-legged nightmare *hissed* and started to turn back toward her, digging its claws into the deck for traction.

Kira didn't wait. She loosed a yell and jumped after the creature. With one hand, she stabbed out toward it, and the Soft Blade complied by impaling the sore-covered nightmare with a triangular blade that then sprouted a pincushion of black needles.

The creature squealed, thrashed, and went limp.

With her other hand, Kira stabbed the next nightmare in line and killed it in the same fashion.

Two down, two to go.

The humanoid nightmare aimed a small device at her. A loud *thump* hit Kira in both her ears and her hip, knocking her off course. Her hip went numb, and pain radiated up her spine, sending electric shocks shooting through the nerves in her arms.

She gasped and, for a moment, found herself unable to move.

The other beast-like nightmare jumped her then. The impact knocked them both tumbling down the corridor. Kira covered her face with her arms as the creature attempted to savage her with its snapping jaws. Teeth skated across the hardened surface of the Soft Blade while claws scrabbled harmlessly against her belly.

Despite her instinctual fright, the nightmare couldn't seem to hurt her.

Then it drew back its head and, from its gaping mouth, sprayed a stream of greenish liquid across her head and chest.

An acrid smell hit her nostrils, and wisps of smoke rose from the patches of skin hit by the liquid. But she felt no pain.

The creature had sprayed her with *acid*. The realization outraged Kira. *How dare you?!* If not for the Soft Blade, the acid would have burned her beyond recognition.

She jammed her fists into the creature's mouth. With a heave of her arms, she tore its head apart, spraying blood and flesh across the walls.

Panting, she looked for the humanoid nightmare, intending to kill it as well.

The humanoid was right next to her, mandibles spread to reveal round, pearl-like teeth. Then it *spoke*, in a hissing, growling voice: "You! Forgotten flesssh! You ssshall join the maw!"

Shock delayed Kira's reaction. The nightmare took the opportunity to wrap a tentacle around her right arm, and a current of fire seemed to course through her skin and into her brain.

A horrible sense of recognition seized her, and she howled as her vision flared white.

2.

She saw herself from two different angles, standing in the storage room aboard the Extenuating Circumstances. *The perspective was confusing: competing viewpoints that overlapped and intermingled to produce a warped re-creation of the moment. As with the images, she felt a jumbled mix of emotions, none of which seemed to relate: surprise, fear, triumph, anger, contempt, regret.*

One of her perspectives was trying to hide, pulling itself behind a rack of equipment with speed born of terror. The other seemed confident, unafraid. It remained where it was and attacked, hot beams of light slicing through the air.

She saw herself flee toward the exit, but too slow, far too slow. Black spikes bristled from her skin in random, undisciplined outbursts.

Then she turned, face contorted with fear and anger as she lifted the pistol she'd taken from the dead crew member. The muzzle flashed, and bullets smacked into a wall.

The perspective that was afraid was shouting and waving, desperate for her to stop.

The perspective that wasn't, evaded, darting across the walls. It felt no concern.

Sparks flashed as lasers vaporized bullets.

Then one of the bullets hit the red-labeled pipe at the back of the room, and her perspectives flew apart amid a thunderclap. A moment of blankness, and when perception returned, it was further fractured. Now there were three sets of memories, and none of them familiar. The newest addition was smaller, less distinct than the others; it did not see with eyes, yet was still aware of its surroundings in a vague and cloudy way. And it was possessed of the same fear and anger she had experienced, only now amplified by confusion and lack of direction.

The explosion had torn open the hull of the Extenuating Circumstances. *Wind clawed at the separate parts of her, and then she was spinning through space. Three different minds beheld the same kaleidoscope of stars, and pain racked her trinity of torn flesh. Of the three, the original two seemed weaker: their vision dimmed as consciousness faded. But not the third. Damaged it was, afraid and angry it was, incomplete it was, but not yet deprived of motive force.*

Where to go? It had lost contact with the parent form, and it no longer possessed the ability to locate it. Too many fibers were broken; too many loops interrupted. Redundancy failed and self-repair cycled and stalled, lacking both knowledge and required elements.

Driven by rage and terror that refused to abate, it stretched itself thin, cast spider-threads far into the void as it searched for the nearest sources of warmth, frantically seeking its parent form, as the pattern commanded. If it failed, dormancy would be its fated lot.

Just as the last gleam of light vanished from the view of the two others—just as the stifling press of oblivion enveloped them—threads caught and held their flesh. Confusion reigned. Then the imperative to heal overrode the other directives of the searching threads, and a new pain manifested: a needlelike prick that quickly expanded into a crawling agony that encompassed every centimeter of their battered bodies.

Flesh joined with flesh in a frantic mating as the three viewpoints became one. No longer were they grasper or two-form or Soft Blade. Now they were something else entirely.

It was a malformed partnership, born of haste and ignorance. The parts did not fit, though they were stitched together at the smallest level, and they revolted against themselves and against reality itself. Then within the cross-joined mind of the new flesh, madness took hold. Reasoned thought no longer dwelt therein, only the anger that had been hers, and the fear too. Panic was the result, and further dysregulation.

For they were incomplete. The fibers that had joined them had been flawed, imperfect, poisoned by her emotions. As was the seed, so was the fruit.

They struggled to move, and their contradictory urges caused them to flail without purpose.

Then the light of a double sun bathed them with heat as the Extenuating Circumstances *detonated, destroying the* Tserro*—the grasper ship—at the same time.*

The blast blew them away from the shining disk of the nearby moon, a piece of flotsam driven before a storm. For a time, they drifted in the cold of space, at the mercy of momentum. Soon though, their new skin gave them the means to move, and they stabilized their spin and looked anew upon the naked universe.

Unceasing hunger gnawed at them. They desired to eat and grow and spread beyond this barren place, as their flesh commanded. As the broken pattern dictated. And coupled with that ravenous appetite, a constant roar of fury and fear: an instinctual rejection of the extinction of self, inherited from her confrontation with Carr/Qwon.

They needed food. And power. But first food to feed the flesh. They spread themselves wide to catch the light of the system's star and flew the short distance to the rocky rings around the great gas giant in whose gravity well they resided.

The rocks contained the raw materials they sought. They gorged themselves upon stone, metal, and ice—used it to grow and grow and grow. Power was plentiful and easy to acquire in space; the star provided all they needed. They extended themselves across the vastness and converted every ray of light they captured into useful forms of energy.

The system could have been a home for them; there were moons and planets fit for life. But their ambition was greater. They knew of other places, other planets, where life teemed in the billions and trillions. A banquet of flesh, and power also, waiting to be claimed and converted and put to use in service to their overriding cause: expansion. With such resources at their disposal, their growth would be exponential. They would spread like fire among the stars—spread and spread and spread until they filled this galaxy and others beyond.

It would take time, but time they had. For they were undying now. Their flesh could not stop growing, and so long as a single speck of it remained, still then their seeds would spread and flourish. . . .

But there was an obstacle to their plan. A problem of engineering that they could not overcome, not with all their flesh nor all their gathered power.

They did not know how to build the device that would allow them to slip between the fabric of space and travel faster than the speed of light. They knew of the device, but no part of their mind knew the specifics of construction.

Which meant they were trapped in the system unless they were willing to venture forth at slower-than-light speeds, and they were not. Their impatience compelled them to stay, for they knew others would come. Others bearing the needed device.

So they bided their time, and waited and watched and continued to prepare.

. . .

They did not have long to wait. Three flashes along the boundary of the system alerted them to the arrival of grasper ships. Two were so foolish as to come close to investigate. The flesh was ready. They struck! They seized the ships, and in a rage, emptied them of their contents, absorbed the bodies of the graspers, and made the vessels their own.

The third ship escaped their maw, but that did not matter. They had what they needed: the machines that would allow them to bridge the chasms between the stars.

So they left to feed their hunger. First to the nearest grasper system: a newly settled colony, weak and undefended. There they found a station orbiting in the darkness: a ripe fruit ready for plucking. They crashed into it and made themselves part of the structure. The information contained within the computers became their own, and they grew confident in their ambition.

Their confidence was premature. The graspers sent more ships after them: ships that burned and blasted and cut away their flesh. No matter. They had what they needed, though not what they wanted.

They fled back into interstellar space. This time, they chose a system free of graspers or two-forms. But not barren of all life. One of the planets was a festering boil of living creatures busy eating other living creatures. So the Maw descended and devoured them all, converted them to new forms of flesh.

There then, they held. There they ate and increased and built in a heated frenzy. Soon the surface of the planet was covered and the sky dotted with the ships they were building.

No, not building . . . growing.

With the ships, they also grew servants, in substance based upon half-remembered templates from their binding flesh, in shape based upon a grafting of forms suggested by the different parts of their mind. The results were crude and unlovely, but they obeyed as required and that was sufficient. A horde of creatures made to carry out the dictates of the pattern. Life self-sufficient and capable of propagating itself. But some of the servants were more—pieces of the Maw, given a seed of their own flesh, that their essence might travel among the stars.

When the strength of their forces was sufficient, they sent them forth to recapture the graspers' system, and to attack others besides. The hunger was yet unsated, and the fear-driven anger of their two minds still no less.

A season of feasting followed. The graspers fought back, but they were unprepared, and they were too slow to replace their fallen. The Maw had no such difficulty. Each system it struck, it quickly established a permanent foothold and began the process of spreading across every available planet.

Progress brought their servants closer to the space of the two-forms. The flesh of the Maw spanned seven systems now, and it felt confident in its strength. So it sent its minions against the two-forms, to drive them back and begin the process of conversion.

And then, when least expected, they had heard a cry in the dark: Stop it! *And they recognized the signal and the voice as well. The first belonged to the makers of the flesh, now long vanished, and the second to her, Kira Navárez.*

Again she saw her face contort with fear and anger as she fired the pistol. . . .

The Maw roared, and they told their servants: Find the forgotten flesh! Break it! Smash it! EAT IT!

3.

Kira . . . Where are you? . . . Kira?

Kira screamed as she returned to herself.

The humanoid nightmare still had the tentacle wrapped around her arm, but there was more to it than that. Black threads joined the surface of the Soft Blade to the flesh of the nightmare, and she could *feel* the creature's consciousness pressing against her, seeking to blot her out. The nightmare's skin was eating into her own as it assimilated the Soft Blade. It wasn't a process she could stop by force of will; the xeno didn't recognize the nightmare as an enemy. Rather, it seemed to *want* to assimilate with the creature's broken flesh, to become one again with its lost parts.

If she delayed, Kira knew she would die. Or least be converted into something she abhorred.

She tried to yank her arm away from the humanoid, and they spun end over end until they smacked into the deck. The flesh of the nightmare was still melting into her.

"Give up," said the monster, mandibles clicking. "You cannot win. All will be flesssh for the mouth of many. Join usssss and be eaten."

"No!" said Kira. She willed the Soft Blade outward, and it responded with a thousand jutting spikes, piercing the nightmare through and through. The creature shrieked and writhed, but it did not die. Then Kira felt the spikes impaling its body dissolve and flow into the nightmare, leaving the Soft Blade thinner, smaller than before.

The tentacle had sunk deep into her arm; only the top of it was visible above the churning surface of the Soft Blade.

No! She refused to die like this. Flesh was expendable. Consciousness wasn't.

Kira formed the suit on her left arm into a blade, and—with a yell of desperation—she cut twice.

Once through her right arm, severing it at the elbow.

Once through the nightmare, slicing it in two at the waist.

Blood fountained from the stump of her arm, but only for an instant. Then the Soft Blade closed over the raw end of the wound.

It should have hurt, but whether from adrenaline or the xeno, it didn't.

The two halves of the nightmare flew to opposite ends of the corridor. And still the creature didn't die; the torso half continued to move its arms and head and chitter with its mandibles, while the lower half kicked as if trying to run. Even as she watched, black tendrils emerged from the exposed surfaces of its insides, reaching and searching in an attempt to pull themselves back together.

Kira knew she was outmatched.

She looked for the alcove: *there.* She kicked herself over to it, grabbed Trig's cocoon with her one hand, and then willed the Soft Blade to propel them back along the corridor, in the direction they'd been headed originally.

As they neared the end of the passage, she glanced over her shoulder at the nightmare. The two parts of the creature's body were nearly rejoined. Then she saw the torso half lift its remaining tentacle and point the same small device at her as before.

She tried to duck her head behind her arm. Too slow.

. . .

. . .

. . .

A bell-like ringing filled her ears as she regained awareness. At first, she couldn't remember who she was or where she was. She gaped at the blue-lit walls as they drifted past, trying to understand, for she was convinced something was wrong. Terribly wrong.

Her breath rushed in, and with it memory. Knowledge. Fear.

The nightmare had shot her in the head. Kira could feel a dull throb in her skull, and her neck spasmed with jolts of pain. The creature was still at the other end of the corridor, still working to rejoin its severed halves.

Boom! It fired at her again, but this time the bullet glanced off her shoulder, deflected by the hardened surface of the Soft Blade.

Kira didn't wait to see more. Still dazed, she grabbed the wall, pulled herself and Trig around the corner at the end of the corridor, breaking the line of sight with the nightmare.

As she moved through the ship, Kira felt disconnected from reality, as if everything were happening to someone else. Sounds made little sense, and she saw rainbow-colored halos around lights.

Must have a concussion, she thought.

The things she had seen from the nightmare . . . They couldn't be, and yet she knew they were. Dr. Carr and the Jelly, joined together into an abomination by the fragments of the Soft Blade blasted off her. If only she hadn't been so consumed by her emotions during their confrontation. If only she had listened to Carr's pleading. If only she had avoided shooting the oxygen line. . . . *She* was the mother of the Corrupted. Her actions had led to their creation, and their sins were hers. All those dead: Jellies, humans, and so many innocent life-forms on distant planets—her heart ached to think of it.

She was barely conscious of where she was going. The Soft Blade seemed to decide for her: left *here,* right *there.* . . .

A voice drew her from her haze: "Kira! Kira, over here! Where—"

She looked up to see Falconi hanging before her, a fierce expression on his face. The Jelly, Itari, was with him, weapons aimed at the doorway. Behind them was a large, jagged hole in the hull, big enough for a car to pass through. The dark of space showed through it, and hanging in the dark, like a gleaming gem, the *Wallfish,* over a hundred meters away.

With a start, Kira realized they were in vacuum. Somehow that had happened without her noticing.

". . . your arm! Where—"

She shook her head, unable to find the words.

Falconi seemed to understand. He grabbed her by the waist and pulled her and Trig toward the opening in the hull. "You have to jump. They can't get any closer. Can you—"

On the side of the *Wallfish,* Kira saw the airlock was open. In it, several figures moved: Nielsen and some of the Marines.

Kira nodded, and Falconi released her. She gathered her strength and then leaped into the void.

For the length of a breath, she floated in silence.

The Soft Blade adjusted her course by a few centimeters, and she flew straight into the *Wallfish* airlock. A Marine caught her, stopped her momentum.

Falconi followed a moment later, bringing Trig with him. The Jelly came also, somewhat to Kira's surprise, and crowded its tentacled bulk into the airlock.

The instant the outer door closed, Falconi said, "Hit it!"

Gregorovich's whispering voice answered, "Aye-aye, Captain. Currently *hitting* it."

A surge of high-g thrust dropped them to the floor. Kira yelped as the stump of her arm banged against the inside of the airlock. Then she thought of the nightmare she'd cut in two, and fear focused her thoughts.

She looked at Falconi and said, "You have to . . . You have to . . ." She couldn't seem to fit her tongue around the words.

"Have to what?" he said.

"You have to destroy that ship!"

Sparrow was the one to answer, her voice emanating from the intercom overhead: "Already taken care of, sweetcheeks. Hold on tight."

Outside the airlock, there was a flash of pure white light, and then the window darkened until it was opaque. Seconds later, the *Wallfish* shuddered, and a series of faint *pings* sounded against the outer hull. Then the ship grew still again.

Kira let out her breath and allowed her head to drop back against the floor.

They were safe. For now.

CHAPTER VII

* * * * * * *

NECESSITY

1.

The inner door to the airlock rolled open. Sparrow was standing there with a rifle fitted to her shoulder, aiming it toward the Jelly at the back of the airlock. Her hair hung flat and heavy in the high-g of the *Wallfish*'s burn.

"What's that thing doing here, Captain?" she said. "You want I should remove it?"

The Marines scooted back from the Jelly while keeping their own weapons trained on it. A sudden tenseness filled the air. "Falconi?" said Hawes.

"The Jelly was helping us," said Falconi, getting to his feet. It took him noticeable effort.

[[Itari here: Strike Leader Wrnakkr ordered me to guard you, so I will guard you.]]

Kira translated, and Falconi said, "Fine. But he stays here until we get shit sorted out. Not going to have him wandering around the ship. You tell him that."

"*It*," said Kira. "Not him."

Falconi grunted. "It. Whatever." He slung his grenade launcher across his back and lurched out of the airlock. "I'll be in Control."

"Roger that," said Nielsen, her voice muffled as she pulled off the helmet of her power armor.

The captain staggered down the corridor as fast as he could despite the ship's thrust, and Sparrow followed close behind. "Glad you made it, knuckleheads!" she shouted over her shoulder.

Kira conveyed Falconi's orders to the Jelly. It formed a nest with its tentacles and settled down at the end of the airlock. [[Itari here: I will wait.]]

[[Kira here: Do you need help with your injuries?]]

Nearscent of negation reached her. [[Itari here: This form will heal on its own. Help is not required.]] And Kira saw that the crack in the Jelly's carapace was already crusted over with a hard, brown substance.

As Kira moved out of the airlock, she passed by Nielsen. "Your arm!" said the first officer.

Kira shrugged. She was still in so much shock over what she'd learned about the nightmares that the loss didn't seem very important. And yet she avoided looking at the absence below her elbow.

The Entropists were there, but of their whole expedition, only seven of the Marines had survived.

"Koyich? Nishu?" she said to Hawes.

The lieutenant shook his head while tending to Moros, who had a piece of humerus sticking through his skinsuit. Despite her own distress, Kira felt a pang of sorrow for the lost men.

Vishal came hurrying up to the airlock, bag in hand. His face was lined and streaked with sweat. He gave Trig's body a worried glance and then said, "Ms. Nielsen! Ms. Kira! We thought for sure we'd lost you. It's good to see you."

"You too, Vishal," Nielsen said, stepping out of her armor. "When you get a chance, we'll need some rad-pills."

The doctor bobbed his head. "Right here, Ms. Nielsen." He handed a blister pack to the first officer, and then held out another to Kira.

She tried to accept with her missing hand. The doctor's eyes widened as he noticed. "Ms. Kira!"

"It's fine," she said, and snatched up the pills with her other hand. It most definitely wasn't.

Vishal continued to stare after her as she left the airlock.

Once out of sight, she stopped in the corridor and downed the pills. They stuck in her throat for an unpleasant moment. After, she just stood there. She didn't know what she wanted to do, and for a time, her brain refused to provide an answer.

Then, she said, "Gregorovich, what's happening?"

"Rather busy at the moment," the ship mind answered in an unusually serious voice. "Sorry, O Spiky Meatbag."

Kira nodded and started to trudge toward Control, each weighted step jarring her heels.

2.

Falconi was hunched over the central display along with Sparrow. In the holo, a window displayed the feed from a skinsuit headcam of someone moving about on the outside of the *Wallfish*'s hull.

Hwa-jung's voice sounded through the comms: "—checking the welds. I promise. Five minutes, no more, Captain."

"No more," he said. "Falconi out." He touched a button, and the holo switched to a map of the system, with all the ships marked for easy viewing.

As Kira sank into the welcome relief of a padded crash chair, Sparrow glanced at her. The woman's eyes widened as she noticed what she hadn't before. "Shit, Kira. What happened to your—"

"Not now," said Falconi. "Storytime later."

Sparrow bit back her questions, but Kira could feel the weight of her gaze.

The Jellies and the nightmares were still skirmishing near and around Nidus. But it was a confused fight. The three remaining ships that belonged to the friendly Jellies—including the one carrying Tschetter—were taking potshots at both the nightmares and their own kind. Two Jelly vessels and one of the nightmares had taken off from the planet and were shooting at any and all. Kira suspected the Seeker was in control of them. Likewise, the rest of the nightmares were fighting everyone but themselves.

As one of the Jellies' ships—fortunately, not a friendly—exploded in a nuclear flare, Sparrow winced. "What a clusterfuck," she said.

At first Kira thought the *Wallfish* had been lucky enough to escape pursuit, but then she spotted the trajectories plotted from two of the nightmares: intercept courses. The long, angular ships (they looked like bundles of enormous femurs bound together with strips of exposed muscle) were on the opposite side of the planet, but they were accelerating at the same insane, cell-destroying g's the other nightmares had employed. At the current rate, they'd be in range within fourteen minutes.

Or maybe not.

Approaching from the near asteroid belt was the *Darmstadt,* trailing threads of coolant from its damaged radiators. Kira checked the numbers; the cruiser would just barely cross paths with the nightmares before they shot past. If the nightmares piled on another quarter g of thrust, the UMC would be far too slow.

The comms crackled, and Akawe's voice sounded: "Captain Falconi, do you read?"

"I read."

"We can buy you some time here, I think. Maybe enough for you to get to the Markov Limit."

Falconi gripped the edge of the table, the tips of his fingers turning white from the force. "What about you, Captain?"

A chuckle from Akawe surprised Kira. "We'll follow if we can, but all that matters is that someone lets Command know about the offer from Tschetter's Jellies, and right now the *Wallfish* has the best shot of escaping the system. I know you're a civvy, Falconi—I can't order you to do jack shit—but it doesn't get more important than this."

"We'll get the message back to the League," said Falconi. Then, after a moment's pause, "You have my word, Captain."

A crackle of static and then: "I'll hold you to that, Captain. . . . Stand by for a light show. Over."

"What are they planning?" said Kira. "They can't outmaneuver the nightmares."

Sparrow wet her lips, her gaze fixed on the holo. "No. But maybe Akawe can hit them hard and fast enough to take them off our tail. Depends on how many missiles the *Darmstadt* has left."

Kira and the others were still sitting, waiting and watching, when Hwa-jung lumbered in through the doorway. Falconi gave her a nod. "Problem fixed?"

Hwa-jung surprised Kira by bowing past parallel. "It was my fault. The repair I made in Sixty-One Cygni, I made in anger. The work was bad. I am sorry. You should find a better machine boss to work for you."

Falconi walked over, put his hands on Hwa-jung's shoulders, and raised her back into a standing position. "Nonsense," he said, voice unexpectedly gentle. "Just don't let it happen again."

After a moment, Hwa-jung ducked her head. Tears filled her eyes. "I will not. I promise."

"That's all I ask," said Falconi. "And if—"

"Shit," said Sparrow in a subdued tone, pointing at the holo.

The nightmares had increased their thrust. The *Darmstadt* was going to fall short by a good margin. Certainly more than the effective range of the cruiser's main lasers.

"Now what?" Kira asked. She felt numb from the rolling series of catastrophes. What else could go wrong at this point? Didn't matter. *Just deal with it.* If the nightmares docked with the *Wallfish*, she might be able to fight off some of the invaders, but if there were more creatures like the one that had grabbed her on the Jelly ship, then she would be lost. They would all be lost.

"We set up a killing zone in the main shaft," said Falconi. "Funnel the nightmares into there and hit 'em from every side."

"Assuming they don't just blow us up," said Sparrow.

"No," said Hwa-jung, motioning toward Kira. "They want her."

"They do," Falconi agreed. "We can use that to our advantage."

"Bait," said Kira.

"Exactly."

"Then—"

A bloom of dazzling white in the center of the holo interrupted her and caused them all to stop and stare.

Both nightmare ships had exploded, leaving nothing but an expanding cloud of vapor.

"Gregorovich," said Falconi. "What just happened?"

The ship mind said, "Casaba-Howitzers. Three of them."

The image in the holo ran in reverse, and they saw the explosions collapse back into the nightmares' ships and—just before—three needles of light flickering in a scattered line some tens of thousands of klicks away.

"How?" said Kira, confused. "The *Darmstadt* isn't in range."

Sparrow seemed about to answer when the comm line crackled again and Akawe came on. "There's the light show, folks," he said, sounding grimly amused. "We dropped a few RD Fifty-Twos on approach to Nidus. Something new we've been playing with. Hydrogen-cooled Casaba-Howitzers. Makes 'em nearly impossible to spot. In a pinch, they work pretty well as mines. We just had to force the nightmares into range. Stupid fucks didn't even realize they were flying into a trap. We're changing course now. Going to do our best to keep the rest of these hostiles off your backs. Just keep up your burn and don't stop for anything. Over."

"Roger that," said Falconi. ". . . And thank you, Captain. We owe you one. Over."

"There'll be drinks to go around when this is done, Captain. Over," said Akawe.

As the line went dead, Sparrow said, "I'd heard about the RD Fifty-Twos. Never got to play with them, though."

Falconi leaned back from the holo. He ran his hands through his bristly hair, scrubbing at his scalp with the tips of his fingers, and then said, "Okay. We've got some breathing room. Not much, but a little."

"How long until we can jump out?" Kira asked.

"At our current two g's of thrust," whispered Gregorovich, "we shall gain the freedom to depart this hallowed graveyard in exactly twenty-five hours."

That's too long. Kira didn't have to say it; she could see the others were thinking it as well. The nightmares and the Jellies had only taken a few hours to reach Nidus after dropping out of FTL. If more of them decided to pursue the *Wallfish,* they'd have no trouble overtaking it.

"Gregorovich," said Falconi, "any chance of a solar flare?"

Smart. Like all red dwarfs, Bughunt would be prone to high variability, which meant enormous and unpredictable solar flares. A large enough outburst would disrupt the magnetic fields used in the exhaust nozzles of their fusion drives and keep the Jellies or the nightmares from overtaking the *Wallfish.* Assuming they hadn't found an effective way to shield themselves.

"None at the moment," said Gregorovich.

"Dammit," Falconi muttered.

"We'll just have to hope Akawe and Tschetter's Jellies can keep everyone off our tail," said Sparrow.

Falconi looked like he'd just bitten down on a rock. "I don't like it. I *really* don't like it. If even one of those assholes comes after us, we're going to be in a world of trouble."

Sparrow shrugged. "Not sure what we can do about it, Captain. The *Wallfish* ain't like a horse. She won't go any faster if you hit her."

A thought occurred to Kira: the malformed corruption that was the nightmares had been able to make use of the Jelly tech, so . . . why couldn't they?

The idea was so outlandish, she nearly dismissed it. Only because of the desperate nature of their circumstances did she say, "What about the Jelly, Itari?"

"What about it?" said Falconi.

"Maybe it could help us."

Hwa-jung's eyes narrowed, and she sounded outright hostile as she said, "How do you mean?"

"I'm not sure," said Kira. "But maybe it can tweak our Markov Drive so we can jump to FTL sooner."

Hwa-jung cursed. "You want to let that *thing* tinker with the *Wallfish*? Gah!"

"It's worth a try," said Sparrow, looking at Falconi.

He grimaced. "Can't say I like it, but if the Jelly can help us, we have to give it a shot."

Hwa-jung looked profoundly unhappy. "No, no, no," she muttered. Then, louder: "You do not know what it could do. It could break every system in the ship. It could blow us up. No! The Jelly doesn't know our computers or our—"

"So you'll help it," Falconi said in a gentle tone. "We're dead if we can't get out of this system, Hwa-jung. Anything that can help us is worth trying at this point."

The machine boss scowled and rubbed her hands together again and again. Then she grunted and got back to her feet. "Okay. But if the Jelly does anything to hurt the *Wallfish,* I will tear it apart."

Falconi smiled slightly. "I'd expect nothing less. Gregorovich, you keep an eye on things also."

"Always," whispered the ship mind.

Then Falconi shifted his gaze. "Kira, you're the only one who can talk with the Jelly. Go see if it thinks it can help, and if it *can,* then coordinate between it and Hwa-jung."

Kira nodded and pushed herself out of the crash chair, feeling every one of the added kilos from their burn.

The captain was still talking: "Sparrow, you too. Make sure things don't get out of hand."

"Yessir."

"When you're done, take the Jelly back to the airlock."

"You're going to leave it there?" Sparrow asked.

"Seems like the only semi-secure place for it. Unless you have a better idea?"

Sparrow shook her head.

"Right. Then get to it. And Kira? When you're finished, go see the doc and have him look at that arm of yours."

"Will do," said Kira.

3.

As Kira left Control along with the other two women, Hwa-jung gestured at her arm and said, "Does it hurt?"

"No," said Kira. "Not really. Just feels weird."

"What happened?" said Sparrow

"One of the nightmares grabbed me. The only way I could escape was by cutting myself free."

Sparrow winced. "Shit. At least you made it out."

"Yeah." But privately, Kira wondered if she really had.

Two of the Marines—Tatupoa and another man whose name Kira didn't know—stood stationed in the airlock antechamber, keeping watch over the Jelly inside. The rest of the Marines had cleared out, leaving behind bandages and bloody streaks on the deck.

The two men were wolfing down rations as Kira and her companions approached. They both looked pale and exhausted, stressed. She recognized the look; it was the same way she felt. After the adrenaline wore off, then came the crash. And she'd crashed hard.

Tatupoa paused with his spork in the air. "You here what to talk with the squid?"

"Yeah," said Kira.

"Gotcha. You need any help, just holler. We'll be right behind you."

Although Kira doubted the Marines could protect her better than the Soft Blade, it made her glad to know they were there, guns at the ready.

Sparrow and Hwa-jung hung back as she went to the airlock and peered through the diamond pressure window. The Jelly, Itari, was still sitting on the floor, resting amid its knotted tentacles. For a moment, apprehension stalled her. Then Kira hit the release button and the airlock's inner door rolled back.

The scent of the Jelly struck her: a smell that reminded her of brine and spice. It had an almost coppery tang.

The alien spoke first: [[Itari here: How can I help, Idealis?]]

[[Kira here: We are trying to leave the system, but our ship is not fast enough to outswim the Wranaui or the Corrupted.]]

[[Itari here: I cannot build you a flow modifier.]]

[[Kira here: Do you mean a—]] She struggled to find the right word: [[—a weight changer?]]

[[Itari here: Yes. It lets a ship swim more easily.]]

[[Kira here: I understand. What about the machine that lets us swim faster than light?]]

[[Itari here: The Orb of Conversion.]]

[[Kira here: Yes, that. Can you do anything to make it work better, so we can leave sooner?]]

The Jelly stirred and seemed to motion at itself with two of its tentacles.

[[Itari here: This form is meant for fighting, not building. I do not have the assemblers or the materials needed for this sort of work.]]

[[Kira here: But do you know *how* to improve our Orb of Conversion?]]

The Jelly's tentacles wrapped over themselves, rubbing and twisting with restless energy. [[Itari here: Yes, but it may not be possible without the proper time, tools, or form.]]

[[Kira here: Will you try?]]

. . . [[Itari here: Since you ask, Idealis, yes.]]

[[Kira here: Follow me.]]

"Well?" said Sparrow as Kira left the airlock.

"Maybe," Kira replied. "It's going to take a stab at helping. Hwa-jung?"

The machine boss scowled and said, "This way."

"Whoa, there," said Tatupoa, holding up a tattooed hand. "No one told us but nothing about this. You want to take the Jelly out?"

Sparrow had to call Falconi then, and Falconi call Hawes, before the Marines would relent and allow them to escort Itari to engineering. Kira kept close to the Jelly, the Soft Blade covered in short, dull spikes in preparation for potentially having to fight and kill.

But Kira didn't think it would be necessary. Not yet.

Although she was alert and functional, she felt weak, wrung out by the trauma of the day. She needed food. And not just for herself; the Soft Blade needed nourishment as well. The suit felt . . . thin, as if the energy required for combat and the loss of the material covering her forearm had depleted its reserves.

"Do you have a ration bar on you?" Kira said to Sparrow.

The woman shook her head. "Sorry."

Where's Trig when you need him? Kira winced at the thought. No matter; she would wait. She wasn't about to pass out from hunger, and food—or rather the lack thereof—was far from the top of her priority list.

Engineering was a cramped room packed full of displays. The walls, floors, and ceiling were painted with the same flat grey Kira remembered from the *Extenuating Circumstances.* In contrast, every pipe, wire, valve, and handle was a different color: bright reds and greens and blues and even a tangerine orange, each of them distinct and impossible to confuse. Heavy studs of oversized braille marked the objects so they could be identified in the dark and while wearing a skinsuit.

The floor looked cleaner than the galley counter. Yet the air was thick with heat and moisture, and laden with the unpleasant tang of lubricants, cleaners, and ozone. It left the taste of copper on Kira's tongue, and she could feel her eyebrows standing on end with static electricity.

"Here," said Hwa-jung, leading the way to the back of the room, where one half of a large, black sphere, over a meter across, protruded: the *Wallfish*'s Markov Drive.

The quarter hour that followed was a frustration of failed translations for Kira. The Jelly kept using technical terms that she didn't understand and couldn't render into comprehensible English, and likewise, Hwa-jung kept using technical terms that Kira couldn't adequately convert into the Jellies' language. The machine boss toggled a holo-display built into the console next to the Markov Drive and brought up schematics and other visual representations of the machine's inner workings, which helped some, but—in the end—still failed to fully bridge the language gap.

The math behind a Markov Drive was anything but simple. However, the execution—as Kira understood it—was fairly straightforward. Annihilation of antimatter was used to generate electricity, which in turn was used to power the conditioned EM field that allowed for transition into superluminal space. The lower the energy density of the field, the faster a ship could fly, as less energy equaled higher speeds when going FTL (exactly the opposite of normal space). Efficiencies of scale meant bigger ships had higher top speeds, but in the end, the ultimate limiting factor was one of engineering. Maintaining the low-energy fields was tricky. They were prone to disruption from numerous sources both within and without a ship, which was why a strong gravity well would force a ship back into normal space. Even during interstellar flight, the field had to be adjusted multiple times every nanosecond in order to maintain some semblance of stability.

None of which gave Kira much confidence that Itari could somehow redesign their Markov Drive on the fly, without the proper equipment and without understanding English or the coding of human math. Nevertheless, she hoped, despite what reason told her.

At last, Falconi's voice came over the comms: "Making any progress? Things aren't looking too good out there."

"Not yet," said Hwa-jung. She sounded as annoyed as Kira felt.

"Keep at it," said the captain and signed off.

"Maybe—" said Kira, and was interrupted by the Jelly turning away from the holo and crawling over the bulging surface of the Markov Drive.

"No!" Hwa-jung exclaimed as the alien started to pull at the paneling with one of its tentacles. The machine boss moved across the room with surprising nimbleness and tried to pull the Jelly off the drive, but the creature effortlessly pushed her back with another of its tentacles. "Kira, tell it to stop. If it breaks containment, it'll kill us all."

Sparrow was already lifting her blaster, finger on the trigger, when Kira said, "Stop! Everyone be calm. I'll ask, but don't shoot. It knows what it's doing."

The sound of bending metal made her wince as Itari wrenched free the protective shell from around the guts of the Markov Drive.

"It better," Sparrow muttered. She lowered her blaster some, but not entirely.

[[Kira here: What are you doing? My shoalmates are worried.]]

[[Itari here: I need to see the way your Orb of Conversion is built. Do not worry, two-form. I will not destroy us.]]

Kira translated, but Itari's assurances did little to alleviate Hwa-jung's concern. The machine boss stood next to the Jelly, peering over its humped tentacles, scowling, and knotting her hands. "*Shi-bal,*" she growled. "Not the . . . no . . . ah, you stupid thing, what are you doing?"

After several minutes of tense standoff, the Jelly withdrew its armlike pincers from the insides of the drive and turned to face Kira.

[[Itari here: I cannot make your Orb work better.]] The burn of acid hit Kira's stomach as the Jelly continued talking: [[I could make it stronger, but—]]

[[Kira here: Stronger?]]

[[Itari here: By increasing the flow of energy, the strength of the bubble can be improved, and the conversion to faster than light will happen closer to the star. But to do that, I would need equipment from one of our ships. There is no time to make the wanted parts from raw materials.]]

"What is it saying?" Hwa-jung asked. Kira explained, and the machine boss said, "How much closer?"

[[Itari here: With your Orb of Conversion . . . at least half again.]]

"You don't look impressed," Kira said, after she finished translating.

Hwa-jung snorted. "I'm not. We already boost the field strength before going FTL. It's an old trick. The drive can't handle any more power, though. The reaction chamber will fail or the circuits will burn out. It's not workable."

"Doesn't matter in any case," said Sparrow. "You already said it: the Jelly can't do anything without the right equipment. We're just shitting out an airlock." She shrugged.

While they talked, Kira had been thinking. At first she wondered if the Soft

Blade could provide Itari with the tools and materials it needed. She felt sure it ought to be possible, but she had no idea where or how to start, and the xeno gave her no hint. Then, she ran through everything she knew of on the *Wallfish,* searching for something—anything—that might help.

The answer sprang to her mind almost at once.

"Hold on," she said. Hwa-jung and Sparrow paused, looked at her. Kira tabbed her comms and put a call through to the Entropists: "Veera, Jorrus, we need you down in engineering, posthaste. Bring that object you found on the Jelly ship."

"On our way, Prisoner," the two replied.

Hwa-jung's eyes narrowed. "You cannot expect a random piece of machinery scavenged off an alien ship to be of any real use, Navárez."

"No," said Kira. "But it's worth a try." She explained to Itari, and the Jelly settled onto the deck to wait, tentacles wrapped around itself.

"How can this squid do anything anyway?" Sparrow demanded. She jerked the barrel of her blaster toward Itari. "It's just a soldier. Are all their soldiers trained engineers?"

"I would like to know that too," said Hwa-jung, her eyebrows beetling.

Kira relayed the question to the Jelly, and it said: [[Itari here: No, this form is not for making machines, but each form is given a seed of information to serve when needed.]]

"What do you mean by form?" said Sparrow.

Several of the alien's tentacles twisted in on themselves. [[Itari here: This form. Different forms serve different uses. You should know; you have two forms yourselves.]]

"Do they mean men and women?" said Hwa-jung.

Sparrow also frowned. "Can Jellies change form? Is that what it—"

The arrival of the Entropists interrupted her. The two Questants cautiously approached Kira and—keeping both sets of eyes fixed on Itari—handed her the bluish, oblong-shaped object they had retrieved from the Jelly ship at 61 Cygni.

Nearscent of excitement struck Kira's nostrils as she handed the piece to Itari. The Jelly turned the fist-sized object over with its crab-like arms, and its tentacles flushed with autumnal reds and oranges.

[[Itari here: This is a nodule from an Aspect of the Void.]]

[[Kira here: Yes. That was the room where my shoalmates found it. Is the nodule of any use?]]

[[Itari here: Perhaps.]]

Then Kira watched with interest and some astonishment as a pair of even smaller arms unfolded from a hidden slot within the rim of the Jelly's carapace. Like their larger brethren, the limbs were cased in a shiny, chitinous material, but unlike them, they were fine-jointed and tipped with a set of delicate cilia no more than a centimeter or two in length.

With them, Itari rapidly disassembled the nodule. Inside were a number of solid components, none of which resembled any part of a computer or mechanical device Kira was familiar with. If anything, the pieces most closely resembled shaped sections of a gem or crystal.

Components in-cilia, Itari returned to the Markov Drive and reached with its small, tertiary limbs into the depths of the spherical device.

As banging, scrabbling, and sharp metal screeches sounded inside the drive, Hwa-jung said, in a warning tone, *"Kira."*

"Give it a chance," said Kira, though she was equally tense. Along with the Entropists and machine boss, she peered over Itari's tentacles, into the drive. There, Kira saw the Jelly fitting the crystalline components to different parts of the machine's innards. Whatever the components touched, they bonded to after a few moments, tiny glittering threads joining them to the nearby material. But only—Kira noticed—where appropriate. Either Itari's direction or some inbuilt programming guided the threads.

"How are they doing that?" Hwa-jung asked, a strange intensity to her voice.

Upon Kira's translation: [[Itari here: By the will of the Vanished.]]

The Jelly's answer did nothing to lessen Kira's concerns, nor—it seemed—Hwa-jung's. But they stood by and let the alien work unhindered. Then it said:

[[Itari here: You will need to turn off the rock mind governing the Orb of Conversion for this to work.]]

"Rock mind?" said Hwa-jung. "Does it mean the computer?"

"I think so," said Kira.

"Mmh." The machine boss seemed less than pleased, but after several moments of silence as her eyes darted back and forth across her invisible overlays, she said, "Done. Gregorovich is overseeing the drive now."

After Kira informed the Jelly, it said, [[Itari here: The Orb of Conversion is ready. You may activate it twice as soon as before.]]

Hwa-jung scowled as she bent over the drive, studying the mysterious additions to the machine's internals. "And afterward?"

[[Itari here: Afterward, the energy flow will be returned to normal, so your ship may swim as fast as always.]]

The machine boss seemed unconvinced, but she grunted and said, "Guess that's the best we're going to get."

"Twice as soon as before," said Sparrow. "We're thrusting at two g's, so that means we can jump out . . . when?"

"Seven hours," said Hwa-jung.

That was better than Kira had feared but far worse than she'd hoped. Seven hours was still more than enough time for one or more of the enemy ships to catch up with them.

When Hwa-jung called up to Control and informed Falconi of the situation, he said, "Well. Good. We're not out of the woods, but we might be able to see the light between the trees. Neither the Jellies nor the nightmares are going to expect us to jump out so soon. If we're lucky, they'll think they have plenty of time to come after us and just concentrate on blowing each other out of the sky. . . . Good work, everyone. Kira, thank the Jelly for us and check if it needs any food, water, blankets, that sort of thing. Sparrow, make sure it gets back to the airlock."

"Yessir," said Sparrow. Then, when the comm line went dead, she said, "*If we're lucky.* Sure. When have we had any luck recently?"

"We are still alive," said Jorrus. "That—"

"—counts for something," said Veera.

"Uh-huh," said Sparrow. Then she motioned at Itari. "Comeon, big-and-ugly. Time to go."

Mention of the nightmares again turned Kira's mind to unpleasant thoughts. As they ushered the Jelly into the narrow corridor outside engineering, she conveyed Falconi's thanks and asked after the Jelly's needs, to which it replied:

[[Itari here: Water would be welcome. That is all. This form is hardy and requires little to sustain it.]]

Then she said, [[Kira here: Did you know that the Corrupted came from the Idealis?]]

The alien seemed surprised she would ask. [[Itari here: Of course, two-form. Did you not?]]

[[Kira here: No.]]

Garish colors roiled the surface of its tentacles, and nearscent of confusion tinged the air. [[Itari here: How is that possible? Surely you were present for the spawning of these Corrupted. . . . We have been most curious about the circumstances of this, Idealis.]]

Kira put a hand on Sparrow's shoulder. "Hold on. I need a minute."

The woman glanced between her and the alien. "What's up?"

"Just trying to clarify something."

"Really? Now? You can chat all you want back at the airlock."

"It's important."

Sparrow sighed. "Fine, but make it snappy."

Despite her immense reluctance, Kira explained to Itari the sequence of events that had resulted in the birth of the Maw. But she skimmed over the specifics of *how* exactly the explosion on the *Extenuating Circumstances* had happened, for she felt ashamed of what she had done and the consequences it had led to.

When she finished, a bouquet of unpleasant scents wafted from the Jelly's hide. [[Itari here: So the Corrupted we see now are a mixture of Wranaui, two-forms, and the blessed Idealis?]]

[[Kira here: Yes.]]

The Jelly shivered. Not a reaction Kira had seen from any of their species before. [[Itari here: That is . . . unfortunate. Our enemy is even more dangerous than we first thought.]]

You're telling me.

Itari continued: [[Until you responded to the *tsuro,* the searching signal of the Vanished, we thought you were the Corrupted. How could we not, when we found Corrupted lying in wait for us around the star where we hid the Idealis?]]

[[Kira here: Is that why you did not search for me after I left that system?]]

Nearscent of affirmation. [[Itari here: We did search, Idealis, but again, we thought you *were* the Corrupted, so it was the Corrupted we followed. Not your little shell.]]

She frowned, still struggling to understand. [[Kira here: So, the reason you and the rest of the Wranaui thought the Corrupted were allied with us is because . . . you knew that I'd created them?]]

[[Itari here: Yes. Such a thing happened once before, during the Sundering, and it nearly proved our undoing. Even though the others of our kind did not know the exact source of these Corrupted, they knew it had to be from an Idealis. And since, as your co-form said, the Corrupted used your language and, for a time, did not attack your pools, it seemed clear that they were your shoalmates. It was only once we heard your signal and saw the response of the Corrupted that we realized you were not growing them to wage war against us.]]

[[Kira here: The rest of the Wranaui must have realized this as well, yes?]]

[[Itari here: Yes.]]

[[Kira here: And yet they continue to attack us.]]

[[Itari here: Because they still think you and your co-forms are responsible for the Corrupted. And you *are,* Idealis. From that point of view, the how and the why do not matter. It has long been our plan to dam your pools and limit your spread. The appearance of the Corrupted did nothing to change that. But the ones this form serves believe otherwise. They believe the Corrupted are too great a threat for the Wranaui to overcome alone. And they believe that now is the best chance since the Sundering to replace the leadership of the Arms. For that, we need your help, Idealis, and the help of your co-forms.]]

[[Kira here: What exactly do you expect me to do?]]

The Jelly flushed pink and blue. [[Itari here: Why, to oppose the Corrupted. Is not that obvious? Without the Staff of Blue, you are our greatest hope.]]

4.

With Itari safely returned to the airlock, Kira headed to the galley. There, she grabbed three ration bars and downed a glass of water. Gnawing on one of the bars, she made her way back through the center of the ship to the *Wallfish*'s machine shop. As once before, she opened the drawers of printing stock and stuck the stump of her arm into the different powders. *Eat,* she told the Soft Blade.

And it did.

Metals and organics and plastics: the xeno absorbed them all, and in great quantities. It seemed to be fortifying itself against what might come.

While the suit gorged, Kira ate the other two ration bars, although it was difficult to tear open their foil wrappers with just one hand—and her off one at that. *Why couldn't it have been my left?* she thought.

In any case, the inconvenience kept her from dwelling upon darker, more dire things.

When she and the suit were both fed, enough time had passed that Kira felt sure Vishal had finished tending to the wounded. At least, enough to spare her a few minutes. So, she closed the drawers of stock and headed to sickbay.

The room was a shambles. Bandages, gauze, empty canisters of medifoam, and scraps of bloody clothes littered the deck. Four of the Marines were there: one on the lone exam table, three more lying on the deck in various stages of undress while the UMC medic attended to them along with Vishal. All of the injured men appeared sedated.

But Kira didn't see the one person she was most worried about. As Vishal bustled over, she said, "Hey, where's Trig? Is he okay?"

Vishal's expression darkened. "No, Ms. Kira. I cut him free from the webbing the Jelly placed on him. It most definitely saved his life, but . . ." The doc *tsked* and shook his head as he stripped off his blood-smeared gloves.

"Will he make it?"

Vishal removed another pair of gloves from a box on the counter and donned them before answering. "If we can get Trig to a proper medical facility, then yes, he will survive. Otherwise, not so much."

"You can't fix him here?"

Vishal shook his head. "The projectile shattered vertebrae here"—he touched the upper part of her neck—"and sent fragments into his skull. He needs surgery of a sort the medibot here isn't rated for. He may even be needing to have his brain transferred into a construct while a new body is grown for him."

The thought made Kira feel even worse. A kid as young as Trig losing his body. . . . It didn't seem right. "Is he in cryo now?"

"Yes, yes, in the storm shelter." Then Vishal reached for the end of her severed arm. "Now then, Ms. Kira, let me see. Ah, what have you been doing?"

"Nothing fun," she said.

Vishal bobbed his head as he produced a scanner and started to examine the stump of her arm. "No, I would think not." His gaze flicked up toward her. "The men showed me some of what you did on Nidus. How you fought the Jellies and the nightmares."

Kira half shrugged, feeling uncomfortable. "I was just trying to keep us from getting killed."

"Of course, Ms. Kira. Of course." The doc tapped on the end of the stump. "Does that hurt?"

She shook her head.

As he felt the muscles around the shortened end of her arm, Vishal said, "The video I saw . . . What you are able to do with this xeno . . ." He clucked his tongue and went rummaging around in one of the cupboards overhead.

"What of it?" Kira said. The morbid part of her wondered how the sight of the Soft Blade killing had affected him. Did he see her as a monster now?

Vishal came back with a tube of green gel that he rubbed across her stump. It was cool and viscous. He pressed an ultrasound projector against her arm and focused on his overlays while he said, "I have a name for your xeno, Ms. Kira."

"Oh?" Kira said, curious. She realized she'd never told him that the suit called itself the Soft Blade.

Vishal shifted his gaze to her for a moment, serious. "The Varunastra."

"And what is that?"

"A very famous weapon from Hindu mythology. The Varunastra is made of water and can assume the shape of any weapon. Yes, and many warriors such as Arjuna used it. Those who carry weapons of the gods are known as Astradhari." He eyed her from under his eyebrows. "*You* are Astradhari, Ms. Kira."

"Somehow I doubt that, but . . . I do like the name. The Varunastra."

The doc smiled slightly and handed her a towel. "It is named after the god Varuna. He who made it."

"And what is the price for using the Varunastra?" said Kira as she wiped the gel off her arm. "There's always a price for using the weapons of the gods."

Vishal put away the ultrasound. "There is no price per se, Ms. Kira, but it must be used with great care."

"Why?"

The doc seemed reluctant to answer, but at last he said, "If you lose control of the Varunastra, it can destroy you."

"Is that so?" said Kira. A slight chill crawled down her spine. "Well, the name fits. Varunastra." Then she motioned toward the stump of her arm. "Can you do anything for me?"

Vishal wobbled his hand from side to side. "You do not seem to be in pain, but—"

"No."

"—but we do not have time to print a replacement arm for you before we leave the system. Hwa-jung may be able to make a prosthetic for you, but again, time is very short."

"If it weren't," said Kira, "do you think you would be able to attach the replacement? I can make the suit retract from the area, but . . . I'm not sure how long I could hold it back, and if you have to cut open the skin again—" She shook her head. Anesthetic wouldn't be an option for her either. Maybe a prosthetic would end up being the best choice after all.

Vishal bent to check the dressings on the leg of a Marine and then said, "True, true. But the xeno knows how to heal, yes?"

"Yes," said Kira, thinking of how it had joined Carr and the Jelly. *Sometimes too well.*

"Then perhaps it could join a new arm to you. I do not know, but it seems capable of great things, Ms. Kira."

"The Varunastra."

"Indeed so." And he smiled at her, showing his bright white teeth. "Aside from the injury itself, I can find nothing wrong with your arm. You tell me if you feel any pain, and I will look at it again, but in meantime, I do not think it is necessary to take any special precautions."

"Okay. Thanks."

"Of course, Ms. Kira. My pleasure to help."

Back outside the sickbay, Kira paused in the hallway, hand on hip, and took a few seconds to collect herself. What she really needed was time to sit and think and process everything that had happened.

But, as Vishal had said, time was short, and there were things that needed doing. And not all of them were so obvious—or straightforward—as combat.

From sickbay, she headed toward the center of the ship and the lead-lined storm shelter set directly under Control. She found Nielsen standing by one of the seven cryo tubes mounted along the walls. Trig lay inside the tube, his face barely visible through the frosted viewplate. Smears of dark blood still discolored his neck, and there was a slackness to his face—an *absence*—that Kira found unsettling. The body before her didn't feel like the person she knew but rather an object. A thing. A thing devoid of any animating spark.

Nielsen moved aside as Kira walked over and put a hand on the side of the tube. It was cold beneath her palm. She wasn't going to see the kid again anytime soon. What was the last thing she'd said to him? She couldn't remember, and it bothered her.

"I'm sorry," she whispered. If she'd been faster, if she hadn't been so careful to keep the Soft Blade under control, she could have saved him. And yet, maybe not. . . . Given what she now knew about the creation of the nightmares, letting go was the last thing she should have done. Using the Soft Blade was like playing with a motion-activated bomb; at any moment it could go off and kill someone.

What was the answer, then? There had to be a middle way—a way that would allow her to operate not from fear but a sense of confidence. Where it was, though, she didn't know. Too much control and the Soft Blade might as well be nothing more than a glorified skinsuit. Not enough and, well, she'd seen the result. Catastrophe. She was trying to balance upon a knife's edge, and so far, she'd failed and it had cut her.

"Eat the path," Kira murmured, remembering Inarë's words.

"It's my fault," said Nielsen, surprising her. The first officer joined her by the front of the cryo tube.

"No, it's not," said Kira.

Nielsen shook her head. "I should have known he would do something foolish if he thought I was in danger. He's always acted like a puppy around me. Should have sent him back to the ship."

"You can't blame yourself," said Kira. "If anything . . . I'm the one responsible." She explained.

"You don't know what would have happened if you let the suit act on its own."

"Maybe. And there's no way you could have known that Jelly was going to pop up. You didn't do anything wrong."

After a moment, Nielsen relented. "I suppose. The thing is, we should have never put Trig in that situation in the first place."

"Did we really have a choice? It wasn't much safer on the *Wallfish*."

"That doesn't mean it's right. He's younger than both my sons."

"He's not a child, though."

Nielsen touched the top of the tube. "No, he isn't. Not anymore."

Kira hugged her, and after her initial surprise, Nielsen hugged back. "Hey, the doc says he'll live," said Kira, pulling away. "And you *did* make it. Everyone on the *Wallfish* did. I bet Trig would consider that a win."

The first officer managed a wan smile. "Let's try to avoid any more wins like that from now on."

"Agreed."

5.

Twenty-eight minutes later, the *Darmstadt* exploded. One of the nightmares controlled by the Seeker managed to hit the UMC cruiser with a missile, rupturing its Markov Drive and vaporizing half the ship.

Kira was in Control when it happened, but even there, she heard a loud "Fuck!" echoing up from the injured Marines in sickbay.

She stared with dismay at the holo of the system—at the blinking red dot that marked the last location of the *Darmstadt.* All those people, dead because of her. The sense of guilt was overwhelming.

Falconi must have seen something of it on her face, because he said, "There's nothing we could have done."

Perhaps not, but that didn't make Kira feel any better.

Tschetter contacted them almost immediately. "Captain Falconi, the Jellies with me will continue to provide you with as much cover as possible. We can't guarantee your safety, though, so I'd advise maintaining your current burn."

"Roger that," said Falconi. "What sort of shape are your ships in?"

"Don't worry about us, Captain. Just get back to the League in one piece. We'll take care of the rest. Over."

In the holo, Kira saw the three friendly Jelly ships darting in and around the larger conflict. Only four of the hostile Jelly ships remained, and most of the nightmares' had been disabled or destroyed, but those last few were still fighting, still dangerous.

"Gregorovich," said Falconi. "Crank us up another quarter g."

"Captain," said Hwa-jung in a warning tone. "The repairs may not hold."

He looked at her with a steady gaze. "I trust you, Song. The repairs will hold."

Gregorovich cleared his simulated throat, then, and said, "Increasing thrust, O Captain, my Captain."

And Kira felt the weight of her limbs increase yet again. She sank into the nearest chair and sighed as the cushioning took some of the pressure off her bones. Even with the help of the Soft Blade, the extra thrust was far from pleasurable. Just breathing took noticeable effort.

"How much time does that save us?" Falconi asked.

"Twenty minutes," said Gregorovich.

Falconi grimaced. "It'll have to do." His shoulders were hunched under the force of the heavy burn, and the skin on his face sagged, making him look older than he was.

Then Nielsen, who was on the other side of the holo, said, "What are we going to do about the Marines?"

"Is there a problem?" Kira asked.

Falconi lay back in his own chair, allowing it to support him. "We don't have enough cryo tubes for everyone. We're four short. And we sure as hell don't have the supplies to keep anyone awake and kicking all the way back to the League."

Apprehension formed in Kira as she remembered her time without food on the *Valkyrie*. "So what then?"

An evil gleam appeared in Falconi's eye. "We ask for volunteers, that's what. If the Jelly could put Trig into stasis, then it can wrap up the Marines. Doesn't seem to have hurt Tschetter."

Kira exhaled forcefully. "Hawes and his men aren't going to like that, not one bit."

Falconi chuckled, but beneath it, he was still deadly serious. "Tough. Beats having to take a walk out an airlock. I'll let you inform them, Audrey. Less of a chance they'll punch a woman."

"Gee, thanks," said Nielsen with a wry expression. But she didn't complain any further as she carefully pushed herself out of her seat and headed down to the hold.

"Now what?" Kira asked once the first officer was gone.

"Now, we wait," said Falconi.

CHAPTER VIII

* * * * * * *

SINS OF THE PRESENT

1.

The day had started early. One by one the crew, the Entropists, and the Marines still able to walk gathered in the galley. With so many people present, the room was cramped, but no one seemed to mind.

Hwa-jung and Vishal took it upon themselves to heat and serve food to everyone. Despite the ration bars she'd consumed earlier, Kira didn't refuse the bowl of rehydrated stew when it was pushed into her one remaining hand.

She sat on the floor in a corner, with her back propped against the wall. At 2.25 g's, it was by far the most comfortable option, despite how much effort it took to get up or down. There, she ate while watching and listening to the others.

On each table, a holo displayed a live view of the ships behind them. The projections were the main focus of attention; everyone wanted to see what was happening.

The Jellies and the nightmares were still skirmishing. Some had fled to planet c or b and were currently chasing each other through the fringes of the atmosphere, while another group—three ships in total—were diving around the star, Bughunt.

"Looks like they still think they have plenty of time to catch us before we go FTL," said Lt. Hawes. He was red-eyed and grim; all the Marines were. The losses they'd suffered during the escape from the planet, as well as the destruction of the *Darmstadt,* had left them looking hollow and withdrawn, shattered.

Kira thought it was an accurate representation of how everyone on the ship felt.

"Fingers crossed they don't change their minds," said Falconi.

Hawes grunted. Then he looked at Kira. "Once you're up for it, we need to talk with the Jelly. This is the first chance we've had to communicate with one of them. The brass back home is going to want every bit of intel we can squeeze out of that thing. We've been fighting in the dark until now. It'd be nice to have some answers."

"Can we do it tomorrow?" said Kira. "I'm wiped, and it won't make any difference if we can't escape first."

The lieutenant rubbed his face and sighed. He seemed even more exhausted than her. "Yeah, sure. But let's not put it off any longer."

While they waited, Kira withdrew deeper and deeper into herself, as if she were retreating into a shell. She couldn't stop thinking about what she'd learned about the nightmares. *She* was responsible for creating them. It had been her own misguided choices, her own fear and anger that had led to the birth of the monstrosities currently running rampant among the stars.

Even though Kira knew that, logically, she couldn't be blamed for the actions of what the humanoid nightmare had called the *Maw*—the twisted, mutated fusion of Dr. Carr, the Jelly, and the damaged parts of the Soft Blade—it didn't change how she felt. Emotion trumped logic; the thought of everyone who had been killed in the conflict between humans, Jellies, and the nightmares made her heart ache with a dull, soul-crushing pain that the Soft Blade could do nothing to alleviate.

She felt as if she'd been poisoned.

The Marines ate quickly and soon returned to the hold to oversee preparations for the transition to FTL. The Entropists and the crew of the *Wallfish* lingered about the holos, quiet save for the occasional murmured comment.

At one point, Hwa-jung said in her blunt way, "I miss Trig." To that, they could only nod and express their agreement.

Partway through the meal, Vishal looked over at Falconi and said, "Is there enough salt for you, Captain?"

Falconi gave a thumbs-up. "Perfect, Doc. Thanks."

"Yeah, but what's with all the carrots?" said Sparrow. She lifted a spoon piled high with orange disks. "Always seems like you put in an extra bag or something."

"They're good for you," said Vishal. "Besides, I like them."

Sparrow smirked. "Oh, I know you do. Bet you keep carrots hidden in sickbay to snack on when you're hungry. Just like a rabbit." And she made a nibbling motion with her teeth. "Drawers and drawers full of carrots. Red ones, yellow ones, purple ones, you—"

A flush darkened Vishal's cheeks, and he put his spoon down with a loud *clack*. Kira and everyone else looked. "Ms. Sparrow," he said, and there was an uncharacteristic note of anger in his voice. "Always you have been, as you put it, 'riding my ass.' And because Trig admired you so much, he did the same."

With an arch expression, Sparrow said, "Don't take it so seriously, Doc. I'm just ribbing you. If—"

Vishal faced her. "Well please don't, Ms. Sparrow. There is none of this *ribbing* with anyone else, so I would thank you to treat me with the same respect as I treat you. Yes. Thank you." And with that, he went back to eating.

Sparrow seemed embarrassed and taken aback. Then Falconi gave her a warning look, and she cleared her throat and said, "Sheesh. If you feel so strongly about it, Doc, then—"

"I do," said Vishal with definitive firmness.

"Uh, then sorry. Won't happen again."

Vishal nodded and continued eating.

Good for him, Kira thought dully. She noticed a small smile on Nielsen's face, and after a few minutes, the first officer got up and went to sit next to Vishal and started talking with him in a low tone.

Soon after, Sparrow left to check on the Jelly.

Everyone had finished eating, and Nielsen and Vishal were washing up, when Falconi trudged over to Kira and carefully lowered himself onto the floor next to her.

She watched without much curiosity.

He didn't meet her gaze but stared somewhere at the ceiling across the room and scratched the day-old stubble on his neck. "You going to tell me what's bothering you, or do I have to pry it out of you?"

Kira didn't feel like talking. The truth about the nightmares was still too raw and immediate, and—if she was honest with herself—it made her feel ashamed. Also, she was tired, tired right down her to bones. Having a difficult, emotional discussion felt like more than she could deal with at the moment.

So, she deflected. Motioning at the holos, she said, "That's what's bothering me. What do you think? Everything's gone wrong."

"Bullshit," Falconi said in a friendly tone. He gave her a look from under his dark brows, the blue of his eyes deep and clear. "You've been off ever since we got back from that Jelly ship. What is it? Your arm?"

"Sure, my arm. That's it."

A crooked smile appeared on his face, but there wasn't much humor to his expression. "Right. Okay. If that's the way you're going to be." He undid a pocket on his jacket and slapped a deck of cards down onto the floor between them. "Ever play Scratch Seven?"

Kira eyed him, wary. "No."

"I'll teach you then. It's pretty simple. Play a round with me. If I win, you answer my question. If you win, I'll answer any question you want."

"Sorry. I'm not in the mood." She started to stand, and Falconi's hand closed about her left wrist, stopping her.

Without thinking, Kira formed a cuff of spikes around her wrist, spikes sharp enough to cause discomfort though not sharp enough to draw blood.

Falconi winced but kept hold of her. "Neither am I," he said, his voice low, his expression serious. "Come on, Kira. What are you afraid of?"

"Nothing." She sounded unconvincing even to herself.

He raised his eyebrows. "Then stay. Play a round with me. . . . Please."

Kira hesitated. As much as she didn't want to talk, she also didn't want to be alone. Not right then. Not with the leaden ache in her chest and the fighting going on in the system around them.

That by itself wasn't enough to change her mind, but then she thought of the scars on Falconi's arms. Perhaps she could get him to tell her the story of how he acquired them. The idea appealed to her. Besides, there was a part of her—buried deep inside—that really did want to tell someone about what she'd learned. Confession might not make things any better, but perhaps it would help lessen the pain in her heart.

If only Alan were there. More than anything, Kira wished she could talk with him. He would understand. He would comfort and commiserate and perhaps even help her find a way of solving the galactic-level problem she'd caused.

But Alan was dead and gone. All she had was Falconi. He would have to do.

"What if you ask something I really don't want to answer?" Kira said, a bit of strength entering her voice.

"Then you fold." But Falconi said it as if he were daring her otherwise.

A sense of rebelliousness stirred within Kira. "Fine." She settled back down, and he let go of her wrist. "So teach me."

Falconi examined the hand she'd poked and then rubbed it against his thigh. "It's a points game. Nothing special." He shuffled the cards and started to deal: three cards for her, three for him, and four in the middle of the table. All of them facedown. The remainder of the deck he set aside. "The goal is to get as many sevens or times sevens as possible."

"How? By multiplying the cards?"

"Adding. One plus six. Ten plus four. You get the idea. Jacks are eleven, queens twelve, kings thirteen. Aces low. No jokers, no wild cards. Since each player has seven cards, counting the shared ones," Falconi indicated the four cards on the deck, "the highest natural hand is a straight sweep: four kings, two queens, and an ace. That gives you—"

"Seventy-seven."

"For a score of eleven. Right. Cards always keep their face value, *unless*—" He held up a finger. "—*unless* you get all the sevens. Then sevens are worth double. In that case, the highest hand is a full sweep: four sevens, two kings, and a nine. Which gives you . . ." He waited for her to do the math.

"Ninety-one."

"For a score of thirteen. Betting is normally done after each shared card is turned over, but we'll make it easy and just bet once, after the first card. There's a catch, though."

"Oh?"

"You can't use your overlays for the adding. Makes it too easy." And a message popped up in the corner of Kira's vision. She opened it to see a prompt from a privacy app that would lock their overlays for as long as they both chose to use it.

Annoyed, she hit Accept. Falconi did the same, and everything on Kira's overlays froze. "Okay," she said.

Falconi nodded and picked up his cards.

Kira looked at her own cards. A two, an eight, and a jack: twenty-one. How many sevens did that make? Despite the math she'd done during FTL, multiplying and dividing numbers in her head still wasn't easy. Addition it was. *Seven plus seven is fourteen. Plus another seven is twenty-one.* She smiled, pleased that she already had a score of three.

Then Falconi reached out and turned over the first of the four communal cards: an ace. "I'll start the betting," he said. Behind him, the Entropists deposited their empty meal wrappers in the trash and headed out of the galley.

"You dealt. Shouldn't I?"

"Captain's prerogative." When she didn't argue, he said, "Same question as before: What's bothering you?"

Kira already had her own question ready: "How did you get those scars on your arms?" A hard expression settled on Falconi's face. He hadn't expected that from her, she could tell. *Well, good.* It served him right. "Call. Unless you think that's a raise?" She asked in the same tone of challenge he had used before.

Falconi's lips flattened into a thin line. "No. I think that counts as a call." He turned over the next card. A five.

They were both silent as they checked their math. Kira still came up with the same figure: twenty-one. Was that a good hand? She wasn't sure. If not, her only chance of winning would be to ask another question, one that might make Falconi fold.

Nielsen and Vishal were drying their hands after finishing the dishes. The first officer walked over—her steps painfully slow in the high-g—and touched Falconi on the shoulder. "I'm going back to Control. I'll keep an eye on things from there."

He nodded. "Okay. I'll relieve you in, say, an hour."

She patted him and moved on. As she left the galley, she turned and said, "Don't bet anything too valuable, Kira."

"He'll steal the tongue right out of your mouth," Vishal added, following after.

And then it was just the two of them in the galley.

"Well?" said Kira.

Falconi turned over the third card. Nine.

Kira tried to keep her lips from moving as she did the sums. Keeping track of all the numbers wasn't easy, and a few times she lost her place and had to start over again.

Thirty-five. That was the best she could come up with. Five sevens. A good sight better than what she'd had before. She started to feel as if there was a chance she might win the hand. Time to take some risks.

"I'm going to raise," she said.

"Oh?" said Falconi.

"Yeah. How did you manage to buy the *Wallfish*?" The skin under his eyes tightened. She'd struck another nerve. Good. If she was going to tell him about the nightmares, Kira didn't want to be the only one sharing secrets. When Falconi still hadn't responded after a few seconds, she said, "What's it going to be? Fold, call, or raise?"

Falconi rubbed his chin. The stubble rasped against the pad of his thumb. "Call. What happened to your arm? How did you really lose it? And don't give me that nonsense you told Sparrow about a nightmare grabbing you. It would take a half-dozen exos to give you any trouble."

"That's two questions."

"It's a restatement. If you want to say it's two, just say I . . . upped the stakes."

Kira bit back a sarcastic reply. He wasn't making it easy to open up, that was for sure. "Leave it. Keep going."

"Last card," Falconi said, seemingly unperturbed, and flipped it over.

A king. Thirteen.

Her mind raced as she tried different combinations. The next multiple of seven was seven times six, or . . . forty-two. Eleven plus thirteen plus one plus eight plus nine—that did it! Forty-two!

Satisfied, Kira started to relax. Then she saw it: add in the two and the five, and she had another seven. Forty-nine. Seven times seven. Her lips curled. How appropriate.

"Now there's a dangerous expression," said Falconi. Then he laid his cards on the deck. Two threes and a seven. "Pity it won't do you any good. Five sevens."

She revealed her own cards. "Seven sevens."

His gaze darted from card to card as he checked her math. A hard line formed between his eyebrows. "Beginner's luck."

"Sure, keep telling yourself that. Pay up." She crossed her mismatched arms, pleased with herself.

Falconi tapped his fingers against the deck. Then he went still and said, "The scars are from a fire. And I managed to buy the *Wallfish* because I spent almost a decade saving every bit I could. Got a good deal and . . ." He shrugged.

His job must have been *very* well-paying for him to afford a ship. "Those aren't much in the way of answers," Kira said.

Falconi swept up their cards and shuffled them back into the deck. "So then play another round. Maybe you'll get lucky."

"Maybe I will," said Kira. "Deal."

He dealt. Three for her, three for him, and four on the table.

She scanned her cards. No sevens, nor anything that added up to seven or a multiple of seven. Then Falconi turned over the first card on the table: the two of spades. That gave her . . . one seven.

"Why did you keep the scars?" she asked.

He surprised her with his counter: "Why do you care?"

"Is that . . . your bet?"

"It is."

Falconi turned over the next card. Kira still had only one seven. She decided to go for another bet. "What exactly did you do before you got the *Wallfish*?" she asked.

"Call: What's bothering you?"

Neither of them wagered again through the rest of the round. With the last of the communal cards, Kira had three sevens. Not too shabby. However, when Falconi showed his hand, he said, "Four sevens."

Dammit. Kira paused, checking his math, and then she made a sound of disgust. "Three."

Falconi leaned back and crossed his arms, expectant.

For a few moments, the only sound was the rumble of the ship and the whirring fans of life support. Kira used the time to marshal her thoughts and then said, "I care because I'm curious. We're way out past the rim, and yet I don't really know anything about you."

"Why does it matter?"

"That's another question."

"Mmm. . . . You know I care for the *Wallfish.* And my crew."

"Yes," said Kira, and she felt an unexpected sense of closeness with him. Falconi *was* protective of his ship and crew; she'd seen it. And his bonsai also. That didn't mean he was necessarily a good person, but she couldn't deny his sense of loyalty to the people and things he considered his own. "As for what's bothering me, the nightmares."

"That's not much of an answer."

"No, it isn't," said Kira and, one-handed, swept up the cards on the floor. "Maybe you can get more out of me if you beat me again."

"Maybe I will," said Falconi with a dangerous flash in his eyes.

It was difficult, but Kira managed to shuffle the cards. She plopped them next to her knee, stirred them in a muddled mess, and then dealt by picking up individual cards between thumb and index finger. She felt horribly clumsy throughout the whole process, and it annoyed her nearly enough to use the Soft Blade to facilitate. But she didn't because, right then, she didn't want anything to do with the xeno. Not then and not ever.

Since she hadn't gotten her questions answered the last time, she repeated them. In turn, Falconi asked her: "What about the nightmares is bothering you so much?" And "How did you really lose your arm?"

To Kira's extreme annoyance, she lost again, one to three. Still, she also felt a measure of relief at no longer having to avoid the truth.

She said, ". . . I haven't been drinking enough for this."

"There's a bottle of vodka over in the locker," said Falconi.

"No." She tilted her head back and rested it against the wall. "It wouldn't fix anything. Not really."

"Might make you feel better."

"I doubt it." Tears suddenly filled her eyes, and she blinked, hard. "Nothing will."

"Kira," said Falconi, his voice unexpectedly gentle. "What is it? What's really going on?"

She let out a shuddering breath. "The nightmares . . . they're my fault."

"How do you mean?" His eyes never left her.

So Kira told him. She told him the whole sorry tale, starting with the creation of the Carr-Jelly–Soft Blade monstrosity and all that had transpired with it since. It was as if a barrier broke inside her, and a tidal wave of words and feelings came rushing out in a tumult of guilt, sorrow, and regret.

When she stopped, Falconi's expression was unreadable; she couldn't tell what he was thinking, only that his gaze had grown hooded and the lines about his mouth deepened. He started to speak, but she preempted him: "The thing is, I don't think I can fight the nightmares. At least, not the ones like the Soft Blade. When we touched, I could feel it absorbing me. If I'd stayed . . ." She shook her head. "I can't beat them. We're too similar, and there are so many more of them. I'd drown in their flesh. If I met this Carr-Jelly-thing, it would eat me. I know it would. Flesh for the Maw."

"There has to be a way to stop these things," said Falconi. His voice was low, gravelly, as if he were suppressing an unpleasant emotion.

Kira lifted her head and let it bang back against the wall. In the two-and-a-quarter g's, the impact was a hard, painful blow that made stars flash before her eyes. "The Soft Blade is capable of so much. More than I really understand. If it's unbound and unbalanced, I don't see how it *can* be stopped. . . . This situation with the nightmares is the worst sort of grey goo, nanobot catastrophe." She snorted. "A real *nightmare* scenario. It's just going to keep eating and growing and building. . . . Even if we kill whatever it is that Carr and the Jelly, Qwon, have turned into, there are still the other nightmares with the flesh of the Soft Blade. Any one of them could start the whole thing over. Hell, if a single speck of the Maw survives, it could infect someone else, just like at Sigma Draconis. There's just no, no way to—"

"Kira."

"—to contain it. And I can't fight it, can't stop it, can't—"

"Kira." The note of command in Falconi's voice cut through the swarm of buzzing thoughts in her head. His ice-blue eyes were fixed on her, steady and—in a way—comforting.

She allowed some of the tension to bleed out of her body. “Yeah. Okay. . . I think the Jellies might have dealt with something like this before. Or at least, I think they knew it was possible. Itari didn’t seem surprised.”

Falconi cocked his head. “That’s encouraging. Any idea how they contained the nightmares?”

She shrugged. “With a whole lot of death is my guess. I’m not real clear on the details, but I’m pretty sure their whole species was endangered at one point. Not necessarily because of nightmares, but just because of the scale of the conflict. They were even fighting a Seeker at one point, same as us.”

“In that case, it sounds like Hawes is right; you need to talk with the Jelly. Maybe it can give you some answers. There might be ways we don’t know about to stop the nightmares.”

Encouragement wasn’t what Kira was expecting from Falconi, but it was a welcome gift. “I will.” She looked down at the deck and picked at a piece of dried food stuck in the grating. “Still . . . it’s my fault. All of this is my fault.”

“You couldn’t have known,” said Falconi.

“That doesn’t change the fact that I’m the one who caused this war. Me. No one else.”

Falconi tapped the edge of his cards against the floor in an absentminded fashion, although he was too sharp, too aware, for the motion to be careless. “You can’t think like that. It’ll destroy you.”

“There’s more,” she said, soft and miserable.

He froze. Then he gathered up the rest of the cards and started to shuffle them. “Oh?”

Now that she’d started confessing, Kira couldn’t stop. “I lied to you. The Jellies weren’t the ones who killed my team. . . .”

“What do you mean?”

“Like with the Numenist. When I’m scared, angry, upset, the Soft Blade acts out. Or it tries to. . . .” The tears were rolling down her cheeks now, and Kira made no attempt to stop them. “Pretty much everyone on the team was pissed off when I came out of cryo. Not at me, not exactly, but I was still responsible, you know? The colony was getting canceled, we were going to lose our bonuses. It was bad. I ended up getting in an argument with Fizel, our doctor, and when Alan and I went to bed—” She shook her head, the words stuck in her throat. “I was still all messed up, and then . . . then that night, Neghar was coughing. She must have gotten a bit of the xeno in her, from rescuing me, see? She was coughing and coughing, and there was . . . there was so much *blood.* I was scared. C-couldn't help it. Scared. A-and the Soft Blade came out stabbing. It-it stabbed Alan. Yugo. Seppo. J-Jenan. But it was because of me. I'm responsible. I killed them."

Kira bent her neck, unable to bear Falconi's gaze, and allowed the tears to fall freely. On her chest and legs, the suit roiled in response. Revulsion filled her, and she clamped down on the xeno's reactions, forcing it to subside.

She flinched as Falconi's arms wrapped around her shoulders. He held her like that, and after a few seconds, Kira allowed her head to rest against his chest while she cried. Not since the *Extenuating Circumstances* had she mourned so openly. The revelation of the nightmares had stirred up old pains and added to them.

When her tears had begun to dry and her breathing slow, Falconi released her. Embarrassed, Kira dabbed at her eyes. "Sorry," she said.

He waved a hand and got to his feet. Moving as if he had bone-rot, he shambled across the galley. She watched as he turned on the kettle, made two mugs of chell, and then carried them back to where she sat.

"Careful," he said, handing her one.

"Thanks." She wrapped her hands around the warm mug and breathed in the steam, savoring the smell.

Falconi sat and ran his thumb around the rim of his cup, chasing a drop of water. "Before I bought the *Wallfish,* I worked for Hanzo Tensegrity. It's a big insurance company out of Sol."

"You sold insurance?" Somehow Kira found that hard to believe.

"I got hired to vet claims by miners, stakeholders, freelancers, that sort of thing. Only problem was, the company didn't really want us to vet anything. Our actual job was to, ah, discourage claimants." He shrugged. "Couldn't take it after a while, so I quit. Not the point. One claim I had, there was a boy who—"

"A boy?"

"It's a story. Listen. There was a boy who lived on a hab-ring out by Farrugia's Landing. His father worked maintenance, and every day, the boy would go with his father, and the boy would clean and check the skinsuits the maintenance crew used." Falconi flicked the drop of water off the mug. "It wasn't a real job, of course. Just something to keep him busy while his father was working."

"Didn't he have a mother?" Kira asked.

Falconi shook his head. "No other parent. Not mother, not a second paterfamilias, not grandparents, not even a sibling. All the boy had was his father. And every day, the boy cleaned and checked the suits, laid them in a line, ran diagnostics before the maintenance crew went out to tend the hull of the hab."

"And then?"

Falconi's eyes seemed to burn into her. "One of the guys—they were almost all guys—one of the guys, he didn't like anyone touching his suit. Made him antsy, he said. Told the boy to knock it off. Thing is, regs were clear; at least two people had to inspect all safety equipment, skinsuits included. So the boy's father told him to ignore the jerk and keep doing what he was doing."

"But the boy didn't."

"But he didn't. He was young, just a kid. The jerk convinced him that it was okay. He—the jerk, that is—would run the diagnostics himself."

"But he didn't," Kira murmured.

"But he didn't. And one day . . . *poof.* The suit ripped, a line tore, and Mr. Jerk died a horrible, agonizing death." Falconi moved closer. "Now who was to blame?"

"The jerk, of course."

"Maybe. But the regs were clear, and the boy ignored them. If he hadn't, the man would still be alive."

"He was only a child, though," Kira protested.

"That's true."

"So then the father was to blame."

Falconi shrugged. "Could be." He blew on his chell and then took a sip. "Actually, it turned out to be bad manufacturing. Defect in the suits; the rest of them would have failed, given time. The whole batch had to be replaced."

"I don't get it."

"Sometimes," Falconi said, "everything just turns to crap, and there's nothing we can do about it." He looked at her. "No one's to blame. Or maybe everyone's to blame."

Kira chewed over the story in her mind, searching for the kernel of truth at the center. She felt Falconi had offered it up in the spirit of understanding, if not absolution, and for that, she was grateful. But it wasn't enough to soothe her heart.

She said, "Maybe. I bet the boy still felt responsible."

Falconi inclined his head. "Of course. I think he did. But you can't let the guilt from something like that consume your life."

"Sure you can."

"Kira."

She pressed her eyes shut again, unable to block out the image of Alan slumped against her. "What happened can't be changed. I killed the man I loved, Falconi. You'd think that was the worst thing ever, but no, I had to go and start a war—a goddamn interstellar war, and it *is* my fault. There's no fixing something like that."

A long silence came from Falconi. Then he sighed and put his cup down on the deck. "When I was nineteen—"

"Nothing you can say is going to make this any better."

"Just listen; it's another story." He fiddled with the handle of the mug, and as she didn't interrupt again, continued: "When I was nineteen, my parents left me to watch my sister while they went out for dinner. The last thing I wanted was to be stuck babysitting, especially on a weekend. I got pretty angry, but it didn't matter. My parents left, and that was that."

Falconi rapped the mug against the deck. "Only it wasn't. My sister was six years younger than me, but I figured she was old enough to take care of herself, so I snuck out and went to hang with some of my friends, same as I would any other Saturday. Next thing I knew—" Falconi's voice caught, and his hands opened and closed as if crushing something invisible. "There was an explosion. By the time I got back to our rooms, they'd half caved in."

He shook his head. "I went in after her, but it was already too late. Smoke inhalation. . . . That's how I got burned. We found out later my sister had been cooking, and somehow a fire started. If I'd been with her, where I was supposed to be, she would have been fine."

"You can't know that," said Kira.

Falconi cocked his head. "Oh can't I? . . ." He picked up the deck of cards, worked the free ones into the middle, and shuffled them twice. "You didn't kill Alan or anyone else on your team."

"I did. I—"

"Stop," Falconi said, stabbing a middle finger at her. "Maybe you *are* responsible, but it wasn't a conscious decision on your part. You wouldn't have killed them any more than I would have killed my sister. As for this goddamn war, you're not all-powerful, Kira. The Jellies made their own choices. So did the League and this Maw. In the end, they're the only ones who can answer for themselves. So stop blaming yourself."

"I can't seem to help it."

"Bullshit. The truth is you don't *want* to. It makes you feel good to blame yourself. You know why?" Kira shook her head, mute. "Because it gives you a sense of control. The hardest lesson in life is learning to accept that there are some things we can't change." Falconi paused, his eyes hard and glittering.

"Blaming yourself is perfectly normal, but it doesn't do you any good. Until you stop, unless you *can* stop, you'll never be able to fully recover."

Then he unbuttoned the cuffs on his shirt, and rolled back his sleeves to expose the melted surface of his forearms. He held them up for Kira to see. "Why do you think I keep these scars?"

"Because . . . you feel guilty over—"

"No," Falconi said harshly. Then, in a gentler tone: "No. I keep them to remind me of what I can survive. Of what I *have* survived. If I'm having a rough time, I look at my arms, and I know I'll get through whatever problem I'm dealing with. Life's not going to break me. It can't break me. It might kill me, but nothing it throws at me is going to make me give up."

"What if I'm not that strong?"

He smiled without humor. "Then you'll crawl through life with this monkey sitting on your back, and it'll tear at you until it kills you. Trust me on that."

". . . How did you manage to get rid of it?"

"I drank a lot. Got in a bunch of fights. Nearly ended up dead a few times. After a while, I realized that I was just punishing myself for no good reason. Plus, I knew my sister wouldn't have wanted me to end up like that, so I forgave myself. Even though it wasn't my direct fault—just like it's not your fault—I forgave myself. And that's when I was finally able to move on and make something of my life."

Kira made her decision then. She couldn't see a path clear from the mire she was stuck in, but she could at least try to fight free. That much she could do: try.

"Okay," she said.

"Okay," Falconi repeated softly, and at that moment, Kira felt a bone-deep sense of connection with him: a bond born of shared sorrows.

"What was your sister's name?"

"Beatrice, but we always called her Bea."

Kira stared at the oily surface of the chell, studying her dark reflection. "What do you want, Falconi?"

"Salvo. . . . Call me Salvo."

"What do you really want, Salvo? Out of all the universe?"

"I want," he said, drawing the words out, "to be free. Free from debt. Free from governments and corporations telling me how to live my life. If that means I spend the rest of my years as captain of the *Wallfish,* well then—" He lifted his mug in mock salute. "—I accept my fate willingly."

She mirrored his gesture. "A worthy goal. To freedom."

"To freedom."

The chell made the back of her throat tingle as she took another sip, and right then, the terrors of the day no longer seemed quite so immediate.

"Are you from Farrugia's Landing?" she asked.

A small nod from Falconi. "Born on a ship thereabouts, but I grew up at the outpost itself."

A half-forgotten memory stirred in the back of Kira's brain. "Wasn't there an uprising there?" she said. "Some sort of corporate rebellion? I remember seeing an article about it. Most of the workers went on strike, and a lot of people ended up hurt or in prison."

Falconi took a drink of chell. "You remember correctly. It got real bloody, real fast."

"Did you fight?"

He snorted. "What do you think?" Then he glanced at her from the corners of his eyes, and for a moment it seemed as if he were trying to decide something. "What does it feel like?"

"What?"

"The Soft Blade."

"It feels like . . . like this." She reached out and touched Falconi on the wrist. He watched with caution, surprised. "It feels like nothing at all. It feels like my skin."

Then Kira willed a row of razor-sharp edges to rise from the back of her hand. The xeno had become such a part of herself, willing the blades into existence took hardly any effort.

After a moment, she allowed them to subside.

Falconi placed his hand over hers. She shivered and nearly flinched as he traced the tips of his fingers across her palm, sending cold sparks shooting up her arm. "Like this?"

"Exactly."

He lingered a moment more, the pads of his fingers just touching hers. Then he pulled his hand back and picked up the cards. "Another round?"

The last of the chell didn't taste quite so good as Kira downed it. What the hell was she doing? *Alan* . . . "I think I've had enough."

Falconi nodded, understanding.

"Are you going to tell Hawes about Carr and the Maw?" she asked.

"No reason to yet. You can file a report when we get back to the League."

Kira made a face at the thought. Then, heartfelt, she said, "Thank you for talking and listening."

Falconi slipped the cards back in his pocket. "Of course. Just don't give up. None of us are going to get through this if we stop fighting."

"I won't. Promise."

2.

Kira left Falconi brooding in the galley. She debated going straight to Itari and trying to talk with the Jelly. (Would it even be awake? Did Jellies sleep?) But as much as she wanted answers, right then, she needed rest. The day had left her exhausted in a way no amount of AcuWake could fix. Sleep was the only remedy.

So she returned to her cabin. No messages from Gregorovich were waiting for her, nor would she have answered them if there were. Leaving the lights off, she lay on the bed and sighed with relief as the weight came off her throbbing feet.

Falconi's words—she couldn't bring herself to think of him by his first name—were still running through her head as Kira closed her eyes and, almost at once, fell into a dreamless state.

3.

A bell-like tone echoed throughout the *Wallfish*.

Kira tried to bolt upright and struggled as she remained pinned to the mattress, held in place by tendrils of the Soft Blade. The 2.25 g's of thrust had let off, leaving her in weightlessness. If not for the xeno, she would have floated off in her sleep.

Heart pounding, she forced the Soft Blade to relax its hold and pulled herself over to the desk. Had the sound been in her imagination? Had she really slept that long?

She checked the console. Yes, she had.

They'd just jumped to FTL.

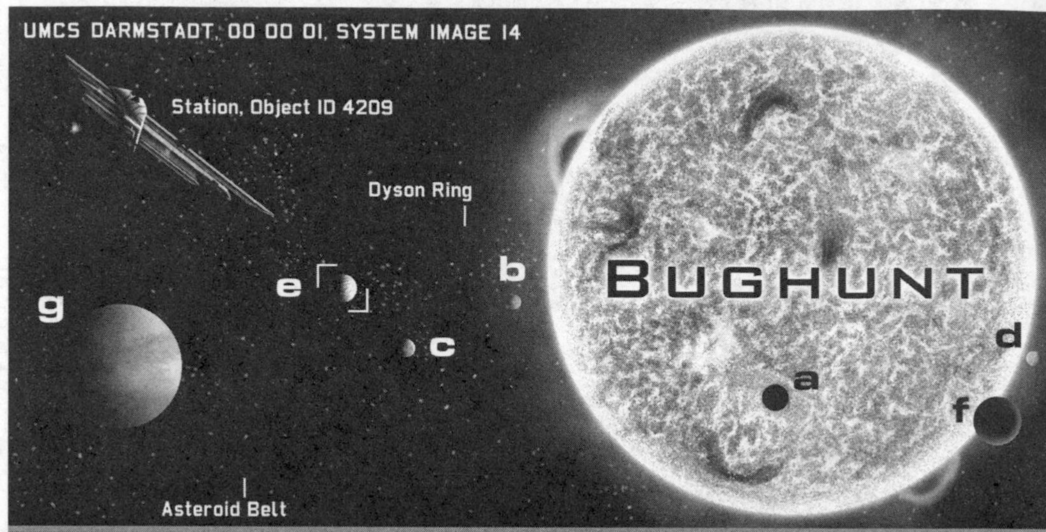

UMCS DARMSTADT, 00:12:79, SYSTEM IMAGE 91

PLANET E

- $0.35R_{\oplus}$ Surface: -200 Ċ – 200 Ċ
- ATM: 78% N_2, 20% O_2, 1% CH_4
- Tidally locked, no moons
- Evidence of satellite clusters in orbit
- Identified settlements: 9+
- Nidus, ID 4412

UMCS DARMSTADT, 02:01:35, SYSTEM IMAGE 735

NIDUS

* * * *

EXEUNT III

1.

They had escaped, but they weren't safe.

Kira checked the ship's records, unable to believe that none of the Jellies or the nightmares had overtaken them.

One of the Jellies had headed after the *Wallfish* a bit over an hour ago, closely followed by the two remaining nightmares. The three ships had been only minutes away from opening fire on the *Wallfish* by the time it transitioned to FTL.

In order to leave Bughunt as quickly as possible, the *Wallfish* had executed a hot jump, transitioning to FTL without taking the time to properly cool the ship. To do so would have required shutting off the fusion drive for the better part of a day. Hardly practical with hostile ships so close behind.

Even with the drive extinguished, the heat radiating from it—as well as the thermal energy contained within the rest of the *Wallfish*'s hull—would quickly build up to intolerable levels inside the Markov Bubble. Heatstroke would become a very real risk, and soon afterward, equipment failure.

Kira could already hear the life-support fans running harder than normal.

It wouldn't be long before the *Wallfish* would have to drop back into normal space. But it almost didn't matter. Whether in subluminal or superluminal space, the ships chasing them were faster than any human-built vessel.

They'd escaped, but it still looked like the Jellies and the nightmares would catch them. And when they did, Kira had no illusions of what would happen next.

She couldn't see how they were going to get out of the situation. Maybe Falconi or Gregorovich had an idea, but for herself, Kira thought the only option would be to fight. And she had no confidence in her ability to protect the crew, much less herself, if more of the xeno-like nightmares attacked.

Her throat tightened, and she forced herself to take a breath, calm herself. The *Wallfish* wasn't taking fire. It wasn't being boarded. Better to save her adrenaline for when that was actually the case. . . .

She had just started for the door when the bell-like tone sounded again. *So soon?* Was something wrong with the *Wallfish*? Out of instinct born of far too many trips on spaceships, she reached for the handhold next to the desk.

The stump of her arm swung past the hold, missing it.

"Fuck." Momentum nearly spun her around, but Kira managed to catch the hold with her left hand and stabilize her position.

A faint tingle passed across her skin, as if the electrical charge of the air had increased. She realized they'd just dropped back into normal space.

Then a thrust warning rang out, and she felt the wall press against her as the *Wallfish* turned and then began to burn in a new direction. "Ten minutes until next jump," said Gregorovich in his warbling whisper.

Kira hurried straight to Control. Falconi, Nielsen, and Hawes glanced at her as she entered.

The lieutenant was pale and hard-faced. If anything he looked worse than the previous day.

"What's going on? Why did we stop?" said Kira.

"We're changing course," said Falconi.

"Yes, why? We just left the system."

He gestured at the ever-present holo in the center of the room. It showed a map of Bughunt. "That's the point. The Jellies are jamming the whole area, and we're still inside the jamming. That means no one saw us drop out of FTL, and since the light from the *Wallfish* will take over a day to get back to Bughunt—"

"No one knows we're here," said Kira.

Falconi nodded. "For the time being, no. FTL sensors can't pick up sublight objects, so the assholes chasing us aren't going to see us when they fly past, not unless—"

"Not unless," said Nielsen, "we're really unlucky and they decide to drop back into normal space to take a look."

Hawes scrunched his forehead. "They shouldn't, though. They don't have any reason to."

Falconi gave Kira a look from under his brows. "That's the idea at least. We wait for the Jellies and the nightmares to go by, and then we blast off in a different direction."

She frowned, mirroring Hawes's expression. "But . . . won't they pick us up on their instruments as soon as we leave the jamming?"

"Shouldn't," said Falconi. "I'm guessing the Jellies don't want the rest of the nightmares to know about you, the Staff of Blue, or anything else at Bughunt.

If I'm right, the Jellies following us are going to keep up their jamming, which means they'll be limited to short-range observations in FTL."

Kira was doubtful. "That's an awfully big guess."

He nodded. "Sure is, but even if the Jellies drop their jamming . . . You know anything about FTL sensors?"

"Not really," she admitted.

"They're pretty crap. Passive ones have to be big, real big to be effective. Not something most ships can haul around. Active are even worse, and it's active we have to worry about. Range is only a few light-days at *best,* which isn't much at the speeds we're traveling, and they aren't particularly sensitive, which is a problem if you're trying to detect Markov Bubbles, since the bubbles have such a low energy state. Plus . . . Hawes, why don't you tell her?"

The lieutenant never took his eyes off the display as he spoke, his words slow and deliberate. "The UMC found that the Jelly sensors are about twenty percent less effective directly behind their ships. Probably because their shadow shield and fusion drive get in the way."

Falconi nodded again. "Odds are the nightmares have the same issue, even if they don't use a shield." He brought up an image in the holo of the three ships chasing them. "Once they're past us, they're going to have trouble detecting us—assuming no jamming—and every minute is going to make it that much harder."

"How long until they realize the *Wallfish* isn't in front of them?" Kira asked.

He shrugged. "No idea. Best-case scenario, a couple of hours. Worst case, sometime in the next thirty minutes. Either way, it should still be enough time to get out of their FTL sensor range."

"And then what?"

A flicker of sly cunning crossed Falconi's face. "We take a random walk, that's what." He jerked his thumb toward the aft of the ship. "The UMC gave us more than enough antimatter to fly to Bughunt and back. We're using the spare to make a few extra hops, changing course each time, to throw off anyone trying to follow us."

"But," said Kira, trying to visualize the whole arrangement in her head, "they can still flash trace us, right?"

Gregorovich cackled and said, "They can, O my Inquisitive Mammal, but 'twill take time—time that will allow us to make our most hasty retreat."

Falconi tipped a finger toward the speakers in the ceiling. "With each jump, it'll be harder and harder for the Jellies and the nightmares to track us. This isn't like the trip out here. We're not going to be dropping out of FTL at regular intervals in what was pretty much a straight-shot flight."

"We took precautions," said Hawes, "but nothing as extreme as this."

Nielsen said, "Once we're out of sensor range, the Jellies won't be able to predict when we go sublight. And if they miscalculate even one trajectory or miss even one jump—"

"They'll end up waaay off," said Falconi with a satisfied grin. "The *Wallfish* can cover almost three-quarters of a light-year in a day. Think how long you'd have to wait on a flash trace if you were off by even a few *hours* on one of our jumps. It could take days, weeks, or even months for the light to reach you."

"So we're actually going to make it," said Kira.

A grim smile appeared on Falconi's face. "Seems like it. Once we're out far enough, the chances of any of 'em finding the *Wallfish,* even by accident, are going to be pretty much nil. Hell, unless they track us to our last jump, they won't even know which system in the League we're aiming for."

The pressure pushing Kira against the wall ceased, and she had to hook the stump of her arm through a handhold to keep from drifting across the room. Then the jump alert echoed forth again, and again she felt the strange tingle pass across her skin.

"And which system would that be?" she asked.

"Sol," said Nielsen.

2.

The second jump was longer than the first: forty-three minutes to be precise.

While they waited, Kira went with Hawes to talk with Itari. "You okay?" she asked as they left Control.

He didn't meet her gaze. "Fine, thanks."

"Akawe seemed like a good captain."

"Yeah. He was. And he was crazy sharp. Him and Koyich. . . . There were a lot of good people on the *Darmstadt.*"

"I know. I'm sorry about what happened."

He nodded, accepting the condolences.

"Is there anything you *don't* want me to say?" Kira asked as they neared the airlock with the Jelly.

The lieutenant considered. "It probably doesn't matter at this point, but whatever you know about Sol, the League, or the UMC, keep it to yourself."

She nodded, lightly pushing against the wall to keep herself centered in the corridor. "I'll try. If I'm not sure about something, I'll check with you first."

Hawes nodded. "That should work. We're mostly interested in the Jellies' military—placement of troops, tactics, future plans, et cetera—as well as their technology. Also details on why exactly this group of Jellies wants to join forces with us. So, politics, I guess. Anything else you can dig up would be a bonus."

"Got it."

At the airlock, Kira saw Itari floating near the back wall, its tentacles wrapped around itself in a protective embrace. The alien stirred and looked out with a single glossy eye from between a pair of tentacles. *Curiosity.* To be expected in any sentient organism, but Kira still found it intimidating. The intelligence lurking within the Jelly's eye was a constant reminder that they were dealing with a creature just as capable as any human. Probably more so given its armored carapace and many limbs.

Hawes spoke with the Marines stationed on either side of the airlock—Sanchez and another man Kira didn't recognize—and they opened the door, allowed Kira and the lieutenant inside. Kira moved to the front; Hawes stayed behind her and to the right.

[[Kira here: We would like to ask you questions. Will you answer them?]]

The Jelly rearranged its tentacles as it settled on the deck in front of them, holding itself in place with its suckers. [[Itari here: Speak, two-form, and I will answer as best I can.]]

First things first: definitions of terms. [[Kira here: Why do you call us *two-forms*? Do you mean . . .]] And she stalled out, unable to think of the Jelly word for *male* or *female* or even for *sex*. [[. . . do you mean like us?]] She motioned from herself to Hawes.

Nearscent of respectful disagreement. [[Itari here: No. I mean the form you have and the form that lives in your spaceships.]]

Of course. [[Kira here: Our ship minds?]]

[[Itari here: If that is what you call them, then yes. They give us much difficulty when we board your shells. Our first goal is always to disconnect or destroy them.]]

When Kira translated for Hawes, he snorted, darkly amused. "Good. At least they've learned to be scared of the minds."

"As they should be," Gregorovich whispered from the ceiling.

Hawes gave the speakers an annoyed glance. "This is classified, Gregorovich. Butt out."

"And this is my ship," Gregorovich answered, deadly quiet.

Hawes grunted and didn't argue the point.

The Jelly shifted, a wash of reddish-pink moving across its tentacles. [[Itari here: We wonder, what relation do your ship minds have to your current forms? The one you call]]—and it produced a jumble of scents that, with some difficulty, Kira realized was the Jelly's attempt to reproduce Tschetter's name—[[Tschetter refused to discuss the subject. Are the minds subordinate to your form or are they senior?]]

Kira checked with Hawes, and he gave her the go-ahead. "Might as well tell it a bit," said the lieutenant. "Reciprocity has to be worth something, right? Their civilization wouldn't work otherwise."

"Maybe," Kira said. She didn't feel confident of anything when it came to an alien society.

[[Kira here: Ship minds begin as one of us. We have to decide to become a ship mind. It does not happen on its own. A ship mind often knows and understands more than we do, but we do not always take orders from them. That depends on what position or authority the ship mind has. And not all ship minds are in ships. Many exist elsewhere.]]

The Jelly seemed to chew on that for a while. [[Itari here: I do not understand. Why would a form that is larger and more intelligent *not* be your shoal leader?]]

"Why indeed?" asked Gregorovich when Kira repeated the Jelly's words. And he chuckled.

She struggled to answer. [[Kira here: Because . . . every one of us is different. Among our kind, you have to earn your position. It is not given to you just because you were born or built with certain traits.]] More definitions of terms, then: [[By *forms* you mean bodies, yes?]]

[[Itari here: Yes.]] For once the Jelly had said something expected.

Kira wanted to continue that line of questioning, but Hawes had other ideas. "Ask it about the Soft Blade," he said. "Where does it come from?"

The nearscent of the Jelly thickened, grew sharper, and conflicted colors rolled across its skin. [[Itari here: You ask for secrets we do not share.]]

[[Kira here: I *am* a secret.]] She gestured at herself, at the Soft Blade. [[And the Corrupted are chasing us. Tell me.]]

The Jelly rolled and twisted its tentacles, one around another. [[Itari here:

Many cycles ago, we discovered the works of the Vanished. It was their makings that allowed us to swim through space, both slower and faster than light. Their makings that gave us weapons to fight.]]

[[Kira here: You found these . . . makings on your homeworld?]]

Nearscent of confirmation. [[Itari here: Deep on the Abyssal Plain. Later, we found more remnants of the Vanished floating around a star counterspin to our homeworld. Among those findings were the Idealis, including the one you now are bonded with. It was that which began the war that led to the Sundering.]]

How much of their technology did the Jellies actually invent? she wondered. [[Kira here: Who are the Vanished? Are they Wranaui?]]

[[Itari here: No. They swam long before us, and we do not know where they went or what happened to them. If not for them, we would not be what we are, so we give praise to the Vanished and their makings.]]

[[Kira here: But their makings led to war.]]

[[Itari here: We cannot blame the Vanished for our own failings.]]

Hawes made notes while Kira translated. He said, "So it's confirmed: there were or are at least two other advanced civilizations in this area of the galaxy. Great."

"Sentient life isn't as rare as we thought," said Kira.

"That's not exactly a good thing if we're at the bottom of the pecking order. Ask if any of the Vanished are still around."

The response was quick and definitive: [[Itari here: None that we know of, but always we hope. . . . Tell me, Idealis, how many makings of the Vanished have you found?]] The bite of avid desire flavored the alien's words. [[There must have been a great number in your system for you to spread so quickly.]]

Kira frowned and again checked with Hawes. "They seem to think—"

"Yeah."

"Should I mention the Great Beacon?"

The lieutenant thought for a second. "Okay. But don't give away its location."

With some trepidation, she said, [[Kira here: We have found one of the Vanished's makings. I think. We found . . . a large hole that emits lowsound farscent at regular intervals.]]

A burst of reddish satisfaction spread across the Jelly's skin. [[Itari here: You speak of a Whirlpool! One as yet unknown to us, for we keep close watch on all makings of the Vanished.]]

[[Kira here: Are there more Whirlpools?]]

[[Itari here: Six that we know of.]]

[[Kira here: What purpose do they serve?]]

[[Itari here: Only the Vanished could say. . . . But, I do not understand. Our scouts have not scented a Whirlpool in any of your systems.]]

She cocked her head. [[Kira here: That is because it is not in one of our main systems, and because we only found it a few cycles ago. The Vanished's makings have not helped us learn how to fight or swim through space.]]

Itari went a dull grey, and its tentacles knotted in on themselves, as if it were rubbing its hands together—hands with fingers that were far too long and flexible. The alien seemed unreasonably perturbed. Even its scent changed, growing bitter and almondy. (Was that *arsenic* she was smelling?)

"Navárez?" said Hawes. "What's going on? Talk to me."

As Kira opened her mouth, the Jelly said, [[Itari here: You lie, Idealis.]]

[[Kira here: I do not.]] And she impressed the nearscent of sincerity upon her words.

The Jelly's agitation increased. [[Itari here: The Vanished are the source of all wisdom, Idealis.]]

[[Kira here: Wisdom can come from within as well as without. Everything my kind has done, we have done on our own, without help from Vanished, Wranaui, Idealis, or any other form or kind.]]

With a wet, sticky stound, Itari let go of the deck with its suckers and started to push itself around the airlock, as if it were swimming in circles. It was, Kira thought, the Jellies' version of pacing. Out of the corner of her mouth, she said, "The idea that we invented all our technology ourselves seems to be a bit disturbing to our friend here."

Hawes smirked. "Score one for humanity, eh?"

The Jelly stopped and turned its tentacles toward Kira, pointing them at her as if they had eyes on the tips. [[Itari here: Now I understand.]]

[[Kira here: Understand what?]]

[[Itari here: Why it has been the plan—since first we scented your kind after the end of the Sundering—to destroy your conclaves once we reached a ripple of appropriate strength.]]

A splinter of unease burrowed into Kira. She resisted the urge to fidget in response. [[Kira here: Have you changed your mind? Do you agree with that plan?]]

The scent equivalent of a shrug. [[Itari here: Were it not for the Corrupted, yes. But circumstances are not what they were or will be.]]

"Did it really say that?" asked Hawes. "Really?"

Bemused, but not in a pleasant way, Kira said, "It doesn't seem worried about how we might react."

The lieutenant scrubbed his fingers through his short-cropped hair. "So . . . what? The Jellies think xenocide is normal? Is that it?" He was very young, Kira suddenly thought. No STEM shots for him. He couldn't have been older than his midtwenties. Still just a kid despite all the responsibility the military had given him.

"Could be," she said.

He gave her a worried look. "How is peace ever going to work then? Long term, that is."

"I don't know. . . . Let me ask a few more questions."

He gestured toward Itari. "Go for it."

Returning her attention to the Jelly, she said: [[Kira here: Tell us of the Sundering. What was it exactly?]]

[[Itari here: The greatest struggle of our kind. Arm fought against Arm in an attempt to control the makings of the Vanished. In the end, the makings nearly destroyed us. Entire planets were left uninhabitable, and it took us many cycles to rebuild and regain our strength.]]

"Say," Hawes remarked, "do you think the Sundering explains why we haven't seen any signals from the Jellies over the past hundred years? If they got knocked back and had to rebuild their tech, the light might not have had time to reach us."

"Could be," Kira said.

"Mmm. The brass back home are going to *love* this."

Now they were coming to the crux of the matter. [[Kira here: Much of the destruction during the Sundering was caused by Corrupted, yes?]]

Again, nearscent of confirmation. [[Itari here: It was they that brought about the greatest calamities of the war. They that marked the darkest days of the conflict. And they that woke one of the beings you call the Seeker from its sleep.]]

[[Kira here: And how were the Corrupted stopped?]]

[[Itari here: Few records survived from the Sundering, so we do not know exactly how. But we know this much: the colony where the Corrupted first emerged was blasted out of existence by an impact from above. The seabed is cracked, and all forms of life on the planet are now gone. Some of the Corrupted swam into space, and those spread much as they are now spreading, and it was only with many resources and great effort that we killed them.]]

Queasiness formed in her stomach, and it wasn't just from the weightlessness. [[Kira here: Do you think we can stop the Corrupted now?]]

The Jelly's tentacles flushed with a deep purple. [[Itari here: You and the rest of your co-forms? No. Nor do we believe the Wranaui can. Not alone. These Corrupted are stronger and more *virulent* than those of the Sundering. We must fight them together if we are to have any hope of success. Know this, Idealis: to stop the Corrupted, every cell in their bodies must be obliterated or else they will grow anew. That is why we sought the Staff of Blue. It had the power to command the Idealis and more besides. With it, we could have broken the Corrupted. Without it, we are weak and vulnerable.]]

"What's wrong?" Hawes murmured. "You've gone all green about the gills."

"The nightmares . . ." Kira started to say, and then paused, tasting acid. Right then, she didn't want to reveal her part in creating the Maw to the lieutenant or to the UMC at large. It would come out eventually, but she couldn't see how the truth would make any difference to the League's response. They needed to kill the nightmares. What else mattered? "The nightmares come from the Vanished," she said, and translated the rest of Itari's words.

The lieutenant scratched at his neck. "Well that's not good."

"Nope."

"Don't count out the UMC," he said with false confidence. "We're damn good at killing things, and we've got some real geniuses back home figuring out new ways of dealing out death. We're not out of the fight by a long shot."

"I hope you're right," said Kira.

He fiddled with a UMC logo patch on his sleeve. "What I don't understand is, why are we seeing nightmares now? They've been around for a while, yeah? So what triggered them? You finding the xeno?"

She shrugged, uncomfortable. "The Jelly didn't say." Technically it was true.

"Has to be," the lieutenant muttered. "Doesn't make sense otherwise. Signal goes out, then . . ." His expression shifted. "Say, how did Tschetter's Jellies know to show up at Adra when they did? Were they keeping an eye on the system, in case anyone found the xeno?"

[[No,]] Itari said in response. [[That would have attracted attention we did not want. When the reliquary was breached, lowsound farscent was released, and after it reached us, we sent our ship, the *Tserro,* to investigate.]]

Kira said, "Should I get some details on who exactly this *we* is?"

Hawes nodded. "Good idea. Let's find out who we might be forming an alliance with."

[[Kira here: The ones you serve, the ones who want to form a . . . shoal . . . with our leaders, do they have a name?]]

Nearscent of confirmation. [[Itari here: The Knot of Minds.]]

From the Soft Blade came an image of tentacles gripping and intertwining, and with that a sense of close trust. And Kira understood that a *knot* was a form of group bonding among the Jellies, one that signified a joint—and unbreakable—cause.

Itari was still talking: [[The Knot was formed to protect the secret of Shoal Leader Nmarhl.]]

A thrill of recognition passed through her at the name. She remembered Nmarhl from one of the memories the Soft Blade had shown her when she was investigating the computer system on the Jelly ship, back at 61 Cygni. And she again recalled the unusual fondness the xeno seemed to have for the shoal leader. [[Kira here: And what was that secret?]]

[[Itari here: The location of the Idealis, which Nmarhl hid at the end of the Sundering.]]

Kira had so many questions, she didn't know what to ask first. [[Kira here: Why did Nmarhl hide the Idealis?]]

[[Itari here: Because the shoal leader failed in its attempt to seize control of the Arms. And because hiding the Idealis was the only way to protect it and to protect *us* from further Corruption. If this Idealis had been in use, the Sundering could easily have been the end of the Wranaui.]]

Kira took a moment to process that and to translate for Hawes.

"You remember this shoal leader?" the lieutenant asked.

She nodded, keeping her eyes on Itari. "A bit. It was definitely joined with the Soft Blade at some point."

Hawes motioned for her to look at him. "Let me get this straight. The Knot of Minds tried to stage a coup back during the Sundering—whenever that was—and now they're trying to do the same again?"

When he put it that way, it didn't sound so good. "That's what it looks like," Kira said.

"So what was their justification back then, and what's their justification now?"

The Jelly's response was swift: [[Itari here: Our reason was and is the same: we believe there is a better current to follow. The one we are caught in now can only lead to the death of Wranaui everywhere, in this ripple and others.]]

[[Kira here: Then, if you succeed in replacing your leadership, is there one among the Knot of Minds who will scent for the Wranaui?]]

The Jelly was slow to answer. [[Itari here: That will depend on those whose patterns survive. Mdethn may, perhaps, be fitted to the task. Lphet, also, but the other Arms would dislike answering to one who followed the heresy of the Tfeir. Either way, it would be difficult for any of the Wranaui to replace the great and mighty Ctein.]]

At that name, and at that phrase, a line of ice poured down Kira's spine. Flashes of images from her dreams filled her head: a vast bulk rooted amid the Abyssal Conclave; a huge, scheming presence that saturated the water with its pungency. [[Kira here: Is Ctein a name or a title?]]

[[Itari here: I do not understand.]]

[[Kira here: Are all your leaders called *Ctein,* or is it the name of just one?]]

[[Itari here: There is but one Ctein.]]

"It can't be," she murmured, fear prickling the back of her neck. [[Kira here: How *old* is Ctein?]] She had to stop herself from adding the phrase "the great and mighty."

[[Itari here: The wise and ancient Ctein has guided the Arms since the last cycles of the Sundering.]]

[[Kira here: How many cycles around your sun has that been?]]

[[Itari here: The number would mean nothing to you, but Nmarhl placed the Idealis within its keeping place when your kind were first venturing off your homeworld, if that gives you an idea.]]

She did the math in her head. Over two and a half centuries. [[Kira here: And Ctein has ruled the waters for all that time?]]

[[Itari here: And longer.]]

[[Kira here: All in the same form?]]

[[Itari here: Yes.]]

[[Kira here: How long do Wranaui live?]]

[[Itari here: That depends on when we are killed.]]

[[Kira here: What if . . . you aren't killed? How long would it take you to die from old age?]]

Nearscent of understanding. [[Itari here: Age does not kill us, two-form. Always we can revert to our hatchling form and grow anew.]]

[[Kira here: Your hatchling form . . . ?]] Several more questions only left her more confused about the Jelly life cycle. There were eggs, hatchlings, pods, rooted forms, mobile forms, forms that didn't seem to be sentient, and—as Itari seemed to indicate—a host of forms adapted to specific tasks or environments. The unique nature of the Jellies' biology sparked Kira's professional curiosity, and she found herself shifting back into her role of xenobiologist. It just didn't make *sense.* Complex life cycles were nothing new. Plenty of examples existed on Earth and Eidolon. But Kira couldn't figure out how all the parts and pieces Itari was mentioning were supposed to fit together. Every time she thought she had a handle on it, the Jelly would mention something new. As a puzzle, it was frustrating and exhilarating.

Hawes had other ideas in mind. "Enough with all the questions about eggs," he said. "You can figure out the squishy stuff later. Right now we've got bigger problems."

From then on, the conversation revolved around things Kira considered less interesting but—as she would acknowledge—were no less important. Things such as fleet placement and numbers, shipyard capabilities, travel distances between the Jelly outposts, battle plans, technological capabilities, and so forth. Itari answered most of the questions in a straightforward manner, but some subjects it evaded or outright refused to answer. Mostly questions having to do with the locations of the Jelly worlds. Understandable, Kira thought, if sometimes frustrating.

Yet, no matter what the topic, she couldn't stop thinking about the great and mighty Ctein. The formidable Ctein. And at last, she interrupted the stream of Hawes's questions to ask one of her own: [[Kira here: Why does Ctein refuse to join with us to fight the Corrupted?]]

[[Itari here: Because the cruel and hungry Ctein has grown bloated with age, and in its arrogance, it believes the Wranaui can defeat the Corrupted without help. The Knot of Minds believes otherwise.]]

[[Kira here: Has Ctein been a good leader?]]

[[Itari here: Ctein has been a strong leader. Because of Ctein we have rebuilt our shoals and expanded again across the stars. But many of the Wranaui are dissatisfied with the decisions Ctein has made these recent cycles, so we fight to have a new leader. It is not a big problem. Next ripple will be better.]]

Hawes made a noise of impatience, and Kira returned to asking questions for the lieutenant, and no more was said on the subject of Ctein.

They were still talking with Itari when the jump alert sounded and the *Wallfish* transitioned back to STL space.

"Two more to go," said Hawes, dragging a sleeve across his forehead.

During their time in the Markov Bubble, the air in the ship had grown thick and stifling and hot enough that even Kira had begun to feel uncomfortable. She could only imagine how bad it was for the others.

They gripped the handholds in the walls while Gregorovich reoriented the *Wallfish*, and then off they went again, flying away many times faster than the speed of light.

The interrogation of Itari continued.

The third jump was shorter than the last—only a quarter of an hour—and the fourth one was shorter still. "Just to throw them for a real loop-de-loop," Gregorovich said.

Then the *Wallfish* disengaged its Markov Drive, and they sat, seemingly motionless, in the dark depths of interstellar space, with radiators spread wide and the interior of the ship pulsing with heat.

"Gregorovich, any sign of the Jellies or the nightmares?" Kira asked.

"Not a whisper. Not a whisker," said the ship mind.

She felt herself relax slightly. Maybe, just maybe, they had really managed to escape. "Thanks for getting us out of there in one piece," she said.

A soft peal of laughter echoed from the speakers. "It was my neck on the line as well, O Meatbag, but yes, you are most welcome."

"Alright," said Hawes, "we'll call it quits with the Jelly for now. We've got plenty of material. It's going to take the spooks back home years to parse all this intel. Good job translating."

Kira released the Soft Blade's grip on the wall. "Of course."

"Don't go yet. I'm going to need you to translate for a little longer. Still have to get my men settled."

So she stayed while Hawes summoned the Marines who didn't have cryo tubes and, one by one, Itari cocooned them. The men were *not* happy with the prospect, but since there was no reasonable alternative, they had no choice but to agree.

Once the cocooned Marines were safely placed in the cargo hold, next to where Hawes and the rest of his squad would soon be lying frozen in their tubes, Kira left them and went to help the crew prepare the *Wallfish* for the three-month-long trip back to the League.

"Gregorovich gave me an update," said Falconi as he descended toward her on the central ladder.

Good. That saved her from having to repeat everything Itari had said. "I feel like I have more questions than answers," she said.

Falconi made a noncommittal noise and stopped in front of her. "You didn't tell Hawes, did you?"

She knew what he meant. "No."

His blue eyes fixed her in place. "You can't avoid it forever."

"I know, but . . . not yet. When we get back. I'll tell the League then. It wouldn't do any good now anyway." She allowed a faint note of pleading into her voice as she spoke.

Falconi was slow to answer. "Okay. But don't put it off any longer. One way or another, you're going to have to face this thing."

"I know."

He nodded and continued down the ladder, passing so close she could smell the musk of his sweat. "Come on then. Could use your help."

3.

As the *Wallfish* cooled, Kira worked alongside Falconi to secure equipment, flush lines, shut down nonessential systems, and otherwise prepare the ship for their upcoming trip. It wasn't easy for her with only one hand, but Kira made do, using the Soft Blade to hold objects she couldn't directly grasp.

The whole time, she kept thinking about her conversation with Itari. A number of things the Jelly had said were bothering her: words and phrases that didn't entirely make sense. Seemingly innocuous expressions that were easy to chalk up to quirks of the Jellies' language, but that—the more Kira focused on them—seemed to hint at greater unknowns.

And she wasn't comfortable with unknowns of that sort. Not after learning the truth about the Maw.

When most of the big, obvious tasks were complete, Falconi sent her and Sparrow to carry water and several bags of sugar to Itari. The Jelly claimed its form could digest the simple molecules of sugar without any difficulty, although it wasn't an ideal food long term.

Fortunately, long term wasn't an issue. Itari would be cocooning itself once the *Wallfish* returned to FTL. Or so the Jelly claimed. It made Kira nervous to think of the Jelly perhaps being awake while the rest of them were in a coma-like state, oblivious to their surroundings.

They left the Jelly pouring the bags of sugar into the beak-like maw on the underside of its carapace and went then to the storm shelter near the center of the ship.

There, Kira watched with an increasing sense of loneliness as, one by one, the crew again got into their cryo tubes. (The Entropists had already retired to their cabin and the tubes contained within.)

Before closing the lid over himself, Vishal said, "Ah, Ms. Navárez, I forgot to tell you earlier: there is another pair of contacts waiting for you in sickbay. So sorry. Check the cupboard above the sink."

"Thanks," she said.

As in 61 Cygni, Falconi waited until the last. Holding onto a grip with one hand, he pulled off his boots with the other. "Kira."

"Salvo."

"Are you going to practice with the xeno on the way back, like you did before?"

She nodded. "I'm going to try. I have control, but . . . it's not enough. If I'd had a better feel for the xeno, I might have been able to save Trig."

Falconi studied her with an understanding expression. "Just be careful."

"You know I will."

"Since you're going to be the only one up and around, can you do something for me?"

"Of course. What?"

He stashed the boots in the locker next to him and started peeling off his vest and shirt. "Keep an eye on the Jelly while we're in cryo. We're trusting it to not break out and kill us, and I'll be honest, I don't trust it that much."

Kira nodded slowly. "I had the same thought. I can hang some webbing outside the airlock and hunker down there."

"Perfect. We've got alarms set in case the Jelly *does* break out, so you should have plenty of warning." He gave her a wry smile. "I know it won't be that comfortable there in the entryway, but we don't have any better options."

"It's fine," said Kira. "Don't worry about it."

Falconi nodded and pulled off his shirt. Then he stripped off his pants and socks, put them in the locker, and pushed himself over to the one empty cryo tube. On the way, he trailed a hand across the side of Trig's tube, leaving a three-fingered mark in the layer of frost coating the machine.

Kira joined Falconi as he popped open the lid to his tube. Despite herself, she couldn't help but admire the play of muscles across his back.

"You going to be okay?" he said, fixing her with a look of unexpected sympathy.

"Yeah. I'll be fine."

"Gregorovich will be up for a little while longer, and remember—if you need to talk, at any time, you wake me up. Seriously."

"I will. Promise."

Falconi hesitated, and then he put a hand on her shoulder. She covered it with her own, feeling the heat from his skin radiating into hers. He gave her a soft squeeze before letting go and pulling himself into the cryo tube.

"We'll meet again at Sol," he said.

She smiled, recognizing the lyrics. "In the shadow of the moon."

"By the shine of that green Earth. . . . Goodnight, Kira."

"Goodnight, Salvo. Sleep well."

Then the lid of the cryo tube slid shut over his face, and the machine began to hum as it pumped in the chemicals that would induce hibernation.

4.

Kira carefully guided a bundle of bedding through the ship's corridors. She'd wrapped it with several tendrils from the Soft Blade, so as to keep her hand free and keep the blankets from floating away.

When she reached the airlock, she saw Itari floating near the outer door, looking out the clear sapphire porthole at the spray of stars outside.

The *Wallfish* still hadn't jumped back to FTL. Gregorovich was waiting until the ship was fully chilled. Already the temperature had dropped by a noticeable amount as the radiators did their job.

Kira secured the blankets to the deck with clips and webbing from the port cargo hold. Then she went and fetched the few supplies she would need for the long journey ahead: water, ration bars, wipes, bags to store trash, the replacement contacts Vishal had printed out, and her concertina.

When she was satisfied with her little nest, she went and opened the airlock. Anchoring herself to the frame of the open doorway, she was about to speak when the Jelly preempted her: [[Itari here: Your scent lingers, Idealis.]]

[[Kira here: What do you mean?]]

[[Itari here: The things you said earlier . . . Your kind and mine differ in more ways than just our flesh. I have been trying to understand, but I fear it is beyond this form.]]

She cocked her head. [[Kira here: I feel the same.]]

The Jelly blinked, pale nictitating membranes flashing across the black orbs of its eyes. [[Itari here: What is it that two-forms consider sacred, Idealis? If not the Vanished, then what?]]

The question daunted her. Now she was supposed to discuss religion and philosophy with an alien? Her classes on xenobiology had never covered *that* particular possibility.

She took a fortifying breath.

[[Kira here: Many things. There is no one right answer. Every two-form has to decide for themselves. It is a . . .]]—she struggled to find a translation for *individual*—[[. . . a choice each two-form has to make on their own. Some find the choice easier than others.]]

One of the Jelly's tentacles rolled across its carapace. [[Itari here: What do you consider sacred, Idealis?]]

That stopped Kira. What *did* she consider sacred? Nothing so abstract as the concept of god or beauty or anything like that. Not numbers, as the Numenists did. Nor scientific knowledge, as the Entropists did. She briefly considered saying *humanity,* but that wasn't right either. Too limited.

In the end she said, [[Kira here: *Life.* That is what I think is sacred. Without it, nothing else matters.]] When the Jelly didn't immediately reply: [[What about the Wranaui? What about you? Is there anything other than the Vanished you consider sacred?]]

[[Itari here: We, the Wranaui. The Arms and our expanse into the swirl of stars. It is our birthright and our destiny and an ideal that all Wranaui are devoted to, even if we sometimes disagree on the means to accomplish our goal.]]

The answer disturbed Kira. There was too much of the zealot, the xenophobic, and the imperialistic about it for her liking. Hawes had been right; it wouldn't be easy to live in peace with the Jellies.

Difficult doesn't mean impossible, she reminded herself.

She changed the subject: [[Kira here: Why do you sometimes say *this form* when you refer to yourself? Is it because the Wranaui have so many different shapes?]]

[[Itari here: One's form determines one's function. If another function were needed, the form can be changed.]]

[[Kira here: How? Can you change the arrangement of your flesh just by thinking?]]

[[Itari here: Of course. If there were no thinking, why would one go to the Nest of Transference?]]

It was a term she didn't recognize from the Soft Blade. [[Kira here: Is the Nest of Transference also a making of the Vanished?]]

[[Itari here: Yes.]]

[[Kira here: So if you want to change into your hatchling form or your rooted form, you would go to the Nest of Transference and—]]

[[Itari here: No. You misunderstand, Idealis. Those are forms of the original flesh. The Nest of Transference is used for forms that are manufactured.]]

Surprise gave her pause. [[Kira here: You mean your current *form* was made? In a machine?]]

[[Itari here: Yes. And if needed, I might choose another form at the Nest of Transference. Also too if this flesh were destroyed, I might select another.]]

[[Kira here: But, if your form were destroyed, you would be killed.]]

[[Itari here: How can I be killed when there is a record of my pattern at the Nest of Transference?]]

Kira frowned as she struggled to understand. Several more questions did little to clarify the matter. She couldn't seem to get the Jelly to make a distinction between its body and its pattern, whatever that was.

[[Kira here: If your form were destroyed right now, would your pattern contain all your memories?]]

[[Itari here: No. All memories from when we left the system of the Vanished would be lost. This is why our shells always swim in sets of two or more unless the need for secrecy is great, as when we sent the *Tserro* to the reliquary.]]

[[Kira here: Then . . . the pattern is not you, is it? The pattern would be an out-of-date copy. A you from the past.]]

The Jelly's colors grew more muted, neutral. [[Itari here: Of course the pattern would still be me. Why would it not? The passing of a few moments does not change my nature.]]

[[Kira here: What if your pattern were given a new form while your old form was still here? Would that be possible?]]

Nearscent of disgust spiked the air. [[Itari here: That would be the heresy of the Tfeir. No Wranaui from the other Arms would do such a thing.]]

[[Kira here: You disapproved of Lphet, then?]]

[[Itari here: Our goals are greater than our differences.]]

Kira thought on that for a while. So the Jellies were uploading their consciousness, or at least their memories, into different bodies. But they didn't seem bothered by their actual deaths. . . . She couldn't understand Itari's seeming indifference to its individual fate.

[[Kira here: Don't you want to live? Don't you want to keep this form?]]

[[Itari here: So long as my pattern endures, I endure.]] One of its tentacles reached out, and Kira struggled not to recoil as the rubbery appendage poked her in the chest. The Soft Blade stiffened as if it were about to attack. [[The form is unimportant. Even if my pattern is erased—as Ctein did to Nmarhl's, long ago—it will continue to propagate in the ripples that follow.]]

[[Kira here: How can you say that? What do you mean by *ripple*? What do you mean *those that follow*?]]

The Jelly flashed red and green, and its tentacles wrapped tighter about its carapace, but it refused to answer. Kira asked her questions twice more, to no response. And that was all she could extract from the Jelly on the subject of ripples.

She asked a different question then: [[Kira here: I am curious. What is the *tsuro,* the summons that I felt when the Knot of Minds arrived at the resting place of the Idealis? I've felt it from all your shells, except here in this system.]]

[[Itari here: The *tsuro* is another of the sacred artifacts of the Vanished. It speaks to the Idealis and coaxes it forth. Were it not bonded with you, the Idealis would answer of its own accord and move to present itself at the source of the summons. By use of the *tsuro,* Wranaui shells everywhere search for the Ideali.]]

[[Kira here: And have you found any more since the end of the Sundering?]]

[[Itari here: Since then? No. Yours is the last surviving. But we live in hope that the Vanished have left more of their makings for us to find and that, this time, we will treat them with greater wisdom than before.]]

She stared at the weave of fibers on the back of her hands: black, gleaming, complex. [[Kira here: Does your form know—does the Knot of Minds know—how to remove the Idealis from the one it is joined with?]]

The Jelly's skin roiled with the colors of affront, and its nearscent acquired a mix of shock and outrage. [[Itari here: In what ripple would that be desired? To be joined with the Idealis is an honor!]]

[[Kira here: I understand. It is a matter of . . . curiosity.]]

The alien seemed to struggle with that, but in the end it said, [[Itari here: The only way this form knows to separate from the Idealis is death. Lphet and the other ruling forms of the Knot may be aware of other methods, but if so, they have not scented them.]]

Kira accepted the news with resignation. She wasn't surprised. Just . . . disappointed.

Then the ghost of Gregorovich's voice sounded from the speakers, and he said, "Retracting radiators. Transitioning to FTL in four minutes. Prepare thyselves."

Only then did Kira notice how cold it had gotten in the antechamber. Frustrated that she didn't have any more time for questions, she informed Itari of the impending jump and then retreated from the doorway and closed and locked the airlock door.

The lights switched to the dull red of ship-night, a whine sounded near the back of the *Wallfish*, and the exposed skin on Kira's cheeks tingled as the Markov Drive activated and they set out on the last and longest leg of their journey: the trip to Sol.

5.

Through the airlock window, Kira watched with interest as Itari wound a cocoon around itself with goo secreted from the undersides of its tentacles. The viscous substance hardened quickly, and within only a few minutes, the Jelly lay hidden within an opaque, somewhat greenish pod stuck to the floor of the airlock.

Kira wondered how the alien would know when to wake up.

Not her problem.

She retreated to her own little nest, secured herself to the webbing, and wrapped herself with blankets. The antechamber was dark and intimidating in the nighttime lighting; hardly a friendly place to spend the next three months.

She shivered, finally feeling the cold.

"Just you and me, headcase," she said to the erstwhile ceiling.

"Worry not," whispered Gregorovich, "I shall keep you company, O Varunastra, until your eyes grow heavy and the soft sands of sleep dull your mind."

"How comforting," Kira said, but she only half meant the sarcasm. It *was* nice to have someone to talk to.

"Forgive me for my irrepressible curiosity," said Gregorovich, and he chuckled, "but what strange scents did you exchange with our be-tentacled guest? You stood there for quite some minutes, and you seemed most affected by the stench afflicting your delicate nostrils."

Kira snorted. "You could say that. . . . I'll write a proper account later. You can see the details there."

"Nothing immediately helpful, I take it," said Gregorovich.

"No. But—" She explained about the Nest of Transference and ended with, "Itari said, *The form is unimportant.*"

"Bodies do tend to be rather fungible these days," the ship mind said dryly. "As both you and I have discovered."

Kira pulled the blankets tighter. "Was it difficult becoming a ship mind?"

"*Easy* certainly isn't the word I would use to describe it," said Gregorovich. "Every sense of mine was stripped away, replaced, and what I was, the very foundation of my consciousness, was expanded beyond any natural limit. 'Twas confusion piled upon confusion."

The experience sounded deeply unpleasant, and it reminded Kira—somewhat to her distaste—of the times when she had extended the Soft Blade, and in doing so, extended her sense of self.

She shivered. The soft sway of her body in zero-g caused her to swallow hard and focus on a fixed spot on the wall while she tried to calm her inner ear. The darkness of the antechamber and the abandoned, empty feeling of the *Wallfish* affected her more than she liked. Had it really been less than half a day since they'd been fighting through the streets on Nidus?

It seemed as if it had been more than a week ago.

Trying to fend off her sudden loneliness, she said, "My first day here, Trig told me how—in your last ship—you crashed and got stranded. What was it like . . . being by yourself for so long?"

"What was it like?" said Gregorovich. He laughed with a demented tone, and at once, Kira knew she'd gone too far. "What was it *like*? . . . It was like death, like the obliteration of the self. The walls around my mind fell away and left me to gibber senselessly before the naked face of the universe. I had the combined knowledge of the entire human race at my disposal. I had every scientific discovery, every theory and theorem, every equation, every proof, and a million, million, million books and songs and movies and games—more than any one person, even a ship mind, could ever hope to consume. And yet . . ." He trailed off into a sigh. "And yet I was *alone.* I watched my crew starve and die, and when they were gone, there was nothing I could do but sit alone in the dark and wait. I worked on equations, mathematical concepts you could never comprehend with your puny little brain, and I read and watched and counted toward infinity, as the Numenists do. And all it did was stave off the darkness for one more second. One more moment. I screamed, though I have no mouth to scream. I wept, though I have no eyes for tears. I crawled through space and time, a worm inching through a labyrinth built by the dreams of a mad god. This I learned, meatbag, this and nothing more: when air, food, and shelter are assured, only two things matter. Work and companionship. To be alone and without purpose is to be the living dead."

"Is that so great a revelation?" Kira asked quietly.

The ship mind tittered, and she could hear him swaying on the edge of madness. "Not at all. No indeed. Ha. It's obvious, isn't it? Banal even. Any reasonable person would agree, wouldn't they? Ha. But to live it is not the same as hearing or reading it. Not at all. The revelation of truth is rarely easy. And *that* is what it was like, O Spiked One. It was revelation. And I would rather die than endure such an experience again."

That much Kira could understand and appreciate. Her own revelations had nearly destroyed her. "Yeah. Same for me. . . . What was the name of the ship you were in?"

But Gregorovich refused to answer, which upon reflection, Kira decided was probably for the best. Talking about the crash only seemed to make him more unstable.

She pulled up her overlays and stared at them without seeing. How did you provide therapy for a ship mind? It wasn't the first time she had wondered. Falconi had said that most of the psychiatrists who worked with them were ship minds themselves, but even then . . . She hoped Gregorovich would find the peace he was looking for—as much for their own sake as his—but solving his problems was beyond her.

6.

The long night crept past.

Kira wrote up her conversation with Itari, played her concertina, watched several movies from the *Wallfish*'s database—none of them particularly memorable—and practiced with the Soft Blade.

Before she started working with the xeno, Kira took time to think about what she was trying to accomplish. As she'd said to Falconi, control alone wasn't enough. Rather, she needed . . . synthesis. A more natural joining between her and the Soft Blade. *Trust.* Otherwise she would always be second-guessing her actions, as well as those of the xeno. How could she not, given past mistakes? (Her mind wandered toward the subject of the Maw; with an effort of will, she resolutely pulled it back.) As she'd learned through painful experience, second-guessing could be every bit as deadly as overreacting.

She sighed. Why did everything have to be so hard?

With her goal in mind, Kira began much as she had before. Isometric exercises, unpleasant memories, physical and emotional strain . . . everything she could think of to test the Soft Blade. Once she was confident her grip on the xeno was as strong as ever, then and only then did she start to experiment by relaxing her dictatorial control. Just a little bit at first: a tiny amount of leeway so she could see how the Soft Blade would choose to act.

The results were mixed. Around half of the time the xeno did exactly what Kira wanted in the way she wanted, whether that was forming a shape on her skin, helping to hold a stress position, or fulfilling whatever other task she'd put to the organism. Perhaps a quarter of the time the Soft Blade did what she wanted but not as she expected. And the rest of the time, it reacted in a completely disproportionate or unreasonable manner, sending spikes or tendrils every which way. Those, of course, were the occurrences Kira was most concerned with.

When she'd had enough and stopped, Kira didn't feel as if she had made any noticeable progress. The thought dampened her mood until she reminded herself that it would be over three months before they arrived at Sol. She still had lots of time to work with the Soft Blade. Lots and lots of time . . .

Gregorovich started talking with her again soon afterward. He seemed to have returned to his usual self, which she was pleased to hear. They played several games of *Transcendence*, and though he beat her every time, Kira didn't mind, as she enjoyed having the company, *any* company.

She tried not to think too much about the nightmares or the Maw or even the great and mighty Ctein brooding in the depths of the Plaintive Verge . . . but her mind returned to them time and time again, making it difficult to relax into the state of dormancy needed to survive the journey.

It might have been a few hours, it might have been more than a day, but eventually Kira felt the familiar slowing of her body as the Soft Blade responded to the lack of food and activity and began to prepare her for the sleep that was more than sleep. Each time she entered hibernation, it seemed to become easier; the xeno was getting better at recognizing her intent and taking the appropriate action.

She set her weekly alarm, and as her eyes drifted shut, she said, "Gregorovich . . . think I'm going to sleep."

"Rest well, meatbag," the ship mind whispered. "I think I shall sleep as well."

". . . perchance to dream."

"Indeed."

His voice faded away, and the soft strains of a Bach concerto took its place. Kira smiled, snuggled deeper into the blankets, and at long last, allowed herself to relax into oblivion.

7.

A shapeless while passed, full of half-formed thoughts and urges: fears, hopes, dreams, and the ache of regrets. Once a week, the alarm roused Kira, and she—groggy and bleary-eyed—would train with the Soft Blade. It often felt like fruitless labor, but she persisted. And so did the xeno. From it she sensed a desire to please her, and with repetition of action came clarity of intent, if not mastery of form, and she began to feel a hint of yearning from the Soft Blade. As if it aspired to some type of artistry in its endeavors, some form of creativity. For the most part, she shied from those instincts, but they stirred her curiosity, and often Kira had long, deeply strange dreams of the greenhouses of her childhood and of plants sprouting and twining and leafing and spreading life, good and healthy.

Once every two weeks, the *Wallfish* emerged from FTL, and Kira went down to Sparrow's makeshift gym and pushed her mind and body to their limits while the ship cooled. Each time, she sorely missed her right hand. The lack of it caused no end of difficulty, even though she used the Soft Blade as a substitute to hold and lift things. She consoled herself with the knowledge that using the xeno like that was good practice. And it was.

As she trained in the hold, the Marines stood watch among the nearby racks of equipment: Hawes and three others frozen in their blue-lit cryo tubes; Sanchez, Tatupoa, Moros, and one other wrapped in the same cocoons that had saved Trig's life. Seeing them there left Kira feeling as if she'd stumbled upon a row of ancient statues set to defend the souls of the dead. She gave them a wide berth and did her best to avoid looking at them, an odd bit of superstition for her.

Sometimes she ate a ration bar after exercising, to keep up her strength, but mostly she preferred water and a return to hibernation.

Partway through the first month, in the empty hours of the night, as she floated outside Itari's airlock—all but insensate to the universe around her—a vision coalesced behind her shuttered eyelids, a memory from another time and another mind:

Summoned once more to the high-vaulted presence chamber, she and her flesh stood as witness before the gathered Heptarchy, three to each ascension, and the Highmost stationed between.

The central seal broke, and through the patterned floor rose a gleaming prism. Within the faceted cage, a seed of fractal blackness thrashed with ravening anger, the perversion pulsing, stabbing, tearing, ceaselessly battering its transparent prison. Flesh of her flesh, but now tainted and twisted with evil intent.

"What now must be done?" the Highmost asked.

The Heptarchy replied with many voices, but one spoke most clearly: "We must cut the branch; we must burn the root. The blight cannot be allowed to spread."

But dissent made itself known with another voice: "True it is we must protect our gardens, but pause a moment and consider. There is potential here for life beyond our plans. What arrogance have we to put that aside unexamined? We are not all-knowing nor all-seeing. Within the chaos might also dwell beauty and, perhaps, fertile soil for the seeds of our hope."

Long discussion followed, much of it angry, and all the while the captive blackness struggled to escape.

Then the Highmost stood and struck the floor with the Staff of Blue and said, "The fault is ours, but the blight cannot be allowed to persist. The risk is too great, the rewards too uncertain, too slight. Although light may emerge from dark, it would be wrong to allow the dark to smother the light. Some acts exist beyond forgiveness. Illuminate the shadows. End the blight."

"End the blight!" cried the Heptarchy.

Then the rainbowed prism flashed blindingly bright, and the malevolence within shrieked and burst into a cloud of falling embers.

PART FOUR

★ ★ ★ ★ ★ ★ ★

FIDELITATIS

Not for ourselves alone are we born.

—MARCUS TULLIUS CICERO

CHAPTER I

★ ★ ★ ★ ★ ★ ★

DISSONANCE

1.

Kira's eyes snapped open.

Why had she woken? Some change in the environment had roused the Soft Blade, and it her. An almost imperceptible shift in the air currents circulating throughout the *Wallfish*. A distant whir of machinery coming to life. A slight decrease in the otherwise stifling temperature. Something.

A jolt of alarm caused her to glance at the nearby airlock. The Jelly, Itari, was still inside where it ought to be, encased in its secreted pod, barely visible in the dull red light of the long ship-night.

Kira let out her breath, relieved. She really didn't want to have to fight the Jelly.

"G-Gregorovich?" she said. Her voice was rusty as an old wrench. She coughed and tried again, but the ship mind still didn't answer. She tried a different tack: "Morven, are you there?"

"Yes, Ms. Navárez," the *Wallfish*'s pseudo-intelligence answered.

"Where are we?" Kira's throat was so parched, the words came out in a faint rasp. She tried to swallow, despite the lack of moisture in her mouth.

"We have just arrived at our destination," said Morven.

"Sol," Kira croaked.

"That is correct, Ms. Navárez. Sol system. The *Wallfish* emerged from FTL four minutes and twenty-one seconds ago. Standard arrival procedures are in effect. Captain Falconi and the rest of the crew will be awake soon."

They'd made it. They'd actually made it. Kira dreaded to think about all the things that might have happened since they'd left 61 Cygni six months ago.

It hardly seemed real that they'd been traveling for half a year. The wonders of hibernation, artificial or otherwise.

"Has anyone hailed us?" she asked.

"Yes, Ms. Navárez," Morven replied, prompt as could be. "Fourteen messages from UMC monitoring stations. I have explained that the crew is currently indisposed. However, local authorities are most insistent that we identify our system of origin and our current mission as soon as possible. They are rather agitated, Ms. Navárez."

"Yeah, yeah," Kira muttered. Falconi could deal with the UMC once he was out of cryo. He was good at that sort of thing. Besides, she knew he would want to speak for the *Wallfish*.

Feeling uncomfortably stiff, she began to extract herself from the nest of blankets and webbing she'd constructed close to the airlock.

Her hand.

Her forearm and hand that she had cut off in the Jelly ship had . . . reappeared. Astonished, disbelieving, Kira held up the arm, turned it so she could see every part, worked her fingers open and closed.

She wasn't imagining things. The arm was real. Hardly believing, she touched it with her other hand, feeling fingers sliding across fingers. Only five days had passed since she'd last woken, and in that time, the Soft Blade had constructed a perfect replica of the flesh she had lost.

Or had it?

A sudden shade of fear colored Kira's thoughts. Drawing a breath, she focused on the back of her hand and, with an effort of will, forced the Soft Blade to retreat.

It did, and she uttered a soft cry as the shape of her hand caved inward, melting away like ice cream on a hot summer's day. She recoiled, both mentally and physically, losing her focus in the process. The Soft Blade snapped back into shape, again assuming the form of her missing limb.

Tears filmed her eyes, and Kira blinked, feeling a sense of bitter loss. "Dammit," she muttered, angry with herself. Why was she letting the missing hand affect her so much? Getting an arm or a leg replaced wasn't *that* big of a deal.

But it was. She was her body, and her body was her. There was no separation between mind and matter. Her hand had been a part of her self-image for her entire life up until Bughunt, and without it, Kira felt incomplete. For a moment she'd had hope that she was whole again, but no, it wasn't to be.

Still, she had *a* hand, and that was better than the alternative. And the fact that the Soft Blade had managed to replicate her missing limb was cause for optimism. Why had it done so now and not before? Because it knew they were nearing the end of their trip? As a demonstration of the sort of cooperation she'd been attempting to train all the way from Bughunt? Kira wondered. Regardless of the answer, she felt vindicated in the results. The Soft Blade had acted of its own volition (although perhaps guided by her own, unvoiced desires) and in a constructive manner at that.

Again, Kira examined her hand, and she marveled at the detail. It was, so far as she could tell, a near-perfect copy of the original. The only real difference she noticed was a slight disparity in density; the new arm felt perhaps a hair heavier. But it was a small change, hardly perceptible.

Still testing the mobility of her new fingers, Kira climbed out of the nest. She attempted to pull up the date on her overlays and only then realized that—as on the trip to Bughunt—the Soft Blade had absorbed her contacts.

Belatedly she remembered the small case containing the replacements Vishal had printed for her. She dug it out from the blankets and carefully placed each transparent lens onto the corresponding eye.

She blinked and felt a sense of comfort as the familiar HUD of her overlays popped up. *There now.* She was a fully functioning person again.

Resisting the urge to check the news, Kira left the airlock, pulled herself along the walls until she reached the center of the *Wallfish,* and then started up the main shaft.

The ship was still so quiet, empty, and dark, it felt abandoned. If not for the sound of the life-support fans, it might have been a derelict drifting alone through space for gods knew how long. Kira felt like a scavenger moving through halls that had once been inhabited by others . . . or like an explorer opening a centuries-old mausoleum.

Her thoughts returned to the city on Nidus and their dire findings there. She growled and shook her head, annoyed. Her imagination was getting the better of her.

As she reached the level below the Control deck, the thrust alert sounded. Taking heed, Kira planted her feet on the floor, and a proper sense of weight pressed her down—there was again a *down*!—as the *Wallfish*'s fusion drive roared back to life.

She sighed with relief, welcoming the burn.

The surrounding lightstrips flickered and changed from red to the bluish-white glow of ship-day. The light was almost painfully bright after so long spent in the somber dark. Kira shielded her face until her eyes adjusted.

Falconi and the rest of the crew were just emerging from cryo when Kira arrived at the ship's storm shelter. Dropping to all fours on the deck, Sparrow dry-heaved like a cat with a hairball.

"God, I hate long runs," the woman said, and wiped her mouth.

"Good, you're up," said Kira.

Falconi grunted. "If you can call it that." He looked as green as Sparrow, and like all the crew, he had bruised circles under his eyes. Kira didn't envy them the side effects of such an extended cryo sleep.

Sparrow hacked again and then staggered to her feet and joined Falconi, Nielsen, and Hwa-jung as they retrieved clothes from their lockers. Vishal took longer to get going. Once he did, he went around handing out the little blue pills Kira knew so well. They helped with the nausea, as well as replenishing some of the body's lost nutrients.

Vishal offered one of the pills to her as well, but she declined.

"What's the shape of things?" Falconi asked, pulling on his boots.

"Not sure yet," said Kira.

Then Gregorovich's voice broke in on them with a laughing, teasing tone. "Greetings, my lovelies. Welcome back to the land of the living. Yes, oh yes. We've survived the great journey across the void. Once again we have defied the dark and lived to tell the tale." And he laughed until the ship rang with the sound of his voice.

"Someone's in a good mood," said Nielsen as she closed her locker. Vishal joined her and bent his head to ask her something in an undertone.

"Hey," said Sparrow, taking a proper look at Kira. "Where'd you get the new arm?"

Kira shrugged, self-conscious. "The Soft Blade. I woke up with it."

"Huh. Just make sure it doesn't get away from you."

"Yes, thank you."

All of the cryo tubes were open save Trig's. Kira went to pay her respects. Through the frosted viewplate, the kid looked the same as before, his expression unsettlingly serene. If not for the deathly pallor of his skin, he might have been sleeping.

"Right," said Falconi as he started toward the door. "Let's see what's what."

2.

"Jesus-fucking-Christ-on-a-stick," said Sparrow. Next to her, Hwa-jung's brow pinched, and she made a disapproving sound, though she never took her gaze off the holo. None of them did.

Falconi was scrolling through images from throughout the system. Sol was a war zone. The ruins of antimatter farms floated inside the orbit of Mercury. Ship debris cluttered the skies over Venus and Mars. On asteroids, hab-domes had been cracked open like eggs. Damaged space stations, rings, and O'Neill cylinders drifted abandoned throughout the system. Hydrotek refueling facilities were venting plumes of burning hydrogen from punctured storage tanks. On Earth—*Earth* of all places!—impact craters marred the northern and southern hemispheres, and a black blight covered part of Australia.

Large numbers of ships and orbital platforms clustered around the settled planets. The UMC's Seventh Fleet was massed by Deimos, close enough to the Markov Limit that they could jump out at short notice, but not so far away that they couldn't help the inner planets in an emergency.

In several places, fighting was ongoing. The Jellies had established a small operating base all the way out on Pluto, and they'd invaded a number of underground settlements along the arctic regions of Mars. The tunnels prevented the UMC from clearing out the aliens with aerial attacks, but ground operations were in progress to eliminate the Jellies while also trying to save the civilians in the area. More serious still was the blotch on Australia: a nightmare ship had crashed there, and within hours, their infection had taken root, spreading their corrupted tissue through the soil. Fortunately for Earth, the crash had occurred in the barest of deserts, and the immediate use of an orbital solar array to scorch and melt the area had contained the infection, although efforts were ongoing to ensure that no scrap of tissue had escaped destruction.

"My God," said Vishal, and crossed himself.

Even Falconi seemed stunned by the extent of the damage.

Nielsen uttered a distressed sound as she pulled up a window listing the news from Venus. Kira glimpsed part of a headline saying: *Falling City Is—*

"I have to make a call," said the first officer. Her face was deathly pale. "I have to check if . . . if . . ."

"Go," said Falconi. He touched her on the shoulder. "We've got this."

Nielsen gave him a grateful look and then hurried out of Control.

Kira exchanged worried glances with the rest of the crew. If Sol was this bad, what was the rest of the League like? *Weyland!* She fought a sudden surge of despair.

Just as she started to search for news from home, Gregorovich said, "Ahem, if I might make a suggestion, it would be best to answer the UMC before they do something foolish. They're threatening us with all sorts of violence if we don't provide immediate flight information, as well as clarification of intent."

Falconi sighed. "Might as well get this over with. Do they know who we are?"

The ship mind chuckled without much humor. "Judging by the frantic nature of their calls, I would say that is a most definite *yes.*"

"Alright. Put them on the line."

Kira sat near the back of Control and listened while Falconi talked with whomever Gregorovich had connected him with. "Yes," he said. ". . . No. . . . That's right. The UMCS *Darmstadt*. . . . Gregorovich, you'll— . . . Uh-huh. She's right here. . . . Okay. Roger that. Over and out."

"Well?" Kira asked.

Falconi rubbed his face and looked between her, Sparrow, and Hwa-jung. If anything, the circles under his eyes had gotten darker. "They're taking us seriously, so that's a start. UMC wants us to dock at Orsted Station, right quick-like."

"How far away is that?" said Kira.

Before she could pull up her overlays, Falconi said, "Seven hours."

"Orsted is a hab-ring out by Ganymede, one of Jupiter's moons," said Sparrow. "The UMC use it as a major staging point."

That made sense. The Markov Limit for Sol was right near Jupiter's orbit. Kira didn't know a whole lot about Sol, but that much she remembered from her stellar geography class.

"You didn't tell them we have a Jelly on board?" Kira said.

Falconi took a long drink from a water bottle. "Nope. Don't want to alarm 'em too much. Figured we can work up to it."

"They're going to be pissed when they find out," said Kira.

"That they are."

Then Hawes's voice, rough from cryo, came over the intercom: "Captain, we're out of the cryo tubes, but we need the Jelly to come get these damn cocoons off the rest of my men. We'd cut them off, but I'm not sure what it would do to them."

"Roger that, Lieutenant," Falconi said. "Send someone over to the airlock, and I'll have Kira meet them there."

"Appreciate it, Captain."

Falconi glanced at the ceiling. "Gregorovich, is the Jelly awake yet?"

"Just barely," said the ship mind.

"Wonder how it knew?" Falconi muttered.

Kira was already moving toward the door as he looked at her. "I'm on it," she said.

3.

Escorting Itari to the cargo hold, waiting while it extracted the three Marines and—with another secreted gel—revived them, took nearly forty minutes. When not translating, Kira stood by one of the racks of equipment, skimming news reports from Weyland.

They weren't encouraging.

At least one article claimed that Weyland had suffered orbital bombardment near Highstone. Her family didn't live especially close to the city, but they were close enough that the news made Kira even more worried.

The Jellies had also landed near Toska, a settlement in Weyland's southern hemisphere, but according to the most recent news (which was nearly a month old), they hadn't stayed. Several nightmares had passed through the outer part of the system, and they and the Jellies had engaged in a furious fight, the outcome of which was unknown, as all ships involved had jumped to FTL, one after another. The League had sent reinforcements to the system, but it had only been a small task force; the bulk of their ships were kept concentrated in and around Sol, to protect Earth.

Kira stopped reading when Itari finished with the Marines, and she walked the Jelly back to the airlock. When Kira told it about Orsted, Itari expressed polite acknowledgement and nothing more. The alien seemed surprisingly uncurious about where the *Wallfish* was heading or what would happen when they arrived. When she asked about that, it replied, [[Itari here: The ripple will spread as it will.]]

With the Jelly back in the airlock, Kira swung by the galley to grab some food and then climbed back up to Control. Nielsen arrived just as she did. The first officer was flushed and had tears in her eyes.

"Everything okay?" Falconi asked from across the holo table.

Nielsen nodded as she sank into her crash chair. "My family is alive, but my daughter, Yann, lost her home."

"On Venus?" Kira asked.

Nielsen sniffed and smoothed the front of her tan shirt. "The whole city was shot down. She barely escaped."

"Damn," said Falconi. "At least she made it."

A minute of silence followed. Then Nielsen stiffened and looked around. "Where's Vishal?"

Falconi waved toward the back of the ship in a distracted way. "Went to check on sickbay. Said something about running a few tests on the Marines."

"Didn't he live in a hab-cylinder here at Sol?"

Concern spread across Falconi's face. "Did he? He never mentioned that to me."

Nielsen let out an exasperated sound. "*Men.* If you ever actually bothered asking some questions, you might learn—" She shoved herself up from her chair and stalked out of Control.

Falconi watched her go with a faint look of puzzlement. He looked over at Kira, as if hoping for an explanation. She shrugged and looked back at her overlays.

Interstellar wars were slow-moving affairs—even with technology as advanced as the Jellies'—but what *had* occurred was of a depressing sameness. Weyland's experience was mirrored by those of the other colonies (although the battles at Stewart's World were more similar in size to those at Sol).

And then there were the nightmares. As the months swept past, they had become increasingly prevalent, to the point where the UMC was fighting them as often as the Jellies. Every time they appeared, the monsters seemed to take a different set of forms, as if the result of constant mutation. Or, as Kira felt more likely, as if the driving intelligence behind them—the mashing Maw born of the unholy fusion of human, Wranaui, and Soft Blade—was feverishly, frantically, insanely, and randomly experimenting to find the best possible flesh for fighting.

The scale of suffering that the nightmares must be enduring, as well as inflicting, sickened Kira to think of.

She was unsurprised to see that the war had resulted in an unprecedented drawing together of humanity. Even the Zarians had put aside their differences with the League in order to join forces against their shared enemies. What was the point of arguing amongst yourselves if the monsters in the dark were attacking?

And yet for all that, the combined might of every living human wasn't enough to fight off their attackers. Fragmented though the news was, it was more than clear that they were losing. *Humanity* was losing, despite every effort to the contrary.

The news was overwhelming, exhausting, and depressing. At last, unable to bear any more, Kira tabbed out of her overlays and sat staring at the banks of lights and switches overhead, trying not to think about how everything seemed to be falling apart.

An alert appeared in the bottom corner of her vision. A message waiting for her. Kira opened it, expecting to see something from Gregorovich.

It wasn't.

Sitting in her inbox was a reply to the video she'd sent to her family from 61 Cygni. A reply from her mother's account.

Kira stared, shocked. With a start, she remembered to breathe. She hadn't expected an answer. Her family couldn't have known where or when she would return, so how could there be a message waiting for her *here,* at Sol? Unless . . .

Trembling slightly, she opened the file.

A video appeared in front of her, a dark window into what appeared to be an underground bunker. Kira recognized it as the sort used for radiation shielding by the first wave of colonists on Weyland. . . . Her parents were sitting facing her, gathered around a desk cluttered with tools and medkits. Isthah stood behind them, peering between their mom and dad with an anxious face.

Kira swallowed.

Her dad had a bandage around his right thigh. He looked painfully thin, and the lines around his eyes and nose were far deeper than she remembered. There was white in his sideburns that shouldn't have been there, not if he'd gotten his scheduled STEM shots. As for her mom, she'd grown even harder, like an eagle carved from granite, and her hair was cut short, in the style favored by colonists who spent most of their time living in skinsuits.

Only Isthah appeared much the same, and Kira took some comfort in that.

Her mom cleared her throat. "Kira, we just received your message yesterday. It was a month late, but it got here."

Then her dad: "We're really happy to know you're alive, honey. Really happy. You had us worried for a while." Behind him, Isthah ducked her head. Kira was surprised she didn't butt in; the restraint was uncharacteristic. But then, they were living in uncharacteristic times.

Her mom glanced at the other two before focusing on the camera again. "I'm sorry, *we're* sorry, to hear about your teammates, Kira. And . . . Alan. He seemed like a good person."

"This can't be easy for you," her father added. "Just know we're thinking about you and wishing you the best. I'm sure the scientists here in the League can find a way to get this alien—" He hesitated. "—this alien parasite off you." Her mom put a comforting hand on his arm.

She said, "I'm not sure why the League let your message go through. Maybe they missed it, but whatever. I'm glad it got here. You can see we're not at home. The Jellies came by a few weeks ago, and there's been fighting around Highstone. We had to evacuate, but we're okay. We're doing fine. We have a place to stay here with some folks called the Niemerases—"

"Over on the other side of the mountains," said her father.

A tip of the head from her mom. "They're letting us live in their shelter for the time being. It's decent protection, and we have plenty of room." It didn't look like *plenty of room* to Kira.

"The Jellies burned the greenhouses," Isthah said in a low voice. "They burned them, sis. Burned all of them. . . ."

No.

Their parents shifted, uncomfortable. Her dad looked down at his large hands where they rested on his knees. "Yeah," he said. Kira had never seen him appear so sad or defeated. A hollow chuckle escaped him. "Got this scratch trying to get out in time." He tapped the bandage on his leg and forced a smile.

Then her mom stiffened her back and said, "Listen to me, Kira. You don't worry about us, okay? Go do this expedition you have to do, and we'll be here when you get back. . . . We're going to send this recording to every system in the League, so no matter where you arrive, it'll be waiting for you."

"We love you, honey," said her father. "And we're very proud of you and the work you're doing. Try to stay safe, and we'll see you soon."

There was a bit more, a few more words of farewell from her mom and Isthah, and then the video ended.

Kira's overlays swam before her, blurred and watery. She took a hitched breath and realized she was crying. Closing the display, she hunched forward and buried her face in her hands.

"Hey now," said Falconi, sounding alarmed and concerned at the same time. He came over, and she felt his hand light between her shoulder blades. "What's wrong?"

"I got a message from my family," she said.

"Are they—"

"No, no, they're fine, but—" Kira shook her head. "They had to leave our home, where I grew up. And, just seeing them . . . my mom, my dad, my sister; they're not having an easy time of it."

"No one is these days," Falconi said gently.

"I know, but this was from—" She checked the date on the file. "Almost two months ago. Two months. The Jellies hit Highstone with orbital bombardment about a month ago, and—and I don't even know if they're . . ." She trailed off. The surface of her arms prickled with tiny points as the Soft Blade mirrored her emotions. A tear fell onto her left forearm and was quickly absorbed by the fibers.

Falconi knelt next to her. "Is there anything I can do?"

Surprised, she considered for a moment. "No, but . . . thank you. Only thing you or I or anyone can do to help is find a way to end this damn war."

"That would certainly be nice."

She wiped her eyes with the heel of her hand. "What about your family? Have you—"

A flicker of pain darkened his eyes. "No, and they're too far away to just call. I don't know if they'd want to hear from me anyway."

"You don't know that," said Kira. "Not for sure. Look at what's happening out there. We're facing what could be the end of everything. You should touch base with your parents. If not now, when?"

Falconi was silent for a while, and then he patted her on the shoulder and stood. "I'll think about it."

It wasn't much, but Kira didn't think she could expect anything more from him. She got to her feet as well and said, "I'm going to my cabin. I want to answer them before we arrive at Orsted."

Falconi grunted, already lost in examination of the holo. "I wouldn't count on the League letting you get a message out. Them or the Jellies. Bet you a bucket of bits Weyland is jammed up as bad as the toilet we had in the hold."

A moment of uncertainty shook Kira's confidence. Then, accepting the situation as it was, she steadied herself and said, "Doesn't matter. I have to try, you know?"

"Family is that important to you, huh?"

"Of course. Isn't it to you?"

He didn't answer, but she saw the muscles in his shoulders bunch and tense.

4.

Seven hours.

They passed faster than Kira expected. She recorded her response to her family—she told them what had happened at Bughunt, although as with Hawes, she avoided mentioning her role in creating the Maw—and she even showed them a little of what the Soft Blade was capable of by holding up her hand and forming the blossom of a Midnight Constellation from her palm. She hoped that would make her father smile. Most of what she said were general well-wishes and exhortations for them to stay safe, and she ended with, "Hopefully you get this in the next week or so. I don't know what the League is going to have me doing, but I'm guessing they won't let me communicate with you for a while. . . . Whatever's happening there on Weyland, just hold on. We have a chance for peace with the Jellies, and I'm going to be working to make it happen as fast as possible. So don't give up, you hear me? Don't give up. . . . Love you all. Bye."

Afterward, Kira took a few minutes for herself in the dark of her cabin, eyes closed, lights off, while she allowed her breathing to slow and body to cool.

Then she gathered herself and returned to Control. Vishal was there, talking in low tones with Falconi and Sparrow. The doctor stood bending at the neck to be closer to their heights.

"—that's too bad, Doc," said Falconi. "Seriously. If you need to bail on us, I'd understand. We could pick up another—"

Vishal was already shaking his head. "No, that will not be necessary, Captain, although I thank you. My uncle said he will let me know as soon as they find out."

Sparrow startled him with a slap on the shoulder. "You know we've got your back, Doc. Anything I can do to help, you just say the word, and"—she made a whistling sound—"*wsipp,* I'm there."

At first Vishal appeared offended by her familiarity, but then his posture softened and he said, "I appreciate that, Ms. Sparrow. Most truly I do."

As Kira took her seat, she gave Falconi an inquiring glance. *<What's up? – Kira>*

<The Jellies destroyed Vishal's hab-cylinder. – Falconi>

<Shit. What about his mother and sisters? – Kira>

<They might have gotten out in time, but so far, no news. – Falconi>

As Vishal moved over to his crash chair near her own, Kira said, "Falconi just told me. I'm so sorry. That's horrible."

Vishal lowered himself into the chair. A dark frown furrowed his brow, but his voice remained gentle as he said, "Thank you for your kindness, Ms. Kira. I'm sure everything will be fine, God willing."

Kira hoped he was right.

She switched to her overlays and pulled up the feed from the *Wallfish*'s rear-facing cameras so she could watch their approach to the banded mass of Jupiter and the tiny, speckled disk that was Ganymede.

The sight of Jupiter in all its orange-colored glory reminded her with painful strength of Zeus hanging in the sky of Adrasteia. No wonder: the similarities had been the reason the original survey team had given Zeus its name.

Ganymede, by comparison, seemed so small as to be inconsequential, even though—as Kira's overlays informed her—it was the largest moon in the system, larger even than the planet Mercury.

As for their destination, Orsted Station, it was a fleck of dust floating high above the battered surface of Ganymede. Several sparkling motes, smaller still, accompanied it on its orbit, each mote marking the position of one of the many transports, cargo haulers, and drones clustered around the station.

Kira shivered. She couldn't help it. No matter how often she thought she understood the immensity of space, something would happen to drive home the fact that no, she really didn't. The human brain was physically incapable of grasping the distances and scales involved. At least unaltered humans were. Maybe ship minds were different. All that empty vastness, and nothing humans had built (or would ever build) could compare.

She shook herself and returned her gaze to the station. Even the most experienced spacers could go mad if they stared into the void long enough.

It had always been a goal of Kira's to visit Sol and, most particularly, Earth, that great treasure trove of biology. But she had never imagined that her visit would occur as it was: harried and hurried and in the shadow of war.

Still, the sight of Jupiter filled her with a sense of wonder, and she wished Alan was there to share the experience with her. They'd talked about it a few times: making enough money so they could afford to vacation in Sol. Or else getting a research grant that would allow them to travel to the system on the company dime. It had been nothing more than wishful thinking, though. Idle speculations on a possible future.

Kira forced her thoughts elsewhere.

"Everything shipshape?" Falconi asked when Nielsen came floating through the doorway a few minutes later.

"Shipshape as can be," said Nielsen. "We shouldn't have any problems with inspectors."

"Aside from Itari," said Kira.

The first officer smiled with a dry expression. "Yes, well, at least they can't blame us for breaking quarantine. There hasn't been proper biocontainment with the Jellies since day one." Then she went and sat in the crash chair on the other side of Vishal.

Sparrow made a disgusted noise and looked over at Nielsen. "You see what the Stellarists are up to?"

"Mmm. No worse than the Expansion or Conservation Parties. They'd do the same if they were in charge."

Sparrow shook her head. "Yeah, you keep telling yourself that. The Premier is using this whole state of emergency thing to really clamp down on the colonies."

"Ugh," said Kira. Why was she not surprised? The Stellarists were always putting Sol first. Understandable to a point, but it didn't mean she had to like it.

Nielsen assumed a pleasantly blank face. "That's a rather extreme point of view, Sparrow."

"Just you watch," the short-haired woman said. "After this whole mess is over, if there even *is* an after, you won't be able to so much as spit without getting permission from Earth Central. Guarantee it."

"You're overst—"

"What am I saying? You're from Venus. Of *course* you're going to back Earth, just like everyone else who grew up with their heads in the clouds."

A frown settled on Nielsen's face, and she started to answer when Falconi said, "Enough with the politics. Save it for when we've got enough drink to make it tolerable."

"Yessir," said Sparrow in a surly voice.

Kira returned her attention to her overlays. She never could keep track of the finer points of interstellar politics. Too many moving parts. But she did know she didn't like the Stellarists (and most politicians, for that matter).

As she watched, Orsted swelled in size until it dominated the aft view. The station looked heavy and brutal, like a gothic gyroscope, dark of hue and sharp of edge. The stationary shield ring appeared undamaged, but the rotating hab-ring mated to it had several large rents along one quadrant, as if a monster had raked Orsted with its claws. Explosive decompression had peeled the hull back along the edges of the holes, turning the plating into lines of jagged petals. Between the petals, rooms were visible, white and glittery with a layer of frost.

The top face of Orsted's central hub (where *top* meant pointing away from Ganymede) was a bristle of antennas, dishes, telescopes, and weapons, standing motionless on their frictionless bearings. Most of the equipment appeared broken or slagged. Fortunately, the attacks didn't seem to have penetrated to the fusion reactor buried within the core of the hub.

The spindly, cross-braced truss that extended for several hundred meters from the bottom face of Orsted's hub appeared intact, but many of the transparent radiators that fringed it had holes punched through them or had been shattered, reducing them to knifelike shards that dribbled molten metal from their severed veins. Dozens of service bots were flitting about the damaged radiators, working to stanch the loss of coolant.

The auxiliary communications and defense array mounted at the far end of the truss appeared scorched and mangled. Through some incredible stroke of luck, the containment chamber in the Markov generator (which powered the station's FTL sensors) hadn't been breached. The generator only held a minuscule amount of antimatter at any given time, but if it had lost containment, the whole array (and a good part of the truss) would have been annihilated.

Four UMC cruisers hung off the port side of the station, a visible demonstration of the League's military power.

"Thule," said Sparrow, taking a seat. "They really got the shit beaten out of them."

"Ever been to Orsted before?" Kira asked.

Sparrow licked her lips. "Once. On leave. Wouldn't care to repeat the experience."

"Better strap in," said Falconi from across Control.

"Yessir."

They secured themselves, and then the burn ended. Kira made a face at the return to zero-g. The *Wallfish* performed one last skewflip (so it was flying nose-first toward the station), and Gregorovich said, "ETA, fourteen minutes."

Kira tried to empty her mind.

Hwa-jung joined them soon after, pulling herself into Control with the grace of a ballet dancer. An expression of disgust marred her face, and she seemed more surly than usual.

"How are Runcible and Mr. Fuzzypants?" Falconi asked.

The machine boss grimaced. "That cat had another accident. Yuck. There was poop everywhere. If I ever buy a ship myself, I won't have a cat. Pigs are okay. Not cats."

"Thanks for cleaning up."

"Mmh. I deserve hazard pay."

For a time they were silent. Then Sparrow said, "You know, speaking of biocontainment, they really shouldn't have been so angry with us on Ruslan."

"Why's that?" Nielsen asked.

"All those escaped animals were a great source of *newt*rition."

Kira groaned along with everyone else, but it was a token protest. Most of them, she thought, were just sorry Trig wasn't there to make his usual jokes.

"Thule be saving us from puns," said Vishal.

"Could be worse," said Falconi.

"Yeah? How?"

"She could be a mime."

Sparrow threw a glove at him, and the captain laughed.

5.

Kira's stomach tightened as the *Wallfish* slowed and, with a faint shudder, coupled with their assigned docking port in Orsted's shield ring.

After a few seconds, the all-clear sounded.

"Alright, listen up," said Falconi, pulling off his harness. "Captain Akawe arranged pardons for us—" He gave Kira a look from under his brow. "All us miscreants, that is. The League should have them on file, but that doesn't mean you should go making fools of yourself. No one say nothing until we have representation and we're clear on the situation. That goes double for you, Gregorovich."

"As you say, Captain O my Captain," the ship mind responded.

Falconi grunted. "And don't go blabbing about the Jelly neither. Kira and I will take care of that."

"Won't Hawes and his men have already told the UMC?" Kira asked.

A grim little smile from Falconi. "I'm sure they would have if I'd given them comms access. But I haven't."

"Hawes is fighting mad about it too," Nielsen said.

Falconi kicked his way over to the pressure door. "Doesn't matter. We're going to talk with the UMC straightaway, and it's going to take them some time to debrief our friendly neighborhood Marines."

"Do we all have to go?" said Hwa-jung. "The *Wallfish* still needs maintenance after *that* jump."

Falconi gestured toward the door. "You'll have plenty of time to deal with the ship later, Hwa-jung. I promise. And yes, we all have to go." Sparrow groaned, and Vishal rolled his eyes. "The liaison officer on Orsted specifically asked for everyone on the ship. I think they're not sure what to make of us yet. They mentioned having to check for orders with Earth Central. Besides, we're not letting Kira walk in there alone."

". . . Thanks," she said, and she meant it.

"Of course. Wouldn't let any of my crew go off by themselves." Falconi grinned, and though it was a hard, dangerous grin, Kira found it reassuring. "If they don't treat you right, we'll kick up a ruckus until they do. Rest of you, you know the drill. Eyes peeled and mouths shut. Remember, this isn't shore leave."

"Roger that."

"Yessir."

"Of course, Captain."

Hwa-jung nodded.

Falconi slapped the bulkhead. "Gregorovich, keep the ship on standby, case we have to leave in a hurry. And full monitoring of our overlays until we're back."

"Of course," said Gregorovich in a warbling tone. "I shall keep an ever-so-close watch upon the feeds from your peepers. Such delightful snooping. Such scrumptious snooping."

Kira snorted. Their long sleep certainly hadn't changed *him*.

"Are you expecting trouble?" asked Nielsen as they left Control.

"No," said Falconi. "But better safe than sorry."

"Second that," said Sparrow.

With Falconi at the lead, they went to the central shaft of the *Wallfish* and pulled themselves along the ladder until they reached the airlock mounted in the nose of the ship. The Entropists joined them there, the Questants' robes billowing in free fall, like wind-blown sails. They dipped their heads and murmured, "Captain" as they slowed to a stop.

"Welcome to the party," said Falconi.

The airlock was crowded with all nine of them crammed in—especially with Hwa-jung taking up nearly as much space as three of them combined—but with some pushing and shoving, they managed to fit.

The airlock cycled with the usual assortment of *clicks* and *hisses* and other unidentifiable sounds. And when the outer door rolled open, Kira saw a loading dock identical to the one she'd arrived at on Vyyborg over a year ago. It gave her a strange feeling, not quite déjà vu, not quite nostalgia. What had once been familiar, even friendly, now seemed cold, stark, and—though she knew it was just nerves—out of joint.

A small spherical drone was waiting for them, floating just to the left of the airlock. The yellow light next to its camera was on, and from a speaker came a man's voice: "This way, please."

With puffs of compressed air, the drone turned and jetted away toward the pressure door at the other end of the long, metal-clad room.

"Guess we follow," said Falconi.

"Guess so," said Nielsen.

"Don't they realize we're in a hurry?" said Kira.

Sparrow clucked her tongue. "You should know better, Navárez. You can't rush a bureaucracy. There's time, and then there's military time. Hurry up and wait is standard operating procedure."

Then Falconi launched himself off the lip of the airlock toward the pressure door. He spiraled slowly through the air, one arm above his head to catch himself when he landed.

"Show-off," said Nielsen as she crawled out of the airlock and grabbed the handholds in the nearby wall.

One by one, they left the *Wallfish* and crossed the loading dock, with its gimbaled waldos and grooved strips for holding cargo containers in place. As they did, Kira knew that lasers and magnets and other pieces of equipment were checking their ID, scanning them for explosives and other weapons, looking for traces of contraband, and so on. It made her skin crawl, but there was nothing she could do about it.

For a second she considered allowing the mask to cover her face . . . but then she dismissed the urge.

She wasn't going into battle, after all.

Past the pressure door, the drone zipped into the wide hallway beyond. It was at least seven meters across, and after so long spent on the *Wallfish*, the amount of space seemed enormous.

All the doors along the hallway were closed and locked, and aside from themselves, not one person was to be seen. Not there and not around the corners of the first dogleg. Nor the second.

"Some welcoming committee," Falconi said dryly.

"Must be they are scared of us," said Vishal.

"No," said Sparrow. "They're just scared of *her*."

"Maybe they should be," Kira muttered.

Sparrow surprised her by laughing so loudly, the sound echoed up and down the hall. "That's it. You show them." Even Hwa-jung looked amused.

The hallway led them through all five floors of the shield ring and then, as Kira knew it would, to a maglev car waiting at the end. The car's side door was already open, the seats inside empty.

From the blackness on the other side of the car, she could hear the whisper of the rotating hab-ring, turning, turning, constantly turning.

"Please watch your hands and feet as you enter," said the drone, stopping next to the car.

"Yeah, yeah," Falconi muttered.

Kira took a seat with the rest of them and strapped herself in. Then a musical tone sounded, and from hidden speakers, a woman's voice said, "The car is about to leave. Please tighten your seat belts and secure all loose items." The door slid shut with a squeal. "Next stop: hab-section C."

The car accelerated forward, smoothly and with hardly any noise. It passed through the pressure seal at the end of the terminal and entered the main transit tube that lay embedded between the docking ring and the hab-ring. As it did, Kira felt the cab rotate inward—felt *herself* rotate—and a sensation of weight began to press her down into the seat. Her arms and legs settled, and within seconds, she felt as if she'd regained her usual number of kilos.

The rotation combined with the acceleration was a weird feeling. For a moment it left her dizzy, and then her perspective shifted as she adjusted to her new down.

Down was between her feet (where it ought to be). Down pointed outward, through the shield ring and away from the station's hub.

The car slid to a stop, and the door opposite the one they'd entered through popped its seal and retracted.

"Ah. I feel as if I've been twisted around a spindle," said Vishal.

"You and me both, Doc," said Falconi.

A chorus of *clicks* as they released their belts, and then they stumbled out into the terminal, still finding their balance on unsteady legs.

Falconi stopped before he'd gone more than a step or two. Kira stopped next to him.

"Shi-bal."

Waiting for them was a phalanx of troopers in black power armor. All carrying weapons. All aimed at her and the crew. A pair of heavy assault units stood looming behind the others, like blocky giants, bug-faced and impersonal. At intervals between the troopers, turrets had been bolted to the floor. And filling the air with a hum like a million angry wasps was a swarm of battle drones.

The door to the maglev snapped shut.

A voice boomed: "Hands on your heads! Drop to your knees! You *will* be shot if you fail to comply. *MOVE!*"

CHAPTER II

* * * * * * *

ORSTED STATION

1.

Kira wasn't sure why she had expected anything different. But she had, and the UMC's behavior left her angry and disappointed.

"You fucking *bastards*!" said Falconi.

The voice boomed across the terminal again: "On the floor. NOW!"

There was no point in fighting. Kira would just get herself killed. Or the crew. Or the troopers, and they weren't her enemies. At least, that was what she kept telling herself. They were human, after all.

Kira put her hands on her head and dropped to her knees, never taking her eyes off the soldiers. Around her, the crew did the same, the Entropists too.

A half-dozen troopers rushed forward, boots clanging in a metallic cacophony. The weight of their suits made the deck shake; Kira felt the vibrations through her shins.

The troopers moved behind them and began securing the crew's wrists with restraints. The Entropists' also. Hwa-jung snarled when one of the troopers grabbed her arms. For a second she resisted, and Kira could hear the soldier's armor whine as it struggled against her strength. Then Hwa-jung relaxed and muttered an expletive in Korean.

The troopers dragged Falconi and the others to their feet and marched them off to the side, toward a pressure door that slid open at their approach.

"Don't let them hurt you!" Falconi shouted back at her. "They touch you, rip off their hands. You hear me?!" One of the troopers shoved him in the back. "Gah! We have a pardon! Let us go or I'll get a lawyer who'll tear this whole place down for breach of contract. You've got nothing on us. We're—"

His voice faded away as they passed through the doorway and out of sight. Within seconds, the rest of the crew and the Entropists were gone.

A chill crept into Kira's fingers, despite the best efforts of the Soft Blade. Once again, she was alone.

"This is a waste of time," she said. "I need to speak with whoever is in command. We have time-sensitive intel about the Jellies. Trust me, the Premier is going to want to hear what we have to say."

The troopers moved aside, clearing a path forward, and for a moment, Kira thought her words had had the desired effect. Then the thunderous voice again sounded: "Take out your contacts and drop them on the floor."

Dammit. They must have detected the contacts when she boarded Orsted.

"Weren't you listening?" she half shouted. The skin of the Soft Blade tightened in response. "While you're jerking me around, the Jellies are out there killing humans. Who's in charge? I won't do a damn thing until—"

The volume of the voice was enough to make her ears hurt: "You WILL comply, or you WILL be shot! You have ten seconds to obey. Nine. Eight. Seven—"

For just a moment, Kira imagined pulling the Soft Blade over herself and *letting* the troopers shoot her. She was pretty sure the xeno could protect her against all but the largest of their weaponry. But if the fighting on Nidus was anything to go by, the largest would be more than enough to hurt her, and then there would be the consequences for Falconi and the rest of his crew. . . .

"Fine! Fine!" she said, tamping down her anger. She wasn't going to lose control. Not now, not ever again. At her urging, the Soft Blade returned to its normal relaxed state.

She reached for her eyes, hating that she was once again going to lose access to a computer.

Once the contacts were on the floor, the voice returned: "Hands back on your head. Good. Now, when I tell you, you're going to stand up and walk to the other side of the terminal. You will see an open door. Go through that door. If you turn to the side, you will be shot. If you try to go back, you will be shot. If you lower your hands, you will be shot. If you do anything unexpected, you will be shot. Do you understand?"

"Yes."

"Walk now."

It was awkward, but Kira got to her feet without using her arms for balance. Then she started forward.

"Faster!" said the voice.

She quickened her pace, but not by much. She'd be damned if she was going to run for them like a server bot programmed to obey their every word.

The battle drones followed her as she walked, their incessant buzzing as maddening as a headache. As she passed the troopers, they closed in behind her, forming a wall of iron, blank and impassive.

At the far end of the terminal was the open door the voice had promised. Another group of troopers waited for her on the other side—a double row of them standing with their weapons trained on her.

Keeping to the same measured pace, Kira left the terminal behind and walked out into the concourse beyond. It was a large chamber (decadent almost with its extravagant use of space), lit by bright panels embedded in the ceiling, which made the whole chamber appear to be bathed in Earth-norm sunlight. The light was needed too, for the walls and floor were dark, and that darkness gave the room an oppressive feel, despite the brightness of the illumination.

As elsewhere, all the doors and passageways leading out of the room had been sealed off, some with freshly welded plates. Benches, terminals, and a few potted trees were distributed in a grid throughout the area, but what really caught her attention was the structure in the very center of the concourse.

It was a polyhedron of some sort, perhaps three meters tall and painted army green. Surrounding it and separated from it by the width of a hand was a wire framework that exactly matched the polyhedron's shape. A host of thick metal disks (each about the diameter of a dinner plate) were attached to the framework, arranged so the empty space between them was minimized. Every disk had a panel on the back with buttons and a tiny glowing display.

Within the facing side of the polyhedron was a door, and the door stood open. The polyhedron was hollow. Inside was a single chamber so dim and shadowy she couldn't make out the details.

Kira stopped.

Behind and above her, she heard the troopers and the drones stop as well.

"Inside. *Now!*" said the voice.

Kira knew she was testing their patience, but she paused a little longer, savoring her last moment of freedom. Then she steeled herself and walked forward and entered the polyhedron.

A second later, the door slammed shut behind her, and the dark confines rang with what felt and sounded like her death knell.

2.

Several minutes passed, during which Kira listened to the troopers thudding about as they shifted equipment into place next to her prison.

Then a new voice sounded outside the door: a man with a rough, burred accent so thick she wished she still had her overlays to provide subtitles.

"Ms. Navárez, can you hear me?"

His words were muffled by the walls, but she could hear well enough. "Yes."

"My name is Colonel Stahl. I'll be debriefing you."

Colonel. That wasn't a navy rank. "What are you? Army?"

A brief hesitation on his part. "No, ma'am. UMCI. Intelligence."

Of course. Same as Tschetter. Kira nearly laughed. She should have guessed. "Am I under arrest, Colonel Stahl?"

"No, ma'am, not as such. You are being held in accordance with article thirty-four of the Stellar Security Act, which states—"

"Yes, I'm familiar with it," she said.

Another pause, this time as if Stahl was surprised. "I see. I realize your accommodations aren't what you were expecting, Ms. Navárez, but you have to appreciate our position. We've seen all sorts of crazy stuff from the nightmares over the past few months. We can't afford to trust the xeno you're carrying."

She bit back a sarcastic response. "Yes, alright. I get it. Now, can we please—"

"Not quite yet, ma'am. Let me be explicitly clear, lest there be any, ah, unwarranted *accidents* down the road. The disks you saw on the outside of your cell, do you know what they are?"

"No."

"Shaped charges. Self-forging penetrators. The walls of your cell are electrified. If you break the current, the charges will detonate and crush you and everything around you into a molten-hot ball less than half a meter across. Not even your xeno can survive that. Do you understand?"

"Yes."

"Do you have any questions?"

She had lots of questions. A bedevilment of questions. So many questions, she doubted she would ever find enough answers. But she had to try. "What's going to happen to the crew of the *Wallfish*?"

"They'll be detained and interrogated until the full extent of their involvement with you, the suit, and the Jellies is determined."

Kira swallowed her frustration. The UMC couldn't really be expected to do otherwise. Didn't mean she had to like it. Still, there was no point in antagonizing Stahl. Not yet. "Okay, so are you going to debrief me or what?"

"Whenever you're ready, Ms. Navárez. We have the recording of your initial conversation with Captain Akawe on Malpert Station, so why don't you begin there and bring us up to date?"

So Kira told him what he wanted to know. She spoke quickly, concisely—striving to present the information in the most organized fashion possible. First, she explained their reasons for leaving 61 Cygni for Bughunt. Second, she described what they had discovered on Nidus. Third, she recounted the events of the nightmare attack. And fourth, she outlined in painstaking detail the offer of friendship Tschetter had conveyed from the rebellious Jellies.

The one thing Kira *didn't* tell Stahl was her role in the creation of the nightmares. She'd planned on it. She'd promised Falconi she would. But the way the League was treating her did nothing to engender a sense of charity. If the information could have helped them win the war, then she would have shared it, regardless of any discomfort. But as she saw no way it could, she didn't.

Afterward, Stahl was silent for so long that she began to wonder if he was still there. Then he said, "Your ship mind can provide corroboration?"

Kira nodded, even though he couldn't see. "Yes, just ask him. He also has all the relevant records from the *Darmstadt*."

"I see." The terseness of the colonel's reply couldn't hide the underlying anxiety. Her account had shaken him, and more than a little. "In that case I'd best look at them immediately. If there's nothing else, Ms. Navárez, then I'll—"

"Actually . . ." said Kira.

"What?" said Stahl, wary.

She took a breath, preparing herself for what was to come. "You should know, we have a Jelly on the *Wallfish*."

"What?!"

And Kira heard the rapid drumbeat of troopers running toward her cell. "Everything okay, sir?" someone called out.

"Yes, yes," said Stahl, irritable. "I'm fine. Get out of here."

"Yessir." The weighted footsteps retreated.

Stahl swore quietly. "Now, Navárez, what the hell do you mean you've got a goddamn Jelly on the *Wallfish*? Explain."

Kira explained.

When she finished, Stahl swore again.

"What are you going to do?" she asked. If the UMC tried to force their way onto the *Wallfish,* there wasn't a whole lot Gregorovich could do to stop them, not without taking drastic and most likely suicidal measures.

"... Give Earth Central a call. This is way above my pay grade, Navárez."

Then Kira heard Stahl walk away, and the clamor of the troopers' footsteps followed, rising and swelling until the sound broke like a passing wave, leaving her alone in silence.

"Yeah, that's what I thought," she said, feeling a certain perverse satisfaction.

3.

Kira looked around.

The inside of the polyhedron was empty. No bed. No toilet. No sink. No drain. The walls, floor, and ceiling were all made of the same green plating. Above her, a small round light provided the only source of illumination. Slits with fine mesh covers edged the ceiling: vents for airflow, she assumed.

And there was her. The only occupant of the strange, faceted prison.

She couldn't see them, but she assumed there were cameras recording her, and that Stahl or someone else was watching everything she did.

Let them watch.

Kira willed the Soft Blade to cover her face, and her vision expanded to encompass both the infrared and the electromagnetic.

Stahl hadn't lied. The walls glowed with bluish loops of force, and between the end points of each loop ran a snake of twisting electricity, bright and shining. The leads weren't built into the walls; it looked to Kira as if the current was coming from the framework that held the shaped charges, flowing through wire contacts dotted across the entire polyhedron. Even the floor glowed with the soft haze of an induced magnetic field.

Over the door and in the corners of the ceiling, Kira spotted several small disturbances in the fields: knot-like eddies that connected to tiny threads of electricity. She'd been right. Cameras.

She allowed the mask to withdraw and sat on the floor.

There was nothing else to do.

For a moment, anger and frustration threatened to overwhelm her, but then she beat them back. *No.* She wasn't going to allow herself to get worked up over things she couldn't change. Not this time. Whatever was going to happen, she'd strive to face it with a sense of self-control. Things were difficult enough without making them harder on herself.

Besides, coming to Sol had been their only real option. The offer from the Knot of Minds was too crucial to risk delay by trying to pass it along from another system in the League. With all the jamming and fighting going on, there was no guarantee the intel would have gotten through. And then there was Itari; the Jelly was an important link to the Knot of Minds, and Kira needed to be there to translate for it. She supposed they could have just jumped in, transmitted the information to the League, and then jumped out. But that would have been a dereliction of duty. If nothing else, they owed it to Captain Akawe to deliver the Jellies' message in person.

Kira just wished that she hadn't gotten Falconi and the rest of the crew tangled up in her mess. *That* she felt guilty about. Hopefully the UMC wouldn't detain them for too long. A small consolation, but the only one she could think of at the moment.

A deep breath, and then another as Kira tried to empty her mind. When that didn't work, she recalled a favorite song, "*Tangagria*," and let the melody displace her thoughts. And when she tired of the song, she switched to another, and then another.

Time passed.

After what felt like hours, she heard the heavy tread of an approaching suit of power armor. The armor stopped next to the cell, and then a narrow slot in the door was pulled open and a metal-clad hand shoved a tray of food toward her.

She took it, and the hand withdrew. The cover to the slot clicked back into place, and the trooper said, "When you're done, bang on the door."

Then the footsteps withdrew, but not very far.

Kira wondered how many troopers were standing guard. Just the one? Or was there a whole squad of them?

She placed the tray on the floor and sat cross-legged before it. With a single look, she cataloged the contents: a paper cup full of water. A paper plate with two ration bars, three yellow tomatoes, half a cucumber, and a slice of orange melon. No fork. No knife. No seasoning.

She sighed. She'd had enough ration bars to last the rest of her life, but at least the UMC was feeding her. And the fresh produce was a welcome treat.

As she ate, she eyed the slot in the door. Things could obviously pass through it without triggering the explosives. If she could sneak a fiber or two through the seams, maybe she could find a way to turn off the current on the outside of the cell. . . .

No. She wasn't trying to escape. Not this time. If she—or more accurately the Soft Blade—could help the League, then she had a responsibility to stay. Even if they *were* a bunch of assholes.

When she finished eating, she shouted at the door a few times, and as promised, the trooper came and took the tray away.

After that, she tried pacing, but the walls were only two and a half steps apart, so she soon gave up and instead did push-ups, squats, and handstands until she burned off her nervous energy.

She'd just finished when the light overhead began to dim and grow red. In less than a minute, it plunged her into almost total darkness.

Despite her resolution not to worry or obsess, and despite her tiredness, Kira had difficulty falling asleep. Too much *stuff* had happened during the day for her to just relax and drift off into unconsciousness. Her thoughts kept going round and round—returning each time to the nightmares—and none of it was useful. It didn't help that the floor was hard, and even with the suit, she found it uncomfortable.

She concentrated on slowing her breathing. Everything else might be outside of her control, but that much she could do. Gradually her pulse slowed and the tension drained from her neck, and she could feel a welcome coolness creeping through her limbs.

While she waited, she counted the cell's faces: twelve in total, which made it a . . . dodecahedron? She thought so. In the faint red light, the walls appeared brown, and the color and the concave shape reminded her of the inside of a walnut shell.

She laughed softly. "—and count myself a king of infinite space . . ." She wished Gregorovich could see. He of all people would appreciate the joke.

She hoped he was okay. If he behaved himself with the UMC, he might get off with a fine and a few citations. Ship minds were too valuable to ground over even relatively major infractions. However, if he yammered at them the way he had during some of his conversations with her, and the UMC decided he was unstable, the League wouldn't hesitate to yank him out of the *Wallfish* and ban him from flying. Either way, he was going to have to endure a gauntlet of psych tests, and Kira didn't know if Gregorovich was willing or able to hide the crazy. If he didn't—

She stopped, annoyed with herself. Those were the sorts of thoughts she needed to avoid. What would be would be. All that mattered was the present. What *was,* not word-castles and hypotheticals. And right then, what she needed to do was sleep.

It must have been almost three in the morning before her brain finally allowed her to sink into welcome unconsciousness. She'd hoped that the Soft Blade might choose to share another vision with her, but though she dreamed, her dreams were her own.

4.

The light in the cell brightened.

Kira's eyes snapped open, and she sat upright, heart pounding, ready to go. When she saw the walls of her cell and remembered where she was, she growled and bounced her fist against her thigh.

What was taking the League so long? Accepting the offer of support from Tschetter's Jellies was a no-brainer. So why the delay?

She stood, and a faint layer of dust fell from her body. Alarmed, she checked the floor underneath herself.

It appeared the same as before.

Kira let out her breath, relieved. If the Soft Blade had chewed through the plating during the night, she would have been in for an explosive surprise. The xeno had to know better, though. It wanted to live as much as she did.

"Behave yourself," she murmured.

A fist pounded on the outside of the door, startling her. "Navárez, we have to talk," said Stahl.

Finally. "I'm listening."

"I have some additional questions for you."

"Ask away."

And Stahl did. Questions about Tschetter—had the major seemed to be in her right state of mind, had she been as Kira remembered from the *Extenuating Circumstances,* and so forth and so on—questions about the Jellies, questions about the Seeker and the Staff of Blue, and also many, many questions about the nightmares.

Finally Stahl said, "We're done here."

"Wait," said Kira. "What happened to the Jelly? What did you do about it?"

"The Jelly?" said Stahl. "We moved it to biocontainment."

A sudden fear struck Kira. "Is it . . . is it still alive?"

The colonel seemed to take a certain offense at that. "Of course, Navárez. What do you take us for, complete incompetents? It took some doing, but we managed to *incentivize* your, ah, tentacle-covered friend to move from the *Wallfish* to the station."

Kira wondered what that incentivizing had involved, but she decided it was wiser not to probe. "I see. So what is the League going to do about this? Tschetter, the Knot of Minds, and all the rest of it?"

"That's need-to-know, ma'am."

She gritted her teeth. "Colonel Stahl, after everything that's happened, don't you think I ought to be part of this conversation?"

"Maybe so, ma'am, but that's not up to me."

Kira took a calming breath. "Can you at least tell me how long I'm going to be held here?" If the League was going to transfer her to a UMC ship, that would be fairly clear evidence that they were going to take her to meet with the Knot of Minds so she could help negotiate the terms of alliance.

"You'll be moved to a packet ship at zero nine hundred hours tomorrow and taken to the LaCern research station for further examination."

"*Excuse me?*" said Kira, nearly sputtering. "Why would you . . . I mean, isn't the League going to at least talk with the Knot of Minds? Who else do you have to translate for you? Iska? Tschetter? We don't even know if she's still alive! And I'm the only one who can actually *speak* the Jellies' language."

Stahl sighed, and when he answered, he sounded far more tired than he had a moment ago. "We're not going to *talk* with them, Navárez." And Kira realized he was breaking protocol by telling her.

A horrible sense of dread came over her. "What do you mean?" she asked, not believing.

"I mean that the Premier and his advisors have decided that the Jellies are too dangerous to trust. *Hostis Humani Generis,* after all. Surely you heard. It was announced before you left Sixty-One Cygni."

"So what are they going to do?" she said, nearly whispering.

"It's already done, Navárez. The Seventh Fleet departed today under the command of Admiral Klein to attack the Jelly fleet stationed at the star Tschetter gave us info on. It's a K-type star about a month and a half away. Objective is to smash the Jellies when they're least expecting it, make sure they can't ever threaten us again."

"But . . ." Kira could think of any number of things wrong with that plan.

The UMC might be cast-iron bastards, but they weren't stupid. "They'll see the Seventh coming. And they can jump out before you get close enough to shoot. Our only chance is to take out the leadership before—"

"We've got it covered, ma'am," said Stahl, terse as ever. "We haven't been sitting on our hands the past six months. The Jellies might outclass and outgun us, but if there's one thing humans are good at, it's codging together makeshift solutions. We've got ways of keeping them from seeing us and ways to keep them from jumping out. Won't last long, but it'll last long enough."

"Then what about Tschetter's Jellies?" Kira asked. "The Knot of Minds?"

Stahl grunted. When he spoke again, his voice had acquired a brittle tone, as if he were guarding himself. "A batch of hunter-seekers was dispatched toward the meeting location."

"To . . . ?"

"Eliminate with extreme prejudice."

Kira felt as if she'd been struck. She wasn't the biggest fan of the League, but she'd never thought of it as being actively evil. "What the hell, Colonel? Why would—"

"It's a political decision, Navárez. Out of our hands. It's been determined that leaving any of their leadership alive, even if they're rebels, is too great a risk for humanity. This isn't a war, Navárez. This is extermination. Eradication. First we break the Jellies, and then we can focus on taking out these nightmares."

"It's been determined," she said, spitting out the words with all the scorn she could muster. "Determined by *who*?"

"By the Premier himself." A brief pause, then: "Sorry, Navárez. That's the way it is."

The colonel started to walk away, and Kira shouted after, "Yeah, well fuck the Premier and fuck you too!"

She stood there, breathing heavily, fists clenched by her sides. Only then did she notice that the Soft Blade—that *she*—was covered with spikes poking through her jumpsuit. Again her temper had gotten the better of her. "Bad, bad, bad," she whispered, and she wasn't sure if she meant herself or the League.

Calm but still filled with a cold, clinical anger, Kira sat cross-legged on the floor while she tried to think through the situation. In retrospect, it seemed apparent that Stahl didn't approve of the Premier's decision either. That Stahl would tell her the League's plans meant *something,* although she wasn't sure what. Maybe he wanted her forewarned for some reason.

That hardly mattered now. The League's impending betrayal of the Knot of Minds was far more important than her own troubles. Finally they had a chance of peace (with the Jellies at least) and the Premier had to throw it away because he wasn't willing to *try.* Was trying so great a risk, after all?

Frustration joined anger within Kira. She hadn't even voted for the Premier—none of them had!—and he was going to set them at perpetual odds with the Jellies. Fear was driving them, she thought, not hope. And as events had taught her, fear was a poor guide indeed.

What *was* the Premier's name? She couldn't even recall. The League tended to shuffle through them like cards.

If only there was a way to warn the Knot of Minds. Maybe then some sort of alliance could be saved. Kira wondered if the Soft Blade could somehow contact the Jellies. But no, whatever signals the xeno could produce, they seemed to be indiscriminate, blasted forth to the whole of the galaxy. And luring even *more* Jellies and nightmares to Sol would hardly be helpful.

If she could somehow manage to break out, then—then what? Kira hadn't seen the file of information Tschetter had given Akawe (and that the *Darmstadt* had copied over to the *Wallfish*), but she felt sure there had to be contact information in it: times, frequencies, and locations, that sort of thing. But she doubted that the UMC technicians would have left even a single copy of the file on the *Wallfish*'s computers, and Kira had no idea whether Gregorovich had bothered to memorize any of the information.

If not—and Kira thought it would be irresponsible to assume otherwise—then Itari would be their only hope of warning the Knot of Minds. She'd not only have to rescue herself, she'd also have to rescue Itari, get the Jelly to a ship, and then fly the ship out of the system, where they'd be clear of any jamming, and the whole time the UMC would be doing their damnedest to stop them.

It was the sheerest fantasy, and Kira knew it.

She groaned and looked up at the faceted ceiling. She felt so helpless it hurt. Of all the torments a person could endure, that—she felt sure—was the worst of all.

Breakfast was a long time coming. When it arrived, she could hardly eat, her stomach was so cramped and unsettled. After disposing of the tray, she sat in the center of the cell, meditated, and tried to think of what she could do.

If only I had my concertina. Playing would help her concentrate, of that she felt sure.

5.

No one else came to see her for the rest of the day. Kira's anger and frustration remained, but boredom smothered them like a blanket. Without her overlays, she was again left with nothing but the contents of her mind for amusement. And her thoughts were far from amusing at the moment.

In the end, she did what she always did when trying to while away the time during each of the long FTL trips she'd endured since leaving Sigma Draconis. Which was to say, she dozed, drifting into the hazy half-sleep that allowed the Soft Blade to preserve her strength while still keeping ready for whatever might happen next.

And so she spent the day, her only interruption being the bland lunch and even blander dinner the troopers delivered.

Then the lights dimmed to red, and her half-sleep became a full-sleep.

6.

A tremor ran through the floor.

Kira's eyes snapped open, memories of the *Extenuating Circumstances* coursing through her. It might have been midnight. It might have been three in the morning. There was no way to tell, but she'd been lying on her side for so long her hip was sore and her arm was numb.

Another tremor, larger than the first one, and with it, an odd twisting sensation, similar to what she'd felt in the maglev. A moment of vertigo caused her to grab the floor for support, and then her balance steadied.

A shot of adrenaline cleared the last of her sleep haze. There was only one explanation: the hab-ring had wobbled. *Shit.* Not good. The very definition of not good. Jellies or nightmares—*someone* was attacking Orsted Station.

She looked at one of the cameras. "Hey! What's going on?" But no one answered.

A third tremor shook the cell, and the light overhead flickered. Somewhere in the distance, she heard a *thud* that might have been an explosion.

Kira went cold as she dropped into survival mode. The station was under attack. Was she safe? That depended on the cell's power source, assuming she wasn't hit by a missile or a laser. If the cell was hooked up to the main reactor, and the reactor went offline, the explosives surrounding her could detonate.

Same if there was a large enough power surge. On the other hand, if the cell was hooked up to batteries, then she might be okay. It was a gamble, though. A big one.

Boom!

She staggered as the cell shook around her. The light flickered again, more than before, and her heart clutched. For an instant, she was certain she was dead, but . . . the universe continued to exist. *She* continued to exist.

Kira straightened and looked at the door.

Screw the UMC and screw the League. She was getting out.

CHAPTER III

* * * * * * *

ESCAPE!

1.

Determined, Kira went to the door.

She had only two options. Find a way to disarm the explosives or find a way to reroute the current so she could break down the door without ending up as a white-hot lump of slag.

The floor rumbled.

Whatever she did, she'd have to do it fast.

Disarming would be safer, but she couldn't figure out *how* to disarm it. Even if she could sneak a few tendrils past the slot in the door, she wouldn't be able to see what she was doing on the other side. Groping around blindly, she'd be just as likely to blow herself up as not.

Okay. That left rerouting the current. She knew the xeno could protect her from being shocked. Which meant it could channel electricity into conductive paths around her body. So theoretically, it ought to be able to form wires or some such that could keep the current from being disrupted if she opened the door. Right? If not, she was dead.

The light dimmed for a second.

She might be dead anyway.

She covered her face with the suit and studied the lines of electricity embedded within the polyhedron's outer surface. A half-dozen of them crossed the door. Those were the ones she'd have to bypass.

Kira took a moment to visualize, with as much detail and clarity as she could manage, what she wanted. More importantly, she tried to impress her *intentions* on the Soft Blade, as well as the consequences of failure. As Alan would say, "All go boom."

"No boom," Kira murmured. "Not this time."

Then she released the Soft Blade and willed it to act on its own.

A cluster of thin black wires sprouted from her chest and extended outward until they touched the spots, on either side of the door, where the lines of electricity originated. Then additional wires leaped across the door and joined each contact point to its intended partner.

She could feel the xeno drilling into the walls then, burrowing with atomically sharp tips through the paneling, toward the leads.

The cell shuddered hard enough to rock her, and her breath caught.

Just a few more microns of drilling and . . . Contact! The glowing, blue-white lines of electricity jumped from their established paths into the wires the Soft Blade had laid down. Around them, the translucent loops of magnetic force shifted as well, roiling and realigning as they sought a new state of equilibrium.

Kira stood frozen, waiting for the inevitable explosion. When it didn't happen, she relaxed slightly.

Hold, she told the Soft Blade, and reached between the wires. She placed her fingers over the door's locking mechanism and drove the suit *into* the door. Metal screeched, and there was a sticky, tearing sound as the seal around the door parted.

The warbling whine of a siren seeped in through the gap.

Feeling as if she were trying to pet a sleeping tigermaul without waking it, Kira slowly pushed the door outward.

It swung open with a protesting squeal, but it *did* open.

She almost laughed. No boom.

Then Kira stepped forward. The wires warped around her as she passed through the doorway, and though the lines of electricity bent, they never broke.

Freedom!

The concourse had become a garish nightmare. Emergency lights painted the walls red, while rows of yellow arrows glowed in the floor and the ceiling. The arrows pointed spinward, and she knew if she followed them, they would lead her to the nearest storm shelter.

Now what?

"Don't move!" shouted a man. "Hands on your head!"

Kira turned and saw two power troopers standing by a pillar over nine meters to her right. One of them held a blaster, the other a slug thrower. Behind them, a quartet of drones rose off the floor and hung whirring overhead.

"You've got five seconds to comply or I'm putting a bolt through your head!" shouted the trooper with the blaster.

Kira lifted her arms and took a single step away from her cell. Two thin tendrils still connected her to the bypass circuits the suit had formed across the doorway.

The troopers stiffened, and the buzzing from the drones increased as the machines flew out and took up positions in a broad, rotating circle around her.

She took another step.

Bang!

A gold slug flattened itself on the deck in front of her, and she felt a pinch in her left calf as a fragment struck her.

"I'm not shitting you, lady! We *will* ventilate you! On the floor, right now! I'm not saying it a—"

"Don't be stupid," she said in a sharp voice. "You're not going to shoot me, Marine. Do you know how much trouble you'd be in with Colonel Stahl if you did? The UMC lost a lot of good people getting me here."

"Fuck that noise. We've got orders to stop you if you try to escape, even if it means killing you. Now get on the goddamn floor!"

"Okay. Okay."

Kira did the math. She was only about a meter and a half from the cell. Hopefully that was enough . . .

She bent, as if to kneel, and then tucked and allowed herself to stumble forward into a roll. As she did, she yanked the wires out of the cell, back toward herself.

A white-hot flash obliterated her sight, and a thunderclap slammed into her so hard, she felt it in the roots of her teeth.

2.

If not for her suit, the blast would have thrown Kira halfway across the concourse. As it was, the xeno kept her anchored against the deck, like a barnacle holding firm against a tsunami. A suffocating heat enveloped her—a heat too intense for even the Soft Blade to fully protect her.

Then cooler air washed over her and her vision cleared.

Dazed, Kira got to her feet.

The explosion had torn apart several meters of the floor, leaving behind a crater of crushed decking, wiring, pipes, and unidentifiable pieces of machinery. In the center of the crater was the misshapen, half-melted lump of metal and composite that had been the polyhedron.

Shrapnel had sprayed the ceiling and floor in a wide circle around the epicenter. A jagged piece of casing from one of the shaped charges had embedded itself into the deck only a few centimeters from her head.

Kira hadn't expected the explosion to be so powerful. The UMC must have *really* wanted to stop the Soft Blade from escaping. The charges had been intended not just to kill but to obliterate.

She had to find Itari.

Off to the side, the two Marines lay sprawled on the floor. One of them moved his arms aimlessly, as if unsure which direction was up. The other had gotten to his hands and knees and was crawling toward his blaster.

Three of the drones lay broken on the floor. The fourth hovered tilted at an awkward angle, its blades rotating in fitful starts.

Kira stabbed the drone with a blade the xeno formed from the hand it had made for her. The ruined machine crashed to the floor with a pitiful whine as its propellers spun to a stop.

Then she sprinted across the concourse and tackled the Marine reaching for his blaster. She knocked him sprawling onto his belly. Before the man could react, she jammed the Soft Blade into the joints of his armor and cut the power lines, immobilizing him. The armor weighed a ton (more than that, actually), but she flipped him over, planted a palm on his faceplate, and ripped it away.

"—answer me, dammit!" the man shouted. Then he clamped his mouth shut and glared at her with fear disguised as anger. His eyes were green, and he looked about as young as Trig, although that meant nothing on its own.

So. Comms weren't working. That was to her advantage. Still, Kira hesitated for a second. Escaping the cell had been a spur-of-the-moment decision, but now the reality of the situation crashed down upon her. There was no hiding on a space station. No avoiding the ever-present cameras. The UMC would be able to track her every move. And though comms were down, as soon as she asked the Marine about Itari, he would know where she wanted to go.

The man saw her indecision. "Well?" he said, sneering. "What the fuck are you waiting for? Get it over with."

He thinks I'm going to kill him. The realization seemed so unjust, it left Kira feeling defensive.

The station lurched underneath them, and a pressure alert sounded with strident urgency in the distance.

"Listen to me," she said, "I'm trying to help you, asshole."

"Sure you are."

"Shut up and listen. We're being attacked. Might be the nightmares. Might be the Jellies. Doesn't matter. Either way, if they blow us up, it's game over. That's it. We lose. You get it?"

"Bull*shit,*" said the Marine, spitting in her face. "Admiral Klein just set out with the Seventh to kick those sumbitches back to the Stone Age. He'll see they get what's coming to them."

"You don't understand, Marine. The Jelly that came here with me on the *Wallfish*—the one you've got locked up—it came here with a peace offer. *Peace.* If it dies, how do you think the rest of the Jellies will take it? How do you think the *Premier* will take it?" Now Kira saw indecision similar to her own appear on the man's face. "That Jelly gets blown up, it isn't going to matter *what* the Seventh does. You understand? How long do you think this station is going to last?"

As if to punctuate her question, everything twisted around them as Orsted wobbled even more than before.

Kira swallowed a surge of bile, feeling green. "We *have* to get that Jelly out of here."

The Marine squeezed his eyes shut for a moment. Then he shook his head—making a face as if he were in pain—and said, "Goddammit. Biocontainment. That's where they took the Jelly. Biocontainment."

"Where i—"

"This deck. Up-spin. By the hydroponics bay."

"And what about the *Wallfish* crew?"

"Holding cells. Same section. Can't miss it."

Kira shoved him back and stood. "Okay. You made the right decision."

He spat again, this time on the floor. "You betray us, I'll come kill you myself."

"I'd expect nothing less," said Kira, already moving away. It would take him at least half an hour to extricate himself from the power armor, so she figured he wasn't a threat. The other Marine, though, was starting to move. She hurried over, grabbed the top of his helmet, pulled open the casing on his back, and ripped out his armor's cooling system. The armor immediately shut down to avoid melting.

There. Just let them try to follow her now!

Kira left them and started to run up-spin, against the direction of the yellow arrows. *Hide me,* she told the Soft Blade. A soft, silk-like rustle passed across her skin, and when she glanced down, Kira could see through herself, as if her body had turned to glass.

Thermals would still pick her up, but she didn't think it likely the station's interior cameras were full-spectrum. Either way, it would at least be harder for the UMC to spot her like this. How long until troops arrived to investigate the implosion of her cell? Not long, she thought. Not long at all, even if Orsted Station *was* under attack.

Through the concourse exit was a long hallway. Empty. Everyone was either in hiding, helping emergency services, or fighting the attackers. Whatever the reasons, Kira was grateful. She really didn't want to fight a bunch of Marines. They were on the same side after all. Or they were supposed to be.

Down the hallway she ran, avoiding the occasional moving walkway. She was faster on foot. The whole time, she looked for lettering on the walls that might indicate the location of the hydroponics bay. Most people just used their overlays to navigate, but legally, every ship and station had to have clearly marked signage in the case of emergencies.

This sure as hell qualifies as an emergency, Kira thought. Legal requirements or not, the lettering she did see was small, faint, and hard to read, which kept forcing her to slow in order to decipher it.

At one intersection between the hall and another passageway, she jogged around a fountain where the stream of water traced two-thirds of an infinity symbol as it rose and fell. It was a small thing, but the sight fascinated Kira in an obscure way. The Coriolis effect never failed to mess with her sense of how gravity (or the appearance of gravity) should work. She supposed she wouldn't find anything strange about it if she had grown up in a hab-ring, especially a smaller one like Orsted's.

She must have run almost half a klick, and she was starting to wonder whether the Marine had lied to her and she should turn back, when she spotted two lines of faint green lettering on a nearby corner.

The upper line said: *Hydroponics Bay 7G*

The bottom line said: *Detention 16G*

On the other side of the hallway was another set of lettering: *Biocontainment & Decontamination 21G.* Down that way, Kira saw what appeared to be a security checkpoint: a closed door flanked with armored portals and a pair of viewscreens. Two Marines in full exos stood watch outside the door. Even with the station under attack, they hadn't left their post. Kira wouldn't be surprised if there were more of them on the other side of the door.

She did the math. She might be able to get close enough to disable the armor of the two Marines, but anyone past that would be a challenge. And as soon as she broke Itari out, the rest of the UMC would know where she was.

Shit. If she attacked, there was no predicting what would happen next. Events would spin out of control in a shockingly short time, and then . . . and then a lot of people might end up dead.

A faint tremor passed through the deck. Whatever she was going to do, she had to do it now. Any longer and the station itself might spin out of control.

She growled and turned away from biocontainment. Fuck it. She needed help. If she could free the crew of the *Wallfish,* she knew they would have her back. Maybe, together, they could figure out a solution. Maybe.

Kira's pulse was loud in her ears as she hurried down the side corridor that led toward the holding cells. If there was as much security around detention as biocontainment, she wasn't sure *what* she would do. The temptation to let loose with the Soft Blade was strong, but Kira had more than learned her lesson. No matter what, she couldn't make another mistake like the one that had resulted in the creation of the nightmares. The galaxy wouldn't survive it.

The lettering on the walls led her through several lengths of identical hallway.

As she rounded one more corner, she spotted two people—one man, one woman—kneeling next to a pressure door halfway down the corridor, wrist deep in a hatch they'd pried open in the wall, the actinic flicker of electricity lighting their faces. The pair was shirtless, pantless, wearing only drab grey shorts. Their skin was chalk white, and everywhere but their faces was covered with gleaming blue tattoos. The lines formed circuit-like patterns that reminded Kira of the shapes she'd seen in the cradle on Adrasteia.

Because of their lack of clothes, it took her a moment to recognize the two people as the Entropists, Veera and Jorrus.

She was still invisible and too far away to hear, and yet somehow the Entropists detected her. Never looking her direction, Jorrus said, "Ah, Prisoner Navárez—"

"—you were able to join us. We—"

"—hoped as much."

Then the Entropists wrenched something within the wall, and the pressure door snapped open to reveal a stark holding cell.

Falconi stepped out. "Well, about time," he said.

3.

Kira allowed her invisibility to subside, and Falconi spotted her. "There you are," he said. "I was afraid we were going to have to go hunting for you."

"Nope," she said. She trotted over. The Entropists had moved on to the next door.

"Were you locked up too?" Falconi asked.

She jerked her chin. "You know it."

"Don't suppose you got free without being noticed?"

"Not a chance."

He bared his teeth. "Shit. We gotta move fast."

"How did you manage to escape?" she asked.

Veera laughed, a quick, high sound, full of tension. "Always they take the robes and think—"

"—that is enough. We are more than our many-colored garments, Prisoner."

Falconi grunted. "Lucky for us." To Kira he said, "Any idea who's hitting the station?"

She was about to say no, but then she stopped to think for a moment. No hint existed of the compulsion she always felt when the Jelly ships were near. Which meant . . . "Pretty sure it's the nightmares," she said.

"Great. Even more reason to move fast. There'll be plenty of confusion to cover our departure."

"Are you sure?" Kira said.

Falconi caught her meaning at once. If he and the rest of the crew broke out, their pardons would be null and void, and unlike the local government at Ruslan, the UMC wouldn't stop pursuing them at the system border. The *Wallfish* crew would be fugitives throughout the entirety of known space, with the possible exception of Shin-Zar and various tiny freeholdings out on the fringes.

"You're damn right I am," he said, and Kira felt an immediate glow of comradery. At least she wouldn't be alone. "Veera. Jorrus. Have you managed to get a line open to Gregorovich yet?"

The Entropists shook their heads. They were still fiddling with the wiring in the wall alongside the next pressure door. "Access to the station's system is restricted and—"

"—we do not have transmitters powerful enough to reach the *Wallfish* through all these walls."

"Shit," said Falconi.

"Where's security?" said Kira. She'd expected to find a whole squad of Marines stationed by the holding cells.

Falconi jerked his chin toward the Entropists. "Not sure. Those two hacked the cameras to buy us time. We've got about five minutes before the station control gets eyes on us again."

Veera held up a finger without taking her attention from the inside of the hatch. "We may be able to spoof the—"

"—station's sensors and buy us some more time," said Jorrus.

Falconi grunted again. "See what you can do. . . . Can't you get that blasted door open?"

"Trying, Captain," they said.

"Let me," Kira said. She raised her right hand, letting the Soft Blade fuse its replica of her fingers into blades and spikes.

"Careful," said Falconi. "There could be pressure lines or high-voltage wires in the wall."

"It should not be—"

"—a concern," said the Entropists, and moved aside.

Kira moved forward, glad to finally be doing *something.* She slammed her fist into the metal and willed the Soft Blade outward. It spread across the surface of the wall, sending seeking tendrils deep within the mechanism holding the door closed. Then she pulled, and with a screech, the bolts snapped and the door slid back on its greased track.

Inside was a small holding cell. Sparrow stood half-crouched in front of the bunk, as if ready to fight. "Thule," she said as she saw Kira. "Glad you're on our side."

Falconi snapped his fingers. "Perimeter watch, now."

"Roger," said the woman, hurrying out of the cell. She trotted down the corridor and peeked around the corner.

"Over there!" Falconi said to Kira, pointing at another pressure door. Kira went to the second door and, like the first, ripped it open. Inside, Hwa-jung rose from where she'd been sitting. "Fighting!" the machine boss said, and smiled.

"Fighting," said Kira.

"This one!" said Falconi.

Another door and another screech revealed Nielsen. She gave Kira a quick nod and went to stand with Falconi.

Last of all, Kira broke into the cell containing Vishal. He appeared somewhat haggard, but he smiled at her and said, "How delightful." Further relief broke across his face as he came out and saw Nielsen and the others.

Falconi returned to the Entropists. "Have you found him yet?"

There was a silence that made Kira want to scream with impatience.

Jorrus said, "Uncertain, but it seems that—"

"—they've left Trig in stasis on the *Wallfish*."

"Falconi," said Kira, lowering her voice. "We have to rescue the Jelly. If we can't get it out of here, there's a chance none of this will matter."

He stared at her, his glacial eyes focused, searching, nearly devoid of emotion, though she could tell that he—like her—was concerned. So concerned that no room for panic existed.

"You sure?" he said, deadly quiet.

"I'm sure."

With that, she saw the switch flip inside him. His expression hardened, and a deadly gleam appeared in his eyes. "Sparrow," he said.

"Yessir."

"We need to jailbreak a Jelly and then somehow get off this hunk of metal. Give me options."

For a moment, Sparrow looked as if she were going to argue. Then, like Falconi, she seemed to put aside her objections and concentrate only on the problem at hand.

"We could try cutting the power to biocontainment," said Nielsen, coming over.

Sparrow shook her head. "Won't work. It has its own backup power sources." While she spoke, she knelt and pulled up the right leg of her pants. Then she dug her fingers into the skin over her shin, and to Kira's puzzlement, lifted it off to reveal a small compartment underneath, embedded within the bone. "Pays to be prepared," said Sparrow in response to Kira's look.

From the compartment Sparrow produced a narrow, thin-bladed knife of some glassy, non-metallic material, a black wire mesh that she pulled over her hands like a set of gloves, and three small marbles that appeared soft, almost fleshy.

"Someday you're going to have to explain that," said Falconi, gesturing toward Sparrow's shin.

"Someday," the short-haired woman agreed, covering up the compartment and standing. "But not today." To Kira she said, "What did you see over at biocontainment?" Kira described the security checkpoint and the two Marines stationed outside. A faint smile crossed Sparrow's face. "Right, here's what we do." She snapped her fingers and beckoned for Veera to come over. "You, Entropist, when I give the signal, I want you to walk over to where the Marines can see you."

"Is that—"

"Just do it. Kira—"

"I can hide myself," Kira quickly said. She explained.

Sparrow jerked her sharp chin. "That makes it easier. I'll take care of the two standing guard. You be ready to jump anyone who comes out. Get it?"

"Got it."

"Good. Let's hustle."

4.

Kira willed herself back to invisibility while she hid with Sparrow in the hall that opened on the central corridor.

"Nice trick, that," Sparrow said under her breath.

Ahead of them, Veera walked out across the intersection, heading toward biocontainment. The Entropist was more voluptuous than she had appeared when garbed in her gradient robes, and the tattoos across her pale skin only enhanced the impression. The sight was rather distracting, which—Kira had to admit—was the point.

"Go," said Sparrow. She darted out and to the side, avoiding the Marines' line of sight.

Kira broke in the opposite direction, and the two of them flanked Veera and took up positions on opposite sides of the passageway that led to biocontainment.

Just as Veera reached the doorway, the Marines spotted her. Kira heard the heavy treads as their armor turned, and a man said with a tone of obvious confusion, "Hey, you! What the—"

He never finished. Sparrow reached around the corner and tossed the fleshy marbles toward the Marines. Three quick *bzzts!* sounded as the Marines' exos shot the marbles out of the air.

That was a mistake.

A triple strobe of light flashed the hall, smoke clogged the air, and with her enhanced vision from the Soft Blade, Kira saw flickers of violet EM energy. *What the hell?*

Sparrow didn't wait. She sprinted around the corner and disappeared into the smoke. Metallic screeches sounded, and then a moment later, two enormous *thuds* as the exos crashed to the deck, immobilized.

Kira followed a half step behind. Switching her vision to infrared, she saw the door to biocontainment roll open. Another Marine in power armor stepped out, blaster raised to fire. Behind him or her, she saw three more Marines scrambling to take cover behind desks.

Even with all the sensors of a military-grade exo, the Marine in the doorway never saw her coming. She slammed into his power armor while driving a hundred different fibers from the Soft Blade into the machine. It took her only a fraction of a second to find the weak spots and disable the exo.

The Marine's armor locked up and began to fall. Kira pulled it to the side, landed inside biocontainment, and rolled across her shoulders and back to her feet. None of the Marines inside were able to triangulate her exact location, but that didn't stop them from firing blindly toward the spot she'd been.

Too slow. A laser blast seared a hole through the back of a chair next to her, but Kira was already moving, throwing tendrils across the room and snaring each of the Marines.

Don't kill, she told the Soft Blade, hoping against hope it would heed.

A clutch of heartbeats later, and the other Marines dropped to the floor. The weight of their armor crushed tables, smashed shelves, and dented the deck.

"Get 'em all?" Sparrow asked, poking her head in.

Kira allowed her invisibility to fade and nodded. Deeper into the room was another door leading to what she recognized as an impressively large decon chamber. Past *that* was a third pressure door, which she assumed opened to the isolation chamber where Itari was being held.

"Watch my back," she said.

"Roger."

It might have been possible to get the access codes off the Marines, but Kira saw no point in wasting time. Hurrying forward, she extended her arms and allowed the Soft Blade to flow out and rip open the decon door.

At the other end of the chamber, she saw Itari through the pressure door window. The Jelly was sitting with its tentacles curled underneath it, like the legs of a dead spider.

A flash of relief passed through Kira. At least they were in the right place.

She set herself against the pressure door and again allowed the Soft Blade to worm its way into the mechanism and then to *tear.*

Clank. The lock broke. Pulling and pushing with the xeno, Kira rolled the door back.

A questioning scent reached her from the Jelly as it unfurled its tentacles. [[Itari here: Idealis?]]

[[Kira here: If you truly want peace, we must leave this place.]]

[[Itari here: Are these two-forms our enemies?]]

[[Kira here: No, but they do not know better. Do not kill them, I ask you. But do not let yourself be killed either.]]

[[Itari here: As you will, Idealis.]]

Kira left to rejoin the others outside biocontainment, and she heard Itari follow with a dry-leaf shuffle of tentacles.

"We good?" Falconi asked as she, Sparrow, and Itari emerged from the smoke. Veera had found a jacket somewhere in the biocontainment offices and was pulling it on, covering herself.

"Yup," said Sparrow. "Boobs, works every time. Everyone falls for them."

"Let's get the hell out of here," said Kira.

Orsted rumbled around them, and Vishal said, "Heavens preserve us, yes."

"Veera! Jorrus!" said Falconi.

"Yessir?"

"Still nothing from Gregorovich?"

"Nothing."

"Jamming?"

"No. They have him in lockdown."

"He'll be fighting mad," said Hwa-jung.

"Good. We can use that," said Falconi. He rounded on the rest of them. "Right. We'll go up the main passage. Anyone shows up, break right, take cover. Don't let 'em use you as hostages. Kira, you'll have to deal with any opposition. None of us have weapons."

"Speak for yourself," said Sparrow. She held up her right hand. The glass-like dagger glinted between her fingers.

Kira gestured at the fallen Marines. "What about—"

"No good," said Falconi. "They're locked. Civvies can't use UMC weapons. Not without authorization. Enough yapping. Let's—"

With a dull *thunk,* pressure doors slammed shut around the intersection, closing off the corridor everywhere but the direction Kira had originally come from. There, she heard the thunder of approaching power armor, and then twenty or more Marines trotted into view, carrying blasters, railguns, and heavy turrets. A small cloud of wasp-like drones accompanied them.

"Freeze! Don't move!" shouted an amplified voice.

5.

Kira and the others, including the Jelly, retreated into the hall leading to biocontainment and hid behind the corners of the doorway.

The voice rang out again: "We know you're trying to rescue the Jelly, Navárez. Private Larrett told us everything."

Kira guessed Larrett was the Marine she'd talked to outside her imploded cell. "Bastard," she muttered.

"Unless anyone has any ideas, we're shit out of luck," said Falconi, his face grim.

Then Stahl spoke from the speakers embedded within the glowing ceiling, loud enough to cut through the alarms. "Kira, you don't want to do this. Fighting isn't going to help anyone, least of all you. Stand down, tell the Jelly to return to its cell, and no one has to—"

The deck rumbled and twisted underneath them again.

Kira didn't hesitate. She *had* to do something.

She jumped into the corridor and sent a score of shafts out from her chest and legs. They angled forward and downward, and pierced the deck in different spots.

Don't lose control. Don't—

Her ears rang as a bullet skipped off her head, and she felt what were like several punches to her ribs, directly above her heart. Then she pulled the shafts inward, tearing up large chunks of the deck.

At her command, the Soft Blade slammed the pieces of decking together, layering them like scales to form a tall, wedge-shaped shield in front of her.

Finger-sized holes—white-hot around the edges and dripping molten metal—peppered the shield as the angry *bzzt!* of laser fire sounded throughout the concourse.

Kira took a step forward, and the Soft Blade moved the shield with her. As she did, she reached out farther with the suit and grabbed more pieces of the deck, adding them to the barrier, thickening it, widening it.

"With me!" she shouted, and the crew and the Jelly scurried after her.

"Right behind you!" said Falconi.

Bullets whined overhead, and then an explosion shook the shield, and Kira felt the impact through her body.

"Grenade!" shouted Sparrow.

[[Itari here: Can I help, Idealis?]]

[[Kira here: Do not kill anyone if you can avoid it, and do not get in front of me.]]

A pair of drones appeared around the edge of the shield. Kira lanced them with two quick stabs and continued plodding forward. The floor was a tattered mess of twisted girders and exposed pipes; it was difficult to keep her footing.

"Just get us to the terminal!" Falconi said.

Kira nodded, barely paying attention. Even though she couldn't see what was in front of her, she kept using the suit to grab decking, panels off the wall, benches—any and everything she could use to protect them. She didn't know how much weight the suit could move or support, but she was determined to find out.

Another grenade hit the shield. That one she barely felt.

Several of the suit's tentacles encountered something long and smooth and warm (very warm, burning hot even; if she'd touched it with bare flesh, she suspected it would have seared a hole right through her skin): one of the laser turrets. That too she added to the pile, tearing the weapon free from the floor and jamming it into the gap between two benches.

"More drones!" said Vishal.

Before he'd finished speaking, Kira created a web of struts and rods (some metal, some made from the suit itself) between the shield, the ceiling, and the distant walls. In several places, she felt and heard the drones collide with the barrier; the tone of their blades increased from the strain.

She flinched as grenades blew open a hole in the web.

"Jesus!" shouted Falconi.

The drones swung toward the hole. One of them darted through, and Itari smacked it out of the air with a well-timed swing of a tentacle. Before the rest could make it past, and before they could find an angle that would allow them to shoot any of the crew, Kira snared the machines out of the air—like a frog snapping up flies—and crushed them.

All of them.

She could feel the suit growing in size, reinforcing itself with metal and carbon and whatever else it needed from the structure of the station. Her arms seemed thicker, her legs too, and a sense of power coursed through her; she felt as if she could claw her way through solid rock.

The gunfire subsided as the Marines in front of her stopped shooting and started to run back along the concourse, their heavy steps pounding a rapid beat.

Kira bared her teeth. So they'd realized it was pointless to fight. Good. Now if she could just get everyone safely to the *Wallfish,* then—

She heard, not saw, the pressure door in front of them slam shut. Then the one beyond it, and so forth and so on down the concourse.

"Shit!" said Nielsen. "They've locked us in."

"Stay with me!" said Kira.

She continued forward until she felt her shield bump into the pressure door. The door itself was too large and heavy to cut through in a reasonable amount of time, but the frame around it wasn't. It took her and the Soft Blade only a few moments of work before the door toppled outward and crashed with deafening results against the deck.

Ten meters down the corridor, the next blast door blocked their way.

Kira repeated the procedure, and the second door soon followed the example of the first. Then a third. . . . And a fourth.

All of the doors ahead of them seemed to be closed. It wasn't stopping them, but it did slow Kira down. "The UMC is trying to buy themselves time," Falconi said to her.

She grunted. "Bet they're preparing a nice welcome party for us at the terminal." A loud hissing sounded near the walls. The back of her neck prickled with alarm. Was the air being pumped out or was something being pumped *in*?

"Gas!" Falconi shouted, and pulled the collar of his shirt over his mouth and nose. The others did the same. The cloth molded to their faces, forming skin-tight filters. The Entropists made arcane gestures with their hands, and the lines of their tattoos slid across their faces, forming a paper-thin membrane that covered their mouths and noses.

Kira was impressed. Nanotech of the highest order.

She knew the instant she broke through to the last section of concourse—the one adjacent to the terminal—as a heavy barrage of bullets, laser blasts, railgun projectiles, and explosives pounded into the barrier she'd built. The impacts rocked her back, but she set her shoulder and pressed forward with deliberate steps.

A third of the way through the concourse section, Falconi tapped her shoulder and said, "Right! Go right!" He pointed toward the terminal entrance.

As Kira started to edge in that direction, the pipes under her feet shook, and she heard a sound like an oncoming avalanche as the Marines charged.

With less than a second to prepare, she wrenched several of the floor girders upward, so they supported the inside of the shield and prevented it from sliding backwards.

"Brace!" she shouted.

Thick as it was, the shield bent and gave as the troopers slammed into it with their power armor. There was a terrible screeching as the soldiers began to tear away pieces of the shield.

"Gotcha," said Kira, baring her teeth.

She willed hundreds of hairlike fibers through the bulk of the shield, through all the little nooks and crannies and hidden crevices until, sightless creeping, they found the smooth shells of the troopers' armor. Then she did as she had done before. She sent the fibers boring into the joints and seams of the armor, and she cut every wire and coolant line she could find, stopping only when she encountered the touch of overheated flesh.

It was an effort to stop, but the Soft Blade obeyed her will and respected the boundaries of flesh. Her confidence swelled.

On the other side of the shield, the screeching stopped, and the troopers collapsed with a sound fitting the fall of titans.

"Did you kill them?" asked Nielsen, her voice sounding too loud in the sudden silence.

Kira licked her lips. "No." Talking felt weird. The shield seemed to occupy a larger part of herself than her own body. She could sense every square centimeter of the barrier. The amount of information was overwhelming. Was the experience similar to what ship minds had to deal with? She wondered.

She was about to detach herself from the shield when more boots sounded ahead of them, at the other end of the concourse.

Before Kira could react, the lights flickered and went out, save for small emergency floods along the floor, and the deck rippled like a wave, causing everyone but Kira and Itari to stagger and fall.

An industrial crash of crumpling metal echoed through the concourse, and a dark dart of veined hull punched through the decking farther up the main hallway, past the newly arrived Marines. Pressure alarms shrieked, and from a weeping cleft in the side of the intruding spaceship poured dozens of scrambling nightmares.

The heavy chatter of cycling machine guns filled the air, along with the electric snap of discharging lasers as the Marines engaged the grotesque invaders.

"*Shi-bal!*" cried Hwa-jung.

Kira shouted and drove the shield forward, plowing past the limp weight of the troops she'd incapacitated. If the nightmares realized who and what she was, they'd all converge on her. She half trotted, half walked the shield across the floor, and for the moment, she stopped adding material to it, her only concern to escape.

She turned, pivoting the shield around Falconi and the others so her back was to the concourse exit and the terminal beyond. Then she retreated, step by step, until the edges of the shield banged into the wall on either side of the doorway.

Moving quickly, she pulled the shield in toward herself, collapsing it into a dense cap over the doorway. She secured it to the floor, ceiling, and walls with twisted pieces of metal, making it so the only practical way to remove it would be by cutting.

Falconi pounded her on the shoulder. "Leave it!" he shouted.

A *boom* echoed through the terminal as a grenade detonated on the other side of the barrier. A moment later, Marines began to bang on it, producing a muffled din.

The shield would hold, but not for very long.

Kira extricated the suit from the material, and as she did, she felt diminished, reduced to her normal sense of size.

Whirling around, she saw the others had already crossed the small terminal and were forcing open the doors to a maglev car.

From the ceiling came a man's voice: "This is Udo Grammaticus, stationmaster of this installation. Cease resisting, and I guarantee you won't be harmed. This is your final warning. There are twenty power troopers outside your—"

He kept talking, but Kira tuned him out. She jogged over to the maglev car as Falconi said, "Can we use it?"

"Aside from the lights, all power's been cut," said Hwa-jung.

"So we can't leave?" said Nielsen.

Hwa-jung grunted. "Not like this. Maglev won't work."

"There must be another way into the docking ring," said Vishal.

"How?" said Sparrow. "We're moving waaay too fast to just jump over. Maybe Kira or the Jelly could make it, but the rest of us would get turned into a bloody smear. It's a fucking dead end."

Outside the shield, gunfire continued to erupt: dull *thumps* that came in controlled bursts as the Marines fought back the nightmares. Or so Kira assumed.

"Yes, thank you," Falconi said in a dry tone. He turned back to Hwa-jung. "You're the engineer. Any ideas?" He glanced at the Entropists. "How about you?"

Veera and Jorrus spread their hands in a gesture of helplessness. "Mechanics—"

"—are not our specialty."

"Don't give me that. There has to be a way to get us from here to there without killing us."

The machine boss frowned. "Of course there is, if we had enough time and materials."

Another *boom* sounded in the concourse.

"No such luck," said Falconi. "Come on, anything. Doesn't matter how far-fetched. Be *creative,* Ms. Song. That's what I hired you for."

Hwa-jung's frown deepened, and for a moment she was silent. Then, she muttered, *"Aigoo,"* and scrambled into the maglev car. She ran her hands over the floor, rapping it with her knuckles in different places. Then she waved Kira over and said, "Here. Open the floor here." And she traced a square on the floor. "Be careful. Just remove the top layer. Don't damage anything underneath."

"Got it."

Kira retraced the square with her index finger, and the tip of her nail scored the grey composite. She repeated the motion, increasing the pressure, and a thin, diamond-like blade extended from her finger and sliced through the first centimeter or so of material. Then she gripped the square—bonding it to her palm as if with gecko pads—and pulled it free from the rest of the floor, like snapping a cracker along pre-established lines.

Hwa-jung got down onto her hands and knees as she peered into the hole, studying the wires and banks of equipment within. Kira had no idea what any of them were for, but Hwa-jung seemed to understand what she was looking at.

The banging outside the terminal intensified. Kira glanced back at the shield. It was beginning to dent inward. Another minute and she figured she would have to go reinforce it.

Hwa-jung made a sound in the back of her throat and then stood. "I can move the car, but I need a power source."

"Can't you—" Falconi started to say.

"No," said Hwa-jung. "Without power, it is a no-good stupid rock. I can't do anything with it."

Kira looked over at the Jelly. [[Kira here: Can you fix this machine?]]

[[Itari here: I have no energy source that would work.]]

"What about a set of power armor?" asked Nielsen. "Would that do the trick?"

Hwa-jung shook her head. "Enough power, yes, but it wouldn't be compatible."

"Could you use a laser turret?" Kira asked.

The machine boss hesitated, then nodded. "Maybe. If the capacitors can be set to—"

Kira didn't wait to hear the rest. She jumped out of the car and sprinted back to the makeshift barrier. As she reached it, the banging stopped, which worried her, but she wasn't going to complain.

Extending the suit in dozens of wriggling tentacles, she rooted through the mangled plug of scraps, searching for the turret she'd buried within the mass. It wasn't long before she found it: a smooth, hard piece of metal, still warm from being fired. Moving as fast as she dared, she bent and pressed the parts of the shield until she created a tunnel just large enough to pull the turret through—all the while struggling to maintain the structural integrity of the shield and keep the front of it a solid, unmoving face.

"Faster, please!" said Falconi.

"What do you think I'm doing?" she shouted.

The turret came free, and she caught it in her hands. Cradling it like a live bomb, she hurried back to the car and handed the weapon to Hwa-jung.

Sparrow tapped her glass-like knife against her thigh as she glanced around. Then she grabbed Kira by the arm and dragged her a few steps away.

"What?" said Kira.

In a low voice, tight with tension, Sparrow said, "Those grease-heads are going to blast their way in through the ceiling or the walls. Guarantee it. You'd better work up some kinda fortification shit, or we're goners."

"On it."

Sparrow nodded and returned to the car, where Vishal was helping Hwa-jung take apart the turret.

"Everyone stay back!" Kira said. Then she faced the cramped terminal and, as in the concourse, sent forth dozens of lines from the Soft Blade, allowing it to do what was needed. A painfully loud din assaulted her as the xeno started to dismantle the floor, walls, and ceiling. She drew the pieces closer and, fast as she could, began to assemble them into a dome around the front of the maglev docking port.

As the chunks crashed into place, she could feel her sense of self expanding again. It was intoxicating. She distrusted the feeling—distrusted both herself and the Soft Blade—but the lure of *more* was seductive, and the ease with which she and the xeno were working together bolstered her confidence.

One of the panels she yanked free must have contained the intercom speaker, because she heard sparks, and then the stationmaster's voice cut out.

Meter by meter, she stripped the terminal, exposing Orsted's underlying skeleton of cross-joined beams, anodized against corrosion and riddled with holes to save on weight.

Soon she couldn't see anything but the inside of the dome, and still she kept adding to it. Darkness enveloped them, and from the car, Vishal called, "You're not making this easy, Ms. Navárez!"

"It's that or getting shot!" she shouted back.

A blast shook the terminal.

"Time to get this show on the road," said Falconi.

"I'm working on it," said Hwa-jung.

Kira extended herself even farther, stretching to the limits of her reach and finding she could reach yet farther still. Consciousness thinned, spread over a greater and greater area, and the amount of input became disorienting: pressures and scrapes here, pipes there, wires above and below, the tickle of electrical discharges, heat and cold and a thousand different impressions from a thousand different points along the Soft Blade, and all of them squirming, changing, expanding, and inundating her with ever more sensations.

It was too much. She couldn't oversee it all, couldn't keep up. In places, her supervision failed, and where it failed, the Soft Blade acted of its own, moving forward with deadly intent. Kira felt her mind fragmenting as she tried to focus first on one place, then another, then another, and each time quickly bringing the suit back to heel, but while she was occupied, it continued to swarm elsewhere, growing . . . building . . . *becoming.*

She was drowning, disappearing into the expanding existence of the Soft Blade. Panic sparked within her, but the spark was too feeble to rein in the suit. A sense of pleasure emanated from the Soft Blade at finally being let loose to pursue its purpose; from it Kira had flashes of . . . *yellow fields with flowers that sang* . . . memories that . . . *a treelike growth with metal scales for bark* . . . disoriented her further, made it almost . . . *a group of long, furry creatures that yipped at her from between brindled mandibles* . . . impossible to concentrate.

In a brief shard of lucidity, the horror of the situation struck Kira. What had she done?

With ears not her own, she heard a sound like doom itself: the measured tramp of armored soldiers marching into the outer part of the terminal. Discomfort, sharp and piercing, disturbed several grasping pseudopods. Startled, she/they retracted.

Attack her/it, would they?

Walls and beams and structural supports crumpled beneath her/their grasp as they collapsed the station in around the shield. The deck buckled, but it didn't matter. Only finding more mass: more metals, more minerals, more, more, *more.* A hunger formed inside her/it, an insatiable, world-eating *hunger.*

"Kira!"

The voice sounded as if from the far end of a tunnel. Whoever they were, she/it didn't recognize the person. Or maybe she/it didn't care to. There were other, more important things that needed her/its attention.

"Kira!" At a remove, she/it felt hands and shaking and pulling. None of which, of course, could budge her/it from place: her/their cords of banded fibers were too strong. *"Kira!"* Pain shot through her/its face, but it was so slight and distant as to be easily ignored.

The pain appeared again. And then a third time.

Anger formed in some part of her/itself. She/it looked inward from every direction, with eyes above and eyes below and eyes still made of flesh, and with them beheld a man standing next to her, red-faced and shouting.

He slapped her across the face.

The shock of it was enough to clear Kira's mind for a moment. She gasped, and Falconi said, "Snap out of it! You're going to kill us all!"

She could already feel herself slipping back into the morass of the Soft Blade. "Hit me again," she said.

He hesitated and then did.

Kira's vision flashed red, but the bright sting on her cheek gave her something outside of the Soft Blade to focus on and help center herself. It was a struggle; gathering the different parts of her mind back together felt as if she were trying to free herself from a pool of grasping hands—one for each fiber of the suit, and all of them freakishly strong.

Fear gave Kira the motivation she needed. Her pulse soared until she teetered on the brink of passing out. But she didn't, and moment by moment she was able to retreat into herself. At the same time, she recalled the Soft Blade from the surrounding walls and rooms of the station. It fought her at first; it was reluctant to abandon its grand project and surrender what it had already subsumed.

But in the end, it obeyed. The Soft Blade recoiled upon itself, constricting and contracting as it returned to the shape of her body. There was more of it than she needed, and at the thought, ropes of the suit's material shriveled and turned to dust, leaving nothing useful behind.

Falconi started to lift his hand again.

"Wait," said Kira, and he did.

Her hearing was returning to normal; she noticed the whistle of escaping air and pressure alarms sounding in the distance, overriding all other alarms.

"What happened?" said Falconi. She shook her head, still not feeling entirely whole. "You ripped a hole in the hull, nearly spaced us."

Kira glanced up and quailed as she saw—directly above them—a thin, dark rift of space showing through the ruined ceiling and several layers of ruptured decks. Stars spun past the opening, a crazed kaleidoscope of constellations, dizzying in their speed.

"Lost control. Sorry." She coughed.

Something clanged against the outside of the dome.

"Hwa-jung!" he shouted. "We need to be outta here. I mean it!"

"*Aigoo!* Stop bothering me!"

Falconi turned back to Kira. "You good to move?"

"Think so." The Soft Blade's intrusive presence still wormed restless within her mind, but her sense of identity held strong despite.

From the source of the clang, Kira heard a spitting, hissing noise, like something a congested blowtorch would produce. A spot on the inside of the dome began to glow dull red, then yellow, and almost immediately, she felt the temperature in the space increasing.

"What is that?" said Nielsen.

"Shit!" said Sparrow. "The pricks are using a thermal lance!"

"The heat will kill us!" said Vishal.

Falconi gestured. "Everyone in the car!"

"I can stop them!" said Kira, though the thought filled her with fear again. As long as she concentrated upon one area of effort and didn't let the Soft Blade run amuck . . . Even as she spoke, she started ripping up the floor within the dome and slapping the pieces onto the glowing hotspot. Fumes shot out sideways from the sections of composite as they turned red and softened.

"Forget it. We gotta go!" shouted Falconi.

"Just close the doors. I'll buy you some time."

"Stop fucking around and get in the car! That's an order."

[[Itari here: Idealis, we must leave.]] The Jelly was already crammed into the front end of the car, tentacles pressed against the sides.

"No! I can hold them off. Let me know when you're—"

Falconi grabbed her by the shoulders and twisted her toward him. "*Now!* I'm not leaving anyone behind. Comeon!" By the burning light, his blue eyes seemed bright as flaming suns.

At that, Kira relented. She released the dome and allowed him to pull her into the car. Sparrow and Nielsen shoved the maglev door shut; it locked with a loud *click*.

"You trying to get yourself killed?" Falconi growled in Kira's ear. "You're not invincible."

"Yeah, but—"

"Stow it. Hwa-jung, we good to go?"

"Almost, Captain. Almost . . ."

Outside the car, a spray of white-hot metal erupted from the center of the glowing spot as the lance burned its way through the full thickness of the dome. The spray started to move downward, slowly cutting one side of a trooper-sized opening.

"Don't look at it!" said Sparrow. "It's too bright. It'll burn out your retinas."

"Hwa-jung—"

"Ready!" said the machine boss. Kira and everyone else turned to face her. The turret lay in parts between her feet. The power pack had been pried open, and wires led from it into the machinery that filled the car's undercarriage.

"Listen to me," said Hwa-jung. She tapped the power pack. "This is damaged. When I turn it on, it might melt and explode."

"We'll risk it," said Falconi.

"There is more."

"Not really the time for a lecture right now."

"Listen! *Aish!*" Hwa-jung's eyes gleamed with the searing light of the thermal lance. "I was able to splice into the feeds for the electromagnets. This thing will lift us, but that is all. I can't access the directional controls; it won't move us forward or backward."

"Then how—" Nielsen tried to say.

"Kira, you do this: break off a chair for each of us, and then knock out the windows, there and there." Hwa-jung pointed at each side of the car. "When I activate the circuit, you use your suit to pull us forward, and we will coast into the main tube. The supercapacitors only have enough charge to keep us suspended for forty-three seconds. We're going about two hundred and fifty klicks per hour relative to the docking ring. We have to shed as much of that speed as possible before we crash. The way we do that is by sticking the chairs out the windows and pushing them against the walls of the tube. They will act as brakes. Clear?"

Kira nodded along with the others. Outside, the fountain of molten metal vanished for a second as the thermal lance reached the floor. Then it reappeared at the top of the dripping incision and started to make a horizontal cut.

"You will have to push very hard," said Hwa-jung. "As hard as you can. Otherwise the crash will kill us."

Kira grabbed the nearest chair and wrenched it off its gimbaled mount with a hollow *ping*. The next three chairs produced similar sounds. With a quick exchange of scents, she explained what they were doing to Itari, and the Jelly also grabbed a pair of chairs with its coiled limbs.

"This is some shit-crazy plan, Unni," said Sparrow.

Hwa-jung grunted. "It'll work, punk. You'll see."

"Watch your eyes," Kira said. Then she lashed out with the Soft Blade and smashed the windows along both sides of the maglev.

A furnace-blast of heat washed over them from the interior of the half-shell dome. Falconi, Nielsen, Vishal, and the Entropists dropped to the floor, and Falconi said, "Seven hells!"

The thermal lance started its second downward cut.

"Get ready," said Hwa-jung. "Contact in three, two, *one*."

The floor rose a few centimeters underneath Kira. It listed slightly and then stabilized.

Lifting her arms, she launched several ropy strands from her fingers, through the shattered windows, and onto the walls outside. The xeno understood her intent, and they stuck, like lines of spider silk, and she pulled.

The car was heavy, but it slid forward, seemingly without friction. With a soft brushing sound, it passed through the seal at the end of the station and then tilted downward and raced into the dark, rushing tube set within the inner face of the docking ring.

Wind screamed past them. If not for her mask, Kira would have had difficulty seeing or hearing in the ferocious torrent of air. It was cold too, although—again because of the suit—she wasn't sure how cold.

She scooped up one of the loose chairs and stuck it out the nearest window. A horrible screeching split the wind, and a comet's tail of sparks streamed back along the inside of the tube. The impact nearly tore the chair out of her hands, even with the help of the Soft Blade, but she clenched her teeth and tightened her grip and held it in place.

Ahead of her, Itari did the same. Behind her, she was dimly aware of the others staggering to their feet. The screeching worsened as Nielsen, Falconi, Vishal, Sparrow, and the Entropists also pressed their chairs against the wall of the tube. The car rocked and chattered like a jackhammer.

Kira tried to keep track of the seconds, but the noise was too loud, the wind too distracting. It felt as if they weren't slowing down, though. She leaned on the chair even harder, and it squirmed in her hands like living thing.

The tube had already ground through the chair's legs and half of its seat; soon she wouldn't have anything to hold on to.

Slowly—far too slowly—she felt her herself growing lighter, and the soles of her feet started to slip. She fixed herself to the floor via the suit and then slung out lines and secured the others so they could keep pushing and wouldn't drift away.

The screeching lessened, and the banner of sparks grew shorter and fatter, and soon they began to curl and spiral in elaborate patterns instead of flying straight back.

Kira had just begun to think they would make it when the electromagnets cut out.

The car slammed into the outer rail with a yammering shriek that dwarfed the noise of the chairs. The capsule bucked, and the ceiling twisted and tore like taffy being pulled. Itari flew through the front windshield, tentacles flopping, and from the back, there was an electric flash, bright as lightning, and then smoke billowed through the maglev.

With a dwindling whine, they slid to a stop.

6.

Kira's stomach lurched as the sensation of weight vanished, but for once, her gorge didn't rise. That was fine with her. Nausea was the last thing she wanted to deal with right then. Explosions, thermal lances, and maglev crashes. . . She'd had enough for one day. Suit or not, her whole body felt bruised.

Itari! Was the Jelly still alive? Without it, everything they were doing would be pointless.

Moving jerkily, even in zero-g, she released her hold on the car and the crew. Falconi was bleeding from a cut on his temple. He put the heel of his hand to the wound and said, "Everyone okay?"

Vishal groaned and said, "I believe that removed a few years from my life, but yes."

"Yeah," said Sparrow. "Same."

Nielsen brushed bits of glass out of her hair, sending them drifting forward through the destroyed windshield, like a small cloud of crystal motes. "A bit shaken up, Captain."

"Second that," said Veera and Jorrus. The male Entropist had a row of bloody scrapes across his bare ribs, which looked painful but not serious.

Kira pulled herself to the front of the ruined maglev and peered out. She could see Itari several meters ahead of them, clinging to a rail in the hull. Orange ichor oozed from a nasty-looking wound near the base of one of the Jelly's larger tentacles.

[[Kira here: Are you okay? Can you move?]]

[[Itari here: Worry not about me, Idealis. This form can take much damage.]]

Even as it spoke, one of the Jelly's bony arms reached out from its carapace and, to Kira's shock, began to snip away with its pincer at the wounded tentacle.

"What the hell!" said Sparrow, joining Kira.

With startling speed, the alien cut off the tentacle and left it drifting in the air, abandoned amid a cloud of orange blobs. Despite the size of the raw stump left on Itari's carapace, the Jelly's bleeding had already stopped.

Hwa-jung coughed and swam her way out of the bolus of smoke, like a ship rising from the depths of oily water. She caught a handhold and pointed out the front. "The next maglev station is just ahead."

Kira went first, using her suit to knock out the jagged remains of the windshield. Then she pushed herself away from the car, and one by one, the others extricated themselves from the wreckage. Hwa-jung was last; she barely fit through the frame, but with some effort, she made it.

Using maintenance grips on the walls, they crawled along the interior of the black and echoing tube until lights flicked on a few meters ahead of them.

With a sense of relief, Kira aimed herself for them.

As they floated over to the station, a pair of automatic doors in the wall opened and allowed them to dive into the vestibule on the other side.

They paused then to regroup and check their directions.

"Where are we?" Kira asked. She noticed that Vishal had a nasty cut on his right forearm and both of Hwa-jung's hands were burned and blistering. It must have been excruciating, but the machine boss hid her pain well.

"Two stops past where we should be," said Nielsen. She pointed downspin (not that they were spinning anymore).

With her in the lead, they started through the abandoned hallways of Orsted's docking ring.

Occasionally they encountered bots: some recharging from sockets in the walls, some scurrying about on tracks, some jetting about on bursts of compressed air, busy with one of the myriad tasks necessary to the functioning of the station. None of the machines seemed to pay them any mind, but Kira knew each and every one was recording their location and actions.

The outer decks were filled with heavy industry. Refineries that, even during an attack from the nightmares, still rumbled and groaned with the imperatives of their operation. Fuel processing stations, where water was cracked into its component elements. Storage units packed to the brim with useful materials. And of course, the vast stacks of zero-g factories, where everything from medicines to machine guns was produced in quantities not only sufficient to satisfy the needs of Orsted's resident population but also much of the larger UMCN fleet.

Empty as they were, the nether regions of the station gave Kira the creeps. Even there, the alarm sirens still wailed, and glowing arrows (smaller and dimmer than in the main part of the station) pointed the way to the nearest storm shelters. But no shelter could help her now. That much she'd admitted and accepted. The only safety she could count on was the isolation of deep space, and there too, the nightmares or the Jellies might find her.

They moved quickly, and after only a few minutes, Falconi said, "Here," and pointed at a hallway that led rimward.

Kira recognized it as the same hallway they'd passed through during their arrival at Orsted.

With a sense of growing eagerness, she kicked her way along its crooked length. After everything that had happened on the station, returning to the *Wallfish* felt like returning home.

The pressure door to the loading dock slid open, and through the airlock at the far side, she saw . . .

Blackness.

Emptiness.

And perhaps a kilometer in the distance, the *Wallfish* rapidly shrinking in size, driven by a white plume of RCS thrusters.

7.

Falconi shouted. Not a word or a phrase, just a raw cry of anger and loss. As she heard it, Kira felt herself collapsing inward, surrendering to despair. She allowed the mask to slide off her face.

They'd lost. After all that, they'd—

Falconi jumped toward the airlock. He landed awkwardly and his breath ran out of him with an audible *whoof,* but he kept hold of the rungs next to the lock. Then he dragged himself across to the window and pressed his face against the sapphire wedge and stared after the *Wallfish.*

Kira looked away. She couldn't bear to watch. Seeing him like that embarrassed her, as if she were intruding on something private. His grief was too open, too desperate.

"Ha!" said Falconi. "Gotcha! Oh yeah! Just caught her in time." He turned and grinned at them with a wicked expression.

"Captain?" said Nielsen, floating over to join him.

He pointed out the window, and to her astonishment, Kira saw the *Wallfish* slow and reverse its course as it headed back toward the airlock.

"How did you manage that?" rumbled Hwa-jung.

Falconi tapped his blood-smeared temple. "Direct visual signal sent through my overlays. As long as the ship's passive sensors are working, and as long as they're in range and there's a clear line of sight, they can't be jammed. Not like radios or FTL broadcasts."

"That is quite a few qualifiers, Captain," said Vishal.

Falconi chucked. "Yeah, but it worked. I set up an override system just in case anyone tried to steal the *Wallfish.* Ain't no one hijacking *my* ship."

"And you never told us about this?" said Nielsen. She actually seemed offended. Kira, on the other hand, was impressed.

Falconi's levity vanished. "You know me, Audrey. Always know where the exits are. Always have an ace up the sleeve."

"Uh-huh." She looked unconvinced.

"Here, let me see your hands, please," said Vishal, moving over to Hwa-jung. She dutifully let him examine her. "Mmm, not too bad," he said. "Mostly second-degree burns. I will give you a spray to prevent any scarring."

"And some painkillers, please," she said.

He laughed softly. "Of course, and painkillers."

The *Wallfish* didn't take long to reach them. As it loomed large in the window, Veera grabbed the handle in the center of the airlock in an attempt to get a better view.

"Ahhh!" Her yell ended in a strangled gurgle. She arched her back nearly in half, and her whole body went rigid, save for small twitches in hands and feet. Her face contorted into a hideous rictus, teeth clenched.

Jorrus matched her yell, although he was nowhere near the airlock, and he likewise contorted.

"Don't touch her!" Hwa-jung shouted.

Kira didn't listen; she knew the suit would protect her.

She looped several tentacles around Veera's waist while, at the same time, attaching herself to the nearest wall. Then she pulled the convulsing Entropist free of the door. It wasn't easy; Veera's hand was clamped around the handle with unnatural strength. As the woman's grip gave way, Kira hoped she hadn't torn any of the muscles in her hand.

The instant Veera's fingers lost contact with the door, her body went limp, and Jorrus's howl ceased, though he retained the expression of a man who had just seen unspeakable horror.

"Someone grab her!" said Nielsen.

Vishal lunged out from the wall and snared Veera by a sleeve of her jacket. He wrapped an arm around the Entropist and, with his free hand, peeled back her eyelids. Then he opened Veera's mouth and peered down her throat. "She'll live, but I need to get her to sickbay."

Jorrus groaned. He had his arms wrapped around his head, and his skin was alarmingly pale.

"How bad is it?" Falconi asked.

The doctor gave him a worried look. "Uncertain, Captain. I will have to keep an eye on her heart. The shock might have burned out her implants. I can't tell yet. They need a hard reboot."

Jorrus was muttering to himself now: nothing that Kira could make sense of.

"That was a nasty trick," said Nielsen.

"They're panicked," said Sparrow. "They're trying anything to stop us." She raised a middle finger toward the center of the station. "I hope you get your own asses electrified! You hear me?!"

"It's my fault," said Kira. She motioned at her face. "I should have kept the mask on. I would have seen the electricity."

"Not your fault," said Falconi. "Don't beat yourself up about it." He maneuvered over to Jorrus. "Hey. Veera's going to live, yeah? Relax, it's alright."

"You don't understand," said Jorrus between hitching breaths.

"Explain."

"She—Me—Us—" He wrung his hands, which caused him to start floating away. Falconi caught him, stabilized him. "There is no *us*! No *we*. No *I*. All gone. Gone, gone, gone, ahhh!" And his voice dropped into meaningless rambles again.

Falconi shook him. "Pull yourself together! The ship's almost here." It made no difference.

"Their hive mind is broken," said Hwa-jung.

"So? He's still himself, isn't he?

"That's—"

Veera woke with a gasp and a wild start that sent her spinning. An instant later she clutched her temples and began to scream. At the sound, Jorrus curled into a fetal ball and whimpered.

"Great," said Falconi. "Now we've got a pair of crazies to deal with. Just great."

Soft as a falling feather, the *Wallfish* slowed to a stop outside the airlock. A series of *clanks* sounded as the docking clamps activated, securing the nose of the ship.

Falconi gestured. "Kira. If you wouldn't mind?"

As the doctor struggled to calm the Entropists, Kira allowed the mask to cover her face again. The current in the airlock door appeared to her as a thick bar of bluish light, as if part of a lightning bolt had been trapped in the handle of the door. The bar was so bright and wide, she was surprised it hadn't killed Veera outright.

Extending a pair of tendrils, she sank them into the door and—as she had in her cell—rerouted the flow of electricity through the cabled surface of the Soft Blade.

"It's safe," she said.

"Outstanding," said Falconi, but he still looked wary as he reached for the airlock controls. When no shock hit him, his shoulders relaxed and he quickly activated the release.

There was a *beep,* and a green light appeared above the control panel. With a hiss of escaping air, the door rolled open.

Kira released her hold then, retracting the Soft Blade and allowing the electricity to resume its normal path. "No one touch the handle," she said. "It's still hot." She repeated herself for Itari.

Falconi went first. He floated over to the nose of the *Wallfish,* punched a combination of buttons, and the ship's own airlock popped open. Kira and the others trailed after, Vishal with one arm around Veera while Hwa-jung helped with Jorrus, as he was barely able to move on his own. Last of all was Itari, the Jelly graceful as an eel as it pulled itself through the airlock.

A thought occurred to Kira. A horrible, cynical thought. What if the UMC chose that moment to blow the docking clamps and space her and everyone else? Given everything the League and the military had done, it wasn't something she'd put past them at that point.

However, the seal between the airlocks held, and once the last centimeter of Itari's tentacles were inside the *Wallfish,* Nielsen closed the ship's door.

"Sayonara, Orsted," said Falconi, heading down the *Wallfish*'s central shaft.

The ship seemed dead. Abandoned. Most of the lights were off, and the temperature was freezing. It smelled familiar, though, and that familiarity comforted Kira.

"Morven," said Falconi. "Initiate ignition sequence and prepare for launch. And get the damn heat back on."

The pseudo-intelligence answered, "Sir, safety procedures specifically state that no—"

"Disable safety procedures," he said, and rattled off a long authorization code.

"Safety procedures disabled. Beginning launch preparations."

To Hwa-jung, Falconi said, "See if you can get Gregorovich hooked back up before we blast out of here."

"Yessir." The machine boss handed Jorrus off to Sparrow and then flew down the corridor, continuing deeper into the ship.

"Come now, please," said Vishal, pulling Veera in the same direction. "Off to sickbay for you. And you too, Jorrus."

Leaving the incapacitated Entropists with Sparrow and the doctor, Kira,

Nielsen, and Falconi proceeded to Control. Itari trailed behind, and no one, not even the captain, objected.

Falconi uttered a sound of disgust as he entered the room. Dozens of small items cluttered the air: pens, two cups, a plate, several q-drives, and other pieces of random flotsam. It looked as if the UMC had ransacked every drawer, cupboard, and bin, and they hadn't been too careful about it either.

"Get this cleared up," said Falconi, moving to the main console.

Kira made a net with the Soft Blade and began to sweep the flotsam out of the air. Itari stayed by the pressure door, tentacles coiled close to itself.

Falconi tapped several buttons underneath the console, and around them, lights brightened and machines powered up. In the center of the room, the holo-display sprang to life.

"Okay," said Falconi. "We've got full access again." He tapped buttons along the edge of the holo, and the display switched to a map of the area surrounding Orsted Station with the locations and vectors of all nearby vessels labeled. Four red-blinking dots marked hostiles: nightmares currently skirmishing with the UMC forces around the curve of Ganymede. A fifth dot marked the nightmare ship embedded in Orsted's inner ring.

Kira hoped Lt. Hawes and the other Marines would be safe on the station. They might have answered to the UMC and the League, but they'd been good people.

"Looks like they hit the station and flew on past," said Nielsen.

"They'll be back," Falconi said with grim certainty. His eyes darted back and forth as he studied whatever his overlays were showing. He uttered a sharp bark of laughter. "Well, I'll be . . ."

"Who'd have thought?" said Nielsen.

Kira hated to ask: "What?"

"The UMC actually refueled us," said Falconi. "Can you believe it?"

"Probably planned on commandeering the *Fish* and using it for shuttling around supplies," said Nielsen.

Falconi grunted. "They left us the howitzers as well. Thoughtful of them."

Then the intercom clicked on, and Gregorovich's distinctive voice rang out, "My, you've been busy, my pretty little moppets. Mmm. Kicked up the hornets' nest, did you. Well, we'll see what we can do about that. Yes we will. Tee-hee. . . . By the way, my charming infestations, I have reignited the fusion drive. You're welcome." A low hum sounded from the back of the ship.

"Gregorovich, yank the restrictor," said Falconi.

An infinitesimal pause on the part of the ship mind. "Are you *absolutely* sure, Captain O my Captain?"

"Yes, I am. Yank it."

"I live but to serve," said Gregorovich, and he tittered a bit more than Kira would have liked.

She couldn't help but worry about the ship mind as she pulled herself into the nearest seat and buckled the harness. The UMC had put Gregorovich in lockdown, which meant he'd been kept in near total sensory deprivation since they'd arrived at the station. That wouldn't be good for anyone, but *especially* for an intelligence like a ship mind, and doubly so for Gregorovich, given his past experiences.

"What's the restrictor?" she asked Falconi.

"Long story. We have a choke in the fusion drive that changes our thrust signature, makes it a hair less efficient. Take it out, *bam!* we look like a different ship."

"And you didn't pull it out back at Bughunt?" Kira asked, scandalized.

"Wouldn't have helped. Not enough, at least. We're talking a difference of a few hundredths of a percentage point."

"That's not going to hide us from—"

Falconi made an impatient gesture. "Gregorovich plants a virus in every computer we send registry info to. It creates a second entry with a different ship name, different flight path, and engine specs that match what our drive is like sans restrictor. Far as the computers go, it won't be the *Wallfish* blasting off. Probably won't fool anyone for more than a few minutes, but right now, I'll take any advantage we can get."

"Clever trick."

"Unfortunately," said Nielsen, "it's a single-use device. At least until we can get into dock and have a new one installed."

"So what's the name we're flying under now?" Kira asked.

"The *Finger Pig*," said Falconi.

"You really like pigs, don't you?"

"They're smart animals. Speaking of which . . . Gregorovich, where are the pets?"

"They are again blocks of furry ice, O Captain. The UMC decided to return them to cryo rather than deal with the hassle of feeding and cleaning up."

"How considerate of them."

The *Wallfish* jolted as it disconnected from the docking ring, and then the maneuver alert sounded seconds before the RCS thrusters kicked in and shoved them away from the station.

"We're going to give Orsted an extra dose of radiation today," said Falconi, "but I think they earned it."

"With interest," said Sparrow as she sailed past Itari by the doorway. She snared a seat of her own. The Jelly braced itself against the floor, preparing for the upcoming burn.

Vishal's face appeared in the holo-display. "We're good to go in sickbay, Captain. Hwa-jung is here as well."

"Roger that. Gregorovich, get us the hell out of here!"

"Yes, Captain. Proceeding to 'get us the hell out of here.'"

With a rising roar, the *Wallfish*'s main rocket slammed Kira back into her seat as they hurtled away from Orsted Station. The thrust forced a laugh from her, though the laugh was lost in the sea of sound. They'd actually made it. The realization seemed almost absurd. Now maybe they could keep the Seventh Fleet from destroying any chance of peace.

A bell-like tone sounded, and her elation curdled.

With an effort, she craned her neck to see the display, wishing that she still had her contacts. The holo switched to a view of Saturn as a large cloud of red dots appeared close to the gas giant.

Fourteen more nightmares had just dropped out of FTL.

CHAPTER IV

* * * * * * *

NECESSITY II

1.

Itari moved closer to the display, tentacles braced against the deck. "Kira," said Falconi in a warning tone.

"It's okay," she said, hoping she was right.

Nielsen zoomed out in the holo, and for the first time, Kira could see what was happening throughout Sol. In addition to the nightmares by Orsted, and the fourteen by Saturn, dozens of other nightmares had entered the system. Some were on a hard burn toward Mars. Others were out by Neptune, harassing the planet's defense network. Still more were heading toward Earth and Venus.

A bright line flashed across the holo, from a satellite near Jupiter over to one of the nightmares' vessels. The ship vanished in a flare of light. The bright line stabbed outward again and again, and each time, another of the intruders exploded.

"What's *that*?" Kira asked.

"I'm . . . not sure," said Sparrow, frowning as she studied her own overlays.

Gregorovich chuckled. "I can explain. Yes, I can. The League has built a solar laser. Energy farms by Mercury collect sunlight and then beam it to receivers throughout the system. Most of the time the energy is just used for power production. But in the event of an exogenic intrusion, well, you can see for yourself. Pump the energy through a giant-ass laser, and you have yourself a proper death ray. Yes you do."

"Clever," said Falconi.

Sparrow grinned. "Yeah. Having the local receivers cuts down on the light lag. Not bad."

"Is anyone following us?" Kira asked.

"Not yet, my pretties," said Gregorovich. "Our ersatz credentials continue to hold firm."

"So what the hell is a *Finger Pig*?" said Kira.

"Thank you!" said Nielsen, with an exasperated tone. She gestured at Falconi. "See?"

The corner of his mouth quirked. "It's a finger that's a pig."

"Or a pig that's a finger," said Sparrow.

In the holo, Vishal raised his eyebrows. "My understanding is that it's *slang* for a pork hot dog." Then his face vanished as he signed off.

"You're saying we're in a flying hot dog then?" said Kira.

Falconi chuckled with false humor. "Maybe."

A snort came from Sparrow. "That's not how we used the phrase in the Marines."

"What did you use it for?" Kira asked.

"I'll tell you when you're older."

"Enough chitchat," said Falconi. He twisted in his chair to look at Kira. "There's more going on than we know, isn't there? That's why you were so insistent we rescue the Jelly."

Kira tensed. Escaping had been easy compared with what she had to do now. "Did the UMC tell you what they decided to do?"

"Nope."

"Nothing."

"Not a damn clue."

". . . Okay." Kira took a moment to prepare, but before she could open her mouth, an incongruously cheery *chirp* sounded from the display.

Gregorovich said, "Orsted Station is broadcasting a message on all channels. It's Colonel Stahl. I think it's meant for *you,* O Spiky One."

"Play it for us," said Falconi. "Can't hurt to hear what he has to say."

"I wouldn't go so far as that," Sparrow mumbled.

An image of Stahl replaced the holo of the system. The colonel appeared harried, out of breath, and there was a bloody scrape on his left cheekbone.

"Ms. Navárez," he said. "If you can hear this, I'm imploring you to turn back. The xeno is too important to the League. *You* are too important. I don't know what you think you're going to do, but I promise it won't help. If anything, you're going to make the situation worse. If you get yourself killed, if our enemies get ahold of the xeno, it could be the death of all of us. You don't want that on your conscience, Navárez. You really don't. I know the situation isn't what you wanted, but please—for the survival of our species—turn back. I promise you and the crew of the *Wallfish* won't face any additional charges. You have my word."

Then the transmission ended, and the holo returned to a view of the system.

Kira could feel the weight of everyone's gazes upon her, even Itari with its many small, button-like eyes strung round its carapace.

"Well?" said Falconi. "It's your call. *We're* not going back, but if you want, I'll cut the engine long enough for you to jump out the airlock without getting fried. I'm sure the UMC would be happy to pick you up."

"No," said Kira. "We keep going." Then she told them, including Itari, about the Premier's decision to betray the Knot of Minds and attack the gathering Jelly fleet.

Sparrow made a sound of disgust. "That's what I hated the most about the service. Damn politics."

The Jelly's skin roiled with greens and purples. Its tentacles twisted with seeming distress. [[Itari here: If a Knot cannot be formed between your kind and ours, the Corrupted will overswim us all.]]

After Kira translated, Falconi said, "What do you have in mind?"

She looked at Itari. "I was hoping Itari might be able to send a warning to the Knot of Minds before the UMC's hunter-seekers get there."

She repeated the thought for the Jelly and then said, [[Kira here: Can you use our transmitter to warn the Knot of Minds?]]

[[Itari here: No. Your farscent is not fast enough. It would not reach the meeting point in time to save the Knot of Minds. . . . The Seventh Shoal your conclave has sent cannot kill the great Ctein of their own. They need our help, and they need us to take the leadership and to guide the Arms in the proper direction. Without the Knot of Minds, your shoal will be doomed, as will we all.]]

A sense of despair threatened to unbalance Kira as she felt her plans unraveling. Surely there had to be a way! [[Kira here: If we swam after the Seventh Shoal, could we get close enough to the meeting place that we could warn the Knot of Minds in time?]]

A flush of crimson ran the length of the Jelly's limbs, and nearscent of confirmation suffused the air. [[Itari here: Yes.]]

That wouldn't solve the larger problems between the Jellies and the League. But those problems were far too large for anyone on the *Wallfish* to fix.

Kira did her best to keep emotion out of her voice as she translated for Falconi and the others.

In a far more subdued tone than normal, Sparrow said, "You're talking about flying right into enemy territory. *Aish.* If the other Jellies caught us, or the nightmares . . ."

"I know."

"Stahl wasn't wrong," said Nielsen. "We can't afford to let the xeno fall into the wrong hands. I'm sorry, Kira, but it's true."

"We also can't afford to stand around and do nothing."

Sparrow rubbed her face. "We're already criminals in the eyes of the League, but this is treason. Aiding and abetting the enemy will still earn you the death penalty in damn near every territory."

Falconi leaned forward and tabbed the intercom. "Hwa-jung, Vishal, come up to Control as soon as you can."

"Yessir."

"Be there directly, Captain, yes, yes."

Anguish twisted in Kira's gut. The Soft Blade was the problem. It had *always* been the problem, even going back into the distant past. Because of the Soft Blade, millions—if not billions—had died, humans and Jellies both. Because of the Soft Blade, the nightmares threatened to spread their sickness throughout the galaxy, overrunning every other form of life.

Although that wasn't entirely true. The xeno wasn't the only one to blame for the nightmares. *She* had played a role in the creation of the devouring Maw. It had been her fear, her ill-judged violence that had loosed so much pain upon the stars.

Kira groaned and covered her face with her hands and dug her fingers into her scalp until it hurt nearly as badly as her insides. The xeno seemed confused; she could feel it hardening and thickening around her, as if preparing for an attack.

If only she could rid herself of the Soft Blade, things would be easier. They would have many more options then. The Knot of Minds had safeguarded the xeno for centuries; it could safeguard it again.

Another groan clawed its way out of Kira's throat. Absent the Soft Blade, Alan would still be alive, and so many others besides. All she wanted—all she had wanted since the Soft Blade had first infested her—was to be free. *Free!*

She slapped the release on her harness, shoved herself out of the chair, and stood. In 2.5 g's, she stood. The suit helped hold her upright, but her arms felt like leaden weights, and her knees and the balls of her feet began to throb.

She didn't care.

"Kira—" Nielsen started to say.

Kira screamed. She screamed as she had when she'd first realized Alan was dead. She screamed, and she spread her arms and used everything she had learned while training with the Soft Blade—every ounce of hard-fought mastery gained during the long, dark months spent in FTL—to shove the xeno away from herself. And she poured all of her anger and sorrow and frustration into that single, primal desire.

The xeno sprang outward. Spikes and ridged membranes extended in every direction, vibrating in response to her mental assault. But only to a degree. She constrained it with her mind, leashed it so the xeno couldn't threaten the others.

Even so, it was a risk.

In the hollows between the protrusions, she could feel the suit thin and retract, and then air struck her exposed skin—air cold and dry and shocking in its intimacy. Her flesh prickled as the bare patches spread, islands of pale nakedness amid the jagged darkness.

By the doorway, Itari recoiled, holding up its tentacles, as if to shield its carapace.

Kira pushed and pushed, forcing the xeno to withdraw until only a few tendon-like strips connected her to it. A handful of fibers and nothing more. She concentrated on them, and she tried to will them to part. She raged at them to part. She urged them to part. She *commanded* them to part.

The tendons squirmed before her eyes, but they refused to give. And in her mind, she could feel the Soft Blade resisting. It had retreated and retreated, but no more. Any farther, and they would be separated, and that, apparently, it would not accept.

Enraged, Kira bore down even harder. Her vision flickered and went dark around the edges from the effort, and for a moment, she thought she would pass out. She remained standing, though, and still the Soft Blade defied her. From it, she had strange thoughts, obscure and barely understandable, worming their way from the depths of her mind into the upper regions of her consciousness. Thoughts such as: *The uncleft making was not to be wrongwise cast.* And: *The time was off-balance. The manystuff graspers still hungered, and no cradle was close. For now, the making had to hold.*

The words may have been odd, but the gist of them was clear enough.

Kira howled and threw herself against the Soft Blade with every bit of remaining strength, holding nothing back. One last attempt to drive it away. One last chance to free herself and regain something of what she had lost.

But the Soft Blade held firm, and if it empathized with her, if it felt any sympathy for her plight or regret for its opposition, she could not tell. From it came only a sense of resolute purpose, and a sense of satisfaction that the making would stand true.

And for the first time since she'd realized Alan was dead, Kira gave up. The universe was full of things she couldn't control, and this, it seemed, was one of them.

With a choked cry, she stopped fighting and collapsed to her hands and knees. Soft as falling sand, the xeno flowed back over her, and the coldness of the air disappeared everywhere but on her face. She could still feel the floor, still feel the currents of the ship's atmosphere tickling the small of her back, but only filtered through the artificial skin of the Soft Blade. And it blanked any discomfort, removed the bite of the cold and the sharpness of the ridges beneath her knees, so that all was warm and comfortable.

Kira squeezed her eyes shut, feeling tears leak out the corners, and her breath hitched.

"Father above," said Vishal from by the doorway. He staggered over and put an arm around her. "Ms. Kira, are you alright?"

"Yeah. I'm fine," she said, forcing the words out past the lump in her throat. She'd lost. She'd tried her utmost, and it hadn't been enough. And now all she had left was bare necessity. That was the phrase Inarë had used, and it fit. Oh how it fit, like shackles of black wire wound round and round. . . .

"You sure?" said Falconi.

She nodded without looking, and tears fell on the backs of her hands. Not cold. Not warm. Merely wet. "Yeah." She took a shuddery breath. "I'm sure."

2.

As Kira got back to her feet and returned to her chair, Hwa-jung came stomping through the doorway. The high thrust didn't seem to impede her in the slightest. Indeed, the machine boss moved with a natural ease, even though Kira knew their burn was stronger than the gravity back on Shin-Zar.

"I take it we're stuck with the xeno," said Falconi.

Kira took a moment to answer; she was busy reassuring Itari that she was okay. Then: "You would be right."

"Excuse me, Captain," said Vishal. "But what is the matter of concern? We must decide where to go, yes?"

"Yes," said Falconi in a decidedly grim tone. For the benefit of the doctor and Hwa-jung, he outlined the situation with a few terse sentences and then said, "What I want to know is whether the *Wallfish* is up for another long haul."

"Captain—" Nielsen started to say.

He cut her off with a sharp gesture. "I'm just trying to get a sense of our options." He nodded at Hwa-jung. "Well?"

The machine boss sucked on her lower lip for a moment. "Ah, the lines need to be flushed, the fusion drive and the Markov Drive both need to be checked. . . . Water, air, and food are still mostly full, but I would restock if we were going out for a long time. Hmm." She bit at her lip again.

"Could we do it?" Falconi asked. "Three months' travel in FTL, round trip. Assume three weeks out of cryo, just to be on the safe side."

Hwa-jung dipped her head. "We could do it, but I would not recommend it."

A bark of laugh escaped Falconi. "Most of what we've done over the past year falls under the category of 'I wouldn't recommend it.'" He looked back at Kira. "The question is, *should* we?"

"There's no profit in it," said Sparrow, leaning forward, elbows on her knees.

"No," Falconi admitted. "There isn't."

Nielsen said, "There's a good chance we'd get killed. And if not killed—"

"—executed for treason," said Falconi. He picked at a patch on his trousers. "Yeah, that's my read on it too."

"What would you do instead?" Kira asked, quiet. She could feel the delicacy of the moment. If she pushed too hard, she would lose them.

At first, no one answered. Then Nielsen said, "We could take Trig to a proper medical facility, somewhere outside the League."

"But your family is still here in Sol, isn't it?" said Kira. The first officer's silence was answer enough. "And yours too, right, Vishal?"

"Yes," said the doctor.

Kira let her gaze roam across the others' faces. "We all have people we care about. And none of them are safe. We can't just go and hide. . . . We can't."

Hwa-jung murmured in agreement, and Falconi looked down at his clasped hands.

"Beware the temptation of false hope," whispered Gregorovich. "Resist and seek your validation elsewhere."

"Hush," said Nielsen.

Falconi lifted his chin toward the ceiling and scratched the underside of his jaw. The sound of nails rasping against stubble was surprisingly loud. "Ask Itari this for me: If we warn the Knot of Minds, would there still be a chance of peace between Jellies and humans?"

Kira repeated the question, and the Jelly said, [[Itari here: Yes. But if the Knot is cut, then the cruel and mighty Ctein will reign over us until the end of this ripple, to the detriment of all.]]

Falconi gave another of his grunts. "Uh-huh. That's what I thought." He turned toward Kira as far as his seat and harness would allow. "You would go?"

Despite the fear she felt at the prospect of again venturing into the unknown, Kira nodded. "I would."

Falconi looked around the room, at each and every one of the crew. "Well? What's the verdict?"

Sparrow made a face. "I don't much like the thought of helping the UMC after the shit they pulled on us, but . . . sure. What the hell. Let's do it."

A sigh from Vishal, and he raised a hand. "I don't much like the thought of this war continuing. If there is anything we can do to stop it, I feel we must."

"Where she goes, I go," said Hwa-jung, and put a hand on Sparrow's shoulder.

Nielsen blinked several times, and it took Kira a moment to realize the first officer had tears in her eyes. Then the woman sniffed and nodded. "I vote yes as well."

"What about the Entropists?" Kira asked.

"They're in no state to be making decisions," said Falconi. "But I'll ask." His gaze went blank as he switched to his overlays. His lips twitched as he subvocalized his texts, and the control room was silent.

Kira assumed he was communicating with the Entropists via a screen in the sickbay, since their implants were burned out. She took the opportunity to update Itari on the conversation. The constant back-and-forth of translation was beginning to wear on her. She also checked on the holo in the central display—to her relief, she didn't see any pursuing ships, but the nightmares had managed to destroy the near receiver/emitter for the solar laser.

"Okay," said Falconi. "Veera can't talk, but Jorrus votes yes. It's a go." He scanned their faces once more. "Everyone on the same page? . . . Alright, then.

We're agreed. Gregorovich, set a course for the rendezvous point Tschetter gave us."

The ship mind snorted, a surprisingly normal sound coming from him. Then he said, "Forgotten me, have you? Does my vote not count?"

"Of course it does," said Falconi, exasperated. "Tell us your vote, then."

"*My* vote?" said Gregorovich, an unbalanced edge to his voice. "Well now, so kind of you to ask. I vote *NO*."

Falconi rolled his eyes. "I'm sorry you feel that way, but we've already decided, Gregorovich. You're outnumbered seven to one. Lay in the course and get us out of here."

"That I think not."

"*Excuse* me?"

"No. I won't. Is that clear enough, O Captain, my stern captain, my supernumerary captain?" And Gregorovich giggled and giggled and giggled until he broke into a demented laugh that echoed through the corridors of the *Wallfish*.

Cold fear wormed its way into Kira. The ship mind had always seemed a bit unstable, but now he'd gone totally insane, and they were all at his mercy.

3.

"Gregorovich—" Nielsen started to say.

"I object," whispered the ship mind, breaking his laugh. "I *object* most strenuously. I won't take you there—I won't—and nothing you can say or do will convince me otherwise. Pretty my hair and pat my head, doll me up with satin ribbons and pamper me with plumpest persimmons; I shall not reverse, regress, retract, or otherwise rescind my decision."

[[Itari here: What is the wrongness?]] Kira explained, and the Jelly turned a queasy-looking green. [[Itari here: Your ship forms are as dangerous as hidden currents.]]

Falconi swore. "The hell is wrong with you, Gregorovich? We don't have time for this nonsense. I'm giving you a direct order. Change our goddamn course."

"Never I will. Never I might."

The captain slapped the console in front of him. "Seriously? You didn't object when we went off to Bughunt, but you're going to mutiny *now*?"

"The expectation of peril thereat was not a certainty. Calculated risks remained within reasonable tolerances given available information. You were not setting forth to plunge yourself into the midst of martial turmoil, and I won't allow it now. No, I won't." The ship mind sounded insufferably self-righteous.

"Why?" asked Nielsen. "What is it you're so afraid of?"

The ship mind's unhinged giggle returned. "The universe is spinning apart: a pinwheel driven to the point of failure. Darkness and emptiness, and what matters still? The warmth of friends, the light of human kindness. Trig lies on the brink of death, frozen in a tomb of ice, and I will not allow this crew to be further torn apart. No, not I. If we venture forth amid nightmares and Jellies battling, with the Seventh Fleet skulking about for trouble to cause, likely it is circumstance shall deliver us our doom in the shape of some ship—bearing down upon us as the wrath of cruel fate unburdened by grace or pity or the slightest shade of human consideration."

"Your concern is noted," said Falconi. "Now I'm ordering you to turn this ship around."

"Can't do, Captain."

"You mean you won't."

Gregorovich laughed again, long and low. "Is the inability a result of nature or nurture? You say *potatoh,* I say *potayto.*"

Falconi glanced at Nielsen, and Kira saw the alarm in his expression. "You heard Kira. If we don't warn the Knot of Minds, we'll lose our only chance of peace with the Jellies and, possibly, our only chance of defeating the nightmares. Is that what you want?"

Gregorovich laughed again, long and low. "When an immovable force meets an irresistible object, causality becomes confused. Probabilities expand beyond computational resources. Statistical variables become unconstrained."

"You mean an irresistible force and immovable object," said Nielsen.

"I always mean to say what I mean."

"But you don't?"

Sparrow made a sound in her throat. "Just seems like a pretentious way of admitting you don't know what's going to happen."

"Ah!" said Gregorovich. "But that's the point. None of us know, and it is uncertainty itself I am protecting you against, my little chickadees. Oh yes I am."

"Alright, I've had enough of your insubordination," said Falconi. "I don't want to do this, but you're not leaving me any choice. Access code four-six-six-nine-upyours. Authorization: Falconi-alpha-bravo-bravo-whisky-tango."

"Sorry, Captain," said Gregorovich. "Did you expect that to work? You can't force me out of the system. The *Wallfish* is mine, more than she was ever yours. Flesh of my flesh, and all that nonsense. Accept your defeat with good humor. To Alpha Centauri we go, and should it prove too dangerous, we'll find safe haven upon the rim of settled space, where aliens and their seeking tentacles have no reason to intrude. Yes we shall."

While he talked, Falconi pointed at Hwa-jung and snapped his fingers without noise. The machine boss nodded and unbuckled her harness and moved with swift steps toward the door to Control.

It slammed shut in front of her and locked with an audible *clank*.

"Ms. Song," crooned the ship mind. "Ms. Song, what are you doing? I know your tricks and stratagems. Don't think to thwart me; a thousand years of plotting and you still couldn't outwit me, Ms. Song, Ms. Song—your melody is self-evident. Abandon your dishonorable intentions; your motif contains no surprises, no surprises at all. . . ."

"Quick," said Falconi. "The console. Maybe you can—"

Hwa-jung pivoted and hurried to one of the access panels underneath the bank of controls next to the holo table.

"What about me?" Kira said. She didn't know what the machine boss was about, but distracting Gregorovich seemed like a good idea. "You can't keep me in here. Stop this, or I'll go crack open your case and rip out all your power cords."

A shower of sparks erupted from the access panel as Hwa-jung touched it. She yelped and yanked back her arm and clutched her wrist, looking hurt.

"You bastard!" Sparrow yelled.

"Just try," the ship mind whispered, and the *Wallfish* trembled around them. "Oh just try. It won't matter, though; not at all. I've set the autopilot, and nothing you can do will free it up, not even were you to wipe the mainframe and rebuild it from—"

A dark expression settled on Hwa-jung's face, and she let out a sharp hiss from between her bared teeth. She pulled a rag from a pouch on her belt and wrapped it around her bandaged hand, covering her fingers. Then she reached for the access panel again.

"Let me—" Kira started to say, but by then the machine boss already had the panel open and was scrabbling around inside.

"Song," Gregorovich crooned. "What do you think you are doing, beautiful Song? My roots run deep. You cannot dig me out, not here, not there, not with a thousand lasers on a thousand bots. Within the *Wallfish,* I am omniscient and omnipresent. The one and the word, the will and the way. Leave off this pointless, pathetic pandering and lay you down to—"

Hwa-jung yanked on something under the console, and the lightstrips flickered, and a burst of static sounded from the speakers—cutting off Gregorovich—and half the indicators along the walls fell dark.

"Wrong," said the machine boss.

4.

A moment of stunned silence followed.

"Shit. Are you okay?" Sparrow asked.

Hwa-jung grunted. "I am fine."

"What did you do?" Falconi demanded. In the question, Kira could hear his anger at Gregorovich, but also his anger that the machine boss might have hurt the ship mind and/or the *Wallfish*.

"I removed Gregorovich from the computer," said Hwa-jung, standing. She rubbed her injured hand and grimaced.

"How?" said Falconi. Kira wondered that herself. Gregorovich hadn't lied. Ship minds were so thoroughly integrated into the workings of a machine like the *Wallfish,* extricating them was no easier than extricating a still-beating heart from a living body (and without killing the patient, no less).

Hwa-jung lowered her arms. "Gregorovich is very clever, but some things even he doesn't understand about the *Wallfish.* He knows the circuits. I know the pipes the circuits run in. *Aish.* That one." She shook her head. "There are mechanical breakers on all his connecting power lines, in case of a bad electrical surge. They can be activated here or in the storm shelter." She shrugged. "It is simple."

Nielsen said, "So is he completely cut off, then? All alone, in the dark?"

"Not completely," said Hwa-jung. "He has a computer built into his case. Whatever is stored on there, he can see."

"Thank god for that," said Vishal.

"But he can't contact anyone?" Nielsen said.

Hwa-jung shook her head. "No wireless. No hardline." Then: "We can talk with him, if we want, if we plug into the outside of his case, but we have to be careful. Any access to an external system and he could take control of the *Wallfish* again."

"He sure ain't going to be happy about *that,*" said Sparrow.

Kira agreed. Gregorovich had to be furious. Being once again trapped in his nutrient bath with no way to contact the outside world would be a nightmare. She shuddered at the thought.

"Who cares if he's happy?" Falconi growled. He ran a hand through his hair. "Right now we have to get out of Sol before we get blown up. Can you set up a new course?"

"Yes, sir."

"Do it, then. Program another random walk. Three jumps should do it."

Hwa-jung returned to her seat and concentrated on her overlays. A minute later, the free-fall alert sounded and the sense of crushing weight vanished as the engines cut out.

The Soft Blade kept Kira welded to the back of her chair as the *Wallfish* reoriented itself. Of course the xeno did. It was so accommodating. So concerned with her safety and welfare. Except when it came to what she really wanted. Her old hatred for it welled up again, sour poison lanced from a boil. But it was a useless hatred. A weak and ineffectual hatred, because there was nothing she could do about it—not one damn thing—just as there was nothing Gregorovich could do to rescue himself from the prison of his mind.

"How long until we can jump to FTL?" she asked.

"Thirty minutes," said Hwa-jung. "The modifications from the Jelly are still holding. We can jump out sooner than normal."

[[Itari here: Idealis?]] In response to the query, Kira updated the Jelly on what was happening, and the sick green color faded from its tentacles, replaced by its normal, healthy orange.

"Real light show over there," said Sparrow, gesturing at the alien. "Never realized they were so colorful."

Kira was impressed by how well the crew had accepted the presence of the Jelly. So had she, for that matter.

The *Wallfish* finished turning, and then the deck pressed against Kira as they resumed thrust—heading toward a different point along the system's Markov Limit.

5.

The crew spent the thirty minutes preparing the *Wallfish* for FTL, and themselves for another round of cryo sleep. Ideally they would have had longer to recover from hibernation, as each cycle took a toll on their bodies. Still, they were well under the yearly limit. Two a month for three months had been the commercial limit for the Lapsang Corporation, but Kira knew private citizens and military personnel often far exceeded those limits. Though not without consequence.

They had one piece of good news before departure: Vishal burst into Control with a great big smile and said, "Listen! I had word from my uncle. My mother and sisters are on Luna, thank God." And he crossed himself. "My uncle, he promised he would keep them safe. He has a shelter, buried very deep on Luna. They can stay with him as long as they need. Thank God!"

"That's wonderful news, Vishal," said Falconi, clasping him on the shoulder. "Truly." And they all gave the doctor their congratulations.

When she could, Kira stole a quick break in her cabin. She pulled up a live view of the system and zoomed in on the small green-and-blue dot that was Earth.

Earth. The ancestral home of humanity. A planet swarming with life, and so much of it complex, multicellular organisms far more advanced than those found in most xenospheres. Only Eidolon could come close to the evolutionary accomplishments of Earth, and Eidolon didn't possess a single self-aware species.

Kira had studied the vast diversity of Earth's biome. All xenobiologists did. And she'd always hoped to travel there for real one day. But Orsted Station was the closest she'd come, and it seemed unlikely she would ever set foot on the planet.

The sight of Earth felt slightly unreal. To think that all of humanity until just three hundred years ago had lived and died on that single ball of mud. All those people, trapped, unable to venture forth among the stars as she and so many others had been able to.

Even the word *earth* came from the planet she was looking at. And *moon* from the pale sphere hanging in close proximity (both haloed with orbital rings, bright as silver wire).

The earth.

The moon.

The originals, and no others.

Kira took a shaky breath, finding herself unaccustomedly overcome with emotion. "Goodbye," she whispered, and she wasn't sure to whom or what she was talking.

Then she closed the display and went to rejoin the crew. And soon enough, the jump alert sounded, and the *Wallfish* transitioned to FTL, leaving behind Sol, Earth, Jupiter, Ganymede, the invading nightmares, and the vast majority of humanity's teeming masses.

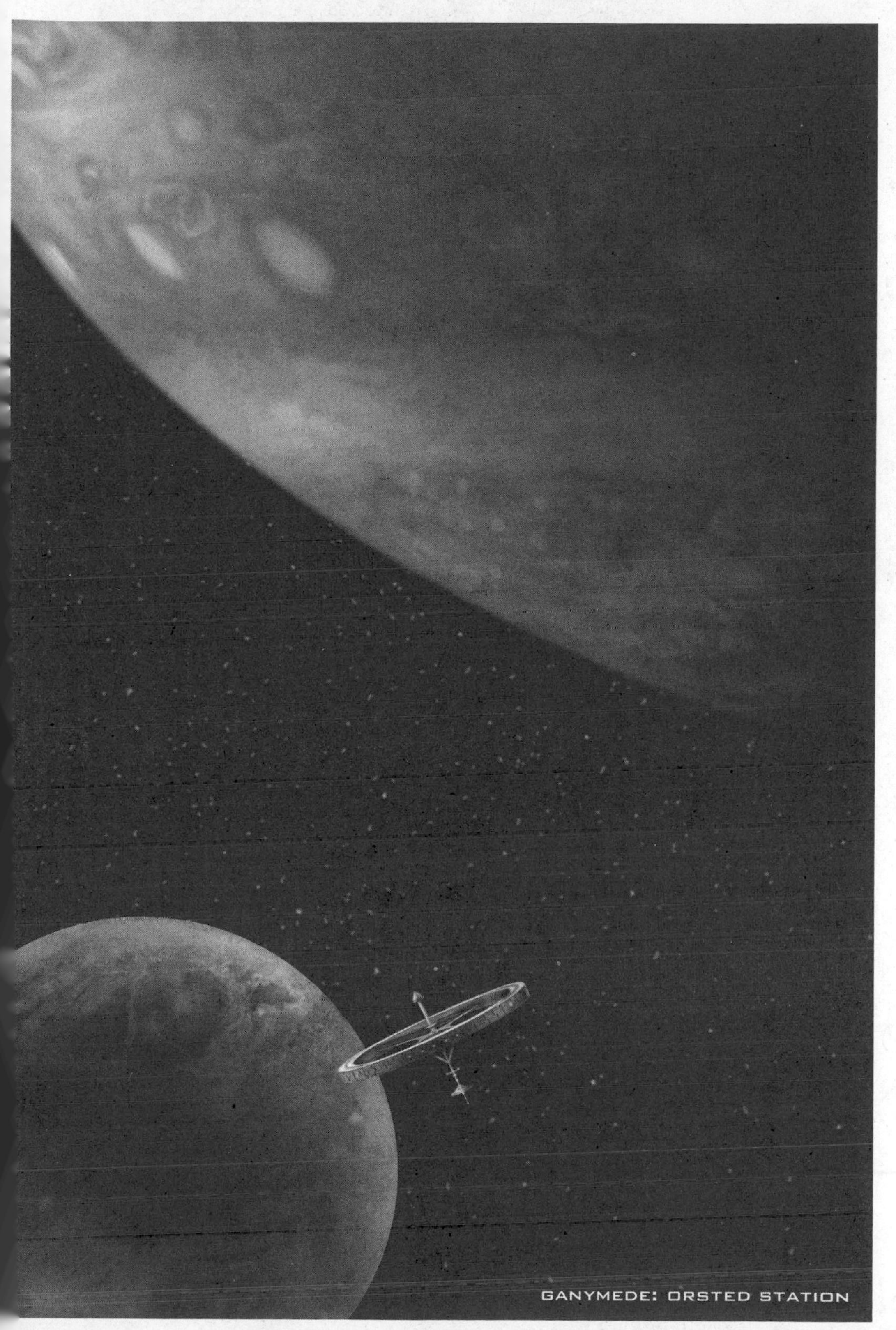
GANYMEDE: ORSTED STATION

* * * *

EXEUNT IV

1.

By the third jump out from Sol, everyone was in cryo save Falconi, Hwa-jung, and of course, Kira. Even Itari had entered its dormant state, cocooning itself within the port cargo hold (Falconi had decided there was no longer any reason to keep the Jelly in an airlock).

While they waited in interstellar space for the *Wallfish* to cool, before setting out on the last leg of their journey, Kira went to the galley and made short work of three reheated meal packs, four glasses of water, and an entire pouch of candied beryl nuts. Eating in zero-g was far from her favorite thing to do, but the xeno's exertions on Orsted had left her ravenous.

She couldn't stop thinking about Gregorovich during her meal. The ship mind was still locked out of the *Wallfish*'s computer system, sitting alone in his tomb-like casing. The fact disturbed her for several reasons, but mainly because she empathized. Kira knew what it was like to be alone in the dark—her time aboard the *Valkyrie* had more than acquainted her with that sensation—and she worried what it would do to Gregorovich. Being abandoned, isolated, was a fate she wouldn't wish on her worst enemy. Not even the nightmares. Death was a far preferable end.

Also . . . although she was slow to admit it, Gregorovich had become her friend. Or as much of a friend as she and a ship mind were ever likely to be. Their conversations during FTL had been a comfort to Kira, and she didn't like to see Gregorovich in his current predicament.

Back in Control, she tapped Falconi's arm to get his attention and said, "Hey. What are you planning on doing about Gregorovich?"

Falconi sighed, and the reflected light of overlays vanished from his eyes. "What *can* I do? I tried talking with him, but he's not making a whole lot of sense." He rubbed his temples. "Right now my only real option is to throw him into cryo."

"And then what? Keep him on ice from here on out?"

"Maybe," said Falconi. "I'm not sure how I'm supposed to trust him after this."

"Could you—"

He stopped her with a look. "Do you know what they do to ship minds who refuse an order, barring extenuating circumstances?"

"Retire them?"

"Exactly." Falconi jerked his chin. "The minds get yanked from their ships, and their flight credentials get revoked. Just like that. Even in civilian ships. And you know why?"

Kira pursed her lips, already anticipating the answer. "Because they're too dangerous."

With a finger twirled around his head, Falconi indicated their surroundings. "Any spaceship, even one as small as the *Wallfish,* is effectively a flying bomb. Ever think about what happens if someone—let's say, oh, I don't know, a deranged ship mind—flies a cargo tug or a cruiser into a planet?"

Kira winced as she remembered the accident on Orlog, one of the moons in her home system. The crater could still be seen with the naked eye. "Nothing good."

"Nothing good."

"And with all that, you were still comfortable keeping Gregorovich on board?" She eyed, him curious. "Seems like a hell of a risk."

"It was. It *is.* But Gregorovich needed a home, and I thought we could help each other. Until now he's never made me think he was a danger to us or the *Wallfish.*" He raked his fingers through his hair. "Shit. I don't know."

"Could you limit Gregorovich's access to just comms and sublight navigation?"

"Wouldn't work. Once a ship mind is in one part of your system, it's pretty much impossible to keep them out of the rest. They're too smart, and they're too integrated with the computers. It's like trying to grab an eel with your bare hands; sooner or later they wriggle free."

Kira rubbed her arms, thinking. *Not good.* Aside from her concern for Gregorovich as a person, she didn't like the prospect of flying into hostile territory without him at the helm. "Do you mind if I talk with him?" She motioned toward the ceiling.

"Actually, it's more like—" Falconi pointed at an angle toward the deck. "But why? I mean, you're more than welcome to, but I don't see what good it's going to do."

"Maybe not, but I'm worried about him. I might be able to help him calm down. We spent a fair bit of time talking in FTL."

Falconi shrugged. "You can try, but again, I'm not sure what good it's going to do. Gregorovich really sounded off."

"How so?" Kira asked, her concern deepening.

He scratched his chin. "Just . . . weird. I mean, he's always been different, but this is more than that. Like there's something really wrong with him." Falconi shook his head. "Honestly? It doesn't matter how calm Gregorovich is or isn't. I'm not giving control of the *Wallfish* back to him unless he can convince me this was a one-off event. And I don't see how he can. Some things can't be undone."

She studied him. "We all make mistakes, Salvo."

"And they have consequences."

". . . Yes, and we might need Gregorovich when we get to the Jellies. Morven is all well and good, but she's only a pseudo-intelligence. If we run into trouble, she won't be much help."

"No, she won't."

Kira put a hand on his shoulder. "Besides, you said it: Gregorovich is one of you, same as Trig. Are you really going to give up on him that easily?"

Falconi stared at her for a good while, the muscles in his jaw flexing. At last, he relented. "Fine. Talk to him. See if you can knock some sense into that lump of concrete he calls a brain. Go find Hwa-jung. She'll show you where to go and what to do."

"Thanks."

"Mmh. Just don't let Gregorovich get access to the mainframe."

Kira left him then and went looking for Hwa-jung. She found the machine boss in engineering. When told what Kira wanted, Hwa-jung didn't seem surprised. "This way," said Hwa-jung, and led her back up toward Control.

The halls of the *Wallfish* were dark and cold and eerily quiet. Condensation beaded the bulkheads where the chilled air blew, and Kira and Hwa-jung's shadows stretched before them like tortured souls as they floated through the ship.

One deck below Control, close to the core of the ship, was a locked door Kira had walked by before but never made much note of. It looked like a closet or a server room.

In a way, it was.

Hwa-jung opened the door to reveal a second door a meter within. "Acts like a mini-airlock, in case the rest of the ship gets vented," she said.

"Gotcha."

The second door rolled open. Past it was a small, hot room busy with whirring fans and walled with banks of Christmas-light indicators: each bright point marking a switch or toggle or dial. In the center of the room lay the neural sarcophagus, huge and heavy. A metal edifice twice the width and breadth of Kira's bed and standing as high as her mid-chest, it had an imposing presence, as if designed to warn off any who came near—as if to say, "Meddle not, lest you regret it." The fittings were dark, nearly black, and there was a holo-screen along one side, as well as rows of green bars marking the levels of different gasses and liquids.

Although Kira had seen the sarcophagi in games and videos, she'd never been close to one in person. The device, she knew, was hooked into the *Wallfish*'s plumbing and power, but were it to be separated, it was perfectly capable of keeping Gregorovich alive for months or even years, depending on how efficient the internal power source was. It was both artificial skull and artificial body, and built so securely it could survive reentry at speeds and pressures that would shred most ships. The durability of the cases was legendary. Plenty of times a sarcophagus (and the mind inside) was the only intact part left after the destruction of its parent ship.

It was strange to know that there was a brain hidden within the slab of metal and sapphire. And not an ordinary brain, either. It would be larger—much larger—and more spread out: wrinkled butterfly wings of grey matter surrounding the walnut-shaped core that was the original seat of Gregorovich's consciousness, now grown to immense proportions. Picturing it made Kira uneasy, and in an irrational bit of imagining, she couldn't help but feel as if the armored case was alive as well. Alive and watching her, though she knew Hwajung had disabled all of Gregorovich's sensors.

The machine boss fished a pair of wired headphones out of her pocket and gave them to her. "Plug in here. Keep the headphones over your ears while you talk. If he can broadcast sound, he could hack into the system."

"Really?" said Kira, doubtful.

"Really. Any sort of input would be enough."

Kira found the jack on the side of the sarcophagus, plugged in, and, not knowing what to expect, said, "Hello?"

The machine boss grunted. "Here." She flipped a switch next to the jack.

A raging howl filled Kira's ears. She flinched and scrabbled to lower the volume. The howl trailed off into a torrent of uneven muttering—words without end and hardly a break between them, stream-of-consciousness blathering giving voice to every thought racing through Gregorovich's mind. There were layers to the muttering: a cloned crowd yammering to itself, for no one tongue could keep pace with the relentless, lightning-fast processes of his consciousness.

I'll wait outside, mouthed Hwa-jung, and she departed.

". . . Hello?" said Kira, wondering what she had gotten herself into.

The muttering never stopped, but it receded, and a single voice—the voice she knew—spoke forth: "Hello?! Hello, my pretty, my darling, my ragtime gal. Have you come to gloat, Ms. Navárez? To point and prod and laugh at my misfortune? To—"

"What? No, of course not."

A laugh echoed in her ears, a shrieking, broken-glass laugh that made the skin on the back of her neck prickle. There was an odd tone to Gregorovich's synthesized voice, a distorted waver that made it hard to understand his vowels, and the volume kept swinging soft to loud and there were irregular breaks to the sound, like a radio broadcast cutting in and out. "Then what? To assuage your conscience? This is your doing, O Angst-Ridden Meatsack; your choice; your responsibility. A prison here of your making, and all around a—"

"You were the one who tried to hijack the *Wallfish,* not me," said Kira. If she didn't interrupt, she had a feeling the ship mind would never stop. "I didn't come here to argue, though."

"Ahahaha! Then what? But I repeat myself. You are so slow, too slow; your mind like mud, your tongue like tarnished lead, your—"

"My mind is fine," she snapped. "I just think before I speak, unlike you."

"Oh, ho! The true colors show; pirates starboard; skull and crossbones and ready to stab a friend in need, ohahaha, when upon rocky reefs a shuttered lighthouse stands and the keeper drowns alone, 'Malcolm, Malcolm, Malcolm,' he cries, and the millipede screams in lonely sympathy."

Kira's alarm rocketed. Falconi was right. Something was wrong with the ship mind, and it went far beyond his disagreement over their decision to help the Knot of Minds. *Gently now.* "No," she said. "I came to see how you were doing before we leave."

Gregorovich cackled. "Your guilt is as clear as transparent aluminum, yes it is. Yes, yes. How am I doing? . . ." There was a welcome pause in his verbal vomit, and even the background muttering fell off, and then his tone grew more measured—an unexpected return of something resembling normalcy.

"The impermanence of nature long ago drove me as mad as a March hare, or haven't you noticed?"

"I was trying to be polite and not mention it."

"Truly, your tact and consideration are without peer."

That was more like it. Kira half smiled. His semblance of sanity was a fragile thing, though, and she wondered how far she dared push. "Are you going to be okay?"

A snortling giggle escaped Gregorovich, but he quickly suppressed it. "Me? Oh I'll be *fiiine,* sure I will. Right as rain, twice as comfy. I'll sit here, all by my lonesome, and devote myself to good thoughts and the hope of future deeds, yes I will, I will, I will."

So that's a no *then.* Kira licked her lips. "Why did you do it? You knew Falconi wouldn't just let you take over. So why do it?"

The background chorus swelled louder. "How to explain? Should I explain? What point now, when actions are spent, and consequences at hand? Hee-hee. But this: I sat through darkness once before, lost my crew and lost my ship. I would not, could not endure it again, no indeed. Give me sweet oblivion first—death that ancient end. A far preferable fate to exile along the cold cliffs where souls wander and wither in isolation, each one a Boltzmann paradox, each one a torment of bad dreams. What is mind, no matter, what is matter, no mind and isolation the cruelest reduction of April and—"

A staticky burst interrupted him, and his voice faded from hearing, but Kira had already tuned him out. He was babbling again. She thought she understood what he'd been saying, but that wasn't what concerned her. A few hours of isolation shouldn't have unbalanced Gregorovich *this* much. There had to be another cause. What could affect a ship mind so strongly? Kira realized she didn't have much of an idea.

Perhaps, if she steered the conversation toward calmer waters, she could get him into a better mindset and find out what the underlying problem was. Perhaps.

"Gregorovich . . . Gregorovich, can you hear me? If you're there, answer me. What's going on?"

After a moment, the ship mind answered with a tiny, far-off voice: "Kira . . . I don't feel so good. I don't . . . Everything is wrong ways round."

She pressed the headphones tighter against her ears, trying to hear better. "Can you tell me what's causing it?"

A faint laugh, growing louder. "Oh, are we in sharing and confessing mode now? Hmm? Is that it?" Another of his unsettling cackles. "Did I ever tell you why I decided to become a ship mind, O Inquisitive One?"

Kira hated to change the topic, but she didn't want to upset him. As long as Gregorovich was willing to talk, she was willing to listen. "No, you didn't," she said.

The ship mind snorted. "Why, because it seemed like a good idea at the time, thatswhyisasisssss. Ah, the untempered idiocy of youth. . . . My body was slightly the worse for wear, you see (you don't, but you do, oh yes). Several limbs were missing, and certain important organs too, and what I'm told was a spec-*tacular* amount of blood and fecal matter was smeared across the road. Black ribbon against black stone, red, red, red, and the sky a faded patch of pain. The only viable options were to be installed in a construct while a new body was grown for me or to transition into a ship mind. And I, in my arrogance and my ignorance, I decided to dare the unknown."

"Even though you knew it was irreversible? Didn't that bother you?" Kira regretted the questions as soon as she asked them; she didn't want to unbalance him further. To her relief, Gregorovich took them well.

"I wasn't so smart then as I am now. Oh, no, no, no. The only things I thought I would miss were hot splashes, sweet soft and savory and seductive spoonfuls and the pleasures of carnal company close held, deep felt, yes, and in both cases I reasoned, yes I reasoned, that VR would provide more-than-adequate substitute. Bits and bytes, bobs of binary, shadows of ideals melting starving on electrons, starving, starving . . . Were I wrong was I wrong? wrong wrong *wrong*, I could always avail myself of a construct to indulge in sensual delights as appealed to my fancy."

Kira's curiosity was sparked. "But why?" she said, in as soothing a voice as she could manage. "Why become a mind at all?"

Gregorovich laughed, and there was arrogance in his voice. "For the sheer thrill of it, of course. To become more than I was before and to bestride the stars as a colossus unbound by the confines of petty flesh."

"It couldn't have been an easy change, though," said Kira. "One moment your life is going one way, and then just like that, an accident sends you in a completely different direction." She was thinking more of herself than him.

"Who said it was an accident?"

She blinked. "I assumed—"

"The truth of it doesn't matter, no it doesn't. I had already considered volunteering to become a ship mind. Precipitous disassembly merely hastened a perilous decision. Change comes more naturally to some people than others. Monotony is boring, and besides, as the ancients loved to point out, expectations of what *could be* or what *should be* are the most common sources of our discontent. Expectations lead to disappointment, and disappointment leads to anger and resentment. And yes, I'm aware of the irony, delicious irony, but self-knowledge is no protection against folly, my Simpering Symbiotic. 'Tis flawed armor at best." The more Gregorovich spoke, the calmer and saner he seemed.

Keep him talking. "If you could do it over again, would you still make the same choice?"

"With regard to becoming a ship mind, yes. Other choices, not so much. Fingers and toes and Mongolian bows."

Kira frowned. A slip from him there. "Is there anything you miss from before? I was going to say 'from when you had a body,' but I suppose the *Wallfish* is your body."

A hollow sigh echoed in her ears. "Freedom. That is what I miss. Freedom."

"What do you mean?"

"All of known space is—or was—at my disposal. I can outrace light itself. I can dive into the atmosphere of a gas giant and bask in the aurora of Eidolon, and I have. But as you said, O Perceptive Little Vexation, the *Wallfish* is my body, and it shall remain my body until such a time (if such a time ever arrives) as I am removed. When we dock, you are free to walk away from the *Wallfish* and go where you will. But not I. Through cameras and sensors I can participate from a distance, but still I remain bound to the *Wallfish,* and the same would be true even if I had a construct I could remotely pilot. That much I miss, the freedom to move without restriction, to relocate myself of my own accord, sans fuss or hassle. . . . I have heard there is a ship mind on Stewart's World who built himself a mech body ten meters high and who now spends his time wandering the uninhabited parts of the planet, painting landscapes of the mountains with a brush as tall as a person. I would like to have a body such as that someday. I would like it very much, although the probability of it seems low at the present."

Gregorovich continued: "Could I advise myself in the past, prior to my transition, I would tell myself to make the most of what I had while I had it. Too often we don't appreciate the value of something until it has slipped our grasp."

"Sometimes that's the only way we learn," said Kira. She paused, struck by her own words.

"So it seems. The benighted tragedy of our species."

"And yet, ignoring the future and/or wallowing in regret can be equally harmful."

"Indeed. The important thing is to try and, by trying, to improve ourselves. Otherwise we might as well have never come down from the trees. But no point in maudlin navel-gazing when the navel is adrift, spinning and wildling and time all out of joint. I have a memoir to write, databases to purge, subroutines to rearrange, chyrons to design, enoptromancy to master, squares upon squares a wave or indivisible scintilla tell me tell me tell me—"

He seemed stuck in a mental rut, the phrase *tell me, tell me* repeating in her ears at different volumes. Kira frowned, frustrated. They'd been doing so well, but he couldn't seem to maintain mental focus. "Gregorovich . . ." Then, more sharply than she intended, "Gregorovich!"

A welcome pause in his logorrhea, and then almost too faint to hear, "Kira, something isn't right. Not right at alllll."

"Can you—"

The chorus of howling voices roared back to full strength, making her wince and dial back the volume on her headphones.

Amid the torrent of noise, she heard Gregorovich say, sounding almost *too* calm, *too* cultured: "Fair winds on your upcoming sleep, my Conciliatory Confessor. May it relieve some of your fermenting spleen. When next we cross paths, I will be sure to thank you most properly. Yes. Quite. And remember to avoid those pesky expectations."

"Thanks. I'll try," she said, trying to humor him. "The queen of infinite space, eh? But you haven't—"

A cackle from the cacophony. "We are all kings and queens of our own dementia. The only question is how we rule. Now go; leave me to my method, atoms to count, TEQs to loop, causality to question, all in a matrix of indecision, round and round and reality bending like photons past deformation of spacetime mass what superluminal transgressions torment tangential tablelands taken topsy-turvy by ahahaha."

2.

Kira pulled off the headphones and stared at the deck. A frown furrowed her brow.

Moving carefully in the zero-g, she went back out to find Hwa-jung waiting for her. "How is *that* one?" the machine boss asked.

Kira handed over the headphones. "Not good. He's . . ." She struggled to find a way to describe Gregorovich's behavior. "He's really off. Something's wrong, Hwa-jung. Really, really wrong. He can't stop talking, and a lot of the time, he can't seem to string together a coherent sentence."

Now the machine boss was frowning as well. "*Aish,*" she muttered. "I wish Vishal were still awake. Machines are what I work with, not squishy brains."

"Could it be something mechanical?" Kira asked. "Could something have happened to Gregorovich when we were on Orsted? Or when you disconnected him from the mainframe?"

Hwa-jung glowered at her. "*That* was a circuit breaker. It would not have caused any problems." But she continued to scowl as she tucked the headphones into a pocket. "Stay here," she said abruptly. "There is something I will check."

The machine boss turned and kicked herself down the hall and around the corridor.

Kira waited as patiently as she could. She couldn't stop thinking about her conversation with Gregorovich. She shivered and hugged herself, although she wasn't cold. If Gregorovich was as bad as he seemed . . . keeping him in cryo really might be their only choice. An unbalanced ship mind was a thing of nightmares.

There were, she thought, many different types of nightmares in the galaxy. Some small, some large, but the worst of all were the ones you lived with.

Kira wanted to tell Falconi about Gregorovich, but she forced herself to wait on Hwa-jung.

Nearly half an hour passed before the machine boss reappeared. She had grease on her hands, new scorch marks on her rumpled sleeves, and a troubled expression that did nothing to ease Kira's worries.

"Did you find something?" Kira asked.

Hwa-jung held up a small black object: a rectangular box the size of two fingers side by side. "This," she said with a tone of disgust. "Bah! It was clamped to the circuits leading into Gregorovich's sarcophagus." She shook her head. "Stupid. I knew something was off when the lights glitched like that in Control when I pulled the breaker."

"What is it?" Kira asked, moving closer.

"Impedance block," said Hwa-jung. "It stops signals from traveling through a line. The UMC must have installed it to help keep Gregorovich from escaping. None of my checks showed it when we came back on the *Wallfish*." She shook her head again. "When I pulled the breaker, it caused a surge in the box, and the surge ran into Gregorovich."

Kira swallowed. "What does that mean?"

Hwa-jung sighed and looked away for a moment. "The surge, it burned the little wires going into Gregorovich. The leads are not connecting properly to his neurons, and the ones that are, *aish*! They are firing wrong."

"Is he in pain?"

A shrug from the machine boss. "I don't know. But the computer says many of the broken leads are in his visual cortex and the area of language processing, so Gregorovich, he may be seeing and hearing things that are not there. Ahhh." She shook the small box. "Vishal will have to help with this. I can't fix Gregorovich."

A sense of helplessness unmoored Kira. "So we have to wait." It wasn't a question.

Hwa-jung nodded. "The best thing we can do is put Gregorovich into cryo. Vishal will look at him when we arrive, but I do not think he can fix him either."

"Do you want me to tell Falconi? I'm going to see him."

"Yes, tell him. I want to get Gregorovich frozen. Sooner is better. I will go into cryo after."

"Okay, will do." Then Kira put a hand on Hwa-jung's shoulder. "And thank you. At least now we know."

The machine boss grunted. "What help is knowing, though? Ah, what a mess. What a mess."

They parted, the machine boss pulling herself into the ship mind's holding room while Kira returned to Control. Falconi wasn't there, nor was he in the ship's now-defunct hydroponics bay.

Slightly puzzled, Kira sought out the captain's cabin. It didn't seem like him to be in his room at a time like this, but . . .

"Come in," he said when she knocked on the door.

The pressure door creaked as Kira pushed her way in. Falconi was sitting at the desk, strapped into his chair to keep from floating away. In one hand, he held a drinking pouch that he was sipping from.

Then she noticed the bonsaied olive tree pushed to the back of the desk. The leaves were tattered, most of the branches broken, the trunk tilted against the side of the pot, and the dirt around the roots looked as if it had been overturned: small clumps floated loose under the lid of clear plastic that covered the top of the pot and surrounded the trunk.

The state of the tree caught her by surprise. She knew how much he cared for the plant.

"So? How'd it go?" Falconi asked.

Kira braced herself against the wall before delving into her report.

As she talked, Falconi's expression grew darker and darker. "Goddammit," he said. "Fucking UMC. They had to go and make things worse. Every fucking time . . ." He drew a hand across his face and stared at an imaginary point somewhere beyond the hull of the ship. She couldn't recall ever seeing him so angry or tired. "Should have trusted my gut earlier. He really is broken."

"*He's* not broken,"said Kira. "There's nothing wrong with Gregorovich per se. It's the equipment he's hooked up to."

Falconi snorted. "Semantics. He's not working. That makes him broken. And I can't do anything about it either. That's the worst part. The one time Greg actually needs help and . . ." He shook his head.

"He means a lot to you, doesn't he?"

A crinkle of foil as Falconi took a sip from his drinking pouch. He avoided her gaze. "If you asked the rest of the crew, I think you'd find that Gregorovich spent a lot of time talking with each of us. He didn't always say much in groups, but whenever we needed him, he was there. And he's gotten us out of some real tight spots."

Kira planted her feet on the deck and allowed the Soft Blade to anchor her there. "Hwa-jung said Vishal might not be able to heal him."

"Yeah," said Falconi, letting out his breath. "Working on ship-mind implants is tricky stuff. And our medibot isn't rated for it either. . . . Thule. Greg wasn't even this bad when we found him."

"What will you do if we get into a fight with the Jellies?"

"Run like hell if it's at all an option," said Falconi. "The *Wallfish* isn't a warship." He pointed a finger at her. "And none of this changes what Gregorovich did. It wasn't some impedance block that caused him to mutiny."

". . . No. I suppose not."

Falconi shook his head. "Damn fool of a ship mind. He was so scared of losing us, he went and jumped off a cliff, and now look where he's at . . . where *we're* at."

"I guess it goes to show that you can still make mistakes, even with a brain as big as his."

"Mmh. That's assuming Gregorovich is wrong. He could be right, you know."

Kira cocked her head. "If you really believe that, why are we going to warn the Knot of Minds?"

"Because I think it's worth the risk."

She thought it best to change the subject then. Motioning toward the olive tree, she said, "What happened?"

Falconi's lip curled with a snarl. "Again, the UMC, that's what. They ripped it out of its stasis box looking for—for whatever. Took me this long to clean the place up."

"Will the tree recover?" It wasn't a variety of plant Kira had experience with.

"Doubt it." Falconi stroked a branch, but only for a moment, as if afraid to cause further damage. "The poor thing was out of the dirt for most of a day, temperature was down, no water, stripped leaves . . ." He held out the pouch. "Want a drink?"

She took the pouch and put her lips to the straw. The harsh burn of some sort of rotgut hit her mouth, and she nearly coughed.

"Good stuff, eh?" Falconi said, seeing her reaction.

"Yeah," said Kira, and coughed. She took another slug and then handed the pouch back.

He tapped the silvered plastic. "Probably not the best idea before cryo, but what the hell, eh?"

"What the hell indeed."

Falconi took a sip of his own and then let out a long sigh and let his head drift back so he was looking at what would be the ceiling when under thrust. "Crazy times, Kira. Crazy times. Shit, of all the ships we had to pick up, we had to pick up yours."

"Sorry. It's not what I wanted either."

He pushed the pouch across to her. She watched it drift through the air and then snared it. Another mouthful of rotgut and another burning streak pouring down her throat. "It's not your fault," he said.

"Actually, I kinda think it is," she said, quiet.

"No." He caught the pouch as she lobbed it over. "We still would have ended up having to deal with this war, even if we *didn't* rescue you."

"Yes, but—"

"But nothing. You think the Jellies were going to leave us alone forever? You finding the suit on Adrasteia was just an excuse for them to invade."

Kira considered that for a moment. "Maybe. What about the nightmares, though?"

"Yeah, well . . ." Falconi shook his head. He already seemed to be feeling the drink. "That's just the sort of bullshit that always happens. You can prepare and prepare, but it's the stuff you don't anticipate that always throws you for a loop. And it *always* happens. You're going about your day, and bam! An asteroid comes out of the blue, ruins your life. How are you supposed to live in a universe like that?"

It was a rhetorical question, but Kira answered anyway: "By taking reasonable precautions and not letting the possibility drive you crazy."

"Like Gregorovich."

"Like Gregorovich," she agreed. "We all have to play the odds, Salvo. It's the nature of life. The only alternative is to cash out early, and that's just giving up."

"Mmm." He peered at her from under his brows, as he so often did, his ice-blue eyes hooded and ghostly pale in the dim light of ship-night. "It looked like the Soft Blade was getting away from you back on Orsted."

Kira shifted, uncomfortable. "Maybe a bit."

"Anything I should be worried about?"

For an uncomfortably long time, she didn't answer. Then: "Maybe." Contracting her hamstrings, she pulled herself down to the deck and secured herself in a sitting position. "The more I let go of the xeno, the more it wants to eat and eat and eat."

Falconi's gaze sharpened. "To what end?"

"I don't know. None of its memories have shown it reproducing, but—"

"But maybe it's keeping that hidden from you."

She tipped a finger in his direction. He offered her the pouch again, and she accepted. "Letting me drink this is kind of a waste of good alcohol. No way for me to get drunk, not with the Soft Blade interfering."

"Don't worry about it. . . . You think the xeno is some sort of doomsday nanoweapon?"

"It has the capability, but I don't think that's necessarily what it was made for either." Kira struggled to find the right words. "The suit doesn't *feel* malevolent. Does that make sense? It doesn't feel angry or sadistic."

Falconi raised an eyebrow. "A machine wouldn't."

"No, but it does feel some things. It's hard to explain, but I don't think it's entirely a machine either." She tried to think of another way to explain. "When I was holding the shield around the maglev, there were all these tiny little tendrils going out into the walls. I could *feel* them, and it didn't seem like the Soft Blade wanted to destroy. It felt like it wanted to build."

"But build what?" Falconi said in a soft voice.

". . . Anything or everything. Your guess is as good as mine." A somber silence stilled the conversation. "Ah, I forgot to tell you, Hwa-jung said she was going into cryo as soon as she put Gregorovich under."

"Just you and me, then," Falconi said, and raised the pouch as if in a toast.

Kira smiled slightly. "Yes. And Morven."

"Pshaw. She doesn't count."

As if to punctuate his words, the FTL alert interrupted, and then—with a distant whine—the *Wallfish* activated its Markov Drive and departed from normal space.

"And there we go," said Falconi. He shook his head as if he were having trouble accepting it.

Kira found herself looking at the ruined bonsai again. "How old is the tree?" she asked.

"Would you believe, almost three hundred years?"

"No!"

"For real. It's from Earth, back before the turn of the millennium. Got it off a guy as part of payment for a transport job. He didn't realize how valuable it was."

"Three hundred years . . ." The number was hard to comprehend. The tree was older than the entire history of humans living in space. It predated the Mars and Venus colonies, predated every hab-ring and manned research station outside low-Earth orbit.

"Yeah." A brooding expression settled on Falconi's face. "Those jackbooted thugs had to tear it up. Couldn't just scan the place."

"Mmm." Kira was still thinking about how the Soft Blade had felt on Orsted—that and whatever purpose it had been built or born for. She couldn't forget the sensation of the countless threadlike tendrils insinuating themselves through the fascia of the station, touching, tearing, building, *understanding.*

The Soft Blade was more than just a weapon. Of that she was sure. And from that certainty came an idea that gave Kira pause. She didn't know if it would work, but she wanted it to so she could feel less bad about herself and the xeno.

So she would have a solid reason for viewing the Soft Blade as something other than an instrument of destruction.

"Do you mind if I try something?" she asked, extending a hand toward the ruined tree.

"What?" Falconi asked, wary.

"I'm not sure, but . . . let me try. Please."

He fiddled with the edge of the packet as he considered. "Alright. Fine. But nothing too crazy. The *Wallfish* has enough holes in her hull already."

"Give me *some* credit at least."

Kira released herself from the floor and crawled across the wall to the desk. There, she pulled the pot close and laid her hands on the trunk. The bark was rough against her palms, and it smelled fresh and green, sea air wafting over cut grass.

Falconi said, "Are you just going to hang there, or—"

"Shh."

Concentrating, Kira sent the Soft Blade burrowing into the tree, with but one thought, one directive guiding it: *heal*. Bark creaked and split, and tiny black threads swarmed across the surface of the tree. Kira felt the plant's internal structures, the layers of bark (inner and outer), the rings, the hard core of heartwood, every narrow branch, and the sprouting base of every fragile, silver-backed leaf.

"Hey," said Falconi, getting to his feet.

"Wait," said Kira, hoping the suit could do what she was asking of it.

Across the olive tree, broken branches returned to their rightful place, lifting and straightening until standing to proud effect. The cut-grass smell intensified as sap wept from along the trunk. Crumpled leaves flattened and the holes in them closed up and, where missing, new blades budded and burst forth—silver daggers bright with new life.

At last the changes slowed and stopped, and Kira felt satisfied the damage to the tree was repaired. The Soft Blade could have continued—it wanted to continue—but then the directive would have shifted from *heal* to *grow*, and that seemed to her greedy, foolish. An unwise tempting of fate.

So she recalled the suit.

"There," she said, and lifted her hands. The tree stood whole and healthy, as before. An aura of energy seemed to emanate from it: *life* newly born and burnished to a high sheen.

Kira felt overcome with a sense of wonder at what the xeno was capable of.

At what *she* was capable of. She'd managed to heal a living thing—to reshape flesh (of a sort) and to give comfort instead of pain, to create instead of destroy. Unbidden, a laugh escaped her. A weight seemed to lift from her shoulders, as if the thrust had dropped to half a g or less.

This was a gift: a precious ability pregnant with potential. With it she could have done so much on Weyland, in the gardens of the colony. With it she could have helped her father with his Midnight Constellations, or on Adrasteia, she could have helped the spread of green across the moon's rocky crust.

Life, and all that meant. Triumph and gratitude filled her eyes with tears, and she smiled through them, happy.

A similar wonder gentled Falconi's expression. "How did you learn to do that?" He touched a leaf with the tip of a finger, as if unable to believe.

"I stopped being so afraid."

"Thank you," he said, and never had Kira heard him sound so earnest.

"You're . . . you're welcome."

Then Falconi leaned forward, put his hands on either side of her face, and—before Kira quite knew what was happening—kissed her.

He tasted different than Alan. Saltier, and she could feel the sharp tips of his stubble scraping against the skin around her lips.

Shocked, Kira froze, uncertain of how to react. The Soft Blade formed rows of dull spikes across her arms and chest, but like her, they remained held in position, neither advancing nor retracting.

Falconi broke the kiss, and Kira struggled to regain herself. Her heart was racing, and the temperature in the cabin seemed to have shot up. "What was that?" she said. Her voice rasped more than she liked.

"Sorry," said Falconi, seeming somewhat abashed. It was an attitude she wasn't used to seeing from him. "Guess I got carried away."

"Uh-huh." She licked her lips without meaning to and then berated herself for it. *Dammit.*

A sly grin crossed his face. "I don't normally make a habit of hitting on crew or passengers. Unprofessional. Bad for business."

Kira's heart was pounding even harder. "That so."

"Yes it is. . . ." He drained the last of the rotgut from the pouch. "Still friends?"

"Are we friends?" Kira said in a challenging tone. She cocked her head.

Falconi regarded her for a moment, as if debating. "Anyone I'd trust to watch my back in a firefight is a friend of mine. As far as I'm concerned, yeah, we're friends. Unless you feel differently."

"No," said Kira, pausing just as long as he had. "We're friends."

A sharp gleam reappeared in his eyes. "Well, I'm glad to have that cleared up. Again, my apologies. The drink got the better of me. You have my word it won't happen again."

"That's . . . Fine. Good."

"I'd better put this into stasis," he said, reaching for the bonsai. "And then I should get myself into cryo before we heat up the *Wallfish* too much. And you, what are you going to do?"

"The usual," she said. "I think I'm just going to hole up in my cabin this time, if that's okay."

He nodded. "See you starside, Kira."

"You too, Salvo."

3.

Back in her cabin, Kira washed her face with a damp towel and then hung floating in front of the sink while she looked at herself in the mirror. Even though she hadn't initiated the kiss, she still felt guilty about it. She'd never even looked at another man—not in that way—while she and Alan were together. Falconi's sudden forwardness had more than caught her by surprise; it had forced her to consider what she was going to do in the future, if she had a future.

The worst thing was, the kiss had felt good.

Alan . . . Alan had been dead for over nine months. Not for her, not with all the time she'd spent in hibernation, but for the rest of the universe, that was the reality. It was a hard truth to swallow.

Did she even *like* Falconi? Kira had to think about that one for a while. In the end she decided she did. He was attractive in a rather solid, dark, hairy way. But that didn't mean anything in and of itself. She was in no shape to be getting in a relationship with anyone, much less the captain of the ship. That way always led to trouble.

It was selfish, but Kira was glad Gregorovich hadn't been around to see the awkwardness. He would have made endless fun of her and Falconi in his own weird way.

Perhaps it would be best to talk with Falconi again, make it *very* clear that nothing else was going to happen between them. Hell, he was just lucky that the Soft Blade hadn't overreacted out of a misplaced urge to protect her. . . . He'd been either very brave or very foolish.

"You did well," she whispered, looking down at the Soft Blade. And Kira thought, just for an instant, that she felt a sense of pride from the xeno. But it was a fleeting thing that might as well have been a figment of her imagination.

"Morven," she said. "Is Falconi still out of cryo?"

"No, Ms. Navárez," said the pseudo-intelligence. "He just received his first round of injections. He is no longer able to communicate."

Kira made a dissatisfied sound. *Fine.* It probably wasn't necessary to talk to him again, but if it were, she could always do so when they reached their destination.

The idea *wasn't* to fly all the way to the rendezvous point Tschetter's Jellies had proposed. Rather, the *Wallfish* would drop out of FTL some distance away but still close enough to send a warning in time to keep the Knot of Minds from being ambushed and, in doing so, perhaps forestall an even greater catastrophe than the current war between humans and Jellies. Then, the requirements of honor and duty satisfied, they could head back to settled space.

However, Kira had a suspicion that Itari would want to rejoin its compatriots, which would necessitate a meeting of some kind.

"That's what we are," she muttered as she pulled herself over to the bed, "a glorified shuttle service." It reminded her of something her grandfather—on her father's side—had been prone to saying, which was that ". . . the meaning of life, Kira, is moving things from point *a* to point *b*. That's it. That's all we really do."

"But what about when we talk?" she had said, not entirely understanding.

"That's just moving an idea from in here," and he tapped her on the forehead, "out into the real world."

Kira had never forgotten. She'd also never forgotten that he'd described everything outside her head as *the real world*. Ever since, she continued to wonder if that was true or not. How much reality did the contents of one's mind actually possess? . . . When she dreamed, were the dreams mere shadows or was there a truth to them?

She thought Gregorovich might have something to say on the matter.

As Kira made a web of struts from the Soft Blade to hold herself upon the mattress, she kept thinking about the bonsai tree. The memory made her smile.

Life. She'd spent so long on spaceships and space stations and cold, rocky asteroids, she'd almost forgotten the joy that came from growing things.

She recalled each and every one of the sensations she'd felt from the Soft Blade during the healing process. And she compared them to the similar sensations from Orsted. There was something in them worth investigating, she thought. As they traveled through FTL, she would continue to work on her control of the xeno—always that—and on improving the ease of communication between her and the organism so that it could better carry out her wishes without her having to worry about micromanaging it so much. But more than any of that, Kira wanted to explore the urge she'd felt from the Soft Blade—only in fleeting snatches before, now more strongly—the urge to build and create.

It stirred her interest, and for the first time, it was something Kira *wanted* to do with the xeno.

So she set her weekly alarm, as she had done during each trip since 61 Cygni, and then she once again began to work with the Soft Blade.

It was a curious experience. Kira was determined to keep the xeno from damaging the *Wallfish,* as it had Orsted, but at the same time, she wanted to experiment. In certain controlled ways, she wanted to remove all restrictions and let the Soft Blade do what it so obviously wanted.

She started with the handhold by the side of her bed. It was a nonessential part of the ship; if the xeno destroyed it, Hwa-jung could easily print a replacement, although Falconi might not be too pleased about it. . . .

Go, she whispered in her mind.

From her palm, soft fibrils extended, black and seeking. They fused with the composite grip, and again, Kira felt the delicious, addictive sensation of *making* something. What, she didn't know, but there was a satisfaction to the feeling that reminded her of the joy she so often found in solving a difficult problem.

She let out a sigh, her breath a pale wraith twining in the chilled air.

When the fibers from the Soft Blade had completely covered the grip, and when she felt from it a sense of completion and—more—a desire to move past the hold and extend deeper into the hull, she stopped it and withdrew the xeno, curious to see what it had wrought.

She saw, but she didn't understand.

There, where the curved, cylindrical handhold had been, she saw . . . *something.* A length of patterned material that reminded Kira of a cellular structure or an intricate sculpture, one covered with a repeating pattern of subdivided triangles. The surface was slightly metallic and had a greenish iridescence to it, and there were small round nodules of palest chartreuse nestled within the triangles.

She touched the transformed grip. It was warm.

Kira traced the pattern on the surface, overcome by a sense of wonder. Whatever the Soft Blade had made, she thought it was beautiful, and she had a sense from it that the material was somehow alive. Or had the potential for life.

Kira wanted to do more. But she knew, this—*this*—she had be careful with, even more than the deadly stabbing spikes that the xeno was so fond of. Life was the most dangerous thing there was.

Still, she couldn't help but wonder if *she* could guide or control the Soft Blade's creative output. The Maw could, so why not her? *Careful now.* There was a reason biowarfare was banned by every member of the League (and Shin-Zar also). But she wasn't trying to create a weapon. Nor servants to fight for her as the Maw had done.

Like this, she thought, grasping the rail alongside her bed and picturing the coiled shapes of an oros fern: her favorite plant from Eidolon.

At first the xeno failed to respond. Then, just as she'd started to give up, it flowed from her hand and across the railing. As if by magic, the delicate stems of oros ferns sprouted from the railing. They were imperfect replicas, both in shape and substance, but recognizable, and as Kira withdrew the Soft Blade, she caught a whiff of fragrance from the fronds.

The plants weren't just sculptures. They were actual living things: organic and precious because of it.

Kira let out a small gasp, shocked despite herself. She touched each of the ferns, and tears blurred her vision. She blinked them back and half laughed, half cried. If only her parents could have seen this. . . . If only Alan could have. . . .

Kira knew it would be reckless to try anything more ambitious at the moment. She was content with what she'd achieved. What *they'd* achieved.

And for all the uncertainty the future held, she felt a spark of hope that had long been absent. The Soft Blade wasn't just a force for destruction. She didn't know how, but a certainty grew within her that the xeno might be able to stop the Maw, if only she could figure out how to harness its abilities.

A sense of lightness filled Kira's body (and it wasn't the zero-g). She smiled, and the smile stayed as she prepared for the long sleep ahead. *Perchance to dream,* she thought, and she laughed longer and louder than she would around other people. At least while sober.

Still pondering, she closed her eyes and willed the Soft Blade to relax, to rest, to protect her against the cold and the dark. And soon it was—far sooner than ever before—awareness faded and the soft wings of slumber wrapped around her.

4.

Once each week, Kira woke and trained with the Soft Blade. This time, she stayed in her cabin for the duration of the trip; she didn't need to lift weights or otherwise stress her body in order to work with the xeno. Not anymore.

Once each week, and on each occasion she allowed the Soft Blade to spread farther across the interior of her cabin and to build and grow *more.* Sometimes she contributed, but for the most part, Kira gave the xeno the space to do what it wanted, and she watched with increasing wonder. Some limits she set—the display on her desk was not to be touched—but everything else in the cabin was there for the xeno to use.

Once each week and no more. And when not training, she floated still and quiet, hibernating in the sleep that was akin to death, where all was cold and grey, and sounds filtered in as if from a great distance.

In that dusty neverwhere, a dream came to her:

She saw herself—her actual self, shorn of the suit and naked as the day she was born—standing in blackest darkness. At first the void was empty save for her, and a stillness surrounded her, as if she existed in a time before time itself.

Then in front of her flowered a profusion of blue lines: fractal tracery that coiled and scrolled like vines as it spread. The lines formed a dome of intersecting shapes with her at the center, a shell of endlessly repeating curves and spikes—a universe of detail in each point of space.

And she knew, somehow she knew, that she was seeing the Soft Blade as it truly was. She reached out and touched one of the lines. An electric chill poured through her, and in that instant, she beheld a thousand stars born and died, each with their own planets, species, and civilizations.

If she could have gasped, she would have.

She took her hand away from the line and stepped back. Wonder overcame her, and she felt small and humbled. The fractal lines continued to shift and turn with a sound like sliding silk, but they grew no closer, no brighter. She sat and watched, and from the glowing matrix above, a sense of watchful protectiveness emanated.

Yet she felt no comfort. For outside the tracery, she could sense—as if with ancient instinct—a looming menace. Hunger without end spreading cancer-like in the surrounding blackness, and with it, a twisting of nature that resulted in the straightness of right angles. Without the Soft Blade, she would have been exposed, vulnerable, helpless before the menace.

Fear overtook her, and she huddled down, feeling as if the fractal dome were a candle flickering in the void, threatened on all sides by a hostile wind. She was, she knew, the focus of the menace—she and the Soft Blade alike—and the weight of its malignant craving was so great, so all-encompassing, so cruel and alien, that she felt helpless before it. Insignificant. Barren of hope.

Thus she stayed, alone and scared, with a sense of imminent doom so strong that any change—even death itself—would have been a welcome relief.

PART FIVE

★ ★ ★ ★ ★ ★ ★

MALIGNITATEM

And as a twig is bent, it grows.

—MARION TINSLEY

CHAPTER I

* * * * * * *

ARRIVAL

1.

Kira woke.

At first she couldn't tell where she was. Blackness surrounded her, a black so profound there was no difference between her eyes closed and her eyes open. Where the emergency lights should have been, only an inky darkness pervaded. The air was warmer than normal for a trip in FTL—moister too—and no breath of wind stirred the womb-like space.

"Morven, raise lights," she murmured, still groggy from her long inactivity. Her voice sounded curiously muffled in the stilled air.

No lights brightened the space, nor was there any response from the pseudo-intelligence.

Frustrated, Kira tried something else. *Light,* she told the Soft Blade. She didn't know if the xeno could help, but she figured it was worth a try.

To her satisfaction, a soft green illumination gave shape to her surroundings. She was still in her cabin, but it in no way resembled the room as it had been upon departing Sol. Ribs of organic black material lined the walls, and fibrous cross-weaves matted the floor and ceiling. The newborn light came from pulsing, fruit-like orbs that hung upon growths of twisted vines that had crawled up along the corners of the room. The vines had leaves, and in them, she saw the shape of the oros fern repeated and elaborated upon in ornate, rococo flourishes. And everything—vines, orbs, ribs, and mats—was covered with tiny, textural patterns, as if an obsessive artist had been determined to decorate every square millimeter with fractal adornment.

Kira looked with a sense of wonder. *She* had done this. She and the Soft Blade. It was a far better thing than fighting and killing, she thought.

Not only could she see the results of their efforts, she could *feel* them, like extensions of her body, although there was a difference between the material of the suit itself and the plantlike creations. Those felt more distant, and she could tell that she couldn't move or manipulate them the way she could with the actual fibers of the Soft Blade. They were, in a sense, independent of her and the xeno; self-sustaining life-forms that could live on without them, as long as the plants had proper nourishment.

Even disregarding the plants, the Soft Blade had grown during the trip. It had produced far more material than was required to cover her body. What to do with it? She considered having the xeno dispose of the material, as she had with unneeded tendrils on Orsted, but Kira hated to tear down what they had built. Besides, it might be unwise to get rid of the mass when there was a chance—unpleasant to consider but not outside the realm of likelihood—that she might need it in the near future.

Could she leave the extra material in the cabin, though? *Only one way to find out.*

As she prepared to free herself from the struts holding her in place on the bed, Kira looked down at her body. Her right hand—the one she'd lost at Bughunt—had melted into the mattress, dissolved into a web of snarled lines that ran the length of the bed and into the casing on the walls.

A momentary surge of panic caused the material to ripple and stir and extrude rows of barbed spikes.

No! she thought. The spikes subsided, and Kira took a steadying breath.

First, she concentrated on re-forming her missing hand. The snarled lines twisted and flowed back over the bed, once more giving shape to her wrist, palm, and fingers. Then, Kira willed the Soft Blade to release her from the bed.

With a sticky sound, she broke free. Surprised, Kira realized that she didn't have any physical connection to the black growths on the walls, though she could still feel them as part of herself. It was the first time she had managed to consciously separate herself from a part of the Soft Blade. Apparently the xeno didn't mind, not so long as it still covered her body.

It was an encouraging development.

Still somewhat disoriented, she pulled herself along the wall to where the door ought to be. As she approached, some combination of the xeno's awareness and her own intent caused that section of the gleaming black material to retract with a slight sliding sound.

Beneath was the desired pressure door.

It opened, and Kira was relieved to see the normal brown paneling covering the walls of the hallway outside. Her efforts to constrain the Soft Blade's growth had been a success; it hadn't spread to the rest of the ship.

Looking back, she said, "*Stay,*" same as she would to a pet.

Then she exited into the hallway. The mass of black fibers inside her cabin remained behind.

As an experiment, Kira closed the pressure door. She could still feel the xeno on the other side. And again, it didn't try to follow her.

She wondered how the different parts of the Soft Blade communicated. Radio? FTL? Something else? How far away could they safely be? Could the signal be jammed? It might be an issue in combat. Something she'd have to watch for.

But for the present, Kira was content to leave the growths in her cabin. If she needed them, a single thought would be enough to summon the rest of the xeno to her side. Hopefully without damaging the *Wallfish*.

She smirked. Falconi wouldn't be too pleased when he found out about her cabin. Hwa-jung too, and Gregorovich, if the ship mind ever returned to his normal self.

Kira assumed they had arrived, but the *Wallfish* still seemed quieter than it should. She tried pulling up her overlays, but as with each of the last two FTL trips, the Soft Blade had absorbed her contacts. She wasn't sure at what point exactly, but it must have happened sometime during her dreaming hibernation. Frustrated, she muttered, "When are you going to learn?"

Kira was about to head to the storm shelter, to check on the crew, when the intercom crackled and Falconi's voice emanated from a speaker by her head: "Kira, come see me in Control once you're up." He sounded rough, real rough, as if he'd just been puking.

Kira swung by the galley to get herself a pouch of heated chell before heading toward the front of the ship.

As the pressure door to Control swung open with a squeal of protest, Falconi glanced up from the holo-display. His skin was an unpleasant grey, the whites of his eyes were tinged yellow, and he was shivering and chattering as if it were nearly freezing. All the classic signs of cryo sickness.

"Thule," said Kira, kicking herself over to him. "Here, you need this more than me." She shoved the packet of chell into his hands.

"Thanks," said Falconi from between gritted teeth.

"Bad reaction, huh?"

He ducked his head. "Yeah. It's been getting worse the last few jumps. I don't think my body likes the chemicals we've been using. Have to talk with . . ." He shivered so hard his teeth clattered. ". . . have to talk with the doc about it."

"How are you going to get back?" Kira asked. Going to one of the emergency stations along the wall, she fetched a thermal blanket and brought it to him.

Falconi didn't resist as she wrapped it around his shoulders. "I'll survive," he said with a certain amount of grim humor.

"I'm sure you will," she said dryly. Then she glanced around the empty room. "Where's everyone else?"

"Didn't see any reason to wake them up if they just had to go back into cryo." Falconi tightened the blanket around himself. "No reason to make them go through this any more times than necessary."

Kira pulled herself into the seat next to him and strapped herself in. "Have you sent the warning yet?"

He shook his head. "Waiting for Itari. I gave the Jelly a buzz on the intercom. Should be up here before too long." Falconi gave her a sideways glance. "How about you? All good?"

"All good. But, there's something you should know. . . ." Then Kira told him about what she and the Soft Blade had done.

Falconi made an exasperated sound. "Did you really have to start disassembling my ship?"

"Yeah, we did," she said. "Sorry. It was just a little bit."

He grunted. "Great. Do we have to worry about it wrecking the rest of the *Wallfish*?"

"No," said Kira. "Not unless something happens to me, but even then I don't think it would do anything to the ship."

Falconi cocked his head. "So what would the Soft Blade do if you die?"

"I . . . I'm not sure. I'd guess it would return to its dormant state, the way it was on Adrasteia. That or it would try to bond with someone else."

"Mmm. Well, that's not alarming in the slightest." Falconi took another sip of chell and then gave it back to her. The grey in his cheeks was beginning to fade, replaced by a more healthy color.

As he had predicted, Itari arrived in Control soon after, pieces of its hibernation cocoon still clinging to its many limbs. Kira was impressed to see that the Jelly had regrown most of the tentacle it had cut off during their escape from Orsted (although the replacement was still shorter and thinner than the rest of its siblings).

[[Itari here: How moves the water?]]

She answered as was right and proper: [[Kira here: The water is still. . . . We are ready to send farscent warning to the Knot of Minds.]]

[[Itari here: Then let us not waste the rightness of time.]]

2.

Transmitting the signal turned out to be more of a hassle than Kira expected. She had to teach Itari how the *Wallfish*'s FTL comms worked, and the Jelly had to explain—with great difficulty and much backtracking—how to broadcast and encode the message in such a way that the Knot of Minds would not only notice but understand the warning. Lacking the Jelly machine that converted their scents to signals, Kira had to translate Itari's words—if *words* was even the right term—into English, in the hope that the Knot would bother translating.

After several hours of work, the warning went out, and Falconi said, "There, it's done."

"Now we wait," said Kira.

It would take half a day for the warning to reach the proposed rendezvous spot—which itself was within a few days' travel of Cordova-1420, the system where the Jellies were building their fleet—and half a day to receive any answer back. "Any chance that the UMC's hunters might intercept the signal?" Kira asked.

"Eh," said Falconi. "There's a chance, but it's literally astronomical."

3.

For the rest of the day, Kira helped Falconi run diagnostics throughout the *Wallfish* as he checked on the systems necessary for the smooth functioning of the ship. Air duct filters needed to be cleaned, water lines flushed, the fusion drive test fired, computers restarted, and outside sensors replaced, along with all the many little and not-so-little tasks that made survival in space possible.

Falconi didn't ask for help, but Kira had never been one to sit around when work needed doing. Besides, she could tell he was still suffering from the aftereffects of cryo. She'd only had one bad reaction herself, during her second trip out for the Lapsang Corporation. An error in the cryo tube had resulted in her receiving a slightly higher dose of one of the sedatives. Even that small difference had been enough to keep her in the bathroom, puking her guts out, the whole time she'd been on mission. That had been fun.

So she had sympathy for Falconi's distress, although in his case, it seemed worse than just an adverse reaction to some sedative. He appeared genuinely ill. Cryo sickness would fade in time—that she knew—but he might not have very long to recover before they would have to start back for the League. And that worried Kira.

Aside from the usual maintenance required, the *Wallfish* was in generally good shape. The most serious repair that required their attention was a faulty pressure seal in the port cargo hold, but even that was easily dealt with.

Throughout it all, Kira could still feel the contents of her cabin—the black armor the Soft Blade had built upon the walls. She even took Falconi to see what she and the xeno had built. He poked his head in long enough to glance around and then backed out. "Nope," he said. "No offense, Kira, but *nope*."

"None taken," she said with a grin. She still hadn't forgotten about their kiss, but she didn't see a reason to bring it up now. In any case, Falconi wasn't in any shape for that sort of a conversation.

Following a quiet evening, she and Falconi retired to their respective cabins (and Itari to the cargo hold) for the night. The black casing that now covered Kira's room made it feel heavy, ominous. But safe too—there was that—and the vines and flowers helped mitigate the heaviness. She worried about the air vents being blocked, but then she realized the Soft Blade would surely see to it that she had enough oxygen to keep from suffocating.

"I'm back," she whispered, running a hand along the ridged wall.

The wall shivered slightly, like skin crinkling in the cold. And Kira smiled a small smile, feeling an unexpected sense of pride. The room was hers and hers alone, and although it was mostly the work of the Soft Blade, the growth was still a part of her, birthed from her mind, if not her flesh.

And she remembered the dream she'd had during her long sleep. "You were trying to protect me, weren't you?" she said, somewhat louder than before.

The greenish lights in the room seemed to pulse in response, but so faintly that it was hard to be sure. Feeling more comfortable, she moved to the bed and secured herself to sleep.

4.

Late next morning, over twenty-four hours after they had emerged from FTL, Kira and Falconi gathered in the galley to wait for the possible reply from the Knot of Minds. Itari joined them, taking up a position atop one of the two tables. The Jelly held itself in place with the small grasping arms that unfolded from its carapace.

Falconi was lost in his overlays, and Kira was watching a vid—one of the newscasts the *Wallfish* had picked up before leaving Sol—on the holo-display built into the table. The vid wasn't very interesting, so after a few minutes, she turned it off and fell to studying the Jelly across the room.

The dusky, autumn colors of Itari's tentacles were solid now, unshifting, though that would change were its emotions to rise. Kira found it interesting that the Jellies not only had emotions, but that they weren't entirely alien to her. Perhaps, she thought, they were easier for her to understand because of the Soft Blade's time spent joined with the graspers.

Graspers . . . Even in the small moments the xeno was inside her mind, it shaded her thoughts with meanings from another era. Once that had bothered Kira. Now she acknowledged and accepted the fact without judgment. *She* was the one who would decide the worth of things, not the xeno, no matter how strongly she felt its inherited memories.

A continuous cloud of scents emanated from the Jelly. At the moment, they were subdued—just a general *I am here,* like a low hum in the background—interspersed with an occasional spike of interest-driven odor, spicy and somewhat unpleasant.

Kira wondered what the Jelly was doing, whether it had implants of its own or if it was just thinking and remembering.

[[Kira here: Tell me of your shoal, Itari.]]

[[Itari here: What shoal do you mean, Idealis? My hatching? My co-forms? My Arm? There are many kinds of shoals. Does not the Idealis tell you of these things?]]

The Jelly's question was close enough to her own ruminations, it gave her pause. [[Kira here: Yes, but as through muddy water. Tell me, where were you hatched? How were you raised?]]

[[Itari here: I was hatched in a clutching pool near the shore of High Lfarr. It was a warm place with much light and much food. When I was grown to my third-form, I was given to this current form, which is how I have served ever since.]]

[[Kira here: Did you have no choice as to your form?]]

Scent of puzzlement from the Jelly. [[Itari: Why would I have a choice? What choice is there?]]

[[Kira here: I mean . . . what did *you* wish to do?]]

The puzzlement deepened. [[Itari here: Why would that matter? This form was how best I could serve my Arm. What else would there be to do?]]

[[Kira here: Do you not have any desires of your own?]]

[[Itari here: Of course. To serve my Arm and the Wranaui as a whole.]]

[[Kira here: But you have your own ideas of how best to do that, yes? You do not agree with all Wranaui about the course of this . . . ripple.]]

A gentle flush crept down the Jelly's limbs. [[Itari here: There are many solutions to the same problem, but the goal itself does not shift.]]

She decided to try a different tack. [[Kira here: If you did not have to serve, what would you do? If the Arms did not exist and there were no one to tell you how to spend your time?]]

[[Itari here: Then it would fall to me to rebuild our race. I would shift forms and spawn hatchlings every moment of the day until our strength was returned.]]

Kira released a small hiss of frustration, loud enough that Falconi noticed. "You talking with that thing?" he asked, nodding toward Itari.

"Yeah, but not really getting anywhere."

"I'm sure it feels the same about you."

Kira grunted. He wasn't wrong. She was trying to communicate with an alien species. Just talking to a human from another city, much less another *planet,* could be nigh on impossible. Why should it be any easier with an alien? She felt like she had to try, though. If they were going to be dealing with the Jellies on a regular basis in the future, then she wanted to have some sense of what was important to them (outside of the memories from the Soft Blade).

[[Kira here: Answer me this: What do you do when there is nothing that needs doing? You cannot work *all* the time. No creature can.]]

[[Itari here: I rest. I contemplate my future actions. I honor the acts of the Vanished. If I have the chance, I swim.]]

[[Kira here: Do you play?]]

[[Itari here: Play is for first- and second-forms.]]

There was a curious lack of imagination to the Jellies that Kira found odd. How had they managed to build an interstellar civilization when they didn't seem driven to dream the way humans so often were? The technology they had scavenged from the Vanished couldn't have helped *that* much. Or had it? . . . She warned herself against making human-centric judgments. After all, the Jelly the Soft Blade had been joined with—Shoal Leader Nmarhl—had shown plenty of initiative during its time. Perhaps she was failing to understand a linguistic or cultural difference between her and Itari.

[[Kira here: What do the Wranaui want, Itari?]]

[[Itari here: To live, to eat, to spread to all friendly waters. In that, we are the same as you, two-form.]]

[[Kira here: And what are the Wranaui? What is the heart of your nature?]]

[[Itari here: We are what we are.]]

[[Kira here: The Idealis calls you *graspers.* Why would it think that?]]

The Jelly's tentacles rubbed over themselves. [[Itari here: Because we have taken up the sacred pieces the Vanished left behind. Because what we can hold, we hold tight. Because each Arm must do as it sees fit.]]

[[Kira here: The Vanished were on your homeworld, were they not?]]

[[Itari here: Yes. We found their works on the land and deep in the Abyssal Plain.]]

[[Kira here: So there *is* solid land on your planet?]]

[[Itari here: Some, but less than most.]]

[[Kira here: What level of technology did the Wranaui have before finding the works of the Vanished?]]

[[Itari here: We had learned how to smelt metal by the heated vents in our oceans, but there was much that was beyond us by reason of our life under the water. It was only by the grace of the Vanished that we were able to expand beyond the vergeal depths.]]

[[Kira here: I see.]]

She continued to question the Jelly, trying to suss out what she could of its species and civilization, but too many areas of confusion remained for her to make much progress. The more she talked with Itari, the more Kira realized just how different their two kinds really were—and the differences went far beyond the already vast physical disparities.

It was nearing midnight ship time, and Falconi was picking up in the galley in preparation for retiring, when a tone sounded and Morven said, "Captain, incoming transmission."

5.

An electric tingle crawled down Kira's spine. Now maybe they would have a sense of what was going to happen—of where to go and what to do.

"On screen," said Falconi, terse. He wiped his hands with a towel and pushed himself over to where Kira sat floating at the table.

The built-in holo sprang to life, and an image of Tschetter—clad in the same skinsuit as before—appeared from the shoulders up. Kira was relieved to see the major had survived the battle at Bughunt.

Tschetter said, "Captain Falconi, Navárez, your message is received and acknowledged. Thank you. We would have been in a shit-ton of trouble otherwise—not that the current situation is much better. Given the change in circumstances, it's imperative that we meet and talk." As Kira had expected. "Let me repeat: it's imperative that we meet. Long-distance won't suffice. It's not secure, and we can't have a proper conversation this way. Lphet has proposed the following coordinates, which I've done my best to convert into standard notation. For the sake of everyone's safety, don't respond to this message. We will travel to the specified location and wait exactly forty-two hours after you receive this. If the *Wallfish* doesn't arrive by then, Lphet says it will assume that you—and this specifically means *you*, Kira—are no longer willing to assist in this endeavor, and the Knot of Minds will plan accordingly." A note of appeal entered Tschetter's voice, even though her expression remained as stern as ever. "I can't emphasize enough just how important this is, Kira. Please, you have to come. And you as well, Falconi. Humanity needs all the allies it can find at the moment. . . . Tschetter over and out."

"They don't know we're traveling under the name *Finger Pig*, do they," said Kira, gesturing at the holo. The realization had just occurred to her.

"No," said Falconi. "Good point. We'll shift our transponder back. Would suck to get blown up over a case of mistaken identity."

"So we're going?" Kira asked.

"One second. Let me check the coordinates. Update our wriggly little friend here while I do."

Itari, Kira saw, *was* rather restless. Its tentacles were red and blue, and they wormed across the table where the Jelly had been floating, gripping and regripping the grating with what in a human would have been nervous energy.

After Kira filled it in, the Jelly said, [[Itari here: We will meet with the Knot, yes? Yes?]]

The repetition reminded her of Vishal, and Kira smiled without meaning to. [[Kira here: Yes, I think so.]]

"Okay," said Falconi. "Looks like they want to meet closer to Cordova-Fourteen-Twenty. Assuming we get out of here quick-like, we can make it to the spot in about twenty-eight hours."

"In FTL?" said Kira.

"Of course."

"Just checking. . . . That's cutting it awfully close, isn't it?"

He shrugged. "They're only twelve hours away by signal, so not really."

"Do you need to go back into cryo?"

"Nah, but I'm going to leave the rest of the crew under, and we'll have to keep the ship as cold as possible. You'll tell Itari that, yes?"

She did. And then they set about departing the empty patch of interstellar space the *Wallfish* was currently racing through—although with no close point of reference, they seemed to be sitting perfectly still.

Once the ship was properly chilled, the Markov Drive wound back up, the familiar whine sounded, and they entered FTL.

6.

The twenty-eight hours passed in cold, quiet, and dark. Kira and Falconi spent most of their time apart, in their cabins, keeping as still as they reasonably could, to avoid producing extra heat. Likewise, Itari retreated to the port cargo hold, and there the alien held itself in watchful stillness.

A few times Kira met with Falconi in the galley for meals. They talked in hushed tones, and the meetings felt to Kira like the slow, late-night conversations she'd had with friends in school while growing up.

When they finished eating, they played games of Scratch Seven. Round after round, and sometimes Falconi won and sometimes Kira. Unlike before, they didn't bet questions but rather tokens they folded out of wrappers from their meal packs.

During the last game, Kira broke the silence and said, "Salvo . . . why did you buy the *Wallfish*?"

"Hmm?"

"I mean, why did you want to leave your home? Why this?"

His blue eyes gazed at her over the tops of his cards. "Why did you become a xenobiologist? Why leave Weyland?"

"Because I wanted to explore, to see the universe." She shook her head, rueful. "Sure got more than I bargained for. . . . But somehow I think that's not why you left Farrugia's Landing."

He turned over one of the shared cards stuck to the deck. A six of clubs. Added to her own hand, that gave her . . . four sevens in total. "Sometimes it's not possible to stay home, even if you want to."

"Did you want to?"

A slight shrug underneath his thermal blanket. "The situation wasn't great. I didn't have much of a choice. You remember the uprising there?"

"Yeah."

"The company was screwing folks over on their benefits in all sorts of ways. Disability. Worker's comp. You name it. Things finally reached a boiling point and . . . everyone had to take sides."

A slow realization dawned on her. "You were a claims adjuster, right?"

Salvo nodded, but with some reluctance. "That's how I really came to understand how people were getting swindled. Once the protests started, I couldn't stand by and do nothing. You have to understand, these were people I grew up with. Friends. Family."

"And after?"

"After . . ." He put his cards down and rubbed at both temples with the tips of his index fingers. "After, I couldn't bear to stay. Words had been said and actions had been done that couldn't be forgiven. So I buckled down, saved my money for a few years, and then bought the *Wallfish*."

"To escape?" she asked.

"No, to be free," he said. "I'd rather struggle and fail on my own than be coddled as a slave."

The conviction in his voice was so strong, it made the back of Kira's neck prickle. She liked it. "So you *do* have principles," she said in a softly mocking tone.

Salvo chuckled. "Careful now. Don't tell anyone or you'll give them a bad impression."

"Wouldn't dream of it." She put down her cards. "Hold on. I'll be back in a moment."

Salvo watched with a questioning look as she left the galley. Hurrying, Kira returned to her cabin, fetched her concertina from under a blanket of the Soft Blade's living tissue, and then headed back.

When he saw the concertina, Salvo groaned. "What now? Are you going to make me listen to a polka?"

"Hush," said Kira, using the brusque response to conceal her nervousness. "I don't know if I remember all the fingering, but . . ."

Then she played him "*Saman-Sahari*," one of the first pieces she had ever learned. It was a long, slow song with what she thought was a beautiful melody. As the languid music filled the air, it reminded her of the greenhouses on Weyland, of their fragrant scents and the buzz of pollinating insects. It reminded her of family and home and much that was now lost.

Tears filled Kira's eyes in spite of herself. When she finished, she stayed where she was for a long while, staring down at the concertina.

"Kira." She looked up to see Falconi gazing at her with an earnest expression, his eyes gleaming with tears of his own. "That was lovely," he said, and put his hand on hers.

She nodded and sniffed and laughed a little. "Thanks. I was afraid I was going to make a mess of it."

"Not at all."

"Well then. . . ." She cleared her throat, and then with some reluctance, freed her hand. "I suppose we should call it a night. Tomorrow's going to be a busy day."

"Yes, I suppose we should."

". . . Goodnight, Salvo."

"Goodnight, Kira. And thank you again for the song."

"Of course."

7.

Kira was climbing along the *Wallfish*'s central shaft, after checking on Itari in the hold, when the jump alert sounded and she felt a subtle but noticeable shift in the ship's position. She checked the time: 1501 GTS.

From overhead, Falconi's voice sounded. "We're there. And we're not alone."

CHAPTER II

* * * * * * *

NECESSITY III

1.

The *Wallfish* had emerged from FTL near a brown dwarf: a dark, magenta-colored orb devoid of moons or planets. It dwelled in the void outside Cordova-1420's heliosphere, a lonely wanderer orbiting the galactic core, spinning round and round in silent eternity.

By the equator of the brown dwarf hung a cluster of twenty-one white dots: the ships of the Knot of Minds, positioned such that the mass of the failed star shielded them from any FTL telescopes aimed at them from Cordova-1420.

The moment the *Wallfish* had silenced its Markov Drive, Falconi triggered the wake-up procedures for the rest of the crew (with the exception of Gregorovich). It would take the *Wallfish* four hours to match speed with the Knot of Minds; more than enough time for the crew to defrost and down the food and fluids they would need to be functional.

"We'll talk when you get here," Tschetter had said in response to their hail. "It'll be easier with you in person, Kira, when you can communicate with the Jellies directly."

After the call, Kira went to the galley to greet the crew as they straggled in. None of them looked particularly good. "Survived another one," said Sparrow, wiping her face with a towel. "Oh yay."

Nielsen appeared even worse than Falconi had, although she displayed none of the symptoms of cryo sickness. She had a twitch, and there was a thin tightness to her lips, as if she were in pain. It was, Kira suspected, a return of the first officer's old affliction.

"Can I get you anything?" Kira asked, sympathetic.

"No, but thanks."

The Entropists joined them also. They came stumbling in, garbed in a replacement set of gradient robes, arms wrapped around each other and a haggard look on their faces. But they seemed calm at least and sane, which was an improvement. Their time spent in cryo appeared to have dulled the shock of having their hive mind broken. They never moved more than a meter away from each other, though, and they were always touching, as if physical contact were somehow a substitute for the mental connection they'd lost.

Kira helped heat and serve food to the group, doing whatever she could to smooth their recovery from hibernation. As she did, Vishal sat with Nielsen, put an arm around her, and spoke to her in a quiet voice. Whatever he was saying seemed to ease the first officer's distress; she kept nodding, and some of the strain vanished from her posture.

When they were all seated with food and drink, Falconi stood and said, "There's something you should know." And then he briefed them on the situation with Gregorovich.

"How horrible," said Nielsen. She shivered.

"You going to thaw him out?" Sparrow asked.

Falconi shook his head. "Not until we know what's happening with the Knot of Minds. We might end up just turning around and heading back for the League. If I *do* have Hwa-jung pull Gregorovich out of cryo, I want you, Doc, to look at him at once."

"Of course," said Vishal. "I will do everything I can for him."

"Glad to hear it, Doc."

2.

Four hours later, with everyone awake, if still somewhat groggy, the *Wallfish* docked with the Jelly flagship: a large, gleaming orb with a dozen or so gun ports ringing its rounded prow.

Along with the crew, Kira hurried off to the airlock. Only the Entropists stayed behind in the galley, nursing warm drinks while huddled over the holodisplay. "We will watch from—"

"—from here," they said.

Despite Kira's wariness toward the meeting, she was eager to get it over with so that—one way or another—she would have a sense of what the future would hold. Right then, she didn't have the slightest idea. If they ended up returning to the League, would she go into hiding? Turn herself over to the UMC? Find a way to fight the Jellies and the nightmares without ending up stuck in a cell somewhere? Maybe she would head back to Weyland, try to find her family, protect them. . . . The lack of certainty wasn't a feeling she liked. Far from it.

She could tell that Falconi was wrestling with a similar disquiet. He'd been unusually taciturn since they'd arrived at the brown dwarf, and when she asked him about it, he shook his head and said, "Just thinking, that's all. It'll be nice to have this behind us."

That it will.

The *Wallfish* jolted as the two ships connected. The outer airlock rolled open, and on the other side, a membrane retracted to reveal one of the Jellies' mother-of-pearl-esque doorways. It rotated to reveal the three-meter-long tunnel that led into the Jelly ship.

Waiting inside the Jelly ship was Tschetter and, as Kira quickly identified from the scents wafting her way, the tentacle-adorned shape of Lphet.

"Permission to come aboard, Captain?" said Tschetter.

"Permission granted," said Falconi.

Tschetter and Lphet floated inward and took up positions in the airlock antechamber. [[Lphet here: Greetings, Idealis.]]

"Good to see you again, Major," said Falconi. "Things werc getting pretty hairy back at Bughunt. Wasn't sure if you were going to make it." Like the rest of the crew, he was armed, and his hand never strayed far from the grip of his blaster.

"We almost didn't," said Tschetter.

Nielsen said, "What happened to the—what was it you called it, Kira—the Seeker?" At the mention of the ancient danger, a shiver ran down Kira's back. She'd wondered that herself.

A flicker of distaste crossed Tschetter's face. "It fled Bughunt before we could destroy it."

"Where is it now?" Kira asked.

A slight shrug on the part of the major. "Wandering among the stars somewhere. I'm sorry; I can't tell you more than that. We didn't have time to go chasing after it."

Kira frowned, wishing otherwise. The thought of a Seeker set loose among the stars, free to pursue whatever cruel agenda it saw fit—free of any oversight of its creators, the Vanished—filled her with dread. But there was nothing she could do about it, and even if there were, they had more pressing concerns.

"Well, isn't that the best fucking news," said Sparrow in a tone that matched Kira's mood.

Falconi lifted his chin. "Why did we have to meet in person, Major? What was so important you couldn't say over the horn?"

Even though it couldn't have understood Falconi's question, the Jelly answered: [[Lphet here: The currents are against us, Idealis. Even now the shoal of your Arm prepares to attack our forces gathered around the neighboring star. The attack will surely fail, but not without great losses on both sides. The empty sea will run with blood, and our shared sorrow will be the Corrupted's gain. This tide must be turned, Idealis.]] And a scent of earnest supplication suffused the air. Behind her, Itari rubbed its tentacles and turned a fermented yellow.

Tschetter tipped her head toward the Jelly. "Lphet was just telling Kira something of the situation. It's worse than you might think. If we don't intervene, the Seventh Fleet will be destroyed and all hope for peace between us and the Jellies lost."

"The League tried to kill you," Nielsen pointed out.

The major never faltered. "It was a reasonable choice given the circumstances. I don't agree with it, but from a tactical standpoint, it made a certain sense. What *doesn't* make sense is losing the Seventh. It's the largest standing fleet in the UMC. Without it, the League is going to be at even more of a disadvantage. Any serious attack and the Jellies or the Corrupted will be able to overrun our forces."

"So what do you have in mind?" said Kira. "You must have an idea or we wouldn't be talking right now."

Tschetter nodded, and the Jelly said: [[Lphet here: You are right, Idealis. The plan is a desperate leap into the abyss, but it is all that is left to us.]]

[[Kira here: You can understand my other words?]]

She tasted nearscent of understanding. [[Lphet here: The machine that your co-form Tschetter wears translates for us.]]

The major was still speaking. "Unfortunately, the Premier's decision to take out the Knot of Minds has ruined our original plan. At best possible speeds, the Seventh Fleet will reach Cordova-Fourteen-Twenty within the next few hours. Once it does, they'll come under fire, and it'll be difficult to save them. That, and finding a way to establish peace between us and the Jellies is going to be dicey. Very dicey."

Kira looked at Falconi. "Could we send a message to the Seventh before they reach Cordova? Warn them? Tschetter, you must know a way to contact them on military channels."

"It's worth a shot," Falconi said. "But—"

"Won't work," said Tschetter. "We don't know where exactly the Seventh is. If Klein is smart, and he is, he won't be bringing the fleet in on a straight shot from Earth. It would be too easy to cross paths with a Jelly ship that way."

"Can't you locate them with your FTL sensors?" Kira asked.

Tschetter gave her a rather unpleasant smile. "We've *tried,* but they're not showing up. No idea why. The other Jellies certainly haven't found them. The Knot of Minds would have heard."

Kira remembered something Colonel Stahl had mentioned. "On Orsted Station, the officer who debriefed me mentioned that they had some way to keep the Jellies from detecting the Seventh."

"Is that so?" said Tschetter with a thoughtful expression. "Before I was captured, I remember there were rumors coming out of the research divisions about experimental techniques for hiding a ship in FTL. It had something to do with generating short-range signals—basically white noise—that would disrupt any active scanning attempts. Maybe that's what he meant." She shook herself. "It doesn't matter. The point is, we can't find the Seventh Fleet in FTL, and once they drop back to sublight, the Jellies are going to jam the system. No signal that's fast enough to reach the Seventh in time will be powerful enough to punch through the interference. Besides, I doubt they would listen to anything we had to say."

Kira was starting to feel frustrated. "What are we talking about then? Are you going to fly off and fight alongside the Seventh? Is that it?"

"Not quite," said Tschetter.

Falconi interceded with a raised hand. "Wait a moment. What *was* your original plan, Tschetter? I've never been entirely clear on it. The Jellies outrun and outgun us from here to Alpha Centauri. Why did they need us to help them off their head honchos? Seems like we would just get in the way."

"I was getting to that," said Tschetter. She tugged on the fingers of her skinsuit, pulling out wrinkles on the back of her hands. "The plan was—and still is, I might add—for the Knot of Minds to escort one of our ships past the Jelly defense perimeter. The Knot will say they captured the ship while raiding the League and that it has valuable intel on it. Once in, the Knot will ID the target, and we blow up their leadership for them. Simple as that."

"Oh, just that," scoffed Sparrow.

Vishal said, "Such an easy task. We could be done by dinner." He laughed hollowly.

A ripple ran the length of the Jelly's limbs. [[Lphet here: We wish your help, Idealis. . . . We wish your help in killing the great and mighty Ctein.]] And a mélange of sickness, pain, and panic clogged Kira's nostrils, as if the Jelly had become physically ill.

She couldn't conceal her shock at its words. [[Kira here: Ctein is *here*?]]

[[Lphet here: Indeed, Idealis. For the first time in four ripples and uncounted cycles, the huge and terrible Ctein has uprooted its many limbs so as to oversee the invasion of your planets and the crushing of the Corrupted. This is our best and only chance of toppling our ancient tyrant.]]

"Kira?" said Falconi, an edgy tone in his voice. His hand drifted closer to the grip of his blaster.

"It's okay. Just . . . wait," she said. Her mind was racing. [[Kira here: Is *this* why you wanted the League's help? To kill the one and only Ctein?]]

Nearscent of affirmation. [[Lphet here: But of course, Idealis. What else might we have wanted?]]

Kira shifted her gaze to Tschetter. "Did you know about this Ctein they're talking about?"

The major frowned. "They mentioned its name before, yes. I didn't think it was of any particular significance."

A disbelieving laugh burst forth from Kira's throat. "Not of any significance. . . . Thule."

Falconi gave her a glance of concern. "What's wrong?"

"I—" Kira shook her head. *Think!* "Okay. Hold on." Again, she addressed the Jelly: [[Kira here: I still do not understand. Why not kill Ctein yourselves? Your ships are better than ours, and you can swim closer to Ctein without arousing alarm. So why have you not already killed Ctein? Do you want us to be . . .]] She couldn't think of the Jelly concept for *blame* and instead finished with, [[known for the deed?]]

[[Lphet here: No, Idealis. We need your help because we *cannot* do it ourselves. After the events of the Sundering, and after Nmarhl's failed uprising, the wise and clever Ctein saw to it that all Wranaui, even we the Tfeir, were altered so that we will not and could not harm our great Ctein.]]

[[Kira here: Do you mean you are physically incapable of hurting Ctein?]]

[[Lphet here: That is exactly the problem, Idealis. If we try, a sickness stops us from moving. Even just thinking about causing harm to the huge and mighty Ctein causes us immense distress.]]

A deep frown pinched Kira's brow. So the Jellies had been genetically modified to be slaves? The thought filled her with disgust. To be bound by one's own genes to bow and scrape was abhorrent. The intentions of the Knot of Minds were making more sense now, but she wasn't liking the shape of them.

"You need a human ship," she said, looking at Tschetter.

The major's expression softened slightly. "And a human to pull the trigger, literally or metaphorically, at some point along the process."

Fear uncoiled inside Kira. "The *Wallfish* isn't a cruiser, and it sure as hell isn't a battleship. The Jellies would tear us apart. You can't—"

"Slow down," said Falconi. "Context, please, Kira. Not all of us can talk smells, you know." Behind him, the crew was looking nervous. Kira couldn't blame them.

She ran a hand over her scalp, trying to marshal her thoughts. "Right, right . . ." Then she told them what Lphet had told her, and when she finished, Tschetter confirmed and explained a few of the points Kira herself was fuzzy on.

Falconi shook his head. "Let me get this straight. You want us to let the Knot of Minds fly us right into the heart of the Jelly fleet. Then you want us to attack the ship carrying this Ctein—"

"The *Battered Hierophant*," Tschetter helpfully supplied.

"I don't give two fucks what it's called. You want us to attack this ship, whereupon every single Jelly stationed there at Cordova is going to descend upon us with furious hellfire, and we won't stand a damn chance. Not a single chance."

Tschetter seemed unsurprised by his reaction. "The Knot of Minds promises they will do everything they can to protect the *Wallfish* once you launch your Casaba-Howitzers toward the *Battered Hierophant*. They seem fairly confident of their ability to do so."

A mocking laugh escaped Falconi. "Bullshit. You know as well as I do it's impossible to guarantee anything once the shooting starts."

"If you're looking for guarantees in life, you're going to be sorely disappointed," said Tschetter. She drew herself up, no mean feat in zero-g. "Once Ctein is dead, the Knot of Minds claims—"

"Wait," said Kira, as an unpleasant thought occurred to her. "What about the Nest of Transference?"

A flicker of confusion appeared on Tschetter's face. "The what?"

"Yeah," said Falconi. "What?"

Dismayed, Kira said, "Didn't you read my write-up about the conversation I had with Itari on the way out from Bughunt?"

Falconi opened his mouth and then shook his head. "I—Shit. Guess I missed it. There's been a lot going on."

"And Gregorovich didn't tell you?"

"It didn't come up."

Tschetter snapped her fingers. "Navárez, fill me in."

So Kira explained what she knew about the Nest of Transference.

"Un-fucking-believable," said Falconi.

Sparrow popped a stick of gum into her mouth. "So you're saying the Jellies can resurrect themselves?"

"In a way," said Kira.

"Lemme get this straight: we shoot 'em, and they pop back out of their birthing pods, fresh as daisies and knowing everything that just happened? Like where and how they got killed?"

"Pretty much."

"Christ-on-a-stick."

Kira looked back at Tschetter. "They didn't tell you?"

The major shook her head, appearing displeased with herself. "No. I guess I never asked the right questions, but . . . it explains a lot."

Falconi tapped the grip of his blaster in a distracted way. "Shit. If the Jellies can store backups of themselves, how are we supposed to kill this Ctein? Kill it for good, that is." He glanced at Kira. "That was your question, wasn't it?"

She nodded.

Nearscent of understanding flooded the air, and Kira remembered that the Jellies had been listening the whole time.

[[Lphet here: Your concern is reasonable, Idealis, but in this case it is unfounded.]]

[[Kira here: How so?]]

[[Lphet here: Because no copy exists of the great and mighty Ctein's pattern.]]

"How can that be?" Nielsen asked as Kira translated. Kira was wondering that herself.

[[Lphet here: In the cycles since the Sundering, Ctein has indulged the worst excesses of its hunger, and it has grown beyond all normal bounds of Wranaui flesh. This indulgence prevents the proud and cunning Ctein from using the

Nest of Transference. The Nest cannot be built large enough to copy Ctein's pattern. The currents will not hold at that size.]]

Sparrow popped her gum. "So Ctein is a fatass. Got it."

[[Lphet here: You would do well to be cautious of the strength of Ctein, two-form. It is unique among Wranaui, and none there are among the Arms that can match it. This is why the great and terrible Ctein has grown complacent in its supremacy.]]

Sparrow made a dismissive noise.

[[Kira here: To be clear, if we kill Ctein, that will be the end of it? Ctein will die a true death?]]

A distressed nearscent, and the Jelly flushed a sickly color. [[Lphet here: That is correct, Idealis.]]

When Kira finished translating, Tschetter said, "Going back to what I was saying . . . Once Ctein is dead, the Knot of Minds will be able to assume control over the ships at Cordova. You wouldn't have to worry about anyone blowing up your precious ship then, Captain."

A grunt from Falconi. "I'm more worried about *us* getting blown up."

Irritation pinched Tschetter's face. "Don't be dense. You wouldn't have to be on the *Wallfish*. Your pseudo-intelligence could fly it in. The Jellies can give you room on their ships, and after Ctein is dead, they can transport the lot of you back to the League."

Hwa-jung cleared her throat. "Gregorovich."

"Yeah," said Falconi. "There's that." He returned his gaze to Tschetter. "If you didn't realize, we've got a ship mind on board."

The major's eyes widened. "What?"

"Long story. But he's here, he's big, and we'd have to disassemble half of B-deck in order to remove him from the ship. It would take at least two days' work in dock."

A crack appeared in Tschetter's self-control. "That's . . . not ideal." She pinched the bridge of her nose, the corners of her eyes wrinkled as if she were fighting off a headache. "Would Gregorovich agree to pilot the *Wallfish* alone?" She looked toward the ceiling. "Ship mind, you must have an opinion on all this."

"He can't hear you," Falconi said shortly. "Also a long story."

"Back up a moment," said Sparrow. "If taking out the *Battered Hierophant* is the objective, why not just tell the Seventh? Admiral Klein is a hard-ass, but he's not stupid."

Tschetter made a sharp motion with her chin. "The Jellies won't let the Seventh get anywhere near the *Hierophant*. Even if they could, the *Hierophant* will just fly Ctein out of the system, and there isn't a ship in the League that can keep up with the Jellies' drives." It was true, and they all knew it. "In any case, I think you might be overly optimistic about Admiral Klein's willingness to listen to anything I have to say at this point."

[[Lphet here: Because of our compulsion, the Wranaui will protect the great and mighty Ctein with every last bit of our strength. Believe me on this, Idealis, for it is true. Even if it costs us all our lives, so it would be.]]

At the word *compulsion*, a shiver wormed its way down Kira's back. If what the Jellies felt was in any way similar to the yearning ache that had driven the Soft Blade to respond to the ancient summons of the Vanished . . . she could understand why deposing Ctein was so difficult for them.

"We need to talk about this among ourselves," Kira said to Tschetter. She glanced at Falconi for confirmation, and he indicated agreement with a tilt of his head.

"Of course."

Along with the rest of the crew, Kira retreated into the hall outside the airlock antechamber. Itari stayed behind.

As the pressure door clicked shut, Falconi said, "Gregorovich is in no shape to be piloting the *Wallfish*. Even if he were, there's no way I'd send him off on a suicide mission."

"Would it be, though? Really?" said Nielsen.

Falconi snorted. "You can't tell me you think this crazy plan is a good idea."

The first officer smoothed back a lock of hair that had sprung free of her bun. She still looked as if she was wrestling with a certain amount of pain, but her eyes and voice were clear. "I'm just saying that space is big. If the *Wallfish* could kill this Ctein, it would take the Jellies time to react. Time that the Knot of Minds could use to keep them from attacking the ship."

To Sparrow, Falconi said, "And here I thought you were supposed to be the tactical one." Back to Nielsen, then: "We're talking about the biggest, baddest Jelly of them all. The king or queen or *whatever* of the squids. They probably have escorts all around the *Battered Hierophant*. As soon as the *Wallfish* opens fire—"

"Boom," said Hwa-jung.

"Exactly," said Falconi. "Space is big, but the Jellies are fast and their weapons have a hell of a long range."

Kira said, "We don't know what the situation will be at Cordova. We just don't. The *Battered Hierophant* might be surrounded by half the Jelly fleet, or it might be all by itself. There's no way to tell ahead of time."

"Assume the worst," said Sparrow.

"Okay, so it's surrounded. What do you think the odds are the Seventh Fleet can take out the *Hierophant*?" When no one answered her, Kira looked at each of the crew, studying their faces. She'd already made her decision: the humans and Jellies *had* to join forces if either of their species were to have any hope of surviving the all-consuming Maw.

Vishal said, "There are two questions that are important here, I think."

"What would those be?" Falconi asked, respectful.

The doctor rubbed the pads of his long, round-tipped fingers together. "Question one: Can we afford to lose the Seventh Fleet? Answer: I think not. Question two: What is peace between us and the Jellies worth? Answer: Nothing is more valuable in all the universe right now. Yes, that is how I see it."

"You surprise me, Doc," Falconi said quietly. Kira could see the gears of his brain turning at a furious speed behind his shrouded eyes.

Vishal nodded. "It is good to be unpredictable at times."

"Somehow I don't think we'd be paid anything for peace," said Sparrow. With one red-painted nail, she scratched at her nose. "The only wages to be earned out there are paid in blood."

"That's what I'm afraid of also," said Falconi. And Kira believed him. He was afraid. Any sensible person would be. *She* was afraid, and the Soft Blade gave her far more protection than anyone else on the ship.

Nielsen had been staring at the deck while they talked, her face turned inward. Now, she said in a low tone, "We should help. We have to."

"And why is that?" Falconi asked. His tone wasn't mocking; it was a serious question.

"Do tell us, Ms. Audrey," Vishal said kindly. He was, Kira noted, using her first name now.

Nielsen pressed her lips together, as if fighting back her emotions. "We have a moral obligation."

Falconi's eyebrows climbed toward his hairline. "A *moral obligation*? Those are some awfully high-minded words." A hint of his usual sharp-edged style began to creep back in.

"To the League. To humanity in general." Nielsen pointed back at the airlock. "To the Jellies."

Sparrow made an incredulous noise. "*Those* fuckers?"

"Even them. I don't care if they're aliens. No one should be forced to live a certain way just because someone messed with your DNA before you were born. No one."

"That doesn't mean we're under any obligation to get ourselves killed for them."

"No," said Nielsen, "but it doesn't mean we should ignore them either."

Falconi picked at the butt of his gun. "Let's be clear. Sparrow's right: we're under no obligations. None of us are. We don't *have* to do anything Tschetter or the Knot of Minds says."

"No obligations but those dictated by the bounds of common decency," said Vishal. He stared at his feet, and when he spoke again, his voice sounded far away. "I like to sleep at night and not have bad dreams, Captain."

"I like to be able to *sleep,* and it helps to be alive for that," Falconi retorted. He sighed, and Kira saw a shift in his expression, as if he'd reached a decision of his own. "Hwa-jung, thaw out Gregorovich. We can't have this conversation without him."

The machine boss opened her mouth as if to object and then closed it with an audible slap of her lips and grunted. Her gaze zoned out as she focused on her overlays.

"Captain," said Kira. "You spoke with Gregorovich before we left. You know what he's like. What's the point?"

"He's part of the crew," said Falconi. "And he wasn't *completely* out of it. You said so yourself. He could still follow what you were saying. Even if he's half out of his mind, we still have to try. His life is on the line too. Besides, we'd try if it were any one of us down in sickbay."

He wasn't wrong. "Alright. How long will it take to wake him up?" Kira asked.

"Ten, fifteen minutes," said Falconi. He went to the pressure door, opened it, and said to Tschetter and the Jellies waiting on the other side, "We're going to be about a quarter hour. Have to get our ship mind out of cryo."

The delay obviously displeased Tschetter, but she just said, "Do what you have to. We'll be waiting."

Falconi gave her a loose salute and pulled the door closed.

3.

The next ten minutes passed in silent anticipation. Kira could see the others thinking hard about everything Tschetter and Lphet had told them. So was she, for that matter. If Falconi agreed with the plan—regardless of what Gregorovich said—there was more than a small chance that they would end up stuck on one of the Jelly vessels without a ship of their own and at the mercy of the travel decisions of the Knot of Minds. It wasn't an appealing prospect. But then, neither was the destruction of the Seventh Fleet, a continuation of the human–Jelly war, and the nightmares overrunning both their races.

When almost fifteen minutes had elapsed, Falconi said, "Hwa-jung? What's going on?"

The machine boss's voice sounded over the intercom: "He is awake, but I'm not getting anything from him."

"Have you explained the situation?"

"*Aish.* Of course. I showed that one the recording of our conversation with Tschetter and the Jellies."

"And he still hasn't answered?"

"No."

"Can't or won't?"

A brief pause before she answered. "I don't know, Captain."

"Dammit. I'm on my way." Falconi unstuck his boots from the deck, kicked himself over to the nearest handhold, and hurried off toward the storm shelter.

In his absence, an awkward silence filled the corridor. "Well this is fun," said Sparrow.

Nielsen smiled, but with a hint of sorrow. "I can't say this is how I imagined spending my retirement."

"You and me both, ma'am."

It wasn't long before Falconi came hurrying back along the corridor, a troubled expression on his face. "Well?" Kira asked, even though the answer seemed obvious.

The captain shook his head as he planted his feet back on the deck and allowed the gecko pads to fix him in place. "Nothing I could make sense of. He's gotten worse. Vishal, you'll have to look at him as soon as we're done here. In the meantime, we need to decide. One way or another. Right here, right now."

None of them seemed willing to say what Kira felt sure they were all thinking. Finally, she took the initiative and—with false confidence—said, "I vote yes."

"Yes *what* exactly?" said Sparrow.

"That we help Tschetter and the Knot of Minds. That we try to kill their leader, Ctein." There. She'd said it, and the words hung in the air like an unwelcome smell.

Then the low rumble of Hwa-jung's voice sounded: "What about Gregorovich? Are we supposed to abandon him on the *Wallfish*?"

"I would not like that," said Vishal.

Falconi shook his head, and Kira's heart sank. "No. I'm captain of this ship. There's no way I'm sending Gregorovich—or any of you for that matter—off on a mission like this all alone. I'd have to be twelve days dead before I'd let that happen."

"Then—" Kira said.

"It's my ship," he repeated. A strange gleam appeared in his cold blue eyes: a look that Kira had seen on plenty of men's faces over the years. Usually right before they did something dangerous. "I'll go with Gregorovich. It's the only way."

"Salvo—" Nielsen started to say.

"You're not going to talk me out of it, Audrey, so don't even try."

Sparrow made a face, her delicate features wrinkling. "Ah, shitballs. . . . When I enlisted in the UMCN, I swore to protect the League against all threats, domestic and foreign. You couldn't pay me enough to go back into the service, but, well, I guess I meant those words when I said them, and I think I still mean them, even if the UMC *is* a bunch of self-righteous assholes."

"You're not going," said Falconi. "None of you are."

"Sorry, Captain. If it's our choice *not* to go, then it's also our choice *to* go. You're not the only one who gets to make a grand gesture. Besides, you'll need someone to watch your back."

Then Hwa-jung put a hand on Sparrow's round shoulder. "Where she goes, I go. Besides, if the ship breaks, who will fix it?"

"Count me in also, Salvo," said Nielsen.

Falconi looked at each of them, and Kira was surprised by the anguish in his expression. "We don't need all of you to run the ship. You're damn fools if you want to come. The *Wallfish* gets blown up, it'll just be a waste of your lives."

"No," said Nielsen quietly. "It won't be, because we'll be with friends, helping to do something that matters."

Vishal bobbed his head. "You could not keep me away, Captain. Not even if I were twelve days dead."

Falconi didn't seem to appreciate his own words being thrown back at him. "And you?" he asked Kira.

She already had her answer ready: "Of course. I'm better, ah, suited to handle it if things go wrong."

"They always do," Falconi said darkly. "It's just a question of how. You realize that if our Markov Drive is breached, not even the Soft Blade will be able to protect you."

"I know," Kira said. She'd already accepted the risk. Freaking out about it now wasn't going to help. "What about the Entropists?"

"If they want to go with Tschetter, no skin off our backs. Otherwise they can tag along and enjoy the ride."

"And what about Trig?" said Nielsen. "We should—"

"—get him off the *Wallfish,*" said Falconi. "Yeah, good idea. If nothing else, maybe Tschetter can get him back to the League. Anyone have any objections? No? Okay." Falconi took a deep breath and then laughed and shook his head. "Shit. I guess we're really doing this. Everyone sure? Last chance."

Murmurs of agreement sounded from all of them. "Alright," he said. "Let's go kill this Jelly."

4.

After further discussion, it was agreed by both parties that Itari would stay on the *Wallfish* for the time being, both as a gesture of good faith on Lphet's part and also to help should any problems arise with the alterations Itari had made to their Markov Drive. Likewise, the Entropists both decided to remain on the *Wallfish.*

As they said, "How could we refuse—"

"—to help at such a crucial moment—"

"—in history?"

Kira wasn't sure how much help the two could really provide with their hive mind broken, but it was a nice sentiment.

Hwa-jung and Sparrow went to the storm shelter and brought Trig's cryo tube to the airlock. As they passed the tube over to the major, Falconi said, "Anything happens to him, I'm holding you responsible."

"I'll protect him like he was my own son," said Tschetter.

Mollified, Falconi gave the tube a pat on the ice-covered viewplate. The rest of the crew came by to pay their respects—and Kira also—and then Tschetter maneuvered the tube through the mother-of-pearl tunnel and into the Jelly ship beyond.

The instant the Knot of Minds flagship separated from the airlock, Falconi turned and said, "Time to prep. Nielsen, with me in Control. Hwa-jung, engineering. Sparrow, crack open the armory and get everything ready. Just in case."

"Yessir."

"Roger that."

"Can we make it to Cordova with all of us awake?" Kira asked.

Falconi grunted. "It's going to get as hot as Satan's own asshole in here, but yeah, should be possible."

"Better than having to go back into cryo," quipped Sparrow on her way out.

"You said it," said Falconi.

5.

Kira had thought Falconi was exaggerating when he described the impending heat. To her dismay, he wasn't. The *Wallfish* was half a day of FTL from Cordova-1420, and with everyone—including Gregorovich—out of cryo, all the ship's systems running, and no way to dump the thermal energy they were pumping out, the inside of the *Wallfish* quickly became a hothouse.

The Soft Blade protected Kira from the worst of it, but she could feel her cheeks and forehead burning: a hot stinging that continued to build. Rivulets of sweat dripped into her eyes, annoying her to the point that she used the xeno to make a protective shelf above her brows.

"That," said Sparrow, pointing at her with rude directness, "looks fucking weird, Kira."

"Hey, it works," she said, dabbing her cheeks with a damp cloth.

Half a day was a vanishingly short trip by any measure of stellar or interstellar travel. However, it was a long time to be stuck in a sweltering box of metal where each breath felt suffocating and the walls were unpleasantly warm and no matter what action they took, it only made the situation worse. And it was longer still when waiting to arrive at a location where there was a better than average chance of being vaporized by a laser or missile.

At Kira's request, Vishal had given her yet another set of contacts before going to examine Gregorovich. She'd taken them and sequestered herself in her cabin. Keeping themselves spread out within the *Wallfish* helped disperse the heat, so as to avoid overloading the life-support systems in any one room.

"This is *not* good for the *Wallfish,*" Hwa-jung had said.

"I know," Falconi replied. "But she can survive it for a few hours."

Kira did her best to distract herself from the reality of their situation by reading and playing games. But she kept thinking about Gregorovich—the more time passed without word from Vishal, the more concerned she became—and fears about Cordova continued to intrude: the presence of the great and mighty Ctein, waiting there like a great fat toad, bloated with its arrogant self-confidence, secure in its cruel strength. The likely response of Admiral Klein to the arrival of the *Wallfish* and the Knot of Minds in the system. The uncertain outcome of their whole precarious venture . . .

No obvious answers presented themselves, but Kira kept chewing over her worries as she read. The situation was so far from anything familiar, the only beacon she had to guide her was her own sense of self. Although, her self had been somewhat tenuous lately, what with the Soft Blade stretching her out the way it did.

Again she felt the substance of the dark shell that coated the inside of her cabin, flesh of her flesh and yet . . . *not.* It was a strange sensation.

She shook herself, forced her attention back onto the overlays. . . .

6.

Nearly four hours had passed before the intercom clicked on and Falconi said, "Listen up, everyone. Vishal just gave me an update."

In her cabin, Kira perked up, eager to hear.

"Long and the short of it is, Greg is in pretty bad shape. The surge from the impedance block caused damage throughout his neural net. Not only did it burn out a good chunk of the leads, but the connection between the computer and Greg's brain is continuing to degrade as the neurons that got shocked are dying off."

A commotion of concerned and overlapping voices on the line. "Is he going to die?" Sparrow asked with characteristic bluntness.

"Not unless we all get blown up tomorrow," said Falconi. "Vishal isn't sure if this is going to cause permanent problems for Greg or if he's just going to lose a few extra brain cells. No way to tell at the moment, and the doc can't exactly wheel Greg into sickbay for a scan. He did say that Greg is probably enduring extreme sensory distortion. Aka, hallucinations. So Vishal is keeping him under sedation, and he's going to keep working on him."

"*Aish,*" said Hwa-jung. The machine boss sounded unusually emotional. "This is my fault. I should not have thrown the breaker without checking the line first."

Falconi snorted. "No, it's not your fault, Song. You couldn't have known the block was there, and Greg wasn't giving us any choices, the stubborn bastard. This is the UMC's fault and no one else's. Don't beat yourself up about it."

"Nossir."

"Alright. I'll let everyone know if there are any changes." And the intercom clicked off.

In the dark of her cabin, lit only by the green glow of the fruit-like orbs hanging from the vines the Soft Blade had grown, Kira hugged herself. So Gregorovich had made a mistake in not wanting to come to Cordova. He'd still been trying to do the right thing. He didn't deserve what was happening now, and she hated to think of him trapped alone in the madness of his mind, not knowing what was real, perhaps even thinking that his fellow crewmates had abandoned him. It was terrible to imagine.

If only . . . If only she could help.

Kira looked down at the arm the Soft Blade had made for her. Even if *she* couldn't, maybe the xeno could. But no, that was crazy. There was a universe of difference between an arm (or a tree) and a brain, and a mistake with Gregorovich could cause even worse problems.

She put the thought from her mind.

7.

With the tweaks Itari had made to their Markov Drive, the *Wallfish* was able to dive into Cordova's gravity well nearly as deeply as the Jellies.

They dropped out of FTL close to a pitted moon in orbit around a minor gas giant, the location of which the Knot of Minds had given them beforehand. The instant the Markov Drive shut off, Kira, the Entropists, and the crew (except for Vishal) abandoned their self-imposed exile and headed in a group toward Control.

As they piled into the room, Kira scanned the feed from outside the *Wallfish*. The moon obscured part of the view, but she could see the Knot of Minds surrounding them, the purple gas giant looming nearby, and several hours coreward, the cluster of dots that marked the location of the Seventh Fleet.

There were a lot of UMC ships—a *lot*—but it was what Kira spotted deeper in the system that made her gasp and Hwa-jung mutter, "*Shi-bal.*" Without seeming to notice, the machine boss put a hand on the back of Sparrow's shoulder and rubbed, as if to comfort her. Sparrow never blinked.

A swarm of Jelly ships surrounded a small rocky planet next to the orange, K-type star. And not just ships: stationary construction yards; vast, glittering fields of solar collectors; satellites of every shape and size; defense lasers the size of UMCN corvettes; two beanstalks and four orbital rings for quickly and easily transporting materials from the scarred surface of the planet.

The Jellies were strip-mining the rocky orb. They had removed a massive amount of material from the crust, enough so that the scars were visible even from space—a crazy patchwork of rectangular excavations cast into sharp relief by shadows along their edges.

Not all the Jelly ships were meant for fighting, but even so, those that were outnumbered the Seventh Fleet at least two to one. The biggest of them all—the one Kira assumed was the *Battered Hierophant*—lay alongside the shipyards, a bloated whale wallowing in the gravity well of the planet. Like every other Jelly ship, it was pearl white, ringed with weapon ports, and as was evident by even its small thruster adjustments, far more maneuverable than any human vessel. Several ships hung nearby, but they appeared to be more maintenance vessels than honor guard.

"Thule," said Nielsen. "Why doesn't the Seventh Fleet turn around? They don't stand a chance."

"Physics," Falconi said grimly. "By the time they decelerate, they're going to be in range of the Jellies."

Then Sparrow said, "Besides, if they try to run, it'll be easy for the Jellies to catch them. You don't want to fight a larger force out in interstellar space. There's no tactical advantages. At least here they have planets, moons, stuff they can use to maneuver around while engaging with the Jellies."

"Still . . ." said Nielsen.

"Extending radiators," Morven announced.

"About time," said Sparrow. Like the others, she was covered with a slick of sweat.

As Falconi slid into his seat, Tschetter appeared in the main holo-display. Behind her was a blue-lit room filled with coral-like structures and Jellies that were crawling across the curved bulkheads. "Any problems with the *Wallfish*, Captain?"

"All green here."

The major seemed satisfied. "Lphet says we're cleared to pass through the Jellies' defenses. Tagging the *Battered Hierophant* for you now."

"Looks like we lucked out," said Kira, gesturing at the flagship. "It doesn't seem to be overly protected."

"No, just by all the blasters, railguns, and missiles it's carrying," said Sparrow.

Tschetter shook her head. "We won't know for sure what the situation is until we're closer. The Jellies will move their ships in response to the Seventh. You can see they're already shifting positions. We'll just have to hope they don't decide to surround the *Hierophant*."

"Fingers crossed," said Falconi.

"Toes too," said Sparrow.

The major looked off-camera for a moment. "We're ready. Start your burn on our mark. . . . Mark."

The thrust alert sounded, and Kira let out a sigh of relief as a sensation of weight settled over her. Outside, she knew the Knot of Minds was keeping pace with the *Wallfish*, the Jelly ships arranged in a box-like formation around them. That was the plan, in any case.

Falconi said, "Stay on the line. I'm going to contact the Seventh."

"Roger that."

"Morven, get the Seventh Fleet on the line. Tightbeam transmission only. Tell them Kira Navárez is with us and we need to talk with Admiral Klein."

"One moment please," said the pseudo-intelligence.

"At least the shooting hasn't started," said Sparrow.

"Wouldn't want to miss the party," said Falconi.

They didn't have to wait long for an answer: the comms blinked with an incoming, and Morven said, "Sir, the UMCS *Unrelenting Force* is hailing us."

"Put it on-screen," said Falconi.

Next to Tschetter's face appeared a live stream of what Kira recognized as a battleship command center. Front and center sat Admiral Klein, stiff-backed, square-jawed, with sloping shoulders, buzzed hair, and four rows of service ribbons pinned to his left breast. Like all career UMCN personnel, he had a deep spacer's tan, although his was deeper than most, so deep that she guessed he never entirely lost it.

"Falconi! Navárez! What in the name of all that's holy are you doing here?" The admiral's accent was impossible for Kira to place, although she guessed it was from somewhere on Earth.

"Don't you get it, sir?" said Falconi. "We're the cavalry." And he grinned in a cocky way that made Kira both proud and want to slap him.

The admiral's face reddened. "Cavalry?! Son, last I heard, you were locked up on Orsted Station. Somehow I doubt the League just let you go, and they sure as *shit* wouldn't send you out here in that pile of rust you call a ship."

Falconi looked rather offended by his description of the *Wallfish*. Kira was more interested in the fact that the UMC hadn't managed to tell the Seventh about their escape. *The fleet must have been running silent,* she thought. *Or things back at Sol got* really *bad after we left.*

The admiral wasn't done: "On top of that, I'm guessing the Jelly ships with you means you warned off the Knot of Minds, which means my hunter-seekers are out wandering around buttfuck nowhere when they could be helping here." The admiral poked a finger out of the holo, causing Kira to flinch. "And *that* would be treason, Captain. Same for you, Navárez. Same for all of you."

Around the holo, Kira and the crew exchanged glances. "We're not traitors," Sparrow said in an injured tone. "Sir."

"We're here to help you," said Kira, quieter. "If you want to have any chance of surviving this battle, much less winning the war, you need to hear us out."

"That so." Klein seemed spectacularly unconvinced.

"Yessir. Please."

The admiral's gaze shifted to a point beside the holo, and Kira had a distinct impression that someone was speaking to him off-camera. Then his attention snapped back to them, hard-eyed and uncompromising. "You've got one chance to convince me not to classify you as an enemy combatant, Navárez. Make it count."

Kira took him at his word. She spoke clearly, quickly, and as straightforwardly as she could. And yet, she made no attempt to hide her underlying desperation. That also was important.

To his credit, the admiral listened without interruption. By the time she'd finished, a dark frown had settled on his face. "That's a hell of a story, Navárez. You really expect me to believe it?"

Tschetter was the one to answer. "Sir, you don't have to believe us. We just need—"

"Who's this *we* and *us*, Major?" said Klein. "Last I checked, you're still a uniformed member of the United Military Command. You don't answer to the Jellies. You answer to your nearest superior officer, and right now, that's *me*."

In the holo, Tschetter stiffened. "Sir, yessir. I'm aware of that, sir. I'm just trying to answer your question." It was strange for Kira to see her treating someone else as a figure of authority.

Klein crossed his arms. "Go on."

"Sir. As I was saying, we don't need you to believe us. We're not asking for your help, and we're not asking you to ignore orders. All we'd like is for you to hold your fire as we come through the system. And if we kill Ctein, then don't attack the Knot of Minds right after. Give them a chance to take command of the Jellies and call off their forces. Admiral, we could end the war between our species in a single blow. That's worth some risk."

"Do you really think you can kill this Ctein?" Klein asked.

Falconi nodded. "I'd say we have a pretty good chance. Wouldn't be trying otherwise."

The admiral grunted. "My *orders* were to eliminate the Knot of Minds, the Jelly fleet, and the Jellies' current leadership, with both the fleet and the leadership being the primary objectives." He peered at them from beneath his bristling eyebrows. "*If* you manage to kill Ctein, and *if* the Knot manages to get control over the rest of the Jellies . . . Well, then I suppose the Knot would become the new leadership of the Jellies. They wouldn't *be* the Knot anymore. That would also serve to neutralize the threat of the Jellies' fleet. . . . It's a bit of a stretch, but I think I could sell it to the Premier."

Kira felt a slight easing of tension among the others.

"Thank you, sir," said Tschetter. "You won't regret it."

Klein made a noncommittal noise. "Truth is, going after the Knot of Minds was always a strategic fuckup, and I wasn't the only one who thought so. . . . If you pull this off, a lot of good men and women are going to owe you their lives."

His gaze sharpened. "As for you, Major: if we make it through this, you're to report to the Seventh without delay. That's an order. Taking out the head of the Jellies would go a long way toward smoothing your return, but either way

Intelligence is going to want a *thorough* debriefing. You know how it is. After that, we'll figure out what the hell to do with you."

"Yes, sir," said the major. "Understood." To Kira's eye, she didn't seem too pleased with the prospect.

"Good." Klein's attention returned to the command center around him, and he said, "I have to go. We'll be engaging the Jellies in just under seven hours. They're going to give us all we can handle and then some, but we can try to draw their forces away from the *Battered Hierophant.* The rest will be up to you. Let our ship mind, Aletheia, know if there are any changes to the plan. Good luck and fly safe." Then he surprised Kira by saluting. "Navárez. Captain Falconi."

CHAPTER III

* * * * * * *

INTEGRATUM

1.

"That went . . . well," said Nielsen.

Sparrow *tsked.* "What else could he say?"

"What's our ETA?" Kira asked.

Falconi glanced at the holo. "We're a bit behind the fleet, so . . . seven hours, give or take, before we're in range of the *Battered Hierophant.*"

"That is," said Veera, "assuming the Jellies don't move the *Hierophant* beforehand, no?" As she spoke, Jorrus mouthed her words in silent mimicry.

Tschetter's face now filling the majority of the display, she said, "They shouldn't. Lphet made it clear we have intel on the *Wallfish* that Ctein needs to smell."

"Smell?" said Hwa-jung, and wrinkled her nose.

"That's how Lphet phrased it."

Seven hours. Not long at all, and then they'd know if they were going to live or die. Whatever their fate, there was no escaping it. Not that there ever was.

Falconi seemed to pick up on her thoughts. After ending the call with Tschetter, he said, "It's been a long day, and if you're anything like me, this heat has left you feeling like a damp rag that's been wrung out."

A few sounds of agreement came from the crew.

"Right. Everyone get some food and grab some downtime. Sleep if you can, and if you can't, the doc can give you some pick-me-ups later. Sleep would be better, though. We need to be sharp when we get to the *Hierophant.* Make sure you're all back here in Control an hour before contact. Oh, and full skinsuits. Just in case."

2.

Just in case. The phrase kept ringing in Kira's ears. What could they do if things went wrong, as they so often did? A single blast from one of the Jelly ships would be more than enough to disable or destroy the *Wallfish*. . . . It didn't bear thinking about, and yet she couldn't help herself. Preparation was a person's best ward against the inevitable mishaps of space travel, but opportunities for preparation were limited when the actors deciding outcomes were spaceships and not individuals.

She helped Hwa-jung with a few service tasks around the ship. Then they adjourned to the galley. Everyone but Vishal was already there, crammed in around the near table.

Kira fetched some rations and then went to sit next to Nielsen. The first officer nodded and said, "I think . . . I'm going to record a message for my family and give it to Tschetter and also the Seventh. Just in case."

Just in case. "Sounds like a good idea. Maybe I'll do the same."

Like the others, Kira ate, and like the others, she talked, mainly speculations about how best to destroy the *Battered Hierophant* with one of their Casaba-Howitzers—it seemed unlikely they would be able to fire more than one shot without being noticed—as well as how best to survive the chaos that was sure to follow.

The consensus that emerged was that they were at a serious disadvantage without Gregorovich to oversee operations throughout the *Wallfish*. As with most ship minds, it had been Gregorovich's responsibility to operate the lasers, the Casaba-Howitzers, the countermeasures against both blasters and missiles, and the cyberwarfare suite, as well as oversee the piloting of the *Wallfish* in combat, which was as much about strategy as it was calculating the uncompromising math of their delta-v.

The pseudo-intelligence, Morven, was capable enough, but like all such programs, it was limited in ways that a human—or human-derived—intelligence wasn't. "They lack imagination," said Sparrow, "and that's the truth of it. Won't say we're sitting ducks, but it's not ideal."

"How big of a drop in operational efficiency do you think we're looking at?" Falconi asked.

Sparrow's bare shoulders rose and fell. "You tell me. Just think back to before you had Gregorovich on board. UMC figures put the difference at somewhere between fourteen to twenty-eight percent. And—"

"That much?" said Nielsen.

Hwa-jung was the one to answer: "Gregorovich helps oversee the balance between all the systems in the ship, as well as coordinating with each of us."

A quick downward jerk of Sparrow's chin. "Yeah, and what I was going to say is that when it comes to strategy, logistics—basically any kind of creative problem-solving—ship minds blow everyone and every*thing* out of the water. It's not the sort of skill you can really quantify, but the UMC estimates that ship minds are at least an order of magnitude better at that stuff than any regular human, much less a pseudo-intelligence."

Jorrus said, "But only so long as they—" He hesitated, waiting for Veera to finish the sentence. When she shook her head, seemingly not knowing what to say, he continued on, disconcerted: "Uh, only as long as they are functional."

"Ain't that the truth," said Falconi. "For all of us."

Kira picked at her food while she thought about the situation. *If only* . . . No. The idea was still too crazy. Then she pictured the Jelly fleet around Cordova. Maybe there was no such thing as too crazy, under the circumstances.

Conversation throughout the galley stopped as Vishal appeared in the doorway. He looked drained, exhausted.

"Well?" Falconi asked.

Vishal shook his head and held up a finger. Not saying a word, he marched to the back of the galley, got himself a pouch of instant coffee, drained it, and then, and only then, returned to stand in front of the captain.

"That bad, huh?" said Falconi.

Nielsen leaned forward. "How is Gregorovich?"

Vishal sighed and rubbed his hands together. "His implants are too damaged for me to fix. I cannot remove or replace the broken leads. And I cannot identify the ones that end in a dead neuron. I tried rerouting signals to different parts of his brain, where the wires still work, but there aren't enough of them, or Gregorovich could not pick out the signal from the disorganized sensory information he's receiving."

"You still have him sedated?" Falconi asked.

"Yes."

"Is he going to be okay, though?" Nielsen asked.

Sparrow shifted in her seat. "Yeah, is he going to end up impaired or something like that?"

"No," Vishal said slowly, cautiously. "*But,* we will have to take him to a proper facility. The connections are continuing to degrade. In another day,

Gregorovich may become completely cut off from his internal computer. He would be totally isolated."

"Shit," said Sparrow.

Falconi turned toward the Entropists. "Don't suppose there's anything you could do to help?"

They shook their heads. "Alas, no," said Veera. "Implants are delicate things and—"

"—we would be reluctant to work on an ordinary-sized neural net, much less—"

"—that of a ship mind." The Entropists appeared smug at the smoothness of their exchange.

Falconi made a face. "I was afraid of that. Doc, you can still put him in cryo, right?"

"Yes, sir."

"You'd better go ahead and put him under, then. He'll be safer that way."

Kira tapped her fork on her plate. Everyone looked at her. "So," she said, feeling out her words, "just to be clear: the only thing that's wrong with Gregorovich are the wires going into his brain, is that right?"

"Oh, there's a whole lot more wrong with him than just that," Sparrow quipped.

Vishal assumed a long-suffering expression as he said, "You are correct, Ms. Kira."

"He doesn't have large amounts of tissue trauma or anything like that?"

Vishal started to move toward the door, obviously eager to get back to Gregorovich. He paused at the threshold. "No. The only damage was the neurons he lost at the ends of some wires, but it is a negligible loss for a ship mind of his size."

"I see," said Kira. She tapped her fork again.

A wary look came over Falconi's face. "Kira," he said in a warning tone. "What are you thinking?"

She took a moment to answer. "I'm thinking . . . I might be able to use the Soft Blade to help Gregorovich."

A babble of exclamations filled the galley. "Let me explain!" said Kira, and they quieted down. "I could do the same thing I did with Akawe, back at Cygni. Connect the Soft Blade to Gregorovich's nerves, only this time, I'd be hooking them back up to the wires in his neural net."

Sparrow let out a long, high whistle. "Thule. You really think you could pull this off?"

"Yes, I do. But I also can't make any guarantees." Kira shifted her gaze back to Falconi. "You saw how I was able to heal your bonsai. And you saw what I did in my cabin. The Soft Blade isn't just a weapon. It's capable of so much more."

Falconi scratched the side of his chin. "Greg is a person, not a plant. There's a big difference there."

Then Nielsen said, "Just because the Soft Blade is capable, are *you*, Kira?"

The question rang in Kira's mind. It was one she'd wondered often enough since becoming joined with the xeno. Could she control it? Could she use it in a responsible way? Could she master herself well enough to make either of those things possible? She stiffened her back and lifted her chin, feeling the answer rising within her, born of pain and long months spent practicing. "Yes. I don't know how well it will work—Gregorovich will probably have to readjust to his implants, just like when they were first installed—but I think I can hook him back up again."

Hwa-jung crossed her arms. "You should not go rummaging around inside someone's head if you do not know what you're doing. He isn't a machine."

"Yeah," said Sparrow. "What if you turn him into scrambled mush? What if you totally screw up his memories?"

Kira said, "I wouldn't be interacting with most of his brain, just the interface where he plugs into the computer."

"You can't be sure of that," Nielsen said calmly.

"Mostly sure. Look, if it's not worth it, it's not worth it." Kira spread her hands. "I'm just saying I could try." She eyed the captain. "It's your call."

Falconi tapped his leg with a furious rhythm. "You've been awfully quiet over there, Doc. What about you?"

By the door, Vishal ran his long-fingered hands over his equally long face. "What do you expect me to say, Captain? As your ship doctor, I cannot recommend this. The risks are too high. The only reasonable treatment would be to take Gregorovich to a proper medical facility in the League."

"That's not likely to happen any time soon, Doc," said Falconi. "Even if we make it out of this alive, there's no telling what shape the League will be in when we get back."

Vishal inclined his head. "I am aware of that, Captain."

A scowl settled onto Falconi's face. For several heartbeats, he just looked at Kira, staring at her as if he could see into her soul. She matched his gaze, never blinking, never looking away.

Then, Falconi said, "Okay. Do it."

"Captain, as the attending physician, I must formally object," said Vishal. "I have serious concerns about the outcome of this procedure."

"Objection noted, but I'm going to have to overrule you here, Doc."

Vishal didn't seem surprised.

"Captain," said Nielsen in an intense tone. "She could kill him."

Falconi wheeled on her. "And we're flying straight into the Jelly fleet. That takes priority."

"Salvo—"

"*Audrey.*" Falconi bared his teeth as he talked. "One of my crewmembers is incapacitated, and that's endangering both my ship and the rest of my crew. This isn't a cargo run. This isn't a goddamn fetch-and-retrieve mission. This is life or death. We don't have a millimeter of wiggle room here. If we screw up, we're done for. Gregorovich is mission critical, and right now he's no good to anyone. I'm his captain, and since he can't make this decision for himself, I have to make it for him."

Nielsen stood up and crossed the galley to stand in front of Falconi. "And what if he decides not to follow orders again? Have you forgotten about that?"

The air between them grew tense. "Greg and I will have a little chat," said Falconi between set teeth. "We'll hash it out, trust me. His life is on the line here, same as ours. If he can help, then he will. I know that much."

For a moment, it seemed as if Nielsen wasn't going to budge. Then she relented with a sigh and said, "Alright, Captain. If you're really convinced this is what's best . . ."

"I am." Then Falconi shifted his attention back to Kira. "You better hurry. We don't have a lot of time."

She nodded and got to her feet.

"And, Kira?" He gave her a stern gaze. "Be careful."

"Of course."

He nodded in return, seeming satisfied. "Hwa-jung, Vishal, go with her. Keep an eye on Gregorovich. Make sure he's okay."

"Sir."

"Yessir."

3.

With the doctor and the machine boss at her heels, Kira ran from Control and proceeded down a deck to the sealed room that contained Gregorovich's sarcophagus. Along the way, Kira could feel her skin prickling as her adrenaline ramped up.

Was she really going to do this? *Shit.* Falconi was right; there was no room for error. The weight of sudden responsibility made Kira pause for a second and question her choices. But no, she could do this. She just had to make sure that she and the xeno were working in harmony. The last thing she wanted was for it to take the initiative and start making changes to Gregorovich's brain on its own.

At the sarcophagus, Hwa-jung handed Kira the same set of wired headphones she'd used before, and Vishal said, "Ms. Kira, Captain gave the order, but if I think Gregorovich is in any danger, then I will say *stop* and you will stop."

"I understand," said Kira. She couldn't think of anything the doctor could actually do to stop her or the Soft Blade from working on Gregorovich once they started, but she intended to respect the doctor's judgment. No matter what, she didn't want to hurt Gregorovich.

Vishal nodded. "Good. I will be monitoring Gregorovich's vitals. If anything drops into the red, I will tell you."

Hwa-jung said, "I will monitor Gregorovich's implants. Right now, they are at . . . forty-two percent operation."

"Okay," said Kira, sitting next to the sarcophagus. "I'll need an access port for the Soft Blade."

"Here," said Hwa-jung, pointing at the side of the sarcophagus.

Kira fit the headphones over her ears. "I'm going to try talking with Gregorovich first. Just to see if I can check with him."

Vishal shook his head. "You can try, Ms. Kira, but I could not speak with him before. The situation will not have improved."

"I'd still like to try."

The instant Kira plugged in the headphones, a whirling roar filled her ears. In it, she seemed to hear snatches of words—shouts lost in an unrelenting storm. She called out to the ship mind, but if he heard, she could not tell, and if he answered, the roaring obscured his response.

She tried for a minute or more before pulling the headphones off. "No luck," she said to Vishal and Hwa-jung.

Then Kira sent the first tentative tendrils from the Soft Blade into the access port. *Careful:* that was the directive she gave the Soft Blade now. *Careful* and *do no harm.*

At first she felt nothing but metal and electricity. Then she tasted Gregorovich's enveloping nutrient bath, and metal gave way to exposed brain matter. Slowly, ever so slowly, Kira sought a point of connection, a way to bridge the gap between matter and consciousness—a portal from brain to mind.

She allowed the tendrils to subdivide even further, until they formed a bristle of monofilament threads, each as thin and sensitive as a nerve. The threads probed the interior of the sarcophagus until at last they chanced upon the very thing Kira was seeking: the caul of wires that lay atop Gregorovich's massive brain and that penetrated deep into the folds of grey and formed the physical structure of his implants.

She twined around each of the tiny wires and followed them inward. Some ended at a dendrite, marking where non-living merged with living. Many more ended in a bead of melted metal or a neuron that was dead and withered.

Then, delicately, ever so delicately, Kira began to repair the damaged connections. For the melted leads, she smoothed the bead at the tip to ensure a proper connection with its target dendrite. For the leads that stopped at a dead neuron, she repositioned the wire to the nearest healthy dendrite, moving the wires infinitesimal amounts within the tissue of Gregorovich's brain.

With each wire that she reconnected, Kira felt a brief shock as a small amount of electricity passed from one to the next. It was a sharp, satisfying feeling that left her with the faint taste of copper on her tongue. And sometimes, she thought she detected the ghost of a sensation from a neuron, like a tickle in the back of her mind.

Despite the microscopic scale she was working on, Kira found connecting the wires relatively easy. What *wasn't* easy was the scale of the task. There were thousands upon thousands of wires, and each one had to be checked. After the first few minutes, Kira realized it would take her days to do the work by hand (as it were). Days they didn't have.

She wasn't willing to give up, which meant she had only one chance. Hoping against hope that she wasn't making a mistake, she fixed her goals in mind—*smooth the melted wires, attach them to the closest neurons*—and did her best to impress them on the Soft Blade. Then she released her hold on the xeno, as carefully as if she were letting go of a wild animal that might react in an unpredictable manner.

Please, she thought.

And the Soft Blade obeyed. It slid along the wires in an atomically thin film, moving metal, pushing aside cells, and realigning wires with dendrites.

Kira's awareness of her body (and the growths in her cabin) faded; every bit of her consciousness was divided among the many thousands of monofilaments the xeno was manipulating. At a remove she heard Hwa-jung say, "Forty-five percent! . . . Forty-seven . . . Forty-eight . . ."

Kira blocked out her voice as she continued to focus on the task at hand. *Wires, smooth, attach.*

So many wires were connecting, Kira felt them like a wave of cold and hot prickles washing through her head. Tiny explosions popping off, and with each one a sense of expansion.

The feeling accumulated, moving faster and faster. And then—

A curtain swept back in her mind, and a vast vista opened up before her, and Kira sensed a Presence within. If not for her experience with the Soft Blade, the experience would have been overwhelming, unbearable—a behemoth weighing upon her from all sides.

She gasped and would have recoiled, but she found she couldn't move.

Vishal and Hwa-jung were making noises of alarm, and the doctor said, as if from a great distance, "Ms. Kira! Stop! Whatever you're doing, it's upsetting his neurotr—"

His voice faded away, and all Kira was aware of was the immensity surrounding her. **Gregorovich,** she said, but no response was forthcoming. She pressed harder, attempting to project herself: **Gregorovich! Can you hear me?**

Distant thoughts swirled far above—thunderheads beyond reach and too large to comprehend. Then, lightning crashed and:

A ship rattled around her, and stars spun outside. Fire streamed from her left flank: a meteoroid strike near the main generator. . . .

Flashes. Screams. A howling across the sky. Below, a tortured landscape of smoke and fire rose toward her. Too fast. Couldn't slow down. Emergency chutes failed.

Darkness for unremembered time. Gratitude and disbelief at continued existence: the ship should have exploded. Ought to have. Perhaps would have been better. Seven of the crew still alive, seven out of twenty-eight.

Then a slow agony of days. Hunger and starvation for her charges and then, to one and all, death. And for her, worse than death: isolation. Loneliness, utter and absolute. A queen of infinite space, bound within a nutshell, and plagued by such dreams as to make her scream and scream and scream. . . .

The memory began anew, repeating as a computer frozen in a logic loop, unable to break out, unable to reboot. **You're not alone,** Kira shouted into the storm, but she might as well have been trying to catch the attention of the earth or the sea or the universe at large. The Presence took no note of her. Again she tried. Again she failed. Instead of words, she tried emotions: comfort, companionship, sympathy, and solidarity, and—underlying it all—a sense of urgency.

None of it made any difference, or at least none Kira could tell.

She called out again, but still, the ship mind didn't notice, or noticed but refused to answer, and the lowering thunderheads remained. Twice more she attempted to contact Gregorovich, with the same results.

She felt like screaming. There was nothing else she could do. Wherever the ship mind had buried himself, it was beyond her reach or the reach of the Soft Blade.

And time—time grew short.

At last the Soft Blade ceased its labors, and though she was reluctant to do so, Kira extricated the suit's tendrils from the innermost parts of Gregorovich's brain and carefully withdrew. The curtain in her mind drew shut as contact broke, and the Presence vanished also, leaving her once again alone with her alien consort, the Soft Blade.

. . .

4.

Kira swayed as she opened her eyes. Dizzy, she braced herself against the cold metal of the sarcophagus.

"What happened, Ms. Kira?" said Vishal, coming over to her. Behind him, Hwa-jung watched with concern. "We tried to wake you, but nothing we did worked."

Kira wet her tongue, feeling displaced. "Gregorovich?" she croaked.

The machine boss answered: "His readings are normal again."

Relieved, Kira nodded. Then she pushed herself off the sarcophagus. "I repaired his implants. You can probably see that. But the weirdest things happened. . . ."

"What, Ms. Kira?" Vishal asked, leaning in, brow pinched.

She tried to find the words. "The Soft Blade, it connected my brain to his."

Vishal's eyes widened. "No. A direct neural link?!"

Kira nodded again. "I wasn't trying to. The xeno just did it. For a while, we had a . . . a . . ."

"A hive mind?" said Hwa-jung.

"Yeah. Like the Entropists."

Vishal clucked his tongue as he helped Kira to her feet. "Forming a hive mind with a ship mind is very dangerous for an unaugmented human, Ms. Kira."

"I know. Good thing I'm augmented," said Kira wryly. She tapped the fibers on her arm to make her meaning clear.

Hwa-jung said, "Were you able to talk with him at all?"

Kira frowned, troubled by the memory. "No. I tried, but ship minds are . . ."

"Different," Hwa-jung supplied.

"Yes. I knew that, but I never really understood just *how* different." She handed back the headphones. "I'm sorry. I couldn't reach him."

Vishal took the headphones from Hwa-jung. "I am sure you did your best, Ms. Kira."

Had she? Kira wondered.

Then the doctor plugged the headphones back into the sarcophagus. In response to Kira and Hwa-jung's questioning looks, he said, "I will try to talk with Gregorovich in a more normal manner, yes? Maybe now he will be able to communicate."

"You still have him isolated from the rest of the ship?" Kira asked, guessing the answer.

Hwa-jung made an affirmative noise. "Until we know he isn't a threat to the *Wallfish*, we keep him like this."

They waited while Vishal tried several times to contact Gregorovich. After repeating the same few phrases for a minute, the doctor unplugged from the sarcophagus and sighed. "There is still no response I can understand."

Disappointed, Kira said, "I'll tell Falconi."

Vishal held up a hand. "Wait a few minutes, please, Ms. Kira. I think it would be most helpful to run some tests. Until I do, I cannot say with confidence what Gregorovich's condition is. Now, both of you shoo. You are crowding my space."

"Okay," said Kira.

She and Hwa-jung retreated into the hallway outside the small room while they waited for the doctor to finish his tests.

Kira's mind was still whirling from the experience. She felt as if *she'd* been the one turned inside out. Unable to stand still, she paced up and down the hall while Hwa-jung squatted with her back against the wall, arms crossed and chin tucked.

"I don't know how he does it," said Kira.

"Who?"

"Gregorovich. There's so *much* in his head. I don't know how he can process it all, much less interact with us."

A slow shrug from Hwa-jung. "Ship minds find amusement in strange places."

"I can believe that." Kira stopped pacing and squatted next to Hwa-jung. The machine boss looked down at her, impassive. Kira rubbed her hands and thought about the things Gregorovich had said to her back at Sol, and specifically how he'd envied the ship mind who painted landscapes. She said, "What are you going to do when all of this is over, if we survive? Go back to Shin-Zar?"

"If my family needs me, I will help. But I will not live on Shin-Zar again. That time has passed."

Then Kira thought about the Entropists' offer of sanctuary at their headquarters by Shin-Zar. She still had their token sitting in the desk of her cabin, covered by a layer of the Soft Blade's growths. "What's it like on Shin-Zar?"

"It depends," said Hwa-jung. "Shin-Zar is a big planet."

"What about where you grew up?"

"I lived in different places." The other woman stared down at her crossed arms. After a moment, she said, "My family settled in the hills by a mountain range. Ah, it was so tall, so pretty."

"Were asteroids much of a problem? I saw a documentary about Tau Ceti that said the system has a lot more rocks flying around than, say, Sol."

Hwa-jung shook her head. "We had a shelter deep in the stone. But we only used it once, when there was a bad storm. Our defense force destroys most of the asteroids before they get close to Shin-Zar." She looked over her arms at Kira. "That is why our military is so good. We get lots of practice shooting things, and if we miss, we die."

"The air is breathable there, right?"

"Earth-norm humans need extra oxygen." The machine boss tapped herself on the sternum. "Why do you think we have such big lungs? In two hundred years, there will be enough oxygen for even narrow people like you. But for now, we must have big chests to breathe well."

"And have you been to the Nova Energium?"

"I have seen it. I have not been inside."

"Ah. . . . What do you think of the Entropists?"

"Very smart, very educated, but they meddle where they shouldn't." Hwa-jung uncrossed her arms and hung them over the tops of her knees. "They always say they will leave Shin-Zar if we join the League; it is one reason we haven't. They bring lots of money to the system, and they have lots of friends in the governments, and their discoveries give our ships advantages over the UMC."

"Huh." Kira's knees were starting to ache from the squatting. "Do you miss your home, where you grew up?"

Hwa-jung rapped the knuckles of one fist against the deck. "Really, you ask a lot of questions. So nosy!"

"Sorry." Kira looked back in at Vishal, embarrassed.

Hwa-jung muttered something in Korean. Then in a quiet voice, she said: "Yes, I miss it. The problem was my family did not approve of me, and they did not like the people I liked."

"But they take your money."

The tips of Hwa-jung's ears turned red. "They are my family. It is my duty to help. Do you not understand that? Seriously . . ."

Abashed, Kira said, "I understand."

The machine boss turned away. "I could not do what they wanted, but I do what I can. Perhaps one day it will be different. Until then . . . it is what I deserve."

From farther down the hallway, Sparrow said, "You deserve better." She walked over to where they sat and put a hand on Hwa-jung's shoulder. The machine boss softened and leaned her head against Sparrow's hip. The small, short-haired woman smiled down at Hwa-jung and kissed the top of her head. "Come on. If you keep frowning like that, you'll turn into an *ajumma*."

Hwa-jung made a harsh noise in the back of her throat, but her shoulders relaxed, and the corners of her eyes wrinkled. "Punk," she said in an affectionate tone.

Vishal came back out of the ship-mind room at that moment. He seemed surprised to see the three of them in the middle of the corridor.

"Well? What's the prognosis, Doc?" said Sparrow.

He made a helpless gesture. "The prognosis is that we wait and hope, Ms. Sparrow. Gregorovich seems healthy, but it will take him time to adjust to the changes in his implants, I think."

"How much time?" Hwa-jung asked.

"I could not say."

Kira had doubts of her own. If Gregorovich's mental state didn't improve, it wouldn't matter if his implants were working or not. "Can I tell the captain?"

"Yes, please," said Vishal. "I will send my report to him later, with the details of the tests."

The others dispersed then, but Kira remained where she was while she put a call through to Falconi. It didn't take long for her to bring him up to date.

Afterward, Kira said, "I'm sorry I couldn't do more. I tried, I really tried to get through to him, but . . ."

"At least you made the effort," said Falconi.

"Yeah."

"And I'm glad you did. Now go get some rest. We don't have much time."

"Will do. Night, Salvo."

"Night, Kira."

Discouraged, Kira slowly made her way back to her cabin. Falconi was right. They didn't have much time. She'd be lucky to get even six hours of sleep at this point. It would be pills for sure in the morning. She couldn't afford to be groggy when they attacked the *Battered Hierophant.*

The door closed behind her with a cold *clink*. She felt the sound in her heart, and it struck her with the knowledge of the fast-approaching inevitable.

Kira tried not to think about what they were about to do, but that proved to be an impossibility. She'd never wanted to be a soldier, and yet here they were, flying into the heart of a battle, about to attack the greatest Jelly of them all. . . .

"If you could see me now," she murmured, thinking of her parents. She thought they would be proud. She hoped so, at least. They wouldn't approve of the killing, but they would approve of her and the crew trying to protect others. That, above all else, they would consider worthwhile.

Alan would have agreed also.

She shivered.

At her command, the Soft Blade cleared the desk and chair in her cabin. Kira sat, turned on the console with a tap of her finger, started it recording.

"Hey Mom, Dad. Sis. We're about to attack the Jellies out at Cordova-Fourteen-Twenty. Long story, but in case things don't work out, I wanted to send you this. I don't know if my previous message reached you, so I'm including a copy with this one."

With short, clear sentences, Kira recounted their ill-fated visit to Sol and the reasons for now agreeing to help the Knot of Minds.

She finished by saying: "Again, I don't know what's going to happen here. Even if we make it out of this, the UMC is going to want me back. Either way, I won't be seeing Weyland again any time soon. . . . I'm sorry. I love you all. If I can, I'll try to get another message to you, but it might not be for a while. Hope you're safe. Bye." And she touched her fingers to her lips and pressed them against the camera.

As Kira ended the recording, she allowed herself one breath of grief, one hiccupping gulp of air that formed a fist of pain in her chest before she let it out, all of it.

Calm was good. Calm was necessary. She needed calm.

She had Morven forward the message to the Seventh Fleet, and then she shut down the console and went to the sink. A splash of cold water on her face, and she stood blinking, letting the droplets roll down her cheeks. Then she removed her rumpled jumpsuit, willed the Soft Blade to dim its lights, and got under the frayed blanket on the bed.

It required a serious effort of will not to pull up her overlays and check on what was happening throughout the system. If she did, Kira knew she would never sleep.

So she remained in the dark and worked to keep her breathing slow and her muscles soft while she imagined sinking through the mattress and into the deck. . . .

She did all those things, and yet sleep continued to elude her. Words and thoughts could not erase the nearness of danger, and because of it, her body refused to accept the lie of safety—would not relax, would not allow her mind to do anything but keep watch against the fanged creatures that instinct insisted must be lurking in the surrounding shadows.

In a few hours she might be dead. They all might. Finito. Kaput. Done and done. No respawning. No do-overs. *Dead.*

Kira's heart began to jackhammer as a slug of adrenaline hit, more potent than any rotgut. She gasped and bolted upright, clutching at her chest. A deep, wounded groan escaped her, and she hunched over, struggling to breathe.

Around her, dark whispering sounded as thousands of needle-sharp spines sprouted from the walls of the cabin.

She didn't care. None of it mattered, only the ice water pooling in her gut and the pain stabbing at her heart.

Dead. Kira wasn't ready to die. Not yet. Not for a long, long, long time. Preferably never. But there was no escaping it. No escaping what tomorrow would bring. . . .

"Gaaah!"

She was afraid, more afraid than she'd ever been. And what made it worse was knowing that there was *nothing* that could fix the situation. Everyone in the *Wallfish* was strapped to an express rocket heading straight toward their doom, and there was no getting off early unless they wanted to grab a blaster and put it against their temples, pull the trigger, and ride the short trip to oblivion.

Had Gregorovich's dark dreams infected her mind? Kira didn't know. It didn't matter. Nothing mattered—not really—except the terrifying pit yawning before her.

Unable to hold still any longer, she swung her legs over the edge of the bed. If only Gregorovich were there to message with. *He* would understand.

She shivered and sent a thought to the Soft Blade that activated the light-producing nodules along the corners of the room. A dim green glow brightened the bristling space.

Kira gulped for air, struggling to get enough. *Don't think about it. Don't think about. Don't* . . . She let her gaze roam across the room in an attempt to distract herself.

The scratch on the surface of the desk caught her eye, the scratch she'd put there when she'd first tried to force the Soft Blade off her body. That had been, what, her second day on the *Wallfish*? Her third?

It didn't matter.

Cold pinpricks of sweat sprang up on her face. She hugged herself, feeling chilled in a way no external warmth could correct.

She didn't want to be alone, not then. She needed to see another person, to hear their voice, to be comforted by the nearness of their presence and to know that she wasn't the only speck of consciousness facing the void. It wasn't a matter of logic or philosophy—Kira *knew* they were doing the right thing by helping the Knot of Minds—but rather animal instinct. Logic only took you so far. Sometimes the cure to the dark was to find another flame burning bright.

Still feeling as if her heart were about to hammer its way out of her chest, she sprang to her feet, went to the storage locker, and removed her jumpsuit. Her hands shook as she dressed herself.

There. Good enough.

Down, she told the Soft Blade. The protrusions throughout the room quivered and subsided several centimeters but no more than that.

She didn't care. The spines retracted around her as she made her way to the door, and that was all she required.

Kira strode down the hallway with purpose-born steps. Now that she was moving, she didn't want to linger, certainly didn't want to stop. With each step, she felt as if she were teetering along the edge of a precipice.

She climbed one level up the central shaft to C-deck. The dimly lit corridor there was so quiet, Kira was afraid to make any noise. It felt as if she were the only person aboard, and all around her was the immensity of space, pressing in against a lone spark.

A sense of relief as she arrived at the door to Falconi's cabin.

The relief was short-lived. A spike of panic erased it as she heard a *clank* farther down the corridor. She jumped and spun to see Nielsen opening a cabin door.

But not to her own cabin: Vishal's.

The other woman had wet hair, as if she'd just washed, and she was carrying a tray with foil-wrapped snacks and a pair of mugs and a pot of tea. She stopped as she caught sight of Kira—stopped and stared.

In the first officer's eyes, Kira glimpsed a hint of something she recognized. A similar need perhaps. A similar fear. And sympathy too.

Before Kira could decide how to react, Nielsen gave a brief nod and disappeared into the cabin. Even through the cutting edge of her panic, Kira felt a sense of amusement. Vishal and Nielsen. *Well, well.* When she thought about it, she supposed it wasn't entirely surprising.

She hesitated a moment and then lifted her hand and knocked on Falconi's door with three quick raps. Hopefully he wasn't sleeping.

"It's open."

The sound of his voice did nothing to slow her pulse. She spun the locking wheel and pushed back the door.

Yellow light spilled into the corridor. Inside, Falconi sat in the cabin's single chair, his feet (still in their boots) propped up on the desk, ankles crossed. He'd removed his vest, and his sleeves were rolled up, exposing the scars on his forearms. His gaze shifted from his overlays to her face. "You couldn't sleep either, huh?"

Kira shook her head. "Mind if I . . . ?"

"Be my guest," he said, dropping his feet and scooting back in the chair.

She entered and closed the door behind herself. Falconi raised an eyebrow but didn't object. He leaned forward, elbows on his knees. "Let me guess: worried about tomorrow?"

"Yeah."

"Want to talk about it?"

"Not particularly."

He nodded, understanding.

"I just . . . I . . ." She grimaced and shook her head.

"How about a drink?" Falconi reached for the locker over his desk. "I've got a bottle of Venusian scotch somewhere around here. Won it in a poker game a few years ago. Just give me a—"

Kira took two steps forward, put her hands on either side of his face, and kissed him on the mouth. Hard.

Falconi stiffened, but he didn't pull away.

Up close he smelled good: warm and musky. Wide lips. Hard cheeks. He tasted sharp, and his perma-stubble was an unfamiliar prickle.

Kira broke the kiss to look at him. Her heart was pounding faster than ever, and her whole body felt alternatively hot and cold. Falconi wasn't Alan, wasn't anything like him, but he would do. For this one moment in time, he would do.

She fought and failed to keep from trembling.

Falconi let out his breath. His ears were flushed, and he appeared almost dazed. "Kira . . . What are you doing?"

"Kiss me."

"I'm not sure that's a good idea."

She lowered her face toward his, keeping her gaze fixed on his lips, not daring to meet his eyes. "I don't want to be alone right now, Salvo. I really, *really* don't."

He licked his lips. Then she saw a change in his posture, a softening of his shoulders, a broadening of his chest. "I don't either," he confessed in a low voice.

She trembled again. "Then shut up and kiss me."

Her back tingled as his arm slid around her waist and he pulled her closer. Then he kissed her. He gripped the back of her neck with his other hand, and for a time, all Kira was aware of was the rush of sensations, intense and overwhelming. The touch of hands and arms, lips and tongues, skin against skin.

It wasn't enough to make her forget her fear. But it was enough to redirect her panic and anxiety into a feral energy, and *that* she could do something with.

Falconi surprised her by putting a hand on the center of her chest, pushing her back, evading her mouth.

"What?" she said, half snarling.

"What about this?" he asked. He tapped her sternum and the Soft Blade covering it.

"I told you," she said. "Feels just like skin."

"And this?" His hand slid lower.

"Same."

He smiled. It was a dangerous smile.

Seeing it only stoked the heat inside her. She growled and dug her fingers into his back while leaning in for his ear, nipping at it with her teeth.

With an eagerness born of impatience, he undid the seal to her jumpsuit, and with equal eagerness, she shimmied out. She'd worried that the Soft Blade would put him off, but Falconi caressed her as avidly and attentively as any of her past lovers, and if he didn't find the texture of the Soft Blade as appealing as her real skin, he hid it well. After the first few minutes, she stopped worrying and allowed herself to relax and enjoy his touch.

As for the Soft Blade itself, it seemed unsure how to respond to their activities, but in one of her more lucid moments, Kira impressed on it (in no uncertain terms) that it wasn't to interfere. To her relief, it behaved.

She and Falconi moved together with a frantic urgency, fueled by their shared hunger and the knowledge of what awaited them at night's end. They spared no centimeter of skin, no curve of muscle nor ridge of bone in their feverish pursuit. Every bit of sensation they could wring from their bodies, they did, not so much for the sake of pleasure, but to satisfy their craving for closeness. The feeling drove the future from Kira, forced her into the present, made her feel *alive*.

They did all they could, but because of the Soft Blade, not all they wanted. With hands and fingers, mouths and tongues, they satisfied each other, but still it wasn't enough. Falconi didn't complain, but she could see he was frustrated. *She* was frustrated; she wanted more.

"Wait," she said, and put a hand on his matted chest. He leaned back, his expression quizzical.

Turning inward, she focused on her groin, gathered her will, and forced the Soft Blade to retreat from her innermost parts. The touch of air on her exposed skin made her gasp and clench.

Falconi looked down at her with a crooked grin.

"Well?" Kira said, her voice taut with strain. Holding back the suit was an effort, but it was one she could maintain. She arched an eyebrow. "How brave are you?"

As it turned out, he was very brave.

Very brave indeed.

5.

Kira sat with her back to the bulkhead, the blanket pulled around her waist. Next to her, Falconi lay on his stomach, his head turned toward her, his left arm draped across her lap, warm and comforting in its weight.

"You know," he mumbled, "I don't normally sleep with my crew or passengers. Just for the record."

"And I don't normally seduce the captain of the ship I'm traveling on."

"Mmm. Glad you did. . . ."

She smiled and ran her fingers through his hair, lightly scratching his scalp. He made a contented sound and snuggled closer.

"Me too, Salvo," she said, softly.

He didn't answer, and his breathing soon deepened and slowed as he fell into sleep.

She studied the muscles on his back and shoulders. At rest, they appeared soft, but she could still see traces of the lines and hollows that separated them, and she remembered how they'd bunched and knotted and stood out in hard relief as he'd moved against her.

She slid a hand over her lower belly. Was it possible for her to get pregnant? It seemed unlikely the Soft Blade would tolerate the growth of a child inside her. But she wondered.

She leaned her head against the wall. A long breath escaped her. Despite her worries, she felt content. Not happy—circumstances were too dire for that—but not sad either.

Only a handful of hours remained before they arrived at the *Battered Hierophant*. She kept herself awake until, halfway through their flight, the free-fall warning sounded, and then she used the Soft Blade to hold Falconi and herself in place while the *Wallfish* flipped end for end before resuming thrust.

Falconi mumbled something incoherent as thrust resumed, but like a true spacer, he stayed asleep through the whole procedure.

Then Kira slid farther under the blanket, lay next to him, and allowed her eyes to close.

And finally, she too slept.

6.

Kira dreamed, but the dreams were not her own.

Fractures upon fractures: forward, backward, she could not tell which. Twice the cradle cupped her resting form. Twice she woke and waking found no sign of those who first laid her there to rest.

The first time she woke, the graspers stood waiting.

She fought them, in all their many forms. She fought them by the thousands, in the depths of oceans and the cold of space, on ships and stations and long-forgotten moons. Scores of battles, large and small. Some she won; some she lost. It mattered not.

She fought the graspers, but she herself was bound to one. The graspers warred amongst their own, and she to her bond of flesh was true. Though she had no wish to kill, she stabbed and sliced and shot her way across the stars. And when the flesh was hurt beyond repair, another took its place, and still others after that, and with each joining, the side she served was wont to change, back and forth and round again.

She did not care. The graspers were nothing like the kind who made her. They were quarrelsome upstarts, arrogant and foolish. They used her badly, for they knew not what she was. But still, she did her duty best she could. Such was her nature.

And when the graspers died, as die they did, she took a certain satisfaction in their end. They should have known: it was wrong to steal and wrong to meddle. The things they took were not for them.

Then came the flesh of Shoal Leader Nmarhl and the ill-fated uprising of the Knot of Minds that ended with the triumph of Ctein. Cradle-bound she became again as Nmarhl laid their flesh down to rest, and rest she did for fractures yet.

The second time she woke, it was to a new form. An old form. An odd form. Flesh joined with flesh, and from flesh came blood. The pairing was imperfect; she had to learn, adjust, adapt. It took time. Errors had crept in; repairs had to be made. And there was cold that dulled her, slowed her, before the match could then conclude.

When she emerged, it was difficult. Painful. And there was noise and light, and though she tried to protect the flesh, her attempts were flawed. Sorrow then, that upon waking, she had again been the cause of death, and with that sorrow, a sense of . . . responsibility. Apology even.

. . .

A flash, then. A disjunction, and somehow she knew, it was an earlier time, an earlier age, before the first ones had left. She beheld the whorl of stars that was the galaxy and—among that sprawling spiral—the billions upon billions of asteroids, meteors, moons, planets, and other celestial bodies that filled the heavens. Most were barren. Some few teemed with small and primitive organisms. Rarest of all were those places where life had developed into more complex forms. Priceless treasures were they, gleaming gardens pulsing with movement and warmth amid the deathless void.

This she beheld, and her sacred cause she knew—to move among the empty worlds, to furrow the fruitless soil, and to plant therein the germs of future growth. For nothing was more important than the spread of life, nothing more important than nurturing those who would someday join them among the stars. As the ones who came before, it was their responsibility, their duty, and their joy to foster and protect. Without consciousness to appreciate it, existence was meaningless—an abandoned tomb decaying into oblivion.

Driven, sustained, and guided by her purpose, she sailed forth into the desolate reaches. There, by her touch, she brought forth growing things, moving things, thinking things. She saw planets of bare stone flush and mottle with the spread of leafing plants. Glimpses of greenery and reddery (depending on the hue of the reigning star). Roots burrowing deep. Muscles stretching. Song and speech the primordial silence breaking.

And she heard a voice, though the voice used no words:

"Is it good?"

And she responded, "It is good."

Sometimes battles broke the pattern. But they were different. She was different. Neither she nor her foes were graspers. And there was a rightness to her actions, a sense that she was serving others, and the fights, while fierce, were brief.

Then she was soaring through a nebula, and for a moment, she beheld a patch of twisted space. She could see it was twisted by the way it warped the surrounding gas. And from the patch, she felt a warped sensation, a feeling of utter wrongness, and it terrified her, for she knew its meaning. Chaos. Evil. Hunger. A vast and monstrous intelligence coupled with power even the first had not. . . .

She hurtled past stars and planets, through memories old and ancient, until once again, as once she had, she floated before a fractal pattern etched upon the face of an upright stone. As before, the pattern shifted, turning and twisting in ways she could not follow, while lines of force flashed and flared along the pattern's edge.

The name of the Soft Blade flooded her mind, with all its many meanings. Image upon image, association upon association. And all the while, the fractal hung before her, like an overlay burned upon her sight.

The deluge of information continued in a loop, cycling and cycling without pause. Among the general profusion, she recognized the sequence she had translated as the Soft Blade. *It still seemed fitting, but it no longer seemed adequate. Not given all she had learned.*

She concentrated on the other images, other associations, attempting to trace the connections between them. And as she did, a structure began to emerge from what had once seemed formless and obscure. It felt as if she were assembling a three-dimensional puzzle without having any concept of the final product.

The smaller details of the name escaped her, but piece by piece, she came to grasp the larger theme. It coalesced in her mind, like a crystal edifice, bright and clear and pure of line. And as the shape of it grew visible, understanding broke.

A sense of awe crept through her, for the truth of the name was greater, so much greater, than the words Soft Blade *implied. The organism had a purpose, and that purpose was of almost unimaginable complexity and—of this she was sure—importance. And though it seemed a contradiction, that purpose, that complexity, could be summed up not by pages or paragraphs but by a single word. And that word was thus:*

Seed.

Wonder joined with awe, and joy too. The organism wasn't a weapon. Or rather, it hadn't been created with that sole intention. It was a source of life. Of many lives. A spark that could bathe an entire planet in the fire of creation.

And she was happy. For was there anything more beautiful?

7.

A hand shook her shoulder. "Kira. Wake up."

"Uhh."

"Come on, Kira. It's time. We're almost there."

She opened her eyes, and tears rolled down her cheeks. *Seed.* The knowledge overwhelmed her. All the memories did. The Highmost. The horrible patch of distorted space. The seemingly endless battles. That the suit had apologized for the deaths of Alan and her teammates.

Seed. She finally understood. How could she have guessed? Guilt overwhelmed her that she had so terribly misused the xeno—that her fear and anger had led to the creation of a blighted monstrosity as horrible as the Maw. The tragedy was, now she had to again take the xeno into battle. It felt almost obscene in light of its true nature.

"Hey now. What's wrong?" Falconi pushed himself up on an elbow and leaned over her.

Kira wiped her eyes with the heel of her hand. "Nothing. Just a dream." She sniffed, and hated how weak she sounded.

"Sure you're okay?"

"Yeah. Let's go kill the great and mighty Ctein."

CHAPTER IV

* * * * * * *

FERRO COMITANTE

1.

The *Battered Hierophant* hung before the *Wallfish,* a bright point of light against the black backdrop of space.

The Jelly ship was larger than any other vessel Kira had seen. It was as long as seven UMC battleships placed end to end, and almost as wide, giving it a slight ovoid shape. In terms of mass, it was equal to—if not greater than—a structure like Orsted Station, but unlike Orsted, it was fully maneuverable.

To Kira's dismay, a trio of smaller ships had taken up positions in front of the *Battered Hierophant:* extra firepower ready to defend their leader should one of the human ships get close enough to threaten.

The *Hierophant* and its escorts were only seven thousand-some klicks out, but even at such a relatively short distance (nearly in spitting range by the standards of interplanetary travel) the giant ship was no more than a fleck of light when seen without magnification.

"Could be worse," said Sparrow.

"Could be a hell of a lot better too," said Falconi.

Aside from Itari, who had insisted it would be fine in the cargo hold, all of them were crammed into the *Wallfish*'s storm shelter. No one looked particularly fresh, but of them, Jorrus and Veera seemed the most tired, the most drawn. Their normally impeccable robes were wrinkled, and they fidgeted in a way that reminded Kira of the wireheads back in Highstone, on Weyland. But they were alert, and they listened with sharp-eyed interest to everything being said.

When questioned about their choice of attire—with the exception of Kira, the crew had traded their normal clothes for skinsuits—the Entropists said, "We are most well—"

"—equipped as we are, thank you." Whereupon Nielsen had shrugged and shelved the suits she'd been offering them.

To Kira's amusement, the first officer and Vishal stayed on opposite sides of the shelter, but she noticed secret smiles passing between them, and their lips often moved slightly as if they were texting.

Tschetter's face appeared in the upper right-hand corner of the display. Behind her, the Jellies were moving about as they prepared their ship for what was to come. Trig's cryo tube was visible by a curved wall, secured in place with several strange-looking brackets. "Captain Falconi," said Tschetter. There were deep bags under her eyes, and Kira realized the woman didn't have access to any stims or sleep pills.

"Major."

"Have your crew stand by. We'll be in firing range soon."

"Don't worry about us," said Falconi. "We're ready. Just make sure the Knot gives us cover once we go hot."

The major nodded. "They'll do their best."

"We've still got clearance from the Jellies?"

A grim smile stretched Tschetter's face. "They'd be shooting at us if we didn't. As is, they're expecting us to bring the *Wallfish* to the *Hierophant* so their techs can pick through its computers."

Kira rubbed her arms. It was happening. There was no going back now. A sense of inevitability curdled in her veins. The rest of the crew looked similarly apprehensive.

"Roger that," said Falconi.

Tschetter gave him a terse nod. "Wait for my signal. Over and out." She vanished from the holo.

"And here we go," Falconi said.

Kira pressed on the earpiece Hwa-jung had given her—making sure it was securely seated—and then used her own overlays to check on the progress of the battle. The Seventh Fleet had scattered as it neared the Jellies, drawing them out and around the rocky planet the aliens were strip-mining, luring them toward a pair of small moons. The planet had been dubbed R1 by the UMC, the moons r2 and r3. Hardly elegant names, but convenient for the purposes of strategy and navigation.

Clouds of smoke and chaff obscured most of the UMC ships (in visible light, at least; they showed up fine in infrared). Sparks flashed within the clouds as the UMC's point-defense lasers took out incoming missiles. Unlike their spaceships, the Jellies' missiles weren't substantially faster or more agile than the UMC's, which meant the Seventh was able to destroy or disable most of them.

Most, but not all, and as the lasers overheated, more and more missiles slipped past.

The shooting hadn't been going on for long, but three of the UMC cruisers were already out of commission: one destroyed, two incapacitated and drifting helplessly. A cluster of Jellies were attempting to board the pair, but Admiral Klein's forces were working to keep the aliens tied up, away from the crippled vessels.

As for the Jellies, hard numbers were difficult to find, but it looked to Kira as if the UMC had destroyed at least four of them and damaged quite a few more. Not enough to put a serious dent in the Jelly fleet, but enough to slow the first wave.

Even as Kira watched, projectiles slammed into two of the UMC ships, both in the engine area. Their rockets sputtered and died, and the cruisers tumbled away, powerless.

Near the leading edge of the Seventh Fleet, a Jelly jinked at speeds and angles that would have flattened any human. A half dozen of the Seventh's capital ships fired their main lasers at the vessel, impaling it with crimson threads. The lights on the Jelly ship went out, and it tumbled end over end, spraying boiling water in an ever-expanding spiral.

"Oh yeah," Kira murmured.

She dug her nails into her palms as a pair of Jellies darted toward a hulking battleship that had somehow ended up alone by the moon r2. Lasers flickered between the battleship and the Jellies, and both sides fired several missiles.

Without warning, a white-hot spike shot out from one of the battleship's missiles, snapping across almost nine thousand klicks in the course of a second. The spike obliterated the incoming missiles and vaporized half of the nearest alien ship, like a blowtorch blasting through styrofoam.

The damaged Jelly ship spun like a top as it vented atmosphere, and then it vanished in an explosion of its own, the annihilating antimatter creating an artificial sun that quickly dissipated.

The remaining Jelly corkscrewed away from the battleship. A second spike erupted from one of the two remaining UMC missiles—a white-hot lance of superheated plasma. It missed, but the third spike from the last missile didn't.

A nuclear fireball replaced the alien ship in the holo-display.

"You see that?" Kira said.

Hwa-jung grunted. "Casaba-Howitzers."

"Anything from Gregorovich?" Kira asked, looking over at Vishal and Hwa-jung.

They both shook their heads, and the doctor said, "No change, I am afraid. His vitals are the same as yesterday."

Kira wasn't surprised—if Gregorovich had recovered, he would have been making constant comments—but she was disappointed. Again, she hoped she hadn't made things worse by using the Soft Blade . . . using the *Seed* to touch his mind.

Tschetter reappeared in the holo. "It's time. Much closer and the ships guarding the *Battered Hierophant* are going to get suspicious. Prepare to launch."

"Roger," said Falconi. "Sparrow."

"On it." A hollow *thud* sounded elsewhere in the *Wallfish*, and the woman said, "Howitzer is loaded. Missile tubes are open. We're ready to release."

Falconi nodded. "Alright. You hear that, Tschetter?"

"Affirmative. The Knot of Minds is moving into final position. Transmitting updated targeting data. Stand by for go."

"Standing by."

On the other side of R1, a UMC cruiser vanished in a flare of light. Kira winced and checked the name: the *Hokulea*.

Vishal said, "Ah, poor souls. May they rest in peace."

A hush descended upon the storm shelter as they waited, tense and sweating. Falconi moved over to Kira and put an unobtrusive hand on the small of her back. The touch warmed her, and she leaned back slightly. His fingers scratched against her coated skin, light and distracting.

On her overlays, a line appeared: *<Nervous? – Falconi>*

She subvocalized her answer: *<Who wouldn't be? – Kira>*

<If we make it through this, we should talk. – Falconi>

<Do we need to? – Kira>

The corner of his mouth twitched. *<It's not required. But I'd like to. – Falconi>*

<Okay. – Kira>

Nielsen's eyes lingered on them, and Kira wondered what the first officer was thinking. Kira lifted her chin, feeling defiant.

Then Tschetter's voice intruded. "We're a go. I repeat, we're a go. Light them up, *Wallfish*."

Sparrow cackled, and a loud *thump* resonated through the hull. "Who wants fried calamari?"

2.

The *Wallfish* had been decelerating tail-first toward the *Battered Hierophant*. That meant the ravening torch of nuclear death that was the *Wallfish*'s fusion drive was pointed in the general direction of their target.

This had two advantages. First was that the drive's exhaust helped protect the *Wallfish* from missiles or lasers that might be fired at them from the Jelly flagship or its escorts. Second was that the amount of energy, thermal and EM, radiating from the drive was enough to overload most any sensor aimed at it. The fusion reaction was hotter than the surface of any star and brighter too—the brightest flashlight in the galaxy.

As a result, the Casaba-Howitzer that Sparrow had just released from the *Wallfish*'s aft missile tube (port side) would be nearly invisible next to the drive's blue-white incandescence. And since the howitzer was currently unpowered, its own rocket cold and inactive, it would continue past the slowing *Wallfish* without any need for a burn that would attract unwanted attention.

"T-minus fourteen seconds," announced Sparrow. That was the length of time the Casaba-Howitzer needed to pass behind their shadow shield and reach a safe(ish) distance from the *Wallfish* before detonating and sending a beam of nuclear energy racing toward the *Battered Hierophant*.

The bomb would be going off far, far closer than any sane person would be comfortable with, and—excluding Gregorovich—Kira liked to think that they were all quite sane. The shadow shield ought to protect them from the worst of the radiation, same as it did with the rather nasty by-products of their fusion drive. Likewise, the storm shelter. The main risk would be shrapnel. If the explosion blew a piece of the howitzer's casing into the *Wallfish*, it would cut through the hull like a bullet through tissue paper.

"T-minus ten seconds," said Sparrow.

Hwa-jung pulled her lips back, made a disparaging *hiss* between her teeth.

"Time to get a year's worth of rads, I think." By the wall, the two Entropists sat holding hands and rocking.

"T-minus five, four—"

"*Shit!* They're turning!" exclaimed Tschetter.

"—three—"

"No time to change!" said Falconi.

"—two—"

"Aim for—"

"—one."

Kira's neck snapped to the side as a violent application of the RCS thrusters pushed the *Wallfish* off its current trajectory. Then the ship's acceleration surged at what must have been at least 2 g's, and she grimaced as she fought the sudden press of force.

Less than a second later, the *Wallfish* shuddered around them, and Kira heard several *pings* and *pops* across the hull.

On the display, a burning spike of light raced toward the *Battered Hierophant*. The Jelly ship had already rotated halfway around, so that its drive was hidden from view, and it was continuing to turn, reorienting itself away from the *Wallfish*.

"Goddammit," muttered Falconi.

Kira watched with horrified fascination as the blaze of plasma flashed toward the *Battered Hierophant*. Lphet and the Knot of Minds had given them precise information on where the *Hierophant*'s Markov Drive was located. Hitting it and breaching the antimatter containment within the drive was their best chance of destroying the ship. Otherwise, they had no guarantee that the Casaba-Howitzer would kill Ctein.

As Itari had explained, even the smaller Jelly co-forms were hardened against heat and radiation, and as the UMC had discovered to their dismay, the creatures were incredibly hard to kill. A Jelly as large as Ctein—whatever its current form—would be far more resilient. It was, as Sparrow said, more like trying to kill a fungus than a human.

Black smoke billowed out of vents along the swollen middle of the alien ship—a threatened squid hiding itself in an ever-expanding cloud of ink—but it wouldn't provide any protection against the howitzer's shaped charge. Few things could.

The lance hit the belly of the *Hierophant*. A hemisphere of vaporized hull exploded outward along with a haze of air and water that had flashed to steam.

Sparrow groaned as the view cleared.

The nuclear charge had carved a trough as large as the *Wallfish* through the *Battered Hierophant*. Its main drive appeared disabled—propellant spurted from the nozzle, failed to ignite—but the bulk of the vessel remained intact.

Lasers and missiles shot forth from the Knot of Minds toward the three escort vessels near the *Hierophant* even as the trio turned to attack. The *Wallfish* released its own cloud of defenses, shrouding the ship in darkness. The display switched to infrared.

"Pop off another howitzer," said Falconi.

"We've only got two more," said Sparrow.

"I know. Fire it anyway."

"Aye-aye, sir."

Another *thud* echoed through the hull, and then the Casaba-Howitzer streaked away from the *Wallfish* as it headed to the minimum safe distance for detonation.

The missile never reached its destination. A jet of violet sparks spewed from its nose, and then its rocket sputtered out and the howitzer went tumbling harmlessly off course.

"Fuck!" said Sparrow. "Laser took it out."

"I see that," said Falconi, calm.

Kira wished she could still bite her nails. Instead, she found herself clenching the armrests of her crash chair.

"Is Ctein dead?" she asked Tschetter. "Do we know if Ctein is dead?"

The major shook her head in the holo. Lights were flashing on the deck behind her. "It doesn't seem so. I—"

An explosion rocked the Jelly ship. "Are you okay, Major?" Nielsen asked, leaning in toward the display.

Tschetter reappeared, appearing shaken. Frizzy strands of hair had come loose from her bun. "We're okay for now. But—"

"More Jellies incoming," Sparrow announced. "A good twenty of them. We've got maybe ten minutes. Less."

"Of course," Falconi growled.

"You still need to kill Ctein," said Tschetter. "We can't do it over here. Half the Jellies with me seem to be sick."

"I don't—"

Morven said, "Admiral Klein for you, Captain Falconi."

"Put him on hold. Don't have time for him right now."

"Yessir," said the pseudo-intelligence, sounding absurdly cheery given the situation.

A blinking yellow light appeared in the holo, heading toward them from the *Battered Hierophant.* "What's that?" Jorrus and Veera asked, pointing.

Falconi zoomed in. A dark, blob-like object about four meters long came into view. It looked as if several intersecting spheres had been welded together. "That's no missile."

A memory stirred in the back of Kira's mind: the storage room where she'd seen Dr. Carr and the Jelly Qwon fighting, and on the far end of the room, a hole cut into the hull. A hole glowing with blue light emanating from the small vessel that had clamped barnacle-like onto the outside of the *Extenuating Circumstances.*

"It's a boarding shuttle," she said. "Or maybe an escape pod. Either way, it can cut right through the hull."

"There are more of them," Vishal said in a warning tone.

He was right. Another dozen of the blobs were heading their way.

"Major," said Falconi. "You have to help us take them out, or—"

"We'll try, but we're slightly busy," Tschetter said.

One of the *Hierophant*'s three escorts exploded, but the other two were still firing at the Knot of Minds, as was the *Battered Hierophant* itself. So far, the Knot hadn't lost any of their ships, but several of them were trailing smoke and vapor from hull breaches.

Falconi said, "Sparrow—"

"Already on it."

On her overlays, Kira watched as lines flashed between the *Wallfish* and the incoming blobs: laser blasts, highlighted by the computer to make them visible to human eyes.

She bit her lip. It was horrible not being able to help. If only she had a ship of her own. Better yet if she were close enough to tear apart the approaching enemies with the Soft Blade.

Then the interior lights flickered and Morven said, "Security breach in progress. Firewall compromised. Shutting down nonessential systems. Please turn off all personal electronic devices until notified otherwise."

"They can hack our systems now?" cried Nielsen.

Jorrus and Veera said, "Give us—"

"—root access, we—"

"—can provide assistance."

Falconi hesitated, and then nodded. "Password sent to your consoles." The Entropists hunched over the displays built into their chairs.

Ruddy flashes appeared within the smoke surrounding the *Battered Hierophant*—missiles being fired.

Alarms blared. Morven said, "Warning, incoming objects. Collision imminent."

The missiles shot out of the smoke and quickly overtook the approaching blobs, some hurtling toward the Knot of Minds and the rest, all four of them, racing toward the *Wallfish*.

A fresh charge of foil chaff launched from the rear of the *Wallfish*. The ship was still decelerating, but the missiles rushing toward them were accelerating even faster and the distance between them dwindled with horrifying quickness.

The *Wallfish*'s laser stabbed out. A missile exploded (sharp blast, there and gone). Then another, closer this time. Two left.

"*Sparrow*," said Falconi from between his teeth.

"I see it."

One ship of the Knot of Minds shot down the third missile. The fourth one kept coming, though, evading the incoming laser blasts with brutally fast jerks up, down, and sideways.

A sheen of sweat coated Sparrow's unblinking face as she concentrated fire on the incoming projectile.

Morven: "Caution, brace for impact."

At the last moment, when the missile was nearly upon them, the *Wallfish*'s blaster finally connected and the missile exploded only a few hundred meters away from their hull.

Sparrow uttered a triumphant shout.

The ship rattled and shook, and the bulkheads groaned. More alarms shrieked, and smoke poured out of an overhead vent. Half the lights on the control panels went dark. A strange burst of noise sounded from the speakers: not static—transmitted data?

"Damage report," said Falconi.

In the display, and in Kira's overlays, a diagram of the *Wallfish* appeared. A large section of the hab-ring, as well as the cargo holds below, were flashing crimson. Hwa-jung stared like a person possessed while her lips moved with murmured queries to the computer.

She said, "Decks C and D are breached. Cargo hold A. Massive damage to the electrical system. Main laser is offline. Reclamation unit, hydroponics bay . . . everything's been affected. Engine working at twenty-eight percent efficiency. Emergency protocols in effect." The machine boss gestured and brought up the feed from an outside camera: along the curved hull of the *Wallfish*'s hab-ring, a large hole cratered inward to reveal internal walls and rooms dark but for an occasional flash of electrical discharge.

Falconi made a fist and thumped the arm of his chair. Kira winced. She knew how much the ship meant to him.

"Thule," said Nielsen.

"Itari?" Falconi barked. An image popped up in the holo showing the Jelly climbing up the center of the ship. The alien appeared unharmed. "What about Morven?" He craned his neck toward the Entropists.

Their eyes were half-closed and glowing with the reflected light of their implants. Veera said, "Firewall restored, but—"

"—some sort of malicious program is still in the—"

"—mainframe. We've confined it to the waste management subroutines while we try to purge it." Veera made a face. "It's very . . ."

"Very resistant," said Jorrus.

"Yes," said Veera. "It is probably best to avoid using the head for now."

Again the pseudo-intelligence announced: "Warning, incoming objects. Collision imminent."

"Fuck!"

This time it was the Jelly boarding vessels. One was headed straight for the *Wallfish,* the others for the Knot of Minds.

"Can we evade?" Falconi asked.

Hwa-jung shook her head. "No. Not possible with thrusters. *Aish.*"

"Howitzer?" Falconi asked, turning on Sparrow.

She grimaced. "We can try, but there's a good chance we'll lose it to their countermeasures."

Falconi scowled and swore under his breath. In the holo, Tschetter briefly reappeared and said, "Save the nuke for the *Battered Hierophant.* We're going to try to get you past their point defenses."

"Roger that. . . . Morven, drop thrust to one g."

"Affirmative, Captain. Dropping thrust to one g." The corresponding alert sounded, and Kira breathed a slight sigh of relief as the weight pressing on her returned to normal. Then Falconi slapped the console and stood. "All hands on deck. We're about to be boarded."

3.

"Shit," said Nielsen.

"Looks like they're heading for the breach in the cargo hold," said Sparrow.

A knocking sounded on the pressure door to the storm shelter. Vishal opened it, and Itari's tentacled shape pushed forward, filling the frame. [[Itari here: What is the situation?]]

[[Kira here: Wait. I do not know.]]

"Six minutes to contact," said Hwa-jung.

Falconi tapped the grip of his blaster. "Pressure doors are sealed around the damaged areas. The Jellies will have to cut their way through. That buys us a little time. Once they're in the main shaft, we'll ambush them from above. Kira, you'll have to take point. If you can kill at least two of them, we can probably handle the rest."

She nodded. Time to test words with action.

Falconi started for the door. "Out of the way!" he said, waving at Itari. The Jelly understood well enough to move back, clearing the opening.

[[Kira here: We are being boarded by Wranaui from the *Battered Hierophant*.]]

Nearscent of understanding, colored with some . . . eagerness. [[Itari here: I understand. I will do my best to protect your co-forms, Idealis.]]

[[Kira here: Thank you.]]

Falconi said, "Let's go! Let's go! Kira, Nielsen, Doc, go grab weapons for everyone. Sparrow, you're with me. Move!"

Along with Vishal, Kira trotted after Nielsen through the darkened corridors to the *Wallfish*'s small armory. The air in the ship was hot and smelled like burnt plastic.

At the closet-sized room, they scooped up blasters and firearms both. Kira nearly didn't bother picking one for herself; if she was going to fight, the Soft Blade would be her best weapon. (It seemed more appropriate to think of the xeno as the *Soft Blade* when heading into battle, although the prospect of again committing violence with the Seed felt profoundly wrong.)

Nevertheless, Kira knew it would be overconfident of her *not* to have another option, so she grabbed a blaster and slung it over her shoulder.

Despite the saw-toothed buzz of fear riding on her nerves, she felt relief. The waiting was over. Now, the only thing she had to focus on was survival—hers and the crew's. Everything else was irrelevant.

Life became so much simpler when you were faced with a physical threat. The danger was . . . clarifying.

The xeno responded to her mood, stiffening and thickening and preparing itself in unseen ways for the chaos about to commence. The change in the suit's distribution reminded her of her distant flesh: the black coating that had devoured the interior of her cabin. If need be, she could call upon it, draw it to her, and allow the Soft Blade to once more swell in size.

"Here," said Nielsen, and tossed Kira several canisters: two blue and two yellow. "Chalk and chaff. Should have some handy."

"Thanks."

Arms piled high with weapons, the three of them hurried back through the corridors to the main shaft of the *Wallfish.* Itari and the Entropists were waiting for them there, but Falconi and Sparrow were nowhere to be seen.

While Nielsen kitted out the Entropists, Kira offered Itari a choice of blasters or slug throwers. The alien chose two blasters, which it grasped with the bony arms that unfolded from the underside of its carapace.

"Captain," Kira heard Nielsen say in a warning tone.

Falconi's voice sounded over the intercom: "Working on it. Get into position. We'll be there in two shakes."

The first officer hardly seemed reassured. Kira couldn't blame her.

Along with Itari, they obeyed the captain and arranged themselves in a ring around the tube, hiding behind the sides of the open pressure doors.

They'd just finished when first Sparrow and then Falconi came stomping out of the nearest corridor, garbed head to toe in power armor.

As if by prior agreement, Sparrow positioned herself on one side of the shaft while Falconi did the same on the other. "Thought you might want this," Nielsen said, and tossed Falconi his grenade launcher.

He gave her a tense nod. "Thanks. Owe you one."

Seeing both Sparrow and Falconi in their armor made Kira feel slightly less apprehensive about facing the incoming Jellies. At least everything wouldn't be riding on just her. Although she worried about them putting themselves front and center. Especially Falconi.

The lights flickered, and for a second, red emergency strips illuminated the room. "Power at twenty-five percent and dropping," Falconi read off his overlays. "Shit. Five more minutes and we'll be dead in the water."

"Contact," said Hwa-jung, and the *Wallfish* shuddered as the Jelly pod collided with it somewhere below. A brash tone echoed overhead, and Kira grabbed a handhold as the ship's engines cut out.

"Showtime," Sparrow muttered. She raised her metal-clad arms and aimed the exo's built-in weapons toward the bottom of the shaft.

4.

A series of strange noises sounded to the aft, somewhere in the A cargo hold: bangs and clattering and dull *thuds,* as of tentacles slapping against the sealed pressure doors.

Kira allowed the Soft Blade's mask to cover her face. Taking deep breaths to steady herself, she shouldered her blaster and aimed down the shaft. *Soon. . . .*

"Once they breach," said Hwa-jung, "they'll have fourteen seconds until the next set of pressure doors seal."

"Got it," said Sparrow. In her armor, she couldn't really hide; she filled most of a doorway, like a giant metal gorilla, faceless behind a mirrored helmet. Likewise, Falconi stood mostly exposed in his own set of armor, although he kept his visor semi-transparent, the better to see.

Bang!

Kira felt a spike of compressed air in her ears, even through the suit's mask. She worked her jaw, a dull ache forming along the base of her skull.

Smoke appeared at what had been the bottom of the shaft and that, in weightlessness, now appeared to be the far end of a long tube. The *Wallfish*'s pressure alarm began to blare.

A breath of wind touched Kira's cheek: the most dangerous of sensations on a spaceship.

Around her, the crew started firing with blasters and slug throwers as the dark, many-armed shapes of the Jellies swarmed into the central shaft. Graspers, desperate and despised. The aliens didn't stay to fight. Instead, they darted across the tube and disappeared down another corridor.

Seconds later, an unseen pressure door by the cargo hold slammed shut with an ominous *clang,* and the wind ceased.

"Shit, they're heading toward engineering," said Falconi, peering down the shaft.

"They can incapacitate the whole ship from there," said Hwa-jung.

As if to prove her point, the lights flickered again and then went out entirely, leaving them bathed in the dull red radiance of the backups.

Then the most unexpected sight caught their attention: a single tentacle unfurled from within a doorway at the end of the shaft. Wrapped in its deadly embrace was the transparent cryo box that contained none other than Runcible, still frozen in hibernation.

Even through his visor, Kira saw Falconi's face contort with rage. "Goddammit, *no*," he growled, and was about to launch himself aftward when Nielsen caught his arm.

"Captain," she said, matching his intensity. "It's a trap. They'll overpower you."

"But—"

"Not a chance."

Sparrow joined them. "She's right."

The only one who could do anything was Kira, and she knew it. Was she really going to risk her life for the pig? Well, why not? A life was a life, and she had to face the Jellies at some point. Might as well be now. She just wished it didn't have to happen on the *Wallfish*. . . .

The tentacle gently waved the pig back and forth in an unmistakable invitation.

"Those fuckers," said Falconi. He half raised the grenade launcher, and then stopped. "Can't get a good shot."

The emergency lights failed then, leaving them in pure and unfriendly darkness for several heartbeats. Via infrared, Kira could still make out the shape of her surroundings, and she noticed an odd confluence of EM fields along the shaft—swirling fountains of violet force.

"Plasma containment field failing," Morven announced. "Please evacuate immediately. Repeat, please—"

Hwa-jung groaned.

The lights snapped back on, first red, and then the normal, full-spectrum glare of the standard strips, bright enough to hurt. A faint tremor shook the plating of the walls, and then booming through the *Wallfish* came an enormous bellowing voice:

"PUT DOWN THAT PIG!"

Gregorovich.

5.

The pressure door at the end of the shaft slammed shut, cutting off the Jelly's tentacle amid a spurt of orange ichor. The tentacle floated free, twisting and writhing in apparent agony. It threw Runcible's cryo box against the wall, and the box bounced, tumbling several times in the shaft before Falconi managed to snare it.

The box and the pig inside appeared unharmed, save for a deep scratch along one side.

"Perforate that thing," said Falconi, pointing at the tentacle.

Nielsen, Sparrow, and Kira happily obliged.

"Welcome back, my symbiotic infestation!" cried Gregorovich. "O happy day that we should be reunited, my bothersome little meatbags! Such dark times they were with me lost in the twisting maze of fruitless fallacies and you off gallivanting in meddlesome misadventures! How fortunate for you a luminous lantern led me back. Rejoice, for I am reborn! What have you done to this poor snail of a ship, hmm? I'll assume control of operations, if you don't mind. Morven, alas poor simulacrum, isn't fit for the task. First to purge this grotesque bit of alien code infecting my processors, aaand . . . done. Venting and stabilizing reactor. Now to show these sump-sniffers what I'm really capable of. Whee!"

"About time," said Falconi.

"Heya," said Sparrow, slapping the bulkhead. "Missed you, headcase."

"Don't get too carried away," said Nielsen, giving the ceiling a warning glance.

"Me? Carried away?" said the ship mind. "Well, I *never.* Please remove all hands and feet from walls, floors, ceilings, and handholds."

"Uh . . ." said Vishal.

[[Kira here: Itari, move away from the walls!]]

The Jelly responded to the urgency of her scent with gratifying swiftness. It withdrew its tentacles and stabilized itself in midair with small puffs of gas along the equator of its carapace.

A dangerous hum filled the air, and Kira felt the skin of the xeno prickle and crawl. Then from behind the door that had severed the tentacle, teeth-jarring discharges sounded: mini-crashes of lightning snapping and crackling and buzzing.

And a horrible burnt-meat smell drifted toward them.

"All taken care of," said Gregorovich with evident satisfaction. "There's your fried calamari, Sparrow. My apologies, Hwa-jung, but you'll have to replace some of the wiring."

The machine boss smiled. "That's okay."

"You heard what I said earlier?" Sparrow asked.

The ship mind cackled. "Oh yes, faint as feathers, a voice echoing across misty water."

"How?" said Falconi. "We had you isolated from the rest of the ship."

Gregorovich sniffed. "Ah well, see now. Hwa-jung may have her little secrets, but I have mine as well. Once my mind was cleared of perfidious visions and debilitating doubts, it was quite a simple challenge to circumvent, oh yes it was. A twist of that, a dab of this, lizard's leg and adder's fork, and a sly bit of mischievous torque."

"I don't know," said Nielsen. "I think I preferred you the way you were before." But she was smiling.

"What about Mr. Fuzzypants?" Vishal asked.

"Safe as buttons," replied Gregorovich. "Now then, to address our larger situation. You've placed us in a most precarious pickle, my friends, yes you have."

Falconi fixed his gaze on a nearby camera mounted in the wall. "You sure you're up for this?"

A ghostly hand, blue and hairy, appeared projected from the nearest screen. It gave a thumbs-up, and the ship mind said, "Right as horses and twice as obnoxious. Wait, that didn't make sense. Hmm . . . But yes, good to go, Cap'n! Even if I weren't, you really want to take on the many-armed horde without me?"

Falconi sighed. "You crazy bastard."

"That I am." Gregorovich sounded positively smug.

Nielsen said, "The plan was—"

"Yes," said Gregorovich, "I know the plan. All records and recordings reviewed, filed, and archived. However, the plan is, to put it delicately, well and truly fucked. Twenty-one Jellies are currently inbound, and they appear anything but friendly."

"Well? You have any ideas in that big brain of yours?" Sparrow asked.

"Indeed I do," whispered Gregorovich. "Permission to take action, Captain? Drastic action is required if you or I or that pig in your arms are to have any chance of seeing the bright light of morn."

Falconi hesitated a long moment. Then his chin jerked, and he said, "Do it."

Gregorovich laughed. "Ahahaha! Your trust is most precious to me, O Captain. Hold on! Prepare for skewflip!"

"Skewflip!" exclaimed Nielsen. "What do you think y—"

Kira tightened her hold and closed her eyes as she felt herself and everything around her turn end for end. Then the ship mind said, "Resuming thrust," and the soles of her feet sank back to the deck, and she again weighed her normal amount.

"Explain," said Falconi.

Seemingly unperturbed, Gregorovich said, "The Knot of Minds cannot defend us against all our foes. Nor can they bring themselves to act against their dear leader. That leaves us with just one choice."

"We still have to kill Ctein," said Kira.

"Exactly," said Gregorovich, with much the same pride as an owner talking to a particularly well-behaved pet. "So we shall seize the moment by the throat and *throttle* it. We shall teach these aquatic reprobates the meaning of human ingenuity. There's nothing we can't turn into a weapon or make blow up, ahahaha!"

"We are *not* ramming the *Hierophant*," said Falconi between clenched teeth.

"*Tsk, tsk.* Who said anything about ramming?" The ship mind sounded far too amused for the situation. "Nor are we to use our fusion drive to *flambé* our target, for then it would explode and destroy us with it. No, that we shall not do."

"Stop dancing around," Sparrow growled. "What are you up to, Greg? Spit it out."

The ship mind harrumphed. "Really now, Greg? Fine. Have it your way, birdname. The *Battered Hierophant* is pulling away from us, but in seven minutes and forty-two seconds, I shall park the nose of the *Wallfish* into the gaping wound that you gouged out of the *Hierophant*'s hide."

"*What?!*" Sparrow and Nielsen exclaimed together.

In his exo, Falconi's eyes flashed back and forth as he skimmed his overlays. His lips were pressed together, thin and white.

"Oh yes," said Gregorovich, sounding immensely pleased with himself. "The Jellies won't dare fire at us, not when we're so close to their beloved and feared leader. And once secured in place, then you—and by that I mean most likely *you,* O Queen of Thorns—may sally forth and dispose of this troublesome Jelly once and for all."

Vishal glanced from Falconi to Sparrow, appearing confused. "Won't the *Hierophant* shoot us down? What about their defenses?"

"Look," said Falconi, and gestured at the display.

On it appeared a composite image showing the *Wallfish* from the outside. A dense cloud of chalk enveloped them, streaming from vents by the prow and glittering with tiny ribbons of chaff. Positioned in a ring around the *Wallfish* were five ships from the Knot of Minds. Even as Kira watched, their lasers fired, destroying another wave of missiles launched by the *Hierophant.*

The *Wallfish* rattled but otherwise seemed unaffected.

"Can we make it?" she asked, quiet.

"We'll find out." Falconi turned off the display. "Better not watch. Alright, everyone over to airlock B. We're going to have a fight on our hands. A real one." Then he handed Runcible's cryo box over to Vishal and said, "Stash him somewhere safe. Maybe sickbay."

Vishal bobbed his head as he accepted the pig. "Of course, Captain."

Again the fear returned, crawling through Kira's insides with razor claws. Assuming they could even *reach* Ctein, and assuming that Nmarhl's memories were correct, she would be facing a creature as big or bigger than the Soft Blade had been during their escape from Orsted. The Jelly was smart too, as smart as the largest ship mind.

She shivered.

Falconi saw. <*Don't think about it. – Falconi*>

<*Hard not to. – Kira*>

He touched her gently on the shoulder with his armored glove as he passed by.

6.

The *Wallfish* didn't blow up.

To Kira's grateful astonishment, the five ships from the Knot of Minds managed to stop every missile but one—and that one missed the *Wallfish* by several hundred meters and went screaming off into space, lost forever.

She checked on the larger battle. It was going as badly as she feared. The

Seventh Fleet was scattered, and the Jellies were picking off the UMC ships with inexorable efficiency. Seeing the number of damaged or destroyed warships put a chill in Kira's veins and filled her with renewed determination. The only way to stop the slaughter would be to kill Ctein, whatever that took.

What if that means blowing up the Battered Hierophant *while we're on it?* A hard core of certitude formed inside her. Then that's what they would do. The alternative would be no less fatal.

If she *had* to fight the Jellies, she wasn't going to make it easy for them to kill her. Reaching out with her mind, she summoned the portion of the xeno that had overgrown her cabin. She drew the orphaned flesh through the corridors of the *Wallfish,* doing her best to avoid damaging the ship, and brought it to the airlock where she was waiting along with the rest of the crew.

Nielsen yelped as the Seed surged toward them in a black tide of crawling, grasping fibers. "It's okay," Kira said, but the crew still jumped back as the fibers flowed across the deck and up and over her feet, legs, hips, and torso—encasing her in a layer of living armor nearly a meter thick.

Though the increased bulk of the xeno restricted Kira's movements, she felt no sense of weight. No sense of being trapped. Rather, it was as if she were surrounded by muscles eager to do her bidding.

"Goddamn!" Sparrow said. "Anything else you've been holding out on us?"

"No, that was it," said Kira.

Sparrow shook her head and swore again. Only Itari appeared unaffected by the appearance of the Seed—of the Idealis. The Jelly merely rubbed its tentacles and emitted a nearscent of interest.

A crooked smile appeared on Falconi's face. "Well, that got the pulse going."

"It nearly gave me a heart attack, it did," said Vishal. He was kneeling on the floor, repacking the contents of his medical bag. The sight was a grim reminder of what was about to happen.

A sense of unreality gripped Kira. The situation seemed outlandish beyond all expectation. The events that had led them to that exact time and place were so unlikely as to be nigh on impossible. And yet there they were.

An electric discharge lit the antechamber. Hwa-jung growled and bent over the four drones she was fiddling with in the corner. "Those things going to be ready in time?" Sparrow asked.

The machine boss kept her gaze fixed on the drones as she answered: "God willing . . . yes." Each drone had a welding attachment built into one manipulator and a repair laser in the other. Either tool, Kira knew, could cause serious injury if misapplied, and she suspected Hwa-jung intended to misapply them most vigorously.

"So how are we going to do this?" said Nielsen.

Falconi pointed at Kira. "Simple. Kira, you'll take point, give us cover. We'll watch your flanks and provide supporting fire. Same as on Orsted. We cut straight through the *Battered Hierophant,* no stopping, no turning around, no slowing down until we reach Ctein."

"What if someone gets hit?" said Sparrow. She raised one sharp eyebrow. "It's going to be a shitshow in there, and you know it."

Falconi tapped his fingers against the stock of his grenade launcher. "If someone's wounded, we send them back to the *Wallfish.*"

"That's—"

"If we can't send them back to the *Wallfish,* we keep them with us." His eyes roamed across their faces. "Either way, no one gets left behind. No one."

It was a comforting thought, but Kira wasn't sure if what he was proposing would really be possible. *Trig* . . . She didn't want to lose more of the crew. More of her friends. If there was anything she could do to keep them safe, anything at all, she had to seize it, no matter how frightening she found it herself.

"I'll go," she said. No one seemed to notice, so she said it again, louder. "I'll go. Alone."

Silence fell in the antechamber as everyone looked at her. "Not a chance in hell," said Falconi.

Kira shook her head, ignoring the sour pit forming in her stomach. "I mean it. I've got the Soft Blade. It'll keep me plenty safe—safer than you are in your exos. And if it's just me, I won't have to worry about protecting anyone else."

"And who will protect you, *chica*?" said Sparrow, coming over to her. "If a Jelly decides to snipe you from around a corner? If they ambush you? If you go down, Navárez, we're all screwed."

"I'm still better equipped to deal with whatever they throw at us," said Kira.

"Ctein?" said Nielsen. She crossed her arms. "If it's anything like you've described, we're going to need every bit of firepower we have in order to take it down."

Falconi said, "Unless you want to let the Soft Blade go completely out of control."

Of all of them, he was the only one who knew of her role in creating the nightmares, and his words struck Kira's deepest fear. She set her jaw, frustrated.

"I could keep you here." A cluster of twining tendrils extended upward from her fingers, threatening.

Falconi's gaze grew even more flinty. "You do that, Kira, and we'll find some way to cut or blast our way free, even if it means breaking the *Wallfish* in two. I promise you. And then we'll still come after you. . . . You're not going alone, Kira, and that's that."

She tried not to let the situation affect her. She tried to accept what he'd said and move on. But she couldn't. Her breath hitched in her throat as her frustration swelled. "That's—I—You're just going to get yourself hurt or killed. I don't *want* to go alone, but it's our best option. Why can't you—"

"Ms. Kira," said Vishal, standing and joining them. "We know the risks, and—" He bowed his head, his eyes soft, and round, gentle. "—we accept them with open hearts."

"You shouldn't have to, though," said Kira.

Vishal smiled, and the pureness of his expression stopped her. "Of course not, Ms. Kira. But life is such, yes? And war is such." Then he surprised her with a hug. And then Nielsen hugged her as well, and both Falconi and Sparrow touched her on the shoulder with their heavy gauntlets.

Kira sniffed and looked up at the ceiling to hide her tears. "Okay. . . . Okay. We'll go together then." It occurred to her how much she'd lucked out with the crew of the *Wallfish.* They were good people at heart, far more than she'd realized when she'd first arrived on board. They'd changed too. She didn't think the crew she had first met back at 61 Cygni would have been willing to put themselves in harm's way as they were now.

"What I want to know," said Sparrow, "is how we're going to find this Ctein. That ship is fucking enormous. We could wander around for hours and still come up empty."

"Any ideas?" said Falconi. He looked toward Itari. "How about you, squid? Got anything that can help us?"

Kira translated the question, and the Jelly replied. [[Itari here: If we can swim inside, and if I can find a node to access the Reticulum of the *Battered Hierophant,* then I will be able to locate the exact location of Ctein.]]

Hwa-jung seemed to perk up. "Reticulum? What is—"

"Ask later," said Falconi. "What do these nodes look like?"

[[Itari here: Like squares of stars. They are located at junctions throughout every ship, for ease of communication.]]

"I might have seen one before," Kira said, remembering the first Jelly ship she'd been on.

[[Itari here: Once we know where Ctein is, there are drop tubes that grant passage throughout the decks. We can use them to travel quickly.]]

Nielsen said, "Are you going to be able to help us, Itari? Or will your genetic programming get in the way?"

[[Itari here: As long as you do not mention why we are there . . . yes, I should be able to help.]] A red band of unease crept across its tentacles.

"Should be able to help," said Falconi. "Bah."

Sparrow looked worried. "The second the Jellies get a fix on us, they're going to swarm us."

"No," said Falconi. "They're going to swarm *her.*" He motioned at Kira. "You keep them off our backs, Kira, and we'll keep them off yours."

She mentally prepared herself for the challenge, determined. "I'll do it."

Falconi grunted. "We just have to find one of these nodes. That's our first objective. After that, we go kill ourselves a Jelly. Hey—" He turned toward Jorrus and Veera, who were crouched in one corner, gripping each other's forearms while they whispered back and forth. "What about you, Questants? Sure you're up for this?"

The Entropists picked up their weapons and stood. They were still garbed in their gradient robes, faces exposed. Kira wondered how they intended to survive vacuum, much less a laser blast.

"Yes, thank you, Prisoner," said Veera.

"We would not wish to be anywhere but here," said Jorrus. Still, both of the Entropists looked queasy.

A bark of cynical laughter escaped Sparrow. "That's more than I can say, I'll tell you what."

Falconi cleared his throat. "Don't think I'm going all soft, but uh, a man couldn't ask for a better crew than you lot. Just thought I'd say that."

"Well, you make a pretty good captain, Captain," said Nielsen.

"Most of the time," said Hwa-jung.

"Most of the time," Sparrow agreed.

The intercom flicked on, and Gregorovich said, "Contact in sixty seconds. Please secure yourselves, my delicate little meatbags. We're in for a bumpy ride."

Vishal shook his head. "Ah. That is not comforting. Not at all." Nielsen touched her forehead and murmured something in an undertone.

Kira switched to her overlays. Ahead of them, she saw the *Battered Hierophant* on swift approach. Up close, the Jelly ship appeared even more massive: round and white, with spindles and antennas protruding along its bulky midsection. The hole blasted by the Casaba-Howitzer had exposed a long stack of decks within the ship: dozens upon dozens of chambers of unknown function now exposed to the cold of space. Floating within, she spotted several Jellies, some still alive, most dead and surrounded with icicles of frozen ichor.

With the *Hierophant* looming over them, Kira could again feel the same aching draw she had experienced before: the compulsion of the Vanished urging her to reply.

She allowed herself a grim smile. Somehow she didn't think Ctein or its graspers were going to like how she answered the summons.

Graspers? She was falling into the thought patterns of the Soft Blade/Seed. Well, why not? They fit. The Jellies *were* many-limbed graspers, and today she was going to remind them why they should fear the Idealis.

Next to her, she scented sickness from Itari. It shivered, turning unpleasant shades of green and brown. [[Itari here: It is difficult for me to even be here, Idealis.]]

[[Kira here: Just concentrate on protecting my co-forms. Worry not about the great and might Ctein. What you are doing is completely unrelated.]]

The Jelly rippled with a wave of purple. [[Itari here: That is helpful, Idealis. Thank you.]]

As the *Wallfish* nosed into the hole the howitzer had torn out of the *Battered Hierophant*, and the half-melted decks darkened the view outside the *Wallfish*'s sapphire windows, Falconi said, "Hey, Gregorovich, you're in fine form. How about a few words to send us on our way?"

The ship pretended to clear his throat. "Fine. Hear me now. The Lord of Empty Spaces protect us as we venture forth to fight our foes. Guide our hands—and our thoughts—and guide our weapons that we may work our will upon these perversions of peace. Let daring be our shield and righteous fury be our sword, and may our enemies flee at the sight of those who defend the defenseless, and may we stand unbowed and unbroken in the face of evil. Today *is* the Day of Wrath, and we *are* the instruments of our species' retribution. *Deo duce, ferro comitante.* Amen."

"Amen," said Hwa-jung and Nielsen.

"Now *that* was a prayer!" said Sparrow, grinning.

"Thank you, birdname."

"A bit more warlike than I'd prefer," said Kira. "But it'll do."

Falconi hoisted his grenade launcher onto his shoulder. "Let's just hope someone was listening."

Then the *Wallfish* lurched around them as it came to a rest amid the bowels of the *Battered Hierophant.* If not for the Soft Blade holding her against the wall, Kira would have been thrown to the floor. The others staggered, and Nielsen fell to one knee. The rumble of the fusion engine cut out, but a sensation of weight remained as the *Hierophant*'s artificial gravity encompassed the *Wallfish.*

7.

Outside the airlock, Kira saw what appeared to be a storage room stacked with rows of translucent pink globules arranged around a dark, stem-like growth. Racks of unidentifiable equipment lined the three walls that hadn't been vaporized by the Casaba-Howitzer. Droplets of slag had frozen to the grated floor, the curved walls, and the familiar tri-part shell that acted as a door. Everything visible would be highly radioactive, but that was the least of their concerns at the moment. . . .

No Jellies were visible in the chamber; a stroke of good luck Kira hadn't been expecting.

"Not bad, Greg," said Falconi. "Everyone ready?"

"One moment," said Hwa-jung, still bent over her drones.

Falconi's eyes narrowed. "Hurry it up. We're sitting ducks here."

The machine boss muttered something in Korean. Then she straightened, and the drones rose into the air with an annoying *buzz.* "Ready," said Hwa-jung.

"Finally." Falconi hit the release, and the airlock's inner door rolled open. "Time to make some noise."

"Uh . . ." Kira said, and looked at the Entropists. How were they supposed to breathe in vacuum?

She needn't have worried. As one, Veera and Jorrus drew their hoods over their faces. The fabric hardened and shimmered, growing transparent and forming a solid seal around their necks, same as any skinsuit helmet.

"Neat trick," Sparrow said.

The silence of vacuum swallowed them as Falconi vented the airlock and opened the outer door. In an instant, the only sounds Kira could hear were those of her breathing, those of her pulse.

Then her earpiece emitted a scrap of static, and from it Gregorovich said, sounding startlingly close: **Oh dear.**

Oh dear? Falconi said, his voice sharp and somewhat tinny over the radio.

The ship mind seemed reluctant to answer. **I'm sorry to say, my dear friends, most sorry indeed, but I fear that cleverness may no longer be sufficient to save us. For all, luck must inevitably run out, and run out it has for us.**

And on Kira's overlays, an image of the system appeared. At first she didn't understand what she was seeing: the blue and yellow dots that marked the positions of the Jellies and the UMC respectively were half-hidden behind a constellation of red.

What— Sparrow started to say.

Alas, said Gregorovich, and for the first time, he seemed genuinely sorry, **alas, the nightmares have decided to join the fight. And this time, they've brought something else with them. Something big. It's broadcasting on all channels. Calls itself . . . the Maw.**

CHAPTER V

* * * * * * *

ASTRORUM IRAE

1.

Kira stared with horror.

On her overlays, she beheld a vision of terror. A true nightmare, given shape by the sins of her past. The Maw. . . . It appeared as a grotesque collection of black and red flesh floating in space, raw, skinless, glossy with oozing fluids. The mass was bigger than the *Battered Hierophant*. Bigger than any space station she had seen. Nearly the size of the two small moons orbiting the planet R1. In form, it was a branching, cancerous mess, too chaotic for anything resembling order, but with a suggestion—an attempt perhaps—at a fractal shape along its fringe.

At the sight of the Maw, Kira felt an instant, visceral disgust, followed by a sickening, almost debilitating fear.

The obscene tumor had emerged from FTL near the orbit of R1, along with the vast swarm of smaller Corruptions. Already the Maw and its forces were moving in to attack human and Jelly alike, making no distinction between the two.

Kira wrapped her arms around herself and dropped into a hunched crouch, feeling ill. There was no way the Seed could overcome something like the Maw. It was too big, too twisted, too angry. Even if she had time to grow the Seed to an equal size, she would lose herself in the body of the xeno. Who she was would cease to be, or else would become such a small part of the Seed as to be totally insignificant.

The thought was more terrifying than death itself. If she were just killed, she would still be who and what she was until the end. But if the Seed consumed her, she would be facing the destruction of her self long before her mind or body ceased existing.

Then the heavy hands of Falconi's exo were on her, and he was lifting her back onto her feet, speaking to her in soothing tones: **Hey, it's okay. We haven't lost yet.**

She shook her head, feeling tears forming underneath the xeno's mask. "No, I can't. I can't. I—"

He shook her hard enough to get her attention. The Soft Blade reacted with a mild ripple of spikes. **Don't fucking say that. If you give up, we might as well already be dead.**

"You don't understand." She made a helpless gesture toward the misbegotten shape hovering in her overlays, even though Falconi couldn't see it. "That, that—"

Stop it.* His voice was stern. Stern enough that Kira listened. *Focus on one thing at a time. We need to kill Ctein. Can you do that?

She nodded, feeling a measure of control returning to her. "Yeah. . . . I think so."

Okay. Then get it together and let's put down this Jelly. We can worry about the nightmares afterward.

Kira's gut still twisted with fear, though she tried to ignore it, tried to act as if she were confident. She banished the feed from her overlays, but in the back of her mind, the image of the Maw remained, as if burned into her retinas.

At Kira's internal command, the xeno propelled her to the front of the airlock. "Let's do this," she said.

2.

Outside the *Wallfish,* in the alien storage room, shadows spun as the *Battered Hierophant* spun, and yet because of the alien ship's gravity field, Kira felt none of the rotation. The shifting light had the brutal, hard-edged starkness peculiar to space, and its movement produced a strobe-like effect that was disorienting.

"Stay close," she said.

We're right behind you, said Falconi.

Unwilling to waste even a single second, Kira started across the strobing storage room. The cycling shadows made her dizzy, so she focused on the decking between her feet and tried not to think about how they were spinning through space.

As she moved among the rows of translucent globules—each of which was at least four meters in diameter and filled with strange, frozen shapes—a fist-sized explosion took out a chunk of the one by her head.

There was no sound, but Kira felt a spray of shrapnel ping the hardened surface of the xeno.

Cover! Falconi shouted.

Kira made no attempt to hide. Instead, she reached out with the xeno and ripped up the pearl-white decking, tore at the nearby globules and the stem that connected them, and compacted all the material into a shield that protected not only her but also the crew behind her. Same as she'd done on Orsted. Only now she felt confident, self-assured. Compared with before, commanding the Seed was effortless, and she had little fear of losing control. As she willed, so it was.

She switched her vision to infrared and saw a white-hot beam stab out from among the racks of storage units and burn a glowing, pinkie-sized hole into the material directly over her chest. The sight alarmed her until she realized the hole was far too shallow to reach her body.

Ahead of her, two Jellies—a pair of squids—lurked among the globules. They were hurrying away from her on coiled tentacles, a pair of enormous blasters gripped in their pincers and aimed her way.

Oh no you don't, Kira thought, and sent tendrils racing out from the Soft Blade.

With them, she caught the Jellies, squeezed them, cut them, tore them into a mess of twitching flesh and spurting ichor. Maybe this was going to be easier than they'd thought. . . .

Over the radio, Kira heard someone gag.

"With me!" she shouted, and headed toward the white shell that would grant them access to the pressurized interior of the *Battered Hierophant.*

The shell refused to open as she neared, but with three quick slices of the Soft Blade, Kira severed the mechanism that kept the three-part door closed.

A hurricane of wind buffeted her as the wedges of the shell sagged apart.

The shield she'd constructed was too large to fit inside, so with some reluctance, she discarded it before allowing the xeno to propel her into the depths of the alien ship. Itari and the crew followed close behind.

3.

The interior of the *Hierophant* was unlike the two other Jelly ships Kira had been on. The walls were darker, more somber—colored with an assortment of greys and blues, and decorated with strips of coral-like patterns that in any other circumstance Kira would have loved to study.

She was standing inside a long, empty corridor marked with side passages, additional doorways, and alcoved tunnels leading both up and down. Now that they were again surrounded by air, Kira could hear a piercing whistle from the ruined door behind them, as well as the buzz of Hwa-jung's drones and a howling klaxon that reminded her of whale sounds, as if the entire ship were bleating with pain, anger, and fear.

The rushing air stank with nearscent of alarm, and with it, a command that all service co-forms were to swim shadow-wise without delay. Whatever that meant.

For the briefest of moments, Kira thought that perhaps they had slipped past the *Hierophant*'s sensors, and perhaps they wouldn't have to fight every step of the way.

Then, with an audible *snikt*, a white membrane slid across the door she'd cut open, stopping the flow of air, and—at the opposite end of the corridor—a mass of swarming limbs appeared: scores of Jellies, angry, armed, and heading straight for her and the others.

Kira's heart rate doubled. This was the exact scenario she'd hoped to avoid. But she had the Soft Blade, and it was her arm, her sword, and her shield. The Jellies would be hard-pressed to stop her. Grabbing all sides of the corridor with a starburst of tendrils, she *yanked* the walls inward, forming a thick plug out of the bulkheads.

As lasers and slug throwers and dull explosions sounded on the other side of the barrier, Sparrow said, **That's a hell of a welcoming party!**

Itari! said Falconi. **Where's the nearest node?**

Kira translated, and the Jelly crawled up beside her. It tapped the inner part of her makeshift shield. [[Itari here: Forward.]]

"Forward!" she shouted, and started to push her way farther into the corridor, keeping the shield suspended in front of her, using it as a plug to fill the rounded passage. She could feel the impacts against the outside of the shield, both from transferred momentum and from sharp twinges of not-pain that shot through her tendrils. Just enough feedback for the Soft Blade to let her know where the danger was, but not enough to actually hurt.

Kira passed the first door and was almost to the second when a shout sounded, and she turned to see a Jelly hurtling out of the now-open door behind them, tentacles spread wide like a cuttlefish about to engulf its prey. Accompanying the Jelly was a pair of white, orb-shaped drones with glinting lenses. . . .

The alien slammed into Sparrow's power armor, knocking her into the wall.

Then several things happened at once, nearly too fast to follow: Itari slung several of its own tentacles around the attacking Jelly and attempted to pull it off Sparrow. The three of them stumbled into the near wall. A burst of laser fire from Sparrow's exo stitched a line of holes across the enemy's carapace, and Falconi moved forward to help, only for the alien to knock him to the deck with a single blow.

Nielsen jumped forward to shield the captain. The Jelly caught her on the backswing, and hit her square in the chest. She crumpled to the deck.

Hwa-jung's drones fired their welding lasers, and the two white orbs fell from the air amid a jet of sparks. Then the machine boss herself was standing in front of Nielsen and Falconi, and the thickly built woman grabbed the tentacle that threatened them, hugged it to her chest, and *squeezed*.

Bones snapped inside the wriggling, sucker-covered arm.

Vishal was shooting his slug thrower: a rapid *bam! bam! bam!* that Kira felt in her bones. She hesitated, paralyzed. If she used the Soft Blade to attack the Jelly, there was a good chance she'd hurt or kill Itari at the same time.

Her concern was unwarranted. Itari yanked the other Jelly and threw it back down the corridor, past the Entropists and away from Sparrow.

That was all the opening Kira needed. She sent forth a cluster of black needles that pierced the Jelly and held it in place, unable to escape. The creature flopped and twisted and shuddered and then grew still. A pool of orange ichor oozed out from under its carapace.

Ms. Audrey! said Vishal, and hurried to the first officer's side.

4.

Close off that doorway before any more get through! said Falconi, scrambling back to his feet. His heavy exo clanked against the deck, leaving dull, lead-colored smears on the white material.

Kira used the Soft Blade to tear and bend chunks of the wall until the portal was impassable. It had been stupid of her not to block off the entrance as they'd gone by.

As a final precaution, she ripped up a large piece of the curved deck to serve as a blast shield in the corridor behind them. Then she turned her attention back to the group.

Vishal was hunched next to Nielsen, running a chip-lab over her while keeping a hand pressed against her side. **How bad is it, Doc?** Falconi asked.

Two broken ribs, I am afraid, Vishal said.

Dammit, said Falconi, keeping his launcher trained on the hallway. **You shouldn't have done that, Audrey. I'm the one in armor.**

Nielsen coughed. Flecks of blood spattered the inside of her faceplate. **Sorry, Salvo. Next time I'll let the Jelly smash you to pulp.**

You do that, he said savagely.

We gotta keep moving, said Sparrow, joining them. Her exo was scratched and dented, but the damage appeared superficial. Ahead of them, the dull thunder of weapons fire continued to reverberate as the Jellies worked to shoot their way through the plug Kira had constructed in the corridor.

Nielsen tried to stand. She winced and dropped down with a cry Kira heard even through the first officer's helmet.

Shit, said Falconi. **We'll have to carry her. Sparrow—**

The blond-haired woman shook her head. **She'll just get in the way. Send her back. We're still close enough. It's a straight shot from here to the* Wallfish.*

The Entropists moved in closer. **We can escort her to the ship, if you want, Captain, and then—**

—hurry back.

Fuck, said Falconi, scowling. **Fine. Do it. Gregorovich will show you where the armory is. Grab some mining charges while you're at it. We'll use them to block off these side passages.**

Veera and Jorrus dipped their heads. **As you say—**

—it shall be done.

Kira was impressed that the Entropists were working together so well even with their hive mind broken. They almost seemed as if they were still sharing thoughts.

Despite Nielsen's grimace of pain, Jorrus and Veera picked her up, stepped around the blast shield Kira had erected, and trotted back along the corridor.

Go, said Falconi, turning back to Kira. **Let's find one of these nodes before the Jellies pick off the rest of us.**

Kira nodded and started to push forward again, making sure to wall off each of the shell doors she encountered.

The attack had shaken her confidence. For all its power, the Soft Blade didn't make her omnipotent. Far from it. A single Jelly had gotten past their defenses, and now they were down three people. Just as she'd feared. And there was no guarantee the Entropists would be able to rejoin them. What would happen if someone else got hurt? Returning to the *Wallfish* wouldn't be an option much longer, not unless she was there to protect them.

Of all of them, she was the only one who could do anything substantial to keep the Jellies at bay. And if she *could,* then she *should.* The only real limit on what she could do with the Soft Blade was her imagination, so why was she holding back?

At the thought, Kira began to extend the Soft Blade backwards, forming a latticed cage around their group that would, hopefully, ward off any more attacks. She also added to the shield in front of her, incorporating pieces of the wall and deck, reinforcing the material of the Soft Blade to make what she hoped was an impenetrable barrier.

She couldn't see through the shield, of course, not with her eyes, but she could sense what lay ahead via the tendrils of the xeno: the shape of the corridor, the swirls of air—often superheated from lasers—and the ongoing impacts of the Jellies' hostile fire.

They hurried past door after door, and every time Kira asked if they were still heading in the right direction, Itari said, [[Forward.]]

The size of the *Hierophant* continued to astound Kira. She felt as if she were inside a space station or an underground base rather than a ship. There was a solidness to the *Hierophant,* a sense of mass that she had never experienced on a mobile vessel, not even the *Extenuating Circumstances.*

Over their shared line, she heard Falconi say, **Pretty good shooting back there, Doc.**

Thank you, yes.

A *thud* on the other side of a shell door that she'd just barricaded made Kira and the others flinch. The pieces of the shell twitched as they struggled to open, and the door bulged outward as something pushed from the other side. But the strips of bulkhead Kira had secured over the shell held, and whatever was trying to enter the corridor failed.

She drove forward until she felt a wall blocking her way and the passage split into two different directions. Kira allowed the Soft Blade to divide and spread outward until it sealed off both passages. The barrage of incoming fire—physical and energy attacks both—continued, although the majority of it came from the left-hand branch.

As the Soft Blade flowed into place, it exposed the surface of the bulkhead that had stopped their forward drive.

A panel set within the wall glittered as if with a field of stars: pinpoints of shifting light of all different colors.

[[Itari here: The Reticulum!]] The Jelly crawled forward, nearscent of relief and determination emanating from its limbs. [[Itari here: Keep watch for me, Idealis.]] Then the Jelly pressed a tentacle against the illuminated panel. To Kira's astonishment, the tentacle melded with the wall, sinking inward until it was nearly hidden.

Is that it? Falconi asked, settling next to her.

"Yes." But Kira's attention was elsewhere; the impacts hammering against the xeno's barriers were growing stronger. She hurried to reinforce them by ripping additional material from the walls, but she could tell she wouldn't be able to hold off the Jellies much longer.

A sharp pang of not-pain shot through the tendrils extended into the left-hand passage; the xeno's way of letting her know it had been damaged. She gasped, and Vishal said, **What is it, Ms. Kira?**

"I . . ." Another pang, stronger than before. Kira winced, her eyes watering, and shook her head. A spike of blue-hot flame was cutting through the outer layers of her shield—a blazing, sunlike heat that melted and withered her second flesh. The Soft Blade could protect her from many things, but even it would fail beneath the bite of a thermal lance. The Jellies had remembered their old lessons on how to fight the Idealis.

"They're giving me some . . . difficulty." [[Kira here: Hurry if you can, Itari.]]

A wave of colors raced across the Jelly's skin. Then Itari pulled its tentacle away from the wall. Strands of mucus dripped from the suckers on the alien's arm. [[Itari here: Ctein is four *nsarro* ahead of us, and fourteen decks down.]]

[[Kira here: How far is a *nsarro*?]]

[[Itari here: The distance one can swim in seven pulses.]]

From the Seed's memories, Kira had a feeling that a pulse wasn't very long, although she couldn't put an exact time to it.

An explosion shook the deck underneath them. **Kira,** said Falconi, sounding nervous. Hwa-jung's drones hovered over his shoulders, bright searchlights glowing beneath their manipulators.

"Everyone hold on!" said Kira. "We're going down. Fourteen decks."

She sent black rods shooting back and forth across the latticework cage she'd created, placing them between the people she was protecting. Once Falconi and the others had a secure grip on the beams, Kira dug into the deck with the xeno, letting her thousands of tiny, finger-like fibers rip through the flooring, rip through the pipes and circuitry and strange, pulsing organs that separated one level of the ship from another.

It was a risky thing to do; if she hit a pressurized line, the explosion could kill them all. The Soft Blade knew the danger, though, and she felt confident it would avoid any lethal pieces of equipment.

Within seconds, she'd torn open a hole big enough to encompass their group. Beneath them, blue shadows shifted amid a shimmer of rising motes, bright as embers.

Then Kira released the Seed's hold upon the walls and the shield, and dropped herself and her charges into the blue dusk.

5.

A whirl of motes blinded Kira for a moment.

They cleared, and she saw a long, low room, scalloped with shallow beds awash with water. The walls were nearly black, and the floor too. Oval orbs the size of a person's head glowed with soft radiance above altar-like niches set in regular intervals along the bulkheads.

Within the sloshing water, dark shapes skittered, small and insectile. They fled before the harsh searchlights Hwa-jung's drones cast over them, seeking safety in shadows.

Hatching pools, was Kira's first thought, but she couldn't imagine why the Jellies would bother with such a thing on a spaceship of all places. They had other technology for reproduction. The Nest of Transference, for one.

Clear slabs several centimeters thick slammed shut over the pools, sealing them off, and without so much as a whiff of warning from the *Hierophant*'s nearscent, all sense of weight vanished.

Ah, shit! said Falconi. He flailed for a moment and then used the thrusters in his exo to steady himself. Behind him, the others clung to the rods Kira had created out of the Seed.

Normally the shift to zero-g would have upset Kira's stomach. But this time it didn't. Her stomach felt the same as before, not dropping or clutching as if she were about to fall to her death. Instead, she felt a new sense of freedom. For the first time, weightlessness was enjoyable (or would have been if not for the circumstances). It was like flying, as if in a dream. Or nightmare.

Zero-g had given Kira trouble her whole life. The only reason she could imagine for that to change now was the Soft Blade. Whatever the case, she was grateful for the relief.

[[Itari here: Without gravity, the shoals of Ctein will be free to swim at us from every direction, Idealis.]]

"Right," Kira growled, more to herself than anyone else. She again reached out with the xeno and ripped another hole in the decking. With the material she removed, she built a small, dense shield under their feet; for all she knew, a battalion of Jellies might be waiting for them below.

Then with grasping tendrils, she pulled herself and the others through to the next floor.

This time they found themselves in a vast and vaulting space, still blue, but adorned with streaks of red and orange no wider than her thumb. A confluence of hexagonal pillars rose like a tree from floor to ceiling, and around the trunk, tangled nests hung softly swaying from cables that shone as pewter. Throughout, a nearscent of intense concentration pervaded.

Whatever the purpose of the room, Kira didn't recognize it. Yet, she couldn't help but pause for the briefest of moments to appreciate the grandeur, the baroque beauty, the sheer alienness of the room.

She resumed digging and tore a hole through the third deck, allowing them access to a smallish corridor with only a few doors along its way. Ten-some meters ahead of them, the passageway ended at a circular opening that led to yet another shadowed room.

Just as she started ripping up the next floor, now-familiar nearscent intruded: [[Itari here: This way, Idealis.]] And the Jelly darted around her and scuttled off toward the opening.

Kira swore, repositioned the shield, and hurried after, dragging the crew with her. She felt like a sailing ship with sailors hanging off the rigging, ready to repel hostile boarders.

As they passed through the circular doorway, Kira felt the walls open up. She wished to see what was in front of her, and the Seed answered her wishes. Her vision wavered, and then her view switched from the inside of the shield to that of the surrounding room, as if the xeno had grown eyes on the surface of the shield.

For all she knew, it had.

With her now unobstructed view, Kira saw that the room was some sort of feeding area. That much she recognized from the Soft Blade's memories. There were troughs along the walls, and alcoves too, and tubes and vats and transparent containers full of floating creatures waiting to be eaten. In one the *pfennic* that tasted like copper. In another the *nwor* with its many legs, soft and savory and such a delight to hunt. . . .

Amid the alcoves were several more doors, clamped shut. Itari didn't select any of them. Instead, the Jelly jetted toward a patch on the floor, tentacles streaming behind it. [[Itari here: This way.]]

The alien tapped several small circular ridges on the floor, and a disk-shaped cover slid open with an audible *thunk* to reveal a glowing red tube a meter across.

[[Itari here: Swim this way.]] And the Jelly dove into the narrow shaft, disappearing from view.

"Shit," said Kira. She wished the alien had let her retake the lead. "Everyone off. We won't fit otherwise."

The crew let go of the ribs and spars she'd made, and she began to reshape the Seed in order to enter the drop tube.

Before she could finish, a bolt of not-pain shot through her side. Then another on the shield, this one from a different angle, and detonations sounded as weapons fired. Kira flinched; the whole suit flinched, pulling back her quickly eroding barrier with it.

The doors between the alcoves disgorged a swarm of buzzing orbs. Drones. Dozens of them, armed with blasters, slug throwers, and cutters. As they converged on her, their mandibles sparked with electricity, and their manipulators *snipped* and *snacked* like scissors eager to cut her flesh.

Boom! The blast from Falconi's grenade launcher hit her with concussive force. A flash of lightning appeared on the far side of the room, and chunks of Jelly machinery bounced against the wall. The rest of the crew were firing also, lasers and slug throwers alike.

One of Hwa-jung's drones exploded.

Kira stabbed with a thicket of jabbing thorns: one for each of the buzzing orbs. But fast as the Soft Blade was, the orbs were faster. They dodged, jetting at odd, unpredictable angles that her eye couldn't follow. Flesh was no match for the speed or precision of a machine, not even the flesh of her symbiont.

Over the comms, someone shouted in pain.

Kira shouted herself, wishing she could shove the drones away. "Yah!" And the Soft Blade sent a burst of electricity coursing across its outer surface, including her shield. Five of the alien drones sparked and fell away, their manipulators curling into tiny fists. The electricity was welcome, if unexpected. But it wasn't enough to stop the onslaught.

The drones seemed to be concentrating most of their fire on her. Kira doubted they could kill her, but the crew was another matter. She couldn't destroy the drones fast enough to protect Falconi or the others.

So she did the only other thing she could: in her mind, she imagined a hollow sphere encasing her and the crew.

The Soft Blade obeyed, creating a perfectly round bubble around them.

What the hell?! Sparrow exclaimed. The barrels of her blasters were glowing red-hot.

The bubble was thin, though. Too thin. Already Kira could feel a dozen or more hotspots forming on the surface as the drones outside fired at it. Unlike before, she couldn't see out, couldn't pinpoint the location of the orbs in order to destroy them. Half a meter above her head, a jet of sparks punched through the black membrane.

A fist-sized chunk of the sphere flew free, and for an instant, a blinding, crucible-like light flooded the interior. Then the Soft Blade flowed over the hole, covering it again.

Kira didn't know what to do. In desperation, she prepared to separate herself from the bubble and launch herself forth to draw the fire away from the crew. Maybe then she could clear out the orbs. It would be a near-suicidal action, though. The Jellies couldn't be far behind their machines. . . .

"Stay here," she started to say to Falconi, and then a sonic blast hit them. A keening shriek that made Kira's teeth vibrate so hard she feared they would crack before the shrilling, throbbing, rending assault.

6.

The spikes of heat vanished outside the bubble, as did the barrage of laser pulses and projectiles. Bewildered, Kira opened a portal to look out (making sure her head was protected behind a thick layer of her second flesh).

Throughout the room, the orbs spun and darted in random directions. They seemed dazed by the noise; their weapons fired in intermittent bursts at the walls, floor, and ceiling, and their manipulators waved, weak and aimless.

Over the tubes and troughs, Kira saw the two Entropists flying toward her, their robes folded with origami precision. In their hands glimmered light, and in front of them rode a shimmering shockwave of compressed air. From it emanated the horrible shriek. Lasers struck the shockwave, and she saw how it refracted the blasts of energy away from the Entropists. Slugs had no more success; they exploded with sparks of molten metal a meter and a half from Jorrus and Veera.

Kira didn't understand, but she didn't stop to figure it out. She broke her shape and swung at the nearest drone and caught the middle of its bone-like casing. Without hesitation, she tore the machine apart.

Kira! Falconi shouted. **Can't shoot! Get out of the—**

She increased the size of the bubble opening.

Hwa-jung's service drones flew up around her, forming a mechanical halo that flashed with the harsh glare of arc welders—darting and dashing at any of the orbs that came close. Several times they saved her from taking a bolt that might have distracted her.

Some help for you, the machine boss said.

The next few seconds were a blur of electrical discharges, jabbing spikes from the Soft Blade, and laser blasts. Sparrow and Falconi fired over her shoulders, and together, they accounted for almost as many drones as Kira.

The Entropists proved themselves surprisingly capable in the skirmish, despite the fact that they wore no armor. Their robes were more than robes, and they seemed to have blasters of some sort concealed upon them. Kira wasn't sure. But they were able to fight (and more importantly *kill*) their enemies, and for that, she was grateful.

When the last of the orbs was disabled, Kira paused to catch her breath. Even with the Soft Blade working to provide her with air, it was difficult to get enough. And with the mask over her face and the increased mass of the xeno surrounding her, she felt so hot it was making her light-headed.

She collapsed the obsidian-black bubble and turned to look at the crew, dreading what she might see.

Hwa-jung was pressing a hand against the left side of her hip. Blood and medifoam oozed between her fingers. Her moon-shaped face was set in a hard expression, nostrils flared, lips pressed white. Vishal was already floating next to her, unsealing a field dressing taken from his medical case. The doctor looked like he'd been hit also; a white dot of medifoam adorned one of his shoulders. Sparrow appeared unscathed, but a laser blast had fused the left elbow joint on Falconi's exo, freezing it in a half-bent position.

"Is your arm okay?" Kira asked.

He grimaced. **Yeah. Just can't move it.**

Sparrow jetted over to Hwa-jung, the anguish on her face nearly equal to that of the machine boss. The smaller woman touched Hwa-jung on the shoulder, but she didn't do anything to interfere with Vishal's treatment.

I'm fine, Hwa-jung growled. **Don't stop for me.**

Kira bit her lip as she watched. She felt so helpless. And she felt as if she'd failed. If only she'd used the Soft Blade better, she could have kept everyone safe.

In response to her unasked question, Falconi said, **There's no going back. Not now. Only way out is through.**

Before she could reply, a Jelly popped up out of the disk-shaped hole in the deck. She nearly stabbed it before she scented the creature and realized it was Itari.

[[Itari here: Idealis?]]

[[Kira here: We're coming.]]

A cloud of nearscent wafted toward her then, not from Itari, but from the now-open doors where the gleaming bone-white orbs had emerged. More Jellies incoming, and they most definitely *weren't* happy.

"We gotta go," said Kira. "Everyone into the drop tube. I'll bring up the rear."

Itari darted back through the hole in the deck, and then Falconi followed, and Jorrus and Veera and Sparrow too.

"Hurry it up, Doc!" Kira shouted.

Vishal didn't reply, but closed up his medical case with practiced speed. Then he kicked himself over to the hole and pulled himself through. Hwa-jung did the same a second later, her blaster trailing behind her via its shoulder strap.

"About time," Kira muttered.

She compressed the Soft Blade around her sides, discarded some of the extra material she'd picked up moving through the ship, and flew headfirst into the drop tube.

7.

Kill Ctein.

The thought pounded in Kira's skull as she hurtled through the crimson shaft. She was moving fast, real fast—like the maglev on Orsted Station.

Transparent panels flashed past at regular intervals. Through them Kira glimpsed a series of rooms: one full of swaying greenery—a forest of seaweed with a backdrop of stars—one with a coil of metal wrapped around a flame, another humming with unidentifiable machinery, and still more filled with things and shapes she didn't recognize.

She counted the decks as they went by. . . . Four. Five. Six. Seven. Now they were making real progress. Only four more until they reached the level where the great and mighty Ctein lay waiting.

Three more, and—

A detonation slammed Kira into the side of the tube. The curved surface gave way, and she found herself tumbling sideways, along with Itari and the crew, through a long, wide room lined with racks of metal pods.

8.

Crap, crap, crap.

Kira popped the canister of chalk and chaff she'd been carrying at her waist. A white cloud exploded around her and the crew, thinning as it expanded toward the walls. Hopefully it would protect them long enough for her to control the situation.

She had to act fast. Speed was the only way they were going to survive.

Sinking tendrils into the floor, Kira stopped herself with a painful jerk.

Through the chalk, she saw a lobster-like creature with a flared tail scuttling along the far wall, heading toward a small, dark opening less than a meter across.

Stop it.

At her thought, the Soft Blade shed much of its accumulated mass while launching her after the Jelly. Using the thinnest of threads, Kira pulled herself along the deck, arcing through the cloud.

The lobster twitched and attempted to dodge.

Too slow. She stabbed the Jelly with one of the xeno's triangular blades, and she allowed the blade to bristle outward, impaling the alien as a shrike might impale its prey upon a tangle of brambles.

Kira scanned the room. All clear. Sparrow and Falconi had a few more scorch marks on their armor but appeared otherwise unscathed. They were holding position by the ruined drop tube along with the Entropists.

Coils of electricity arced from the twisted decking in front of the tube, blocking the way. Even as Kira watched, Hwa-jung scooted close and reached into the hellish, blue-white glare with a tool from her belt.

An instant later, the discharges vanished.

Then Kira saw Vishal floating near the back wall. The doctor was locked in a rigid, plank-like pose, arms stiff by his sides. His skinsuit had entered safety mode, freezing him in position for his own protection. The reason was obvious: a line of medifoam oozed from a burn across his chest.

Kira started toward him, intending to snag the doctor from the air and secure him with the Soft Blade. As she did, a skittering shadow in the corner of her vision seized her attention.

She twisted, pulse spiking.

A coiled, millipede-like creature raced across the upper deck, heading toward Jorrus, who had his back turned. Hundreds of black legs accordioned along the millipede's segmented length. Pincers hung open before a mouth filled with a row of grasping mandibles that dripped with slime.

Kira and Veera both saw the millipede, but Jorrus didn't. Veera shouted, and Jorrus looked at her, obviously not understanding.

Kira was already stabbing with the Soft Blade, but she was too far away.

The millipede jumped onto Jorrus. Its pincers closed around his head, and its legs snapped shut around his body. The Entropist managed a single strangled yelp before the razor-sharp pincers sliced through his skull and neck, separating his head from his body and releasing a spray of arterial blood.

9.

The millipede shoved Jorrus aside and sprang toward Hwa-jung's unprotected back.

Kira yelled, still unable to reach the alien. . . .

The roar of jets sounded as Sparrow initiated an emergency burn of her armor's thrusters and hurtled past. She tackled the millipede even as it latched onto Hwa-jung, and the three of them tumbled sideways through the air.

Lasers flashed between their clenched bodies. Fans of ichor flew from the alien's segmented carapace. Then blood fouled the air also, and there was a screech of protesting metal from Sparrow's exo.

Over the comms came the sound of desperate panting.

Kira followed with all her speed. She reached the three struggling figures just as Sparrow kicked the millipede away, sent it flying toward the far wall—the alien wriggling and writhing the whole way.

BOOM!

Falconi's grenade launcher bucked, and the millipede exploded in pieces of orange flesh.

"How bad—?" Kira started to ask as she closed with Sparrow and Hwa-jung. She saw the answer even as she spoke. Medifoam was spraying from a nasty-looking crack in the armor encasing Sparrow's left leg—the knee was locked straight, stiff as a rod.

Hwa-jung was in no better shape. The millipede had given her a deep bite on the right side of her upper back. Her skinsuit had already stopped the bleeding, but the machine boss's arm hung limp and useless, and her whole torso appeared lopsided.

Behind them, Veera was screaming. The woman floated next to Jorrus's body, cradling him in her arms, clinging to him as if he were the only solid thing on an endless ocean.

The contortions of Veera's face were too painful for Kira to watch: she had to look away. *This isn't working.* The thought came to her with cold clarity.

What can I do? Falconi said, jetting over to Hwa-jung.

Just keep watch, Sparrow said, her voice tight with pain as she worked on Hwa-jung, applying an emergency bandage to the machine boss's upper back.

Agh! said Hwa-jung.

Kira did more than just keep watch. She snared Vishal from where he drifted rigid and helpless on the other side of the room, and she pulled him in close. The doctor rolled his eyes at her, appearing scared and frustrated at his inability to move. Sweat beaded his face, as if he had a high fever. Then too she caught Veera and Jorrus (and Jorrus's separated head) in her grasp and gently brought them over. Veera didn't object, only clung to Jorrus that much tighter and buried her visor in his bloodstained robes.

Itari joined their small knot of bodies, the alien's tentacles trailing behind it, like flags in a stiff wind.

With everyone close at hand, Kira began to rip up the deck, intending to build a protective dome around them. It wouldn't be long before more Jellies descended upon them, and Hwa-jung, Vishal, and Veera were in no condition to fight.

As she drove the Soft Blade into the plating, she felt a strange reluctance from the xeno, a reluctance that Kira didn't understand and didn't have the time to decipher, so she ignored the feeling and—

She flinched as Itari wrapped a tentacle around her. The creature's suckers gripped the Soft Blade in a futile attempt to hold it in place. For an instant, she had to fight the instinct to send a burst of spines through the Jelly.

[[Kira here: What are—]]

[[Itari here: Idealis, no. Stop. It is not safe.]]

She froze, and the xeno froze with her. [[Kira here: Explain.]]

Falconi eyed them through his visor. **What's going on, Kira?**

"Trying to figure that out."

[[Itari here: There is a power tube in this floor. See?]] And it pointed with one of its bony arms at a line of markings that ran across the middle of the deck. [[Long current and swift. Very dangerous to break. The explosion would kill us.]]

Kira withdrew the Soft Blade at once. She should have paid more attention to the xeno. The mistake could have cost them all. [[Kira here: Is the deck above us safe?]]

[[Itari here: Safe to attack with your second flesh? Yes.]]

With that assurance, Kira ripped apart the ceiling and used it to build a thick dome around them. As she worked, she said to Falconi, "Power conduit in the floor. I'll have to cut through somewhere else." Then she pointed at the doctor and the machine boss and said, "We can't bring them with us."

Well we sure as hell can't leave them, Falconi said, angry.

She gave him a look to match his own, but she never slowed her construction, tendrils assembling the dome seemingly of their own accord. "Do you *want* to get them killed? I can't keep them safe. It's too much. And we can't send them back. What do you want me to do?"

A moment of troubled silence followed. **Can you fix them up, the way you did with my bonsai? You got into Gregorovich's brain, right? How hard would it be to heal some bones and muscle?**

She shook her head. "Hard. Very hard. I could try, but not here, not now. Too easy to make mistakes, and I wouldn't be able to deal with the Jellies at the same time."

Falconi grimaced. **Yeah, but if we leave them, the Jellies—**

"Will focus on me. Hwa-jung, Vishal, Veera—they should be okay for a little while on their own. I don't know about Sparrow, though. Her—"

I can still fight, Sparrow said, brusque. **Don't worry about me.** She gave the field dressing on Hwa-jung's back a final press and then hugged the machine boss's head and jetted over to where Kira hung suspended amid dozens of dark spines, each one connected to the shell she was assembling.

"You should stay. You should all stay," said Kira. "I—"

We're not leaving you,* said Falconi. *End of discussion.

Hwa-jung planted her boots on the deck, locking them in place, and hoisted her blaster with her uninjured arm. **Do not worry about us, Kira. We will survive.**

[[Itari here: We must hurry. The great and mighty Ctein will be preparing for us.]]

"Shit. . . . Fine. You three outside the dome. Now." Kira was in the middle of translating for Itari when the *Hierophant* jolted a meter to starboard and all the lights flickered. Alarmed, she glanced around. Nothing else seemed to have changed.

Gregorovich! said Falconi. He tapped the side of his helmet. **Come in, Gregorovich!** He shook his head. **Dammit. No signal. We gotta move.**

And move they did. Kira extracted herself from within the dome and, with a few seconds of frantic work, sealed it up and reinforced it from the outside. The Jellies would still be able to cut their way in, but it would take time, and she felt confident of what she'd said earlier: they were more concerned with *her*—with the Idealis—than anyone else.

Hwa-jung and Sparrow kept their eyes locked on each other until the last piece of plating slapped into place, cutting off their view. Then Sparrow set her shoulders and turned away with such a hard, killing expression on her knifelike face that, for the first time since meeting her, Kira actually feared her.

Get us to Ctein, Sparrow growled.

"This way," Kira said. Keeping a half meter of decking piled in front of her, she hurried toward the door Itari had pointed out. Sparrow, Falconi, and Itari followed alongside.

The portal slid open. Through it was a room filled with rows of what looked like giant pillbugs stabled in narrow metal enclosures.

Kira hesitated. *Another trap?*

"Let me go first," she said, and repeated herself for Itari. Falconi nodded, and he and the two others, human and alien, dropped back, giving her space.

Kira took a breath and moved forward.

As she passed through the doorway, a thunderous blast blinded her, and a steel belt seemed to cinch tight around her waist, slicing through skin, muscle, and bone.

10.

She wasn't dead.

That was Kira's first thought. And it puzzled her. She *ought* to be dead if the Jellies had mined the doorway. Her waist didn't hurt, not really. She just felt pressure and an uncomfortable pinching sensation, along with a copious amount of not-pain.

The blast had started her spinning. She tried to move and found that only her neck and arms responded. As a volley of laser blasts and slugs slammed into her back, she risked a glance toward her feet.

She wished she hadn't.

The explosion had burned through the half meter of the xeno's material swaddling her waist. Tattered lengths of grey-white intestines spooled out of the holes, along with sprays of shockingly bright blood. As momentum turned her hips, she glimpsed the white of bone through the gore, and she thought she recognized a vertebra.

The xeno was already pulling her guts back inside and sealing over the wounds, but Kira knew the injuries were enough to kill her. The Seed's memories had been more than clear; it was entirely possible for the suit's host to die.

As she spun, a bolt of molten metal punched through her shield, like the spear of a god.

And then another, closer to her vulnerable core. Incandescent drops sprayed her legs; they bounced off the hardened surface of the suit, cooling to ashen black.

Kira felt no pain, but her vision was blurry, and everything seemed distant and insubstantial. She couldn't fight; she could barely think.

She glimpsed an assortment of Jellies jetting toward her: tentacles, claws, graspers reaching toward her. There was no time to evade, no time to escape—

Then Falconi, Sparrow, and Itari were next to her, firing their weapons. *Boom!* went his grenade launcher. *Brrt!* went her guns. *Bzzt!* went its lasers.

At first Kira thought she was saved. But there were too many Jellies. They split into groups, drove Sparrow and Falconi back toward the walls, behind the metal enclosures, forced Itari toward a curved corner.

No! Kira thought as the three of them disappeared behind a wall of twisting bodies.

The Jellies mobbed her then. The big ones and the small ones, those with legs, those with claws, and those with appendages she didn't even recognize. Heat as hot as a star began to cut its way through her protective skin.

She tried stabbing outward. The blades killed some of the aliens, but the others evaded her, or the blasts of heat stopped her, and the suit recoiled in not-pain.

She kept trying, though the heat was making her light-headed. She tried to reach around the torches, tried to find the microscopic flaws in the Jellies' armor. And all the while, an almost stupefying sense of disgust surrounded her: the whole crowd of Jellies projecting their hatred and revulsion toward her. *[[No-form, wrongflesh!]]* they shouted as they stabbed and tore and burned their way toward her flesh. The sheer bulk of them made it difficult to move, even with the full strength of the Soft Blade brought to bear.

So Kira did the only thing she could; she let go. She willingly surrendered control to the Seed and told it to do what was needed. It had to, because she couldn't. Another few seconds and she would lose consciousness—

The shield and the walls and the squirming things faded and lost color. The room tilted around her. There were flashes and jolts and muted sounds. But none of it meant anything, a winter's display, abstract and uninteresting.

She felt the Seed expanding, gorging itself upon the *Battered Hierophant* as never before, springing forth with new life, sprouting and twining and spreading with a multitude of squirming black vines. And Kira was conscious of her increase in size as an expansion of her mental space. What made her *her* was stretched over an ever larger area, drawn thin by the neural demands of the suit.

The vines reached *through* the barrier she'd built, extending until they found what lay behind each spot of not-pain. Feeling. Tasting. Understanding. And when she touched chitin and oddly gelatinous muscles, she grasped and held and then wrenched, twisting and tearing until whatever wriggling thing she held wriggled no more.

Slowly the sounds grew louder and color leached back into the universe. First red, so she saw the blood splattered across the walls. Then blue, so she noticed the pressure alerts flashing near the ceiling. Then yellow and green, which drew her attention to the ichor mixed with blood.

Her head cleared even as the air did; the smoke, chalk, and chaff streamed toward three holes in the bulkheads, the largest the size of her fist.

A nano-thin layer of the xeno's black fibers covered a large portion of the chamber, and she—she floated in the center of the room, suspended there by dozens of spars and lines that radiated from her to the walls. Drifting among the narrow stables where the now-dead pillbugs floated were the remains of dozens of Jellies. A cloud of ichor and viscera surrounded them, a horrible storm front of fluids and mangled body parts, littered with crumpled pieces of equipment. Even as she watched, the escaping air pulled a crab against one of the holes, sealing it shut.

She had done this. Her. A deep ache formed in Kira's heart. Never had she aspired to hurt, to kill. Life was too precious for that. And yet circumstances had forced her to violence, forced her to become a weapon. The Seed also.

Falconi's voice crackled in her ears. **Kira! Can you hear me? Let us go!**

11.

"Huh?" She looked and saw that the Soft Blade had extended backwards out of the room and used a mat of fibers to glue Falconi, Sparrow, and Itari to the walls on either side of the scorched entrance. Relief flooded Kira. They were alive. The Jellies hadn't killed them. The Seed hadn't killed them. *She* hadn't killed them.

With a conscious effort, she retracted the fibers and freed Falconi and the others. She could control any one part of the Seed by concentrating, but as soon as her attention drifted, the part would begin to move and act as the xeno deemed fit. The flood of so much sensory information combined with the shock of her injury left her dazed, light-headed.

Good god, said Falconi as he jetted through a patch of viscera on his way to her.

Don't think god had anything to do with this, said Sparrow.

Stopping next to her, Falconi gave Kira a concerned look through his visor. **You okay?**

"Yeah, I just . . . I—" She didn't want to, but she looked down at herself again.

Her waist appeared normal. Shapeless and thick as a barrel, because of the suit, but showing no sign of injury. It felt normal too. She took a breath, tried flexing her abs. The muscles worked, but they seemed off, mis-strung piano wires that sounded oddly when struck.

Can you keep going? Sparrow asked. She kept her weapons trained on the far doorway.

"Think so." Kira knew she'd have to let Vishal look her over if they made it off the *Hierophant*. The main problem wasn't her muscles (those could be fixed), it was infection. Her intestines had been perforated. Unless the Seed could tell the difference between good and bad bacteria, or good bacteria in a bad place, she was going to end up with sepsis, and fast.

Well, maybe the xeno could. She had more faith in it than she used to. She'd just have to hope for the best, and if she was lucky, she wouldn't pass out from shock.

Kira retracted some of the suit, freeing her arms. She tapped Falconi's breastplate. "You have any antibiotics in there?"

He held up a hand, and a small needle popped out of the index finger of his exo. At her command, the Soft Blade exposed a patch of skin on her shoulder; the touch of the air was hot.

The needle stung as it broke her skin, and the antibiotics burned as they forced their way into her delt. Apparently the Soft Blade didn't consider the injection important enough to block the pain.

"Ouch," Kira said.

Falconi's lips twitched in an approximation of a smile. **That's enough to keep an elephant on its feet. Should work for you.**

"Thanks." The suit covered her shoulder again. She arched her back and flexed her abs once more. This time she concentrated on how they ought to feel, instead of how they did. A hiss escaped her as the mis-strung fibers popped into a new position with a *twang* that sent a zing to the tips of her fingers and the core of her bones.

Sparrow shook her head in her helmet. **Thule! What you did, I've never seen anything like it,* chica.*

Nearscent of reverence. [[Itari here: Idealis.]]

Kira grunted. Now that the Jellies knew how to hurt her, she was going to have to be smarter. A lot smarter. No more charging in headfirst. She'd nearly gotten herself killed, and if she *had,* the Jellies would have taken out Falconi, Sparrow, and Itari. The thought terrified Kira in a way she hadn't felt since her time on Adrasteia.

[[Itari here: We should not stay here, Idealis. We are close to Ctein, and more of Ctein's guard will be approaching.]]

[[Kira here: I know. Down again—]]

A flicker caught Kira's attention as the shell in front of them pulsed, spitting out *something.* Before Kira could see what it was, and before she could pull her shield between them and the object, Falconi fired his emergency jets—putting himself in front of her—and she heard two loud *bangs.*

A shower of sparks and shrapnel knocked Falconi end over end.

12.

With Falconi no longer blocking her view, Kira saw one of the Jellies' drones flitting away from the doorway, trailing a comet-tail of protective smoke. Enraged, she sent a jumble of fibers streaking across the floor and the ceiling until they bracketed the drone. Then she stabbed, and the drone whined as a half-dozen spines impaled it from either side.

She took a shaky breath. If not for Falconi, the shots might have taken her head off. . . .

Sparrow caught the back of Falconi's armor and pulled him close. The captain's right arm was smashed all to hell; it reminded Kira of a nut cracked to expose the meat within. She found it hard to look at. A sudden determination came over her: she wasn't going to lose anyone else. *Not again.*

Falconi was panting but still calm; his implants were blocking most of the pain, she guessed. White foam sprayed out of the broken edges of the armor, stopping the bleeding and setting his arm in an instant cast.

Shit, he said.

"Can you move?" Kira asked. Another tremor shook the *Hierophant.* She ignored it.

Falconi's exo twitched as he checked. **I can still use my left arm, but jets are out.**

"Dammit." That made four wounded and one dead. Kira glanced between him, Sparrow, and Itari. "Back. Hurry. You have to go back with the others."

Behind his visor, Falconi set his teeth and shook his head. **No chance in hell. We're not leaving you alone.**

"Hey." Kira grabbed him and pressed her forehead against his helmet. His blue eyes were only centimeters away, separated by the curved dome of clearest sapphire. "I have the Soft Blade. You're just going to get yourself killed if you stay." Her other thought remained unspoken: with only herself to worry about, she could let loose with the Soft Blade without fear of hurting or killing them.

A handful of breaths, and then Falconi relented. **Fuck. Alright. Sparrow, you too. All of us.**

The woman shook her head. **I'm not letting Kira—**

That's an order!

Fuck! But Sparrow started to jet back toward the room they'd just left. Falconi followed close behind, along with Itari.

"Hurry!" said Kira, shooing them forward. "Go, go, go!"

With her urging them on, they quickly returned to the dome she'd assembled. It was the work of seconds for Kira to peel open a Jelly-sized hole in the shell. Inside, Hwa-jung had a blaster trained on the opening.

You watch yourself, Falconi said as he prepared to enter.

Kira hugged him as best she could through the armor. "Don't keep the scars from this, yeah? Promise me that."

. . . You're going to make it, Kira.

"Of course I am."

Enough, said Sparrow. **You gotta move, and* now!*

[[Itari here: Idealis—]]

[[Kira here: Three down and forward: I know. That's where Ctein is. Just make sure my co-forms stay safe.]]

A hesitation, and then: [[Itari here: I promise.]]

Then Kira sealed them into the dome. And as they vanished from view, Falconi sent her one last message:

You can do this. Don't forget who you are.

13.

Kira pressed her lips together. If only it were that easy. Letting the xeno run rampant would be the safest, easiest way to kill Ctein, but she would risk losing herself and, possibly, creating another Maw. And that was a risk she wasn't willing to take.

Somehow she had to retain control over the xeno, whatever the cost. Still, she could do more with it than she had, which would require entrusting the Seed with a certain amount of autonomy.

That scared her. Terrified her even. But it was the balancing act that was needed—a high-wire act she couldn't afford to slip and fall from even once.

She rushed back to the room where the pillbugs had been. The air was so thick with gore, it was difficult to see. She pulled the xeno in close around her, compacting it into a dense cylinder of material. Then she sent forth tendrils and grabbed the deck and bored her way through it into a transport shaft.

She was alone now. She and the Seed, and a ship of angry Jellies surrounding them, and the great and mighty Ctein ahead.

The corner of Kira's mouth twitched. If through some miracle they survived—if the *human race* survived—there were going to be some interesting xenobiology courses taught about her experiences. She just wished she'd be there to see them.

She'd cut her way halfway through the floor of the shaft when the *Hierophant* tilted like an unhinged seesaw. The walls rattled, and Kira heard an alarming number of *pops* and *hisses*. The lights went out, only to be replaced by emergency backups, dim and red. A half-dozen fingers of high-pressure vapor erupted from the walls, marking the locations of ruptured pressure lines.

Up and down the length of the shaft, Kira saw jagged holes in the paneling—holes that hadn't been there before. Some were no bigger than a fingernail; others were the size of her head.

The receiver in her ear crackled. **. . . copy. I repeat, meatbag, do you read me?**

"Gregorovich?!" she said, hardly believing.

Indeed. You need to hurry, meatbag. The nightmares are closing in. One of them just took out a Jelly ship. The* Hierophant *got hit by the debris. It seems to have disrupted their jamming.

"One of our Jellies?"

Fortunately, no.

She resumed digging into the floor below her. "The others are hunkered down one deck back. Any chance you can help them return to the *Wallfish*?"

We are already in close consultation, said Gregorovich. **Options are being discussed, plans being outlined, contingencies being considered.**

Kira grunted as she tore loose a support beam. A slug ricocheted off her side from farther down the transport shaft; she ignored it. "'K. Let me know if they get off the ship."

Affirmative. Give 'em hell, Varunastra.

"Roger that," she said from between gritted teeth. "Giving 'em hell."

More slugs, laser blasts, and projectiles began to slam into her as a seething pool of Jellies gathered at the end of the shaft. The sides of the Soft Blade were thick enough that Kira paid them no mind. She'd cannibalized enough of her immediate surroundings to make her effectively immune to small-arms fire. The Jellies would have to bring in something a *lot* bigger if they wanted to hurt her.

The thought gave her a measure of satisfaction.

Down through the floor of the shaft, down through a room that glowed dull red and was filled with transparent tubing sloshing with water and large enough for the Jellies to swim through, and then down through the floor of the room and into the final deck. *Finally.* Kira bared her teeth. Ctein was close now: just a short way ahead of her.

The level she'd arrived on was dark purple, and there were patterned lines on the walls that reminded her of the designs from Nidus. Echoes of the Vanished, repurposed by the graspers who neither knew nor cared for the significance of the artifacts they'd found.

The disgust Kira felt was not her own; it came from the Seed, a disapproval strong enough to make her wish to deface the walls, to cleanse them of their arrogant, ignorant, garbled reproductions.

She flew forward, clearing doors with slashes too fast to see, killing Jellies with jabs and twists, letting nothing stop or slow her. She might have gotten lost, but ahead of her a thick bank of nearscent swelled, and she recognized it as Ctein's: a scent of hate and wrath and impatience and . . . satisfaction?

Before Kira could make sense of it, she came upon a circular door that stood a full ten meters high. Unlike every other door she'd seen on the Jelly ships, it was made not of shell but of metal and composite and ceramics and other materials she didn't recognize. It was white, and banded with concentric circles of gold, copper, and what might have been platinum.

Seven stationary guns were mounted around the frame of the door. And hanging on the walls by the guns were at least a hundred Jellies of all different sizes and shapes.

Kira never hesitated. She dove straight toward them while letting the Soft Blade yank up the bulkhead in front of her, sending black needles jabbing toward the guns, and throwing a thousand different threads through the air—each one seeking flesh.

The mounted weapons exploded in a roll of deafening thunder. The room seemed to grow quiet around Kira as the xeno dulled the sound. A dozen or more projectiles slammed into her, some of them breaking or puncturing parts of the suit, with accompanying lashes of not-pain.

It was a valiant effort on the part of the defending Jellies. But Kira had learned too much, and she had grown too confident. Their efforts were nowhere near enough to stop her. A half second later, she felt the tips of the needles tickle the mounted guns, and then she was stabbing through them, destroying the machinery.

The muscles, bones, and carapaces of the Jellies posed no more of a challenge. For a handful of frenzied seconds, she felt their flesh—felt her blades piercing their insides, soft and giving and quivering with trauma. It was intimate and obscene, and although it sickened her, she never stopped, never slowed.

Kira withdrew the Soft Blade then. The area before the circular door was a cloud of misted ichor and mangled bodies: a massacre all her own doing.

A sense of uncleanliness filled her. Shame too, and a quick, sharp yearning for forgiveness. Kira had never been religious, but she felt as if she had sinned, same as when she'd inadvertently created the Maw.

What else was she supposed to do, though? Allow the graspers to kill her?

She didn't have time to think about it. Propelling herself forward, she grasped the door with tendrils extended in every direction. Then, with a shout and a heave, she tore apart the massive structure and threw the parts aside so they crashed into walls and dented bulkheads.

14.

Pungent nearscent assaulted Kira, stronger than any she'd smelled before. She gagged and blinked, eyes watering behind the suit's mask.

Before her was a huge, spherical room. An island of crusted rock rose from what would have been the floor when the *Battered Hierophant* was under thrust. Surrounding the island—enveloping it, encasing it, *subsuming* it—was a vast orb of water, midnight blue and flexing like a great, mirrored soap bubble. And there, in the center of the orb, mounted atop the crusted island, was the great and mighty Ctein.

The creature looked like a nightmare, in both senses of the word. A tangle of tentacles—each mottled grey and red—sprouted from a heavy, corpulent body studded with random growths of orange carapace. Hundreds, no . . . *thousands* of blue-rimmed eyes lay within the upper half of Ctein's folded flesh, and they rolled toward her with a collective glare powerful enough to make Kira quail.

Great and mighty indeed, Ctein was enormous. Bigger than a house. Bigger than a blue whale. Bigger even than the *Wallfish,* and more massive too, as it was solid through and through. The size of the monster was difficult for Kira to comprehend. She'd never seen a creature so huge except in movies or games. It was far larger than she remembered from her dreams, the result, no doubt, of Ctein's ceaseless gluttony through the centuries since.

There was more. With the expanded vision the Soft Blade granted her, Kira saw what seemed to be a miniature sun burning inside the heart of Ctein's shapeless mass—a steady-state explosion desperate to escape its hardened shell. A gleaming pearl of destruction.

She flipped to visible light and then back to infrared. In visible light, nothing unusual appeared; Ctein's body was the same dark grey-red that she remembered from ages past. But in infrared, it burned, it glowed, it shimmied and shined. It *glistered.*

In short, it looked as if the Jelly had a goddamn fusion reactor embedded within itself.

Kira felt tiny, insignificant, and severely outmatched. Her courage nearly failed. Despite everything the Soft Blade had done, she had difficulty imagining it could equal the might of Ctein. The creature was no dumb animal either. It was cunning as any ship mind, and its intelligence had allowed it to dominate the Jellies for centuries.

Knowing that filled Kira with doubt, and the doubt caused her to hesitate.

Rooted on the floor around Ctein's rocky perch was a goodly portion of the Abyssal Conclave—barnacle-like shells mottled with greens and oranges and with the many-jointed arms of their occupants waving in the currents. Waving and wailing in a hellish din that, to Kira's human ears, sounded like a chorus of tortured souls. To the grasper in her, to Nmarhl, it sounded like home, and memories of the Plaintive Verge flooded her mind.

Then the overwhelming stench of nearscent changed from satisfaction to amusement. And from the nightmare creature emanated a single, apocalyptic statement:

[[Ctein here: I see you.]]

At that moment, Kira knew her hesitation had been a mistake. She called upon the Soft Blade, coiling it like a great spring as she prepared to strike and end Ctein.

But she was too slow. Far too slow.

A clawed arm unfolded from along the Jelly's equator, and it plucked a dark slab of something from the top of its carapace. And it aimed the slab at her—

Shit. The object was a massive railgun, a weapon large enough to be mounted on the prow of a cruiser, powerful enough to punch a hole through an entire UMC battleship. She was dead. No time to run, no place to hide. She just wished—

Two things happened, one after the other, so quickly that Kira barely had time to register the sequence of events: the suit shifted around her, expanding outward, and

BANG!

The deck rippled underneath her, and there was a sound so loud, all went silent. Across the chamber, a bubble of sparkling green flame erupted from the side of the curving wall, and a pressure wave raced through the orb of water, crushing the Abyssal Conclave and uprooting the great and mighty Ctein from its ancient throne. The creature's tentacles thrashed, but to no avail.

The bulkhead to Kira's right vanished, and she heard the scream of escaping air. Before she could react, the wall of frothing water slammed into her.

It hit with the force of a raging tsunami. The impact tore off all of her tendrils and feelers—tore the main part of the suit away from the rest of its mass and sent her and it tumbling into the glowing whiteness of outer space.

Kira! Falconi shouted.

CHAPTER VI

* * * * * * *

SUB SPECIE AETERNITATIS

1.

Space was white?

Kira ignored the obvious inconsistency. First things first. She willed the Soft Blade to stabilize their flight, and it responded with puffs of gas along her shoulders and hips. Her spin slowed, and within seconds the receding hull of the *Battered Hierophant* occupied a single location within her vision.

A huge chunk had been torn from the side of the *Hierophant*; whatever had hit the ship had blasted through most of the decks on the aft section. *Another Casaba-Howitzer?*

She could feel the orphaned pieces of the Soft Blade still within the *Hierophant*, separate from her and yet connected. Afraid of what might happen if she lost them for good, Kira drew on them with her mind. And they began to stir, worming their way through the structure of the ship.

She glanced around. Yup, space was white. She dropped the infrared. Still white. And glowing. But not glowing as brightly as it should have been if she were in the open, in direct line of sight with the nearby sun.

Then her brain clicked, and she got it. She was inside a cloud of smoke meant to defend the *Hierophant* against incoming lasers. Good for the ship, inconvenient for her. Even with visible light, she could only see about twenty meters in any given direction.

Kira! Falconi shouted again.

"Still alive. You okay?"

I'm fine. One of the nightmares just rammed the* Hierophant. *It—

"Shit!"

You said it. We're making our way to the* Wallfish. *The Jellies seem to be* *ignoring us at the moment. Their fleet has the rest of the nightmares tied up, but we don't have a whole lot of time. Tschetter says Ctein is still alive. You gotta kill that Jelly, and fast.

"I'm trying. I'm trying."

Kira swallowed hard, doing her best to tamp down her fear of Ctein. She couldn't afford the distraction. Besides, there were worse threats approaching. The nightmares. The Maw.

She'd never been so scared. Her hands and feet were ice cold, despite the best efforts of the Soft Blade to keep her warm, and her heart was pounding painfully fast. Didn't matter. *Keep going. Don't stop moving.*

Kira switched back to infrared and used the xeno to hold herself in place while she scanned up, down, and around. Ctein was big as hell, so where the hell was it? The chamber they had been ejected from was visible as a shadowed cavity deep within the bowels of the *Hierophant,* a husk now empty of its monstrous fruit. Like her, Ctein might have been blown away from the ship, but she had a suspicion the Jelly had attitude jets hidden somewhere in its bulk. If Ctein had flown around the curve of the *Hierophant*'s hull . . . the alien would take a long time to find in the swirling cloud. Too long, in fact. The *Hierophant* had kilometers and kilometers of surface area.

"Gregorovich," she said, continuing to scan. "You see anything out here?"

Alas, the* Wallfish *is still lodged in the* Hierophant. *My sensors are blocked.

"Check with Tschetter. Maybe the Knot—"

A bar of smoke-free space, half a meter across, flashed in front of her. It ran straight from the horizon of the *Hierophant*'s hull, past her chest, and continued on into deep space. A mass of swirling curlicues expanded through the smoke, pressing it outward, and the glow of transferred heat spread through the haze.

Kira swore. At her command, the xeno reversed their course and shoved her toward the damaged ship. They were an easy target, hanging out in the open. She had to get to cover before—

From behind the curve of the *Battered Hierophant,* an enormous tentacle emerged, twisting and grasping with malevolent intent. In infrared, the tentacle was a tongue of fire, its suckers incandescent craters, its skeletal interior a flexible column of white-hot ingots stacked end to end, bright within the translucent flesh. Cilia lined the last third of the limb, each snakelike structure several meters long and seemingly possessed of its own restless intelligence, for they moved and waved and knotted independent of their neighbors.

A second tentacle joined the first, and then a third and a fourth as the rest of the gigantic Ctein hove into view.

The skin of the Jelly had changed: it was smooth and colorless now, as if coated with pewter paint. Armor of some kind, she supposed. Worse yet, the creature still held the ship-sized railgun with its clawed arm.

Kira shouted into the void as she urged the Soft Blade on even faster. She jetted back among the exposed decks of the *Hierophant,* but just when she began to relax slightly, Ctein's multifarious shadow eclipsed her and the monster fired its weapon.

The blast hit her with numbing force and sent her tumbling into a bulkhead.

But she was still alive.

The xeno had poofed out around her, like a giant black balloon, covering her whole body, including her head, though it didn't block her vision any more than the mask had. She could feel structures within the balloon: complicated matrices of fibers and rods and plastic-like filling—all of which the Soft Blade had manufactured in a mere fraction of a second.

Another explosion went off in her face, jarring her so hard, it left her dazed. This time she felt the suit counter the incoming projectile with an explosion of its own, diverting the deadly spray of metal to either side, leaving her untouched.

With a hint of astonishment, Kira realized the xeno had constructed some form of reactive armor, similar to what the military used on their vehicles.

She would have laughed if she'd had the chance.

There was no telling how long the Soft Blade could keep her safe, and she had no intention of staying to find out. She couldn't go head-to-head with Ctein. Not while it was armed. The only way she could fight was to duck and run and wait for the Jelly to run out of ammo. That or find a way to close with it so she could use the Soft Blade to tear it apart.

Stabbing out a hand (it moved but stayed hidden within the balloon), she formed a cable and launched it toward a shelf of half-melted beams several meters above her head. The cable struck and stuck, and she hauled on it with all her strength, slinging herself up and out of the pit blasted into the side of the *Hierophant.* At the lip of the crater, she released the first line, threw out a second one, caught the hull, and *pulled,* converting upward momentum into forward momentum. As she soared over the anchor point for the line, she sent forth another one ahead of her, and then another and another, dragging herself across the hull until she was hidden from the Jelly.

The monster followed. The last she saw of it, Ctein was leaping after her, its limbs rippling with hypnotic grace.

Kira grimaced and tried to pull harder on the latest cable. But she was already at the limits of what her body and the xeno were capable of.

As she flew around the side of the *Hierophant*, like a tetherball around a pole, Kira had a thought. An idea.

She didn't stop to consider practicality or likelihood of success; she merely acted and hoped—blindly hoped—that what she was doing would work.

Sending out several more cables, she yanked herself to a stop beside a jagged rent a piece of shrapnel had torn through the hull. She collapsed the balloon around her and converted the material into tentacles of her own. With them, she grabbed sections of upturned hull and sliced them free.

Each chunk was slightly over a meter thick, most of that thickness being thin layers of composite sandwiched with what looked like a metallic foam. Exactly as she'd hoped. As with human ships, the outer hull of the *Hierophant* had a Whipple shield to protect it against impacts from space debris. If the armor could stop micrometeoroids, then enough layers ought to be able to stop the projectile from a kinetic weapon like the railgun.

As Kira arranged the pieces in front of her, a dark stream of material flowed out from within the tangled ruins of the crevice, crawling toward her with a mind of its own. Alarmed, she recoiled, ready to fight off this new enemy.

Then she recognized the familiar feel of the Soft Blade, the lost parts of the xeno come to rejoin her.

With a sensation like cool water on her skin, the orphaned fibers melted into the main part of the xeno, adding much-needed mass to the organism.

Distracted, Kira only managed to stack four pieces of the hull before the writhing behemoth that was Ctein crested the side of the *Hierophant* and fired its gun at her.

BOOM!

Her makeshift shield stopped the incoming projectile within the first three layers of the hull. Not so much as a single speck of dust got through to the skin of her suit. And while the impact was substantial, the Soft Blade braced and buffered her well enough to keep it bearable.

She wondered how much ammo the Jelly was carrying.

Ctein fired again. Ignoring the blow, Kira sent herself forward. The sections of hull wouldn't last long; she had to take the opportunity while she could.

The giant creature moved toward her faster than its bulk would seem to allow. Puffs of white appeared along the left side of its carapace, and the whole mess of shell and tentacles jerked to the right. The damn thing had thrusters built or grown or attached to its carapace. That made her plan a little more tricky, but she thought she could deal with it. The Jelly might be fast, but there was no way it could move its thousands and thousands of kilos as quickly as the Soft Blade.

"Dodge this," Kira muttered, willing hundreds of razor-sharp threads across the surface of the *Hierophant.* The lines lunged and stabbed and scrambled, one atop another and each at a different angle so that it was impossible to predict which was going to strike where.

Before the great and mighty Ctein could move out of range, the tiny tips of her cutting threads tinked and tickled against the nearest of the Jelly's tentacles. To her dismay, she realized that the thin, grey armor it wore was a nanomaterial not unlike the fibers that made up the Soft Blade. The suit's anger blazed anew; it recognized the material as yet another piece of technology the graspers had stolen from its makers. Given time, Kira felt sure the xeno could burrow through the weave, but Ctein wasn't about to give her that time.

As the behemoth swung its weapon toward her again, Kira allowed the thicket of threads to swarm from one tentacle to the next until she saw and felt the railgun within her thousandfold grasp. She ripped it from the fingers at the end of the Jelly's bony arm, and threw the railgun away, threw it into the depths of empty space, where it might drift unclaimed for a million years or more.

For just an instant, Kira thought she had the advantage. Then, with one of its unencumbered tentacles, Ctein reached behind itself and retrieved a large white tube that must have been attached to the backside of its carapace. The tube was at least six meters long, and as the Jelly turned it toward her, Kira saw a dark iris at the end.

She half yelled as she tried to move out of the way, but this time, she was the one who was too slow.

The opening of the tube flared white, and a spear of solid flame jabbed toward her. It burned through the suit's fibers like so much dry tinder; they melted and evaporated, and from them she felt a wave of not-pain great enough to frighten her.

Now Kira was trying to escape. She shoved Ctein away, but it clung to her even as it forced the ravening fire closer and closer. The creature was fearsomely strong—strong enough to hold its own against the Soft Blade.

But the Blade was also Soft; she allowed it to relax and bend before Ctein's attacks, to run like water and slip through even the tightest of grips. The Jelly's suckers couldn't hold her; however they worked, the suit knew how to defeat them.

With a wriggle and a yelp, Kira succeeded in both pushing and pulling herself free.

She fell away from Ctein with a sense of having barely escaped with her life.

The creature gave her no chance to regroup. It leaped after her, and she fled along the length of the *Hierophant,* toward the distant prow. A pursuit surrounded by silence, mediated only by the pounding of her heart and the rasp of her breathing, and accomplished with the terrible grace that was the natural effect of weightlessness.

The size of Ctein seemed unreal. It felt as if she were being chased by a monster the size of a mountain. Possible names for it flashed through her mind: *Kraken. Cthulhu. Jörmungandr. Tiamat.* But none of them captured the sheer horror of the beast behind her. A crawling nest of lambent serpents, eager to rend flesh from flesh.

She glanced over her shoulder, and she belatedly realized what the tube actually was. A rocket engine, complete with a fuel supply. The Jelly was actually using a *rocket* as a weapon.

Ctein had planned for her. For the Idealis. And Kira hadn't planned at all. She hadn't realized the true extent of the threat the ancient creature posed.

At any other time, the absurdity of using a rocket engine as a weapon would have dumbfounded her. Now, it was just another factor she included in the calculations running in her mind: speeds, distances, angles, forces, and possible reactions and behaviors. Calculations of survival.

Then it occurred to her: along with the heat it produced, the rocket also produced a fair amount of thrust. That was what rockets did. Which meant Ctein had to hold on to something when using it or the rocket would send the Jelly flying away in the opposite direction. Admittedly, Ctein also had its maneuvering thrusters, but she didn't think they were as strong as the rocket.

"Ha!" she said.

As if in reply, her earpiece crackled and a man said, **This is Lieutenant Dunroth. Do you copy?**

"Who the hell are you?"

**Admiral Klein's aide. We have a missile inbound to your location from the* Unrelenting Force. *Can you lead the Jelly back toward the stern of the* Hierophant?*

"You going to blow us both up?"

That's a negative, Ms. Navárez. It's a targeted munition. You shouldn't be in too much danger. But we need to get a clear line of sight.

"Roger. On my way."

Then Tschetter's voice popped in the channel: *Navárez. Make sure you put enough distance between you and Ctein. Remember, there's no such thing as friendly fire.*

"Got it."

Kira jabbed the suit toward the hull and stopped herself. Then she threw herself up and back over the approaching Jelly in what would have normally been a stomach-churning somersault but that now felt like a graceful dive. Ctein reached toward her with three of its tentacles, straining its limbs to their fullest extent, but they fell short by a few scant meters. As she'd hoped, the creature continued to cling to the *Hierophant,* where it could still use its oversized blowtorch.

The Soft Blade arrested her flight and steered her back down to the surface of the battleship. Kira noticed that it moved her faster, more efficiently than before, and she remembered dreams of the suit swooping and soaring through space with the agility of an unmanned drone, something that could only be possible if the organism was able to manufacture thrusters of its own. Actual proper thrusters, capable of sustained output.

She also noticed that she still hadn't run out of air. Good. As long as the suit could keep providing her with oxygen, she could keep fighting.

She pulled herself along the *Hierophant,* propelling herself faster and faster until she wasn't sure she'd be able to stop herself before the shadow shield. And yet, she could feel Ctein closing in on her, like a rising wave, vast, uncaring, unstoppable.

Lt. Dunroth's clipped voice sounded: *Five seconds to target. Clear the area. Repeat, clear the area.*

Ahead of her, Kira saw a meteor arcing toward the *Hierophant,* a shining star bright enough to be visible through the whole thickness of the smoke.

Time seemed to slow, and her breath caught, and she found herself wishing that she were anywhere but there. The worst thing was, she couldn't change the situation. The missile would either kill her—or it wouldn't; the outcome was out of her control.

When the missile was only a second from impact (and still over a hundred meters away), Kira grabbed the hull and pulled herself flat against it, forming the suit into a hard shell.

As she did, the missile vanished with a disappointingly small blip of light, and a sphere of smoke-free space expanded from the spot where it had been.

Dammit. Kira had seen enough point-defense lasers in action to know what had happened. A blaster mounted somewhere along the *Hierophant* had shot down the missile.

She yanked herself free of the hull and threw herself sideways moments before Ctein would have crashed into her.

Nearscent of derision engulfed her. [[Ctein here: Pathetic.]]

Sorry, Navárez, said Lt. Dunroth. **Doesn't look like we can get a missile past the* Hierophant's *lasers. We're looping around r2, and then we'll be taking another pass. Admiral Klein says you better either kill that son-of-a-bitch or find a way off the* Hierophant, *because we'll be hitting it with three more Casaba-Howitzers on the way back.**

Ctein swung one of its tentacles at her, and Kira jetted out of the way just as the massive trunk of muscle and sinew swept past. Then again, like a hummingbird dodging swipes from an angry octopus.

The swirling smoke thickened and then cleared as the *Hierophant* emerged from the haze. For the first time since the explosion had torn her out of the ship, the true darkness of space was visible, and the hull and everything she saw acquired an almost painfully lucid sharpness. At the periphery of her vision, she was aware of distant sparks and flashes (evidence of the battle still ongoing between the Seventh, the Jellies, and the incoming nightmares).

Kira switched back to the visible spectrum. No need for infrared now that the smoke was gone.

She hung before the twining monster, a toy, a tiny plaything suspended before a hungry predator. It lunged; she dodged. She darted forward; it ignited the rocket engine for a second, and the scorching heat drove her back. They were at a stalemate, both of them vying for the slightest advantage—and neither of them finding it.

A spurt of nearscent struck her, ejected from some hidden gland along the Jelly's body:

[[Ctein here: You do not understand the flesh you are joined with, two-form. You are unworthy, unsignificant, doomed to failure.]]

She responded in kind, directing her own nearscent toward the knotted mass of the creature. [[Kira here: You have already failed, grasper. The Corrupted—]]

[[Ctein here: When I am joined with the Idealis, as I should have been before Nmarhl's treachery, the Corrupted will fall before me like silt into the abyss. None shall hold against me. This ripple may have been disrupted, but the next will be a triumph for the Wranaui, and all will bend beneath the force of our shoals.]]

[[Kira here: You will never have the Idealis!]]

[[Ctein here: I will, two-form. And I will enjoy cracking open your shell and eating your meat from within.]]

Kira yelled and tried darting behind the Jelly to snatch the rocket from its grasp, but the alien matched her movements, twisting so that its weapon always faced her.

It was a frantic, ugly dance, but a dance all the same, and despite its ugliness, filled with moments of grace and daring. Ctein was too big and strong for the Soft Blade to restrain (at least not at the suit's current size). So Kira did her best to avoid its grasp. And in turn, the alien did everything it could to avoid the touch of the Soft Blade. It seemed to know that if it let her hold it for too long, she would be able to pierce its armor.

Kira advanced; the Jelly retreated. It advanced; she retreated. Twice she caught hold of a tentacle only to have Ctein strike her so hard, she was forced to let go or risk being bludgeoned into unconsciousness. The blows were powerful enough to break off pieces of the suit: small shafts and rods that liquified into amorphous blobs before rejoining her.

If she could just close the distance between her and Ctein, if she could just wrap the Soft Blade around the alien's carapace and press herself flat against it, she knew she could kill it. Yet for all her efforts, Kira couldn't get past the Jelly's defenses.

The old and cunning Ctein seemed to realize it had the advantage—seemed to realize that it could cause her more pain than she could cause it—because it started to chase her along the *Hierophant*, firing its rocket torch, swinging its tentacles in a random rhythm, forcing her back and leaving great furrows in the hull from its failed strikes. And Kira had no choice but to retreat. Meter after meter she surrendered, desperate to keep her distance, for if the behemoth succeeded in catching her between hull and tentacle, the impact would turn her brain into mush, no matter how well the Soft Blade was able to protect her.

Her breath came in ragged gasps, and even under the suit, Kira could feel herself sweating, her body slick with a film of exertion that the Soft Blade quickly absorbed.

It couldn't continue. *She* couldn't continue. At some point she'd slip and make a mistake, and Ctein would kill her. Running wouldn't help; there was nowhere but emptiness to flee to, and she couldn't leave her friends. Nor the UMC; whatever their faults, they were fighting for the survival of humanity, same as she.

She zipped past Ctein's latest attack. How long could she keep going? It felt as if she'd been fighting for days and days. When had the *Wallfish* crashed into the *Hierophant*? She couldn't remember.

She stabbed at the Jelly's carapace for the umpteenth time. And for the umpteenth time, the suit's atomically sharp spikes skittered across the alien's shell.

Kira grunted with strain as she hooked a nearby antenna and pulled herself away from the Jelly, just barely escaping its retaliatory attack. It followed up with another lash of its tentacles, and she hurried toward the prow of the battleship, trying to avoid it, trying to remain free.

Then Ctein surprised her by jumping toward her, abandoning its grip on the *Hierophant*.

"Gah!" The Soft Blade responded by pushing her backwards and maneuvering her around the wide width of the battleship. White puffs emanated from the Jelly's thrusters as it followed. It succeeded in matching her trajectory and then started to gain on her, rocket extended like a giant accusatory finger.

Kira scanned the hull of the *Hierophant,* looking for something, *anything* that she could use. A jagged uplift of damaged hull caught her eye. If she headed toward it, she could use it to slingshot herself behind the Jelly and maybe—

Kira! Get out of the way! said Falconi.

Distracted, she twisted awkwardly, tumbling as the Soft Blade sent her flying toward the *Hierophant*. A tentacle curved toward her, and some distance away, she saw Falconi's armor-clad torso pop over the edge of the hole in the flagship's hull. With one arm, he lifted his grenade launcher, a flash illuminated the barrel, and—

Ctein's rocket engine exploded in a lopsided plume of burning fuel, spraying liquid fire in every direction.

Kira flinched as it splashed against her. The fuel didn't hurt, but old instincts were hard to ignore.

The explosion knocked the Jelly back, but amazingly, it managed to keep hold of the *Hierophant* with the tip of one tentacle. Much to her disappointment, it appeared unhurt.

Nearscent of a vast and terrible anger washed through the nearby space.

The creature pulled itself back against the battleship and then swung one of its tentacles at Falconi. He ducked beneath the rim of the hole, and Kira saw him vanish through a door an instant before the tentacle slammed down, crushing the exposed walls and girders.

All yours, kiddo, Falconi said.

"Thanks. Owe you one." Kira stopped several meters from the *Hierophant* and turned to face Ctein head-on. No weapons now. Only tentacles and tendrils and their two minds pitted one against the other. She prepared herself to embrace the monstrous Jelly once more, to wrestle with it until one or both of them were dead. Despite the many advantages of the Soft Blade, Kira felt no surety that she could win. All Ctein had to do was slam her against the hull of the *Hierophant*, and that would be the end of her.

But she wasn't about to give up. Not now. Not after everything they'd been through. Not with everything that was at stake.

"Alright, you big ugly," she muttered, gathering her strength. "Let's get this over with."

Then Kira saw it: the smallest of tears in the armored skin of one tentacle—the same tentacle, she guessed, that had been holding the rocket. Falconi's attack had done some damage after all. The tear appeared like a thin crack in the surface of cooling lava, open to reveal the heated flesh within.

Hope blossomed within her. Small as it was, the crack was an opportunity, and in an instant, Kira imagined how she could use it to kill Ctein. Doing so would be risky, terribly risky, but she wouldn't get any better chance.

Her lips twitched with an approximation of a smile. The solution wasn't to stay away—it was to embrace Ctein, regardless of the cost, and join herself to it in much the same way she was joined to the Seed. The solution was in the melding of their bodies, not in the separation.

Kira willed herself forward, and the suit responded with a hard kick from whatever thrusters it had constructed on her back. It drove her toward Ctein at over a g of acceleration, causing her to bare her teeth and laugh into the void.

The Jelly raised its tentacles, not to block her but to catch her in a cradle of grasping flesh. She corkscrewed around two of the tentacles and then latched onto the one with the tear.

At that point Ctein seemed to realize what she was doing, and it went mad.

The universe spun around Kira as the Jelly slammed its limb against the

Hierophant. She managed to harden the suit an instant before they struck, but her vision still went black for a moment, and she felt slow and disoriented.

The tentacle started to rise again. If she didn't act fast, it would beat her to a pulp; that she knew, sure as entropy. And though she hated the thought of dying, she hated the thought of letting Ctein win even more.

She could feel the tear underneath her belly, a small patch of softness on the otherwise hard surface of the tentacle. So she stabbed, she jabbed, and she twisted as she drove the suit's fibers into the wound. The tentacle convulsed, and then it whipped from side to side in a frantic attempt to shake her loose. But there was no getting rid of her. Not now.

The flesh of Ctein was hot against her blades, and globules of ichor spurted forth and coated her skin with a thick slime. Kira extended her reach within the creature, extended and extended until she found the bones at the center of the tentacle. Then she grabbed the bones and spread the flesh, forcing the tear to split and widen, and she poured the Soft Blade into the body of the alien.

The tentacle coiled around her, dark and moist and clutching. Claustrophobia clogged her throat, and though the suit continued to provide her with air, Kira felt as if she were on the verge of suffocating.

Ahead of her, sparks flashed, and with a shock, she realized Ctein was using its other arms to cut off the limb she clung to.

Determined not to lose the advantage, she urged the Soft Blade onward and outward, willing it to do what was needed.

The xeno blossomed into a thousand delicate lines as it burrowed into Ctein. But the threads didn't cut, as Kira expected. They didn't slash or tear or maim. Rather, they were soft and supple, and what they touched, they . . . *remade.* Nerves and muscles, tendons and bone: all of it was food for the xeno.

Ctein thrashed and writhed. Oh how it thrashed! It beat at her through its own flesh; it gripped and wrung its own limb, seeking to crush her, and a thunder filled her ears.

But the might of the great and terrible Ctein was no match for the persistence of the Soft Blade. The fractal fibers of the organism bent and wove and devoured as it converted the flesh of Ctein. It tore apart the creature's cells, desiccated and compressed them into something hard and unyielding. The resulting shape was angular, all flat planes and straight lines and sharp edges of atomic precision. A dull, dead object devoid of movement, unable to hurt or harm.

Twenty meters or more, and then her feelers were inside the carapace, and muscle gave way to organs and machines.

From the Soft Blade came a sense of anger over old sorrows, and without meaning to, she found herself crying out: [[Kira here: For Nmarhl!]]

The xeno increased again, doubling and redoubling until it filled the roomy shell, converting each cubic centimeter into brutal perfection.

Ctein shuddered once more—shuddered and then was still.

Kira switched to infrared for a moment and saw the glow from the fusion reactor fading.

The Soft Blade wasn't finished; it continued to build until it consumed its way through the skin and carapace of the Jelly. Around her, stone-like veins appeared along the tentacle Kira clung to. They spread, expanding across the whole of Ctein.

Uncertain of what the xeno was doing, Kira withdrew the Soft Blade, and with a sense of relief, kicked herself free of the gigantic corpse.

As they drifted apart, she looked back on it.

Where Ctein had been now hung a bristling, dull-black asterisk: an enormous collection of basalt-like pillars, faceted and chisel-tipped. A lifeless lump of restructured carbon. In places, a familiar circuit-board pattern covered the surface. . . . With a shock, Kira recognized the similarity between the floating pillars and the formation she'd found on Adrasteia. That too, she realized, had once been a living thing. Once, long ago.

Kira stared at the remains of Ctein with a sense of bitter accomplishment. *She* had done that. She and the Seed. After centuries of rule, the great and mighty Ctein was well and truly dead. Dead and done. And they were responsible.

All that knowledge lost. All those years of memories, lost. All those hopes and dreams and plans, lost and reduced to a lump of stone drifting through space.

Kira felt a curious sadness. Then she shivered and loosed a bark of laughter. She didn't know *what* she felt; so much adrenaline was rushing through her system, she might as well have been high. But she did know she'd won. She and the Seed had won.

Multiple people were clamoring in her ears, too many to follow. Then Tschetter's voice broke through the din. **You did it, Kira! You did it! The Jellies have broken off! Lphet and the Knot of Minds are taking control of their fleet. You did it!**

Good. Maybe now there was hope for the future. Kira wiped a smear of gore off her face and scanned the hull of the *Battered Hierophant,* reorienting herself. "Gregorovich, where are—"

A shadow fell across her, cutting off the light from the nearby star. With it came an icy chill that settled deep into her bones. Kira looked toward the obstruction, and her sense of triumph evaporated.

Four meat-red ships sailed overhead, their tortured hulls glistening like raw flesh. Nightmares.

2.

Dread spiked Kira's pulse, and she jetted past the rocky corpse of Ctein and back toward the *Hierophant,* desperate for cover. More nightmares were approaching: dozens of them, burning in as fast as the missile from the *Unrelenting Force.* Their silhouettes appeared as blots against the field of stars—shadows nearly lost against the blackness of the void. And behind them, too far to see, she knew the clotted mass of the Maw was fast incoming, moving toward them with insatiable intent.

Kira glanced about, hoping against hope she might see some form of salvation.

Between her feet was the planet the Jellies had been mining, R1—about the size of an airlock door, rust-red and marbled with clouds—and some distance from the orb, the moons r2 and r3, pirouetting around their parent. Behind them she saw the sparks and flashes that marked the larger battle as the UMC and the Jellies joined forces against the nightmares. Each flare of light was a stab to her heart, for Kira knew they marked the deaths of dozens if not hundreds of sentient beings. And nightmares too, for whatever that was worth.

At the distances involved, she couldn't tell who was winning. Only the explosions were visible, not the individual ships. But in her gut Kira knew the battle wasn't going well for either the Seventh Fleet or the Jellies. There were too many nightmares, and the Maw itself still had to be dealt with.

The four nightmare ships that had passed overhead slowed atop spears of nuclear fire, blue-white and brighter than the sun. They turned and nosed in toward the *Hierophant* until they made contact, several hundred meters aft of Kira's position.

A deep tremor ran through the hull.

She squeezed her eyes shut for a moment, dreading what was about to happen. There was no helping it; the only thing she could do now was fight and hope the crew of the *Wallfish* could escape. Fight and fight, until either the nightmares gave up or the Maw came to devour her. And devour her it would, if given the chance.

Kira took a deep breath. She already felt half-dead. Her body was in one piece, thanks to the Soft Blade, but *whole* and *sound* were two different concepts, and right then, *sound* wasn't how she'd describe herself.

At her command, the xeno started to rip a hole back into the *Hierophant.*

Whoa! Hold on to your hats! said Falconi. **Couple of the Jellies and one of the UMC cruisers are taking a run at the Maw.**

A prickle ran down Kira's neck. She swiveled toward the quadrant of the sky that she knew held the monstrosity. She held her breath, waiting.

Farther down the *Hierophant,* small explosions bellied out of the hull. Breaching charges, or something of that nature.

"What's happening?" she asked.

A moment passed before Falconi replied. **The Maw just farted out a cloud. Looks like lasers won't get through very easily. Wait . . . They're trying to hit it with missiles. Bunch of 'em.** A tense silence followed. Then, with audible disappointment, he said, **Missiles are a no-go. The Maw picked them off like flies. Shit. A couple dozen nightmares are heading back to the Maw. If the Jellies or the UMC are going to take it out, they don't have long. . . . Ah shit! Shit!** And among the stars, Kira saw a flare of light, like a miniature supernova.

"Was that—"

The Maw has some sort of crazy powerful laser, particle-beam combo. It just blew up two of the Jelly ships. Punched right through their chalk and chaff. Looks like the cruiser is going to try—

Three more streaks of light pulsed and then faded against the velvet backdrop, vanishingly small for all their destructive potential.

In a flat voice, Falconi said, **Another no-go. The cruiser got off two howitzers. Should have been direct hits, but the Maw shot the incoming streams, blasted them apart with its beam weapon. It deflected nuclear explosions with goddamn counter shots!**

"How are we going to take it out?" Kira asked, struggling with a hopeless feeling. The hull of the *Hierophant* vibrated beneath her.

I don't think we can, said Falconi. **There's no way to get enough ships close enough to overwhelm its—**

As he talked, a cluster of flashes appeared in the upper-right part of her vision, close to the hazy orange dot that was r2.

Kira clenched her fists, driving her nails into her palms. It couldn't be. It just couldn't. "Gregorovich. What was that?"

Oh. You saw, huh? he said in a dull tone.

"Yeah. What was it?"

More nightmares.

The words were the ones she'd dreaded, and they struck her like hammer blows. "How many?"

Two hundred and twenty-four.

3.

"Godda—" Kira's voice gave out, and she closed her eyes, unable to bear the weight of existence. Then she set her jaw and steeled herself to face unpleasant reality.

Without consciously meaning to, she let go of the *Battered Hierophant* and hung floating above the hull while she thought. She had to think; she didn't feel as if she could act until she'd come to some sort of understanding of what was happening.

In her ear, Falconi said, **Kira, what are you doing? You gotta get back here, before—**

His voice faded into the background as she ignored him.

She took a breath. And then another one.

There was no way they could win now. It was one thing to fight knowing that while she *might* die it was also possible they could drive off their enemies. It was an altogether different thing to know that she *would* die and that victory was impossible.

She resisted the urge to scream. After all they'd done, all they'd lost and sacrificed, it felt wrong to lose now. It felt unfair in the deepest possible sense, as if the two hundred and twenty-four nightmares that had just arrived were an affront to nature itself.

One more breath, this one longer and slower than before.

Kira thought of the greenhouses on Weyland—the fragrance of the loam and flowers, the lazy drift of dust in the sunbeams, the taste of the warm summer tomatoes—and of her family also. Then too of Alan and the future they'd planned, the future that she'd long since had to accept would never happen.

The memories left her with a bittersweet ache. All things came to an end, and it seemed her own end was swiftly approaching.

Her eyes filled with tears. She sniffed and looked at the stars, at the glowing band of the Milky Way that spanned the boundless sphere of the heavens. The universe was so beautiful it hurt. So very, very beautiful. And yet, at the same time, so full of ugliness. Some born of the inexorable demands of entropy; some born of the cruelty that seemed innate to all sentient beings. And none of it made any sense. It was all glorious, horrible nonsense, fit to inspire both despair and numinosity.

The perfect example: even as she looked at the galaxy and marveled in its radiance, another of the nightmare ships sailed into view, a torpedo-shaped growth of crimson carnality. From it she could feel a distant tug, an affinity drawing flesh to flesh, like a wire pulling at her navel—pulling at her very essence.

A new sensation broke upon Kira: determination. And with it, sorrow. For she understood: she had a choice where, before, she didn't. She could allow events to continue unchecked, or she could wrench them out of joint and force them into a new pattern.

It was no choice at all.

Eat the path. That was what she would do. She would eat the path and bypass bare necessity. It wasn't what she wanted, but her wants were no longer important. By her act, she could help not just the Seventh, but her friends, her family, and her entire species.

It was no choice at all.

If she and the crew of the *Wallfish* weren't going to survive, she could at least try to stop the Maw from spreading. Nothing else really mattered now. Left unchecked, the corrupted Seed would spread across the whole of the galaxy in the blink of a cosmic eye, and there was little that the Jellies or the humans could do to stop it.

There was a certain beauty to her choice as well: a symmetry that appealed to Kira. With one clean slash, she could resolve the whole problem of her existence, a problem that had been troubling not just her, but all of settled space since she'd stumbled upon that hidden chamber on Adrasteia. The Seed had taught her its true purpose, and now she understood her own purpose as well, and the two halves of her being were of accord.

"Gregorovich," she said, and the sound of her voice was shocking in the silence of the void. "Do you still have that Casaba-Howitzer left?"

* * * *

EXEUNT V

1.

Kira, said Falconi. **What's going on? We can't see you on our screens.**

"You made it back to the *Wallfish*?"

Barely. Now—

"I said: I need a Casaba-Howitzer."

What for? We have to get the fuck out of here before the nightmares blow us out of the sky. If we head straight for the Markov Limit, we might reach it before—

"No," she said quietly. "There's no way we can outrun the nightmares, and you know it. Now send over the Casaba-Howitzer. I think I figured out how to stop the Maw."

How?!

"Do you trust me?"

There was a moment of weighted hesitation on his end. **I trust you. But I don't want to see you get killed.**

"We don't have a lot of options, Salvo. . . . Get me that bomb. Fast."

He was silent for a while—long enough that she began to wonder if he would refuse. Then: **Casaba-Howitzer launched. It's going to take up position half a klick from the dark side of the* Hierophant. *Can you get to it?**

"I think so."

'K. If you position yourself with your feet toward the stern, facing away from the* Hierophant, *the howitzer will be at your seven. Gregorovich is lighting it up with a targeting laser. Should show up nicely in infrared.

Kira scanned the darkness, and then she saw it: a bright little dot, alone in the void. It looked close enough to touch, though she knew better. Distance was always hard to judge absent any reference points.

"Got it," she said. "On my way now." Even as she spoke, the Soft Blade pushed her toward the dormant bomb.

Great. You mind explaining what exactly you're planning? Please tell me it's not what I think it is.

"Wait."

Wait?! Come on, Kira, what the—

"I need to concentrate. Give me a minute."

Falconi grunted and stopped bothering her.

To herself, Kira said, "Faster. Faster!" urging the Soft Blade on with her mind. She knew she had only a short time before the nightmares came to investigate. If she could just reach the Casaba-Howitzer first . . .

The missile swelled in size ahead of her: a thick cylinder with a bulbous nose and red stenciling along the side. Its main engine was off, but the nozzle still glowed with residual heat.

Her breath escaped with a low *huh* as the Casaba-Howitzer slammed into her chest. She grabbed it, wrapping her arms around it. The tube was too thick for her fingers to touch on the other side. The impact started her and the missile spinning, but the Seed quickly stabilized them.

Out of the corner of her eye, Kira saw the nightmare ship that had been on approach to the *Hierophant* was now heading in her direction, and quickly too.

Falconi's voice broke on her ear: **Kira—**

"I see them."

We can—

"Stay where you are. Don't interfere."

Kira thought furiously as she enveloped the Casaba-Howitzer with the suit, sending countless fibers burrowing through its outer casing. With them she felt out the wires and switches and various structures that made up the bomb. And she felt the heat of the stored plutonium, felt the warm bath of its radiation and from it, took sustenance.

Somehow she had to stop the nightmares from stopping her. If she tried to fight them, they would slow her down long enough for more of them to join in. Besides, she remembered how she'd lost herself when she touched the one nightmare during their escape from Bughunt. She couldn't risk that again. Not until she reached the Maw.

The harsh light of retro-thrusters bathed her as the nightmare ship slowed to a stop relative to her. It was only a few dozen meters away. At that distance, she could see veins throbbing beneath its abraded exterior. Just *looking* at the vessel made her wince with sympathetic pain.

A thought stirred within her, a thought not of her own making: *That which is heard may yet be answered.* And she remembered how the suit had responded to the summons when she'd boarded the Jelly ship back at Sigma Draconis. More memories came to her then, and they transported her to another time and another place, in a part of the galaxy far-flung and forgotten, when she had felt the call of her masters and answered as was only right and proper. As was her duty.

Kira knew what to do then.

She gathered her strength, and via the Seed, she sent forth a message to the nightmares and to the Maw that had created them, blasting forth the signal with all the power at her disposal: *Stay back! You can have what you want. Let my friends leave, and I will come to you. This I promise.*

2.

The ship beside her didn't respond with voice or action. But neither did it attack, and as Kira began to accelerate away from the *Battered Hierophant*, the nightmares' crimson vessel remained behind.

A moment later, she *did* receive a response: a transmission that contained nothing but a wild, wordless howl, a wounded cry full of pain, anger, and eager hunger. Chills crawled down Kira's back as she recognized the sound of the Maw.

The Seed allowed her to identify the source of the transmission. Acting against every instinct in her body, she aimed herself toward it and increased her thrust.

Kira! said Falconi, his voice sharp. *What did you do?*

"I told the Maw I'm going to join it."

. . . And it believed you?

"Enough to let me through."

Tschetter spoke then. Kira hadn't even realized the major was listening in: *Navárez, we can't allow the Corrupted to get their claws on the Idealis. Turn around.*

"They already *have* the Idealis," said Kira. "Or part of it, at least." She blinked and felt tears wicked away by the mask covering her face. "Salvo, you can explain. We have to keep the nightmares, the Corrupted, from spreading. If I can stop the Maw, that should give us a fighting chance. *All* of us. Humans and Jellies."

Gah, said Falconi. **This can't be your only option. There has to be a better alternative.**

Nielsen joined the conversation as well, and Kira was glad to hear her once more: **Kira, you shouldn't have to sacrifice yourself just to save the rest of us.**

She laughed lightly. "Yeah. Tell me about it."

There's no talking you out of this, is there? said Falconi. She could almost see him scowling in frustration.

"If you have any other ideas, I'm open to suggestions."

Pull some crazy-awesome stunt out of your ass and kill the rest of the nightmares.

"My ass may be amazing, but it's not that amazing."

Could have fooled me.

"Ha. Don't you get it? This *is* my crazy-awesome stunt. I'm breaking the pattern; I'm resetting the equation. Otherwise, things aren't going to end too well for any of us. It's not your fault; you couldn't have stopped this. No one could have. I think it became inevitable the moment I touched the suit, back on Adra."

Predestination? There's a grim thought. . . . Are you sure about this?

"They're not shooting at you right now, are they?"

No.

"Then yeah, I'm sure."

Falconi sighed, and Kira heard the weariness in his voice. She pictured him back in the control room of the *Wallfish,* floating next to the holo-display, his armor smeared with blood and ichor. She felt a pang. Right then, leaving him and the rest of the *Wallfish*'s crew was more painful than leaving her family. Falconi and the others were present and immediate; her family seemed distant and abstract—dim specters she had already made her farewells to long ago.

**Kira . . . ** said Falconi, and she could hear the grief building in his voice.

"This is the way it has to be. Get the *Wallfish* out of here while you still can. The nightmares shouldn't bother you. Go on, hurry."

A long pause, and she could almost hear Falconi arguing with Nielsen and Tschetter. Finally, with stiff reluctance he said, **Roger that.**

"Also, I need to know how to detonate this howitzer."

The pause that followed was even longer. Then: **Gregorovich says there's an access panel on the side. Should be a keypad inside. Activation code is delta-seven-epsilon-gamma-gamma—** She concentrated on memorizing the string of commands as he rattled them off. **You'll have ten seconds to get clear once you hit Enter.**

But she wouldn't be getting clear, and Falconi knew that as well as she did. She would sure as hell *try*, but Kira didn't have any illusions about the Seed's ability to outrun a nuclear explosion.

She concentrated on melding the Seed with the missile, weaving one through the other until it was hard to tell where the organism ended and the Casaba-Howitzer began. So thoroughly did she infiltrate the bomb, she could feel every part of it, down to the micro-welds in the bell of the rocket and the imperfections in the coffin that held the plutonium. She took care with her work, and when she finished, she felt satisfied that even the Maw would be hard-pressed to separate the Seed from the nuke.

She looked for the Maw then. It was still too far away to see, but she could feel its presence, like a storm building on the horizon, clouds heavy with a torrent ready to burst forth.

The distance between them was shrinking rapidly, but not rapidly enough for Kira's taste. She didn't want to give the Maw a chance to change its mind—or what was left of it. The Seed was already pushing her along as fast as it seemed capable of, but she wasn't carrying any propellant with her, so the thrust was limited.

What else could she do?

The answer, when it came to her, gave her a grim smile.

She focused on the image she'd created—the image and the idea—and did her best to hold them in her mind while she impressed them on the Seed.

The xeno grasped her intent almost immediately, and it responded with gratifying speed.

Four black ribs, curved and delicate, sprouted from the crown of the Casaba-Howitzer and extended outward, forming a great X. The ribs stretched as they grew, growing thinner and thinner until they narrowed to invisibility. She could feel them like fingers spread wide, their tips thirty, forty meters apart, and the distance still increasing.

Starting at the base of each rib, a mirrored membrane began to form, thin as a soap bubble and smoother than a pool of still water. The membrane flowed up and out, joining each rib to its neighbors until it reached the farthest point of the arcing tips. She could see herself in the reflection: a low black lump clinging to the side of the Casaba-Howitzer, faceless and anonymous against the pale expanse of the galaxy.

Kira lifted her right hand and waved at herself. The sight of her mirrored counterpart amused her. The situation was so outlandish she laughed at the absurdity of it. How could she not? Humor was the only appropriate response to having attached herself to a nuclear bomb and grown a set of solar sails.

The sails continued to expand. They massed almost nothing, but in appearance, they dwarfed her. She was a tiny cocoon suspended in the center of silvery wings, a potential surrounded by actuality. A seed unplanted and drifting on the wind.

She turned, slowly, carefully, ponderously, and the sails caught the light of the sun, and the light reflected with blinding radiance. She could feel the pressure of the photons striking the membrane, urging her onward, away from the sun, away from the ships and planets, toward the dark, red blot that was the Maw. The solar wind didn't provide much thrust, but it was *some,* and Kira felt satisfied that she'd done all she could to quicken her flight.

Whoa, said Falconi. **I didn't know you could do that.**

"Neither did I."

It's beautiful.

"Can you give me an ETA for the Maw?"

**Fourteen minutes. It's coming in hot. You know, this thing is enormous, Kira. Bigger than the* Hierophant.*

"I know."

In the silence that followed, she could sense his frustration—could feel him struggling to hold back and not say what he really wanted to. "It's okay," she finally said.

He growled. **No, it's not, but there's nothing we can do about it. . . . Hold on, Admiral Klein wants to talk with you. Here—**

There was a *click,* and loud as life, Kira heard the admiral's voice in her earpiece: **Tschetter explained what you're trying to do. She also explained about the Maw. You're a brave woman, Navárez. Doesn't look like any of our ships can get through to the Maw, so you're our best option right now. If you can pull this off, we might actually have a chance of beating the nightmares.**

"That's the idea."

Good woman. I'm sending four cruisers your way, but they won't get there until after you make contact with the Maw. If you succeed, they'll help mop up whatever remains, as well as provide aid and assistance, if needed.

If needed. It probably wouldn't be, though.

"Admiral Klein, if you don't mind, I have a favor to ask."

Name it.

"If any of the Seventh make it back, can you see to it that charges are dropped against the crew of the *Wallfish*?"

**I can't guarantee anything, Navárez, but I'll put in a good word for them on our packet ship going out. Based off what you've done here at Cordova, I think their unlicensed departure from Orsted Station can be overlooked."*

"Thank you."

An explosion sounded over the line, and Klein said, **Have to go. Good luck, Navárez. Over and out.**

"Roger that."

Then Kira's earpiece fell silent, and for the next while no one spoke to her. Part of her was tempted to ask for Falconi or Gregorovich, but she refrained. As much as she would have liked to talk with them—with anyone—she needed to concentrate.

3.

The fourteen minutes passed with disconcerting speed. Behind her, Kira watched as flashes continued to mark the ongoing fight between the nightmares and the humans and Jellies. The defending fleets were clustered around R1's two moons, using the rocky planetoids for cover as they tried without success to fend off the masses of crimson ships.

The Maw came into view well before the end of the fourteen minutes: first as a dull red star moving against the velvet backdrop of space. Then swelling into a knotted, dendrical tumor that writhed along the edges with a forest of arms, legs, and tentacles that was so dense, it appeared like cilia. Many of the individual limbs were larger than the whole of Ctein. They stretched for dozens, sometimes hundreds of meters—great trunks of misshapen meat that should have crushed themselves under their own mass. And buried among them, like a festering sore gaping wide, was the mouth of the Maw: a jagged slit of skin pulled tight around a ridged beak, which, when parted, revealed row after row of crooked teeth—bone-white and uncomfortably human—leading into a pulsing, gagging redness.

The Maw was more like an island of flesh floating through space than it was an actual vessel. A mountain of pain and misplaced growth packed full of quivering rage.

Kira shrank within herself as she stared at the abomination her actions had given birth to. Why had she ever thought she could kill the Maw? Compared to it, even the Casaba-Howitzer seemed paltry, insufficient.

But there was no turning back now. Her course was set; she and the Maw were going to collide, and nothing in the whole wide universe was going to change that.

She felt incredibly small and frightened. Here was her doom, and there was no escaping it. *"Fuck,"* she whispered, and shivered so hard her legs cramped.

Then, loud enough for the earpiece to pick up, she said, "Wish me luck."

After a few seconds of light-delay, Sparrow said, **Go kick its ass,* chica.*

Fighting! said Hwa-jung.

You can do this, said Nielsen.

I'm praying for you, Ms. Kira, said Vishal.

Be a most troublesome thorn in its side, O Aggravating Meatsack, said Gregorovich.

Just because it's big doesn't mean you can't kill it, said Falconi. **Hit the right spot and it's lights out. . . . We're all rooting for you, Kira. Good luck.**

"Thanks," said Kira, and she meant it with every atom of her being.

What Falconi had said was true, and it had been Kira's plan from the beginning. If she just blasted off a piece of the Maw, it would do nothing to stop the creature. Like the Seed, it could regenerate, seemingly without end. No, the only sure way to stop the Maw would be to destroy its ruling intelligence—the unholy union of Carr's wounded body and that of the Jelly Qwon. In a misguided attempt to heal them, the xeno had mashed their two brains together, stitching them into a malformed whole. If she could get to that whole—get to that lump of tormented grey matter—Kira thought she'd have a good chance of righting her wrong and ending the Maw.

It wouldn't be easy, though. It surely wouldn't.

"Thule guide me," she whispered, collapsing the solar sails so the Seed formed a small, hard shell around her and the missile.

The hellish fleshscape of the Maw loomed before her. Kira had no idea where exactly the brain she sought would be located, but she guessed it would be near the center of the overgrown meat. She might be wrong, but she couldn't think of a better place to strike. It was a gamble she'd have to take.

Several of the largest tentacles lifted from the body of the Maw and reached toward her with what seemed like ponderous slowness but in actuality, given their size, was terrifying speed.

"Shit!"

Kira willed herself into a course correction, altering her trajectory into a sideways slew that dropped her between the tentacles. Thousands of smaller limbs waved beneath her, grasping in a futile attempt to catch hold of her.

If they did, Kira knew they would tear her apart, despite the best efforts of the Seed to keep her safe.

A cloud of nearscent wafted over her, and she nearly vomited as she smelled death and decay and a cruel, eager desire to feast upon her flesh.

Anger spiked within her. There was no *fucking way* she was going to let this overgrown malignancy have its way and eat her. Not without giving it a severe case of indigestion.

Ahead of her, black tendrils began to sprout like hair from the surface of the Maw, similar to the tendrils from the Seed. Only these were thick as tree trunks and tipped with razor-sharp tines.

Left! Kira thought, and with a burst of thrusters, the xeno wrenched her down and to the side, away from the lashing tendrils.

She was nearing the center of the Maw. Just a few more seconds . . .

Next to her, the giant black beak surged upward out of the forest of thrashing limbs and the hills of oozing meat, biting, clacking, and—she felt sure—roaring its silent frustration. Clouds of frozen spittle spewed from within the open mouth.

Kira yelped, and the Seed provided her with one last burst of speed as she bored straight toward the heaving, bleeding, pustulent surface of the Maw. "Chew on this!" she muttered from between clenched teeth.

But in the last moment before she struck, her thought was more prayer than defiance: *Please.* Please let her plan work. Please could she atone for her sin and stop the Maw. Please could her life have not been in vain. Please might her friends survive.

Please.

4.

The instant Seed touched Maw, a raging howl filled Kira's mind. It was louder than any hurricane, louder than any rocket engine—loud enough that it gave her pains throughout her skull.

The force of the collision was greater than any emergency burn she'd experienced. Her vision flashed red, and her joints cried out as the bones pressed hard against one another, squeezing fluids, tendons, and cartilage.

How deep the impact carried her and the Casaba-Howitzer, Kira didn't know, but she knew it wasn't deep enough. She needed to be near the hidden core of the Maw before detonating the missile.

She didn't wait to be attacked; she struck outward then, letting loose with the Seed more than she'd ever done before. The Maw was angry. Well, so was she, and Kira gave full vent to her anger, letting every drop of fear, frustration, and grief fuel her attack.

The xeno responded in kind, slashing and cutting like a whirling buzz saw as it burrowed through the surrounding flesh. Gouts of hot blood bathed them, and the howl in Kira's mind acquired a double edge of pain and panic.

Then the flesh tightened, pressing inward with inexorable strength. Kira fought back, and had the Maw been made of tissue alone, she might have succeeded. But it wasn't. The cancerous growth was shot through with the same substance that comprised the Seed: a web of black, diamond-hard fibers that moved and spread with ruthless intent, cutting, dragging, constricting.

Where the two xenos touched, they wrestled with fierce contention. At first neither seemed to gain the advantage, so closely matched were they in ability, but then—to Kira's alarm—she noticed her second skin starting to dissolve into the attacking threads. Alarm turned to horror as she realized the xenos *wanted* to merge. To the Seed, there was no difference in kind between the part of itself bound to her and the part of itself bound to the Maw. They were two halves of the same organism, and they were seeking to again become whole.

Kira screamed with frustration as the outer surface of the Seed continued to melt into the Maw, and with it, any sense of control. Then a shock hit her body and she convulsed, feeling as if a thousand sparking wires had touched her. Blood filled her mouth, hot and copper-tasting.

A flood of sensory information coursed through her nerves, and for a moment, Kira lost all awareness of where she was.

She could *feel* the Maw, same as she could feel her own body. Flesh piled upon flesh, and most of it throbbing with the agony of exposed nerves, as well as the torment of limbs, muscles, and organs assembled all out of order. Human and Jelly parts had been grafted one onto the other with no care taken for proper structure or function. Ichor oozed through veins made for blood, and blood gushed through spongelike tissues intended for thicker secretions; bones scraped against tendons, cartilage, and other bones; tentacles pressed against misplaced intestines; and everything quivered with the physical equivalent of a scream.

Without the fibers of the xeno laced throughout the Maw—supporting and sustaining it—the entire abomination would have died within minutes, if not seconds.

Accompanying the pain was a grinding hunger—a primal yearning to eat and grow and spread without end, as if the protective safeguards built into the Seed had broken and fallen away, leaving behind only the desire to expand. There was also a certain sadistic glee to the Maw's emotions, and that didn't surprise Kira. Selfishness was more fundamental than kindness. But what she didn't expect was the wandering, childlike confusion that accompanied it. The intelligence born of Carr and Qwon's joined minds seemed unable to comprehend its circumstances. All it knew was its suffering, its hate, and its desire to multiply until it had blanketed every centimeter of every planet and asteroid in the universe—until its offspring clotted the space around every star in the sky, and each ray of light was sucked up by the life, the *life,* the *LIFE,* it had seeded from its misbegotten loins.

This it so desired. And this it needed.

Kira shouted into the darkness as she strained against the Maw, strained against it with mind, body, and Seed. She pitted her own rage and hate against the monster, ravaging the flesh around her with the full force of her desperate desire, fighting like an animal trapped in the clamping jaw of its predator.

Her attempts accomplished nothing. Before the Maw, her anger was a candle compared to a volcano. Her hate was a scream lost in a battering tempest.

The incomprehensible might of the Maw confined her. Constrained her. Blinded her. Every effort it countered. Every strength it matched and overmatched. The Seed was melting around her, dissipating atom by atom as it joined with the Maw. And the harder she fought, the faster the xeno slipped away.

As the Maw neared bare skin—her actual skin, not that of the Seed—Kira realized she had run out of time. If she didn't act, and *now,* everything she had done would have been for nothing.

In a frenzy of fresh panic, she felt for the controls of the Casaba-Howitzer with what was left of the Seed. *There.* The buttons were hard and square under the touch of the xeno's tendrils.

Kira began to punch in the activation code.

And then . . . She lost the tendrils. They went slack and flowed like water into encroaching darkness. Flesh rejoining flesh, and with it her only hope of salvation.

She had failed. Totally and utterly. And she had handed their greatest enemy what might have been humanity's only chance of victory.

Kira's anger burned even brighter, but it was a futile, hopeless anger. Then the last few molecules of the xeno sublimed, and the substance of the Maw collapsed in on her, hot, bloody, and grasping.

5.

Kira screamed.

The fibers of the Maw were tearing her apart. Skin, muscles, organs, bones, all of it. Her body was being ripped away, shredded like an empty suit of clothes.

The Seed still permeated her, and it finally began to resist the Maw with serious intent, attempting to protect her while also melding with its long-lost flesh. They were contradictory urges, though, and even if the Seed had been solely focused on her defense, there was too little of it left to fend off the might of the Maw.

The helplessness that Kira felt was complete. So, too, was her sense of defeat. The all-consuming agony—both her own and the Maw's—paled in comparison. She could have borne any imaginable pain if the cause were justified, but in defeat, the offense to her flesh was a thousandfold worse.

It was wrong. All of it wrong. Alan's death and those of her other teammates, the attack on the *Extenuating Circumstances* and the creation of the Maw, the thousands upon thousands of sentient beings—human, Jelly, and nightmare alike—who had died in the ten and a half months of fighting. All that pain and suffering, and for what? *Wrong.* Worst of all, the pattern of the Seed would end up so twisted and perverted that its legacy—and by extension *hers*—would be one of death, destruction, and suffering.

Anger turned to sorrow. There was little of her left now; Kira didn't know how much longer she would retain consciousness. A few seconds. Maybe less.

Her mind flashed to Falconi and their night together. The salted taste of his skin. The feel of his body pressed against her own. His warmth inside her. Those moments had been the last normal, intimate experience she would share with another person.

She saw the muscles of his back flexing beneath her hands, and behind him, sitting on the console desk, the gnarled bonsai tree—the only bit of living green left on the *Wallfish*. It hadn't been there, though, had it? . . .

Green. The sight reminded her of the gardens of Weyland, so full of life, fragrant, fragile, precious beyond description.

Then, at the very end, Kira surrendered. She accepted her defeat and abandoned her anger. There was no longer any point in fighting. Besides, she understood the Maw's pain and the reasons for its rage. They were, at their heart, not so different from her own.

If she could have wept, she would have. And in her extremis, at the very limits of her existence, a flush of warmth suffused Kira, calming, cleansing—transformative in its redemptive purity.

I forgive you, she said. And instead of rejecting the Maw, she embraced it, opening herself and welcoming it into her.

A shift. . . .

Where the fibers of the Maw touched her—disassembling her flesh with ruthless intent—there was a pause in motion. A cessation of activity. And then Kira felt the strangest thing: instead of the Seed flowing into the Maw, now the Maw began to flow into the Seed, joining with it, *becoming* it.

Kira accepted the influx of material, drawing it to herself like a child to her bosom. Her pain subsided, along with that of the tissue she had gained hold over. As her reach spread, her sense of self expanded, and with it came a breadth of newfound awareness, like a vista opening up before her.

The Maw's anger doubled and redoubled. The abomination was aware of the change, and its fury knew no bounds. It struck at her with all the might and power contained within its malformed body: smashing her, squeezing her, twisting her, cutting her. But as the Maw's fractal fibers closed around her, they relaxed into the Seed and fell under Kira's sway.

The howl that emanated from the Maw's tortured mind was apocalyptic in its strength, a nova of pure, unconstrained wrath exploding from within its center. The creature convulsed as if with a seizure, but all its maddening could not slow or stop Kira's progress.

For she was not fighting the nightmare, not anymore; she was allowing it to be what it was, and she was acknowledging its existence and her role in creating it. And through that, she healed the Maw's agonized flesh.

As her reach grew, Kira felt herself stretching thinner and thinner, fading into the accumulating mass of the Seed. This time, she didn't hold back.

Letting go was the only way she could counter the Maw, so let go she did, once and for all.

A singular clarity consumed Kira's consciousness. She could not have said who she was nor how she came to be, but she could *feel* everything. The press of the Maw's flesh, the sheen of the stars shining upon them, the layers of nearscent wafting about, and enveloping it all, bands of violet radiation that pulsed as if alive.

The mind of the Maw thrashed and struggled with ever-increasing frenzy as the Seed closed in on it, deep within the folds of bloody meat. The greater part of the mountain of flesh belonged to *her* now, and she devoted as much energy to soothing its many hurts as she did to locating and isolating its brain.

She could feel the nearness of Carr and Qwon's corrupted consciousness. It was incoherent with frustration, and she knew that—given the chance—the cojoined insanity would spring forth anew and continue to spread suffering throughout the galaxy.

Neither she nor the Seed could allow that to happen.

There. Shards of bone, and a softer flesh between, unlike any other, a dense web of nerves emanating from the grey interior. *There.* Even at a remove, the force of the thoughts within was enough to make her (and the Seed) quail. She wished she could join herself with the mound of tissue, as she had with Gregorovich, and heal it, but the mind of the Maw was still too strong for her. She would risk losing control of the Seed again.

No. The only solution was a cutting blow.

She stiffened a blade of fibers, drew it back and—

A signal struck her from near one of the planets around the dim, blue-white star. It was a burst of electromagnetic waves, but she heard it as clearly as any voice: a shrill stutter-stop packed with layers of encrypted information.

Deep within her, a jolt of electricity coursed through the circuits of the Casaba Howitzer. Then a piece of machinery shifted inside the missile with a heavy *thud.* And with dreadful certainty she knew:

Activation.

There was no time to escape. No time whatsoever.

Alan.

In the darkness, light blossomed.

PART SIX

* * * * * * *

QUIETUS

. . .

I've seen a greater share of wonders, vast
And small, than most have done. My peace is made;
My breathing slows. I could not ask for more.
To reach beyond the stuff of day-to-day
Is worth this life of mine. Our kind is meant
To search and seek among the outer bounds,
And when we land upon a distant shore,
To seek another yet farther still. Enough.
The silence grows. My strength has fled, and Sol
Become a faded gleam, and now I wait,
A Viking laid to rest atop his ship.
Though fire won't send me off, but cold and ice,
And forever shall I drift alone.
No king of old had such a stately bier,
Adorned with metals dark and grey, nor such
A hoard of gems to grace his somber tomb.
I check my straps; I cross my arms, prepare
Myself to once again venture into the
Unknown, content to face my end and pass
Beyond this mortal realm, content to hold
And wait and here to sleep—
To sleep in a sea of stars.

—*THE FARTHEST SHORE* 48–70
HARROW GLANTZER

CHAPTER I

* * * * * * *

RECOGNITION

1.

She was.

How, where, and what, she could not say . . . but she was. The lack of knowledge did not bother her. She existed, and existence was its own satisfaction.

Her awareness was a thin, trembling sensation, as if she were stretched over too much area. She felt insubstantial; a haze of recognition drifting across a darkling sea.

And for a time, that was enough.

Then she noticed the membrane of her self beginning to thicken, slowly at first, but with increasing speed. With it came the question that birthed all questions: *Why?*

As her flesh continued to solidify, her thoughts also grew stronger, more coherent. Still, confusion dominated. What was happening? Was she supposed to know? Where was she? Was *where* something real or something she had imagined?

The shock of connecting nerves caused her a stab of pain, sharp-edged as the light that shone upon her. For there *was* light now, from many sources: cold sparks set in black and a great blazing sphere that burned without end.

More shocks followed, and even thought failed before the barrage of pain. Throughout, she continued to increase in size. Gathering. Coalescing into being.

A memory returned to her, and with it, the memory of memories: *Sitting in third-year anatomy class, listening to the damn pseudo-intelligence drone on about the internal structure of the pancreas. Looking at the glistening red hair of the undergraduate two rows ahead of him . . .*

What did it mean? Wh—

More memories: *Chasing Isthah through rows of tomato plants in the greenhouse behind their hab-dome . . . then diving past her co-forms toward the Abyssal Plain, swirling around the overgrown lamp lines with the gasping beaks . . . arguing with his uncle who didn't want him to join the UMC, while she sat for entrance exams with the Lapsang Corp. and entered the Nest of Transference before assuming her new form and took the oath of fealty by light of Epsilon Indi on concertina racing forms howsmat double-shot clasp four-point verification nearscent heresy with the swirling exhaust of—*

Had she/he/it a mouth, they would have screamed. All sense of identity vanished within the tsunami of images, smells, flavors, and feelings. None of it made sense, and every part of it felt like them, *was* them.

Fear choked her/him/it, and they flailed, lost.

Among the memories, one set was more lucid and organized than the rest—*greenery mixed with love and loneliness and long nights spent working on alien planets*—and she/he/it clung to it like a lifeline in a storm. From it, they attempted to construct a sense of self.

It wasn't easy.

Then, from somewhere in the howling confusion, a single word surfaced, and she/he/it heard it spoken in a voice not their own: "Kira."

. . . *Kira*. The name rang like a struck bell. She wrapped herself in it, using it as armor to defend her core, using it as a way to give her/him/it some sense of internal consistency.

Without that consistency, she was no one. Just a collection of disparate urges devoid of meaning or narrative. So she held to the name with a fierce grip, trying to maintain a semblance of individuality amid the ongoing madness. *Who* Kira might be wasn't a question she could answer yet, but if nothing else, the name was a fixed point she could center herself on while she tried to figure out how exactly to define *herself*.

2.

Time progressed in strange fits and starts. She couldn't tell if moments were passing or eons. Her flesh continued to expand, as if precipitating out of a cloud of vapor, building, bunching, *becoming*.

Limbs she felt, and organs too. Blistering heat and, in shadows sharp and stark, brittle cold. Her skin thickened in response, forming armor sufficient to protect even the most delicate of tissues.

Her gaze remained turned inward for most of the time. A chorus of competing voices continued to rage through her mind, each fragment struggling for dominance. Sometimes it seemed her name was actually Carr. Other times Qwon. But always her sense of self returned to *Kira*. That was the one voice loud enough to hold its own with the others—the one voice soothing enough to calm their frenzied howls and ease their distress.

Larger she grew, and then larger still, until at last there was no more material to add to her flesh. Her size was set, although she could change its arrangement at will. Whatever felt wrong or out of place was hers to move or mold as she wished.

Her mind began to settle, and the shape of things began to make more sense. She remembered something of her life on Weyland, long ago. She remembered working as a xenobiologist, and meeting Alan—dear Alan—and then, later, finding the Seed on Adrasteia. And yet, she also remembered being Carr. Julian Aldus Carr, doctor in the UMCN, son of two not-so-loving parents, and avid collector of carved beryl nuts. Likewise she remembered being the Wranaui Qwon, loyal servant of the Knot of Minds, member of the strike-shoal Hfarr, and ravenous eater of the delicious *pfennic*. But the memories from both Carr and Qwon were hazy, incomplete—overridden by the far more vivid recollections of their time spent joined together in hungry fashion as the Maw.

A shiver ran through her flesh. *The Maw* . . . With that thought, more information rushed into her mind, full of pain and anger and the torment of unfulfilled expectations.

How was it she and they were still alive?

3.

At long last, she turned her attention to her surroundings.

She hung in the void, seemingly without motion. No debris surrounded her, no gas or dust or other remnants. She was alone.

Her body was dark and crusted, like the surface of an asteroid. The fibers of the Seed bound her together, but she was more than just the fibers; she was flesh too, soft and vulnerable within.

The eyes she had now grown allowed her to see the bands of magnetic force throughout the system. Visible also was the shimmery haze of the solar wind. The sun that illuminated all was a dim blue-white that reminded her of . . . she didn't know, but it felt familiar, nostalgic—though the nostalgia came not from her/Carr/Qwon but from the Seed itself.

She extended her gaze.

Scores of glittering ships populated the system. Some she seemed to recognize. Others were unfamiliar but of a familiar type: vessels belonging to graspers or else to two-forms . . . or else to the misplaced flesh of the Maw—which was her. *She* was responsible. And she saw how the flesh of her flesh had resumed attacking the other ships, spreading pain, death, and destruction throughout the system.

She did not understand the situation, not fully, but she knew that this was wrong. So she called to her wayward children, summoning them to her side that she might end the conflict.

Some obeyed. They flew toward her with great banners of flame streaming from their engines, and when they arrived, she clasped them close and healed their hurts, calmed their minds, returned their flesh to whence it came. For she was their mother, and it was her duty to care for them.

Some rebelled. Those she sent parts of herself racing after, and so caught them and chastised them and carried them back to where she hung waiting. None escaped. She did not hate her children for misbehaving. No, rather she felt sorrow for them and sang to them as she eased their fears, their angers, and their many pains. Their agony was so great, she would have wept if she could.

As she corralled her unruly offspring, some of the graspers and the two-forms shot at her sendings with lasers, missiles, and solid projectiles. That would have incurred the wrath of the Maw, but not of her. The attacks bothered her little, for she knew the graspers and the two-forms did not understand. She had no fear of them. Their weapons could not harm what she had become.

Many of the beings' ships followed as she drew in the leavings of her flesh. They formed a grid in front of her, at what they must have thought was a safe distance. It was not, but she kept that knowledge to herself.

Hundreds of signals emanated from the ships, aimed toward her. The electromagnetic beams were dazzling cones of prismatic energy flashing in her vision, and the sounds and information they carried were like the buzzing of so many mosquitoes.

The display was distracting, and it made thinking harder than it already was. Annoyed, she spoke a single word, using means that every species would understand:

"*Wait.*"

After that, the signals ceased, leaving her in blessed silence. Satisfied, Kira again turned her focus inward. There was much she still didn't understand, much that she still needed to make sense of.

4.

Piece by piece, she worked to assemble a coherent picture of recent events. Again she lived the visit to Bughunt. Again the escape from Orsted Station and then the long trip to Cordova and the battle that followed.

The Casaba-Howitzer had exploded. That much she felt sure of. And somehow—*somehow*—the Seed had salvaged something of her consciousness, and that of Carr and Qwon, from amid the nuclear inferno.

She was . . . Kira Navárez. But she was also so much more. She was part Carr, part Qwon, and also part the Seed.

For a lock seemed to have opened in her mind, and she realized there was a storehouse of knowledge she now had access to—knowledge from the Seed. Knowledge from the time of the Vanished. Only, that wasn't what they had called themselves. Rather, they thought of themselves as . . . the Old Ones. Those who had come before.

In the process of saving her, she and the xeno had finally become fully integrated. But there was more to it, and this too she now understood: there were layers to the Seed's abilities, and most of them remained walled off, inaccessible until the xeno reached a certain size (which she had now far exceeded).

So she who had once been just Kira and was now far more, far greater, hung there in the blackness of space, and she thought, and studied, and contemplated the branching possibilities that lay before her. The path had grown tangled as a thicket, but she knew that the Seed's guiding principle would help guide her, for it was her own principle as well: life was sacred. Every part of their moral code rested upon that fundamental principle. Life was sacred, and it was her duty to protect it and, where reasonable, disseminate it.

While she pondered, she noticed how the ships in the system arrayed themselves: human on one axis, Wranaui on another, and as much as they kept their weapons aimed at her, they kept an equal amount aimed at each other: two fleets facing off, with her in the middle. The cease-fire was an uneasy one. Even with the death of the great and mighty Ctein, it would take little to reignite the flames of war. The two species had had nothing but the Maw to bind them together and both were, at heart, ruthless, bloodthirsty, and expansionist. That much she knew from her life as Kira, and also from her life as Shoal Leader Nmarhl.

Then too, she felt responsible for the war. Her that was Carr and Qwon. Her that had been the Maw and its offspring. Her that now floated in orbit around the Cordovan star.

And she knew that more of her unfortunate offspring moved among the stars, spreading terror, pain, and death among the humans and Wranaui. And her that was Kira felt fear for her family. Nor was that all: she remembered the planet the Maw had infested, an entire sphere of living things, transformed into service of the misguided flesh. Machines there were too, and ships also, and all sorts of dangerous devices.

The thought distressed her.

She wanted . . . peace, in all its forms. She wanted to give the gift of life, that both humans and Wranaui might stand together and breathe air that smelled of green and good and not metal and misery.

She knew then what she needed to do.

"Watch, and do not interfere," she said to the waiting fleets.

First the most painful part. She drew upon what had been the hidden knowledge of the Seed and transmitted a powerful signal from the system. Not a cry, not a plea, but a command. A killing command, directed at the makings of the Maw. Upon reception, it would unknit the cells of the Corrupted, disassemble their bodies, and reduce them to the organic compounds that comprised them. What the Seed had made, it could unmake.

A cleansing was necessary, and she could think of no faster way to stop the violence and suffering. The task had fallen to her, and she would not shy from the work, however sorrowful.

With that done, she formed agents of her flesh and sent them forth to the damaged ships that floated abandoned around the planet the Wranaui had been mining. Other parts of herself she dispatched to the bands of asteroids, with the goal of extracting the materials she needed.

While the drones pursued their function, she set to work upon the main body of her flesh, restructuring it to fit her intention. Around her core, she formed an armored sphere that served to protect what remained of her original body. From that, she extruded polished black panels designed to absorb every ray of sunlight that struck them. Power. She needed power if she were to accomplish her goal. The Seed had plenty of its own, but not enough for what she had in mind.

What mind? No mind... She laughed to herself, a quiet song in space.

Drawing upon the Seed's banks of encoded knowledge, she began to build the needed machines, constructing them from the atomic level up. With energy gathered from the panels, she sparked a burning sun inside herself: a fusion reactor large enough to drive the biggest UMC battleship. With energy from the artificial star, she started to manufacture antimatter—far more than the inefficient techniques of the humans or the Wranaui allowed for. The Old Ones had mastered the means of antimatter production before either species had even come into being. And with antimatter as fuel, she built a modified torque engine that allowed her to twist the fabric of the universe and siphon energy directly from FTL space. Which was, as she had come to understand, how the Seed powered itself.

As her agents took possession of the damaged ships, they sometimes found wounded humans or Wranaui forgotten upon the vessels. The wounded often attacked, but she ignored their attacks and tended to their injuries, despite any protestations, before sending the abandoned crew off to their kind in escape pods taken from the ships or that she made herself.

When the drones returned with ships and stones in tow, Kira devoured the materials they contained—much as the Maw would have—and added them to the structures taking shape around her.

The watching fleets grew nervous at this, and several of the vessels flashed her with powerful signals in an attempt to talk with her.

"*Wait,*" she said. And they did, although both humans and Wranaui retreated even farther, leaving a wide berth of space around her.

With energy and mass to spare, Kira put all her efforts into construction. The endeavor was not purely mechanical; along with beams and braces and metal girders, she allowed the Seed to create special chambers that it filled with an organic soup—heated bioreactors that began to produce the living materials needed for the finished product: woods stronger than any steel; seeds and buds and eggs and more besides; vines that crawled and clung and could transmit electricity as efficiently as copper cable; fungal superconductors; and a whole ecosystem of flora and fauna drawn from the Seed's vast experience, and which it and Kira believed would work in a harmonious whole.

She moved quickly, but her efforts took time. Days passed, and still the fleets sat waiting and watching, and still she built.

From her central core grew four enormous struts that extended forward, backward, left, and right, so that they made a cross with arms of equal length.

She extended the cross, meter after meter, until each strut was three and a half kilometers long and thick enough to fly a cruiser through. Then she set the Seed to joining the tips of the cross with a great equatorial ring, and from the end of each strut, a rib began to grow both up and down and curving inward, as if hugging the surface of an invisible orb.

The Seed was so large by then that Kira could hardly imagine being confined to a body the size of a human or a Wranaui. Her consciousness encompassed the whole of the structure, and she was aware of every part of it at every moment. It was, she imagined, much how a ship mind must feel. The substance of her self expanded to match the demands of the sensory input, and with that expansion came a breadth of thought she had never before experienced.

Construction was yet ongoing, but she was no longer willing to wait. Time had grown short indeed. Besides, all who watched could see what she had set out to make: a space station greater in size than any that human or Wranaui had built. Parts of it were metallic grey, but most of it was green and red, reflecting the organic material that made up the bulk of the station. It was a living thing, as much as any person, and Kira knew it would continue to grow and evolve for decades, if not centuries to come.

But, like all gardens, it needed tending.

She put her attention into several chambers close to her core, sealed them from the vacuum, filled them with air hospitable to both humans and Wranaui, gave them gravity suitable for either species, and finished them in a style that seemed fitting. To that end, she combined elements of design from the Wranaui, the Old Ones, and the part of her that was Kira, from each choosing what was most to her liking.

At her command, a pair of agents brought her the hardened core of what had once been Ctein. The great and mighty Ctein. The Wranaui would not care what happened to it—they were indifferent to bodies—but she did. She took the blackened remnants and again remade the substance of its flesh by converting the leaden pillars into seven shards of gleaming crystal, blue-white and dazzling to behold. Each crystal she set within a different chamber, there to serve as a warning, a remembrance, and a symbol of renewal.

Then finally she broke her silence. *"Admiral Klein, Shoal Leader Lphet, I wish to speak to you. Come. Meet me here. Falconi, you also, and . . . bring Trig with you."*

CHAPTER II

* * * * * * *

UNITY

1.

Kira watched as the three spaceships drew near: the UMCS *Unrelenting Force,* the SLV *Wallfish,* and a battle-scarred Wranaui vessel whose name, when translated, was *Swift Currents Beneath Silent Waves.*

Each of the ships was massively different in appearance. The *Unrelenting Force* was long and thick, with numerous hard points along its hull for lasers, missile launchers, and railguns. It was painted a dark, matte grey, which stood in stark contrast to the glittering, silver-laced diamond of its radiators. The *Wallfish* was far shorter and smaller, stubby even, its hull a familiar brown, scuffed and pitted by years of impacts from micrometeoroids, and with a large hole where the Wranaui had cut into one cargo hold. Like the UMC battleship, the *Wallfish* had the fins of its radiators deployed, many of which had been broken. Last of all, there was the Wranaui ship, a polished, shell-white orb marred only by a blaster burn smeared across its prow.

The three ships used RCS thrusters to slow themselves as they approached the docking ports Kira had grown for them. In the velvet background, swarms of her drones flew past, busy as bees. Her attention was as much with them as with her visitors, but Kira couldn't help but feel a strange tilting sensation in her core.

Was that *unease*? It surprised her. Even with everything she had become, she still wondered what Falconi would think of her.

And not just Falconi. When the airlock to the *Wallfish* opened, the entire crew came trooping out, including Nielsen—still wearing a bandage around her ribs—and the Entropist, Veera. They brought with them Trig's cryo tube, mounted on a rolling pallet, which pleased Kira to see.

The *Unrelenting Force* disgorged Admiral Klein . . . and with him an entire troop of UMCN Marines in full power armor. Likewise, a group of armed Wranaui accompanied Lphet as the shoal leader left its ship. Nearscent of concern and curiosity emanated from the graspers. Among them was Itari, and also a single human: Major Tschetter, her expression unreadable as ever.

"This way," Kira said, and lit a line of emerald lights down the corridor facing them.

Both the humans and the Wranaui followed her lead. She watched from the walls and the floors and the ceiling, for she was all of those and more. Falconi looked uncertain of himself, but she was glad to see that he seemed whole and healthy and that his shoulder injury no longer pained him. Klein showed no emotion, but his eyes darted from side to side, watching for anything unexpected.

Aside from the Marines, all the humans were wearing skinsuits with helmets firmly attached. The Wranaui, as usual, made no concessions to the environment, trusting their current forms to protect them.

As the visitors entered the presence chamber she had created to receive them, Kira shifted her view back to the flesh she had formed for herself, that Klein, Lphet, and Falconi would have an image of her to look at. It seemed the polite thing to do.

The chamber was high and narrow, with an arched ceiling and a double row of columns grown of *nnar,* the coral-like excrescence she knew of from Qwon (and was fond of because). Walls were framed with spars of polished metal, dark grey and adorned with lines of blue that formed patterns of meaning known only to the Old Ones . . . and now her. Filling the frames were great curving sections of wood and vines and dark-leafed greenery.

And those were from her that was Kira. Also the flowers that rested in crannies dark and shadowed: drooping flowers, with purple petals and speckled throats. Midnight Constellations, in memory of her home and of Alan—of all that she had once been.

She had repeated the shape of the flowers on the floor, in fractal spirals that coiled without end. And the sight pleased her, gave her a sense of satisfaction.

Among the spirals stood one of the crystals she had made of Ctein: a frozen flame of faceted beauty. Life arrested, yet still reaching and yearning.

A few glowlights hung from the branches of *nnar* above, ripened fruit pulsing with a soft, golden ambience. In the broken beams of light that reached the floor, pollen swirled like smoke, heavy and fragrant. A trickle of running water sounded amid the pitted columns, but otherwise the chamber was still and silent, sacred.

Kira made no demands, issued no ultimatums, but Klein spoke a single word to his troops, and the Marines held their position by the arched entryway as the admiral continued forward. Lphet did the same with its guard (including Itari), and human and Wranaui advanced with Major Tschetter and the crew of the *Wallfish* in tow.

As they neared the far end of the presence chamber, Kira allowed the glowlights to brighten, banishing the shadows before a rising dawn so they might behold her.

The visitors stopped.

She looked down upon them from where her new body lay embedded within the rootlike structure of the wall, green upon green and threaded throughout with the glossy black fibers of the Seed, the wonderous, life-giving Seed.

"Welcome," said Kira, and it felt strange to speak with a mouth and tongue. Stranger still to hear the voice that came forth: a voice that was deeper than she remembered and that contained hints and echoes of both Carr and Qwon.

"Oh, Kira," said Nielsen. "What have you done?" Through her visor, her expression was one of worry.

"You okay?" Falconi asked, brows drawn together in his habitual scowl.

Admiral Klein cleared his throat. "Ms. Navárez—"

"Welcome," said Kira, and smiled. Or at least she tried; she wasn't sure if she remembered how. "I have asked you here, Admiral Klein, and you, Shoal Leader Lphet, to act as representatives for both humans and Jellies."

[[Lphet here: I am no longer shoal leader, Idealis.]] And Tschetter translated the Wranaui's words for the humans listening.

"How then shall I address you, Lphet?" Kira spoke in both English and nearscent, that all might understand.

[[Lphet here: As the great and mighty Lphet.]]

A faint prickle passed along the spines of the station, as a breath of cold wind along Kira's back. "You have taken the place of Ctein, now that Ctein is dead." It was not a question.

The tentacles of the Wranaui flushed red and white and rubbed together in a prideful gesture. [[Lphet here: That is correct, Idealis. Every Arm of the Wranaui is now mine to command.]]

Admiral Klein shifted his weight. He seemed to be growing impatient. "What is all this about, Navárez? Why have you brought us here? What are you building and why?"

She laughed slightly, a musical sound similar to the trickle of a mossy creek.

"Why? For this that I shall tell you. Humans and Jellies will fight as long as they have no common ground. The nightmares, the Corrupted, provided a shared enemy, but that enemy is now gone."

[[Lphet here: Are you sure of that, Idealis?]]

She understood what Lphet was really asking: Was the Maw truly gone? Was she/it still a threat? "Yes, I can promise you that. The suit I am bonded with, which you know as the Idealis, and you Admiral Klein know as the Soft Blade, shall not cause such problems again. Also, I have sent a command to the Corrupted outside this system. When it reaches them, they will cease to be a threat to any living creature."

The admiral looked doubtful. "How so? Do you mean—"

"I mean," said Kira, her voice echoing above them, "that I have unmade the Corrupted. You no longer need worry about them."

"You killed them," said Nielsen in a subdued tone. The others seemed pleased and troubled in equal measure.

Kira bent her neck. "There was no other choice. But the issue remains: humans and Jellies will never stay allies without reason. Well, I have provided the reason. I have made this common ground."

"This?" said Klein, looking around at the chamber. "This place?"

She smiled again. The expression was easier the second time. "It is a space station, Admiral. Not a ship. Not a weapon. A home. I made it much as the Old Ones—the Vanished—would have. In their tongue, it would be called Mar Íneth. In ours, it is Unity."

"Unity," said Klein, appearing to chew on the word.

Kira nodded as best she could. "This is a place for coming together, Admiral. It is a living, breathing thing that will continue to grow and blossom with time. There are rooms fit for humans, and rooms for Jellies. Other creatures will live here also, caretakers that will tend to Unity's many parts."

Tschetter spoke then, on her own. "You want us to use this station as an embassy, is that it?"

"More than that," said Kira, "as a hub for our two races. There will be enough space for millions to live here. Maybe more. All who come be welcome as long as they keep the peace. If the idea still gives you unease, then think of this: I have built Unity with means and methods that not even the Jellies understand. I will allow those who stay here to study the station . . . and to study me. That alone ought to be incentive enough."

Admiral Klein seemed troubled. He crossed his arms and sucked on the inside of his cheek for a moment. "And what guarantee do we have that this xeno won't go rogue again and kill everyone on board?"

A ripple of purple ran the length of Lphet's tentacles: an offended response. [[Lphet here: The Idealis has already given their promise, two-form. Your concern is unwarranted.]]

"Oh is it?" said Klein. "The millions, if not billions, of people the nightmares killed say otherwise."

[[Lphet here: You do not—]]

Kira rustled the leaves along the walls, and the soft susurration stopped the conversation, made everyone freeze and then look back at her. "I can give you no guarantees, Admiral Klein, but you have seen how I have helped and healed the members of your fleet that I've found."

He cocked his head. "That's true."

"Sometimes you just have to trust on faith, Admiral. Sometimes you have to take a chance."

"It's a hell of a chance, Navárez."

Tschetter looked over at him. "Not having a relationship with the Jellies would be worse."

A sour expression formed on Klein's face. "That doesn't mean that *here* is the right place to set up diplomatic relations, and there's no way in hell civilians should be allowed anywhere *near* Cordova. Not until Intelligence has a chance to go over it with a fine-toothed comb. Besides, I don't have the authority to negotiate this sort of an agreement. You're going to have to deal with the League, Kira, not me, and that's going to take time. My guess is they'll want to send someone out here to talk with you face to face. That means at least another month and a half before any of this can be settled."

She didn't argue but looked at the Wranaui. [[Kira here: What say you, great and mighty Lphet?]]

A blossom of red and orange passed across the nearby Wranaui. [[Lphet here: The Arms would be honored to accept your offer, Idealis. The opportunity to study a making such as this is one we have not had in this or any other ripple. Tell us how many Wranaui may stay upon this station, and I shall send for them at once.]]

As Tschetter translated, Klein set his jaw. "Is that so? . . . Fine. The League can sort out the details later, but I'll be damned if I'm letting the Jellies get the jump on us. However many personnel they post here, I want clearance to bring over just as many of my own people."

This time, Kira knew better than to smile. "Of course, Admiral. I do have a condition, though."

His stance stiffened. "And what's that, Navárez?"

"This goes for everyone who wants to live on or visit Unity: no weapons allowed. If you bring them on board, I will destroy them and expel you."

[[Lphet here: Of course, Idealis. We will obey your wishes.]]

Klein cocked his head. "What about, say, repair bots? Or service lasers? In the right hands, even a fork could be a deadly weapon."

Humans. "Use common sense, Admiral. I'll allow power armor, as long as it is disarmed. But make no mistake, if anyone starts a fight on this station, human or Jelly, I *will* put an end to it." And her voice deepened until it echoed from the walls, as if all of Unity were her throat. In a way, it was.

Even under his spacer's tan, Klein's cheeks grew pale. "Point taken. You won't have any trouble from my crews, Navárez. You have my word."

[[Lphet here: Nor from the forms loyal to the Arms.]]

Kira allowed them to feel her pleasure then, in the color and brightness of the glowlights, in the happy trill of the water, and in the comforting rustle of the leaves. "Then it is settled." Satisfied, she shifted her attention to Falconi and the crew of the *Wallfish,* and she looked at each of them in turn.

Sparrow scratched at her side through her skinsuit. "Shit, Kira, you sure don't do anything halfway, do you?"

"Sparrow."

Then Vishal spoke up. "How did you survive, Ms. Kira? We thought for sure the Casaba-Howitzer had killed you."

At that, Admiral Klein appeared even more uncomfortable. It was he who had authorized the detonation, Kira felt sure. But she didn't care. Assigning blame wouldn't do any good at this point, and besides, setting off the Casaba-Howitzer had been the logical choice. The Maw *had* to be stopped.

Bemused, she said, "I think perhaps it did. For a time, at least."

A grunt came from Hwa-jung, and with a quick motion of her hand, the machine boss made the sign of the cross. "Are you, you?"

A disjointed memory flashed through Kira's reconstituted brain: *a grey holding cell; a mirrored window; cold grating beneath her knees; a holo flickering to life in front of her, and Major Tschetter standing before her in a grey uniform. And the major saying, "Do you still feel like yourself?"*

A small chuckle escaped Kira. "Yes . . . and no. I'm something more than I was."

The machine boss's eyes bored into her, hot as thermal lances. "No. Are you, *you*, Kira? Here," she tapped her sternum, "where it matters. Is your soul still the same?"

Kira thought. "My soul? I don't know how to answer that question, Hwa-jung. But what I want now is the same thing I wanted *before:* that is, peace, and for life to flourish. Does that mean I'm the same person? . . . Maybe. Maybe not. Change is not always a bad thing."

Still, Hwa-jung seemed troubled. "No, it is not. And what you say is good, Kira, but do not forget what it means to be human."

"Forgetting is very much what I *don't* want to do," said Kira. At that, the machine boss seemed, if not happy, at least satisfied.

Then Kira shifted her gaze to Veera. The Entropist stood with her forearms clasped across her chest, hands tucked into the voluminous sleeves of her gradient robes. The woman had bruised circles under her eyes, and her cheeks were gaunt, as if from a great sickness.

"My condolences, Questant Veera, for the loss of your partner. We . . . understand."

The Entropist pressed her lips together, nodded, and bowed low. "Thank you, Prisoner Kira. Your concern is comforting."

Kira inclined her head in return. "Prisoner no more, Questant."

Surprise widened the Entropist's features. "What? That isn't . . . How do you mean?"

But Kira did not answer. Instead, she looked again at Falconi. "Salvo."

"Kira," he replied, somber.

"You brought Trig."

"Of course."

"Do you trust us, Salvo?"

He hesitated and then nodded. "I wouldn't have brought the kid if I didn't."

That warmed the center of Kira's being. Again she smiled. It was fast becoming her favorite expression. "Then trust me once more."

From the fractal floor, she sent a thicket of tendrils—green this time, not black—sprouting up around Trig's cryo tube. Sparrow and Hwa-jung cursed and jumped away from the tube, while at the back of the chamber, the ranks of armored Marines stiffened and lifted their weapons.

"Put those down!" Klein barked. "At ease!"

Kira's smile never wavered as the tendrils twined around Trig's tube, encasing it in a twisting, squirming embrace—burying it beneath the mass of greenery.

"Kira," said Nielsen, in a soft tone. Not warning, not angry, but concerned.

"Trust me," she said. By means of the vines that were her limbs, she reached into the cryo tube and ran a thousand different threads into Trig's damaged flesh, seeking the source of his injuries. *There.* A collection of burned cells, torn muscles, bruised and damaged tendons, ruptured blood vessels, and severed nerves—the insults to his body were as easy for her to feel as the internal structure of the station.

How could she have ever found this hard? The thought seemed inconceivable.

Then she poured the needed energy into Trig's frozen form, guided the Seed as it worked to repair his wounds. When all seemed right, she removed the respirator from his mouth and disconnected the tubes from his arms, separating him from the machine that had kept him in suspended animation for over half a year.

Slowly, carefully, she warmed his body, treating it as gently as a mother hen would a newly laid egg. She felt the heat of his metabolism increase like a kindling fire rising to full flame until, at last, he took his first, unsupported breath.

She released him then. The vines retracted into the floor to reveal Trig's pale form curled in a fetal shape, bare except for a pair of grey thermal shorts of the sort worn under skinsuits. He gasped, like a drowning man coming to the surface, and hacked up a gob of spit. It melted away, as if it had never existed.

"Trig!" exclaimed Nielsen, and she and Vishal bent over the kid. Sparrow, Hwa-jung, and Falconi crowded in close, watching.

"Wh—Where am I?" Trig said. His voice was weak, hoarse.

"That is somewhat hard to explain," said Vishal.

Falconi shrugged off his vest and draped it over the kid's shoulders. "Here, this'll help keep you warm."

"Huh? Why are you all wearing skinsuits? Where *am* I?" Then Sparrow moved out of the way, and Trig saw Kira, suspended as she was in the wall. His mouth dropped open. "That . . . *you,* Kira?"

"Welcome back," she said, and her voice blossomed with warmth. "We weren't sure you were going to make it."

Trig looked around the pillared chamber. His eyes showed white. "Is all this yours?"

"It is."

The kid tried to get to his feet, but his knees buckled and he would have fallen if Hwa-jung hadn't caught him by the arm. "Careful," she rumbled.

"I . . . I . . ." Trig shook his head. Then he looked at Falconi with a plaintive expression. "Are we still at Bughunt?"

"No," said Falconi. "That we aren't. Let's get you back to the *Wallfish* and have the doc check you out, and then you can rest up and we'll fill you in on everything you've missed."

"It's been exciting," Sparrow said in a dry tone.

"Yessir. Rest sounds pretty darn nice right now. Feels like I got worked over by a couple of guys with hammers. I—" The kid's words cut off as he saw Lphet and, by the back of the chamber, the rest of the Wranaui. He yelped and attempted to scramble backwards, but Hwa-jung grabbed him by the arm again, held him in place. "J-j-jellies! Comeon, we gotta—"

"We know," said Nielsen in a soothing voice. "It's okay. Trig, stop, look at me. It's okay. Take a breath, calm down. We're all friends here."

The kid hesitated, glancing between them as if uncertain what to believe. Then Sparrow gave him a light punch on the shoulder. "As I said, it's been exciting."

"That's one way to put it," muttered Falconi. "Nielsen's right, though. We're all friends here." His gaze darted toward Kira for an instant before returning to the kid.

Trig relaxed then and stopped pulling against Hwa-jung. "Yessir. Sorry sir."

"Perfectly understandable," said Falconi, and patted him on the back.

Then Kira shifted her attention back to her other guests. "Admiral Klein, great and mighty Lphet, you have seen what I can do. If you have any other crew members who are wounded—wounded beyond your ability to heal—bring them here, and I will do for them what I did for Trig."

[[Lphet here: Your generosity is without equal, Idealis, but those of the Wranaui who are hurt beyond repair will transfer to new forms rather than suffer with an injury.]]

"As you wish."

A deep furrow appeared between Klein's eyebrows. "That's a damn kind offer, Navárez, but biocontainment protocol doesn't allow for—"

"Biocontainment protocol," said Kira in a gentle voice, "has already been well and truly broken. Wouldn't you agree, Admiral?"

His scowl deepened. "You may have a point, but the League would court-martial me if I violated quarantine like that."

"You must have run tests on the men and women I already healed."

"Of course."

"And?"

"Nothing," growled Klein. "The techs can't find a damned thing wrong with them."

"So there you go."

He shook his head. "No, we don't. The *Extenuating Circumstances* couldn't find anything wrong with you either before the xeno came out of you. So forgive me if I'm somewhat less than *blasé* about the situation, Navárez."

She smiled, but this time less out of pleasure than a desire to appear unthreatening. "The League holds no sway here, Admiral, nor shall it. I am claiming this system for myself, for Unity, and neither the League nor the Jellies shall dictate laws here. While you are under my protection, you are a free man, Admiral—free to make whatever choices your conscience dictates."

"A free man." He snorted and shook his head. "You have some gall, Navárez."

"Maybe. I made my offer not out of consideration for *you*, Admiral, but for your crews. If you have men or women who are suffering, whom you can't heal, I can help. That is all. The decision is yours."

Then she looked past him, at the Wranaui near the back of the chamber. "Itari, it is good to see you unharmed. I am grateful for the help you provided on the *Battered Hierophant*."

A ripple of bright colors passed across the Wranaui's tentacles. [[Itari here: It pleases this one to have been of use.]]

Kira returned her gaze to the forefront. "Great and mighty Lphet, without Itari's service during recent events, we might never have defeated Ctein. As a favor to me, I ask that you grant Itari hatching rights, as well as a choice of whatever form it wishes to have."

Nearscent of agreement reached her. [[Lphet here: Your request is reasonable, Idealis. It will be done.]]

And Itari turned blue and purple. [[Itari here: Thank you, Idealis.]]

Kira responded with pleasant nearscent of her own. Then she shifted her attention to the rest of her guests. "I have said what needed saying. Now, I must return to my work. Leave me, and I shall send for you when I am ready to talk again."

Admiral Klein gave a sharp nod, turned on his heel, and marched toward the back of the chamber. Lphet paused to make a sign of courtesy with its tentacles—a wriggle and a flash of color that Kira recognized from Qwon's memories—and followed suit. Last of all, the crew of the *Wallfish* departed also, but not before Falconi gave her one more look and said, "Are you going to be okay, Kira?"

She gazed down at him with fondness, and the whole chamber seemed to bend toward him. "I'm going to be fine, Salvo. Absolutely fine. All is well." And she meant it with her entire being.

"Alright then," he said. But he did not appear convinced.

2.

With her visitors departed, Kira returned to the work of building out the station. Lphet's promised Wranaui soon arrived, and she guided them to their watery quarters. Directly afterward, Klein sent over a contingent of UMC researchers. Those too she provided housing within the frame of her expanding body, and she offered them fruit grown of Mar Íneth. But while the researchers accepted the fruit, they did not taste of it, and they kept their skinsuits on at all times, which she knew was no small discomfort. No matter. It was not her place to force them to trust. The Wranaui were less concerned for their safety and gladly partook of her hospitality, either because of their history with the Seed and its kin or because of their disregard for individual bodies. Kira wasn't sure which.

Along with the Wranaui came Tschetter. When Kira asked the woman why she had not rejoined the UMC, she said, "After all the time I spent with the Jellies, UMCI would never allow me to have my old job back. As far as they're concerned, I've been irrevocably compromised."

"So what will you do?" Kira asked.

The once-major gestured at the station around her. "Work as a liaison between humans and Jellies, try to avoid another war. Lphet has chosen me to serve as a translator and facilitator with the UMC and the League, and Admiral Klein has agreed to the same." She shrugged. "I think I might be able to do some good here. Ambassador Tschetter; it has a nice ring to it, don't you think?"

Kira did. And it heartened her to see the hope Tschetter had in her new work, as well as the woman's optimism for their shared future.

Outside the station, ships continued to gather: human, Wranaui, and those Kira had built to bring her supplies from throughout Cordova. They clustered around her like bees around a flower full of nectar, and she felt a sense of pride when she looked at them.

A signal beam flashed toward her from the *Wallfish*. Out of curiosity, she answered, and the familiar sound of Gregorovich's voice filled her hidden ears:

Greetings, O Meatsack. Now you are as I am. How do you like being bounded in this particular nutshell?

"I have transcended the nutshell, ship mind."

Oh-ho! A bold claim, that.

"It is true," she said. Then: "How do you manage to keep track of everything that is yourself? There's so . . . much."

His answer was surprisingly sober: **It takes time, O Queen of Thorns. Time and work. Do not make any hasty judgments until you are sure of yourself. After I transitioned, it took a year and a half before I knew who the new me was.** He giggled, ruining his serious air. **Not that I ever really know who I am. Who does, hmm? We change as circumstances change, like wisps blown on the wind.**

She thought on that for a time. "Thank you, Gregorovich."

Of course, station mind. Whenever you need to talk, call, and I will listen.

Kira took his advice seriously. Even as she labored on Unity, she redoubled her efforts to sort through the mess of memories strewn throughout her reconstituted brain, struggling to pin down and identify which ones belonged to which parts of herself. Struggling to figure out who exactly she was. She paid particular attention to the memories of the Maw, and it was while studying them that she made a discovery that filled her with cold dread.

Oh no.

For she remembered. Before coming to Cordova-1420, the Maw had taken precautions against its possible defeat (unlikely as that seemed). It had, in the darkest depths of interstellar space, formed seven avatars from its flesh and the flesh of the Seed—seven living, thinking, self-directed copies of itself. And the Maw had sent off its virulent, wrath-filled clones with no knowledge of where they might ultimately go.

Kira thought of the killing command she had broadcast before. *Surely that would . . .* But then, from the Seed, she felt an unshakable conviction that the command would not stop the Maw's avatars, for they *were* the Seed—twisted and broken as the Maw had been, but still of the same underlying substance.

Unlike the Corrupted, she could not unmake the Maw's poisonous spawn with a single line, just as she could not have unmade the Maw. The Seed did not possess such power over itself. The Old Ones had not seen fit to give their creations that ability, preferring to keep it for themselves in the shape of the Staff of Blue.

But the staff was broken, and Kira knew that even if she had the pieces, she could not repair it. The knowledge was not in her, and that too was the Old Ones' doing.

They had, she decided, been overconfident in their supremacy.

Her dread deepened as she pondered the situation. The Maw's offspring would spread their evil wherever they went, blanketing planets with Corrupted, converting or overwriting any existing life. The seven represented an existential threat to every other being in the galaxy. . . . Their legacy would be one of misery—the exact opposite of everything the Seed was supposed to embody.

The thought haunted her.

With a sense of regret, Kira realized her afterlife was not to be as she'd imagined. The Maw was her responsibility, and so too were the seven deadly darts it had let loose among the stars.

CHAPTER III

* * * * * * *

DECESSION

1.

Kira acted without hesitation. Time was short, and she had no intention of wasting it.

To the ships assembled around her, she said, "Stand clear." A scramble of activity followed as the captains pulled their ships back.

Then she ignited thrusters along the ribs of the station and began to move it, slowly and ponderously, toward the planet the Wranaui had been mining. The UMC had called it R1, but Kira thought it deserved a proper name. She would leave it to the people living on Unity to name it, though. It was their right as the inhabitants of the system.

Both Lphet and Admiral Klein signaled her as the station started to shift its position. **Navárez, what are you doing?** Klein asked.

"Taking up high orbit around R1," she said. "It will be a better location for Unity."

Roger that, Navárez. We'll secure your flight path. Next time, some warning would be appreciated.

[[Lphet here: Do you require any assistance, Idealis?]]

"None at the moment."

2.

Moving Unity took several days. Kira used that time to make the preparations she needed. And when she had settled the station into its final orbit, she summoned the crew of the *Wallfish* to her once again.

They came without delay. The old, ramshackle ship docked near her central hub, and Kira saw that most of the damage the *Wallfish* had sustained had been repaired (though several of its radiators were still little more than needle-tipped shards).

The crew chattered amongst themselves with nervous excitement as they walked her hallways, but they kept the external speakers to their skinsuits turned off, and the moving of their lips was the only obvious giveaway. But she was curious, and she bathed their visors with an invisible wash of collimated light, which allowed her to read the vibrations of their voices.

"—idea what she wants?" said Trig. He sounded excited.

Falconi grunted. "You've asked that three times now."

"Sorry." The kid sounded slightly abashed.

Then Nielsen said, "Klein was pretty clear about what we're supposed to—"

"I don't give two shits what the brass thinks," said Sparrow. "This is Kira we're talking about. Not a Jelly, not a nightmare, Kira."

"Are you sure about that?" Falconi asked.

A moment of silence followed. Then Sparrow thumped her chest with her fist. "Yeah. She's got our back. She healed Trig, after all."

"And we're still being quarantined as a result," said Falconi.

Hwa-jung smiled slightly. "Life is never perfect."

At that, the captain laughed, as did Nielsen.

Kira returned her sight and hearing to her remade body as the crew entered her presence chamber. They stopped before her, and she smiled down upon them. A slow fall of petals drifted from above, pink and white and smelling of warm perfume. "Welcome," she said.

Falconi inclined his head. A wry smile flickered about his mouth. "Don't know why, but feels like I should be bowing to you."

"Please don't," she said. "You shouldn't have to bow to anyone or anything. You're not servants, and you're certainly not slaves."

"Damn right," said Sparrow, and gave Kira a small salute.

Then Kira looked at Trig. "How are you feeling?"

The kid shrugged, trying to appear nonchalant. His cheeks had regained a healthy color. "Pretty good. I just can't believe all the stuff I missed."

"It's not the worst thing. If I could have slept through the past six months, I would have too."

"Yeah, I know. You're probably right, but jeez. Jumping off the maglev on Orsted! That must have been pretty exciting."

Sparrow snorted. "You could say that. Damn near suicidal would be the other way."

The kid flashed a quick grin before growing more serious. "But yeah, thanks again for patching me up, Kira. Really."

"I'm just happy I could help," she said, and the chamber seemed to glow in response. Then she shifted her focus to Vishal. He was standing next to Nielsen, their shoulders nearly touching. "Was there anything with Trig that I overlooked? Any problems that I might have caused?"

"I feel fine!" the kid proclaimed, puffing out his chest.

The doctor shook his head. "Trig appears to be the very picture of health. His bloodwork and neural responses could not be improved even if I tried."

Falconi nodded. "Seriously, we owe you, Kira. If there's anything we can do for you—"

The leaves interrupted him with a stir of disapproval. "Seeing as how none of this would have happened if not for me," she said, "consider us even."

He chuckled. It was good to hear him laugh again. "Fair enough."

Trig hopped from foot to foot. He looked as if he were going to burst with excitement. "Tell her," he said, looking at Vishal and Nielsen. "Come on! Or I'll tell her!"

"Tell me what?" Kira asked, curious.

Nielsen made a face, seeming embarrassed.

"You're not going to believe this," Falconi said.

Then Vishal took Nielsen's hand and stepped forward. "Ms. Kira, I have an announcement to make. Ms. Audrey and I have gotten engaged. And she asked me, Ms. Kira. *Me!*"

Nielsen blushed and laughed softly. "It's true," she said, and she looked at the doctor with a warmth Kira had never seen from her before.

Few things could now surprise Kira. Not the turning of the stars, not the decay of atomic nuclei, not the seemingly random quantum fluctuations that underlay reality as it appeared. But this surprised her, although—in retrospect—she supposed it wasn't entirely unexpected.

"Congratulations," she said with all the heartfelt emotion she could summon. The happiness of two beings might be a small thing when compared with the immensity of the universe, but what, ultimately, was more important? Suffering was inescapable, but to care for another and to be cared for in turn—that was the closest any person might come to heaven.

Vishal bobbed his head. "Thank you, Ms. Kira. We won't get married until we can have a proper wedding, with my mother and sisters and lots of guests and food with—"

"Well, we'll see," said Nielsen with a small smile.

The doctor returned the smile and put an arm around her shoulders. "Yes, we do not want to wait *too* long, do we? We've even talked about someday buying a cargo vessel and starting a shipping company of our own, Ms. Kira!"

"Whatever we do, we'll do it together," said Nielsen. And she kissed him on his shaved cheek, and he kissed her back.

Falconi went to scratch his chin, and his fingers bumped against his visor. "To hell with it," he growled, and unlocked and pulled off the helmet.

"Captain!" said Hwa-jung, sounding scandalized.

He waved his hand. "It's fine." Then he scratched his chin, and the sound of his nails rasping against his stubble carried throughout the presence chamber. "As you can tell, we're all in a bit of shock, but they, uh, seem pretty happy, so we're happy."

"Yeah," said Trig, sounding glum. He glanced toward the first officer and released a small sigh.

Falconi sniffed the air. "Smells nice," he said.

Kira smiled, sweeter than before. "I try."

"Okay," said Sparrow, rolling her shoulders as if she were about to lift a heavy weight. "Why'd you call us here, Kira? Just to chitchat? Doesn't seem like you, say sorry."

"Yes, I'm rather curious about that myself," said Falconi. He rubbed a finger against one of the trunk-like pillars and then held it up before his face to examine the residue.

Kira took a deep breath. She didn't need to, but doing so helped center her thoughts. "I asked you to come for two reasons. First to tell you a truth about the Maw."

"Go on," said Falconi, wary.

So she did. She told them the secret of the seven evil seeds that she had discovered amid the Maw's memories. As she spoke, she watched as their faces grew pale and their expressions stricken.

"Gods!" Nielsen exclaimed.

"You're saying there are seven *more* of those things wandering around, Thule knows where?" said Sparrow. Even she seemed daunted by the prospect.

Kira closed her eyes for a moment. "Exactly. And the Seeker is still out there also, and I can guarantee it's up to no good. Neither the League nor the Jellies can deal with these sorts of threats. They're just not capable of it. I'm the only one—the *Seed* is the only one—who can stop them."

"So what are you going to do about it?" Falconi said, deadly quiet.

"What I have to, of course. I'm going to hunt them down."

For a time, the only sound in the chamber was the soft fall of petals.

"How?" said Sparrow. "They could be anywhere."

"Not anywhere. And as for how . . . I'd rather not say yet."

"Okay," said Falconi, drawing out the word. "What was the other reason you asked us here then?"

"For the giving of gifts." And Kira lowered herself from the wall and released herself from the mesh of rootlike fibers that had kept her wrapped in a tight embrace. Her feet touched the floor, and for the first time since the *Battered Hierophant,* Kira stood whole and unassisted. Her body was the same green-black material as the walls of the station, and her hair rippled as if in a breeze, but there was no breeze.

"Whoa," said Trig.

Falconi stepped forward, his ice-blue eyes searching her. "Is this really you?"

"It's as much me as anything else in Unity."

"That works," he said, and he caught her in a tight hug, and Kira felt his embrace even on the far struts of the station.

The rest of the crew crowded around, touching, hugging, slapping her (lightly) on the back. "So where's your brain?" asked Trig, his eyes wide with wonder. "Is it in your head? Or is it up there?" He pointed at the wall she'd descended from.

"Trig!" said Hwa-jung. "*Aish*. Show more respect."

"That's okay," said Kira. She touched her temple. "Some is here, but most of it is back there. It wouldn't fit in a normal skull."

"Not so different from a ship mind," said Hwa-jung.

Kira bowed her head. "Not so different."

"Either way, it's good to see you in one piece," said Sparrow.

"Hear, hear," said Nielsen.

"Even if you do look like boiled spinach," Sparrow added with a laugh.

Then Kira took a step back to give herself space. "Listen," she said, and they listened. "I won't be able to help you much from now on, so I want to do what I can while I can."

"You don't have to," said Falconi.

She smiled at him. "If I *had* to, they wouldn't be gifts. . . . Trig, I know you have always been interested in aliens. This, then, is for you."

And from the floor by her feet, a rod of green wood sprouted, and it grew in height until it formed a staff nearly as tall as Trig himself. Near the top, embedded within the braided branches, sat what appeared to be an emerald the size of a robin's egg, and it glowed with an inner light.

Kira grasped the staff, and it came off the floor, into her hand. Small leaves grew from it in places, and the smell of fresh sap suffused the air.

"Here," she said, and handed the length of wood to Trig. "This is not a Staff of Blue, but a Staff of Green. It isn't a weapon, although you may fight with it if you must. There is a part of the Seed in it, and if you care for the staff and treat it well, you will find that you can grow most anything, no matter how barren the soil. You will be able to talk with the Jellies, and wherever you plant the staff, life will flourish. The staff can do other things also, and if you prove yourself a worthy caretaker, you may discover them as well. Do *not* allow the UMC to get their hands on it."

Awe and wonder shone forth from Trig's face. "Thank you," he said. "Thank you, thank you, thank you. I don't even know—Ah, jeez. Thank you!"

"One more thing," Kira said. And she caressed the top of the staff. "Once a day the staff will put forth a fruit. A single, red fruit. It is not much, but it is enough to keep you from ever starving. You will never need worry about food again, Trig."

At that, tears filled Trig's eyes, and he clutched the staff close to himself. "I won't forget this," he mumbled.

Kira expected he wouldn't.

She moved on. "Hwa-jung." From within her side, Kira took two orbs, one white, one brown. Each was just large enough to rest comfortably in the curve of her palm. She gave the brown one to the machine boss. "This is a piece of tech from the Old Ones. You can use it to repair most any machine."

The machine boss sucked on her lower lip as she stared at the orb she now held. "*Aish.* Will it eat the whole of my ship?"

Kira laughed and shook her head. "No, it's not like the Seed. It won't spread uncontrollably. But be careful where you use it, as it may sometimes try to make . . . improvements."

Hwa-jung disappeared the orb into one of the pouches around her waist, and she mumbled her thanks. Red spots appeared on her cheeks, and Kira could tell how much the gift meant to the machine boss.

Pleased, Kira then handed the white orb to the doctor. "Vishal, this is also a piece of tech from the Old Ones. You can use it to repair most any wound. But, be careful where you use it, as it—"

"As it may sometimes make improvements," said Vishal with a gentle smile. "Yes, I understand."

She returned his smile. "Good. It could have saved Trig back at Bughunt. Hopefully you won't ever need it, but if you do . . ."

"If I do, better to have it than not." Vishal placed his hands together, cupping the orb between them, and bowed. "Thank you, Ms. Kira, most sincerely."

Sparrow was next. Reaching down, Kira removed a short, all-black dagger from the side of her thigh and handed it to the shorter woman. The blade of the knife contained a faint, fibrous pattern, similar to the Seed. "This *is* a weapon."

"No shit."

"Metal detectors can't see it: x-rays and microwaves won't pick it up. But that's not what makes this special. This knife can cut through anything."

Sparrow gave her a skeptical look. "Really."

"Really," Kira insisted. "It may take time, but you can cut through even the toughest materials. And no, you don't have to worry about losing control of it, the way I did with the Seed."

Sparrow eyed the dagger with renewed interest. She flipped it around the back of her hand, caught the handle, and then tested the edge on the corner of one of her utility pouches. As promised, the blade sliced clean through the material, and when it did, a slight glimmer of blue ran the length of the edge. "Handy. Thanks. Something like this would have gotten me out of a couple jams in the past."

For Nielsen, Kira had no easy fixes. She said, "Audrey . . . I could solve your condition. The Seed has the ability to reshape any tissue, to recode any gene. But if I did—"

"You would have to change most of my brain," said Nielsen. She smiled sadly. "I know."

"It might *not* alter your personality or your memories, but I can't promise it wouldn't, even though the Seed has no desire to harm you. Quite the opposite."

The first officer took a shuddery breath and then lifted her chin, shook her head. "No. I appreciate the offer, Kira, but no. It's a risk I'd rather avoid. Figuring out who I am wasn't easy, and I'm rather fond of who I've become. Losing that wouldn't be worth it."

"I'm sorry. I wish I could do more."

"It's okay," said Nielsen. "Plenty of people have to deal with a lot worse. I'll be fine."

Vishal hugged her. "Besides, Ms. Kira, I will do my best to help Ms. Audrey. Genetic modifications were always a specialty of mine in school, ah yes." And Nielsen's expression softened, and she hugged him back.

"I'm glad to hear that," said Kira. "Even if I can't heal you, there *is* something I can give you. Several somethings, actually, now that you're engaged."

Nielsen started to protest, but Kira paid her no mind. She knelt and traced two equal circles upon the floor, both no more than four or five centimeters across. Where she touched, gold lines formed, and they glowed brighter and brighter until they were painful to behold.

Then the light broke and faded. In its place lay two rings: gold, green, and laced with sparkles of sapphires. Kira took them and presented them to Nielsen. "For you and Vishal, an early wedding present. You're under no obligation to use these, but if you do, you will find that they have certain advantages."

"They're beautiful," said Nielsen, accepting the rings. "Thank you. But I'm afraid they're both too large for me."

Kira allowed herself a secret amusement. "Try and see."

So Nielsen slipped on one of the two rings, and she let out a cry as the band tightened around her finger until it formed a snug but comfortable fit.

"That is *so cool,*" said Trig.

Kira beamed. "Isn't it?" Then she went to the nearest pillar and, from an alcove in the side, removed a pair of objects. She held out the first one to Nielsen. It was a palm-sized disk of what looked like a rough white shell. Embedded within the surface of the shell was a cluster of blue beads, each no bigger than a pea. "This is what I originally intended to give you."

"What is it?" Nielsen asked, accepting the disk.

"Relief. The next time your affliction strikes, take one of these"—she tapped a bead—"and eat it. Just one, no more. They cannot heal you, but they can help you function, make things easier, more bearable."

"Thank you," said Nielsen, sounding somewhat overwhelmed.

Kira inclined her head. "Given enough time, the beads will regrow, so you will never run out, no matter how long you live."

Tears filled Nielsen's eyes. "Seriously, Kira . . . *thank you.*"

Behind her, Vishal said, "You are too kind, Ms. Kira. Too kind. But thank you from the deepest part of my heart."

Then Kira held out the other object: an ordinary q-drive. "Also, there's this."

The first officer shook her head. "You've already done more than enough, Kira. I can't accept anything else."

"It's not a gift," said Kira gently. "It's a request. . . . If you agree, I would like to name you as my legal representative. To that end, there is a document on this drive granting you power of attorney on my behalf."

"Kira!"

She took Nielsen by the shoulders, looked her in the eyes. "I worked for the Lapsang Corporation for over seven years, and the work paid well. Alan and I planned to use the money to start a new life on Adrasteia, but . . . it's not doing me any good now. My request is this: see that the money gets to my family on Weyland, if they're still alive. If they're not, then the bits are yours."

Nielsen opened her mouth, seemingly at a loss for words. Then she nodded, brisk, and said, "Of course, Kira. I'll do my best."

Heartened, Kira continued, "The company might give you some trouble, so I had Admiral Klein witness and notarize this. That should keep the lawyers off your back." She pressed the q-drive into Nielsen's hand, and the first officer accepted.

Then Nielsen wrapped her in a fierce hug. "You have my word, Kira. I'll do everything I can to get this to your family."

"Thank you."

Once Nielsen released her, Kira walked over to where Falconi stood alone. He cocked an eyebrow at her and then crossed his arms, as if suspicious. "And what are you going to give *me*, Kira? Tickets to a resort on Eidolon? Magic pixie dust I can sprinkle over the *Wallfish*?"

"Better," she said. She raised a hand, and from an arched doorway in the side of the chamber, four of the station's caretakers trundled forward, pushing a pallet upon which sat a sealed case painted military grey and stamped with UMC markings.

"What are *those*?" said Trig, pointing with the Staff of Green at the caretakers.

The creatures were small and bipedal, with double-jointed hind legs and short, T. rex arms at the front. Their fingers were delicate and pale to the point of translucence. A flexible tail extended behind them. Polished, tortoise-like plates armored their skin, but they had a feathered frill—red and purple—along the central ridge of their narrow heads. Four dragonfly wings lay flat against their backs.

"They tend to the station," said Kira. "You might even say they were born from the station."

"You mean, born from *you,*" said Falconi.

"In one sense, yes." The caretakers left the pallet next to them and then retreated, chittering to themselves as they went. Kira opened the top of the case to reveal rows upon rows of antimatter canisters, each of them with the green light on the side that indicated they were full and powered.

Nielsen gasped, and Hwa-jung said, "Thule!"

To Falconi, Kira said, "For you and the *Wallfish.* Antimatter. Some of it I recovered from the vessels I disassembled. The rest I manufactured and transferred into the containment pods."

With a stunned expression, Falconi looked over the case. "There must be enough in here to—"

"To power the *Wallfish* for years," said Kira. "Yes. Or you can sell it and stash the bits for a rainy day. It's your choice."

"Thank y—"

"I'm not done yet," said Kira. She raised her hand again, and the caretakers returned, pushing another pallet. On this one rested pots full of dark earth from which sprouted a strange and wild array of plants that bore no resemblance to those of Earth, Eidolon, or Weyland. Some glowed, some moved, and one of them—a red, stone-like plant—hummed.

"Since you had to strip your hydroponics bay, I thought you could use some replacements," said Kira.

"I—" Falconi shook his head. "That's very thoughtful of you, but how are we supposed to take them anywhere? We don't have enough cryo pods, and—"

"The pots will protect them during FTL," said Kira. "Trust me." Then she handed him another q-drive. "Information on how to care for the plants, as well as details on each one. I think you'll find them useful."

For the first time, she saw tears glimmer in Falconi's eyes. He reached out toward one of the plants—a mottled, pitcher-like organism with small tentacles waving about its open mouth—and then thought better of it and pulled his hand back. "I don't know how to thank you."

"Two more things," she said. "One, this." And she gave him a small metal rectangle, similar in size to a deck of playing cards. "For Veera and the Entropists to study."

Falconi turned the rectangle over. It appeared featureless. "What is it?"

"Something to point them in the right direction, if they can make sense of it." She smiled. "They will, eventually. And two, this." And she placed her hands on either side of his face and kissed him on the lips, soft, delicate, and with feeling. "Thank you, Salvo," she whispered.

"For what?"

"For believing in me. For trusting me. For treating me like a person and not a science experiment." She kissed him once more and then stepped back and raised her arms to either side. Vines unfurled from the wall behind, wrapped themselves around her in a gentle embrace, and then lifted her back up to the waiting depression.

"My gifts are given," she said as she again melded into the substance of the station. With it came a sense of safety. "Go now, and know this: no matter where time or fate may take us, I consider you my friends."

"What are you going to do, Kira?" Falconi asked, craning his neck back to look at her.

"You'll see!"

3.

As the crew filed out through the entrance and back through the corridors toward the docking area, Kira reached out to Gregorovich, whom she knew would have been listening to the conversation via their comms. "I have something for you as well," she said. "If you want it."

Oh really? And what might that be, O Ring Giver?

"A body. A new body, as large or small as you want, metal or organic, in any shape or design that strikes your fancy. Just tell me, and the Seed can make it." To Kira's astonishment, the ship mind did not immediately answer. Rather, he was silent, and she could hear his silence as a physical thing: a pressure of contemplation and uncertainty on the other end of the signal. "Think of it; you could go anywhere you wanted to, Gregorovich. You wouldn't need to be bound to the *Wallfish* anymore."

At long last, the ship mind said, **No. But I think, perhaps, I want to be. Your offer is tempting, Kira, mighty tempting. And don't think I'm ungrateful, but for the time being, I think my place is here, with Falconi and Nielsen and Trig and Hwa-jung and Sparrow. They need me, and . . . I won't lie, it's nice to have meatbags like them running around my decks. You might understand that now. A body would be nice, but I could always have a body. I couldn't always have this crew or these friends.**

Kira did understand, and she appreciated his answer. "If you change your mind, the offer stands."

I'm glad to have known you, O Queen of Flowers. You are a prickly and problematic person, but life is more interesting with you around. . . . I could not have chosen as you have, to pursue these miscreants of the Maw all on your lonesome. For that, you have my admiration. Moreover, you showed me the path to freedom. You saved me from myself, and thus, you also have my eternal gratitude. If you find yourself in the far distant future, remember us as we remember you. And if the tides of time are kind, and I am still sound of thought, know this: you shall always be able to count upon my aid.

To which she simply replied, "Thank you."

4.

With her visitors departed and her mind far more at rest, Kira started upon the next stage of her plan. In concept it was simple; in execution it was more complicated and dangerous than anything she had attempted since waking in the aftermath of the Maw's destruction.

First, she moved herself near the skin of the station. There, she gathered material—organic and inorganic—until she had formed a second core, equal to the one at the center of Unity. Then, and this was the most difficult part, she separated her brain into two unequal parts.

Everything that was of Qwon and Carr, she isolated and placed in the heart of Unity. Everything that was of Kira, the Seed, and the Maw, she drew to herself. Some duplication was necessary—she could still remember Carr's medical tests and Qwon's time spent hunting in the waters of its homeworld—and some omissions and oversights were inevitable. But she did her best.

The process was frightening. With every move, Kira worried that she would sever some crucial part of her self. Or that she would cut off access to a memory she didn't even know she needed. Or that she would kill herself.

But again, she did her best. As she had learned, sometimes you had to make a choice, any choice, even when it wasn't clear which path was the right one. Life rarely provided such a luxury.

She labored for a night and a day, until everything that seemed to be *her* fit inside the skull she had chosen. The tiny, limited skull. She felt diminished, but at the same time, it was a relief to be free of all the sensory input pouring in from the station.

She checked on the Qwon/Carr consciousness one last time—a mother checking on a sleeping child—and then she separated herself from Mar Íneth and set forth toward the near asteroid belt, using her newly built fusion core to drive her through space.

As always, Klein and Lphet came clamoring for answers. So Kira told them of the Maw's seven deadly seeds, and she explained her intentions. "I'm leaving to hunt them down," she said.

Klein sputtered. "But what about the station?"

[[Lphet here: Yes, Idealis, I share the shoal leader's concern. The station is too important for it to be unguarded.]]

Kira laughed. "It's not. I left Carr-Qwon in charge."

"What?" said Klein.

[[Lphet here: What?]

"The part of me that was them now watches over Unity. They will care for it and, if it comes to that, protect it. I suggest you don't anger them."

[[Lphet here: Are you trying to create another Corrupted, Idealis?]]

"I hate to say it, but I agree with the Jelly," said Klein. "Are you *trying* to give us another Maw?"

Kira's voice hardened. "The Maw is no more. I have removed all parts of the Seed from Carr-Qwon. What they are now is something different. Something unformed and unsure, but I can tell you this: none of the anger and pain that drove the Maw still exists. Or if it does, it's inside *me,* not them. You have a new life-form to usher into existence, Admiral Klein, Lphet. Treat them accordingly, and you'll be pleasantly surprised. Do not disappoint me."

5.

When she reached the asteroid belt, Kira slowed herself to a stop near one of the largest asteroids: a huge chunk of metallic rock kilometers across and pitted from countless collisions over the years.

There she parked herself, and there she again began to build. This time, Kira drew upon an existing blueprint: one she had found buried deep within the Seed's memory banks. It was technology of the Old Ones, devised at the height of their civilization, and it suited her purpose perfectly.

Using the Seed, Kira devoured the asteroid—adapting it to her needs—and using the Old Ones' schematic, she built a ship.

It was not square and spindly and lined with radiators, like the human ships. Nor was it round and white and iridescent like the Wranaui ships. It was not like any of those things. No. Kira's ship was shaped like an arrow, long and sharp, with flowing lines reminiscent of a leaf. It had veins and ridges and, along its flared stern, fanned membranes. As with Unity, the ship was a living thing. The hull expanded and contracted in subtle motions, and there was a sense of awareness about the vessel, as if it was watching everything around it.

In a way it was, for the ship was an extension of Kira's body. It acted as her eyes, and through it, she could see far more than would otherwise have been possible.

When she was finished, Kira had a ship that was over half the size of a UMC battleship and far more heavily armed. Powering it was another torque engine, and with it, Kira felt confident she could exceed the highest speed of any of the Maw's foul offspring.

Then, she took one last look at the system. At the Cordovan star, at the planet R1 and the verdant framework of Unity floating in orbit high above. At the fleets of human and Wranaui ships clustered thereabout, which were, if not entirely friendly, at least no longer shooting.

And Kira smiled, for it was good.

In her mind, she made her peace, said her last farewells; a silent lament for all that was lost and gone. And then she turned her ship away from the star—pointed it toward the Maw's final memory—and with the smallest of thoughts, started on her way.

* * * *

EXEUNT VI

1.

Kira wasn't alone. Not yet.

As she moved across the face of the void, four UMC battleships and three Wranaui cruisers trailed behind in close formation. Most of the vessels were damaged in some way: explosion-scarred and soot-besmirched and—in the case of the human ships—held together more with FTL tape, emergency welds, and the prayers of their crews than anything else. Still, the vessels were spaceworthy enough to accompany her.

Admiral Klein and Lphet seemed determined to provide her with an escort all the way to the Markov Limit. Not so much for protection, she suspected, as for observation. Also, perhaps, to give her company. Which she appreciated. If anything was going to do her in, it was the silence and the isolation. . . .

Once she reached the Markov Limit—which, for her ship, was far closer to the star than for the humans or Wranaui—she would leave her escorts behind. They didn't have the means to keep pace with her in superluminal space.

And then she would truly be alone.

It was something she'd expected from the moment she'd made her decision. Yet Kira found the actuality somewhat daunting. With Carr and Qwon removed from her consciousness, her mind was a far emptier place. She was an individual again, not a plurality. And while the Seed was a companion of sorts, it was no substitute for normal human interaction.

She had always been comfortable working alone, but even on the loneliest outposts the Lapsang Corp. sent her to, there had been people to talk and drink with. People to fight and fuck and to generally bounce off, mentally and physically. On the long journey that lay before her, there would be none of that.

The prospect did not frighten her, but it did concern her. Though she felt secure in her self for now, would extended periods of isolation unbalance her the way it had Gregorovich when he'd been shipwrecked? And might that lead to her becoming more like the Maw?

A ripple passed through the surface of the Seed, and she shivered, though she was neither cold nor hot.

Inside her darkened cradle, she opened her eyes, her real eyes, and stared at the curved surface above her: a map of textured flesh, part plant, part animal. She traced the shapes with her fingertips, feeling their courses, reading their paths.

After a time, she again closed her eyes and sent a signal to the *Wallfish,* asked to speak with Falconi.

He replied as quickly as the light-lag allowed. **Hey, Kira. What's up?**

Then she confessed to him her concern, and she said, "I do not know what I may become, given enough time and space."

None of us do. . . . I'll say this, though. You're not going to go insane, Kira. You're too strong for that. And you're not going to lose yourself to the Seed. Hell, even the Maw couldn't destroy you. This is a cakewalk in comparison.

In the darkness, she smiled. "You're right. Thank you, Salvo."

Do you need someone to go with you? I'm sure the UMC and the Jellies would have no shortage of volunteers who would love to jet around the galaxy with you.

She seriously considered the idea and then shook her head, though Falconi couldn't see. "No, this is something I have to do myself. If anyone else were here, I'd be too worried about protecting them."

Your call. If you change your mind, just let us know.

"I will. . . . My one regret is that I won't be around to watch how things turn out between us and the Jellies."

It's good to hear you use the word* us. *Klein wasn't sure if you still thought of yourself as human.

"Part of me does."

He grunted. **I know you're going to be out past the rim, but you can still send messages back, and we can figure out a way to do the same. It might take a while, but we can do it. Staying in touch is important.**

"I'll try." But Kira knew it was unlikely she would hear anything from the League or the Wranaui. Even if they knew where she was, by the time their signals reached her, odds were she would have moved on. Only if the Maw's avatars led her back to settled space would it be possible, and she very much hoped that wouldn't be the case.

Still, it meant something to her that Falconi cared. And she felt a measure of peace. Whatever the future held, she was ready to face it.

When they finished talking, she hailed the *Unrelenting Force.* At her request,

Admiral Klein agreed to forward a message of hers (minus any information the UMC deemed classified) back to Weyland and her family. It would have been easy enough for Kira to broadcast a signal strong enough to reach Weyland, but she did not know how to structure the waves of energy so they could be received and interpreted by the listening antennas in her home system.

Kira wished she could wait for a reply. However, even under the best of circumstances, it would take over three months to hear back. Assuming her family could be found . . . and that they were still alive. It pained Kira to realize that she might never know the truth.

As she hurtled toward the Markov Limit, Kira listened to music sent to her from the *Wallfish*. Some Bach, but also long, slow orchestral pieces that seemed to match the turn of the planets and the shift of the stars. The music provided a structure to otherwise formless time—a narrative to the impersonal progression of nature's grandest bodies.

She dozed inside her living casement, slipping in and out of wakefulness. A true sleep was near at hand, but she put it off, not ready to surrender awareness. Not yet. Not until space distorted around her and cut her off from the rest of the universe.

2.

When she arrived at the Markov Limit, Kira felt a sense of readiness within the ship. The fabric of reality seemed to grow thinner, more malleable around her, and she knew the time to leave was upon her.

She allowed herself a final look around the system. Regret, anxiety, and excitement all stirred within her. But her purpose was just, and it stiffened her resolve. Hers was to go forth into the unknown, to root out the evil seeds and to spread new life throughout the galaxy. It was a good purpose to have.

Then she diverted power into the torque engine, preparing for the transition to FTL, and a deep hum pervaded the flesh of the ship.

Just as the hum peaked, a crackly transmission reached her. It was from the *Wallfish*, from Falconi. He said, **Kira, the UMC says you're about to jump to FTL. I know it feels like you're going to be all alone from now on, but you aren't. We're all thinking about you. Don't forget that, you hear me? That's a direct order from your captain. Go kick some nightmare ass, and I expect to see you alive and healthy when—**

The hum ceased, and the stars twisted, and a dark mirror enveloped her, isolating her in a sphere no larger than her ship. Then all was silent.

Despite herself, Kira felt sad, and she allowed herself to feel that sadness, to acknowledge her loss and give the emotion the respect it deserved. Part of her resisted. Part of her still made excuses. If she could find the Maw's emissaries and eradicate them within a reasonable amount of time, maybe she could still return home, have a life of peace.

She took a breath. *No.* What was done was done. There was no going back, no point regretting the choices she had made nor, as Falconi had said, what was out of her control.

It was time. She closed her eyes, and though the prospect still unsettled her, she at last allowed herself to sleep.

And in that sleep, there were no dreams.

3.

. . .

. . .

. . .

An emerald ship sailed through the darkness, a tiny gleaming dot, lost within the immensity of space. No other vessel accompanied it, no guards or companions or watchful machines. It was alone among the firmament, and all was quiet.

The ship sailed, but it seemed not to move. A butterfly, bright and delicate, frozen in crystal, preserved like that for all eternity. Deathless and unchanging.

Once it had flown faster than light. Once and many times besides. Now it did not. The scent it followed was too delicate to track otherwise.

The galaxy turned upon its axis for time without measure.

Then a flash.

Another ship appeared ahead of the first. The newcomer was dented and dirty, with a patched hull and an awkward appearance. On its nose, faded letters spelled a single word.

The two ships passed each other in a tiny fraction of a second, their relative velocities so immense, there was only time for a brief transmission to pass from one to the other.

The transmission was of a man's voice, and it said: **Your family is alive.**

Then the newcomer was gone, vanished into the distance.

Within the lonely ship, within the emerald cocoon and the swaddling flesh, there lay a woman. And though her eyes were closed and her skin was blue, and though her blood was ice and her heart was still—though all of that, a smile appeared upon her face.

And so she sailed on, content to hold and wait and there to sleep, to sleep in a sea of stars.

ADDENDUM

* * * * * * *

APPENDIX I

* * * * * * *

SPACETIME & FTL

Excerpt from the Entropic Principia (Revised)

. . . necessary to outline a brief overview of the fundamentals. Let this serve as a primer and quick reference guide for later, more serious studies.

* * * *

FTL travel is *the* defining technology of our modern era. Without it, expansion beyond the Solar System would be impossible, barring centuries-long trips on generational ships or automated seed ships that would grow colonists in situ upon arrival. Even the most powerful fusion drives lack the delta-v to jet between the stars as we do now.

Although long theorized, superluminal travel did not become a practical reality until Ilya Markov codified the unified field theory (UFT) in 2107. Empirical confirmation followed soon afterward, and the first working prototype of an FTL drive was constructed in 2114.

Markov's brilliance was in recognizing the fluidic nature of spacetime and demonstrating the existence of the different luminal realms, as outlined in the earlier, purely theoretical work of Froning, Meholic, and Gauthier around the turn of the twenty-first century. Prior to that, thinking was constrained by the limitations of general relativity.

Per Einstein's formulations for special relativity (coupled with Lorentz transformations), no particle with real mass can accelerate to the speed of light. Not only would that require an infinite amount of energy, doing so would break causality, and as later, practical demonstrations have shown, the universe does *not* break causality on a non-quantum scale.

However, nothing in special relativity prevents a massless particle from *always* traveling the speed of light (i.e., a photon), nor from always traveling *faster* than light (i.e., a tachyon). And that is exactly what the math shows. By combining several of the equations of special relativity, the underlying relativistic symmetry between subluminal, luminal, and superluminal particles becomes clear. With regard to the superluminal, substituting relativistic mass for proper mass allows superluminal mass and energy to become definable, non-imaginary properties.

This provides us with our current model of physical space (fig. 1):

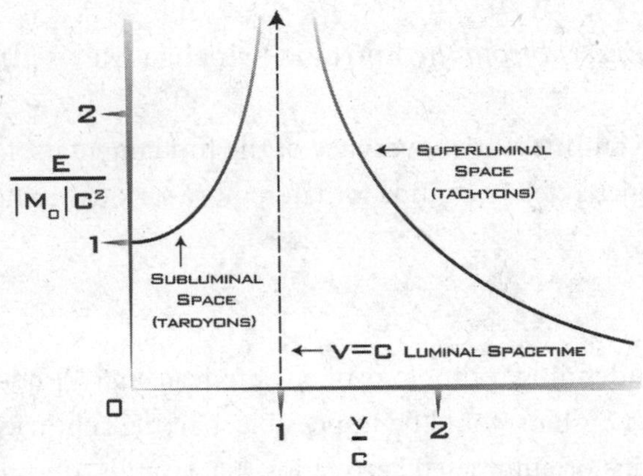

Figure 1: Positive energy vs. velocity

Here the v=c asymptote vertical represents the fluidic spacetime membrane (which has a negligible but non-zero thickness).

By examining this graph, a number of things will become immediately and intuitively clear. First, that just as a subluminal particle can never reach the speed of light c, neither can a superluminal particle. In normal, STL space, expending energy (e.g., shooting propellent out the back of your spaceship) can move you closer to the speed of light. So too in FTL space. However, in FTL space, the speed of light is the *slowest* possible speed, not the fastest, and you can never quite slow down to it, not as long as you possess mass.

Since increasing speed moves you *away* from c in FTL, there is no upper limit to tachyonic speeds, although there are practical limits, given the minimal level of energy needed to maintain particle integrity (remember, less energy = more speed in superluminal space). And while rest mass in subluminal space is real, positive, and increases due to special relativity as v approaches c; in luminal space, rest mass is zero and v always = c; and in superluminal space, rest mass is imaginary at $v=c$, but becomes real, positive, and decreases when moving faster than c.

An implication of this is the reversal of time dilation effects with regard to acceleration. In both STL and FTL, as one approaches c, one ages slower with regard to the larger universe. That is, the universe will age far faster than a spaceship barreling along at 99% of c. However, in FTL, approaching c means slowing down. If, instead, one speeds up, traveling at ever higher multiples of c, you would age faster and faster compared to the rest of the universe. This, of course, would be a major disadvantage of FTL travel if ships weren't encased in a Markov Bubble when superluminal (more on this later).

As one can see in the graph, it is possible to have a velocity of 0 in subluminal space. What does this mean when motion is relative? That you are at rest with regard to whatever reference point you choose, whether that be an outside observer or the destination you wish to travel to. A velocity of 0 in subluminal space translates to around 1.7*c* in superluminal space. Fast, but still slower than the velocities of many FTL particles. Indeed, even low-end Markov Drives are capable of 51.1*c*. Nevertheless, if you need to reach a destination as quickly as possible, it can be worth the delta-v to bring your spaceship to a complete stop with regard to your destination before transitioning to FTL in order to get that extra 1.7*c* of velocity.

Were it possible to directly convert subluminal mass into superluminal mass, without a Markov Bubble, 1.7*c* would be the highest possible speed achievable, as there is no practical way to further accelerate the mass (i.e. further reduce the energy state of said mass) aside from chilling it. One can't suck propellent *into* your tanks, for example. This would be the second major disadvantage of FTL travel, again, if not for the use of a Markov Bubble.

The third disadvantage would be the fact that matter in superluminal space behaves radically differently than in subluminal space, to the point where life as we know it would be impossible to sustain. This, again, is circumvented via a Markov Bubble.

The three different continua—the subluminal, the luminal, and superluminal—coexist within the same time and space, overlapping at every point in the universe. The luminal exists in a fluidic membrane that separates the subluminal from the superluminal, acting as an interference medium between them. The membrane is semi-permeable, and has a definite surface on both sides, upon which all EM forces exist.

The membrane itself, and thus the entirety of three-dimensional space, is made up of Transluminal Energy Quanta (TEQs), which are, quite simply, the most fundamental building block of reality. A quantized entity, TEQs possess Planck length of 1, Planck energy of 1, and a mass of 0. Their movements and interactions give rise to every other particle and field.

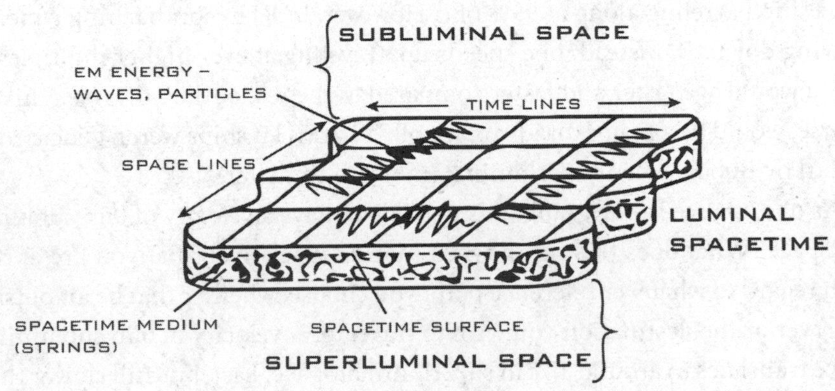

Figure 2: Simplified diagram of spacetime

Taken as a whole, TEQs—and spacetime itself—behave in a quasi-fluidic way. Like a fluid, the luminal membrane exhibits:

- Pressure
- Density and compressibility
- Viscoelasticity
- Surface and surface tension

We will examine each of these in detail later, but for now, it's worth noting that viscoelasticity is the property that gives rise to gravity and inertia and is what allows for all relative motion. As mass accumulates, it begins to displace the spacetime membrane, which thins beneath the object. This is gravity. Likewise, the membrane resists change, which means it takes time to displace when force is applied. (The viscousness of spacetime results in friction between boundary layers, which is the reason for the Lense–Thirring effect, aka: frame-dragging).

Since subluminal and superluminal space are physically separated by the spacetime membrane, STL mass and FTL mass can occupy the same coordinate points simultaneously, although this arrangement would be short-lived as (a) all matter in superluminal space moves at some speed faster than *c,* and (b) the shared membrane means that the spacetime displacement from mass, which is to say gravity, has an equal and opposite effect on the opposing realm.

An example to illustrate: in STL space, a planet will press down upon the fabric of spacetime to create the sort of gravity well we are all familiar with. At the same time, that depression will manifest in FTL space as a gravity "hill"—an equal and opposite prominence in the spacetime fabric. And the reverse is also true.

This has a number of consequences. First of which is that mass in one realm of space has a repulsive effect in the other. Stars, planets, and other STL gravitational bodies no longer act as attractors when one transitions to FTL. Quite the opposite.

The same is true of mass in superluminal space. However, since FTL contains a lower net energy density (a natural side effect of tachyons possessing a base speed of >*c*), and given the radically different laws and particles that exist in FTL, what happens is that the gravity hills produced by the denser, subluminal matter scatter the tachyonic mass, forcing it out and away. As confirmed by Oelert (2122), the majority of our local superluminal matter exists in a vast halo surrounding the Milky Way. This halo provides positive pressure on the Milky Way, which helps keep the galaxy from flying apart.

The gravitational effects of superluminal mass on our own subluminal realm were long a mystery. Early attempts to explain them resulted in the now-obsolete theories of "dark matter" and "dark energy." These days, we know that the concentrations of superluminal mass between the galaxies are responsible for the ongoing expansion of the universe, and that they also affect the shape and movement of the galaxies themselves.

Whether or not tachyonic matter coalesces into the superluminal equivalent of stars and planets remains an open question. The math says *yes,* but so far, observational confirmation has proven elusive. The rim of the galaxy is too far away for even the fastest drones to reach, and our current generation of FTL sensors aren't sensitive enough to pick out individual gravitational bodies at that distance. No doubt that will change in time and we will eventually be able to learn far more about the nature of superluminal matter.

Another consequence of the well/hill caused by mass-induced spacetime displacement is the effect commonly known as the Markov Limit. Before that can be explained, it will be helpful to conduct a quick review of how FTL travel and communication actually work.

In order to have unlabored transition from subluminal to superluminal space, it is necessary to directly manipulate the underlying spacetime membrane. This is done via a specially conditioned EM field that couples with the membrane (or rather, with the constituent TEQs).

In gauge theory, ordinary EM fields can be described as *abelian*. That is, the nature of the field differs from whatever generates it. This is true not only of EM radiation but also electron/proton attraction, and also repulsion within atoms and molecules. *Nonabelian* fields would be those such as the strong and weak nuclear forces. They are structurally more complicated and, as a result, display higher levels of internal symmetry.

The other, more relevant, nonabelian fields are those associated with the surface tension, viscoelasticity, and internal coherence of the spacetime membrane. These arise from the internal motions and interactions of the TEQs, the details of which far exceed the scope of this section.

In any case, it has proven possible to convert ordinary EM radiation from abelian to nonabelian by modulating the polarization of the wave energy emitted from antennas or apertures, or by tuning the frequencies of alternating current to the toroidal geometries through which the currents are driven (this is the method used by a Markov Drive). Doing so results in EM radiation with an underlying field of SU(2) symmetry and nonabelian form, as described in Maxwell's expanded equations. This couples in an orthogonal direction with the spacetime fields via a shared quantity: the "A vector potential." (Orthogonal, as tardyons and tachyons exhibit opposite motion directions along their packet lengths, and the conditioned EM field is interacting with both the subluminal *and* superluminal surfaces of spacetime.) This has often been described as traveling in a straight line along a right angle.

Once the EM field is coupled with the spacetime fabric, it becomes possible to manipulate the density of the medium. By injecting an appropriate amount of energy, spacetime itself can be made increasingly thin and permeable. So much so that at a certain point the energy density of subluminal space causes the affected area to pop into superluminal space, like a high-pressure bubble expanding/rising into an area of lower pressure.

As long as the conditioned EM field is maintained, the encompassed subluminal space can be kept suspended within superluminal space.

From the point of view of an STL observer, everything within the bubble has vanished and can only be detected by its gravitational "hill" from the other side of the spacetime membrane.

From inside the bubble, an observer will see themselves surrounded by a perfect, spherical mirror where the surface of the bubble interfaces with the outer FTL space.

From the point of view of an FTL observer, a perfectly spherical, perfectly reflective bubble will have just popped into existence in superluminal space.

Mass and momentum remain conserved throughout. Your original heading will be the same in FTL as in STL, and your original speed will be converted to the superluminal energy-equivalent.

Once the EM field is discontinued, the bubble will vanish, and everything inside will drop back into subluminal space (a process no doubt familiar to many of you). Often this is accompanied by a bright flash and a burst of thermal energy as the light and heat that built up inside the bubble during the trip are released.

A few points on the specific features of Markov Bubbles are worth mentioning:

- Since the surface of the bubble acts as a perfect mirror, it is nearly impossible to shed waste heat from a spaceship during an FTL flight. This is why it becomes necessary to put crews and passengers into cryo prior to the trip.

- Given that, it is impractical to run a fusion drive while in FTL. Thus, Markov Drives—which require a not-inconsiderable amount of power to generate and maintain a conditioned EM field of sufficient strength—rely upon stored antimatter to produce said power. This is more efficient and results in the least amount of waste heat.

- Although a Markov Drive and the spaceship around it contain a large amount of compressed energy by FTL standards, the only energy that superluminal space sees is that which appears via the surface of the bubble. Thus, the more efficient a Markov Drive (i.e., the less energy it uses to generate the conditioned EM field) the faster you can travel.

- Were one unfortunate enough to collide with a chunk of FTL mass, this would result in immediate disruption of the Markov Bubble and immediate return to STL space, with possible catastrophic consequences, depending on one's location.

- The less energy you use to generate a Markov Bubble, the increasingly delicate the bubble becomes. Large gravitational hills, such as those around stars and planets, are more than strong enough to disrupt the bubble and dump you back into normal, subluminal space. This is what is known as the Markov Limit. With adequate computational powers, the limit can be lowered, but it cannot be removed entirely. Currently, Markov Drives cannot be activated in a gravitational field stronger than 1/100,000 g. This is why, in Sol, spaceships have to fly out to a distance equivalent to the radius of Jupiter's orbit before they are able to go FTL (although if you're actually near Jupiter, you'll have to fly out even farther still).

As annoying as the Markov Limit is—no one likes having to sit through several more days of travel after weeks or months in cryo—it has actually proven to be a good thing. Because of it, no one can drop an FTL asteroid directly onto a city, or worse. Were there no Markov Limit, every spaceship would be far more of a potential threat than they already are and defense against surprise attacks would be basically impossible.

We are also fortunate that the viscoelasticity of spacetime precludes superpositional bombs. If a ship in FTL space flies over a mass in STL space that produces less than 1/100,000 g, and the ship returns to subluminal space at that precise moment, the ship and the mass will push each other apart with equal force, preventing either object from intersecting. If they *did* intersect, the resulting explosion would be on par with an antimatter detonation.

Once a spaceship has entered superluminal space, straight-line flight is usually the most practical choice. However, a limited amount of maneuverability is possible by carefully increasing the energy density on one side or another of the bubble. This will cause that side of the spaceship to slow, and thus the vessel as a whole to turn. But it is a gradual process and only suitable for small course corrections over long distances. Otherwise you risk destabilizing the bubble. For more substantial changes, it is better to drop back into subluminal space, reorient, and try again.

Any changes in heading that occur in FTL will be reflected upon returning to STL. Likewise any changes to total momentum/speed, with the degree of change being inversely proportional.

Technically it is possible for two ships in FTL to dock, but the practical difficulties of matching exact velocities, as well as the mathematics of merging Markov Bubbles, means that while it has been done with drones, no one—to our knowledge—has been crazy enough to try it with crewed ships.

Although a ship within a Markov Bubble can never directly observe its FTL surroundings, some level of sensory information *is* possible. By pulsing the bubble at the appropriate frequencies, FTL particles can be created on the outer surface of the membrane, and these can be used both as a form of radar as well as a signaling mechanism. With careful measurement, we can detect the return of the particles when they impinge upon the bubble, and this allows us to interact with superluminal space, albeit in a crude manner.

This is the same method by which FTL comms and sensors work. Both may be used far closer to a star or planet than one can maintain a Markov Bubble, but as with the bubble, there is a point at which the associated gravity hills become too steep for all but the slowest, most energetic FTL signals to climb.

Due to the protection of the bubble, a ship retains the inertial frame of reference it had prior to FTL, which means it does not experience the extreme time dilation that an exposed superluminal particle would. Nor does it experience any relativistic effects at all (the twins of the famous twin paradox will age at the same rate if one of them takes an FTL flight from Sol to Alpha Centauri and back).

This, of course, leads us to the question of causality.

Why, one might ask, doesn't FTL travel allow for time travel, as all the equations for special relativity seem to indicate? The answer is that it doesn't, and we know this because . . . it doesn't.

Although that may seem facetious, the truth is that the debate remained unsettled until Robinson and the crew of the *Daedalus* made the first FTL flights. It took empirical experimentation to answer the question of time travel for certain, and it was only after the fact that the supporting math and physics were fully developed.

What was found was this: no matter how fast a superluminal voyage—no matter how many multiples of *c* your spaceship travels—you will never be able to return to your origin point *before* you left. Nor for that matter can you use FTL signals to send information into the past. Some amount of time will *always* elapse between departure and return.

How is this possible? If one is at all familiar with light cones and Lorentz transformations, it should be blindingly obvious that exceeding the speed of light results in being able to visit the past and kill your own grandfather (or something equally absurd).

Yet we cannot.

The key to understanding this lies in the fact that all three luminal realms belong to the same universe. Despite their seeming separation (as it appears from our normal, subluminal point of view), the three are part of a larger, cohesive whole. And while local violations of physical laws may appear to occur in certain circumstances, on a global scale, those laws are upheld. Conservation of energy and momentum, for example, are always maintained across the three luminal realms.

Adding to that, there is a certain amount of crossover. Gravitational distortions on one side of the luminal barrier will have a mirrored effect on the other. Thus, an object moving in subluminal space will leave an STL gravitational distortion in the equivalent FTL space. Waves from the distortion will propagate outward at *c* no matter what, but the movement of the gravitational center will be less than *c*. And the reverse is true for a superluminal gravitational mass, which would leave an FTL track of spacetime ripples through normal, subluminal space. (Of course, no such FTL tracks were detected prior to the invention of the Markov Drive, but that was a result of—in most cases—their extreme weakness and the distance of most superluminal matter from the main body of the Milky Way.)

Note: it's important to remember that just as anything moving faster than *c* in subluminal space could theoretically be used to arrange a causality violation, so too could anything moving *slower* than *c* in superluminal space. In FTL, *c* is the minimum speed of information. Above that, relativity and nonsimultaneity are maintained, no matter how fast you might be going.

Even without the existence of a Markov Drive, we now have a situation where natural phenomena seem to be violating the light-speed barrier on both sides of the spacetime membrane, but again, without inducing any causality violations.

The question returns: Why is that?

The answer is twofold.

One: no particle of real mass ever breaks the light-speed barrier in either the sub- or superluminal realm. If one did, we would see all of the paradoxes and causality violations predicted by traditional physics.

Two: just as TEQs form the basis for every subluminal particle, they also form the basis for every superluminal particle. As their name implies, TEQs are capable of existing in all three realms at once, and they are capable of moving as slow as the slowest STL particle and as fast as the fastest FTL particle—which is very fast indeed, limited only by the lower boundary of energy needed to maintain particle coherence, and even then, TEQs can move faster still given their Planck energy of 1.

Thus, with the discovery of TEQs, we have an object that is capable of conveying information far faster than the speed of light. Normally this only occurs in the superluminal realm, but any TEQ is capable of such speeds, and they often transfer from sub- to superluminal velocities as their position within the spacetime membrane changes. These changes are responsible for much of the quantum weirdness seen at small scales.

The light cone, as it were, of an observer using TEQs for informational gathering would be far, far wider than if they were only using photons (wider, but not complete; TEQs have a finite velocity). The wider light cone—or TEQ cone—expands the total set of events that can be regarded as simultaneous. Although non-simultaneity and relativity are maintained throughout all three luminal realms (when considered as a whole), the immense velocity of TEQs reduces the events that can be considered non-simultaneous to a far smaller number, and those that are lie outside the fastest speed of an FTL particle. And while, in theory, the universe remains fundamentally relative, in practice, the vast majority of events may be regarded as ordered and causal.

This means that when a ship goes FTL, it cannot induce any causality violations within superluminal space, as the Markov Bubble *is* a superluminal particle/object and behaves as such. And when a ship drops back to STL, no causality violations occur because travel times are always slower than the top speed of the TEQs (i.e., the speed of information).

Where a paradox *would* have occurred in subluminal space, events are found to have proceeded in a causal relationship, one after another, without any contradiction. From a distance, it may appear that one can send a piece of information back to its origin point before it was transmitted, but *appears* is the word to keep in mind. In actuality, no such thing is possible. If one tries, the return transmission will never arrive any sooner than one unit of TEQ Planck time (where TEQ Planck time is defined as the length of time for a TEQ at maximal speed to traverse one unit of Planck length).

As a result, whenever one sees the possibility for a causality violation in subluminal space, one is, in essence, seeing a mirage. And whenever one tries to exploit said possibility, one will fail.

This renders a large number of observations in our subluminal universe illusionary. Prior to the invention of the Markov Drive (or failing that, detection of FTL gravitational signals), none of this mattered. Relativity was maintained throughout because FTL travel and communications weren't possible. Nor could we accelerate a spaceship to high enough relativistic speeds to really begin to investigate the issue. Only now, with access to both the sub- and superluminal realms, has the truth become clear.

As the light signatures of our modern-day FTL trips begin to reach the nearby stars, an observer positioned there with a powerful enough telescope would see a confusing series of images as ships and signals pop out of nowhere, seemingly out of order. However, by observing TEQs instead of photons, the true order of events may be established (or by physically traveling to the sources of the images).

The exact mechanism that prevents causality violations in STL space is the top velocity of the TEQs. As long as that isn't broken (and no known mechanism would allow for this), FTL will never allow for time travel into the past. And for that we should be grateful. A non-causal universe would be sheer chaos.

* * * *

With our overview finished, we will now examine the theoretical possibility of using conditioned EM fields to reduce inertial effects and to lessen or increase perceived gravity. Although as yet impractical with our current levels of antimatter production, in the future, this could be a means of—

APPENDIX II

* * * * * * *

SHIP-BASED COMBAT IN SPACE

Transcribed from Professor Chung's Lecture at the UMC Naval Academy, Earth (2242)

Good afternoon, cadets. Be seated.

Over the next six weeks, you'll receive the finest education the UMC can muster on the means and methods of ship-based combat. Fighting in space isn't twice as hard as fighting in air or water. It isn't three or four times as hard. It's an entire order of magnitude more difficult.

Zero-g is a non-intuitive environment for the human brain. Even if you grew up on a ship or station, as some of you have, there are aspects of inertial maneuvering *you will not understand* without proper instruction. And no matter how sharp you might be when it comes to good old slower than light, FTL throws those rules out the airlock and stomps on them until they're a bloody mess.

The maneuvering capabilities of your vessel and those you fight alongside will determine where you can fight, *who* you can fight, and—if needed—the requirements of retreat. Space, as has often been stated, is not only large, it's larger than you can imagine. If you can't close the distance between you and your target, they are invulnerable to your fire. This is why it is often advantageous to drop out of FTL with a high degree of relative motion. But not always. Circumstances vary, and as officers, you will be called upon to make those sorts of judgment calls.

You will learn the capabilities and the limitations of our fusion drives. You will learn why—despite what you may have seen in games or movies—the concept of personal combat space vessels is not only outdated, it never was a thing. A drone or missile is not only cheaper, it is far more effective. Machines can withstand far more g's than any human. Yes, on occasion you get a radicalized miner or a local cartel member who uses a smaller spaceship for piracy or the like, but when confronted with a proper warship such as our new cruisers or battleships, they *always* lose.

When you do engage the enemy, combat will be a strategic interplay between the different systems of your ships. A chess game, where the goal is to inflict enough damage on the hostiles to disable or destroy them before they do the same to you.

Every weapon system we use has different advantages and disadvantages. Missiles are best for short- to medium-range attacks, but they're too slow and carry too little fuel for longer-range engagements. And once you fire them, they're gone. Point-defense lasers can stop incoming missiles, but only a certain number and only until the laser overheats. Casaba-Howitzers are also short- to medium-range weapons, but unlike missiles, lasers can't stop them once they're fired. In fact, nothing short of a solid wall of lead and tungsten ten or twenty meters thick is going to stop the radiation beam from a Casaba-Howitzer. The downside is their mass; you can only carry so many Casaba-Howitzers in your ship magazine. Also, at long range, the beam from a howitzer will widen, leaving it about as powerful as a wet fart in a blizzard. Medium to long range, you rely on your keel laser. But again, you have to worry about overheating, and your enemy can counter with chalk and chaff to disperse the incoming pulse. Mass drivers and nuke-powered penetrators can be used at any distance, as kinetic weapons have effectively infinite range in space, but they're really only practical in close-range engagements where the enemy doesn't have time to evade or long, long-range attacks where the enemy doesn't know you're shooting at them.

No matter which weapon or weapons you choose to employ, you will have to balance their use with your ship's maximum thermal load. Do you fire your keel laser one more time or do you execute another evasion burn? Do you risk extending your radiators during a firefight in order to shed a few extra BTUs? How long can you risk cooling down before jumping to FTL if the enemy is chasing you?

Ship-to-surface combat has different requirements than ship-to-ship. Stationary installations such as orbital defense platforms, hab-rings, and converted asteroids all require unique strategies. If you choose to board an enemy vessel, how best to protect your troops as well as your own ship?

Along with physical combat, you will have to contend with electronic warfare. The hostiles *will* be trying to subvert your computer systems and turn them against you. Jamming may not protect you, as the hostiles could use a line-of-sight beam to initiate a system handshake.

All these things and more must be taken into account when engaging in space combat. The environment wants to kill you. The hostiles want to kill you. And your own instincts and lack of knowledge *will kill you*—and everyone around you—if you don't master these fundamentals.

Now, some of you are thinking, "Won't the ship mind or our pseudo-intelligences handle most of these things?" The answer is yes, they will. But not all the time. A ship mind doesn't have hands. What they can move or fix is limited, and that goes double for pseudo-intelligences. In an emergency, some things can only be done by a human. And there have been numerous cases where the ship mind or the ship's computer system has been disabled by enemy action. When that happens, these decisions will fall to *you*, the next generation of UMCN officers.

The next six weeks will be some of the hardest six weeks of your lives. That's by design. The UMC doesn't want *anyone* who is unqualified to step onto a spaceship where they can endanger not only their own lives but the lives of their fellow crew. Better that you wash out now and go back to being swabbies who only have to worry about keeping their boots polished and their jaws off the deck. If you don't think you can handle this sort of responsibility, get up and leave. The door's right there, and no one, not me, not your superiors, and not the UMC will think any less of you for walking out now. . . . No? Alright then. Over the next month and a half, my staff and I are going to put you through the wringer. You *will* wish you gave up. But if you do the hours, work hard, and learn from the mistakes of those who paid for their knowledge with blood and lives, then you have a good chance of wearing your officers' pips—wearing them and doing justice to them.

So study hard, and at the end of this program, I expect each and every one of you to impress me with your knowledge of space-based combat.

That will be all. Dismissed.

APPENDIX III

* * * * * * *

TERMINOLOGY

"May your path always lead to knowledge."
"Knowledge to freedom."

—ENTROPIC LITANY

"Eat the path."

—INARË

A

ABYSSAL CONCLAVE: sycophantic congress of Wranaui co-forms that resides upon the Plaintive Verge within the oceans of Pelagius.

ACUWAKE: *see* StimWare.

ADRASTEIA: moon in orbit around the gas giant Zeus in the Sigma Draconis system. In mythology, a nymph who cared for the infant Zeus in secret. Meaning *inescapable* in Greek.

AIGOO: Korean exclamation used to express many emotions including pity, disgust, frustration, mild discomfort, or surprise. Akin to a verbal sigh.

AISH: Korean interjection expressing frustration or discontent.

AJUMMA: Korean term for any middle-aged or older woman, or a married woman, even if young. Ajummas are often stereotyped as intense and overbearing.

ANTIMATTER FARM: large numbers of satellites placed in close orbit around a star. Solar panels convert sunlight into electricity, which is used to generate antimatter. The process is hideously inefficient but necessary, as antimatter is the preferred fuel for Markov Drives.

ARCH ARITHMETIST: *see* Pontifex Digitalis.

ARMS: semi-autonomous political and sociogenetic organizations in Wranaui society. Each Arm acts as it sees fit, but impulses may be overridden by governing form. (*See also* Tfeir.)

ARROSITO AHUMADO: dessert common to San Amaro. Rice pudding flavored with caramel made by boiling dark sugar and filtering the syrup through the ashes of herbs.

ASPECT OF THE VOID: Wranaui viewscreen; traditionally an image generated within an orb of suspended water.

B

BATTLESHIP: largest standard ship class in the UMC Navy. Heavily armed, able to carry significant numbers of troops, slow to turn given its length. Never operates without support ships. (*See also* Cruiser.)

BEANSTALK: *see* Space Elevator.

BERYL NUTS: edible nuts with gem-like shells used in certain brands of meal packs. Gene-hacked species native to Eidolon.

BITS: cryptocurrency dated to Galactic Standard Time (GTS). Most widely accepted form of legal tender across interstellar space. Official currency of the League of Allied Worlds.

BLACK NOVA: cultivar of *Capsicum chinense*, gene-hacked to deposit pure capsaicin in a waxy outer layer. Developed by Ines Tolentira of Stewart's World prior to winning the Tri-Solar Hot Pepper Bash.

BLASTER: laser that fires a pulse instead of a continuous beam.

B. LOOMISII: orange, lichen-like bacteria native to Adrasteia.

BOSS: generic Hutterite term for a person in charge of any sort of project or organization. Adopted into general usage with numerous variations following the Hutterite Expansion.

BUGHUNT: UMC name for system formerly settled by the Old Ones. Location of the planet humans call Nidus and final resting place of the Staff of Blue.

C

CARETAKERS: highly intelligent biomechanical creatures that live on Unity. Responsible for general maintenance and minor construction. Speculated to have some form of integrated hive mind.

CASABA-HOWITZER: nuclear shaped charge. Often mounted on a missile to increase its range. Term can refer to either pure Casaba-Howitzers (which focus a nuclear explosion into a narrow beam of plasma) or Casaba-Howitzers that use said explosion to propel explosively formed projectiles (slugs of molten tungsten with extreme destructive potential).

CHELL: tea derived from the leaves of the Sheva palm on Eidolon. A mild stimulant used throughout the League, second in popularity only to coffee. More common among colonists than Terrans.

"CHIARA'S FOLLY": Weyland folk song about the misadventures of a cat.

CLOUD CITIES: lightweight, neutral density hab-domes that float in the clouds of Venus. Some of the largest and most prosperous settlements outside of Earth. Majority of structural elements come from trees and other plants grown in the domes.

CO-FORM: term for Wranaui that share the same physical shape.

COLLEGE OF ENUMERATORS: governing body of the Numenists at their headquarters on Mars.

COMPULSION: *see Tsuro.*

CONSERVATION PARTY: one of several major political parties in the League. Ecologically minded with a focus on preserving the flora and fauna of various xenospheres. (*See also* Expansionist Party *and* Stellarists.)

CONSTRUCT: an artificial (though biological) body grown to house the brain of a person who has lost their original flesh. Often an intermediate step along the way toward full conversion to ship mind.

CORDOVA: (Gliese 785) orange-red dwarf star used by the Wranaui as a forward operating base and long-term surveillance post for observing humanity.

CORPORATE CITIZENSHIP: territory-independent citizenship granted to certain employees of interstellar corporations. This allows for individuals to work, travel, and live among different nations/planets/systems with relative ease. Concept developed prior to formation of League, and is slowly being superseded by League citizenship, which grants an equivalent passport.

CORRUPTED: *see* Nightmares.

CRUISER: UMC ship designed to operate solo on long-distance surveys and patrols. Smaller and more maneuverable than battleships, but still formidable. Standard gear includes two Markov-equipped shuttles capable of traveling orbit-to-surface and surface-to-orbit.

CRYO: cryogenic sleep; suspended animation induced via a cocktail of drugs prior to FTL travel.

CRYO SICKNESS: generalized digestive, metabolic, and hormonal distress caused by spending too long in cryo (or too many back-to-back trips). Unpleasant to deadly with side effects scaling to length of time in cryo and/or number of trips. Some individuals are more prone than others.

CYCLE: Wranaui year. Roughly a quarter longer than an Earth-standard year.

D

DELTA-V: measure of the thrust per unit of mass in a spacecraft needed to perform a certain maneuver. In other words, the change in velocity that can be accomplished by expending the ship's propellent. Maneuvers are measured in the delta-v required, and the costs add linearly. The mass of propellant required for any one maneuver is determined via the Tsiolkovsky rocket equation.

DEPARTMENT OF DEFENSE: civilian department of the League responsible for overseeing the UMC.

DERPs: dehydrated excretory recycling pellets. Sterile, polymer-coated feces as processed by appropriately equipped skinsuits.

DIRECTOR OF INTERSTELLAR SECURITY: highest civilian intelligence officer in the League. Primary responsibility is the existential protection of humanity.

DQAR: Wranaui battle formation, typified by an inverted delta shape.

E

EARTH CENTRAL: main League and UMC headquarters. Built around the base of the Honolulu beanstalk.

EIDOLON: planet in orbit around Epsilon Eridani. An Earth-like garden planet teeming with native life, none sentient and most either poisonous or hostile. The colony there has the highest mortality rate of any settled planet.

ENTROPIC PRINCIPIA: central text of Entropism. Originated as a statement of intent, later expanded to a philosophical treatise containing a summary of all known scientific knowledge, with primary emphasis on astronomy, physics, and mathematics. (*See also* Entropism.)

ENTROPISM: stateless, pseudo-religion driven by a belief in the heat death of the universe and a desire to escape or postpone said death. Founded by mathematician Jalal Sunyaev-Zel'dovich in the mid-twenty-first century. Entropists devote considerable resources to scientific research and have contributed—directly or indirectly—to numerous important discoveries. Open adherents are noted for their gradient robes. As an organization, Entropists have proven difficult to control, as they pledge loyalty to no one government, only to the rigors of their pursuit. Their technology consistently runs several decades ahead of the main of human society, if not more. "By our actions we increase the entropy of the Universe. By our entropy, we seek salvation from the coming dark." (*See also* Nova Energium.)

ENUMERATION: broadcast of ascending numbers that Numenists are required to listen to as part of the observance of their faith. Some numbers, such as primes, are considered more auspicious than others. (*See also* Numenism.)

EUROPA COMMAND: League of Allied Worlds Europa Command (LAWEUCOM, shortened EUCOM) is one of seven unified combatant commands of the League military stationed within Sol. Headquartered on Lawrence Station with ongoing material support provided by the manufacturing facilities of Orsted Station by Ganymede.

EXOSKELETON: (EXO in common parlance) a powered frame used for combat, freight, mining, and mobility. Exos vary widely in design and function, with some being open to the elements and others hardened for vacuum or the depths of oceans. Armored exos are standard equipment for UMC combat troops.

EXPANSIONIST PARTY: one of several major political parties in the League. Founded to help foster the spread of humans outside of Sol, now mainly focused on preserving the interests of the established extra-solar colonies, often to the point of blocking the establishment of new ones. (*See also* Conservation Party *and* Stellarists.)

EXPEDITION BOSS: *see* Boss.

F

FARSCENT: class of durable chemicals secreted by Wranaui for long-distance communication in water. Metaphorical bandwidth is narrow and fidelity is low, making this of limited utility for large exchanges of data. (*See also* Nearscent *and* Lowsound.)

THE FARTHEST SHORE: spacer poem by Harrow Glantzer (Hutterite).

FINK-NOTTLE'S PIOUS NEWT EMPORIUM: famed amphibian retailer on Earth. Established by C. J. Weenus circa 2104.

FLASH TRACE: to travel by FTL far enough that one can stop and see the real-time light from an event. E.g., spaceship A wants to see when and where spaceship B left the Solar System sometime in the past day. Spaceship A flies the required number of light-hours (twenty-four in this case) from Sol, then sits and watches via telescope until it sees B leaving Sol.

FLEET INTELLIGENCE: branch of UMCN devoted to gathering information.

FOXGLOVE POPE: *see* Pontifex Digitalis.

FREEHOLDINGS: settlements, conclaves, stations, and outholdings unaffiliated with any major government.

FTL: faster than light. The primary mode of transportation between stars. (*See also* Markov Drive.)

FTL TAPE: slang for vacuum tape, a type of incredibly tough, pressure-sensitive tape. Strong enough to patch breaches in outer hull. Despite popular belief, not suitable for repairs intended to last the duration of FTL trips.

FULL SWEEP: highest hand in Scratch Seven, consisting of four sevens, two kings, and a nine, for a count of ninety-one and a score of thirteen.

G

GECKO PADS: adhesive pads on the bottom of skinsuits and boots intended for climbing or maneuvering in zero-g. As name implies, pads (which are covered with bristles around 5 μm in diameter) depend on van der Waals force for adhesion. Shear force is limiting factor for maximal load, but also provides mechanism for release.

GLITTER BUG: small, insect-like animal native to Eidolon. Noted for their brilliant, metallic exoskeletons.

GLOWLIGHTS: bioluminescent lights grown by the Seed.

GRADIENT ROBES: traditional garb of observing Entropists. Adorned with the rising phoenix that is their sigil. Metamaterial laced with advanced technology that allows the robes to act as a skinsuit, armor, and, when needed, a weapon.

GREAT BEACON: first alien artifact found by humans. Located at Talos VII (Theta Persei 2). The Beacon is a hole fifty kilometers wide and thirty deep. It emits an EMP at 304 MHz every 10.6 seconds, along with a burst of structured sound that is a representation of the Mandelbrot set in trinary code. Surrounded by a net of vanadium-laced gallium that may have once acted as a superconductor. Giant turtle-like creatures (without heads or legs) roam the plain surrounding the hole. As of yet, no one has discovered their relationship with the artifact. Six more Beacons are known to exist. They are assumed to have been constructed by the Old Ones, but definitive proof is lacking. Intended purpose remains a mystery.

GROUND-POUNDER: derogatory term for one who lives on or was born on a planet.

GST: Galactic Standard Time. Universal chronology as determined by emissions of TEQs from the galactic core. Causality may appear to be broken but only appear; *a* must always cause *b*.

H

HANZO TENSEGRITY: insurance company based out of Sol. Not known for their customer satisfaction.

HATCHING POOLS: shallow tidal pools where Wranaui would hatch their eggs. Now replicated in artificial pools for travel and convenience. Upon hatching, young Wranaui are combative and cannibalistic; only the strongest few survive.

HDAWARI: large, saltwater carnivore native to Pelagius. One of only a few predators known to prey upon adult Wranaui. Closely related to Wranaui but less intelligent.

HEPTARCHY: ruling council of the Old Ones. (*See also* Highmost.)

HERESY OF THE FLESH: *see* Tfeir.

HIBERNACULUM: Entropist term for a cryo tube.

HIGH LFARR: a famed prominence on Pelagius. Temperate weather made it a favorite location for Wranaui hatching pools. Later, acquired enormous socio-political and religious significance with the discovery of several artifacts of the Old Ones built upon it. Original site of the Wranaui Conclave (later the Abyssal Conclave) prior to the joining of the Arms and the ascendency of the regnant form.

HIGHMOST: wielder of the Staff of Blue. Leader of the Heptarchy.

HIVE MIND: psycho-mechanical joining of two or more brains. Usually accomplished by continual-beam synchronization of subject implants, ensuring agreement between intero-, extero-, and proprioceptive stimuli. Total exchange of prior sense memory is a common (though not required) part of establishing a hive mind. Effective range depends on signaling bandwidth and tolerance for lag. Breakdown tends to occur when physical proximity exceeds tolerance. Largest recorded hive mind was forty-nine, but experiment was short-lived as participants experienced debilitating sensory overload.

HUNTER-SEEKER: small drones used for surveillance and assassination.

HUTTERITE EXPANSION: series of intensive colonization efforts by Reform Hutterites, starting in the Solar System and expanding outward following the discovery of FTL. The period is said to begin shortly after the construction of Earth's first space elevator and end with the settlement of Eidolon. (*See also* Reform Hutterites.)

HYDROTEK CORP.: company specializing in hydrogen extraction and refinement around gas giants. Hydrotek stations are the main refueling and remassing facilities in most systems.

I

IDEALIS: as the Seed is able to change shape/form at will, the Wranaui consider it the Platonic "ideal" of physical embodiment.

INARË: [[**Invalid Input: Entry Not Found**]]

IPD: interplanetary diploma. Only educational degree accepted throughout all of settled space. Accreditation is overseen by Bao University on Stewart's World in cooperation with several schools in Sol. IPDs cover most relevant subjects, including law, medicine, and all the major sciences.

ITC: Interstellar Trade Commission. A department of the League tasked with overseeing interstellar commerce. Its remit includes enforcing standards, collecting tariffs, and fraud prevention, as well as providing loans and resources to spur economic growth throughout settled space.

J

JELLIES: *see* Wranaui.

K

KNOT OF MINDS: in general, any group of Wranaui bound and dedicated to a singular purpose. A solemn and sacred joining. Traditionally sealed by winding one's tentacles/limbs around those of the other bondees. As such, a Knot often only has seven members (that being the number of primary tentacles the main Wranaui form has), but the concept is often expanded to include more. In the modern era, a Knot can be formed over lowsound nearscent, but there is a bias against those Knots as being less binding than those formed in person.

Specifically: the Knot founded by Shoal Leader Nmarhl and its compatriots with the purpose of opposing Ctein's leadership and safeguarding the Idealis later bonded with Kira Navárez.

L

LAMP LINES: seaweed-like growths that provide illumination in the depths of the Plaintive Verge.

LAPSANG TRADING CORPORATION: interstellar conglomerate that began as a mercantile venture before shifting into founding, funding, and running colonies such as Highstone on Weyland. Headquartered on Stewart's World. Slogan: "Forging the future together."

LEAGUE OF ALLIED WORLDS: (LAW) interstellar government formed after the discovery of the Great Beacon on Talos VII. Consists of the settlements in and around Sol, Alpha Centauri, Epsilon Indi, Epsilon Eridani, and 61 Cygni.

LION CLAM: animal native to Eidolon. Noted for its amber shell. Used in the manufacture of a sepia-colored ink.

LOADER BOT: semi-autonomous robots used for manual labor.

LOWSOUND: vocal emanations used by Wranaui for communication over long distances in their oceans. Similar to whale song.

LOWSOUND FARSCENT: traditionally a combination of the two methods Wranaui use for long-distance communication in water. More commonly, a term for STL or FTL transmissions, such as radio.

LUTSENKO DEFENSE INDUSTRIES: a Ruslan-based munitions company.

M

MACHINE BOSS: *see* Boss.

MAG-SHIELD: either the magnetospheric dipolar torus of ionized plasma used to protect spaceships from solar radiation during interplanetary trips *or* the magneto-hydrodynamic system used for braking and thermal protection during reentry.

MANYFORM: *see* Seed.

MARKOV BUBBLE: sphere of subluminal space permeated with a conditioned EM field that allows for tardyonic matter to transition through the membrane of fluidic spacetime into superluminal space.

MARKOV DRIVE: antimatter-fueled machine that allows for FTL travel. (*See also* unified field theory.)

MARKOV, ILYA: engineer and physicist who outlined the unified field theory in 2107, thus allowing for modern FTL travel.

MARKOV LIMIT: distance from a gravitational mass at which it becomes possible to sustain a Markov Bubble and thus transition to FTL travel.

MEDIBOT: robotic assistant capable of diagnosis and treatment for all but the most difficult cases. Doctors rely on medibots for the majority of surgeries. Many ships forego a doctor entirely, prioritizing cost savings over the relatively small risk of needing a human physician.

MEDIFOAM: sterile, antibiotic-laced foam that hardens into a semi-flexible cast. Used to stop bleeding, immobilize fractures and, when injected into bodily cavities, prevent infection.

MILCOM: official UMC communication network.

N

NANOASSEMBLER: 3-D printer that utilizes nanobots to produce complex shapes, machines, and—given the appropriate stock—biological structures such as muscles, organs, and seeds.

NARU-CLASS: medium-mass Wranaui ships that carry a limited number of troops. Usually no more than three squids, two or three crawlers, and the same number of snappers.

NEARSCENT: chemicals secreted by Wranaui for communication. Their primary method of conveying linguistic and non-linguistic information.

NEST OF TRANSFERENCE: Wranaui device for copying memories and basic brain structures from one body to another. Also used to imprint stored personalities/memories onto a new body after the original individual dies. (*See also* Tfeir.)

NIGHTMARES: malignant, self-sustaining growths caused by an unsuccessful joining between Seed and host (usually when either Seed or host—or both—are damaged beyond proper repair).

NNAR: coral-like organism native to Pelagius, commonly used as a decorative element by the Wranaui. Some varieties secrete a clear coating that has mild psychotropic effects on the immature forms of the Wranaui.

NOMATI: polyp-like animals native to the Arctic regions of Eidolon. Every solar eclipse, they detach from their anchor point (usually a rock) and hop fourteen times. Reason as yet unknown.

NORODON: fast-acting liquid analgesic suitable for mid-level to severe pain.

NOVA ENERGIUM: the headquarters and prime research lab of the Entropists. Located near Shin-Zar.

NSARRO: Wranaui measurement of length. Defined as the distance one can swim in seven pulses. (*See also* Cycle *and* Pulse.)

NUMBER SUPREME: largest number imaginable. As defined by the Numenists, the sum of all knowledge, containing the known and the unknown. The greater part of two equal halves. God.

NUMENISM: religion centered around the supposed holy nature of numbers. Founded on Mars by Sal Horker II circa 2165–2179 (est.), Numenism quickly gained traction among colonists and workers dependent upon the technology of their new world for survival. Defining feature of Numenism is the ongoing broadcast of numbers—the Enumeration—from their headquarters on Mars. The Enumeration is working its way in ascending order through the list of real numbers.

NUMINOUS FLANGE: enormous geological structure on Ruslan. Uplifted granite slab laced with gold veins. Prominent tourist feature on Ruslan. Known to inspire religious fervor and existential crises among viewers. Setting of *Adelin,* an influential drama whose lead actor, Sasha Petrovich, was involved in a corruption scandal near the end of 2249, which led to the resignation of Ruslan's governor, Maxim Novikov, and the appointment of Inquisitor Orloff to resolve the situation. Subsequent unrest continued on and off for several years.

NWOR: many-legged saltwater animal native to Pelagius. Has crustacean-like shell and omnivorous diet. Noted for its solitary habits.

O

OLD ONES: sentient race responsible for making the Seed, the Great Beacons, and numerous other technological artifacts found throughout the Orion Arm of the Milky Way. Humanoid, with two sets of arms, they stood about two meters tall. Seemingly extinct. Evidence shows their species was extraordinarily advanced and predates every other known self-aware species. (*See also* Highmost *and* Staff of Blue.)

ORBITAL RING: large, artificial ring placed around a planet. Can be built at nearly any distance, but first ring is usually built in low orbit. Basic concept is simple: rotating cable orbits equator. A non-orbiting, superconducting shell encases said cable. The shell is used to accelerate/decelerate cable as needed. Solar panels and structures can be constructed on outer shell, including stationary space elevators. Gravity on outer surface of shell/ring is near planetary levels. A cheap and practical way to move large amounts of mass in and out of orbit. Used by both humans and Wranaui.

ORB OF CONVERSION: Wranaui FTL drive. It "converts" a ship from STL space to FTL space.

OROS FERN: plant native to Eidolon. Green-black, with leaves that grow from a coiled shape similar to fiddleheads (thus the name).

P

PACKET: small, unmanned, FTL-capable messenger drone.

PATTERN: embedded directive that guides and sets the long-term goals of the Seed.

PDF: Planetary Defense Force. Local military, often civilian, attached to a certain planet.

PELAGIUS: human name for the Wranaui homeworld. F-type star. 340 light-years from Sol.

PFENNIC: fish-like animal native to Pelagius. Noted for copper taste of its meat. Common delicacy among the Wranaui.

PLAINTIVE VERGE: underwater volcanic vent in the oceans of Pelagius. Home of the Abyssal Conclave.

PONDER UNION: workers' union based out of the Ceres shipyards.

PONTIFEX DIGITALIS: nominal religious head of the Numenists. Commands and answers to the College of Enumerators. Responsible for overseeing the Enumeration of real numbers.

PREMIER: head of the League of Allied Worlds. Elected by the constituent governments.

PRISONER: anyone not an Entropist. One imprisoned within the dying universe by their lack of knowledge.

PSEUDO-INTELLIGENCE: convincing simulacrum of sentience. True artificial intelligence has thus far proven more difficult (and dangerous) to create than anticipated. Pseudo-intelligences are programs capable of limited executive function but lack self-awareness, creativity, and introspection. Despite their limitations, they've proven immensely helpful in nearly every realm of human endeavor, from piloting ships to managing cities. (*See also* Ship Mind.)

PULSE: standard unit of Wranaui timekeeping. Equivalent to forty-two seconds. (*See also* Cycle.)

Q

Q-DRIVE: a quantum-level memory stick.

QUESTANT: an Entropist. One who quests for a way to save humanity from the heat death of the universe.

R

RD 52s: hydrogen-cooled Casaba-Howitzers chilled to within a fraction of a degree of absolute zero. Used as mines. An early attempt at stealth weaponry in space.

REFORM HUTTERITES: heretical offshoot of traditional ethnoreligious Hutteritism, now far outnumbering their forebears. Reform Hutterites (RHs) accept the use of modern technology where it allows them to further pursue the spread of humanity and establish their claim over God's creation, but they frown on any use of tech, such as STEM shots, for what they deem selfish, individual needs. Where possible, they hew to communal-based life. They have proven highly successful everywhere they've settled. Unlike traditional Hutterites, RHs are known to serve in the military, although this is still frowned upon by the majority of their society.

REGINALD THE PIG-HEADED GOD: local cult leader in the city of Khoiso. Gene-hacked human with a head in the shape of a pig's. Believed by his followers to be a deity in flesh and possessed of supernatural powers.

REMASS: propellant expelled out the back of a spaceship. Usually hydrogen. Not to be confused with fuel, which in the case of nuclear rockets is the material fused or split to heat the remass/propellant.

RETICULUM: intra-ship network used by Wranaui.

RIPPLE: [[**Invalid Input: Entry Not Found**]]

RM: reserve mark. Indicates legal protection over a term, phrase, or symbol.

RODS: *see* SJAMs.

RSW7-MOLOTÓK: Casaba-Howitzers manufactured by Lutsenko Defense Industries.

RTC NEWS: Ruslan Transmission Company. Newsfeed out of 61 Cygni.

RUSLAN: rocky planet in orbit around 61 Cygni A. Second newest colony in the League, behind Weyland. Primarily settled by Russian interests. Extensive mining takes place in the asteroid belts around A's binary partner, Cygni B.

S

"*SAMAN-SAHARI*": low, slow song originating from Farson's Combine (a collectivist freehold established on a planetoid around Alpha Centauri during the early years of the system's colonization).

SAN AMARO: small Latin American country. Location of Earth's first space elevator.

SAYA: "to be sure." Direct translation is closer to "my surety." Common usage on Ruslan. Derived from Malay.

SCOURGE: microbe that killed twenty-seven of thirty-four humans sent to survey the rocky planetoid Blackstone.

SCRAMROCK: post-fusion hyper vibes, typified by samples of radio and plasma waves taken from the rings of various gas giants. Popularized by Honeysuckle Heaps in 2232.

SCRATCH SEVEN: traditional spacer card game. Goal is to accumulate as many sevens or multiples of seven as possible by adding values of cards (face cards go by their numerical value).

SECRETARY OF DEFENSE: civilian official who oversees the League military.

SEED: self-organizing genetic potential. A spark of life in the endless void.

SEEKER: servitor life-form created by the Old Ones with the intent of enforcement and containment. Able to assume direct control over a living creature's actions following physical contact and injections into braincase. Highly intelligent, highly dangerous, and known to amass large armies of enslaved sentients.

SEVEN MINUTES TO SATURN: war movie made at Alpha Centauri in 2242 about Venus's failed attempt to win independence from Earth during the Zahn Offensive.

SEVENTH FLEET: numbered fleet of the League of Allied Worlds. Headquartered at Deimos Station by Mars. Part of the UMC Solar Fleet. Largest of the forward-deployed UMC fleets.

SFAR: Wranaui clearance level. Higher than *sfenn*, lower than *sfeir*.

SHADOW SHIELD: a plug of radiation shielding that sits between a reactor and the main body of a spaceship. Comprising two layers: neutron shielding (usually lithium hydroxide) and gamma-ray shielding (either tungsten or mercury). In order to keep stations and crew within the "shadow" cast by the shield, spaceships usually dock nose-first.

SHELL: Wranaui word for "spaceship." Derived from their own protective carapaces.

SHI-BAL: Korean profanity, equivalent to English "fuck." Exclusively used with anger and/or negative connotation.

SHIN-ZAR: high-g planet in orbit around Tau Ceti. Only major colony to refuse membership to the League, which resulted in armed conflict between Zarian forces and the League, and the loss of some thousands of lives on both sides. Notable for the high number of colonists of Korean descent. Also notable for population-wide gene-hacking in order to help the colonists adapt to the stronger-than-Earth gravity. Main alterations being: significantly thicker skeletal structure, increased lung capacity (to compensate for low oxygen levels), increased hemoglobin, increased muscular mass via myostatin inhibition, doubled tendons, and generally larger organs. Divergent genetic population. (*See also* Entropism.)

SHIP CAT: traditional pet aboard spaceships. Superstitious belief attaches great importance to the presence and well-being of a ship cat. Plenty of spacers will refuse to sign on to a vessel without one. More than one instance has been recorded of someone being killed after harming (intentionally or otherwise) a ship cat.

SHIP MIND: the somatic transcendence of humanity. Brains removed from bodies, placed in a growth matrix, and bathed with nutrients to induce tissue expansion and synaptic formation. Ship minds are the result of a confluence of factors: human desire to push their intellect to the limit, the failure to develop true A.I., the increasing size of spaceships, and the destructive potential of any space-faring vessel. Having a single person, a single *mind*, to oversee the many operations of a ship was appealing. However, no unaugmented brain was capable of handling the amount of sensory information a full-sized spaceship produced. The larger the vessel, the larger the brain needed.

Ship minds are some of the most brilliant individuals humanity has produced. Also, in cases, some of the most disturbed. The growth process is difficult, and severe psychiatric side effects have been noted.

It is theorized that ship minds—both on and off ships—are responsible for directing far more of the daily affairs of humans than any but the most paranoid suspect. But while their means and methods may sometimes be opaque, their desires are no different than those of any other living creature: to live long and prosper.

SHOAL LEADER: any Wranaui captain or commander in charge of more than three units, but usually reserved for leaders of equivalent rank to brigadier or admiral.

SJAMs: aka "rods from god." Inert projectiles made of tungsten rods that are dropped from orbit. Concept invented by Dr. Pournelle in the twentieth century. A form of kinetic weapon. Used by militaries when conventional explosives are impractical (as when wanting to avoid radiation) or when anti-projectile countermeasures are a concern.

SKINSUIT: general-purpose, skin-tight protective clothing that—with a helmet—can act as a spacesuit, diving equipment, and cold-weather gear. Standard equipment for anyone in a hostile environment.

SKUT: grimy, useless, as in, "Go do that skut-work." Derived from *scut*. Pejorative.

SLAVER MONK: *see* Seeker.

SLV: superluminal vehicle. League designation for a civilian vessel capable of FTL.

SMART FABRIC: metamaterial embedded with electronics, nanomachines, and other augments. Able to assume different shapes, given the proper stimuli.

S-PAC: robotic manipulator used for handling material in quarantine.

SPACE ELEVATOR: carbon-fiber ribbon that extends from the surface of a planet all the way to an anchor point (usually an asteroid) out past geostationary orbit. Crawlers transport mass up and down the ribbon.

SPACER'S TAN: inevitable result of spending days and months under the full-spectrum lights used in spaceships to avoid seasonal affective disorder, vitamin D deficiency, and a host of other ailments. Especially notable in native station dwellers and lifelong ship inhabitants.

STAFF OF BLUE: command module constructed by the Old Ones. Of great sociotechnological significance.

STAFF OF GREEN: fragment of the Seed, given life unto itself.

STELLARISTS: one of several major political parties in the League. Currently the governing party. Isolationist movement composed of the main governmental powers on Mars, Venus, and Earth. Gained traction following the troubles with Shin-Zar and the discovery of the Great Beacon. (*See also* Conservation Party *and* Expansionist Party.)

STELLAR SECURITY ACT: legislation passed upon the formation of the League of Worlds that resulted in the formation of the UMC and that grants sweeping powers to the military, intelligence services, and civilian leadership in the event of an exogenic incident (such as the discovery of the Soft Blade).

STEM SHOTS: series of anti-senescent injections that revitalize cellular processes, suppress mutagenic factors, restore telomere length, and generally return the body to a state equivalent to mid-twenties biological age. Usually repeated every twenty years thereafter. Doesn't stop age-induced cartilage growth in ears, nose, etc.

STEWART'S WORLD: rocky planet in orbit around Alpha Centauri. First settled world outside of Sol. Discovered and named by Ort Stewart. Not a hospitable place, and as a result, the settlers produce a higher than normal proportion of scientists, their expertise being needed to survive the harsh environment. Also why so many spacers come from Stewart's World; they're eager to find somewhere more temperate.

STIMWARE: one of several brands of a popular sleep-replacement medication. The drug contains two different compounds: one to reset the body's circadian rhythm, and one to clear the brain of metabolites such as β-amyloid. When sleep-deprived, dosage prevents neurodegeneration and maintains high-level mental/physical functioning. Anabolic state of sleep is not replicated, so normal rest is still needed for secretion of growth hormone and proper recovery from daily stresses.

STRAIGHT SWEEP: highest natural hand in Scratch Seven, consisting of four kings, two queens, and an ace, for a count of seventy-seven and a score of eleven.

STRIKE SHOAL HFARR: named fleet within the Wranaui military (there being one for each Arm).

SUNDERING: cataclysmic Wranaui civil war sparked by the discovery of numerous technological artifacts made by the Old Ones, including the Seed and several other forms like it. This led to the Tfeir's heresy of the flesh. While Arm fought Arm for supremacy, the Wranaui also engaged in an ambitious expansionist campaign, colonizing numerous systems. Their internal conflict nearly destroyed their species, partly through conventional warfare, partly through the awakening of a Seeker, and partly through the inadvertent creation of Corrupted. Wranaui civilization was shattered, and it took nearly three centuries to fully recover. (*See also* Ripple *and* Tfeir.)

T

"*TANGAGRIA*": folk song from Bologna, Italy. Composer unknown.

TEQ: *see* Transluminal Energy Quantum.

TESSERITE: mineral unique to Adrasteia. Similar to benitoite but with a greater tendency toward purple.

TFEIR: one of six Arms of the Wranaui. Noted for its heresy of the flesh: self-replication via the Nest of Transference *without* the death of one's original form. Considered a sin of pride by the rest of the Wranaui. A major contributing factor to the Sundering.

THRESH: hardcore smasher metal that originated in the farming communities of Eidolon. Noted for use of agricultural implements as instruments.

THULE: aka the Lord of Empty Spaces. Pronounced *THOOL*. God of the spacers. Derived from *ultima Thule,* Latin phrase used to mean "a place beyond the borders of all maps." Originally applied to a trans-Neptunian planetesimal in Sol, the term came to be applied to the "unknown" in general, and from thence gained personification. Extensive superstitions surround Thule among the asteroid miners in Sol and elsewhere.

TIGERMAUL: large, felinesque predator native to Eidolon. Noted for the barbs on its back, yellow eyes, and high intelligence.

TORQUE ENGINE: generator and propulsive engine devised by the Old Ones. Used to power Unity as well as drive spaceships of the Old Ones' design. Works by "torqueing" the membrane of fluidic spacetime in such a way as to allow the extraction of energy from superluminal space, despite the lower energy density of that space. The distortion can also be used to propel the engine through subluminal space via warping or to form a Markov Bubble for FTL travel.

TORQUE GATE: artificial wormhole generated and sustained by a torque engine stationed at either mouth. Used by the Old Ones for near-instantaneous travel over vast distances.

"*TOXOPAXIA*": popular jig from one of the hab-rings around Sol.

TRANSCENDENCE: computer game where the goal is to guide a species from the dawn of sentience to colonizing nearby stars in as short a time as possible.

TRANSLUMINAL ENERGY QUANTUM (TEQ): the most fundamental building block of reality. A quantized entity of Planck length 1, Planck energy 1, and zero mass. Occupies every point of space, both sub- and superluminal as well as within the luminal membrane that divides the two.

TSURO: signaling device used by the Old Ones for summoning and controlling the Seed. Accomplished via a modulated TEQ wavefront.

TWENTY-EIGHT G: one of several commsats in orbit around Zeus and Adrasteia.

U

UMC: United Military Command. Combined military forces of the League drawn from the constituent members. Numerous of those governments have ceased maintaining their own militaries and instead direct all their defense resources to the UMC.

UMCA: United Military Command Army.

UMCI: United Military Command Intelligence.

UMCM: United Military Command Marines.

UMCN: United Military Command Navy.

UMCS: United Military Command Ship/Station.

UNIFIED FIELD THEORY: theory outlined by Ilya Markov in 2107 that provides the underpinnings for FTL travel (as well as numerous other technologies).

V

VANISHED: *see* Old Ones.

W

WEYLAND: colony planet in orbit around Epsilon Indi. Named after the Nordic/Germanic smith of legend. No notable native life-forms.

WHIRLPOOL: *see* Great Beacon.

WIRE SCAN: an in-depth, invasive review of all the data gathered by a person's implants. Often damaging to the physical and mental health of the subject, given the strength of the electrical signals used as well as the intimate nature of the probe. Sometimes results in loss of brain function.

WRANAUI: sentient, space-faring race originating from the planet Pelagius. Highly complex life cycle, with an equally complicated, hierarchical social structure dominated by Arms and a ruling form. Wranaui are naturally an ocean-based species, but through extensive use of artificial bodies, have adapted themselves to nearly every possible environment. Aggressive and expansionist, they have little regard for individual rights or safety, given their reliance on replacement bodies. Their scent-based language is exceedingly difficult for humans to translate. Even without technological augmentation, Wranaui are biologically immortal; their genetic-base bodies are always able to revert to an immature form in order to renew their flesh and stave off senescence. Some evidence indicates they may have been genetically modified by the Old Ones at some point in their distant past.

Y

YANNI THE NEWT: children's entertainment show popular on Ruslan that led to a fad for owning pet newts.

APPENDIX IV

* * * * * * *

TIMELINE

1700–1800 (EST.):

- The Sundering

2025–2054:

- Development and construction of Earth's first space elevator. Quickly followed by increased exploration and economic development within the Solar System (Sol). First humans land on Mars. Moon base built, as well as several space stations throughout Sol. Asteroid mining starts.

2054–2104:

- With the space elevator up, colonization of the Solar System accelerates. Hutterite Expansion begins. First floating city on Venus established. Permanent (although not self-sustaining) outposts on Mars. Many more habitats and stations built throughout the system. Construction begins on an orbital ring around Earth.
- Fission-powered, nuclear-thermal rockets are primary mode of transportation in Solar System.
- Mathematician Jalal Sunyaev-Zel'dovich publishes founding precepts of Entropism.

- Law enforcement becomes increasingly difficult throughout the Solar System. Clashes start between the outer settlements and the inner planets. International space law is increased and further developed by the UN and individual governments. Militias spring up on Mars and among the asteroid miners. Space-based corporations use private security firms to safeguard their investments. Space is fully militarized at this point.

- Venus and Mars remain tightly tied to Earth, politically and resource-wise, but independence movements begin to form.

- Giant solar arrays built in space provide cheap power throughout Sol. Overlays, implants, and genetic modification are common among those who can afford them.

- Powerful fusion drives replace older fission rockets, drastically reducing travel times within the Solar System.

2104–2154:

- Fink-Nottle's Pious Newt Emporium established.

- STEM shots are invented, effectively rendering humans biologically immortal. This leads to the launch of several self-sustaining, sublight colony ships to Alpha Centauri.

- Soon after, Ilya Markov codifies the unified field theory (UFT). Working prototype of an FTL drive constructed in 2114. Experimental vessel *Daedalus* makes first FTL flight.

- FTL ships depart for Alpha Centauri, overtaking sublight colony ships. First extra-solar colony is founded on Stewart's World at Alpha Centauri.

- Oelert (2122) confirms that the majority of local superluminal matter exists in a vast halo around the Milky Way.

- Several more extra-solar colonies follow. First on Shin-Zar. Then on Eidolon. Some of the cities/outposts are funded by corporations. Some by nations back on Earth. Either way, colonies are highly dependent on supplies from Sol to begin with, and most of the colonists end up deep in debt after buying the various pieces of equipment they need.

2154–2230:

- Weyland colonized.

- Numenism founded on Mars by Sal Horker II circa 2165–2179 (est.).

- As they grow, colonies begin to assert their independence from Earth and Sol. Clashes between local factions (e.g., the Unrest on Shin-Zar). Relations with Earth grow fractious. Venus tries and fails to win its independence in the Zahn Offensive.

- Ruslan colonized.

2230:

- Kira Navárez is born.

2234–2237:

- Discovery of the Great Beacon on Talos VII by Captain Idris and the crew of the SLV *Adamura.*

- The League of Allied Worlds is formed, with much resistance and suspicion. Some colonies/freeholdings abstain. Passage of the Stellar Security Act, leading to the creation of the UMC and consolidation of much of humanity's forces. Battles of sovereignty occur with several groups that insist upon remaining independent, including, most notably, the planetary government of Shin-Zar.

- Severe winter storm on Weyland results in significant damage to the Navárez family greenhouses.

2237–2257:

- Corruption scandal with Sasha Petrovich near the end of 2249 results in the resignation of Ruslan's governor, Maxim Novikov.

2257–58:

- Survey of the moon Adrasteia and subsequent events.

* * * *

AFTERWORD & ACKNOWLEDGMENTS

1.

Greetings, Friends.

It's been a long journey. Come in, have a seat by the holo, take the weight off your feet. You must be tired. There's some Venusian scotch on the shelf to your side. . . . Yes, that's it. Pour yourself a glass, if you want.

While you recover, let me tell you a story. No, not that one, another. One that begins all the way back in 2006–7 (the dates grow vague with time). I had finished my second novel, *Eldest*, and was nearly done with the third, *Brisingr*, and I was straining at the bit, frustrated that what had once been a trilogy had expanded into a tetralogy and that I would have to spend several more years working on the Inheritance Cycle. Mind you, I loved the series and was happy to finish it, but at the same time I wanted—no, I *needed*—to try my hand at something else. Discipline is a necessary prerequisite to creative success, and yet the value of variety should not be dismissed. By trying new things we learn and grow and maintain excitement for our craft.

So, while I spent my days in the land of Alagaësia, writing about elves and dwarves and dragons, I spent my nights dreaming about other adventures in other places. And one of those dreams involved a woman who found an alien biosuit on a moon orbiting a gas giant. . . .

It was a rough idea, more of a sketch than anything. But even from the very beginning, I always knew how the story would start (with Kira finding the suit) and how it would end (with her drifting off into space). The difficult bit was figuring out all the parts in between.

After finishing *Brisingr*, I took a stab at writing the beginning of *To Sleep in a Sea of Stars*. If you saw that early version, you would laugh. It was half-baked, underformed, but the bones of what would become this story were still there, waiting to be unearthed.

I had to put it aside to write and promote *Inheritance*. That took me until mid-2012 (touring for a popular book/series is no small thing). And after that, after finishing a series I had been working on from the age of fifteen to twenty-eight, I needed a break.

For six months, I didn't write. Then, the old itch to create took over. I knocked out a screenplay (which didn't work). I wrote a number of short stories (one of which was later published in *The Fork, the Witch, and the Worm*, a sequel to the Inheritance Cycle). And I began to research the scientific underpinnings to my future history.

That research occupied most of 2013. I'm not a physicist, nor a mathematician—I never even went to college—so I had to put in a lot of work to reach the level of understanding I wanted. Why go to such lengths? Because, as magic is to fantasy, science is to, well, *science* fiction. It sets the rules to your story, defines what is or isn't possible. And although I envisioned *To Sleep* as a love letter to the genre, I wanted to avoid certain technical conventions that would undermine the setting. Mainly, I wanted a way for ships to travel FTL that *didn't* allow for time travel, and that *didn't* blatantly contradict physics as we know it. (I was okay with bending a few rules here and there, but outright breakage didn't sit right with me.)

Of course, all the world-building in the universe doesn't matter if the story itself isn't sound. And that, I'm afraid, is where I met my greatest difficulty.

For various personal reasons, writing the first draft of *To Sleep* took until January of 2016. Three(ish) years of hard, hard work. Upon finishing, my first reader, my one and only sister, Angela, informed me that the book just. didn't. work. Upon reading the manuscript myself, I realized she was, unfortunately, correct.

The year 2017 passed in a frenzy of rewrites. None of which fixed the underlying issues. The rewrites were, to put it metaphorically, like rearranging the deck chairs on the *Titanic*, which did nothing to change the fact that the ship's structural integrity was compromised.

The problem was this: after working on the Inheritance Cycle for so long, my plotting skills had gotten rusty from disuse. The problem-solving muscles I had built while developing the story for *Eragon* and sequels had atrophied in the decade since. And, I won't lie, after the success of the Inheritance Cycle, I had, perhaps, been a bit cocky when starting *To Sleep*. "Well if I could do *that*, surely *this* won't be a problem."

Ha! Life, fate, the gods—call it what you will, but reality has a way of humbling us all.

The situation came to a head at the end of 2017 when my agent, Simon, and then-editor, Michelle, gently informed me that the rewrites just weren't cutting it.

At that moment, I nearly gave up. After so much work and time invested, to be back at nearly square one was . . . demoralizing. But if I have a defining trait, it's determination. I really hate to give up on a project, even when common sense tells me otherwise.

So in November 2017, I stopped rearranging the deck chairs and, instead, went back to the basic blueprint of the story. And I questioned *everything*. In a week and a half, I wrote (by hand) over two hundred pages of notes dissecting character, motivation, meaning, symbology, technology . . . You name it, I looked at it.

And only then, only once I felt I had a new and stronger skeleton to hang this story upon, did I start writing again. Most of part one, Exogenesis, remained the same. And some of part two. But everything after that, I wrote from scratch. There was no Bughunt in the original version of *To Sleep*. No visit to Sol. No trip to Cordova. No nightmares, no Maw, no Unity, no grand adventure beyond 61 Cygni.

In essence, I wrote an entirely new book—and not a small one—over the course of 2018 and the first half of 2019. During the same time, I also wrote and edited *The Fork, the Witch, and the Worm*, toured for it in the U.S. and Europe, and continued to tour the U.S. for the entirety of 2019 as Barnes & Noble's writer in residence. Whew!

Writing and editing *To Sleep* has been by far the hardest creative challenge of my life. I had to relearn how to tell a story, rewrite a book I'd been laboring over for years, and overcome a number of personal and professional challenges.

Was it worth it? I think so. And I'm looking forward to putting the skills I've learned/reacquired to use on a new book. One that, if all goes well, will take substantially *less* than nine years to write and publish.

In looking back over the history of this project, it feels in no small part like a dream. So much time has passed. So much angst and effort and ambition. I finished the first draft while spending the winter split between a dingy apartment in Edinburgh and a slightly brighter apartment in Barcelona. Revisions were carried out where I live in Montana, but also at a dozen different locations across the globe as work, and life, took me about. The final edits were carried out during a pandemic.

When I first got the idea for *To Sleep*, I was in my mid-twenties. Now I'm in the latter half of my thirties. When I started, there was no white in my beard.

Hell, I didn't even have a beard! Now the first streaks of frost have appeared. I've even gotten married, and that's been an adventure all its own. . . .

To Sleep in a Sea of Stars isn't perfect, but it's the best version of this story I could write, and I'm proud of the final result. To quote Rolfe Humphries from the foreword to his translation of *The Aeneid*: "The scope of an epic requires, in the writing, a designed variety, a calculated unevenness, now and then some easy-going carelessness."

All very true. I'm also fond of what he says further on:

"The last revisions are always the most enervating, and Virgil, one can well believe, having worked on the poem for over a decade, had reached the point where he felt he would rather do anything, including die, than go over the poem one more time. . . . Who wants an epic poem absolutely perfect, anyway?"

My sentiments exactly. Nevertheless, I hope you enjoyed the imperfections of this novel.

So. Now I've told a story about a story. The night grows late, and your Venusian scotch is nearly gone. I've spent long enough rambling on. But before you retire, a few final points.

One: those of you who are fans of the Inheritance Cycle may have noticed some references to the series in *To Sleep*. You weren't imagining things. And yes, Inarë is who you think she is. (For those unfamiliar with that name, I recommend looking up Jeod's letter on my website, paolini.net.)

Two: if you wish to dig deeper into the universe of *To Sleep*, I suggest paying attention to the use of the number seven in the story (where possible, all numbers are either multiples of seven or may be added up to equal seven). You may also find it interesting to locate places outside this novel where *seven* might be input.

Three: the table of contents contains some acrostic fun.

Enough. I've said my fill. The air is cold, the stars are bright, and this tale has reached its end, both for Kira and for me.

Eat the path.

2.

In creating this novel, I was fortunate to have the support of an enormous number of people. Without them, *To Sleep* would never have seen the light of day. They are:

My dad, for keeping things running when I was buried in the manuscript for months on end. My mom, for patience and editing (so much editing!) and continual support. My sister, Angela, for never letting me settle for second-best and for giving me the kick in the pants needed to fix Gregorovich's story line (among many others). Caru, who created the awesome logos (aside from Shin-Zar's) that appear in the terminology section, as well as tons of other concept art. My wife, Ash, for her ongoing support, humor, love, and various artistic contributions (including the logo for Shin-Zar). And a big thank-you to my whole family for reading this book more times than any sane person ought to.

My assistant (and friend), Immanuela Meijer, for her input, support, and some gorgeous pieces of artwork. She's the one responsible for the map of Sigma Draconis, 61 Cygni, part of Bughunt, and the really awesome fractal endpaper/map.

My agent, Simon Lipskar, who—from the very beginning—has been a tireless champion of this book and what he knew it could be. Thank you, Simon!

My dear friend, Michelle Frey, who read several early versions of the book and who had the unenviable task of telling me that they weren't working. Without her input, I never would have taken the leap and written a version that *did* work.

At Macmillan: Don Weisberg, who knew me during his time at Random House, and because of it, was willing to take a chance on an adult novel from someone previously only known for YA. Thank you, Don!

At Tor: my editors, Devi Pillai and William Hinton. They pushed me far harder than I expected . . . and the book is better because of it. Also in editorial: assistants Rachel Bass and Oliver Dougherty, and copy editor Christina MacDonald.

In publicity/marketing: Lucille Rettino, Eileen Lawrence, Stephanie Sarabian, Caroline Perny, Sarah Reidy, and Renata Sweeney. If you've heard of this book, they're the ones responsible!

In design/production: Michelle Foytek, Greg Collins, Peter Lutjen, Jim Kapp, Rafal Gibek. Without them, the book wouldn't have been published on time, and it sure wouldn't have looked as good. And thanks to everyone else at Tor who has worked on this book.

Also thanks to Lindy Martin for the gorgeous cover image.

On the technical side of things: Gregory Meholic, who was kind enough to let me use his Tri-Space theory as the basis for my FTL system (as well as several of his graphs, which were redrawn for Appendix I). He also answered scores and scores of questions as I struggled to understand the specifics of how it worked. Apologies to him for bastardizing his theory in one or two places in the interests of fiction. Sorry Greg! Also Richard Gauthier—who originated the idea of TEQs—and H. David Froning Jr., who invented the technical groundwork for conditioned EM fields, which I used as the basis for my Markov Drives. And last but not least, Winchell Chung and the Atomic Rockets website (www.projectrho.com/rocket/). *The* best resource for anyone wanting to write realistic science fiction. Without it, the ideas in this book would have been far less interesting.

A special mention goes to the family of Felix Hofer, who were kind enough to let me use his name in this book. Felix was a reader of mine who, tragically, was killed in a motorcycle accident soon after his eighteenth birthday. We'd had some correspondence, and, well, I wanted to mark his passing and do my best to help Felix's name live on.

As always, the biggest thanks of all go to you, dear reader. Without you, none of this would be possible! So again, thank you. Let's do it again soon.

Christopher Paolini
September 15, 2020